MW00657211

The MX Book of New Sherlock Holmes Stories

Part XXIV – Some More Untold Cases (1895-1903)

THE MX BOOK OF NEW
SHERLOCK HOLMES
STORIES
PART XXIV: SOME MORE
UNTOLD CASES
1895-1903
SOUTHAMPTON
STREET
359
EDITED
By
David
Marcum
OFFICES
TRADITIONAL HOLMES
ADVENTURES
COMPILED FOR THE
BENEFIT OF THE
RESTORATION OF
UNDERSHAW

First edition published in 2020
© Copyright 2020

The right of the individuals listed on the Copyright Information page to be identified as the authors of this work has been asserted by them in accordance with the Copyright, Designs, and Patents Act 1998.

All rights reserved. No reproduction, copy, or transmission of this publication may be made without express prior written permission. No paragraph of this publication may be reproduced, copied, or transmitted except with express prior written permission or in accordance with the provisions of the Copyright Act 1956 (as amended). Any person who commits any unauthorised act in relation to this publication may be liable to criminal prosecution and civil claims for damage.

All characters appearing in this work are fictitious or used fictitiously. Except for certain historical personages, any resemblance to real persons, living or dead, is purely coincidental. The opinions expressed herein are those of the authors and not of MX Publishing.

ISBN Hardback 978-1-78705-664-0
ISBN Paperback 978-1-78705-665-7
AUK ePub ISBN 978-1-78705-666-4
AUK PDF ISBN 978-1-78705-6671

Published in the UK by
MX Publishing
335 Princess Park Manor, Royal Drive,
London, N11 3GX
www.mxpublishing.co.uk

David Marcum can be reached at:
thepapersofsherlockholmes@gmail.com

Cover design by Brian Belanger
www.belangerbooks.com and *www.redbubble.com/people/zhahadun*

CONTENTS

Forewords

Adventures

(Continued on the next page . . . .)

(Continued on the next page . . . .)

These additional adventures are contained in

Part XXII: Some More Untold Cases (1877-1887)

The Philosophy of Holmes (A Poem) – Christopher James
The Terror of the Tankerville – S.F. Bennett
The Singular Affair of the Aluminium Crutch – William Todd
The Trifling Matter of Mortimer Maberley – Geri Schear
Abracadaver – Susan Knight
The Secret in Lowndes Court – David Marcum
Vittoria, the Circus Bell – Bob Bishop
The Adventure of the Vanished Husband – Tracy J. Revels
Merridew of Abominable Memory – Chris Chan
The Substitute Thief – Richard Paolinelli
The Whole Story Concerning the Politician, the Lighthouse, and the Trained Cormorant – Derrick Belanger
A Child's Reward – Stephen Mason
The Case of the Elusive Umbrella – Leslie Charteris and Denis Green
Introduction by Ian Dickerson
The Strange Death of an Art Dealer – Tim Symonds
Watch Him Fall – Liese Sherwood-Fabre
The Adventure of the Transatlantic Gila – Ian Ableson
Intruders at Baker Street – Chris Chan
The Paradol Chamber – Mark Mower
Wolf Island – Robert Stapleton
The Etherage Escapade – Roger Riccard
The Dundas Separation Case – Kevin P. Thornton
The Broken Glass – Denis O. Smith

These additional adventures are contained in

Part XXIII: Some More Untold Cases (1888-1894)

The Housekeeper (A Poem) – John Linwood Grant
The Uncanny Adventure of the Hammersmith Wonder – Will Murray
Mrs. Forrester's Domestic Complication– Tim Gambrell

(Continued on the next page . . . .)

These additional Sherlock Holmes adventures can be found in the previous volumes of

The MX Book of New Sherlock Holmes Stories

(Continued on the next page . . . .)

PART III: 1896-1929

PART IV – 2016 Annual

(Continued on the next page . . . .)

(Continued on the next page . . . .)

PART VI – 2017 Annual

(Continued on the next page . . . .)

PART VII – Eliminate the Impossible: 1880-1891

PART VIII – Eliminate the Impossible: 1892-1905

(Continued on the next page . . . .)

(Continued on the next page . . . .)

Part X – 2018 Annual (1896-1916)

Part XI: Some Untold Cases (1880-1891)

(Continued on the next page . . . .)

Part XII: Some Untold Cases (1894-1902)

PART XIII: 2019 Annual (1881-1890)

(Continued on the next page . . . .)

PART XIV: 2019 Annual (1891 -1897)

(Continued on the next page . . . .)

PART XV: 2019 Annual (1898-1917)

Part XVI – (1881-1890)

(Continued on the next page . . . .)

Part XVII – (1891-1898)

Part XVIII – (1899-1925)

(Continued on the next page . . . .)

Part XIX: 2020 Annual (1892-1890)

(Continued on the next page . . . .)

Part XX: 2020 Annual (1891-1897)

Part XXI: 2020 Annual (1898-1923)

(Continued on the next page . . . .)

The following contributions appear in this volume:
The MX Book of New Sherlock Holmes Stories
Part XXIV – Some More Untold Cases (1895-1903)

"Another Case of Identity" ©2020 by Thomas A. Burns. All Rights Reserved. First publication, original to this collection. Printed by permission of the author.

"The Adventure of the Abergavenny Murder" *and* "The Adventure of the Refused Knighthood" ©2020 by Craig Stephen Copland. All Rights Reserved. First publication, original to this collection. Printed by permission of the author.

"The Adventure of the Nile Traveler" ©2020 by John Davis. All Rights Reserved. First publication, original to this collection. Printed by permission of the author.

"An Act of Faith" ©2020 by Harry DeMaio. All Rights Reserved. First publication, original to this collection. Printed by permission of the author.

"Conan Doyle's Legacy in 2020" ©2020 by Steve Emecz. All Rights Reserved. First publication, original to this collection. Printed by permission of the author.

"The Adventure of Parsley and Butter" ©2020 by Jayantika Ganguly. All Rights Reserved. First publication, original to this collection. Printed by permission of the author.

"The Case of Indelible Evidence" ©2020 by Dick Gillman. All Rights Reserved. First publication, original to this collection. Printed by permission of the author.

"The Man from Deptford" ©2020 by John Linwood Grant. All Rights Reserved. First publication, original to this collection. Printed by permission of the author.

"The Adventure of the Conk-Singleton Forgery" *and* "The Adventure of Mr. Fairdale Hobbs" ©2020 by Arthur Hall. All Rights Reserved. First publication, original to this collection. Printed by permission of the author.

"The Case of the Impossible Assassin" ©2020 by Paula Hammond. All Rights Reserved. First publication, original to this collection. Printed by permission of the author.

"The Case of Vanderbilt and the Yeggman" ©2020 by Stephen Herczeg. All Rights Reserved. First publication, original to this collection. Printed by permission of the author.

"Fond of Queer Mysteries" ©2020 by Roger Johnson. All Rights Reserved. First publication, original to this collection. Printed by permission of the author.

"A Simple Matter" ©2020 by Susan Knight. All Rights Reserved. First publication, original to this collection. Printed by permission of the author.

"The Case of the Consulting Physician" ©2020 by John Lawrence. All Rights Reserved. First publication, original to this collection. Printed by permission of the author.

"Editor's Foreword: Watson's Obfuscations" *and* "The Hammerford Will Business" ©2020 by David Marcum. All Rights Reserved. First publication, original to this collection. Printed by permission of the author.

"Foreword" ©2020 by Otto Penzler. All Rights Reserved. First publication, original to this collection. Printed by permission of the author.

"The Chinese Puzzle Box" ©2020 by Gayle Lange Puhl. All Rights Reserved. First publication, original to this collection. Printed by permission of the author.

"The Tragedy of Woodman's Lee" ©2020 by Tracy J. Revels. All Rights Reserved. First publication, original to this collection. Printed by permission of the author.

"The Case of the Accused Cook" ©2020 by Brenda Seabrooke. All Rights Reserved. First publication, original to this collection. Printed by permission of the author.

"A Word From Stepping Stones" ©2020 by Jacqueline Silver. All Rights Reserved. First publication, original to this collection. Printed by permission of the author.

"Sherlock Holmes and the Return of the Missing Rhyme (*A Poem*)" ©2020 by Joseph W. Svec III. All Rights Reserved. First publication, original to this collection. Printed by permission of the author

"The Murdered Millionaire" ©2020 by Kevin P. Thornton. All Rights Reserved. First publication, original to this collection. Printed by permission of the author.

"The Curious Case of the Crusader's Cross" ©2020 by DJ Tyrer. All Rights Reserved. First publication, original to this collection. Printed by permission of the author.

"The Comet Wine's Funeral" ©2020 by Marcia Wilson. All Rights Reserved. First publication, original to this collection. Printed by permission of the author.

The following contributions appear in the companion volumes:

The MX Book of New Sherlock Holmes Stories
Part XXII – Some More Untold Cases (1877-1887)
Part XXIII – Some More Untold Cases (1888-1894)

"The Adventure of the Transatlantic Gila" ©2020 by Ian Ableson. All Rights Reserved. First publication, original to this collection. Printed by permission of the author.

"The Adventure of the Nonpareil Club" ©2020 by Hugh Ashton and j-views Publishing. All Rights Reserved. Hugh Ashton appears by kind permission of j-views Publishing. First publication, original to this collection. Printed by permission of the author.

"The Whole Story Concerning the Politician, the Lighthouse, and the Trained Cormorant" ©2020 by Derrick Belanger. All Rights Reserved. First publication, original to this collection. Printed by permission of the author.

"The Terror of the Tankerville" ©2020 by S.F. Bennett. All Rights Reserved. First publication, original to this collection. Printed by permission of the author.

"Vittoria, the Circus Bell" ©2020 by Bob Bishop. All Rights Reserved. First publication, original to this collection. Printed by permission of the author.

"Merridew of Abominable Memory" *and* "Intruders in Baker Street" ©2020 by Chris Chan. All Rights Reserved. First publication, original to this collection. Printed by permission of the author.

"The Case of the Elusive Umbrella" ©1945, 2020 by Leslie Charteris and Denis Green. First publication of text script in this collection. Originally broadcast on radio on January 22, 1945 as part of *The New Adventures of Sherlock Holmes* radio show, starring Basil Rathbone and Nigel Bruce. First text publication, original to this collection. Printed by permission of the Leslie Charteris Estate.

"The Adventure of the Singular Worm" ©2020 by Mike Chinn. All Rights Reserved. First publication, original to this collection. Printed by permission of the author.

"The Incident of the Dual Intrusions" ©2020 by Barry Clay. All Rights Reserved. First publication, original to this collection. Printed by permission of the author.

"Introduction – The Case of the Elusive Umbrella" ©2020 by Ian Dickerson. All Rights Reserved. First publication, original to this collection. Printed by permission of the author.

"The Adventure of the Tired Captain" ©2012, 2020 by Matthew J. Elliott. All Rights Reserved. First publication of text script in this collection. Originally broadcast on radio on October 21, 2012 as Episode No. 107 of *The Further Adventures of Sherlock Holmes*.

"Mrs. Forrester's Domestic Complication" *and* "The Smith-Mortimer Succession" ©2020 by Tim Gambrell. All Rights Reserved. First publication, original to this collection. Printed by permission of the author.

"The Secret of Colonel Warburton's Insanity" ©2020 by Paul D. Gilbert. All Rights Reserved. First publication, original to this collection. Printed by permission of the author.

"The Housekeeper (*A Poem*)" ©2020 by John Linwood Grant. All Rights Reserved. First publication, original to this collection. Printed by permission of the author.

"The Adventure of the Drewhampton Poisoner" ©2020 by Arthur Hall. All Rights Reserved. First publication, original to this collection. Printed by permission of the author.

"The Crimes of John Clay" ©2020 by Paul Hiscock. All Rights Reserved. First publication, original to this collection. Printed by permission of the author.

"The Philosophy of Holmes (*A Poem*)" ©2020 by Christopher James. All Rights Reserved. First publication, original to this collection. Printed by permission of the author.

"The Adventure of the Loring Riddle" ©2020 by Craig Janacek. All Rights Reserved. First publication, original to this collection. Printed by permission of the author.

"The Case of the Un-Paralleled Adventures" ©2020 by Steven Philip Jones. All Rights Reserved. First publication, original to this collection. Printed by permission of the author.

"Abracadaver" ©2020 by Susan Knight. All Rights Reserved. First publication, original to this collection. Printed by permission of the author.

"The Secret in Lowndes Court" *and* "The Rhayader Legacy" ©2020 by David Marcum. All Rights Reserved. First publication, original to this collection. Printed by permission of the author.

"A Child's Reward" ©2020 by Stephen Mason. All Rights Reserved. First publication, original to this collection. Printed by permission of the author.

"The Paradol Chamber" ©2020 by Mark Mower. All Rights Reserved. First publication, original to this collection. Printed by permission of the author.

"The Uncanny Adventure of the Hammersmith Wonder" *and* "The Repulsive Matter of the Bloodless Banker" ©2020 by Will Murray. All Rights Reserved. First publication, original to this collection. Printed by permission of the author.

"The Substitute Thief" ©2020 by Richard Paolinelli. All Rights Reserved. First publication, original to this collection. Printed by permission of the author.

"The Adventure of the Vanished Husband" *and* "The Adventure of Merridew of Abominable Memory" ©2020 by Tracy J. Revels. All Rights Reserved. First publication, original to this collection. Printed by permission of the author.

"The Etherage Escapade" ©2020 by Roger Riccard. All Rights Reserved. First publication, original to this collection. Printed by permission of the author.

"To the Manor Bound" ©2020 by Jane Rubino. All Rights Reserved. First publication, original to this collection. Printed by permission of the author.

"The Trifling Matter of Mortimer Maberley" ©2020 by Geri Schear. All Rights Reserved. First publication, original to this collection. Printed by permission of the author.

"Watch Him Fall" ©2020 by Liese Sherwood-Fabre. All Rights Reserved. First publication, original to this collection. Printed by permission of the author.

"The Adventure of the Forgotten Brolly" ©2020 by Shane Simmons. All Rights Reserved. First publication, original to this collection. Printed by permission of the author.

"The Broken Glass" ©2020 by Denis O. Smith. All Rights Reserved. First publication, original to this collection. Printed by permission of the author.

"Wolf Island" ©2020 by Robert Stapleton. All Rights Reserved. First publication, original to this collection. Printed by permission of the author.

"The Adventure of the Tired Captain" ©2020 by Dacre Stoker and Leverett Butts. All Rights Reserved. First publication, original to this collection. Printed by permission of the author.

"The Strange Death of an Art Dealer" ©2020 by Tim Symonds and Lesley Abdela. All Rights Reserved. First publication, original
to this collection. Printed by permission of the author.

"The Dundas Separation Case" ©2020 by Kevin P. Thornton. All Rights Reserved. First publication, original to this collection. Printed by permission of the author.

"The Singular Affair of the Aluminium Crutch" ©2020 by William Todd. All Rights Reserved. First publication, original to this collection. Printed by permission of the author.

"The Affair of the *Friesland*" ©2020 by Jan van Koningsveld. All Rights Reserved. First publication, original to this collection. Printed by permission of the author.

"The Affair of the Hellingstone Rubies" ©2020 by Margaret Walsh. All Rights Reserved. First publication, original to this collection. Printed by permission of the author.

"The Adventure of the Abducted Bard" ©2020 by I.A. Watson. All Rights Reserved. First publication, original to this collection. Printed by permission of the author.

"The Forgetful Detective" ©2020 by Marcia Wilson. All Rights Reserved. First publication, original to this collection. Printed by permission of the author.

Editor's Note:
Duplicate Untold Cases

In some instances, there are multiple versions of certain Untold Cases contained within this volume. Each of these are very different stories and do not contradict one another, in spite of their common jumping-off place. As explained in the Editor's Foreword, no traditional and Canonical versions of the Untold Cases are the definitive versions to the exclusion of the others. They simply require a bit of additional pondering and rationalization to consider what was going on in Watson's thinking, and why he chose to present them in this way.

In this volume, the reader will encounter several versions of "The Two Coptic Patriarchs", "Mr. Fairdale Hobbs", and "The Refused Knighthood" – *Enjoy!*

SP

Editor's Foreword:
Watson's Obfuscations
by David Marcum

<u>*Obfuscate:*</u>

Merriam-Webster –

1 – a: to throw into shadow, darken;
b: to make obscure

2 – Confuse

Dictionary.com –

The act or an instance of making something obscure, dark, or difficult to understand

Watson obfuscated. Without a doubt. To pretend that he did otherwise would be rather naïve.

We have obvious evidence or this, and also that which is much more indirect and must be inferred.

That isn't to say that Watson is an actual *liar*, with the habitual and intentional regular misrepresentations that this word implies. A true liar cannot help him or herself. Such a person chooses falsehoods over truth with the same lack of thought as when taking a breath. Some liars do so occasionally, while others do it dozens of times per day in the very visible public eye, regardless of the damage that they cause.

When Watson obfuscated, it was for a reason.

Consider: Watson wanted to record his Sherlock Holmes's various investigations so that the public would be aware of his friend's abilities, and so that credit for the solution of his investigations would be properly pointed in Holmes's direction. At the end of their first shared adventure, after Holmes explains how he followed the scarlet thread of murder through the tangled skein to a correct solution, Watson cries: *"It is wonderful! Your merits should be publicly recognized. You should publish an account of the case. If you won't, I will for you."*

Holmes replies, *"You may do what you like, Doctor."* – likely little realizing just what he had let himself in for.

A moment later, Watson added, *"I have all the facts in my journal, and the public shall know them."* And so they would – but it would be nearly seven years before that occurred. Watson made that promise in early March 1881, but *A Study in Scarlet* wouldn't be published until late November 1887, in *Beeton's Christmas Annual.*

In the meantime, Holmes continued to investigate, and Watson continued to assist him – more and more as his health improved following his grievous mid-1880 war injury, and also as Holmes's practice continued to grow and thrive. We view those cases now as something from a long-ago time, stirring within us longings for those mysterious gaslit streets and foggy nights. Sometimes we tend to forget that when Watson first began publishing in 1887, those stories were essentially contemporary. Adventures might occur in streets or locations that no longer exist, but they certainly existed then. Our Heroes made their way across London in hansom cabs and growlers, and while those are long gone, that was the norm then. And when Watson was writing about Holmes's cases, they weren't recountings of events that had occurred decades before – some had happened only a few months before they were published.

Consider "The Red-Headed League", which took place in October 1890. (There is a bit of confusing contradiction within the story regarding this date, but that will be addressed in a moment.) Watson, then married for a couple of years and living in nearby Paddington, relates how he'd stopped by to visit Holmes and found him in consultation with Mr. Jabez Wilson concerning the rather comical pawnbroker's recent connections to the mysterious aforementioned League, and his subsequent grievances against them – for they had been paying him steadily for months to spend his mornings copying the *Encyclopaedia Britannica*, and just that morning he'd found that this unusual post had been terminated without any previous warning.

As expected, the matter resolved satisfactorily, and Watson recognized that this was a tale that should be shared. He probably wrote up his notes to a certain degree within a matter of days, and added them to an ever growing stack of narratives. Then, just a few months later – specifically on May 4th, 1891 – Holmes was presumed to have died at the Reichenbach Falls, which gave Watson even more motivation to recall the promise that he'd made on March 6th, 1881, at the end of *A Study in Scarlet*: "*Your merits should be publicly recognized. You should publish an account of the case. If you won't, I will for you.*"

As of the spring of 1891, Watson had only published two accounts of Holmes's cases, *A Study in Scarlet* (in late 1887, in the aforementioned *Beeton's*), and *The Sign of the Four* (in February 1890, appearing first in *Lippincott's Monthly Magazine*). With the idea of paying tribute to his fallen friend, Watson, assisted by his friend and literary agent, Dr. – and later Sir – Arthur Conan Doyle, approached the publisher of the recently formed *Strand* magazine – itself only in business since January 1891 – and arranged for some short sketches of Holmes's cases to be published, beginning with "A Scandal in Bohemia" on June 25th, 1891. The world was electrified – and soon after the obfuscations began to creep in – sometimes from carelessness or accidentally, and sometimes because Watson had no choice.

For example, from the distance of so many years, it's difficult to know exactly which names within The Canon are accurate, and which have been *adjusted* due to Watson's effort to protect the players. It's entirely possible that Jabez Wilson's identity was true as presented – for there is some argument that his modest pawn shop could only have benefitted by being associated with such an interesting story – Wilson could have dined out for the rest of his life on his version of it, were he able to overcome the personal embarrassment at his own gullibility. But as those initial two-dozen stories were published in *The Strand* between June 1891 and December 1893 (when "The Final Problem" appeared to a stunned and dismayed public), it's obvious that some facts must have been changed to protect those involved.

For instance, "The Boscombe Valley Mystery", which occurred in June 1889, was published in October 1891, just a little over two years later. It ends with a dying murderer's confession that is to be kept secret – and yet, here is Watson publishing it to great interest in a widely read magazine when the events were still somewhat fresh in the public mind. But some delicate obfuscation was occurring here. Try finding Boscombe Valley on a map. And if the location was disguised, then it's likely that the names were as well. What other information was smudged and altered to hide the specifics while providing the gist of the cases, while also making sure to highlight Holmes's brilliance?

Of course, if locations and the names of involved parties could be changed, then dates could be altered as well. There are a number of chronological inconsistencies within The Canon that can be blamed on all sorts of reasons – a misreading of Watson's handwriting by a careless typesetter is always likely. Certainly similar carelessness by Watson's Literary Agent was another reason, as he failed to pay enough attention to the preparation of Watson's works for publication while he was instead distracted by his own lesser-known efforts. And of course, Watson certainly made some intentional changes for reasons of discretion.

As early as the publication of *The Sign of the Four* in 1890, there are unexplained discrepancies. We know that the case occurs in 1888, because it says that 1882 was six years earlier. But then a letter, supposedly sent that first day of the investigation, is postmarked "*July*", while just a couple of chapters later, Watson comments that it's a "*September evening*". The internal evidence seems to set this case in September 1888, and the reference to July is likely a printer's error – Watson's short-hand notes probably said "*9*" when referring to the month that the letter was postmarked, but the printer read it as a "*7*".

Other dating errors can be found elsewhere in The Canon – simply examine "The Red-Headed League", where Watson says that he had called upon Holmes "*one day in the autumn of last year*". Since this adventure was published in *The Strand* in August 1891, most chronologicists place it in 1890. (This year is later confirmed in the story.) But then it gets tricky. Watson said it was "*in the autumn*". And yet, in regard to publication of the first advertisement for the League, Watson writes: "*It is* The Morning Chronicle *of April 27, 1890. Just two months ago.*" April is *not* two months ago from the autumn – and in just a few lines "*autumn*" is narrowed down to "*October*". The hapless client, Jabez Wilson, then reports that eight weeks have passed from his initial interview and hire by the curious League to that very same morning, when he decides to visit Holmes, after discovering this notice pinned at the office where he has been laboring:

The Red-Headed League
is
Dissolved
Oct. 9, 1890

For a Sherlockian chronologicist, this ought to be pure gold: An actual firm date as a jumping-off place. The day that Jabez Wilson visited Holmes was October 9th, 1890. But . . .

. . . the events of the story clearly take place on a *Saturday* – in fact, they *have* to occur on a *Saturday* to make any sense – and October 9, 1890 was a *Thursday*! So our solid date, the one fixed point we can grab when trying to date this case, is ephemeral.

And that throws the whole thing open to interpretation or adjustment. All of the major chronologicists still agree that "The Red-Headed League" occurs in October, and most – but not all – still put it in 1890. But in October 1890, some favor October 4th, or 11th, or the 18th – all Saturdays, but *not* October 9th. Gavin Brend will only say October 1890 without picking a specific day. Others choose entirely different years – Baring-Gould 1887 and Ernest Bloomfield Zeisler 1889 – and even then, they don't set it on October 9th, instead picking October 29th or October 19th respectively, because both are Saturdays.

And what to do about that pesky April reference when Jabez Wilson was initially hired, eight weeks before his visit to Holmes? It can't have been *April* as listed, but it could have been *August*. That fits, and the realization that someone – again, the typesetter at The Strand? The Literary Agent? – mis-read Watson's notes, perhaps taking the abbreviation *Au* for *Ap*, becomes the most likely explanation for this inconsistency.

So is this tempest in a chronological teapot due to careless errors, or did Watson have some reason for deliberately confusing the facts? Sidney Paget's original *Strand* illustration had the October date, which serves as a confirmation, seemingly showing *Oct. 9, 1890*:

was shut and locked, the name was new to him."

with a little square of cardboard hammered on to the middle of the panel with a tack. Here it is, and you can read for yourself."

He held up a piece of white cardboard, about the size of a sheet of notepaper. It read in this fashion:—

"THE RED-HEADED LEAGUE IS DISSOLVED. Oct. 9, 1890."

Sherlock Holmes and I surveyed this curt announcement and the rueful face behind it, until the comical side of the affair so completely over-topped every other consideration that we both burst out into a

"THE DOOR WAS SHUT AND LOCKED."

"'Well,' said I, 'the gentleman at No. 4.'

"'What, the red-headed man?'

"'Yes.'

"'Oh,' said he, 'his name was William Morris. He was a solicitor, and was using my room as a temporary convenience until his new premises were ready. He moved out yesterday.'

"'Where could I find him?'

"Oh, at his new offices. He did tell me the address. Yes, 17, King Edward-street, near St. Paul's.'"

"I started off, Mr. Holmes, but when I got to that address it was a manufactory of artificial knee-caps, and no one in it had ever

But a closer look (see next page) even brings that into question, as it isn't clear if the month is *Oct.* or something that maybe starts with an "*A*", or if the date is a *9* or a *4*. (As the image isn't reproduced brilliantly here, an independent investigation by the reader is strongly encouraged.)

And the date isn't the only possible obfuscation in this story. Jabez Wilson is initially interviewed by "the League" and subsequently employed for eight weeks at *7 Pope's Court, Fleet Street*. No such location can be found. (A much more likely candidate is Mitre Court, leading from Fleet Street to King's Bench Walk.) Strangely, while this address is changed, as is the location of Wilson's pawnshop in "Saxe-Coburg Square" (probably Charterhouse Square), another address listed in the narrative, 17 King Edward Street, is accurate and can be visited today – although the buildings look nothing like what was there in 1890.

In some cases, such as "The Second Stain", Watson avoided giving a year at all, being careful to avoid any hints as to when this sensitive matter occurred. (Sharp Sherlockian chronologicists, however, have mostly settled the question anyway.) In other cases, Watson provides specific dates that must be disregarded.

For instance, there's "Wisteria Lodge", which begins with Watson's statement that, "*I find it recorded in my notebook that it was a bleak and windy day towards the end of March in the year 1892 . . . .*" – which is clearly impossible, as at that point in 1892, Holmes had been presumed dead for ten months and was somewhere in the area of Tibet. This, too, is likely a misreading of Watson's notes, seeing the "*5*" in *1895* as a "*2*".

In *The Hound of the Baskervilles*, the inscription on Dr. Mortimer's walking stick indicates that it was presented in *1884*, and a little bit later,

Holmes refers to this date as "*five years ago*". Easy enough to do a little math and come up with a time-frame for *The Hound*: Autumn *1889*. And yet . . . .

If Watson met Mary Morstan in *The Sign of the Four* in September 1888, and certainly married her not long after (as well as purchasing a medical practice which would consume some of his time – although not all of it!), then how is it that he's still living in Baker Street in Autumn 1889, eating breakfast and with plenty of time to leave both Mary and his practice to go away for weeks, journeying indefinitely to Dartmoor in Sir Henry Baskerville's company?

And then there's "A Scandal in Bohemia", in which Watson states that he hadn't seen much of Holmes since his marriage, and he says that he's stopped by to visit "*on the twentieth of March, 1888*". So if he didn't meet Mary Morstan until *September 1888*, who exactly had he recently married several months before that?

And then there's "The Noble Bachelor", in which Lord St. Simon – Was that his real name, or was it obfuscated? – is listed as having a birth-date of 1846, and Holmes says that he's forty-one years old. A little basic math then tells us that this adventure occurs in 1887 – but at the start of the narrative, Watson explains that "*It was a few weeks before my own marriage, during the days when I was still sharing rooms with Holmes in Baker Street . . . .*" So we know that Watson met Mary Morstan in September 1888, but Autumn 1887 was just a short time before his marriage (NOBL), and he was already married in March 1888 (SCAN), and he was able to go away for weeks in Autumn 1889 (HOUN). Clearly there is conflicting information.

As a Sherlockian Chronologicist, I've long been satisfied with the obvious solution that Watson had a *first* wife before Mary Morstan. This first wife's existence somewhat clears up some of these chronological problems. It was William S. Baring-Gould who initially posited this first-wife's existence in *Sherlock Holmes of Baker Street* (1962), his brilliant biography of Holmes, naming her Constance Watson *née* Adams. Baring-Gould speculated that Watson, at the time of publication, adjusted the dates of those stories that occurred while Constance was alive, or didn't mention her by name, in order to protect the feelings of his second wife, Mary. Without knowing what was in Watson's heart, this explanation is as good as any – and goes to show that the Good Doctor was willing to obfuscate when necessary.

And now, turning this lumbering ship of an essay toward the theme of this current set of books, another obfuscation was used when discussing what has come to be known as *The Untold Cases*.

In "The Problem of Thor Bridge", Watson tells us that:

> *Somewhere in the vaults of the bank of Cox and Co., at Charing Cross, there is a travel-worn and battered tin dispatch box with my name, John H. Watson, M.D., Late Indian Army, painted upon the lid. It is crammed with papers, nearly all of which are records of cases to illustrate the curious problems which Mr. Sherlock Holmes had at various times to examine. Some, and not the least interesting, were complete failures, and as such will hardly bear narrating, since no final explanation is forthcoming. A problem without a solution may interest the student, but can hardly fail to annoy the casual reader . . . Apart from these unfathomed cases, there are some which involve the secrets of private families to an extent which would mean consternation in many exalted quarters if it were thought possible that they might find their way into print. I need not say that such a breach of confidence is unthinkable, and that these records will be separated and destroyed now that my friend has time to turn his energies to the matter. There remain a considerable residue of cases of greater or less interest which I might have edited before had I not feared to give the public a surfeit which might react upon the reputation of the man whom above all others I revere. In some I was myself concerned and can speak as an eye-witness, while in others I was either not present or played so small a part that they could only be told as by a third person.*

Thank heavens Watson maintained this amazing tin dispatch box, wherein can be found so many more incredible Sherlockian adventures beyond the pitifully few sixty of them that came to us by way of a detour across the First Literary Agent's desk. By some counts, there are over one-hundred-and-forty additional *Untold Cases* referenced in The Canon – the number goes up or down based on the interpretation of what was truly one of Holmes's cases, or if he was just referring to some affair in which he wasn't associated, or even if a missing comma means one case or two, (as in "*the repulsive story of the red leech and the terrible death of Crosby the banker*", which may be one case or two, and the same for "*the Addleton tragedy and the singular contents of the ancient British barrow*").

Over the decades, as lost Watsonian manuscripts have been discovered all around the world, some confusion has occurred when multiple versions of an Untold Case appear, leading some Sherlockians to wonder which is the actual *true* version, and which is a clever *fake*? As I explained in the foreword to *The MX Book of New Sherlock Holmes Stories: Some Untold Cases* (Parts XI and XII, 2018), there are over two-dozen legitimate versions of that most famous Untold Case *The Giant Rat of Sumatra* (as mentioned in "The Sussex Vampire"), and more have been added since then (listed here, in no certain order, except for the first):

- *The Giant Rat of Sumatra* – Rick Boyer (1976) *(Possibly the greatest pastiche of all time)*
- "*Matilda Briggs* and the Giant Rat of Sumatra", *The Elementary Cases of Sherlock Holmes* – Ian Charnock (1999)
- *Mrs. Hudson and the Spirit's Curse* – Martin Davies (2004)
- "The Giant Rat of Sumatra" – Leslie Charteris and Denis Green. [Originally broadcast on radio on July 31, 1944 as part of the *Sherlock Holmes* radio show, script reprinted in *The MX Book of New Sherlock Holmes Stories: XI – Some Untold Cases (1880-1891)* (2018)]
- *Sherlock Holmes' Lost Adventure: The True Story of the Giant Rats of Sumatra* – Laurel Steinhauer (2004)
- *The Giant Rat of Sumatra* – Paul D. Gilbert (2010)
- "The Giant Rat of Sumatra", *The Lost Stories of Sherlock Holmes* – Tony Reynolds (2010)
- *The Giant Rat of Sumatra* – Jake and Luke Thoene (1995)
- "The Adventure of the Giant Rat of Sumatra", *Mary Higgins Clark Mystery Magazine* – John Lescroart, (December 1988)
- "The Case of the Sumatran Rat", *The Secret Chronicles of Sherlock Holmes* – June Thomson (1992)
- "Sherlock Holmes and the Giant Rat of Sumatra", *More From the Deed Box of John H. Watson MD* – Hugh Ashton (2012)
- "The Case of the Giant Rat of Sumatra", *The Secret Notebooks of Sherlock Holmes* – Liz Hedgecock (2016)
- "The World is Now Prepared" – "slogging ruffian" (Fan Fiction) (Date unverified)
- "The Giant Rat of Sumatra", *Sherlock Holmes: The Lost Cases* – Alvin F. Rymsha (2006)
- "The Giant Rat of Sumatra" *The MX Book of New Sherlock Holmes Stories: XII – Some Untold Cases (1894-1902)* – Nick Cardillo (2018)
- "The Giant Rat of Sumatra", *The Oriental Casebook of Sherlock Holmes* – Ted Riccardi (2003)

- *Sherlock Holmes and the Limehouse Horror* – Phillip Pullman (1992, 2001)
- *Lestrade and the Giant Rat of Sumatra* – M. J. Trow (2014)
- "No Rats Need Apply", *The Unexpected Adventures of Sherlock Holmes* – Amanda Knight (2004)
- *The Shadow of the Rat* – David Stuart Davies (1999)
- *The Giant Rat of Sumatra* – Bob Bishop (2019)
- *The Giant Rat of Sumatra* – Daniel Gracely (2001)
- "The Giant Rat of Sumatra", *Resurrected Holmes* – Paula Volsky (1996)
- "The Mysterious Case of the Giant Rat of Sumatra", *The Mark of the Gunn* – Brian Gibson (2000)
- *Sherlock Holmes and the Giant Rat of Sumatra* – Alan Vanneman (2002)
- "The Giant Rat of Sumatra" – Paul Boler (2000)
- "The Giant Rat of Sumatra" [Radio Broadcast, April 20th (or June 9th), 1932, July 18th, 1936, and March 1st, 1942] – Edith Meiser (Now Sadly Lost)
- "The Case of the Missing Energy", *The Einstein Paradox* – Colin Bruce (1994)
- "All This and the Giant Rat of Sumatra", *Sherlock Holmes and The Baker Street Dozen* – Val Andrews (1997)

The list shown above is by no means a complete representation of all the Giant Rat narratives. These are simply the ones that I found when making a pass along the shelves of my own Holmes Collection. The thing to remember is that *in spite of every one of these stories being about a Giant Rat, none of them contradict one another or cancel each other out to become the only true Giant Rat adventure.*

The fact is that there are lots of different versions of the Untold Tales. Some readers, of course, don't like this and will never accept *any* of them, since the First Literary Agent didn't handle them between Watson and the light of day. Others, however, only wish to seek out the sole and single account that satisfies them the most, therefore dismissing the others as "*fiction*" – a word that I find quite distasteful when directed toward Mr. Sherlock Holmes. Quite a few are more interested in favoring one version or the other because some certain author wrote it, and they hope that naming this work as their favorite will earn them a fleeting glance for their flattery.

My approach is that if the different versions of the Untold Cases are Canonical, and don't violate any of the same rules that define what types of tales appear in these anthologies – no parodies, no anachronisms, no actual supernatural encounters, and no portrayals of Holmes as a murderous sociopathic creep with absolutely no redeeming value whatsoever – then they are legitimate.

Some people can't get their minds around the fact that there were a lot of Giant Rats (in one form or another) causing mayhem in London during Holmes's active years. In fact, each of the Giant Rat adventures listed above is very different – comedy or tragedy, police procedural or gothic horror, London-based or set in the country – and in any case – and here's the point – *Watson obfuscated!*

Not counting printer's errors or Literary Agent carelessness, Watson changed all kinds of things to make the story interesting to general readers – as compared to how Holmes wished his cases could be presented: Dry factual studies for the interested study. ("*You have attempted to tinge it with romanticism,*" he complained some months after the publication of *A Study in Scarlet*, "*which produces much the same effect as if you worked a love-story or an elopement into the fifth proposition of Euclid.*")

Watson brilliantly knew his audience, and he wrote the narratives in a way that would immediately capture the reader's attention, and yet not cloud the issue with too much of the lesser-known tedium of detective work, and also leaving out other unrelated matters which would cause confusion.

For example, when preparing a story for publication, he would often give the impression that it was the only thing currently on Holmes's plate, and possibly the only matter to occupy his attention for weeks, when in fact Our Heroes were constantly busy, and the many cases in which they were involved were truly a *tangled skein.* Watson sometimes gave the impression that Holmes went for weeks in fits of settee-bound depression between cases, when in fact he was constantly working in this or that direction upon a number of cases, each intertwined like incredibly complex threads in *The Great Holmes Tapestry*.

In spite of constructing the stories so that they were self-contained, some mentions of other cases – the Untold Cases – were unavoidable, and as students of The Master's life and methods, we can only be grateful for the small bits that we've been given and what we can glean from them. And one thing that we know by way of stories from Watson's Tin Dispatch Box is that sometimes he obfuscated by naming different cases with the same general catch-all title – an obfuscation that, for whatever reason, was important to him.

For example, there have been many different and varied stories about Holmes and Watson's 1894 encounter with Huret, the Boulevard Assassin, as mentioned in "The Golden Pince-Nez". Confusing? Contradictory? Not at all. Holmes simply rooted out an entire nest of *Al Qaeda*-like French assassins during that deadly summer. There are a lot of tales out there relating the peculiar persecution of John Vincent Harden in 1895. No problem – there were simply a lot of tobacco millionaires in London during that time, all peculiarly persecuted – but in very different ways – and Watson lumped them in his notes under the catch-all name of *John Vincent Harden.* Later Literary Agents, not quite knowing how to conquer Watson's personal codes and reverse-engineer who the real client was in these cases, simply left the name as written.

There is no need, as some do, to pick a favorite version of the Giant Rat or the Abergavenny Murder. There's no reason to think that only one of the variations is true, thus negating or neglecting the others. A previous favorite iteration doesn't have to be scrapped because some other later Literary Agent's attention and approval must be sought and curried. Watson took the time to record *all* of these versions, and all can be respected and enjoyed as part of the overall life of Sherlock Holmes. There are many already out there to read, and over sixty more of them in this collection, and still others to come in days ahead. Enjoy, and take Watson's Obfuscations as an important part of playing The Game.

* * * * *

"Of course, I could only stammer out my thanks."
– The unhappy John Hector McFarlane, "The Norwood Builder"

As always when one of these sets is finished, I want to first thank with all my heart my incredible wonderful wife of over thirty-two years, Rebecca, and our amazing son and my friend, Dan. I love you both, and you are everything to me!

Also, I can never express enough gratitude for all of the contributors who have donated their time and royalties to this ongoing project. I'm constantly amazed at the incredible stories that you send, and I'm so glad to have gotten to know all of you through this process. It's an undeniable fact that Sherlock Holmes authors are the *best* people!

The contributors of these stories have donated their royalties for this project to support the Stepping Stones School for special needs children, located at Undershaw, one of Sir Arthur Conan Doyle's former homes. As of this writing, these MX anthologies have raised nearly $70,000 for the school, with no end in sight, and of even more importance, they have helped raise awareness about the school all over the world. These books are making a real difference to the school, and the participation of both contributors and purchasers is most appreciated.

Next is that group that exchanges emails with me when we have the time – and time is a valuable commodity for all of us these days! I don't get to write as often as I'd like, but I really enjoy catching up whenever we get the chance: Derrick Belanger, Brian Belanger, Mark Mower, Denis Smith, Tom Turley, Dan Victor, and Marcia Wilson.

There is a group of special people who have stepped up and supported this and a number of other projects over and over again with a lot of contributions. They are the best and I can't express how valued they are: Larry Albert, Hugh Ashton, Derrick Belanger, Deanna Baran, S.F. Bennett, Craig Stephen Copland, Matthew Elliott, Tim Gambrell, Jayantika Ganguly, Paul Gilbert, Dick Gillman, Arthur Hall, Stephen Herczeg, Craig Janacek, Mark Mower, Will Murray, Robert Perret, Tracy Revels, Roger Riccard, Geri Schear, Brenda Seabrooke, Shane Simmons, Robert Stapleton, Kevin Thornton, Charles Veley and Anna Elliott, I.A. Watson, and Marcy Wilson.

I also want to particularly thank the following:

- *Otto Penzler* – I've been aware of Otto for ages, and I owe him so much in so many ways. When I was a lad, I obtained, by way of my parents as gifts, two of his reference books, *The Private Lives of Private Eyes, Spies, Crime Fighters, and Other Good Guys* (1977) and *Detectionary* (1977). These books provided incredibly useful information to me, an urgent mystery fan living in a part of the country where such information was rare. Later, when I had my first job, I used my very first pay check to purchase *The Solar Pons Omnibus* from Otto's justly famous Mysterious Bookshop.

  In the mid-1980's while in college, my deerstalker and I were able to visit New York and the store (in its original location) for the first time, and it was something of a religious experience. At some point I was brave enough to correspond with Otto (back in the days of letters instead of emails), and later, when I wrote my own first book of Holmes pastiches, *The Papers of Sherlock Holmes* (2011), he sold copies of that mostly unseen original edition in his store.

  Over the years I've been back to New York on a few occasions, always stopping in at The Mysterious Bookshop – which, along with West 35th Street to see Nero Wolfe-related locations, and the same for Ellery

Queen's house on West 87th Street, were really the only places I cared about visiting in NYC. In January 2020, I was able to visit Manhattan again, for the first time in over a decade, for my first journey to the Sherlock Holmes Birthday Weekend celebration.

Each year at that time, there's an Open House at The Mysterious Booskshop for Sherlockians, and that, along with the famed BSI Dealer's Room, were the main reasons that I'd always wanted to go during the January event. The Open House was planned for Friday, but I went to the store on Thursday afternoon, so I could look around at my leisure – particularly along the entire back wall of the store, covered entirely in Sherlockian shelves – in order to accumulate a stack of Holmesian items for my collection.

When I was finished, I rather timidly asked an employee if Otto was there, and if I could say hello. In a moment the man himself came out and greeted me most wonderfully, making me feel at home and as if I'd been a weekly in-person visitor to the store for decades. Before that afternoon was over, he had me sign a massive stack of books that I'd written or edited – fulfilling a personal bucket list item of being able to autograph books at The Mysterious Bookshop – and he'd also taken me down to the incredible basement collection of still more Sherlockian items. I was also able to visit with him some the next day during the more hectic official Open House.

I'd tried for years to recruit him to write a foreword for these books, and I'm very happy that I've finally succeeded. Otto Penzler is a living legend, and has done so much for so many. It's wonderful to have him be part of these books, and a personal thrill for me. Thank you, Otto.

- *Roger Johnson* – I'm more grateful than I can say that I know Roger. His Sherlockian knowledge is exceptional, as is the work that he does to further the cause of The Master. But even more than that, both Roger and his wonderful wife, Jean Upton, are simply the finest and best kind of people, and I'm very lucky to know both of them – even though I don't get to see them nearly as often as I'd like, and especially in these crazy days! In so many ways, Roger, I can't thank you enough, and I can't imagine these books without you.

- *Steve Emecz* – When I first emailed Steve from out of the blue back in 2013, I was interested in MX re-publishing my previously first book. Even then, as a guy who works to accumulate *all* traditional Sherlockian pastiches, I could see that MX (under Steve's leadership) was *the* fast-rising superstar of the Sherlockian publishing world.

  The publication of that first book with MX was an amazing life-changing event for me, leading to writing and then editing more books, unexpected Holmes Pilgrimages to England, and these incredible anthologies. When I had the idea for these books in early 2015, I thought that it might, with any luck, be one small volume of perhaps a dozen stories. Since then they've grown and grown, and by way of them I've been able to make some incredible Sherlockian friends and play in the Holmesian Sandbox in ways that I'd never before dreamed possible.

  All through it, Steve has been one of the most positive and supportive people I've ever known, letting me explore various Sherlockian projects and opening up my own personal possibilities in ways that otherwise would have never been possible. Thank you Steve for every opportunity!
- *Brian Belanger* – Brian is one of the nicest and most talented of people, and I'm very glad that I was able to meet him in person during the 2020 Sherlock Holmes Birthday Celebration in New York. His gifts are amazing, and his skills improve and grow from project to project. He's amazingly great to work with, and once again I thank him for another incredible contribution.

And last but certainly *not* least, **Sir Arthur Conan Doyle**: Author, doctor, adventurer, and the Founder of the Sherlockian Feast. Present in spirit, and honored by all of us here.

It was particularly unusual editing this collection through the spring and summer of 2020, as the world faced a deadly globe-spanning pandemic. Many people ended up being stuck at home, and my first thought was that a number of them will take advantage of that newly carved-out time – although for terrible reasons – to write. However, it soon became apparent that everyone's lives were turned upside down to greater or lesser degrees, and even if they had the *time* to write something, they didn't necessarily have the *heart* to do so. I was concerned that this set of anthology volumes might not have enough stories – at least not to the level which many have come to expect and look forward to.

But as people found their footing and their spirits, the stories began to arrive, more and more of them – both for these books, and also for other Sherlockian anthologies that I'm editing at the same time. It's been amazing, and it showed that in these dark times, people have found great comfort in writing about Holmes and Watson and those bygone days, and also that they want to share those tales with others who will find comfort as well.

For everyone who dug deep and found a way forward and is a part of this collection, and for all of you who will be reading it, thank you so much.

As always, this collection has been a labor of love by both the participants and myself. As I've explained before, once again everyone did their sincerest best to produce an anthology that truly represents why Holmes and Watson have been so popular for so long. These are just more tiny threads woven into the ongoing Great Holmes Tapestry, continuing to grow and grow, for there can *never* be enough stories about the man whom Watson described as "*the best and wisest . . . whom I have ever known.*"

David Marcum
September 25th, 2020
The 132nd Anniversary of Holmes asking Watson what he makes of Dr. Mortimer's walking stick . . . .

Questions, comments, or story submissions may be addressed to David Marcum at

thepapersofsherlockholmes@gmail.com

Foreword
by Otto Penzler

Everyone reading this extraordinary series of books discovered Sherlock Holmes in his or her own way. No one wrote of that magic moment more compellingly than Ellery Queen (in this case, Frederic Dannay, one of the two cousins who collaborated under that memorable pseudonym) in his essay collection, *In the Queen's Parlor*.

When I was ten years old, P.S. 9, my elementary school in the Bronx, offered what I imagine was common in those long-ago days but which I fear may be less common now: A library class. Once a week, our teacher would walk us down to the school library, where Miss Gibson would talk about how to use about books. We were shown the proper way to open a book, learned the rudiments of the Dewey Decimal System, and absorbed her cheerful talks about the wonders of reading.

For the second half-hour of the class, we were allowed to take any book we wanted off the shelf and read. I pulled down an anthology (title unknown, now), scanned the table of contents, and was intrigued by the title "The Red-Headed League."

I was instantly captivated by this Sherlock Holmes fellow and by the utterly bizarre notion of someone with a particular hair color being hired to copy the *Encyclopaedia Britannica*. Totally immersed, I was crushed when the bell rang, signaling the end of the class.

No, no, no. Wait. I have to know what this all means.

Mercilessly, the class was herded back to home room. Never was a class so eagerly anticipated as the following week's library hour.

Eventually, I learned that there were more stories like this one. I bought *The Complete Sherlock Holmes*, the Doubleday edition with that magical introduction by Christopher Morley, read it more than once, and lamented that there weren't more stories about that odd but curiously likable detective.

Happily, I was wrong. There *are* more stories, and this volume – all the volumes in this worthy series – prove that life always offers hope.

Otto Penzler
New York
April 2020

"Fond of Queer Mysteries"[1]

by Roger Johnson

We're all fond of queer mysteries, of course, or we shouldn't bother with this book. And among the queerest (strangest, oddest, most curious) are those that are merely referred to by John H. Watson in the chronicles of his friend Sherlock Holmes. We're familiar with sixty of the great detective's cases – the number of which we know nothing is potentially infinite, of course, but these particular volumes are concerned with the investigations that are tantalisingly hinted at, sometimes with a little detail.

That detail can provide the spark that our imagination needs to re-create one of those unpublished stories. Who among us hasn't wondered what could possibly link a politician, a lighthouse, and a trained cormorant? Or just why Holmes claimed that world was not yet prepared for the story of the giant rat of Sumatra?

Some of the hints relate to the solving of a crime. There's the Camberwell poisoning case, "*in which, as may be remembered, Holmes was able, by winding up the dead man's watch, to prove that it had been wound up two hours before, and that therefore the deceased had gone to bed within that time – a deduction which was of the greatest importance in clearing up the case*." That's reasonably straightforward. More problematic is the "*dreadful business of the Abernetty family, which was first brought to Holmes's attention by the depth which the parsley had sunk into the butter upon a hot day*". Naturally we wonder what was so dreadful, and what the parsley in the butter had to do with it – but more puzzling yet is how the "*dreadful business*" was *first* brought to Holmes's attention by that seemingly trivial matter. (The essential clue, I fancy, is that the parsley *did* sink into the butter. Real parsley would tend to float, even on melted butter, which suggests that there was something very wrong with one or the other on the Abernetty dining table.)

A few of the unpublished accounts fall into the category of the seemingly impossible, such as that of the cutter *Alicia*, "*which sailed one spring morning into a patch of mist from where she never again emerged, nor was anything further ever heard of herself and her crew*." Or the enigma of Mr. James Phillimore "*who, stepping back into his own house to get his umbrella, was never more seen in this world*".

Even more nightmarish is the mental image of "*Isadora Persano, the well-known journalist and duellist who was found stark staring mad with a match box in front of him which contained a remarkable worm said to be unknown to science*". (The female name "*Isadora*" has encouraged more than a few to assume that Mr. Persano was a cross-dresser, ignoring the obviously correct explanation that it's a persistent mis-spelling of the male "*Isadore*".)

The hints that Watson offers range from the sensational to the apparently mundane. On the one hand, for instance, are the "shocking affair of the Dutch steamship, *Friesland*, which," he says, "so nearly cost us both our lives", and "*the repulsive story of the red leech*", which may or may not be connected with "*the terrible death of Crosby the banker*". On the other are the case of Mrs. Etherege, who recommended Holmes to Mary Sutherland because he had found her husband so easily "*when the police and everyone had given him up for dead*", and that of Mary Morstan's employer Mrs. Cecil Forrester, whom he helped "*to unravel a little domestic complication*". They all offer the opportunity to take up residence at 221b Baker Street, where we can let our imaginations work in tandem with the logical methods of Sherlock Holmes

Roger Johnson, BSI, ASH
Editor: *The Sherlock Holmes Journal*
July 4th, 2020

NOTES

1. "Well, Mr. Holmes, what do you make of these?" he cried. "They told me that you were fond of queer mysteries, and I don't think you can find a queerer one than that." (Hilton Cubitt, in "The Dancing Men")

Conan Doyle's Legacy in 2020
by Steve Emecz

Undershaw
Circa 1900

The MX Book of New Sherlock Holmes Stories has now raised over $65,000 for Stepping Stones School for children with learning disabilities and is by far the largest Sherlock Holmes collection in the world.

Stepping Stones is located in Undershaw, the former home of Sir Arthur Conan Doyle and the fundraising has support many projects continuing the legacy of Conan Doyle and Sherlock Holmes in the amazing building.

One of the amazing projects we have funded is to enable Stepping Stones to be a broadcast location for video using Zoom, including live events. This has proved to be incredibly timely with the global pandemic restricting movement and access. We have even broadcast a live Sherlock Holmes play *A Scandal In Nova Alba* by Orlando Pearson from Undershaw, including fans from over a dozen countries around the joining live!

The Doyle Room at Stepping Stones, Undershaw
Partially funded through royalties from
The MX Book of New Sherlock Holmes Stories

MX Publishing is a social enterprise – all the staff, including me, are volunteers with day jobs. The collection would not be possible without the creator and editor, David Marcum, who is rightly cited multiple times by *Publishers Weekly* and others as probably the most accomplished Sherlockian editor ever.

In addition to Stepping Stones School, our main program that we support is the Happy Life Children's Home in Kenya. My wife Sharon and I have spent seven Christmas's with the children in Nairobi. Due to the global pandemic we won't be visiting Africa this year.

It's a wonderful project that has saved the lives of over 600 babies. You can read all about the project in the second edition of the book *The Happy Life Story.*

There are very interesting parallels between our work in Africa and the UK – we have Zoom video enabled Happy Life, saving them tens of thousands of dollars in saved travel between their locations. In 2020 we're very proud of our *#bookstotrees* program where every book bought on our *www.mxpublishing.com* website results in a tree being funded at Happy Life. We reached our target of 1,000 trees (and still going) in August.

Our support of both of these projects is possible through the publishing of Sherlock Holmes books, which we have now been doing for twelve years.

You can find out more information
about the Stepping Stones School at:

www.steppingstones.org.uk

and Happy Life at:

www.happylifechildrenshomes.com

You can find out more about MX Publishing
and reach out to us through our website at:

www.mxpublishing.com

Steve Emecz
August 2020
Twitter: *@steveemecz*
LinkedIn: *https://www.linkedin.com/in/emecz/*

A Word From Stepping Stones
by Jacqueline Silver

Undershaw
September 9, 2016
Grand Opening of the Stepping Stones School
(Photograph courtesy of Roger Johnson)

"*Life is infinitely stranger than anything which the mind of man could invent.*"

– Arthur Conan Doyle

Apt words to describe current times.

Amidst the uncertainty and ongoing challenges, I have been fortunate enough to have recently joined the wonderful community here at Stepping Stones School, where we spend our days in this wonderful building, steeped in literature and history. Now that the school has re-opened after lockdown and we are reunited at Undershaw, we appreciate our school, our surroundings, and each other even more than ever. It is a privilege to lead the school and its students into the future in this most treasured setting, and we remain ever-grateful to you for your ongoing support.

Jacqueline Silver
Headteacher, *Stepping Stones,* Undershaw
September 2020

Sherlock Holmes (1854-1957) was born in Yorkshire, England, on 6 January, 1854. In the mid-1870's, he moved to 24 Montague Street, London, where he established himself as the world's first Consulting Detective. After meeting Dr. John H. Watson in early 1881, he and Watson moved to rooms at 221b Baker Street, where his reputation as the world's greatest detective grew for several decades. He was presumed to have died battling noted criminal Professor James Moriarty on 4 May, 1891, but he returned to London on 5 April, 1894, resuming his consulting practice in Baker Street. Retiring to the Sussex coast near Beachy Head in October 1903, he continued to be associated in various private and government investigations while giving the impression of being a reclusive apiarist. He was very involved in the events encompassing World War I, and to a lesser degree those of World War II. He passed away peacefully upon the cliffs above his Sussex home on his 103rd birthday, 6 January, 1957.

Dr. John Hamish Watson (1852-1929) was born in Stranraer, Scotland on 7 August, 1852. In 1878, he took his Doctor of Medicine Degree from the University of London, and later joined the army as a surgeon. Wounded at the Battle of Maiwand in Afghanistan (27 July, 1880), he returned to London late that same year. On New Year's Day, 1881, he was introduced to Sherlock Holmes in the chemical laboratory at Barts. Agreeing to share rooms with Holmes in Baker Street, Watson became invaluable to Holmes's consulting detective practice. Watson was married and widowed three times, and from the late 1880's onward, in addition to his participation in Holmes's investigations and his medical practice, he chronicled Holmes's adventures, with the assistance of his literary agent, Sir Arthur Conan Doyle, in a series of popular narratives, most of which were first published in *The Strand* magazine. Watson's later years were spent preparing a vast number of his notes of Holmes's cases for future publication. Following a final important investigation with Holmes, Watson contracted pneumonia and passed away on 24 July, 1929.

Photos of Sherlock Holmes and Dr. John H. Watson courtesy of Roger Johnson

The MX Book of New Sherlock Holmes Stories

Part XXIV: Some More Untold Cases (1895-1903)

Sherlock Holmes and the Return of the Missing Rhyme

by Joseph W. Svec III

Once upon an evening dreary, while I pondered, not much weary,
Over quaint and enthralling volumes of my favorite lore –
While I read – avoiding sleeping – suddenly there came a peeping,
of the circus."

Sherlock Holmes and the Return of the Missing Rhyme

Once more I sat with pen in hand
Staring out across the land.
The rhyme was gone, completely lost.
It must be found, at any cost!

To complete the poem, unfinished still,
It seemed an ever endless hill.
The night was quiet as a mouse.
Somewhat like an Empty House.

I could turn to the Norwood Builder,
Even though it would bewilder,
More than a troop of Dancing Men,
If not now, who knows when.

Perhaps a Solitary Cyclist
T'would be an arbitrary catalyst.
Or if I see the Priory School
I'd have a really fiery tool.

I could perhaps ask Black Peter
If he has a right crack meter.
Or maybe Charles Augustus Milverton,
Per chance an agent of justice, Pinkerton.

If numbers increase the odds from lowly ones

I could then hire Six Napoleons,
Or maybe only Three Students.
Then I could claim or plea prudence.

If I found a Golden Pince-Nez,
It could lead to the rhyme I says.
But just like the Missing-Three Quarter,
I don't have it like I ought'er.

I could look in the Abbey Grange,
To get there, take a cabby strange.
But just like a Second Stain,
My rhyme, it must be reckoned slain.

Again I stand, my rhyme is lost.
It must be found at any cost.
When things do look their utmost bleak,
Sherlock Holmes is the one to seek.

The Comet Wine's Funeral
by Marcia Wilson

(The following was hand-written with a badly bent pen on paper of low quality, typical for the market following The Great War, and fastened by a copper pin to a document that exists as a torn fragment with the letters 'A' *and* 'el' *remaining.)*

Executor's Prelude:

Readers familiar with the inimitable style of Dr. Watson and his worthy agent will notice this account falls out of true for the usual typical style of Sherlock Holmes's cases. It would be a stale writer who did not explore in different formulae – the recipe for success in everything is the desire to press against one's own limitations. Circumstances of the case are much of the reason why this tale is both of interest, yet deemed by Mr. Holmes "petty enough" to be consigned to the oblivion of Dr. Watson's dispatch-box. This case is thus presented for its unique qualities, for we feel that here, Mr. Holmes is being unduly harsh upon himself. We agree that the artist is his own worst critic, and that this may not be the stuff of international legend. Nevertheless, it does stand on its own merits, and its relationship to The Bruce-Partington Plans (however tenuous) ought to persuade you of its worth. Do recall, my friend, that Watson ably wrote of terra firma *he had never walked upon – the wild salt flats and harsh eastern hollows of North America became real to his readers.*

Do forgive this argument and understand that I am not disagreeing with your assessment. It is quite correct should it be a case that stands alone. I humbly propose this is not the case. This is one of Mr. Holmes's "mayfly cases" that served to challenge his intellect and please him with its unexpected twists and turns. We in the field of intelligentsia can happily read written accounts of masterly chess-games and puzzles of logic worthy of Heraclitus. This transition between characters in the role is no different.

With Warm Regards,

I observe with the flawless clarity of looking backwards that Sherlock Holmes's brain was starved for cases in the years following his miraculous return. He spoke rarely of his exile, yet he could not have been idle, as his powers were never greater as they were in 1895. He had managed to keep his intellect whet against whatever stones came his way, but they were often unfulfilling, limited, and dangerous for his secrecy. He permitted me the honour of naming myself his physician, but I ought not to have been clouded by the happiness of having my old friend back. I did not see the signs and thought him too prone to work himself into a state of exhaustion, not understanding the terrifying stagnation that threatened his brain.

Holmes was in such a state and confined to convalescent rest when Inspector Lestrade came to call late, dropping into his lap a case that had given him a nesting-doll of aggravation piled upon aggravation. There was nothing for it, he groaned, but to move to the final aggravation: Could Sherlock Holmes possibly solve a case without leaving his chair?

"That remains to be seen," Holmes replied testily, though his grey eyes sparkled with the hopes of a puzzle that for his *ennui*. "I have not heard this hypothetical case yet." He leveled his pipe-stem to our guest with a stern frown. "Presuming I do, Lestrade, I ask only that you refrain from any comparisons to Poe."

"Who?"

"Excellent. Tell me what happened."

Lestrade pulled out a small purse and placed it on the table to the side – his usual method of paying Holmes without broaching the vulgar topic of money.

Holmes plucked up the fee and returned it to the surprised man's hand. "My fee, Friend Lestrade, will be the release you give me from this intolerable prison. Now: Begin!"

Contrary to common belief, a police inspector does not spend his entire life orbiting around his desk and leaving it only when he is firmly leashed to a case. He is often about in the crowd, but alas, often set apart by his plainclothes, which Holmes has described disparagingly as "boring enough to stand out, no matter what crowd he stands in!"

There is stone-cold truth to this observation, and that day Lestrade resented the requirements of his duties which had him wearing the same slatey-blue suit that "half of London's roughest" associated with a policeman's uniform-in-mufti. He was tired and aching, but knew himself fortunate: A collision with his own police-cab and an out-of-control milk-cart had sent a packed cab (including his two constables) to the surgeon's care. Case concluded, Lestrade was headed back for the office alone.

In some parts of the world a man can wander freely. Regretfully for Lestrade, he was not in one of those mythical kingdoms.

It began, he noted grimly, with a side-glance caught through the swarm of humans. The glance became a blink. First one, then two faces turned away. These were small but important things to notice if a copper did not want to find himself in hard circumstances on the wrong side of

Borough High Street – an innocent enough neighborhood but beleaguered. It was a convenient thoroughfare for less pleasant elements.

Lestrade aimed to blend in rather than seek trouble. He kept his head down slightly, his brim low in the fashion of a struggling shop-keeper who must dress slightly above his income if he is to command respect and customers. He pushed his way through the muddled anarchy of the crowd, shoulder tilted forward, one hand on his plain walking-stick, and the other hand discreetly stuffed into the side-pocket where most men kept their valuables. Above all, he carried the demeanor of a man who had no intention to linger. He had business elsewhere. This recipe normally worked well, but the entire day had felt "off-kilter", and he was anxious to be done with it.

Lestrade had at least another ten minutes' walking left to reach the safety of the nearest station: It was a negligible address on Rope Walk Street in the epicenter of the Red Kings' Territory.

He was beginning to think hard about his options – and his odds. The Red Kings were a normally discreet gang of thieves, gamblers, smugglers, and intelligence-collectors. It is criminal coalitions like these that give the larger fiends their power, in the same way a man is a greater sum of potential trouble-making when he has all his limbs and faculties in working order. In return, the Kings saw themselves as a pleasant, gentlemanly organisation, a crust above the usual "low thugs" that used the Borough as a right-of-way. They were not an overly violent collection, but a recent invasion by their rivals, The Hangmen, had left them bloodied and spoiling for revenge.

Lestrade knew almost nothing about The Hangmen. They were one of the countless criminal groups sprouted in the wake of Moriarty's death and resultant power-vacuum. Inspector Gregson would know, what with his growing collection of cases off Saffron Hill, but Gregson wasn't here.

What Lestrade did know of The Hangmen was grisly and inspired him to buy his produce from the vegetable-beds of trusted grocers. He began returning the gazes in the crowd, his hidden hand clenched tight.

There – he almost missed it. A flash of white cloth poking out of the top of a man's coat: Two white carnations in the button-hole – an emulation of the crumpled white cap of the Crown's Hangman – the mark of the gang! That man was swallowed up in the crowd, but he was replaced by another. The nervous citizens of the Borough were making room. Women pressed closer to their menfolk. An old man clutched his hand around the leash-loop he held against a weathered old fighter of a mastiff. Lestrade shuddered. The rough street-urchins simply vanished. A new trouble was glimpsed in the sea – an everyday labourer, underdressed for the cold weather with a buttonless coat. A red scarf hung around his neck tied with a diamond-knot: One of the Kings. His eyes were blue and hard and unforgiving and, to Lestrade's unbelieving horror, contemptuous of a passing Hangman. He spat before the man's shoes and sneered.

The little detective could smell war. It was as thick as a laundry room, and the King had just punched a bull in the nose!

Seconds later, the inspector's world burst into a stew of screams, shouts, and fists. Shop-glass shattered. Those who weren't fighting for blood or escape were joining in the mindless free-for-all. Whatever could be picked up from the street (including pieces of the street) flew in all directions. Lestrade was almost relieved – the wait was over. He pushed hard against the bodies squashing him in all directions and held his walking-stick in both hands like a bar. He was small, but no larger than the underfed folk he fought. He struggled until his shoulder hit the wall of someone's shop – *Yankee Photography*. The window was already smashed, but iron gates locked out looters. He strained to see some sort of order in the boiling crowd.

The gangs were openly fighting. Carnations clashed with blood-red neck-ties and cravats tied in heart or diamond knots. Metal flashed in a King's fist – a German military half-sword broken at the tip and filed to an icepick point. The owner was a Red King and he grinned from ear to ear as he struck upwards, punching the tip of the blade through the bottom of a Hangman's jaw and into the throat, coring it with the ease of a housewife with an apple. The body gushed blood as it hit the road to be trampled underfoot with the other unfortunates. The rectangular street-stones flowed red.

Lestrade was horrified at the merry murderer, but by the most misfortunate happenstance the King glanced his way. The two locked gazes and with it passed a complete understanding: The King turned to Lestrade. Those who did not get out of the way in time were fodder.

Lestrade put his back to the shop and raised his stick. He could faintly hear the alarm of police-whistles but knew many of the coppers were inexperienced in riot control. They were too likely to act impulsively, with no more design than the rioters flinging fists and street-brick. His first thought was to remove this dangerous man from the crowd.

Lestrade side-walked with his back to the shop, unable to go faster than a crawl. He had to fight through panicky bodies. He heard cries for help, and it went against his grain to not respond. More important, he knew, to get this killer away from the others. If he was marked for assassination, so be it.

He was far slower than the King but at last he hit a corner. The alley-way held the fringe of the crowd and boiled with people running away (or to) the centre. He risked another look behind. The short sword was gone from the King's hand. Its hard outline shaped the assassin's coat under an arm. Lestrade continued to back away, caring less about the King's constant, evil smiling than he was with getting them both away from vulnerable civilians.

The alley opened. Lestrade took a risk and ran through the open spot, glancing behind him to find the King hounding his heels. He was lengthening his legs as he stalked his prey on the balls of his feet. Lestrade ran almost to Rope Walker Street before he could stop and face him.

A church-bell chimed, and Lestrade was astonished to realize the better part of an hour had passed in the melee. The King was growing near, shoulders hunched forward, almost prancing in a silent, straight line to the inspector. The killer's hat was gone. His red scarf hung messily off his throat in a horrid imitation of a slit throat. He had a jagged scar down one side of his face, the skin silvery against a nasty looking rash of dark purpling skin, like a port-wine stain birthmark, spreading up from under his collar to circle both ears. The left hand was missing the first two fingers, and for the first time Lestrade could see the man limping similarly to himself.

Lestrade moved his stick to a defensive pose and jammed his police-whistle to his lips. The shrill blast burnt his own ears. The King ignored the sudden risk and dropped a clasp-knife out of his sleeve and into his right palm. The knife clicked open to reveal a small sheep's-foot blade. He would have to get very close to Lestrade. They were made for slicing, perfect throat-cutters, easily hidden and discarded.

"You will halt," Lestrade announced. "You are under arrest for murder – "

The King only shrugged, which Lestrade found quite insulting. He frowned at the strange, overweening confidence of the man. He had seen the man strike first. How would he react if he were placed on the defence? He decided to find out and closed the distance between them, keeping his eyes firmly on the man's face as he continued with the process of law and declared the Right to Silence.

The King was unaffected by Lestrade's recitation, and only looked impatient. Lestrade made his last step into the zone of combat a half-step backwards, digging his heel into the street and swinging his walking-stick in an interceptive arc to the man's hand. The King had assumed Lestrade would strike at his weapon, not the hand that held it. He growled when the full force of Australian bull-oak deadened the nerves in his wrist and Lestrade saw a flash of gold teeth inside the thug's mouth. How very odd, Lestrade had time to marvel as the blade clattered to the street. He kicked it away as the King pulled his good hand into his coat and returned his original murder weapon to duty.

The man had shown full confidence with his right hand and now he was showing every bit of comfort with using his left. Lestrade disliked fighting left-handed men as they seemed to have an advantage against him, but little about his situation spoke in his favour. The King had clearly decided it worth the risk to kill a policeman and if he were to escape custody for it, he would have to move very quickly. Someone might answer Lestrade's whistle.

Lestrade winded it again and kept the whistle between his teeth as the man suddenly leaped to Lestrade's right side, his weapon sliding into an upwards arc for the wrist. It was too like the killing-stroke Lestrade had witnessed and he jumped backwards blindly, hoping he would stay upright.

For the first time, the King made a sound – a thin, choked-up sort of laugh, and his sword came full force on the middle of Lestrade's stick. The stunned expression that followed almost made Lestrade laugh hysterically, for the weight of the sword had not hacked the stick in half as he had expected. The break in concentration was barely enough time for Lestrade to answer him with a blow to the head. The King stumbled, and Lestrade finished him with a *coupe de vache*.

"And that," Lestrade concluded wearily, "is why I am here today: To say, 'Thank you again, Dr. Watson, what a wonderful Christmas-present.'" He then faced me with the full force of his considerable scowl as he pointed to a tiny chip in the wood. "Followed by, 'It would have been nice if you had told me it could take a direct sword-stroke!'"

"It had not crossed my mind," I admitted. "I chose it because it is the hardest wood in the world."

"Really? I thought you chose it because my wife told you I needed a stick 'harder than his own yed if it exists'."

"I could hardly disappoint a lady."

Through our exchange Holmes had been smoking his pipe and making no secret of his amusement. "Has the riot dispersed?"

"Oh, very much. The Office suspects it was a calculated instigation on part of the Kings to humble The Hangmen." Lestrade managed to imitate the stultified tones of a detached bureaucrat.

"Ah, that was not in the news." Holmes picked up the evening *Times*, which had managed to typeset the event before printing.

"I doubt the morning papers will add much more than what we've got." Lestrade leaned back in his chair and accepted Holmes's cigar and my ice-pack to the black eye he could not recall collecting in the riot. "There were five reported casualties and more we won't know about. They are a proud sort over there. They'll crawl home and heal themselves or die without telling anyone." His mouth tightened. "And this pleasant fellow we call 'Goldtooth', because he will not give his name and doesn't seem to be in any of our records of past offenders."

Holmes grunted. "His pockets?"

"Full of money, paper chemist packets all broken-up and leaking, and some oddities. Speaking of pockets: he had more than he had any right to have done."

"Professional thief?" I wondered.

"A courier, more likely," Holmes said. "One who delivers the goods. He doesn't sound subtle enough for light-fingered detail."

"Yes," Lestrade agreed. "We found a few objects of interest, and we confiscated his clothing – it reeked!" He held up his notebook. "I made a list of everything."

With the sobriety of an anatomist, Holmes dissected the written list that described the man's clothing and holdings. The man's shabby suit was riddled with pockets of all possible sizes.

Many of the chemist packets were in poor shape. Moisture had collected inside the coat and the contents were leaking.

"And there was no name to identify the chemist?"

"None. We even looked inside the packets."

I tapped the page where it listed *Erythroxylum Coca, Pur. Ref.*

"This explains why your murderer had no fear. Enough of this may confuse the brain into a delusion of immortality. I should not speculate without testing, but the actions of your killer suggest the cocaine has been purified to the highest possible level."

"How high would that be?" Lestrade asked uneasily.

"Higher than what you may find in advertised products. You are aware that cocaine in various strengths are easily purchased in medicines and quacksalvers' bottles. Most of these are in a lowered dosage – just enough to cultivate a warm, pleasant experience that will encourage the buyer to return for more."

"This fellow's packets are higher and worser."

"Yes. A chemist will always use the lower dose when mixing, should he have the choice – he wants his fee but also to use up as little of his stock as possible. With something as insidious as cocaine, the higher the dose the more the patient is at risk for unpleasant, debilitating, and even fatal effects."

I expected Holmes to make a comment, for I was keeping myself professionally focused on Lestrade's case and not speak a poor word on Holmes's own use of the drug, but he was busy frowning at a chip of wood that had fallen out of Lestrade's notebook.

"Oh, that." Lestrade shrugged. "I found that in one of the pockets. It didn't seem poisoned, so I brought it with me. Do you know what it is, Mr. Holmes?"

Holmes plucked up the card as though to wring free its secrets. It was a pressed and stiffened veneer of rose-stained wood at the dimensions of a calling-card. Holmes tipped it back and forth under the lamp so we could see a small design: A rude woodcut rendition of a tree with large, fleshy leaves on the left side, and a blocky house on the right.

"Lestrade," Holmes cleared his throat, "your investigation may improve at the Orchid Hotel."

"What! Why, that's Gregson's case!"

I was watching Holmes's face and thus saw his sharp, grey eyes ignite. "Gregson!" he shouted. "Lestrade, you haven't told us everything!"

"Well, I . . . I didn't think," Lestrade muttered, completely red-faced.

Holmes leaned forward with a childlike anticipation. "Pray tell us what you know of Gregson's case."

Lestrade openly hesitated. "I could," he said with trepidation, "but if you'd rather hear it from Gregson himself, I can get him here posthaste."

"Splendid! Do so at once! Watson – summon Mrs. Hudson if you please. I may be confined to my rooms but there is no reason not to invite a few policemen to supper."

I believe I was the only one to hear Lestrade under his breath, "Oh, this will be a charming supper indeed."

It was the previous day from Lestrade's collision with the King. Inspector Gregson was walking to work when a boy jumped out of a cab and raced to his side.

"Sir," the boy breathed. "I was told to get straight to Mr. Gregson, and you're the only one I know."

Gregson frowned into the boy's face, memorizing the details, and matching them up in his memory. "Why, you're Jacky. Old Catercorner's son!"

"Yes, sir. 'S him who needs you, sir. 'S important. At the Orchid Hotel. A dead man. Mr. Woodhouse says it was just an accident, but he – me da – he says it ain't and nobody won't believe him! Please, come quick sir!"

Gregson tightened his hat about his head. "We'll go there now." He ordered the cab to wait as he collected some bobbies. He needed PC's familiar to his methods before the hotel tried to clean up the evidence. Hotel murders were a policeman's migraine, as the stakeholders were desperate to keep good reputations. Gregson thought them fools – a murder properly verified and advertised was the stuff to bring in patrons, not chase them out.

(Gregson was a man of the world – or, in Lestrade's words, "cynical as an eel but mercifully prettier" – and Gregson never wanted Lestrade to know how touched the compliment left him).

Catercorner, or, "Cade Corner", never asked for police help. He had started out as a bobby and would have risen if he had not made a terrible mistake. Coming to work reeking of beer was grounds for anyone's dismissal, and the poor sot had accepted enough pints to qualify for bribery.

Dismissal and disgrace brought the weak and corruptible former PC to sobriety, and if none of his fellows in blue would be caught dead with him after his kick, a stream of anonymous donations had brought him to the Temperance Halls, his first ribbon, and a new life running a coffee-stall. The Brotherhood kept to its own, and he had not named names in his downfall.

Over the pots of corrosive black drink, Corner found a new calling in setting up his stall in the vulnerable space between the Orchid Hotel's front steps by the south-facing corner that wended to the alley and servant's entrance. He profited from more than the hotel's staff: The Orchid's guests worked long hours in the gentlemanly arts of Opera, horses, dogs, cards, and drink. A hotel made money on thirsty patrons, but the good men needed to sober up, fast, between their social engagements. His sharp eyes were an excellent judge of character for transactions, and he accepted all currencies. Many a foreign diplomat had taken advantage of his policy, unaware that their miniscule zloty or ban dropped from an anxious hand in an improper hour was an excellent forecast of Embassy rumblings. He took any payment with a daft smile, poured coffee into their trembling hands, and memorised the faces clutching his cups to their lips. The police scolded him in public for small grievances and smuggled bags of coffee-beans under his table to keep the news and caffeine going.

Gregson was grudgingly familiar with the Orchid Hotel. It was an ageing dowager duchess, the sort of yellow stone architecture that had seen absolutely everything the world had to offer and still managed to look almost completely respectable. It had always been owned by the Woodhouses, a "money-royal" dynasty descended from Elizabeth's era when it was the new fashion to live in a house of wood. It was almost as old as the days when Saffron Hill worked in saffron.

The farmers, workers, and the Woodhouses (the merciless graders of the precious red thread), drank infinite cups of cinnamon and milk thickened with flour of the common *orchis mascula* tuber. It supplied the need for a warm, nourishing drink and a reliable succession of sturdy sons. (Properly treated it also magically granted daughters and fought off evil.)

As the saffron business died, the hotel sprang from the foundations of the original counting-house. The Woodhouse clan turned their specialty into Turkish *salep* and charged a healthy price per cup to maintain London's virile male successions. * Thus did the hotel thrive as a respectable curio of the past, and the rooms suited its clientele of spies, barons (of industry, not title), ambassadors, exiled foreign nobles, and diplomats surviving on their country's narrow budget or looming dismissal.

One would have to go to the Isle of Dogs to see a more successful stew of mischief jumping like so many fleas out of human brains. Gregson consoled himself that at least it had a decent glass of red – Woodhouse's own creation, a planted vineyard carved out of an abandoned lot and walled in.

He did not like the current reigning heir, Kermit Howard Woodhouse. The man was too bland to be real, with his bloodless passions dedicated to his comet wine. He had to be hiding something – It was only a matter of time before his name emerged in a bloody crime, and Gregson ached to be the man to crack him.

The cab pulled up and everyone poured out. Catercorner's tiny coffee-stall was unattended by the steps so he must still be holding the fort down. Gregson marched into the front entrance of the hotel with Jacky anxiously leading. The doorman instinctively tried to block him for his name and purpose, but a single glance of Gregson's glacier eyes froze him in place. He gulped and backed down.

Gregson took in the foyer and its connecting steps to the upper levels of rooms. Catercorner was standing with his arms folded over his caved-in chest and a rare stern expression popping from his dark eyes between his deep brow and deeper line of black beard. By stance and glower he forced a weakly circling satellite of hotel staff from getting closer to a sprawled lump of canvas on the road-wide marble steps. It said more than it ought that the guests were ignoring the scene. A few curious glances were all they gave it on their way to business. With each passing foot-fall, more evidence walked away.

"I held 'em off as much as I could," Catercorner warned. "Good to see you, Mr. Gregson." Like a magician's spell, the words broke the will of the orbiting staff – they fled.

Gregson sighed for the loss of evidence. The staff had covered the dead man with a tarpaulin (small favours), but things were obviously very wrong. He turned the full force of his eyes on the Orchid's guard and concierge. John Baker, a poorly-chosen knight of his realm who enforced his own morality on the quaking staff even as he pocketed the tips and gratuities for the boot-blacks, maids, and bellhops.

"Who moved the body!"

Baker, half Gregson's age but deluded in his assessment as an equal, bristled. "We did not move it!"

"Oh, really? He was found dead, nicely draped over the front steps on his back, straightened out with his feet together and arms folded over his chest? I say, were you hoping I'd bring you a white lily and a set of candlesticks to complete the scene?"

Baker flinched. "Well, I wasn't here when he fell."

"Ah, he *fell*." Gregson nodded sagely, then paused as a thought appeared to strike him. "Who told you he fell?"

"Er . . . no one! I – I – just – "

"You have gloves on, I see. Nice and clean, I take it?"

"Wh – of course!"

"Put him back."

"Eh?"

"*Put. Him. Back.* I want him in the same position, in the same place, in the same way as he was when you 'found' him. Now."

Unbelievingly, Baker looked at the covered corpse, then at Gregson.

"Before he stiffens up if you please! Sometime between yesterday and Easter!" To Jacky: "Find Woodhouse. I want to talk to him now. It is a police investigation and if I have to find him, I shall arrest him for obstruction!"

Baker and the boy leaped to obey.

Catercorner observed this with nostalgia misting his eye. "I'd forgotten what a pleasure it was to see you at work, sir."

Breathing hard and looking faint, Baker stumbled backwards from his task and fell against the rail.

"You there!" Gregson growled at Catercorner. "Does that look the same?"

"It does, sir."

"It'll have to do."

Gregson knelt for a closer look. The man was tall and well-shaped with a patchy brown scalp and his hat upside-down on the step above his left outflung hand. Suffused with congealing blood in the lowest point, the dry, peeling grey flesh was already a sorry sight, the mouth locked open in a last gasp.

Gregson had been in the force long enough that he often wondered if he had seen more dead men than not, and the bluish asphyxiation was a familiar sign of a man struggling to breathe around a heart attack. The purpled rash that clustered like a bunch of grapes was unusual. In the meantime, he tightened his own gloves about his fingers and carefully went through his usual examination of pockets, neck, wrists, ears, and chin. The necktie interested him – it was old silk overdyed to a vulgar red and tied in a heart-knot. When he lifted the knot for a better look, cheap dye blushed his gloved fingertips.

But it was the pockets of the man's coat that stirred his cold heart: Large square packets of thinly waxed paper, much-wrinkled and cracked. The seal was violated and an ugly, milky discolouration like cream cheese left in the sun had soaked through the paper and through the pockets and stained cakes of its unknown matter into the man's trousers. Unlike Lestrade's packets, the writings on these papers were rubbed and soaked to illegibility.

Gregson ignored the protests over his head and unbuttoned the man's shirt. The skin was akin to the face: Dry, blotchy, peeling . . . and again, the queer purpling rash like clusters of grapes.

As a man who had occasionally brought home more than his work, Gregson was familiar with all crawling pests, and even if one dipped bedbugs in thistles, none caused this sight. If this was poison, he needed to know.

Fortunately, the hotel was forward-thinking enough to employ a doctor, and he was just now scrambling to the scene, still chewing breakfast. He wrested a napkin off his neck whilst balancing a General Surgeon's stone-heavy medical bag. The man had every appearance of a fussy old maid, and already shaved, combed, and brushed. Gregson cheered to see it. Such men were fiends for detail.

"Jacky found me," the doctor panted. "You are Mr. Gregson? I would be pleased to make your acquaintance in happier circumstances. I am Dr. Bald Nordstrom, the consultant for this hotel."

They shook hands over the corpse – not a first for Gregson. "Pleased to make your acquaintance. If you feel confident enough in giving me your medical opinion Johnny-on-the-spot, it may point us in the right direction." With that he pointed to the rash.

Dr. Nordstrom's black eyes widened. "Vasculitis in such a young man?" He stroked his yellow beard and leaned until his nose almost touched the dead man. "Oh, dear." He hastily pulled a pen from his pocket and timidly poked at the packet. "Sir, you have not touched this?"

"Certainly not."

"This is . . . ." Again he leaned over, almost touching his nose and sniffing loudly like a very strangely shaped bloodhound. "This is powdered cocaine. So much! Why would he carry it in paper? It needs to be in glass!"

“Interesting,” Gregson drawled. “This man needs a quick autopsy, and we need a room. Where is your practice?”

“Stop!” Lestrade lifted his hand. “Are you telling me Woodhouse actually pulled money out of his own pockets and paid for a doctor to live on-site in his hotel?”

“Horrible, isn’t it?” Gregson agreed. “I hate to think of him in possession of any human grace outside of unctuous.”

His little rival shook his head in scorn. “Either the worm’s turned or a head-injury got him some morality.” He suddenly brightened at a new thought. “Or a ruse to hide something worse.”

“That’s the spirit. Think positively, Ratty.”

“It isn’t like you to just trust a man that fast.” Lestrade’s eyes narrowed shrewdly. “What did you have on him?”

Gregson grinned. “He could dye his hair yellow and keep out of the sun and wear a northern name, but he was a caste from somewhere. Probably a quarter-Lascar. That slice of the eyelid gave him away. He knew I knew, and he about fell over me to make me happy. Scared of Woodhouse, that’s clear.”

Holmes grunted. “I have a little knowledge of the man, Woodhouse. Watson and I attended his lecture on crop-bearing plants and their relationship to Man. He was as accurate as a scalpel and sadly as sterile.”

“He lacks the ability to see Man’s altruistic motivation,” I explained, for I had almost no memory of him, save for how offended his words had left me. Even now, I recalled my thunderclap of realization: Woodhouse did not bother with the starving peasant struggling to feed his family with infected rye, or the grief of unending drought that inspired savages to desperate means.

“I believe it, gentlemen,” Gregson mused thoughtfully when we gave him our observations. “His only passions are his wines. Got to admit, it’s excellent, considering the disadvantage of our English Vintages.”

“Hah! Just a moment.” Holmes rose to his feet and pursued his collection of notes. As it had been a month since I last urged him to re-audit the system known only to him, I stayed out of the *paperkrieg*. “Continue your narrative, Gregson. I am listening.”

“Eh, well, I know a few things about wine,” Gregson bragged. “Woodhouse lived in Naples and made a fortune on top of his family’s fortune by discovering a new method of wasp pollination for figs. When his grandfather died and left him the hotel, he used the sales proceeds to return home. He loves grapes, but this is the worst climate for growing wines south of Hadrian’s. Blight, mildew, disease – you name it, our wine must pass through the fires of crop failures, frosts, and droughts. He allegedly named his winery for '*comet wine*' because of the superstition that wines are their best in comet years."

Gregson was rattling off an interesting subject easily, but Lestrade quietly pinched himself on the wrist to stay awake.

"Anyroad, that's his story. No matter how poorly his rivals, he always manages a small, fine crop of red wine in that postage-stamp-sized vineyard, and he will not give up his secret, beg though his competitors do." He smirked at Lestrade's baffled expression. "Are you following this?"

"Possibly."

"I forget. Your people never did learn to love the grape."

"I'm sorry, Euclid. Was there a reason to love Romans enough to give up the cider besides underfloor heating and plumbing?"

Lestrade's riposte was spoiled by a knock on the door. It was the boy with a message addressed directly to him, a large black '*A*' slashed with china marker over the paper.

"Time to see what the old bonecutter says." Lestrade braced himself and sliced the lip open with his knife.

"Good God, man, you couldn't do better than Archer?" Gregson was stunned. To us: "Archer's the Yard's antediluvian fossil-ancestor of your profession, Doctor. Legend has it he uses messenger-pigeons. Don't even think of putting him in the same room as a telegraph – or a telephone!" To Lestrade he shook his head, knowing there are few things as grating as an enemy's pity. "You couldn't find anyone else?"

"No," Lestrade said curtly. "I think he ate them."

"How did you convince him to use a runner – and good heavens, is that type?"

"It was easy," Lestrade said tightly as he unfolded quires of paper. "I told him to move with the times and have Bibber transcribe. It makes him feel good to have his own secretary." He read quickly, frowning as he tapped his fingers against the knife.

"Lestrade," I felt moved to ask, "is that a sheep's-foot blade?"

"Yes." Lestrade said without looking up. "I found it in a gutter on Rope Walk." He met Gregson's amused eyes with an excellent card-player's gaze. "Goldtooth expressed to me it wasn't his and he'd never seen it before in his life."

"And you took the word of a murderous assassin," the other drawled.

"Well, we're not all savages."

Gregson struggled to keep his composure. "True, that."

"It is possible I may have misunderstood him." Lestrade admitted. "I've gotten out of practice with signing language. But if he wants it back he can ask – " He slapped the papers down with a sudden curse. "No! Can you believe it?" he shouted. "He waited until the end to tell me that Goldtooth died of a heart attack during examination! Now how am I supposed to find out who he is?"

"At least you got a good knife out of it," Gregson commiserated. "Might want to take it to church and get the sins cleaned off first."

Holmes had surfaced from the Sea of Papers. With his elbow he pushed aside his plate and dropped a stack of notes and scrap-books in its place. "He may still be useful, Lestrade. Keep your letter close. I shall read it in a moment. Watson, what do you say for the rash?"

"If this were a classroom-exercise, my teachers would expect me to declare it a negative and severe reaction to prolonged exposure to cocaine. The problem is accumulative. A small amount every week can eventually cause this rash. It is a common-enough sight for any physician, but the severity? That is what makes it so unusual. Gregson, what was Nordstrom's summary?"

Gregson shrugged. "I thought it odd the hotel would hire their own doctor, but not give him an office bigger than a hat-box. We were moved to a side-room down the hall where the servants come in and out – it leads from the back of the hotel through the gardens and out the gate in the wall. I should add that the gate is solid wood and no one can see in or out of it.

"Nordstrom examined him on the table. I didn't tell him he was likely a Red King. His verdict was accidental poisoning by the leaking envelope of cocaine. He says there was enough in each packet to kill an ox. The damp soaked it out and into his skin it went. He suspects the man was a previous victim of the drug, and so it hit him harder than normal.

"But what really got him was when he put a bit of that powder under the microscope. I'm an old knacker, Mr. Holmes, but I don't mind telling you I was surprised."

"Look, look, look! Here!" Dr. Nordstrom grabbed Gregson and tried to pull him to the lab-table. "Look please!"

Gregson sighed and lumbered to the table. Privately he was tickled that the man had found something – but it would never do to show he was pleased about it. He set his best eye to the piece and squinted. "What am I looking for?"

"Mites! Legs!"

Gregson scowled, played about with the ocular adjustment, and found the sample was packed with little oval bodies garlanded with many short, translucent legs.

"Charming. What are they?"

"Mites! Flour mites!"

Gregson stared at him. "Did you say . . . *flour mites*?"

“The cocaine itself is dangerously pure. But somehow it mixed with bread-flour.” Dr. Nordstrom bobbed his head up and down in his eagerness. He looked so much like a street-urchin stuffed full of sweets and strong coffee that Gregson tried not to slap him.

Gregson stopped speaking and drank a long glass of water. Lestrade had been in the middle of pouring honey on a roll. He looked hard at it, and carefully returned it to his plate with a frozen expression.

“I asked him how he knew the cocaine was contaminated with flour and not the other way around,” Gregson continued drily.

“Dare I ask?” Lestrade muttered.

“‘Because the mites are all dead.’”

“This is a grave matter,” I said angrily. “The chemists mix doses according to set standards of weight. If drugs are being stretched it may not appear significant, but it will be many times as dangerous as it ever was.” In my agitation I jumped to my feet. “Where is this poison going? Patients will confuse their physicians with abnormal effects. Chemists will supply the wrong dosage! Weakened drugs are often cheaper, and this hurts the honest chemist! I have seen too many cases where a cheap chemist gives the customer exactly what they pay for! And for what? The poor folk are not wealthy enough to complain and their very poverty makes their protests immaterial!”

“Be at peace, Doctor.” Lestrade lifted both hands. Gregson followed suit. The two were united in devotion to their craft. “We understand the severity – it has taken three lives that we know of, for I consider the murdered Hangman a victim of this trade.”

“It is a hard thing to not have answers,” Gregson added. “I fear more will die.”

“Perhaps,” Holmes interjected. “We may request the local morgues for unusual deaths. Both men had the grape-cluster purpling typical of acute cocaine vasculitis. Gregson, Lestrade led us to your case, but it is my belief that your hotel will be crucial to this investigation.

“Lestrade, if I may ask this of you – your tenacity in digging answers from barren soil could be put to the test. Can you go to the morgues?”

“I can.”

“We are looking for deceased Red Kings with vasculitis or other signs of severe cocaine exposure. I habitually partake, but not in the quantity or quality that is murdering these men.

“For now let us continue with the story. Gregson, I believe you were contemplating violence upon Dr. Nordstrom?”

The urge to slap Dr. Nordstrom was halted when, without a knock, Mr. Woodhouse walked into the room.

The hotel's owner was a tall, healthy man with clear, unblemished skin typical of those who may leave the fumes of London at will. His hair was the same bronze as his hazel-lit eyes, and a short, prim mustache his only adornment. He was dressed for a morning-out in a dove gray suit with tails and white gloves, hat in hand, with his tie-pin, cufflinks, and watch-chain of palest white gold. There are those who argue the validity of the phrase "too handsome", and Mr. Woodhouse was the argument's exhibit.

"Baldy," he said without introduction, "I hear there's been some trouble?" He lazily turned his gaze to Gregson. "Ah. Are you the police?"

Gregson ignored the insult. "A man has dropped dead in your hotel. That makes it a police matter."

Woodhouse shrugged. "The man was not one of my guests. We host a different standard."

Behind Woodhouse, Catercorner was standing behind him pretending to puff an invisible pipe: In the signals of the Brotherhood the message was clear: Woodhouse was "full of puffery" – lying.

"Excellent," Gregson said coolly. "I'll be sure to bring that up as I question your guests."

This was not met happily. "I beg your pardon? Have I not just told you – ?"

"This is the 'slow season' for your hotel. You should have less than a hundred souls, not including your staff and groundskeepers."

"Winery," Woodhouse snapped in dismay. "I have vintners."

It was Gregson's turn to shrug. "We'll be taking the body with us in due time. The sooner we finish, the sooner you can return to your affairs."

"Well! I am confounded that our government is so willing to pour its funding into such paltry matters."

"Ah, but is that not what vintners do? Pay a day's wage, no matter if they show up early or late?" He smiled. "PC Bradley will accompany you. He's more than capable of fending off any pests that might want to plague you with questions. I hear the journalists are on their way." The perfect face paled and Gregson mentally congratulated himself on cruelty well spent.

"You're a man in a thousand, Gregson," Lestrade saluted ironically.

"Course I am." Gregson lit one of his small cigarettes. "I've held enough cards to know when a man's overplayed. He wouldn't look at the dead man."

"Well, if he wasn't a patron, how did he get inside the hotel?"

"Catercorner says he stumbled past him and up the steps like he was shaking-drunk, pouring everything he could into getting inside the hotel, like he was trying to get help. Pushed Baker aside like a fly."

"And he died before he could find the help he sought."

"Which was most likely Woodhouse, even if there's nothing to pin on his donkey. No name or identity, but he wore the knot of a Red King's Heart Faction. Their territory's over an hour-and-a-half on foot from Rope Walk. We've seen the gang in Camden – not many, but enough.

"Our man of mystery was seen around the hotel, and twice he bought coffee from Catercorner. He thinks the man was one of the seasonal hands for Woodhouse's harvests."

Holmes rubbed his jaw in thought. "Most interesting."

"I'm now I'm all plumbed out of news until tomorrow when my contacts return with their reports." Gregson flicked his dead tobacco into the grate with a pout. "Stuck waiting – it's feast or famine."

Lestrade nodded with his eyebrows, agreeing at the aptness of Gregson's cynicism.

"I shall do what I can from my prison, gentlemen. Will you return tomorrow? Excellent! Come again for supper if you please – and send word if anything emerges beforehand."

"A sad case peppered with wasted lives." Holmes passed me a rueful look. "If only my physician would approve a small journey outside."

"Your physician would bar the door," I said sternly. "Come, Holmes! This problem cannot be beyond you. Be patient and feel the frustration and aggravation our friends must endure – you may be temporarily limited in your journey for information, but that is the definition of their very work."

"All solutions need data," he grumbled, but I could tell he was flattered.

Having bound him to his word, I put the rest of my evening to a new novel by the fire, leaving Holmes to pore over his notes. He was still reading through his scrapbooks of crime when I retired for bed, but the effects of a peaceful night were shattered at five o'clock the following morning: Gregson had returned, pounding on the door with the terrified hotel doctor and a tearful Jacky. Catercorner was missing and believed dead.

Dr. Nordstrom had given Jacky a restorative on the way. He was beginning to feel his effects as Holmes ushered the boy to the settee where he could rest with his feet up. To my eye, the lad was grieving sorely and trying too hard to be brave.

"First thing I did when they found me was search the hotel again," the big Yarder growled. "And I went over the vineyard with a comb! But we found nothing. Let them tell you what happened."

"He found something, Mr. Gregson," Jacky persisted as he wrung his cap. "I dunno what. He picked something off the floor right by the dead man – I think it was under him – and he saw it when he was moved. And then I had to find the doctor and Mr. Woodhouse, an' I forgot it a bit."

"Keep going, Jacky," Holmes soothed. "We are listening. Remember everything you can."

"I ast' him when we were both back outside and he said, 'Don't worry, it's for Gregson.' So we went back to sellin' coffee, and it was startin' to get dark. The lamps lit on the hotel first, then the street, and he told me to finish packing up and he'd be back soon. He went around the corner o' the hotel where the servants come in – it leads 'em through the gardens you know – An' a few minutes later, I heard a gun go off!" He looked at Dr. Nordstrom helplessly.

"I was closing up my practice." Dr. Nordstrom looked hardly calmer than his patient. "I passed Mr. Corner in the hall and said a good-evening, and he said, 'It is for some,' and I thought he was strange, but he kept walking and opened up the door to the gardens as if he owned the place."

Gregson looked achingly sad. "He forgot he wasn't a copper."

"He shut the door to the gardens after him very quiet and careful, and I thought I should go see . . . and I went as far as to touch the knob on the door when I heard a pistol." Dr. Nordstrom went chalk-white at the memory. "I could not move. I was frozen-cold. Then I thought there might be an accident and I was the doctor.

"I flung the door open, and Mr. Woodhouse was standing in the vineyard with his hands in his coat. I could see him because he was still in his morning-clothes and he was very pale in the darkness. He asked me what I wanted. I told him I heard a shot. He said I imagined it. I asked where Mr. Corner was and he said I was a fool, there was no one else there."

The poor man gulped. "The . . . the vineyard was all shadow and l-lumps of blackness on the ground. I didn't see him, but I smelled powder in the air. I know I heard a revolver. A small one. Like a *.32*."

"That is specific," Holmes said in surprise.

"There have been duels in the vineyard," the doctor answered darkly. "I was in military. I think I was hired to treat secret wounds. I have treated duelists. And . . . card-sharps. They use guns that are small – small as toy." He held his fingers about four inches apart.

Gregson cursed. "Those damned Belgian poppers! They started making 'em back in the '70's. Nasty things – Lestrade got shot by one in his first year on the force."

"I did what?" Lestrade said from the door. He limped in the room, leaning heavily on his stick. "Good Lord, I was feeling guilty about waking you up."

"A moment please, Lestrade." Holmes excitedly moved to the doctor again. "What happened next?"

"He asked me if I had a match. He had come out for smoking and forgot his match-book. I – I was afraid. I said no, I was sorry. I shut the door. I ran outside, and Jacky was trying to run inside the hotel but Baker – kicked him away!"

"Da always said to run to you if there was trouble," Jacky sniffed.

"I could not leave him," Dr. Nordstrom explained.

"Lestrade," Gregson sighed. "Catercorner's missing. He went on a hunt for clues at the vineyard and never came back. I hope you have better news."

Lestrade's sallow face turned grey. "I don't know," he confessed. "It isn't good. I communicated to every morgue I could find between the hotel and Rope Walk. I found three more Kings with the same rash."

"Most curious," Holmes muttered. "What else did you learn?"

"Well, one of the men was mute. He used a bit of roof-slate and an old bit of lump chalk to write with. We used them in our old school . . . they're useful enough and you can nick them off a building-site, but they scratch more. I had a hunch and rubbed some regular chalk over the slate." Lestrade held out the sliver, and on it we could see a jumble of glyphs, the strongest being the most recent: A childish rendition of the very same card Holmes had found in Lestrade's notebook, and a cluster of dots with a trailing tail – the sort seen in children's books on shooting stars or comets.

"Woodhouse is easily read," Gregson set a thick finger to the second image. "A flying bunch of grapes? – ah, no! *Comet wine!*"

"Gentlemen, it is time for a search warrant."

"That's all I needed to hear," Gregson boasted. "We're off."

"What about Jacky?" Lestrade blurted. "Dr. Nordstrom can come with us."

"Jacky will stay here," Holmes said. "Mrs. Hudson is unlikely to have gone back to bed. A little food and the fireplace can do wonders for calming the nerve."

Holmes's advice was sound, but a string of nonstop communications between the inspectors and ourselves melted from confident to angry, and then finally hopeless. If Catercorner hadn't been a devoted father to his child, the procedure would have been delayed, but Gregson and Lestrade risked every contact as well as their reputations to push for a warrant. He had left behind his only livelihood and son.

That was reason enough for foul play, but though the police searched the hotel from tip to toe, there was no sign of the missing man nor any of foul play. Nor was there a single gun found that could fit Dr. Nordstrom's confident description.

Discussing a man's murder within earshot of his child was not acceptable. Jacky was sent to a bolthole where his safety was guaranteed.

For two days this was endured by all. Through it smiled Woodhouse, and if Lestrade could admit to temper, Gregson was at the boil. At last, Lestrade begged Holmes to think of something.

"We've searched every inch of that hotel. Even the crawlspaces, the attics, and the sewer-lines. If we don't find him – " The little professional clapped his mouth shut and looked away.

"He's laughing at us!" said Gregson. Red with rage, the big man held out a bottle of wine. "Oh, and when someone told him you were a consultant to the case, he asked me to pass on his regards to you!"

Holmes's brow rose. "May I open it?"

Gregson's jaw dropped. Lestrade forgot he was lighting a cigar and yelped as the match burned to his fingers.

"No, by all means. Have it with my blessings!"

"I would not make light of your comrade's fate. It is still information, and who knows what may trip Woodhouse? Gentlemen, you know my methods. I have hopes that our foe will think himself too clever. If I am to expose him, I must examine all clues." The policemen nodded, mollified and a little ashamed for their low spirits.

"I'm sorry, Mr. Holmes." Gregson sank into the nearest chair like a man approaching his own death. He fumbled for his bottle-flask, which I knew contained tea boiled down to a thick syrup instead of strong drink.

"No, you don't." Lestrade pulled it away. "You do not need any more of that," he scolded. "Not if you want to keep your stomach."

"Says the man who can drink cider without dying." Gregson tried to taunt, but his heart was gone.

Holmes examined the bottle thoroughly, then carefully opened the capsule. His sharp nose bent close and he sniffed the cork, frowning.

"Does anyone know which grapes are cultivated?"

Lestrade threw a confused glare at Gregson, who responded dully. "Reds. His advertisements claim they're from South Wales, where the Romans originally planted."

"White wines were for elites," I supplied.

"Hmm. Watson, do you recognise this bouquet?"

I smelled the cork and confessed myself baffled. "A sweet red with an odd . . . how to describe it? This wine has been . . . mixed with something . . . floral."

"Fortified?" Lestrade spread his hands to show he was completely in the dark.

Holmes slowly straightened. His gaze had changed from focussed to distant. The cork dangled in his fingers. I was used to this sudden change in thought, but our comrades were not, and their gaze grew ever more concerned as the clock ticked.

"Lestrade!"

The policemen jumped at the whip-crack of Holmes's voice.

"The card in your notebook. Give it here!"

Lestrade fumbled to obey and managed to hand the card of the Orchid Hotel to Holmes without dropping it.

Holmes snatched it up and glared in fury. He took another sniff of the cork and when he lifted his head again, his pale face had gone flat and cold.

"You are looking at the greatest fool in England."

Now we all stared at him. Holmes whirled. His tails struck his watch-chain, and he marched to one of the open books scattered on the floor. *Agriculture of England and Ireland* was flipped from page to page until he stopped, reading something with his lips moving silently.

"Go back." Holmes slapped the tome shut. "And this time, take shovels to the vineyard."

"We saw no disturbed earth," Lestrade protested.

"This is a fig tree." Holmes pointed to the crude woodcut of the tree on the card. The fleshy shaped leaves were indeed fig. "Woodhouse was growing figs and grapes. Figs in London!"

"Here," Gregson exclaimed. "I saw no fig trees!"

Holmes stabbed the book with his long fingers. "Woodhouse blended his grapes with figs – how better to ensure he would have a crop every year when the others failed? You gave me the facts and like a fool I failed to see them!"

Holmes's white face was flushed with colour. "In my years of exile, gentlemen, I wandered through the wonders of the globe, but I was never so surprised as the day I stumbled into a small market in a valley in northern Germany. There I bought a punnet of figs so fresh and soft they glowed with dew.

"'How is it,' I begged, 'that figs can be brought from the south so quickly?' The farmers roared with laughter and explained they were local. 'Funeral Figs'.

"'Funeral Figs' was their play on words, and it delighted them to show me the trick of their Roman forefathers. When growing fig-trees in a cold climate, they must be buried like a loved one every winter and returned to life in the spring.

"First, one wraps the tree in cloth like a shroud, and with three-quarters of its roots cut, the tree is lowered backwards into its 'grave' – a trench lined with an osier-woven casket and packed with straw. After that, it is well-covered with more insulation, and boards crown the top. Sometimes a farmer will take advantage of his root-bound greensward and cut the sod, roll it up like a carpet, and roll it back when the tree is buried for its winter's sleep." Holmes scowled. "I fear you will find Catercorner's body – and evidence – in a fig-tree's caskets, beneath a carefully rolled carpet of lawn."

The Yarders wasted no time in altering their search. There was nothing we could do but sit and wait for news.

We sat in silence, for the desire to speak had left us both. It was a vigil we were keeping for an old friend of our friends, a disgraced man who had tried to make amends to his Brotherhood and lost his life in the doing.

"Holmes," I said when I could think no more, "what do you think poor Corner found?"

"Proof that would lead the police to the fig caskets where – I am speculating along the lines of existing data – Woodhouse was hiding goods for the Kings' distribution.

"The murder weapon is missing. So is whatever Corner found. It will surprise me if they do not find Woodhouse has been keeping caches of amended drugs. You are honest, old friend, and only buy the best medicines at the chemists you stake your good name against. A low price for a low product is the resort of many, and the poor may as well be created for exploitation, for how often are their voices heard?"

At the rattle of the telephone-bell downstairs, Holmes leaped to his feet. I stopped him with a look. He gnashed his teeth and fell back to his chair as I jumped down the stairwell to answer. It was Lestrade on the other end.

Holmes was standing again by the time I returned to our rooms. He held his body still as a waiting hunter's, but his eyes betrayed the vibrating nerves inside.

"You were right, Holmes. There were twelve mature fig-trees. They found Catercorner in one of the caskets. He was shot through the heart at close range. A four-inch gun was under his body. Most of the caskets were full of waterproofed caches with packages of chemicals, jewellry, some gold. Woodhouse was letting the Kings hide their stolen goods on his land in return for a percentage. Lestrade even found a living Red King who confessed the packets were supposed to be pure and they were trimming it down with flour. The Kings were uneducated of the proper procedures, and its dangers."

"Woodhouse?" Holmes asked impatiently.

"Caught. Gregson and Lestrade have promised to provide you with the details, and hope for your assistance in tracking the owners of some 'objects of interest'."

Holmes sniffed, and collapsed into his chair before the fire. A reluctant smile tugged at his lips. "Assistance in yet more little puzzles? Now that, Watson," he said as he reached for his violin, "is a proper gentleman's payment for my service."

Woodhouse never hung for the murder of Corner, or for his participation for the violent deaths amongst the Red Kings. He sits in Broadmoor thanks to a courtroom performance that was, Lestrade grudgingly admitted, "worth a few award ribbons". His cell allows him books and plants, and he gives every indication of being content.

Holmes visited him once and declared that was more than enough. "That is a dangerous man, Watson, upon my word. I have tangled with Moriarty, but Woodhouse is a different species! It pleases him to play the role of a madman, and so long as he is pleased, there he will stay. I do not envy the warden for the day he grows bored and leaves his cell!"

"Do have some faith in the men guarding him," I urged. "Woodhouse murdered a former policeman. To Gregson and Lestrade, Catercorner was still one of their own – they encouraged Dr. Nordstrom to take in poor Jacky."

"Faith!" Holmes sneered. "I have faith – in humanity's weaknesses, which is strong enough to exploit the most minute cracks and fissures in the walls erected for its own protection. No, Watson, I shall be watching Woodhouse."

He pulled his violin to his chin and poised the bow over the strings.

It was only by accident that I heard him murmur, "Just as he shall be watching me."

> *"Suppose that I were Brooks or Woodhouse, or any of the fifty men who have good reason for taking my life, how long could I survive against my own pursuit?"*
>
> – Sherlock Holmes
> "The Bruce-Partington Plans"

NOTE

* Gregson had once found Lestrade in mufti at the Orchid Hotel, drinking a cup of the cinnamon-infected brew with a puzzled expression.

"I asked for something against the cold and I got this."

"You know they sell that mud to men so they can sire sons, don't you?" Gregson had informed him with great glee.

Lestrade had blinked, scowled and responded, "That's all the world needs. More Lestrades."

Gregson had never forgiven him for beating him to the punch.

The Case of the Accused Cook
by Brenda Seabrooke

The greatest risk to life at 221b Baker Street – aside from Mrs. Hudson's occasional visits away, necessitating foraging for food – was tedium. Holmes didn't handle tedium well – unlike me, a former military doctor who relished long stretches without limb removal, fatal fevers, and unknown maladies. The excessive cold and abundance of late-winter snow had prevented clients from visiting with cases to occupy the mind of the famed consulting detective, and the results were increasingly harder to tolerate in the rooms we sometimes shared. Holmes smoked too much without eating much at all, despite Mrs. Hudson's tempting meals. Holmes lost weight while I gained. The situation should've been the reverse. I needed no extra padding while the rail-thin detecting machine did.

He'd attempted to engage himself with bringing his casebooks up to date, which meant sorting any number of newspaper clippings and papers covered with notes, and now a paper blizzard lay strewn around him, far too close to the fire for comfort. Indeed, the flames behind him crackled and spat by turns and threatened to leap out and gobble up the debris.

When I mentioned the hazard behind him, he replied, "It will have to come through me first, and I'm certain I should feel it immediately."

I didn't share his certainty but felt too desultory to attempt to change his mind, though I have no doubt that I could have done so. Holmes was a man of determination but quick to change direction once he perceived the wind had turned.

For some time, unseasonal snow had hit the window panes with the soft determination of a kitten wanting in, but the knock on the downstairs front door was both loud and determined. I sat up and hoped for a case.

Inspector Lestrade of Scotland Yard entered with his bowler hat in his hand and most of the snow brushed from the shoulders of his overcoat.

"Lestrade!" Holmes greeted him as though he were the first guest at a party. "Some refreshment, Watson?"

I poured whisky for the inspector. He removed his coat and took the glass with a look of gratitude.

"Come warm yourself by the fireside chair." Holmes nodded toward the basket chair, while I poured a wee dram for myself. Holmes hadn't asked for one. If he wanted it, he knew where we kept it.

"What brings you out on a snowy Sunday afternoon?" I said after a restorative sip.

"It's personal."

I pulled up a chair while the inspector warmed himself inside and out.

Holmes leaned forward with interest. "Go on. What's happened?"

"It's my wife's cousin. Second cousin, or maybe third. She's from a large family."

"Come on, man," I said before Holmes could. "Out with it!"

Lestrade's nose twitched as if he could barely form the words. "Iris Jakes is a cook at Netherhill House, in Gloucestershire. She's a widow – nearly five years now. She's been accused of stealing valuables."

"What kind of valuables?" Holmes asked.

"Snuff boxes. Silver and gold, and inlaid with jewels."

"Why was she accused? Were the boxes found on her?"

"No, nor in her things."

"Cooks don't normally come into contact with the upstairs," I said, "which is where such objects are presumably kept."

"To show off the wealth of the owner," Holmes said.

"A message came for one of the maids and no one else was about, so Iris went upstairs herself. That put her in the vicinity of the boxes."

I snorted. "Slender evidence indeed."

"It was enough for Lord Acton. I need to hire you to find the truth. She's an honest woman. Never had a day's trouble in her life unless the bread didn't rise or the pudding fell. The wife's that worried about it."

"I'm not for hire to you, Lestrade," Holmes said.

"Here, Holmes – " I started when he interrupted me.

"I shall do it *gratis*, for the many cases you have brought to me."

"I'm that grateful," Lestrade said looking more relieved now that Holmes was taking the case.

"Give Watson the particulars. We'll be on the first train in the morning." He went to pack while I made notes for the journey.

The day was fine, not a sign of yesterday's fitful snow when we left on the earliest train. We secured a compartment to ourselves. Mrs. Hudson had returned the night before, and that morning had packed us a sumptuous lunch which we ate earlier than usual, there not being much to talk about after we'd done with the newspapers as the train took us west to Gloucestershire.

Netherwold was a small village, but a few shops lined the high street at one end and a pleasant inn, the Nether Royal, where Holmes had secured rooms for us, stood nearby We left our things and set off immediately for the constabulary to interview Mrs. Jakes.

The constable was surprised to see us. He rose quickly from his tea, buttoning his tunic. "We don't get many gents from London in these parts, sir," he said. "I'm Constable Rigdon."

"Sherlock Holmes, and this is my associate, Dr. Watson. We have come on behalf of Mrs. Jakes. Why is she here?"

"She is accused of stealing snuff boxes from Netherhill." He spoke with confidence. "That's the great house just beyond the village."

"Indeed. Were any found on her person?"

"No sir."

"Nor any found in her rooms?"

"No sir."

"On what evidence did you make the arrest?"

Constable Rigdon's confidence began to drain. "Why, Lady Acton said so."

"And if Lady Acton had said that you stole the snuff boxes, would you have arrested yourself?" Holmes's tone hovered above a sneer.

"Well, no sir. I would know I didn't do it. I wasn't nowhere near the house when the theft happened."

"Excellent. We're getting somewhere. Why did Lady Acton accuse Mrs. Jakes?"

"She were seen above stairs where she hadn't no need to be."

"I wish to speak to her."

He looked like he wanted to say that this wasn't convenient, but couldn't quite bring himself to oppose Sherlock Holmes. I wondered if he'd heard of my friend, or was just reacting to his imperious ways. Instead he rose and took a key off a hook and led us to the cells behind a stout wooden door. We followed him down the short hall to the second cell. He knocked and said, "These two gents has come to talk to you, Mrs. Jakes." Then he unlocked the door and allowed us to enter, adding," Give us a shout when you're done."

He closed the door behind him. The afternoon was waning. Not much light entered from the high window, but even from the doorway, I could see the poor woman with red-rimmed eyes sitting in front of a minimal tea of bread and butter and pickles. A small Brown Betty held her allotment of two cups of tea, half-a-cup cooling in front of her.

She turned her head slightly but didn't look at us.

"Mrs. Jakes," Holmes said gently, "your cousin's husband asked us to take your case." He introduced us.

She looked at us now. Her eyes were wide with surprise. "Mr. Holmes?" she whispered. "Sent by Inspector Lestrade?"

"The one," I said.

"I'm so ashamed." She looked down at the cup.

"Don't let us interrupt your tea," I said. "You need to keep your strength up. Have a sip now." She lifted the cup to her lips and drank. I had seen falsely accused people lose their will to live.

"Excellent," I said. I buttered a slice of the bread and wrapped a pickle in it. Bite by bite, I coaxed her to eat.

"Now," Holmes said when the bread was gone. "Tell me about life in Netherhill. How long have you been cooking there?"

"Almost a year."

"Is it a good house in which to work?"

"I thought so. Lady Acton seemed to like my cooking. The staff is all right. Not as many as the house should have."

"Where were you before Netherhill?"

"Silverwell. That's in Kent."

"Why did you leave?"

"The lady died. Her nephew inherited and brought in his own staff."

"Inspector Lestrade said somebody came to the kitchen door with a message for one of the maids?"

"That's right. Wednesday morning. Early it were. The kitchen boy wasn't about. The maids was all at their tasks. Lucy hadn't come back from polishing the fireplace fenders. I went up to find her. She were in the room where they keep them snuff boxes. I didn't pay no attention to them – just told Lucy to come down. She ran ahead of me. I were in no hurry. The breads was all in the ovens. I had a little free space. I planned to have a cuppa before I started on the next meal."

"Who was this messenger?" Holmes asked.

"That's the funny part. When I reached the kitchen, Lucy was standing at the door looking out. 'Ain't nobody here,' she said. I looked out and nobody was around."

"When were the snuff boxes discovered missing?"

"That were on Saturday."

"Tell me about the week before that."

"Nothing much to tell. They had a dinner party on the previous Saturday. Sunday the staff were off – "

"Tell me about the dinner party. Who were the guests?"

"Sir Selwyn and Lady Jellicoe from Bladenoaks. The vicar and his wife and daughter. The doctor and his wife and daughter. Them two military men – "

"Colonel Carruthers and Major Fenton?" Holmes interrupted.

She nodded. "I think there was some matchmaking hopes for the two young ladies and them."

"So twelve altogether," I said, making a note.

She nodded. “Her Ladyship don’t like to entertain for fewer than that. She likes lively talk.”

“That was Saturday. Sunday did you go out?”

“Yes. Me and the housekeeper Mrs. Long went to tea in town.”

“Did you enjoy the tea?”

“It were a treat to eat somethin’ I didn’t cook,” she wrinkled her nose, “but it weren’t as good as mine.”

“And the day the messenger came?”

“That were Wednesday, like I said. I made lemon chicken soup that day.”

“Describe the messenger for me.”

“He were an ordinary bloke. Hairy. Hunched over like.”

“What did he wear?”

“Some kind of shapeless coat. Boots. I think he wore boots.”

“And what day were you accused?”

“That were the next Saturday. His Lordship brought friends from the city on Friday for the weekend and he showed off his snuff boxes the next morning.” She dabbed at her eyes with her napkin.

“What happened then?”

“They searched the house and couldn’t find nothing. His Lordship questioned everybody. Everybody said they saw the snuff boxes up ‘til Wednesday. They said they would’ve noticed if they was missing. They think I made up the story about the messenger so I could steal the snuff boxes.”

“What do they think you did with them?”

“They think I might’ve slipped ‘em to the messenger later. Maybe that night, but I didn’t. I wouldn’t know what to do with old snuff boxes.” Tears slid out of her pale blue eyes.

Holmes didn’t say anything. Then to my great amazement, he patted her arm and told her not to worry, and that we had work to do. “We’ll come back tomorrow with news,” he added.

“You know that she’s innocent,” Holmes said to the constable on leaving.

“She’s a nice lady,” he said.

“Indeed,” Holmes said.

It was too late to call at Netherhill. We dined at the inn and went to bed early. I read a mustard yellow-backed book I’d picked up at the train station. I expected the tale of derring-do would keep me awake, but those pages couldn’t compete with the fresh air of Netherwold.

After a substantial breakfast, we hired a cart and driver named Edrik to take us to Netherhill and wait for us. “You be that Zherlock Holmez and Dr. Watzon, I reckon.”

We acknowledged we were.

"I hope you can help Miz. Jakez. She'z a nice ooman. Not like that awld crater at the big house."

I assumed he meant Lady Acton.

Netherhill was a middle-sized great house built of grey stone, with a pair of towers added on each end of the front which gave it the look of ears. A belvedere, perched on top looking like a nanny's white cap, afforded a splendid view of the village below and countryside beyond. The driver stopped at the front door where we asked him to wait. He drove the cart over to the side as Holmes applied himself vigorously to the knocker.

"Lord or Lady Acton," Holmes said to the man who opened the door, a butler by the look of him.

"Do you have an appointment?"

"I do not. Mr. Sherlock Holmes and Dr. John Watson of London. We've been asked by Scotland Yard to look into the recent theft at – " He glanced around as if assuring himself of the place. " – Netherhill."

"Very good, sir. If you will just wait in the hall."

Holmes strode in with me behind him. The butler left us in the narrow, dark hall which dated it somewhat earlier than the Jacobean hints of the façade. Dark, somber paintings hung on the carved walls.

The butler returned shortly. "Lady Acton will see you now. If you will follow me."

Lady Acton was seated in the morning room in a chair that contrived to look like a throne without any gilt but plenty of plush crimson. She was a thin haughty woman with a sharp nose and bulging eyes, dressed in a dove-colored morning gown with rose touches here and there.

The butler announced us.

"Thank you, Parkins. That will be all." Parkins withdrew.

No offer of tea or morning coffee. Or even a chair.

"Good morning, Lady Acton. My colleague and I have been asked by Scotland Yard to look into the theft of snuff boxes."

She scowled and laid down a book. "The case is solved. The thief has been apprehended."

"Someone has been *arrested*, Lady Acton, but Scotland Yard isn't satisfied the case has been *solved*. If you will recount the events for us."

Her story agreed with Mrs. Jakes'. Dinner party on Saturday. Snuff boxes missing on the following Saturday. She only had second-hand knowledge of the events of Wednesday when Mrs. Jakes left her post in the kitchen below stairs. "I ask you – a cook in the parlor!" Lady Acton sniffed.

"How long has Mrs. Jakes cooked at Netherhill?" I asked, simply to put my oar in.

"I don't know. Six months. Maybe longer. Ask the butler."

"Was she satisfactory?" I asked.

"Satisfactory?" She raised a dark eyebrow.

"A good cook."

"I suppose so. I don't know what we're to do without a cook. None of the maids know how. Lord Acton has sent for one in London, but who knows how long that will take?"

She looked from one to the other of us as if we might somehow produce a cook, or even do it ourselves.

"In due time," I murmured.

She threw her hands out in appeal and seemed younger now that she had dropped some of her haughty airs. "Meantime, what are we to eat? The kitchen maid can't read Mrs. Jakes's recipes. The upstairs maid has to read them to her, and they forget. The food from that kitchen has been a hodgepodge since Cook was taken away."

"We'll need to see the rooms involved and to collect the cook's things," Holmes said.

Lady Acton rang for the butler, who must have been loitering on the other side of the door that he'd immediately opened. "My Lady."

"Take these men to see the rooms and collect the cook's things."

"Very good, my Lady. Follow me, sirs."

We saw the dining room where the men would've had their brandy and cigars the night of the dinner party – a long polished mahogany table, crimson brocade chair seats, paintings of dead animals on the dark walls – and the parlor where the ladies could withdraw, and finally the snuff box room where only three boxes of lesser value remained.

"Tell me about the night of the dinner party."

"The guests arrived promptly at half-seven. Dinner was served soon after. Just before ten, the ladies withdrew for coffee and tea while the gentlemen had brandy and cigars until they joined the ladies. The moon had risen by then and they went up into the belvedere to see the view. They remained until half-eleven."

"Did they stay in a group going to the belvedere?"

"I couldn't say, sir."

"Show us the belvedere, if you will, Parkins."

"Sir, Mrs. Jakes never went up there."

"Nevertheless, we need to see it."

The climb was long, and the view spectacular when we reached the glassed room. The stairs were behind us as we stood at the front looking down on the village, the inn, and the fields beyond. Holmes steepled his fingers, mulling. What facts was he putting together? What theories to exonerate the cook? I'd no doubt his agile brain, stimulated by the climb, was working like a well-oiled machine. I'd often noticed one's thoughts were clearer after vigorous exercise – especially Holmes's.

"On a cloudless day, one might even see Wales up here," I said.

"One might think so, yes," Holmes said. He turned to Parkins. "One might also think guests who have imbibed a good deal might have straggled up so many stairs."

"I went ahead to prepare the champagne for serving so yes, you are correct. It was some time before they all assembled in the belvedere."

"We'll need to see the kitchen next," Holmes said.

Going down was far more pleasurable. I don't know how the guests felt, or if they felt anything after sherry, various wines to compliment the dishes served, brandy, port, coffee, tea, and finally champagne. They probably all thought they saw Wales and maybe Ireland

To reach the kitchen we went through the baize door to the hall and down the stairs to the kitchen. The pretty wallpapers, carpeting, and appointments stopped at that door. On the other side, the hall was painted a pale brown color with dark trim. The floor had a runner the color of coffee with milk but that would be to muffle the noise of the servants' hurried steps from the kitchen, many carrying heavy trays and dishes.

In the stone-flagged kitchen, Holmes barely glanced at the huge ovens, the stoves, the larder, the array of herbs and condiments, and the many implements needed to cook sumptuous meals. Two young women struggled to open the oven door and cram a haunch of something into it.

"Lucy, that should've gone in an hour ago," Parkins said.

"Oh sir, Mullins was late with the delivery," Lucy said.

"I would like a word with you, Lucy," Holmes said.

"I'm that rushed, sir," she said as she pushed her hair under her cap and straightened her apron.

"'Twill take but a moment," he said. "Tell me what happened when Mrs. Jakes came into the room."

"I telled it all to the police, sir."

"Nevertheless I want to hear it from you."

"I was doing the fender in the fireplace. Mrs. Jakes came in and said a messenger was at the kitchen door for me. Well, I run down there and opened the door. Nobody was there."

"Did you look around?"

"Yes, sir. I didn't see nobody."

"Did you see any footprints?"

"No, sir. Them stones was swept clean."

"You stepped out the door." Holmes opened the door and beckoned Lucy to join him.

With a pleading look at Parkins, she took two steps outside the door.

"How far did you go? This far?" Holmes took four long strides.

"'Bout that, sir."

He took two more. She nodded.

"That's right, sir."

"What did you do then?"

"I called out. Nobody answered. I looked around and went back in the kitchen."

"Did Mrs. Jakes follow you to the kitchen?"

"No sir, not at first. Then she come in about the time I came back from looking for the messenger. There ain't no messenger, I tells her."

"Did she seem surprised?"

"She said where did he go then."

I looked out the door at the stoop. I saw nothing that might cast a more favorable light on the cook's dilemma.

"I think we've seen everything here. I'll trouble you for Mrs. Jakes's things."

Parkins sent Lucy and the kitchen boy Ike to the lumber room to get Mrs. Jakes's belongings. They had packed them for her in two boxes.

"That's everything?" I said.

"Yes, sir. There's a list made by the housekeeper."

I noticed a thick book on the deal table. "Are those Mrs. Jakes's receipts?"

Lucy nodded.

"We'll take that as well," Holmes said, closing the book and tucking it under his arm.

Lucy looked like she wanted to protest.

"No doubt the replacement cook will have her own receipt book," I said.

"Quite right, Watson."

They loaded the boxes onto the cart. We climbed in and drove down the hill to the town. The driver let us off at the constabulary and helped us with the boxes.

"'Ere now, I can't have boxes cluttering up my jail," the constable said as we maneuvered them into an empty cell.

"These are Mrs. Jakes's things," I said.

"Oh well, then, that's all right."

I glanced through the bars to see how Mrs. Jakes was taking this. Her cell was empty. "Where is Mrs. Jakes?"

"In the kitchen, sir. She was feeling useless so I let her cook some dinner for us. Would you care to join us?"

"Thank you, no," Holmes interrupted. "We have more calls to make, but give her this book. Come, Watson."

“Where are we going now?” I asked when we had gained the street.

“Why, to the inn for a spot of lunch,” he replied.

I wanted to know what Holmes made of the morning’s intelligence, but he wasn’t inclined to talk beyond compliments to the innkeeper.

When we had finished eating, I asked. “Do you have any idea who took the snuff boxes?”

“Oh yes. I’ve known from the beginning.”

“Are you planning to tell me?”

“Think, Watson. What new events occurred in this village in the last year?”

“I’m sure that there are no end of events that have occurred here, and that we would think nothing of them, but they become phenomena in a village of this size.”

“Astute observation. We can walk to our remaining interviews. We’ll start with the vicarage.”

As were the other village houses, the vicarage was built of the local grey stone softened by swathes of early blooms in the front garden. I recognized hellebores, camellias, snowdrops, and rhododendrons. A young lady with a basket on her arm clipped a twig here, a leaf there, and dropped them into the basket.

“Are you Miss Atlee?” Holmes asked.

“I am. Do you wish to speak to my father?”

“We do. I am Sherlock Holmes, and this is my associate Dr. Watson.”

“Follow me, please.” She seemed rather plain, her most notable feature being her plump rosy cheeks.

She led us into a plush hall to a sitting room with flowers everywhere – in pictures, upholstery, carpets, and curtains. “Please be seated. I’ll tell my father you’re here.”

The vicar was a rotund man with blue eyes almost as bright as his daughter’s. She introduced us and made to withdraw.

“Stay, please,” Holmes said, and she sank onto a rose-printed settee.

“What can we do for you, Mr. Holmes?” The vicar asked expectantly.

“We’ve been asked by Scotland Yard to look into the matter of the missing snuff boxes.”

The vicar nodded as if he already knew. News travels fast in a village. “A most unfortunate affair.” He shook his head. “I cannot believe that Mrs. Jakes would steal from her employer. She is a faithful attendant at services.”

Holmes asked them to go through their movements at the dinner party. They had arrived at the same time as the others. “Punctuality is important to a vicar,” Miss Atlee said.

They had chatted until seated for dinner, which was long. Afterwards, they had gone up to the belvedere. No, he hadn't seen anything. Jane and her mother had gone ahead.

"Gone up where?" We were joined by the vicar's wife.

"These gentlemen are inquiring about the dinner at Netherhill, my dear," the vicar said. "They want to know the order in which we ascended to the belvedere."

"We went straight up the stairs, all the way to that silly thing on top of the house. Built by Acton's grandfather to make his house taller when he found out another story would be too much weight without enormous expense. He wanted a grander house. He's the one who started that snuff box collection. The church could use some of the money spent on those things. Jewelled snuff boxes when the church roof was leaking. And now it's leaking again."

"My wife takes personal responsibility for the condition of the church," the vicar said with a chuckle.

"Jane and I do what we can keeping the church filled with flowers, but in winter its starkness is noticeable. Those snuff boxes would pay for commemorative stained glass windows. Snuff boxes, indeed."

They hadn't seen anyone go into the room with the snuff boxes, or anything suspicious. "Besides, the boxes were stolen later by the cook," Mrs. Atlee said.

"That may be." Holmes didn't look as if he thought so. "How long have Colonel Carruthers and Major Fenton lived in the village?"

"They moved here about a year ago," the vicar said.

"That was when the colonel moved here, March a year ago," Miss Atlee said. "Major Fenton moved in September. The last day of the month."

"What do they do in the village" I asked. "Regular attendees at church?" I could have never settled myself to live in such a quiet village after my short army career.

"The colonel wanted somewhere quiet. He's writing a book, I believe," the vicar said.

"And the major?" Holmes asked. "Is he also writing one?"

"I have not heard so," the vicar replied.

Holmes thanked them for their information and stood up.

"I do hope that you find some miscreant passing through made off with the snuff boxes," the vicar said.

"I'm sure we will," Holmes said.

Miss Atlee saw us to the door. "My mother tends to get worked up over the condition of the church. Really, the roof leaks in only one spot and it is scheduled to be repaired this week. Maybe next winter's storms will veer around our village. The light in the church is lovely even without colored glass windows. Stop in if you have time."

"She seems pleasant," I said when the door closed behind us and we were back in the street. "Indeed, her eyes seemed to sparkle when she talked of the officers."

"I suspect she may have designs on one of them."

"Whatever would make you think that?"

"The way she glanced across the street a number of times and the great care she takes with the plantings in front of the vicarage. The innkeeper said Major Fenton lives across the street. The colonel lives around the corner."

"Shall we cross and call on the major next?"

"Let's continue on this side to the doctor's residence."

Dr. Vidal was out but his wife and daughter agreed to answer some questions. Their comments were similar to the Atlees'.

"We had already seen the snuff boxes a number of times when his Lordship was showing them off," Avril said, suppressing a smile. "We didn't need to see them again."

Avril Vidal appeared to be several years younger than Jane Atlee, a younger, prettier version of her mother, who was pleasant with brown hair drawn back and brown eyes. She was knitting a baby garment of cream wool for her son's first baby.

Miss Vidal sat between the two military men at the dinner party with Miss Atlee on the other side of the colonel.

"The colonel, I believe is writing a book about his military exploits," Dr. Vidal said as he joined us.

"Yes, he is," Miss Vidal said, "and so is the major. He told me so at the dinner party."

"Did he now?" I said. "By Jove, that is a coincidence."

"Isn't that the reason retired military men move to small villages?" Holmes said.

"That," Avril said, "and less expensive living."

Lord and Lady Jellico of Bladenoaks left on the Monday after the dinner for a wedding in Carlisle. "But they've seen the snuff boxes far more than we have," Mrs. Vidal said.

"Yes, the Actons' dinner guests fall into a caste system," Miss Vidal added. "The town people such as the officers, the vicar, and the doctor must be entertained periodically to keep relations pleasant. Jellico is only a baron, so is put in with the rest of us. The more exalted guests will include those higher than a mere baron. A fete will be held for the townspeople on the grounds of Netherhill in the summer. We only see the county lords and ladies when they are in need of something – a doctor, religion, a spool of thread. The Jellicoes' son is meeting them at the wedding."

"Don't sound so cynical, Avril," Mrs. Vidal admonished her. "William is at Oxford – or is it Cambridge?"

"They're hoping Billy Jelly will meet some potential brides there," Avril said. "He needs to marry well so the Jellicoes will dine exclusively with the county families and never see the likes of us again."

"That was an interesting turn from Avril," I said when we were back on the street.

"No doubt she knows Billy quite well, and is bitter not being considered for a wife. She didn't seem interested in the two military chaps."

"I daresay she thinks she has more time to find a husband," Holmes said, "than to settle for a much older retired officer."

We'd now talked to everyone in attendance at the dinner except the absent Jellicoes and the two officers. We walked up the street on the side opposite the vicarage and made the turn to the colonel's cottage on the side street.

This cottage was larger than others in the community with a windowed third floor, no doubt with a perfect view of the entire village. A busybody could keep an eye on everyone without leaving the house. The house's unimaginative name – *Greystone* – was chiseled into the bottom of the step. The shrubbery bore evidence of periodic clipping. No flowers lifted their untidy heads.

I raised the brass doorknocker in the shape of a grenadier. Before it had sounded twice the door was opened by the colonel himself. "I wondered when you would get to me," he said. "Word gets around in a village this small. Come in, gentlemen."

The cottage smelled of lemon and beeswax and hearth-fire. Though the day was fine, there was a fire in the fireplace. Holmes glanced at the flames. The colonel noticed. "Just some papers I'm burning. They tend to pile up."

He led us into a parlor furnished like a gentlemen's club: Leather seating, framed maps on the walls, a spent cannon shell on a highly polished tabletop, a bronze cast of the Duke of Wellington astride a horse – no doubt at Waterloo.

"What brings you to this quiet village?" I asked.

"Just that. It's a quiet village. After the noise of battlefields, I find my hearing is not what it once was. I relish the peace of this green place far from the hurly-burly of life in a city and the smoke of a battlefield. You gentlemen, I take it, are from London."

"Yes. I was an army doctor. Maiwand."

The colonel nodded with understanding. "Nasty business, that."

"I understand you're writing a book," I said.

"I am. What about yourself? Have you been tempted to write of your military experiences?"

"I have, but I've found other areas that currently occupy my time. I'm a practicing doctor in London. What about Major Fenton? We heard he is also writing about his army life. Do you compare notes?"

"Is he now? I'm not surprised. After we retire, we rethink our experiences in war, and writing sometimes helps us put it aside and get on with our lives. I suspect we shall be comparing notes, though merely from a technical standpoint. I can't speak for him, but my experiences were sobering and not for whiling away the hours."

I nodded with understanding. I never discussed my battlefield experiences, although bits and pieces sometimes found their way into comments.

Holmes had been quiet. Now he started on the usual questions. What did the colonel do at the dinner? What did he observe?

"Did you see the snuff boxes?"

"I did."

No one else had admitted seeing them that night. "Had you seen them before?"

"Many times, but this was Major Fenton's first visit to Netherhill, and he hadn't seen them, so I took him to the room where they are displayed on our way to the stairs to the belvedere."

"I wonder Acton didn't show them to him," I said.

"Was the room lit or dark?" Holmes asked after a second.

He looked puzzled for a moment. "Oh I see. You want to know how we were able to see the boxes. The room was lit with several candles in globes."

"What did the Major say about them?"

"Haven't you asked him?"

"He's next on our list," I explained.

"He was stunned. Said he never expected to see anything so grand in a country house like Netherhill. Said they belonged in a museum. I quite agree with him, but the little Lord does love to show them off, especially to his grand guests from afar."

"Afar?" I asked.

"Last month a maharajah and a duke visited to see them. The duke is a collector himself, as is the maharajah. He was particularly taken with the emerald box. I told Acton he should have the collection photographed for insurance purposes. He allowed the Vidal girl to paint water colors of the boxes, but the venture didn't end well. Something to do with their son, I gather. She is a fetching young lady."

"Are you interested in her yourself?" I asked.

"Are you?" He cocked his head and smiled.

"Too young for me."

"Likewise."

"Miss Atlee has a few more years on her," I said, leading him on.

"She is a nice young lady, but I am not, despite Miss Austen, in want of a wife."

We determined the colonel left the dinner party at the same time as the other guests.

"Yes, we departed *en masse*, some tipsier than others from the plethora of wines and spirits. I must say I slept soundly that night. The next day I took the train to London and returned only yesterday."

"May I ask what was your business in London?" Holmes asked.

"You may. Nothing exciting, I can tell you. Research. I needed to refresh my memory on some military history and background in the Reading Room at the British Museum. Dined at some good restaurants. I confess I miss good cuisine in the village. Dinners at Netherhill were noted for the excellent cooking, but I gather that has come to an end with the arrest of the cook. Pity."

"It is more than a pity," I began, but Holmes interrupted

"We need not take up any more of your time, Colonel. Good day sir." Holmes stood up and I followed suit. I thought of more questions, but Holmes was already at the door.

"I say, did you see his desk?" I said when we had walked back to the high street.

"What about it?"

"Neat and tidy. When I'm writing, I have papers strewn all over the room, and you're even worse. How can he be writing a book and not have a single paper on his desk, or in evidence?"

"I suspect you've hit it on the first try, Watson. He's not writing a book. He just tells everybody he is to explain his eccentricities. Or he might be an excessively neat man. I've seen a few of them in the military, present company excepted."

"From the look of his cottage, he could be one of them, though he's been away for over a week."

Around the corner we turned up the walk to Alders Drift. The shrubbery behind the low stone wall was the antithesis of Greystone. Wild, unpruned, the trees and bushes rose to the second story of the Tudor-style cottage. Holmes lifted the tree-shaped knocker.

"Two military men. Judged by their dwelling places, they couldn't be more different, and yet they both chose this village and both are writing their memoirs and battle stories. The major would have been better served in a smaller village where he is the only military inhabitant."

"Quiet, Holmes. He'll hear you."

"It's sound advice. His hearing may not be so sound. Perhaps too close to the artillery?"

He plied the knocker again.

And we waited. After awhile I said, "Maybe he's gone out."

"I hardly think so."

"How do you know that?"

He inclined his ahead. Across the street Miss Atlee pruned the front garden of the vicarage. "Would she be doing that if he had gone out?"

"No, she would work on the overgrown back garden if she knew he was away. You think he's in the cottage then?"

"My faith in Miss Atlee's ability is unerring. I know that he is."

"In a bath?"

"Odd time of day for it."

"Perhaps he has had an accident."

"Excellent supposition, Watson. Let's check the back and see if we can find a way in that doesn't involve the breakage of glass or the splintering of doors."

We made our way through the jungle overgrowth and found a door slightly ajar. As we approached the stoop, the door opened another inch or two, apparently blown by the slight breeze. Holmes looked around and picked up a stick. Neither of us had brought our revolvers to pay calls on the villagers. I broke off a stout leafy branch and followed Holmes inside.

We found him where he had fallen, a mug of tea splashed across the flagstone hall floor where it had dropped from his hand and rolled. He lay face-down, half in the adjacent study, a pool of blood still fresh from the battering of the back of his head. The body was not yet cold.

"Shall I go for the constable?"

"Let's look around first."

"What are we looking for? Not for the battering instrument." An elephant carved from ebony lay on the floor, a smear of blood bright against the dark wood.

"Whatever the murderer came for," Holmes said.

The room, while not quite as neat as the Colonel's, bore no other traces of crime.

"What are we missing here? Holmes said.

"For a man writing a book, he doesn't have any evidence of it. No manuscript pages. No books. No speed of notes. His desk is as. Lean as the Colonel's yet they both professed to be writing books."

"Curiouser and curiouser. I suspect one of them was lying."

Just then we heard the sound of letters falling through the mail slot in the hall. We rushed in to see a sheaf of them dropping onto the floor. Holmes reached for them, removed one, and put the others on the desk. He picked up the letter opener lying on the blotter.

"That's a *choora,* or *pesh-kabz,*" I said, "an armor-piercing dagger used by the Mahsuds in the Khyber Pass area between India and the Pashtun. The handle is horn set in silver with a steel blade. A lethal weapon. I wonder why the murderer didn't use it."

"Perhaps he did." Holmes held up the blade. It had been wiped but along the edges, but clear evidence of blood adhered. "There's a slit in the back of his coat. There's a stab wound there as well, but I believe that he was killed first by the blows to the head."

I examined the man's back and found the wound. "You're right. The blow with the knife was unnecessary. Perhaps something ceremonial. Live by the *choora*, die by the *choora*."

"Or he didn't want to take the time to assure his victim was dead."

Holmes checked the major's pockets. "Ah." He drew out a velvet bag and removed its content. In the palm of his hand lay a silver snuff box with a design of coral and turquoise flowers.

"Case solved," I said.

"Perhaps. Or perhaps the killer wants us to think so."

"Either way, Mrs. Jakes is exonerated."

"Indeed. That is true. Get the constable, will you? I've seen all I need to here."

Across the street, Miss Atlee stared as I emerged from the front door of Alders Drift. I nodded to her and set off for the constabulary.

Constable Rigdon snoozed at his desk when I entered. "I was just working on reports," he said when he jerked awake. "Mrs. Jakes is well, sir."

"Major Fenton isn't. You will need to come at once."

"What's happened?" He rose from his chair and buttoned his tunic.

"He's been murdered."

"Murdered! No one gets murdered in Netherwold. Sir."

"Nevertheless, it has happened."

He grabbed his hat."Are you sure, sir?"

"The back of his head has been battered, and there is evidence that he's been stabbed."

He stopped and looked at me. "I'll have to telegraph for an inspector."

"Excellent. Do so. I'll return to Alders Drift. Holmes is there now."

As I approached the house, Miss Atlee walked across the street to intercept me, her eyebrows drawn together in concern. "Dr. Watson, is something wrong?"

"Yes, Miss Atlee, but I can't discuss it now. I'll call later."

She returned to the vicarage garden, but all pretenses at gardening had left her.

"Rigdon is on the way," I reported to Holmes.

"Excellent. See that nothing is disturbed. I must send telegrams now."

He met the constable at the door. "The inspector is coming, sir. It won't be long."

"Good, man. I'll return as quickly as I can."

Rigdon snatched off his cap and stared at the body of the major. "Do you know who did this, sir?"

"Oh yes. Yes, indeed. I even know why."

"Sir?"

"All in good time, Constable."

At half-four, Holmes returned, followed by Inspector Yarbro, who had arrived by train with a sergeant and two more constables. "Police vehicles are on the way. Never had a murder in Netherwold."

After introductions, Holmes held a private conversation with the inspector, who nodded and then turned away toward his men.

"Come, Watson," said Holmes to me. "We are in need of sustenance."

"You know everything, do you?"

"I do. Even before I received confirmation."

"I should break the news to Miss Atlee," I said.

"She will have watched the removal, Watson. I'm sure she has worked it out."

"I think I should tell her anyway."

He waved a hand. "As you wish. I'll order tea."

Miss Atlee stood at her gate watching when I reached her. "It's the major, isn't it?"

"Yes."

"What happened?"

"He has been killed."

"An accident?"

"No."

"You don't mean – "

"He has been murdered."

"Oh." She put her hand on her cheek and ran to the door of her house, calling for her mother, then her father.

Our tea was ready by the time I reached the inn. We didn't speak, but applied ourselves to food and drink, both needed.

"I've asked the inspector to assemble everyone who was present at that dinner at Netherhill at seven," Holmes said, "excluding the Jellicoes."

"Did her Ladyship agree to that?"

"I assume she did. When an inspector asks . . . ."

We prepared ourselves, and later that evening, we drove up the hill with the inspector.

"Bad business, this," the inspector said. "Man serves his country honourably, only to be struck down in that vicious way."

Her Ladyship didn't look at all pleased by this impromptu assembly. She wore a gown of some dark shade, no doubt as close to mourning for a mere major as she could allow herself. Lord Acton entered the drawing room after the seven guests had been seated. Slightly below average height with thinning greying hair, he wore the haughty air that many of the titled class affected. He pulled his watch out of a flowered waistcoat pocket several times, as if that could bring this intrusion to an end.

The inspector stood at the front of the room. He was slightly taller than his Lordship and had a full head of russet brown hair. "Good evening. I am Inspector Yarbro of the Gloucestershire Constabulary. I regret the necessity of assembling you in the place of a happier occasion over a week ago when you all attended a dinner at Netherhill, but we need to discover some truths which will lead us to the murderer of another guest that night, Major Phillip Fenton. Lord and Lady Acton have graciously allowed us to return to discover who the murderer is. I will now turn the meeting over to the renowned London detective, Sherlock Holmes."

Holmes took his place. "Two crimes were committed here in the last week. Scotland Yard asked me to come to Netherwold to solve the first one, the theft of Lord Acton's valuable snuff boxes. The second one, the murder of the major, occurred because the first one afforded the perfect opportunity to solve the murderer's problem.

"You had all been here before except the victim, Major Fenton, who had only moved to the village a few months ago. I would like for each of you to adhere as closely as possible to your actions that night when you left the table to climb the stairs to see the view from the belvedere. Dr. Watson will take the part of the major. Lord and Lady Acton, will you lead the way to the dining room?" At the reverend's questioning look, he added, "Yes, only from the dining room to the stairs. It will not be necessary to climb them."

He followed us into the dining room, and as the first group left the room, he and the inspector went out another door – to the hall, I assumed.

When all had gone but the Colonel and me, he held out his arm as if offering to escort me. "Shall we?"

"Is that what you said to the major?"

"No, of course not."

He was silent as we proceeded to the study where the three remaining snuff boxes were on display by candlelight. I saw him glance at the boxes as we continued to the stairway where the others waited.

"We're all here," Holmes said, "including the stragglers. Good. Now let's return to the drawing room."

The group seemed good-natured now, as if we had taken part in a parlor game. We resumed our original seats.

"That night the guests drifted in twos and threes to the stairs and began to climb them. Two guests lagged behind. What was the reason for that, Colonel Carruthers?"

"I suppose it might have been the major returning to the dining room for his cigar case. I showed him the snuff boxes, which he hadn't seen before. They reminded him he had left his cigar case behind. He returned to the dining room while I waited."

"What did you do while you waited?"

"I looked at the snuff boxes. I'd seen them several times before, but there's always something new to discover when observing a work of art."

"What was the something new you discovered that night?"

"The ball the black dog is running after is a large opal."

"And you didn't notice this on other occasions when you viewed the boxes?"

"No. The boxes are stunning works of art. Their jeweled brilliance eclipsed the opal."

"Indeed, they are museum-worthy."

Lord Acton looked somewhat gratified on hearing his collection praised, though it in no way made up for losing them.

"Did the major return to the study where you waited?"

"He did not."

"What happened then?"

"I waited a minute or two more then continued to the stairs and started up them."

"Did the major catch up with you?"

"He did not. He arrived in the belvedere sometime after I did."

"Did anybody see the colonel enter the belvedere before the major?" Holmes looked around at the assembled dinner guests.

"I believe, sir, that we were all enthralled with the view," the vicar said. "The stairs enter the belvedere at the back. We were all looking to the front at the panorama of village and field and wood before us."

Holmes nodded as if he had known this all along which I am sure he had. "You all returned home, leaving at half-eleven."

A murmured assent followed.

"Colonel," Holmes continued, "you rode with the Vidals, I believe."

"That is correct."

"And the major rode with the Atlees?"

"Yes, he did," Miss Atlee said.

"And Netherwold went to sleep that night – everybody but one of its denizens. One person dressed in dark clothing, hurried up the hill path, the shortcut to Netherhill if one is traveling by foot. That person retrieved the snuff boxes, wrapped in a napkin where they had been lowered out of a window. That person hurried home with his treasure."

He reached into his pocket and pulled out the velvet bag. He removed the coral and turquoise snuff box and held it up for all to see.

Lord Acton leaped to his feet. "Where did you get that? That's one of the stolen boxes!"

"In good time, your Lordship. Neither you nor your staff noticed the snuff box collection had dwindled?"

Lord Acton scowled. "It hadn't. The boxes were stolen by that cook."

"Yes, the case of the accused cook. On Wednesday morning when the cook, Mrs. Jakes, was alone in the kitchen, a man came to the door with a message for Lucy. Mrs. Jakes went to fetch Lucy from the parlor where she was working. When she returned to the kitchen, Lucy was outside the door looking around. No one was there. The messenger had disappeared. No note, no message, no package of any kind was found. Lord Acton, if you could tell us what happened on the next Saturday?"

In a surly tone, Lord Acton said, "I returned from a week in London, bringing guests with me. We arrived late and went straight to bed. When I showed them the snuff boxes the next morning, they looked at me strangely. I glanced at the shelves where the boxes are kept and saw only three. I summoned Lady Acton and asked if she had had them moved. She had not. I then questioned the staff and discovered the strange occurrence on Wednesday. I concluded that the messenger had been a ruse to give Mrs. Jakes time to remove the boxes. Perhaps the messenger was a confederate, and later when she had a chance, she passed the boxes to him."

"Thank you, your Lordship. You summoned the constable, who arrested Mrs. Jakes on your say-so alone."

"Here now. Are you calling me a liar? She had to have done it. Nothing else fits."

"No indeed. Far be it from me to call a Lordship a liar. No, you merely theorized ahead of the facts, a not-uncommon occurrence. It was a mistake. I once had a client who saw a wet patch on the ceiling and concluded her roof was leaking. She was prepared to re-roof the house until I talked to her children and discovered her smallest son had thrown his wet soapy bath flannel as high as he could and hit the ceiling just before she came to tuck him in bed.

"These Netherhill crimes are far more serious. The thief retrieved the napkin of valuable snuff boxes and took them home that night. The major's fate was sealed. The only variable was when. The thief kept one box and took the rest to London the next day. Eight snuff boxes, most inlaid with costly jewels, emeralds, rubies, sapphires, diamonds, and pearls.

"Are you saying the major had a partner in this thievery?" Inspector Yarbro said.

"No, not at all," Holmes said.

"But what happened to the major?" Miss Vidal asked. "Who killed him? Was he the thief and someone murdered him for his ill-gotten loot?"

I suspected she read those yellow-backed railroad books of crime and derring-do.

"The thief now carried out the second part of his diabolical plan," Holmes said. "He returned to Netherwold, hoping that the theft had been discovered while he was away, but it hadn't. I suspect he disguised himself in rough clothes and went to Netherhill to leave a message for one of the maids. As soon as Mrs. Jakes the cook closed the kitchen door to fetch the maid, the thief left the way he'd come and returned to London. If the inspector checks with the nearby stations, he will find a passenger disembarked on Tuesday and left the station again on Wednesday. He then returned on Sunday to find his theft of the snuff boxes had been discovered and the cook arrested.

"On Monday, he heard that Scotland Yard had sent me to look into the matter of the snuff boxes. Today he saw Dr. Watson and me calling at the vicarage and on the way to the doctor's house. It was time to act. His quarry was alone at home having a cup of tea when he called at the back door, hidden from the village by the overgrown shrubbery. The major turned to make a cup of tea for his murderer when he was struck savagely from behind with the ebony elephant. The first blow may have killed him, but to make sure, the murderer stabbed him with a ceremonial dagger, wiped it clean, and then returned it to the desk. All of this occurred instantly and without a sound.

"He searched the desk until he found what he sought. Then he removed the coral and turquoise snuff box from his pocket – this one here, the only one that he hadn't yet sold – and slipped it into the major's pocket. He had what he had come for, and he'd left the false evidence to give the impression that the major had been the man who had stolen the boxes. He returned home to burn the papers that he'd sought and retrieved, telling some of his history, and the smell of ashes greeted us when we called on Colonel Carruthers to hear his version of the dinner party." Holmes held it up the inlaid snuff box. "You have heard of the work Francis Galton? A man's finger-marks are unique – that they are like no others. When the finger-marks on this snuff box are compared with yours – "

The colonel leaped to his feet. "Here, now, I had nothing to do with the theft of that snuff box or any others! And I did not kill the major! On what evidence do you base this canard? That I was burning some papers when you arrived? I often do that. Papers pile up. Burning them takes the chill off the room and decreases the rubbish. My char can tell you that."

"We'll be speaking to your char," Holmes said. "She also does for the major, I believe. What is her name, please?"

The colonel's face turned red. "You have no right!" he sputtered.

"It's Maisie Veazey," Miss Atlee said, triumph in her voice. The colonel had killed her hopes of the major, even though no hope had ever been there, but at least she felt better.

"Whatever Maisie Veazey says is of no interest to me. You have no evidence."

"When Dr. Watson and I called on the major, the back door was slightly ajar. We entered and found the major lying dead. The afternoon post arrived while we were there. Included was a letter from the major's old messmate. Shall I read it now?" He took the letter from his inner pocket on the other side.

"I'll take that," the inspector said.

Holmes handed it over. "It seems to be a reply to a letter from the major. It says that the major is correct, and that his neighbor is in fact the same Colonel Cholmondelay Carruthers, or 'Chummy' as he was known, who was cashiered while serving in India four years ago for stealing from the officers' mess, along with other crimes. It seems the major had remembered knowing or hearing about Colonel Carruthers in the past. I'm sure we can verify, by getting in touch with his old mess mate, what else he wrote concerning his suspicions. I suspect he let something slip that alerted Carruthers – and it was only a matter of time before the Colonel would find a way to remove him. The case of the missing snuff boxes gave him the opportunity to shift the blame for their theft onto his victim."

"He had lost his pension and everything else. His life had been the army, but only for what he could take from it. He made his way back to England, living by his wits from card games and thieving, and possibly worse. He gained a reputation, and several gangs were on the lookout for him. He found it prudent to bury himself in a small village and wait. I doubt we'll find any evidence of writing a book. Meanwhile, his funds dwindled and he began plotting to steal the snuff boxes. They would finance another move to a more enjoyable place where he wasn't known. America perhaps. It's a big continent."

"Colonel Caruthers," interrupted the inspector, "I am arresting you in the name of the Queen. Sergeant?"

The sergeant stepped up to handcuff the colonel, who began to struggle until it took the two constables who had arrived with the inspector to restrain him.

"Allow me," Constable Rigdon said. The sergeant handed him the handcuffs and Rigdon applied them with a great deal of satisfaction.

"Take him to the station and free Mrs. Jakes," the inspector said.

"With pleasure, sir," Rigdon said.

"Do we get the cook back?" Lady Acton asked.

"I don't see why not," Lord Acton said.

The Colonel fought as the three propelled him out of the room.

"What about my snuff boxes?" his Lordship said.

"I've had telegrams from Scotland Yard. They've all been recovered, but one. Carruthers sold them to the same duke who had visited last month – Colonel Carruthers had identified him as a likely buyer – and he was only happy to do the right thing. The money will be returned to him, and the boxes to you, your Lordship."

"You say that they were all recovered but one," said Lord Acton. "Which one?" His Lordship looked as if he knew which one was lost to him.

Inspector Yarbro pulled a sheaf of telegrams from his pocket and consulted them. "The one with the emeralds."

"He can't keep that box!" he cried. "It belongs to me! He knows it does!"

"It wasn't the duke who kept it, sir. It were the maharajah. He'd already sailed for India. We've sent wires, but the chances are . . . ." He shrugged.

His Lordship was livid. "This is unacceptable! The maharajah knows that's my snuff box! I told him I would never sell any of them. I'll cable the army! The East India Company! The Queen!" He rushed out of the room, followed by Lady Acton.

The villagers looked as if they had been the audience at a play and it was still going on.

"Perhaps his Lordship has forgotten the East India Company disbanded in 1867," Inspector Yarbro said.

"He'll find out," Holmes said.

The villagers laughed.

"Excellent work, Mr. Holmes," the inspector said.

Holmes inclined his head.

Our job was done. We repaired to the inn for a hearty meal. In the morning we were surprised to see Mrs. Jakes at breakfast there.

"Sit with me, sirs."

We took our seats. She held out her hand. On her left ring finger a tiny diamond winked in the morning light. "I spent the night here at the inn. I'm engaged. Constable Rigdon didn't think it seemly for me to stay at the jail since I'm free. So I come here. He said to send the bill to his Lordship. We're to be married at half-ten – we obtained a special license, by way of making up for things. Would you gentlemen stand up with me?"

And that is how we came to stand with the bride in marriage to Constable Rigdon. Inspector Yarbro heard of the nuptials and returned on the early train with the same two constables. She was marrying one of his men and she was also the relative of a Scotland Yard inspector. Miss Vidal and her mother arrived with a large bouquet of winter roses and snowdrops from their garden. Miss Atlee gathered armfuls of greenery and camelias for the church altar. The church was filled with the villagers. The doctor made it just before the vows were spoken. After punch and a light repast in the vicarage parlor, we wished the happy couple well and caught the London train.

Lestrade called late the next day to thank us for saving his relative.

"I'm glad she won't go back to cooking at Netherhill," I said. "Lord and Lady Acton don't deserve her grand dishes, but it's a shame she'll not be creating her excellent cuisine for more than Rigdon and the occasional miscreant."

"I don't know about that. She has plans to put in a shelf of baked goods in the village shop," Lestrade said. "She's noted for her pies and scones."

"She and the constable had a lot of time to talk," Holmes said.

"And to fall in love," I said.

"Oh Watson, you romantic," Holmes said. "I suspect that her cooking had a lot to do with it."

The next week he received a note from the new Mrs. Rigdon, thanking him for the lovely rose-patterned Royal Doulton tea set.

"Now who's the romantic?" I said

> *"My dear Watson, you know how bored I have been since we locked up Colonel Carruthers. My mind is like a racing engine, tearing itself to pieces because it is not connected up with the work for which it was built. Life is commonplace, the papers are sterile, audacity and romance seem to have passed for ever from the criminal world."*
>
> – Sherlock Holmes
> "The Adventure of Wisteria Lodge"

The Case of Vanderbilt and the Yeggman
by Stephen Herczeg

As I drew the curtains on another mid-spring evening, I couldn't help but shiver. The temperatures during the day had been mild to warm, but the chills of winter had not yet removed themselves completely from the night.

Turning back to survey the mess I'd made of the day's *Telegraph*, I realised that a stranger could only draw one conclusion from reading its contents: A heat wave was blasting the great city, given the panic contained in every story. Such was the dread that gripped the media and political class over incidents occurring thousands of miles away in Afghanistan.

The outcome of another skirmish between Russian and Afghani forces threatened to bring British forces into play. Such an expansion was too close to the Indian border for the locals to accept.

Coupled with veiled threats emanating from Russia, the events had placed the British Defence Forces, both home and abroad, on notice for immediate deployment to the region. Contracted arrangements to finish several new British Ironclads had been brought forward. The Prime Minister had formed a war committee and was in the process of requesting additional funding for defence spending.

I shook my head as I gathered up the scattered pages of the newspaper. The sabre-rattling affairs of state always brought back flashes of my time in Afghanistan. I tried to dispel such remembrances, but a small squeal of pain in my shoulder answered the siren song.

I stretched to full height, trying to ease the throb through movement. Placing the newspaper on the settee, I paced about the sitting room in an attempt to stop the ache. I put it down to the chill, or the silly way I had stooped down to pore over the newspaper.

Holmes was out on a case to which I hadn't been made privy, so I had occupied my time with the news, attempting one of his techniques of cross-matching articles to build a deeper picture of the story – something for which I now berated myself as I stepped around the room, bringing the fire in my shoulder under control.

I paced past the door to Holmes's bedroom and then the fireplace, and found myself at Holmes's chemical bench. It was there I saw some of His private paraphernalia: Two slim glass syringes were filled with brown-tinged liquid, resting in an open red silk lined case.

"Oh, Holmes," I said out loud, a hint of exasperation on my lips. I picked up one of the syringes and looked closely at the contents. Pursing my lips, I peered around for any other evidence of Holmes's cocaine habit. Finding none, I replaced the syringe and snapped the case shut.

I've failed to stop you in the past, but at least I can delay any future use for a little while.

I stepped away from Holmes's table just as the door to the sitting room opened. Surprised, I quickly slipped the syringe case into my jacket pocket and promptly forgot about it.

The tall aquiline features of Sherlock Holmes poked through the doorway and glanced across at me.

"Ah, Watson, good man," he said. "Grab your coat. Lestrade needs us at the Yard. *Tout de suite*, it seems."

Even though the traffic at that time of night was rather light, it still took the hansom a good twenty minutes cover the distance to the Yard. I had lost count of the number of times Holmes and I had journeyed along the same route over the last few years. The hansom pulled to a stop outside the front entrance, where we alighted. As always, I turned and paid the driver before joining Holmes.

"What is this about?" I'd waited to ask, as Holmes was disinclined to converse during our journey.

"Lestrade's telegram was non-specific on that point."

He pulled out a small folded paper and read aloud. "*Come now. Have arrested supposed friend of yours. Will only talk to you.*"

"Very strange," I said.

"Hopefully," answered Holmes. I caught sight of a slight smile on his face. He did love a good mystery, and given the amount of information he had to hand, I hoped this one kept him intrigued.

"What friend of yours could he have arrested?"

Holmes turned towards me, that grin still in place, "On that note, Watson, I can honestly say I have no idea. The telegram didn't give me enough information, and I certainly have no knowledge of any friends or acquaintances that have come under the suspicions of the police of late."

I looked up at the imposing edifice of Scotland Yard, the nearby gas lamps casting a pallid glow across the orange-and-grey bricks. We stepped through the great oak doors and stopped in the small reception area. The gap above the small wooden counter provided the only view into the inner workings of the Metropolitan Police.

At that time of night only a few bobbies were on duty, either moving around with sheafs of paper or sitting at their desks and filling out reports.

We stepped up to the counter and rang the small metal bell.

A young constable looked up and approached the counter. He recognised us straight away and nodded to the door to the side of the counter. Stepping through as he opened it, we followed him through the uniform work area and into a corridor beyond.

"The inspector's down in the basement," he said. "We've got a right strange one this time."

"The basement?" I said to Holmes in surprise. He simply smiled and held up a single finger to silence any further questions.

We went down a short flight of steps just outside the work room and walked along a long corridor that ran past storage cupboards and finally into the area reserved for small holding cells. From our past experience, I knew that there were also some unfurnished rooms specifically set aside for interviewing suspects.

I'll admit that I've never enjoyed entering this part of the building. It reeks of a misery from an older time, almost as if we had entered a medieval dungeon complete with torture chamber. Admittedly, the only criminals brought here are those charged with crimes against the Crown. The Yard's location means that miscreants captured near the Houses of Parliament, or worse, Buckingham Palace itself are most likely to be brought there

Finally, the young constable stopped and knocked on a solid wooden door. The knob turned and the door opened a crack, revealing the familiar face of Inspector Lestrade.

"Excellent," he said before stepping back and opening the door fully, allowing us to enter. The constable withdrew, and Holmes and I stepped into the sparsely furnished room.

The only other occupant of the room was a rat-faced little fellow who looked to be in his mid-forties. I could add or subtract a decade though due to the light. He sat on a chair in the middle of the room, his hands shackled behind him.

His features were amplified by the fearful look on his face and the way his eyes darted around the room and across both of us as we entered. A hint of recognition dawned on that face as he saw Holmes and he broke into a wide grim.

"Mr. 'Olmes," he said. "God bless you, sir!"

Holmes peered down his long nose and returned the smile. "Hello, Nobby," he said, "What trouble have you got yourself into this time?"

Nobby looked mortified. "Oh, no, sir, I done nuffin', 'onest. I've been tellin' the inspector 'ere just that. It's all a stitch-up."

Holmes turned to Lestrade, whose expression held the look of someone that lived his life being lied to by criminals.

"What is Nobby here meant to have done?" Holmes asked.

Lestrade pulled out a small notepad and made a big deal out of flipping to the requisite page, whilst eyeing the man in the chair with a healthy level of disdain.

"Arnold Brown, known on the street as 'Nobby', was caught coming out of the back entrance of Number Ten Downing Street – an address I'm sure you are familiar with."

I was aghast. My eyes darted back to look at Nobby again. I studied him more closely and realised that beneath his slightly grubby coat, he wore a neatly pressed dinner suit, with a white low-cut waistcoat and matching white bowtie. If I were to have met Nobby in a mansion house, I would have mistaken him for the butler or a simple valet.

Lestrade continued, "Two uniformed constables were on duty patrolling the grounds when they came upon this fellow skulking across the rear lawns."

"I wasn't skulking," said Nobby, "I 'ad an errand to run for my master."

Lestrade harrumphed. He'd obviously heard this before we arrived.

"And who would that master be?" asked Holmes.

"I shouldn't really say," said Nobby.

"Fine, then. It's the cells for you," said Lestrade, fed up with Nobby dodging the question, "You wanted Sherlock Holmes. Well here he is. If you're not going to answer the questions then you'll spend time in the lockup." He stepped towards Nobby, whose face lit up in fear.

"All right, all right," he said, peering back at Holmes hoping for some sympathy from my friend. When Holmes remained stoically still, Nobby relented, dropped his head and continued. "I'm workin' as man-servant to Mr. Johan Vanderbilt."

"Who?" asked Lestrade.

"Johan Vanderbilt," repeated Nobby, "He's an attaché to the German ambassador. I been workin' out of the London residence. It's a good job, been there for the last six months. On the straight and narrow, me."

"Well that's very good to see, Nobby," said Holmes.

I was quite intrigued. From experience, I knew that Holmes had a large sphere of acquaintances across London, and indeed the country. I assumed that Nobby fell into one of the various coteries that circled Holmes, or vice-versa.

"How exactly do you know Nobby here?" I asked.

"I'd like to know as well," said Lestrade.

"Ah," said Holmes, a wry smile on his lips. He stepped closer to Nobby, stared down at him for a moment before turning back to us. "Nobby here taught me everything I know about safe-cracking. He's been at it for well over twenty years. One of the best in London."

Lestrade's face lit up. "A yeggman, aye." He rubbed his hands together in glee. "Must be good at his job, 'cause I don't know him, but a yeggman caught coming out of the Prime Minister's residence – you might be going down for a long time, my boy."

Nobby cried out in terror, "I done nuthin'! I was working for Vanderbilt, 'onest, I was. Talk to 'im. He'll vouch for me!"

Holmes remained stoic, surveying the scene, searching for clews and digesting all. I'll admit my heart went out to the little man. His demeanour suggested sincerity, but I could tell that Holmes, himself, wasn't convinced. Lestrade was ready to hang the safe-cracker.

Holmes pondered for a while longer, leaving the room in silence, before he turned to Lestrade. "I assume, Inspector, you haven't searched Nobby as yet?"

"No. When he started going on about only talking to you, I thought I'd better wait."

"I've got nothin' on me, 'onest, Mr. 'Olmes. We've known each other for years. I wouldn't ask for you to vouch for me if I'd done somefin' bad, now would I?"

Holmes stood, peering at Nobby's face for several moments before turning to Lestrade. "Inspector, if you would be so kind, could you please undo Nobby's handcuffs?"

Nobby's face lit up. I was taken aback. Grumbling to himself, Lestrade stepped behind Nobby and undid the cuffs.

The yeggman rubbed his wrists to restart the blood flowing. "Thank you so much for trusting me, Mr. 'Olmes. You're a saint, I've always said that," he stated as he stood and headed towards the exit door.

Holmes waited until Nobby put a hand on the doorknob before speaking.

"Ah, not so fast Nobby." The former safe-cracker stopped in his tracks and turned slowly to face Holmes. "It might be prudent to inspect your garments before you head off. Just to satisfy the inspector. I wouldn't want him to think that there was anything untoward about this affair," Holmes said. I felt that there was something unsaid in his statement that would become evident quite soon.

Holmes held out a hand, I could tell he was holding his smile in check, "I'd like to have a quick look at your coat if I may." He shrugged, "Just as a matter of course."

Nobby's face was aghast. He slowly peeled off the coat and handed it to Holmes. My friend took it without taking his eyes off Nobby's expression. My eyes flicked between them, and I finally saw what Holmes saw. As Nobby's eyes dropped to the bottom of the coat, Holmes nodded, turned the coat around, and examined the lining inside. He let out a small, "A-ha!" and stepped over to the chair. Laying the coat across it, with the inner lining revealed, he ran a finger down the stitching in the centre and found a small unsewn section.

"If I'm mistaken, Nobby, I apologise in advance and will repair your coat," he said, before jamming a finger inside and pulling at the thread. It came away easily, revealing a larger section that had evidently been unpicked. The hole created was large enough for his entire hand. Holmes stood and reached into an inner pocket of his own coat and slipped out a pair of fine kid-skin gloves.

Wearing them, he thrust a hand deep inside the lining of Nobby's coat and fished around for a moment. A smile crossed his face and he brought out a folded sheaf of stiff parchment held together with a bright red ribbon. I caught sight of a seal on the outer page. I'm sure that there was a crown, and possibly a lion or unicorn.

"Good Lord!" said Lestrade. "What in the blazes is that?"

Holmes straightened and examined the papers for a moment, mumbling to himself before looking at Nobby and shaking his head.

"Nobby, you've been a very bad boy," he said.

The (now it seemed) active safe-cracker, looking much more presentable in full valet uniform, dropped his head in shame.

As Mycroft Holmes looked up from his work, his mouth dropped open in surprise as he spied his brother's silhouette in the doorway. "Sherlock? What in blazes are you doing in here? And how did you get in?"

A pale face at Holmes's shoulder looked past us and addressed Mycroft. "I'm sorry, sir. I did recognise your brother and was about to come for you, but it's what he was holding that made me bring him straight to you."

Mycroft stared at the man, a flush of anger ran across his cheeks. "Fine, Johnson, but that's not the proper process is it?"

Johnson's face went bright red. "No, sir. Sorry, sir." He backed away and virtually ran away down the corridor.

Holmes moved across to the large oaken desk and *plonked* his prize on the desk before his brother's eyes. Mycroft peered at the parcel of parchment wrapped in red ribbon. He looked from the papers to Holmes, confusion writ large his face. Slowly he pulled at the bow of the ribbon and freed it. He unfolded the sheaf of papers and read the opening words on the first page.

His face turned from confusion to horror.

"Sherlock, where did you get this? You could be in serious trouble."

Holmes took one of the chairs before Mycroft's desk and motioned for me to join him. Mycroft watched in silence as I walked over and sat down.

"I'll admit, dear brother, that I didn't open the papers. I realised as soon as I saw the seal, and was informed of the original location, that it would be tantamount to treason. I could have left the papers with the constabulary, but we agreed that it might be best to bring them to someone of your – how should I put it? – *station* within the Government."

Mycroft pursed his lips and read the first page again. He shook his head. "Where did this come from?"

"I think you already know that."

"Yes. I do."

I piped up, "Well, I don't, so please explain to those of us who are still in the dark."

Mycroft glanced at Holmes for a moment, then turned his face towards me. As always, he treated me with respect. "Well, Doctor, I would think you already know this came from the Prime Minister's residence." I nodded. "Neither of you could have known though, that these are the PM's personal notes to be read out in Parliament on Monday morning. Once presented, they will be taken away and typed up to form an appropriations bill to be tabled at Parliament later in the week. The final bill," he patted the sheaf of papers, "is set to rock the country to its core."

"Why?" I asked, leaning forward in an attempt to make out the wording and figures evident on the parchment.

"This country is on the brink of war – with Russia of all places."

I nodded. "It's all through the newspapers."

Mycroft harrumphed. "Reporters," he spat, "Until they got wind of it, there was nothing but a simple border skirmish. It would have resolved itself in a week and England would have had no reason to be involved. Our papers have blown it up to the point that the Russians have been emboldened and are pushing ever further into Indian territory. This," he smacked the papers, "is the result. Our pacifist Prime Minister is suddenly egged on by his constituency and taking us towards conflict. This outlines the amount of money he will request from Parliament, and the armaments and troops that it will pay for. All to be sent into Afghanistan and into this conflict."

"But surely we have learnt from the past," I said, imploring Mycroft.

He smiled back at me. "Doctor, you should know better than any of us here the futility of combat – combat that results when our ill-informed superiors begin to rattle their sabres."

Holmes finally spoke up. "I'm surprised, brother. I thought you fully supported the decision-making processes of our Government."

Mycroft sighed, "No, I fully support our Government. It just leaves me a little exasperated when those decisions go awry through unsupported opinions rather than actual facts."

He looked down at the parchment and thought for a moment before peering up at us once again.

"Enough of my own opinions, I can only assume that this parcel came from the safe in Number Ten." Holmes and I nodded. "Given the lack of excitement, I can also assume that it hasn't been found to be missing."

"Worse than that," Holmes said. "It has been replaced." He pointed towards the desk. "It seems that the miscreant that stole the original was also tasked with substituting another set of papers. I haven't seen them yet, but I assume they have revised figures created to mislead the Prime Minister and possibly embarrass him, or at worst, lead us to implement an incorrect regime of military acquisitions."

Mycroft thought for a moment, flipping through the notes and murmuring under his breath before looking back at us. "You may be right, Sherlock, but as to misleading the Government, that won't happen. The PM's figures would have been distributed to the Ministries of Defence and Finance already, plus to the Under-Secretaries to prepare the actual bill for tabling in Parliament. This action could embarrass the Prime Minister if he was to read them out in the House, but I feel that there is something far more sinister behind this." He stared at Holmes for a moment before the younger brother answered.

"Espionage," he said, a slight smile on his face.

"Why are you smiling?" Mycroft asked. "You could have just admitted that you already knew. I assume you know who then?"

"The Germans, it seems, but I'm unsure why. The man who stole these papers was doing so under contract to a member of the German diplomatic corp."

"Who?" said Mycroft, a look of confusion on his face. "I'm quite familiar with the Ambassador, Baron Egor."

"The papers were purloined by one Arthur 'Nobby' Brown, a yeggman from Soho," started Holmes.

Mycroft interrupted, "Sorry, did you say that he was an '*eggman*'?"

"No, *yeggman*," said Holmes, placing particular emphasis on the first syllable, "It is street slang for a safe-cracker. Anyway, Nobby Brown was hired by Johan Vanderbilt, an assistant to the Ambassador. Nobby was arrested outside of Number Ten whilst the Prime Minister was entertaining several European ambassadors, including Baron Egor Staal. Nobby went in with Vanderbilt, slipped away from the dining room, opened the safe, switched notes, and exited the building. It was only through sheer luck that a pair of bobbies were checking the rear of the property when Nobby crossed their path."

"Vanderbilt? I don't think I've met him."

"Well, you might have an opportunity tomorrow. He's to meet with Nobby to lay claim to these notes."

"It will be no good if it's on the Embassy grounds."

"With that we are quite fortunate. Our captive yeggman was to meet this Vanderbilt in a small pub in Covent Garden to hand over the papers."

"What time?" asked Mycroft.

"Twelve-thirty, a half-hour after opening. Good idea, that. They should be able to hide amongst the lunch time crowd," said Holmes.

Mycroft stood and picked up the parcel of papers and walked around the desk. "I need to get these back into the PM's safe before he becomes aware and – " He stopped and tapped Holmes on the shoulder. " – I don't understand what interest these Germans have in our defence movements, but we should use everything at our disposal to upset their attempt."

"What are you thinking?" I asked, my eyes darting across to Holmes and seeing a familiar sly grin on his face.

"Who would have written up the PM's notes in the first place?" Holmes asked.

"That would be Miss Marsden, the PM's personal assistant," Mycroft said shaking his head, "She would be long gone."

"Do you have anyone else on staff that can draft up a set of mock papers?" asked Holmes.

"Perhaps, but I think we need to keep the number of people within these walls that know about this to a minimum," Mycroft said.

"I believe I may know someone that can help. We'll need to borrow those," Holmes said pointing at the sheaf of papers, "Or at least an example of Miss Marsden's handwriting, for authenticity's sake. We will also, of course, need some official stationary, including some more of that ribbon."

"More than easy to arrange," said Mycroft.

Within half-an-hour, Mycroft had the wheels turning throughout the Houses of Parliament. At Number 10, Mycroft himself led us down a corridor and into the Prime Minister's outer offices. Using his own key, he rummaged through the personal filing cabinet of Miss Marsden and retrieved another batch of the PM's reading notes.

Back in his office, all three of us crowded around his desk to view the spoils.

Miss Marsden's notes were written out in a spidery thin scrawl, very reminiscent of the delicate hand of woman. The fake notes consisted of similar penmanship but had a slightly heavier look to them.

Mycroft read through the faked papers, murmuring and mumbling to himself as he did so. Finally he burst out, "Preposterous! Whoever wrote this has no idea about the workings of Parliament, or indeed the Defence force."

"Would the PM have gotten far into the figures before realising?"

Mycroft thought for a moment and shook his head. "Sadly, he would have probably read them all out and only realised once the guffaws broke out from the cross-benches."

"As I thought," said Holmes. He then pointed to the script and commented, "This was drafted by a man. The downstrokes on the pen are much heavier than Miss Marsden's, but overall, it is a very good likeness. The forger obviously had access to a set of notes such as ours."

"I agree," said Mycroft. "That worries me quite a bit."

"Why?" I asked.

"It would appear that the forger is working within these walls."

My eyes opened in surprise and I nodded in response. Such an act by a member of Parliament or the Civil Service was tantamount to an act of treason in the eyes of the law.

Finally Mycroft sat back and closed the papers. He looked exhausted. I think it was mostly due to the gravity of the situation, rather than any physical exertion.

"Would it have been as bad as you thought?" Holmes asked.

"If the PM had read this out without examining it first, which is most likely, he would have seemed a fool, and would certainly have stumbled within a couple of pages. The scandal surrounding the theft and replacement that would soon erupt would be far worse." Mycroft peered up at his hawk-faced brother. "I can't thank you enough, I really can't."

"It's not us you have to thank," Holmes said, "I think you should send your regards, and possibly something a little more substantial, to Inspector Lestrade and the two bobbies that caught Nobby."

"Yes, yes, you're right. I will see to it. But first – " He pulled a few sheets of paper from his desk drawer and scrawled several lines whilst flipping through the sheaf of fake papers. I looked across at Holmes, a perplexed look on my face. He simply smiled and shrugged.

Mycroft laid down his pen, gathered up his notes and the fake papers, and stood up. He strode from the room with a rare sense of purpose.

Holmes kept pace with him easily, but I found myself falling back. Luckily, the journey downstairs and into the sub-basement area was short.

We entered a large room packed with shelves and cupboards. A lone desk sat near the doorway and acted as a counter. A young man of barely twenty years sat behind the desk. He was working away on a sort of long handwritten document when he noticed us. His eyes went wide as we entered, he dropped his pen and shot to his feet.

A nervous voice peeped out of his mouth. "Mr. Holmes, sir. What can I do for you?"

"Ah, Atherton, good lad," he said. "Surprised you're here."

"Um, I took the opportunity to learn more about work, sir," he answered with a smile.

Mycroft returned his smile and nodded, "Good man. You'll go far with that attitude. Now, back to business, I need ten pages of the PM's stock paper, a length of red ribbon, a pen, and ink."

Atherton looked confused for a moment. "I'm only meant to give that out to Miss Marsden," he said.

"And normally that would be fair," said Mycroft, "But I have been asked to prepare some reading notes for the PM on Monday and know that he prefers all his notes to be on the same paper stock."

The young man nodded. "I can't argue with that." He turned and disappeared into the depths of the rows of shelves. The sound of his rummaging filtered back to us.

I pivoted and noticed Holmes taking a special interest in what Atherton had been working on. From where I stood, I could see that it was writing, some large, some small, some heavy, some verging on spidery. It was then I noticed Atherton's jacket hanging on a coat rack near the aisles of shelving. My eye was drawn to the pin on the lapel. It was composed of a small silver bar on a red and green striped ribbon. If I wasn't mistaken I would say it was the Afghanistan medal, I had a similar one myself for services in the war. I thought to myself that the lad was far too young to have served and assumed it was a father's or grandfather's pin.

I was about to comment to Holmes when the young lad returned. He *plopped* the supplies down on the desk and handed a wooden clipboard with an attached sheet of paper to Mycroft.

"Just need you to sign for these, sir. Normally, I wouldn't need to ask, but I've been told to keep a close watch on our more special items."

Mycroft nodded and signed. Atherton took the clipboard away and handed over the stationary. He nodded slightly, before saying, "A good night to you, gentlemen."

"And you to Atherton, and thank you," said Mycroft before ushering us out of the room. I looked back as I exited and noted Atherton's gaze intently fixed on the three of us. I was confused as to his expression – it appeared to be part concern, part fear, and part suspicion.

Within moments we had been ushered back into the cold London night. The fake notes, loose sheaf of papers, pens and ribbon – all contained in an official leather satchel.

Mycroft had expressed his concerns about our next steps but wanted to be kept up to date as things progressed. I admit I was still at a slightly loose end. I had faith that the Holmes brothers knew what they were doing, but as always would have liked some inkling of the plan going forward.

Holmes hailed a hansom and as we climbed aboard I peered back to find that Mycroft had already disappeared back inside the building. By the time I turned forward, Holmes had given the driver our destination, so I simply sat and watched as we navigated the virtually empty streets.

After about fifteen minutes of travelling along the edge of the river, we turned right then onto the Kings Road. I felt it was time to ask, "Holmes, where the devil are we going?"

"To visit an old associate," he said in that enigmatic way of his.

"Another one?" I asked, the question disappearing into the ether. Grumbling to myself, I sat back in the seat and remained silent. After another few minutes and we turned into the Fulham Palace Road and headed towards Hammersmith. I was certainly intrigued by now, even more so when we pulled up in front of a dark four-storey Georgian building on the Hammersmith High Street. Holmes leapt from the hansom and made his way towards the ground floor entrance, leaving me to pay the cabbie.

"You might want to get him to stay for a while," Holmes said over his shoulder. "Say two hours."

I heard the heavy knocker hammer away as I was negotiating the fee with the driver and managed to join Holmes just as the door was opened by a crook-backed old man who looked to be in his seventies. He peered up at Holmes's darkened face and I saw a grin appear on his face.

"Sherlock Holmes! My word, it's been well over ten years, hasn't it?"

"Yes, Clive, yes it has," Holmes said.

The old man stepped back and allowed us both to enter. He looked me up and down, before Holmes introduced me. "Ah, this is my associate, Dr. John Watson. Watson, this is Mr. Clive Trimble."

I held out my hand, but Trimble shied away, preferring to nod instead.

"Ah, yes, Clive doesn't shake hands. Do you, Clive?" Holmes asked as the old man nodded. "He is very protective of his hands. Any damage may affect his craft."

"Craft?" I asked.

Before I received an answer, Holmes strolled down the corridor, followed by the old man. I closed the door and chased after them, catching up in a room at the back of the house consisting of several draughtsman's tables, each with a gas light situated above them. An ornate table sat at the end of the room, with two lights shining nearby.

Holmes and Trimble stood next to a normal flat table. Holmes withdrew the sheaf of parliamentary stationary, notes, and other paraphernalia from the satchel and placed them on the bench.

Holmes pointed to the figures that Mycroft had drafted, then the fake notes and Miss Marden's scribbles.

"Clive, I haven't asked for a return of the favour I gave you all those years ago, but tonight I am."

Clive's face dropped into a stern expression. "Nothing illegal is it?" He shook his head and backed away a step. "I don't want to be doing nothing illegal again. I've left all that behind. I'm too old to go back inside Wandsworth. It'd be the death of me."

"It's all right Clive. Nothing about this is illegal. In fact, you would be helping your country." Holmes pointed to the fake notes. "I need you to write up a set of notes like these – " Then at Mycroft's figures. " – using these numbers instead – " Finally, he pointed at Miss Marsden's writings. " – in the handwriting style of this young lady."

Clive looked at each in turn, his eyes lit up at the prospect of what he was to do. "And this is nothing illegal?"

"I assure you, this is all above board. Would I lie to you?"

The old man peered up at my good friend, a small smile crossed his lips and he shook his head. "No, no, you wouldn't lie to me, Mr. Holmes." He picked up the pages and moved across to the ornate draughtman's board and began to delve into his craft. I was intrigued and watched from several feet away as he practiced the strokes from the PM's secretary's scribblings before creating another set of notes with Mycroft's figures.

I almost started when I heard Holmes's voice in my ear. "The man is an artist. He is renowned for recreating historical documents and notations in almost the exact replication of the original's hand-writing and calligraphy."

"But that could so easily be seen as fraud or forgery," I said.

"Ah, yes. Sadly, Clive did stray onto the other side of the law on one occasion. We crossed paths when I was asked to help investigate a case of illegal forgery."

I must have looked confused, as Holmes smiled and said, "Oh, before your time, Watson, before your time. Not an overly exciting adventure, but I'd be happy to relate it to you at another time. Anyway, I tracked the original documents and the miscreants that had ordered the work to be done, and I managed to convince the police that our Clive here had been duped into committing a crime. They reduced his sentence by five years, which – given his age – probably saved his life."

"Was he innocent?"

"That question requires further discussion, as there was a lot of additional information that you would need to make your own judgement, and this isn't the appropriate time or place to expand fully."

We went silent as we saw Clive turn towards us with a disparaging look. I wandered away and perused the works on the other draught boards. One towards the far end of the room held a large sheet of parchment upon which were the letters *A*, *J*, and *S*, written in various styles and sizes. As I studied it, I noticed Holmes standing beside me.

"Ah, Clive has himself an apprentice, it seems," he said.

Confused, I asked, "How so?"

"Well the first thing one is taught is to practice your calligraphy using familiar text. The letters of the alphabet, your name, address, things like that. Most students use their own initials the most," he said, before turning away and rummaging through a large pile of seemingly forgotten sheets of parchment in the far corner. Finally, he stood and brought across a single but very dusty page. He placed it on the draught board next to the object of my interest.

It was a similar page, but it was covered from edge to edge with variations of the letters *S* and *H*. As I stared at the lettering, the penny dropped. I turned to face Holmes.

"You were a student?"

He smiled., "Why yes, Watson, I was. Clive never throws anything away. After her was released from Wandsworth, I helped him to set up this shop, and then engaged his services to learn the art of calligraphy and script replication."

"Forgery, you mean."

Holmes chuckled, "Well, yes, forgery if you like, but it was all in the interests of education. One must understand the criminal mind and their techniques to be able to interpret and judge the distinction between real and fake."

Before I could reply, Clive looked up from his work and harrumphed. "I believe I have finished."

We hurried over and glanced at the finished notes. I was amazed. To my layman's eye, the delicate feminine scrawl of the PM's assistant was reproduced as if by the same hand. I glanced at Holmes. A small grin told me that he seemed just as impressed.

"Excellent work, my good friend," he said. "Excellent work."

Holmes, Lestrade, and I arrived at The Lamb and Flag pub dead on midday. The wonderfully bright sunny day did nothing to heighten the drab look of the external façade of the building. It was nestled down Rose Street in Covent Garden, a street by name only, as in reality it was little more than a dimly lit back-alley that curved around connecting Floral to Garrick street.

The three of us had affected the look of everyday workers, shunning any trappings of finery and dragging out our oldest, shoddiest clothing. Holmes had any number of costumes from which to choose. I simply picked my oldest clothes that I had kept on hand in case Holmes dragged me off on another undercover adventure. It was Lestrade that looked the most out of place amongst the three of us. He obviously had to delve into the back of his cupboard and drag out some very old and well-worn clothing that must have been in everyday use once due to its wear, but they hadn't graced his body in years.

The interior of the pub was no different from the outside in terms of décor and refinement. It was a simple room with a series of booths along the walls, consisting of hard wooden benches and tables, and a scattering of small wooden tables and stools across the central area. A bar ran along one wall, with the dour-looking landlord the only worker in sight.

This was simply a drinkers' pub, servicing the workers from the nearby markets, and one could assume, at night, the more questionable local trade.

As we sat nursing our pints of watery beer and avoiding the suspicious eyes of the landlord, Holmes and Lestrade told tales of their knowledge of the place.

"There's a room upstairs," began Lestrade, "that they call 'The Bucket of Blood', on account of the bare-knuckle fights they hold on the first Saturday night of every month."

"That's barbaric," I said, "Surely the constabulary should shut it down."

Holmes harrumphed to remind me to stay in character, while Lestrade chuckled. "The local bobbies know well to leave this place alone. The locals keep each other in check. The law only steps in when someone gets well out of line. It's a balancing act, but it works."

I crossed my arms at the thought.

Holmes piped up, "From my reading, this place has an even longer and stranger history. It was once a more genteel establishment attracting some of the local poets, such as Dryden and Wilmott. In fact, poor John Dryden was attacked by ruffians not far from here, supposedly in revenge for a satirical poem he wrote about Charles the Second's mistress at the time."

"I thought you said that it was more genteel?" I asked.

"Yes, but one must not vilify the King or his mistress. The intriguing fact was that Dryden didn't even write the poem. It was John Sheffield, the Third Earl of Mulgrave."

"So, he was assaulted for no reason, except mistaken identity," I said.

"As it would seem. Very difficult to bring a grievance against the King – especially someone held in such high regard as Charles the Second."

My comment was stopped short as the front door opened and in stepped a tall, slender figure. He was immaculately dressed in a morning suit, with a calf-length frockcoat over it. He took off his top hat and tucked it under his arm. His hair was dark and neatly trimmed, as was his full-faced beard.

He took one look around the room, regarding the three of us briefly before stepping over to the landlord. He held up his index and middle finger and placed some coins on the bar, before moving to the rear of the room and taking a seat in a booth that looked directly at the entrance.

Holmes stared down at his beer and spoke under his breath. "I do believe that is our man."

I directed my own comment at Lestrade. "I do hope you have things in hand outside?"

"Don't worry about that. I've got some of the best keeping their eyes on this place – one either end of Rose Street, and one across the road on Floral Street." He nodded towards the man we believed to be Vanderbilt. "Just in case he goes out the back."

"And Nobby?" Holmes asked.

"He has his own minder, making sure he plays his part."

"Good," said Holmes.

"I assume that you have your own helpers well advised," I said.

"Of course, Watson, of course. Wiggins and Tommy are on the case, with a couple of extras thrown in for good measure. They have Nobby's description, and using his depiction of Vanderbilt, they should have no problems picking up the trail, just in case."

"Surely," Lestrade added, "he'll be headed back to the German Embassy."

"That would be the logical choice, but something disturbs me about all this. The whole German connection, for a start. The Germans have had no interest in Afghanistan, or the sub-continent for decades, so I'm confused why they should show interest now." He took a sip of his beer before looking up as the door opened. "Ah, here we are now, I believe."

The small stature and rat-like features of Nobby Brown entered the pub. He stood in the entrance way while his eyes grew accustomed to the gloom before looking around the room. His eyes fell on the three of us and grew wide in fear. Holmes simply nodded at him before resuming his examination of the tepid contents of his glass.

The landlord piped up from behind the bar. "Hello, Nobby! Usual is it?"

I watched as Nobby peered over at him, before spying the man in the corner with the two beers before him. "Nah, thanks Harold," he said. "I have an appointment." Harold simply nodded and went back to drying glasses. Nobby made his way to the smartly dressed man's booth and sat opposite. The man we presumed to be Vanderbilt, and whom Nobby knew, leaned forward and spoke in a tone too quiet to hear. Nobby was galvanised into action and quickly reached into his coat pocket, extracting the sheaf of pages wrapped in the red ribbon and sliding them across.

The man drew the ribbon, unknotted the bow, and quickly perused the documents. I noticed a small smile come to his face before he closed the documents, retied the ribbon, and slipped them inside his own jacket pocket. From the other side he withdrew a small envelope which he slid across to Nobby. I barely had time to register the colour of the envelope before Nobby had performed a disappearing act with it.

I leaned into Lestrade and spoke, "You might want to make sure to relieve Nobby of that."

"Already on it," he replied.

The two men held up their beers and clinked glasses before taking long draws in celebration. Their rejoicing was short lived as Vanderbilt rose, put on his coat, and strode towards the entrance.

The three of us remained unmoved until he had left the building, and then we were a flurry of activity. Holmes and I headed towards the entrance doorway, while Lestrade moved towards Nobby, nabbing him by the collar just as the little yeggman was hightailing it towards the rear exit.

"Not so fast, my lad," I heard Lestrade say before following Holmes into the bright sunshine outside.

Vanderbilt was rapidly disappearing down the right-hand alleyway, heading towards the hustle and bustle of Floral Street. I noticed Holmes peer down the left-hand alleyway and cock his head for a moment before striding after the tall German diplomat.

"Intriguing," I heard him mutter under his breath as I struggled to keep up with him.

As we reached Hart Street, we saw the tall figure of Vanderbilt climbing into a hansom cab. Holmes turned to his right and waved. Immediately, a similar vehicle wound its way through the traffic toward us. We quickly climbed in as Holmes addressed the driver.

"Granton, you saw him?" he asked.

The undercover police officer nodded. "Yes, Mr. Holmes. He fits the description that Brown gave us. Don't worry, I won't let him lose us."

"Good man," said Holmes sitting back and relaxing only slightly.

"What troubles you?" I said. "The man grabbed a cab. Nothing unusual in that."

"Ah, but it is, Watson. Prussia House, which now serves as the German Embassy since unification in 1871, is located in St. James Square. It's barely half-a-mile from Covent Garden. A tall man such as Vanderbilt could walk it easily in ten minutes. I don't believe that's where we're headed," he said.

As I looked out of the cab, I realised we were passing along Piccadilly, well north of St. James.

"Where could we be heading then?" I asked.

Holmes had a broad smile across his face.

"Care to enlighten me?"

"You'll find out very soon," he answered. "It will be more interesting to see how Mycroft takes the news."

Still intrigued, I glanced outside and realised that we were then passing Wellington Arch and heading towards Belgravia. The houses and buildings had an air of elegance and expense about them that was a world away from The Lamb and Flag.

We passed many buildings proudly displaying flags of other nations outside. I recognised Austria, Hungary, and Italy before we turned into Chesham Street and stopped facing an ornate building that displayed a flag with yellow, black, and white horizontal stripes.

"The Russian Embassy," Holmes said before I could blurt it out myself.

We watched as Vanderbilt stepped from his cab and walked to the front entrance. I was shocked to see the two guards, standing at the front, step back and allow him unmolested entry to the building. This was a diplomat from another embassy – surely they would need some form of identification.

"Well, that was interesting," said Holmes, almost speaking for myself.

"They didn't even stop him. It's as if they know him," I said.

"Yes, so it would seem," Holmes agreed. He reached up and knocked on the roof. "Granton, pull up behind that other hansom. We're about to set a trap for this Vanderbilt chap."

As Granton pulled the hansom up in front of the embassy, Holmes and I alighted. Holmes strode over to the other cab and chatted with the driver. The driver peered back at Granton, who undid his coat and showed the police uniform beneath. The other driver needed no more convincing and left quickly.

Holmes and I moved away from the building but stayed within sight of both the cab and the entrance. The two men stationed either side of the front entrance eyed us suspiciously for a few moments before turning away.

I leaned into Holmes and asked, "Why would Vanderbilt be allowed such unfettered entry to the Russian embassy? He's a German diplomat, isn't he?"

"That seems to be his station, but then we must delve into his history. Something is unknown to us," he said in that annoyingly deceptive way of his, "but becoming quite apparent." Before I could ask another question, Vanderbilt emerged from the building and strode straight to Granton's cab. We peeled away from our position and hurried after him.

"*Dobryy den' Gospodin* Vanderbilt," said Holmes (Good afternoon Mr. Vanderbilt), as we squeezed in either side of the shocked man, "I assume you are more familiar with your native language." Holmes rapped on the roof and the cab drew away and joined the light traffic.

"Vat is the meaning of this?" Vanderbilt blurted out. Holmes and I placed our arms across him bodily to restrict any chance of his escape. "I will call the police. This is an outrage. I am a German diplomat. Let me go at once."

Holmes smiled, "Sit back and relax, my good man. A policeman is already here, driving the cab. As for you being German – we will get to the bottom of that soon."

When Vanderbilt resisted once more, I pushed my hand into my pocket and pressed the barrel of my service revolver into his side. His eyes went even wider, but all fight quickly left him. Resigned, he sat back and awaited the journey's end.

The taller, straight-backed figure of Vanderbilt presented a far different sight in that small sparsely furnished room than did the object our earlier attention. Lestrade mentioned that Nobby had been sequestered to his own cell in Wandsworth for the time being. Holmes reminded Lestrade that Nobby had been helpful in snaring our new culprit, and with passing on the forged notes.

Regardless, he mentioned to me in passing that Mycroft would be informed of everything, which would hopefully have more weight with the judiciary.

Vanderbilt eyed us with both disgust and vile hatred. He retained an upright posture, in spite of the discomfort that he must have felt. I sensed it was more of an act to sway our opinion of him than anything.

"Who are you?" Lestrade asked him for the fourth time.

The familiar response followed, "I am Herr Johan Vanderbilt. I am a member of the German diplomatic corp. I ask for diplomatic immunity and wish to speak to my consular attorney."

Holmes, apparently fed up with the misdirection, finally spoke up. "But that's not altogether true is it, Ivan? I assume it's Ivan, as that is the Russian equivalent of Johan."

Vanderbilt's face turned to rage as he stared towards Holmes.

"I am Johan Vanderbilt. I am German. I was born in – "

Holmes cut him off, "Again, that isn't true, is it? I've been patient, but let us look at the facts, shall we?" He counted off on his fingers, deliberately using his thumb to start with. "One, you employed a local safe-cracker, Nobby Brown, to break into the Prime Minister's personal safe and replace private papers detailing troop numbers and financial information for an ongoing operation on the Afghanistan border between English and Russian troops."

He extended his index finger and tapped it. "Two, you personally delivered those papers to the Russian Embassy. Three, you understand Russian. Four, you wear a close-cropped full faced beard, very rare in Germany, but very common in western Russia at this time. Five, in The Lamb and Flag, you signalled the number two to the bartender using your index and middle fingers. Any purebred German, worth his salt, would use his thumb and index finger for such a gesture. A mistake like that could get you shot amongst the spy community."

Holmes waited for any reaction. When there was none, he continued. "All we're interested in is who you gave those papers to among the Russian staff, who your accomplice is inside the Government, and how long this has been going on."

"I will never speak. I have diplomatic immunity. You can't prove anything."

"To be honest, we don't need to prove anything. Once those forged papers reach Russia, the fallout will unveil the agents within their embassy, and they will deal with them accordingly. As for you, we have accepted your diplomatic immunity and you will be handed over to the German Embassy staff, who I'm sure will have many questions of their own."

At that moment the door opened and two tall, well-built men in ill-fitting suits entered. They had the square jawed, blonde hair, blue-eyed look of Continental Germans. They took one look at Vanderbilt and stepped forward.

"Ah, they seem to have arrived," said Holmes.

Vanderbilt's eyes widened in fear and his mouth dropped open. He quickly thrust a hand toward his mouth. I was closest and threw out my hand, knocking whatever he'd held to the floor. It was a capsule of some sort. By now two burly men were holding Vanderbilt, but he kept lunging toward the object. Holmes reached down and picked it up. Sniffing it, he quickly turned his head away. Then he held it toward me and I took a careful smell as well. Bitter almonds. *Cyanide.* Vanderbilt had attempted to avoid our questions, but fortunately he had been prevented.

"Well done, old chap," said Holmes.

It was an early morning a few days later that found Holmes and me perusing the papers whilst finishing off another sumptuous breakfast prepared by our wonderful landlady, Mrs. Hudson.

As I sipped my morning coffee, I mused out loud that the last word we had received from Mycroft was over three days previously.

"I'm still a little shocked at the identity of the German agent within the Home Office," I said.

Holmes looked up from his paper. "Well, the lad had a grudge against Her Majesty's Government."

"I can understand, given that his father died in Afghanistan. Losing one's father so early in life leaves scars, as it did young Atherton."

"Sadly, yes. He brooded on it for years. He wasn't working late to improve his prospects – he was copying classified documents, as I saw on his desk when we surprised him the other day. He'd managed to position himself somewhere that nobody would take any notice of him, learning the ins-and-outs of the Home Office and the Prime Minister's office, because nobody would think twice about talking around the person in charge of stationery. Such a person is always invisible in such an organisation."

"What will happen to him?"

"Hopefully he will only be treated as a dissident, and not charged with treason," Holmes said, "Well, that's to be hoped for anyway. His biggest mistake was falling in with Vanderbilt. Young minds are so impressionable, especially when they bear a grudge against authority. It will be for Her Majesty's authorities to decide." Holmes turned back to his newspaper.

I did the same and began to read *The Times*, coming across an article that smacked of a result of our recent adventure. The headline read *Russia Calls for Talks*. The article indicated that sources within the Government stated that the Russian ambassador to England had visited the Foreign Secretary to begin talks aimed at easing tensions on the Afghanistan-Indian border.

I peered across at Holmes and held the paper so he could read the headline. “It seems as if Mycroft’s little ploy worked.”

Holmes looked up from his own reading and smiled. “He will be pleased.”

Our attention was diverted by the ring of the doorbell downstairs. A murmur of conversation filtered up to us, which gave me the impression that Mrs. Hudson knew our visitor, followed by a series of heavy footfalls on the steps that led from the entrance to our door.

“I believe we will be able to ask Mycroft all about it,” Holmes said.

The door opened and admitted Mycroft with a slightly red-face, but possessing a very pleased expression.

“Good morning,” he said, removing his coat and placing it on a nearby chair. His eyes darted towards the open newspapers on our table and he nodded. “Ah, so you already know then. Remarkable that something so simple could have such an impact.”

“What did you write in those notes?” I asked.

“Nothing ground-breaking,” he said, “I merely doubled the number of ground troops, and added a second division of artillery to the figures that the Prime Minister was already requesting. His original numbers were drawn from the intelligence gathered on the Russian’s available forces in Afghanistan, and I simply made it appear that England was prepared to overwhelm them with troops and engines of war.”

“The bluff worked,” said Holmes.

“Yes, yes, it did,” Mycroft added, “All I really wanted was to paint a picture that said we were prepared for a protracted campaign. It’s something that neither side would really want, and obviously the Russians wanted it even less than us.” He shook his head at the futility of it all. “Especially when one considers that there’s nothing there. It’s all just ground that even the locals don’t really care that much about.”

“And Vanderbilt?” I asked.

He nodded towards Holmes and said, “Ah, yes. Everything that my dear brother deduced was correct. The Germans were able to sweat a lot of information out of Mr. Vanderbilt. It seems he had been working under a false name with a false identity for quite a number of years. His real name was in fact Ivan Letorovski, born in St. Petersburg. He moved to Germany twenty years ago and worked his way into the diplomatic corps over that time.”

“Do we have any agents of that type?” asked Holmes, a sly grin on his lips.

I knew he was having a dig at Mycroft, and his brother didn’t disappoint. “If I told you that, you would end up in the same place as Vanderbilt,” he said.

"And where is that?" I asked, a sudden prickle of fear rising up my spine.

"Ah," said Mycroft, "the Germans told me that once they had finished interrogating him, he was going to be returned to Germany." He paused for a moment. "In the diplomatic bag."

I winced. "That sounds nasty."

I leaned back and took down the great index volume to which he referred. Holmes balanced it on his knee, and his eyes moved slowly and lovingly over the record of old cases, mixed with the accumulated information of a lifetime.

"Voyage of the Gloria Scott," he read. "That was a bad business. I have some recollection that you made a record of it, Watson, though I was unable to congratulate you upon the result. Victor Lynch, the forger. Venomous lizard or gila. Remarkable case, that! Vittoria, the circus belle. Vanderbilt and the Yeggman. Vipers. Vigor, the Hammersmith wonder. Hullo! Hullo! Good old index. You can't beat it . . . ."

– Dr. John H. Watson and Sherlock Holmes
"The Adventure of the Sussex Vampire"

The Tragedy of Woodman's Lee
by Tracy J. Revels

Yesterday, I received a letter, its contents terse but not unkind:

> *It has been most gallant of you to keep our family secret for so long,* [it read] *but all those who could be harmed are now beyond the pale, and those who loved her deserve the truth about her sad demise. I absolve you from your oath and give you permission to tell the world how Mr. Holmes brought light into our darkness at Woodman's Lee.*

It took me a moment to recall that obscure little village. Then, with a shame that I could have forgotten it, the memories of two different cases that Holmes and I shared there came rushing back. Both had occurred in 1895 – the terrible murder of Black Peter Carey in the hot summer, and then our return there for a second investigation near the end of the year. Glancing at the published version of "Black Peter", which had appeared in *The Strand* in 1904, I realized that my indifferent punctuation might have given the impression that Holmes and I only traveled to Woodman's Lee once, in connection with Peter Carey. (I should have known to check more carefully after my literary agent caused quite a bit of confusion with his mishandling of commas in relation to Crosby the Banker and the red leech, and the Addleton tragedy and the ancient British Barrow.)

In any event, the affair was now fresh once again in my mind, and so I turned to my old notebooks and cast my mind back to a cold and cheerless late December day, when, just as we were enjoying a morning pipe, Mrs. Hudson interrupted our smoky meditation with the announcement of a visitor.

"Not Father Christmas, unless he is extremely tardy," Holmes chuckled. "And heaven forbid it be another gem-laden goose." He took a single glance at the proffered card before flinging it in my direction. "Yes, Mrs. Hudson, do show the lady up."

"So sad to see a girl newly bereaved at the holiday," our gracious landlady said.

"Newly bereaved?" Holmes asked. "What leads you to that conclusion?"

"Why, I can smell the dye. Her mourning clothes are just from the store."

Holmes elevated his eyebrows as Mrs. Hudson shuffled out. "I may have competition in the consulting detective business. Quickly, Watson, what can you gather from the card?"

I could gather nothing except for the lady's name – Agatha Corbin – and a faint trace of lemon perfume, a perfectly ordinary scent. A moment later, a young woman glided into our rooms and anxiously shook my friend's hand. She wore a very new mourning dress of the cheapest fabric, which had already bled into dark stains around her wrists. She was no more than twenty, with a thick wreath of auburn hair artfully pinned and coiled beneath a little black hat. She would have been attractive under other circumstances, but the unnatural pallor of her face and a pair of silver-rimmed spectacles perched on her thin nose gave her the look of a much older woman, one weighed with cares and gravitas.

"Thank you for seeing me, Mr. Holmes. I hope I am not intruding on what should be a most joyous season. I come bearing a heavy heart and horrible suspicions. Her death haunts me, now even more than it did five days ago. Sometimes, in the darkness, I think I hear her calling to me, begging me to find the truth, to name her murderer. I can bear it no longer, and I come to unburden myself to one who I trust will understand my delicate predicament."

"Who is this ghost?" Holmes asked.

"My niece – the late and most beloved English Lily."

It is difficult to describe the effect her simple statement had on us, and how we were suddenly eager to hear her story. It is possible that some future reader might not know of the English Lily, but in 1895 she was the wonder of the age. An exceptionally beautiful infant, Lily Lewis was discovered in her pram by an artist who had been commissioned to do an engraving for a soap company. Within a month, the baby's cherubic face was appearing on everything from flower vases to tea pots. As she grew into a toddler, developing deep dimples and a crown of golden curls, her likeness and endorsement was sought by a host of British, American, and Continental companies.

Plucked from obscurity by their daughter's remarkable features, her parents took her on a grand tour, during which she was petted and pampered by female royals across Europe. It was during this tour that an insane woman attempted to steal the child from her father, and during the ensuing tussle, the little girl was nearly thrown through the window of a moving train. After this shocking event, the family purchased a large country home and the English Lily was rarely seen in public, though her image remained ubiquitous on advertising copy.

But this fairy tale story had recently taken a heart-wrenching turn. On the morning of Boxing Day, the child was missing from her chamber. The family at first thought she was having a lark, as she was known to be a very playful youngster, but when she did not appear for breakfast, a search commenced. Her father discovered her inside his favorite horse's stall. The child had met with a gruesome fate, her skull crushed by a single kick from the beast's hoof. The afternoon before our client's arrival, the English Lily had been buried with almost regal state in Highgate Cemetery, her funeral cortege made up of over a hundred little girls, all carrying her namesake flower.

"The newspapers would have us believe it was a tragic accident," Holmes observed.

"So would the police," the lady said. "An Inspector Barlow was brought in. Do you know him, sir?"

"Not well," Holmes replied. Only I, who had spent so many years in Holmes's company, would have noted the slight downturn in his lip, the hardening in his eyes. He had a low opinion of the man.

"I know nothing of police work," Miss Corbin continued, "but it seemed to me that he could have been more careful in his duties. He spent less than an hour at the house, asked only a handful of questions about what time Lily had been put to bed and at what time her body was found, and then advised Charlie to shoot the horse. He said Lily's death was clearly an accident."

Holmes leaned back in his chair. "Yet you disagree. Is this merely a woman's intuition, Miss Corbin?"

There was intense resolution in her features. "No, Mr. Holmes. I confess my nerves are on edge, but it is no idle feminine fancy that has brought me to you. It is something I tried to tell Inspector Barlow, but he dismissed without a hearing."

"And what is that?"

"Dearest Lily would never have climbed into that stall. She was utterly terrified of horses."

Within an hour we were on board a train, making our way to Woodman's Lee. At Holmes's encouragement, the lady gave us a very complete narrative of the sad affair.

"Amanda, Lily's mother, is my elder sister. We grew up poor but respectable people – both our parents were in service. She married Charles – Charlie to us, for we had all played together as neighborhood children – when she was twenty-five. He was a gardener on Lord Wiltmore's estate, and she was a seamstress, until the afternoon when Lily was discovered.

"Lily's sudden fame took us all by surprise. It pains me to speak so of my own flesh and blood, but Lily's celebrity turned both Amanda and Charlie into utter fools. They moved from one expensive flat to the next before they purchased their country home. They spent lavishly on things they had gawked at when they were humbler people: Horses, a carriage, fine furniture, and the latest in fashions. All this I could have excused if not for what happened to my nephew, poor little Norris."

"I was not aware there was another child in the family," I said.

"That was by design," the lady answered. "Norris, who has just turned ten, does not favor his little sister. He is dark-haired, rather sallow in complexion, and has small, almost-black eyes. He is a bit underdeveloped in physique, as he has no companions to roughhouse with, but he is still perfectly healthy. Shortly after Lily's rise to fame, Mr. MacAllister, the agent who managed Lily's contracts and appearances, advised Charlie to keep Norris hidden, lest he take some of the luster from Lily. Amanda quickly agreed to this – she has always been amenable to arrangements that will enlarge her coffers, and she was never a doting parent. Charlie suffered pangs of guilt, but he yielded to Amanda's badgering, and I fear that my nephew has been a prisoner of his sister's fame for the last six years. There have been nurses and governesses, of course, but no schooling or outings or anything resembling a normal childhood. I made the mistake of voicing my concerns to Amanda two years ago, when I noticed how Norris would sit for hours, playing silently with his toys, only occasionally looking up with eyes as dull as stones. Amanda took offense at my observation and forbid me to visit."

"What brought you back into the family circle this particular Christmas?" Holmes asked.

"At first I thought Amanda was merely in a forgiving spirit when she summoned me," Miss Corbin said. "I arrived a week before Christmas and was surprised by what I found. All of the servants except for the housekeeper, the handyman, and one maid had been dismissed. Amanda demanded that I assume the duties of the governess for the children. I was tempted to depart as quickly as I had arrived, but Lily seemed glad to see me, and poor Charlie looked at wit's end, so I agreed to stay.

"I knew it was not my place to meddle in their affairs, but it quickly became clear to me that something very dire was afoot. Lily, who had always been active, was becoming very rambunctious and less willing to submit to her mother's commands without a show of spirit. Norris was a virtual cypher, refusing to play with his sister, showing affection only to horses and the fearsome mastiffs. Amanda was shrill and spiteful, while Charlie smelled of liquor by mid-afternoon. It hurt me to see a family so out of sorts with Christmas only days away, so I screwed up my courage and bearded the lion in his den. Charlie had always been a sensible fellow with me, and to my relief, instead of tossing me out on my ear, he began to confide his troubles.

"'We're done for, Aggie,' he moaned. 'There's no more work for Lily, no more money for all of us. Her looks are gone!'"

"Was this true?" Holmes asked. "Had something happened to the child?"

"Only what God and nature intended, sir. Lily had begun to grow rapidly, as many girls do at that age. She was all arms and legs, her hair had straightened, and her baby teeth had shed irregularly. In October, she had contracted a case of measles, and there were still some small blemishes on her skin. But this was deemed a disaster by the purveyors of her image. Charlie showed me cancelled contracts. It seemed that Lily's days as a professional beauty were over."

"And I take it that Mr. Lewis had not invested the proceeds of his daughter's fame wisely?" Holmes said.

"Charlie told me that he was heavily in debt. The house and its staff were too expensive, and Amanda's every foolish whim had been indulged for years. Charlie insisted that unless some miracle occurred, the family would be cast into the poorhouse. He had dismissed most of the servants and was selling off the trinkets given to Lily by royal admirers in order to pay the mortgage. Also, to make matters worse, Mr. MacAllister had defrauded Charlie completely, stealing the money that was supposed to have purchased an insurance policy for Lily."

Holmes raised an eyebrow. "There was no insurance on the child?"

"None. But Charlie bid me not to reveal this to Amanda, and I kept my word. My sister cares for little beside her own pleasures, and even at that moment was plotting ways to improve Lily's appearance, forcing her to rub her face with caustic creams and sleep with her hair knotted tightly into papers. Amanda seemed certain that with enough beauty treatments, Lily could return to the spotlight. Charlie was hoping to hide the bad news from all of them until the holidays were over. He wished the children to have one last happy memory."

"Was it a jolly Christmas morning?" I asked.

"It was a strange one. Somehow, Charlie had scraped up the money to buy toys for the children, and a pair of pearl earrings for Amanda. No one seemed to have thought of poor Charlie, though I had wrapped up a book of poems for him."

Holmes, who had for a moment seemed distracted by the passing winter scenery, turned with suddenly bright eyes.

"Tell me about the toys," he said. The lady's face indicated she found the question a strange one.

"Norris was given a set of wooden soldiers – I overheard him grumble that he had asked for a gun. I scolded him for being ungrateful. Honestly, it was such a nasty comment that I found myself wishing the Saint had left coal in his stocking instead." Miss Corbin shook her head ruefully. "As to Lily's gift, it was a remarkable thing: A porcelain doll that looked exactly as Lily had appeared in her cradle. It was clearly rather costly, but Charlie whispered to me that he feared this might be the last year his daughter craved a doll, and he wanted it to be a special one.

"Afterward, Norris spent much of the day outside, playing with the dogs, while Lily tended to her new doll. We dined at five. At the table, however, the joy of that day turned to ashes. Amanda began to speak of all the things she would be doing to improve Lily's looks, including cutting her hair short in the hopes it would curl again. Lily announced that she wouldn't have it, nor would she wash her face again with the 'special rinse' nor wear the 'baby clothes' that Amanda remained determined to dress her in. It was a most defiant proclamation. Amanda ordered Lily to her room and, as she rose to leave, Lily stuck out her tongue at her mother.

"Before I could intervene, Amanda seized Lily, turned her over her knee, and spanked her unmercifully. Norris laughed loudly. Charlie finally ordered Amanda to stop beating Lily, and quickly sent Norris on to his room with a stern rebuke. I gathered my dear niece into my arms and carried her to her nursery. As you can imagine, it was nearly impossible to calm her. Amanda had never struck her before. At last, I got Lily changed into her nightgown, tucking her new doll beside her in bed. Amanda and Charlie remained downstairs, but I had no heart for keeping company with them. I took a book and retired to my room, where I read until about nine, and then quickly fell asleep."

"Did anything awaken you during the night?" Holmes asked

The lady hesitated.

"I fear you have come too far to shield someone now," Holmes said firmly.

"I am not certain as to the exact time," Miss Corbin said, her voice barely above a whisper, "but I heard Charlie and Amanda in the hallway. I heard Amanda say, 'I know a way to get what we need, though you will not like it!' Charlie made no reply, though shortly afterward I heard their bedroom door slam shut. I dozed off and sometime deep in the night, I was roused by what I thought was the quick patter of footsteps and a slight squeak on the old stairs. Charlie used to joke, in better days, that the house was haunted, and I merely dismissed the sounds as the ghost, or a figment of my imagination."

Holmes leaned forward with his chin perched on his woven fingers. "The arrangement of the bedrooms is along one passage?"

"That is correct, sir. George and Amanda have the largest chamber, at the far end of the hall. There is a little playroom, then Lily's nursery. Next is Norris's room, then a tiny office, and then my bedroom. All open onto the hallway, and the only access to them is the old staircase, which creaks and groans when anyone heavier than a child moves upon it."

"Intriguing," Holmes said. "There was no alarm was raised in the night?"

"None, sir. The inspector said he found no sign of footprints, nor any indication anyone had scaled the high fence that protects the house. Brutus and Cato, the two mastiffs, were loose of course, and would certainly have barked if a stranger had entered the property. And even if some person had come into the house, why would they do such a horrible thing?"

"Perhaps the intent was to abduct the little girl," I said.

Holmes frowned. "Would Lily have cried out if awakened by a stranger?"

"Of course," our client said. "Lily was growing bolder as she aged, but she was still shy around outsiders. I think the experience on the train, when she was just a toddler, had stayed with her. She would have screamed."

Holmes nodded. "I must put an unsavory question to you, Miss Corbin. Were there marks upon the body? Did you see bruises or indications that Lily might have been restrained or gagged – handled in a rough way?"

The lady sighed. "I will never be able to wipe the image from my mind, of Charlie carrying her into the kitchen, her arms and legs already stiff with death. She was dressed only in her nightgown, but as you might imagine it was befouled with blood and muck from the stall. I helped the housekeeper and the maid clean her poor body – Amanda was quite useless, screaming hysterically when she was not in a faint. But no, there was no discernable mark upon her, other than the wound to the head which had claimed her life and some bruises from the beating that Amanda had given her at dinner."

"How did Norris react to his sister's demise?" Holmes asked.

"Norris was frightened by the sight of Lily's corpse, and he ran away. I later found him hiding beneath his bed. The policeman asked him a few questions, but he was of little use, for he had gone to sleep promptly upon retiring and had not awakened until breakfast. I was the one who woke him up, and I will vouch that he was deeply asleep."

"Did you perchance observe the soles of his feet?"

"No."

"Hmm," Holmes murmured. "How does he comport himself now?"

"Much the same as he did before," the lady answered. "He keeps to himself, muttering orders to his toy soldiers."

"And the father and mother?"

"Charlie is broken-hearted. I fear this may kill him. Amanda was hysterical at first but recovered in time to orchestrate Lily's immense funeral and play the role of chief mourner. Just this morning, she mentioned that there was some money to be made in doing interviews with the newspapers, and that Charlie should sober up and look into these opportunities."

Holmes nodded and gestured toward the window. "I believe we have arrived."

It occurred to me as we disembarked that I had only Miss Corbin's word for what had happened. What if, for some reason, she wanted to implicate someone in the household in the little girl's death? As offensive as the thought was, I could not push it aside. Holmes had often warned me not to judge truth by appearances. The lady seemed honest and concerned, but perhaps some darker motive lurked beneath her veneer of sorrow.

An ornate carriage, painted in gaudy shades of blue and gold, waited outside the station. The coachman was a simple looking fellow, with a wide face and a vacant stare. Miss Corbin had to speak to him twice before he came down and admitted us to the vehicle.

"Have you told anyone that you were consulting me?" Holmes asked as our conveyance pulled into the road.

"Yes – I told Charlie my intentions. He agreed readily enough, though he warned me that he couldn't reimburse your fees. I have a little savings, sir, and I would gladly hand over every penny to know who did this monstrous thing to dear Lily."

Holmes waved away her concern. "Let us discuss that at some future date. For now, we must seek justice for an innocent child. One final question: Do the servants have any grievances or grudges against the family?"

"None to my knowledge. Mrs. Dawson, the housekeeper, is quite devoted to the children, and the maid, Laurie, is Mrs. Dawson's daughter. They are both utterly respectable."

"And the handyman?"

Our client frowned. "Grimes – he is our diver, so you have an impression of him, I suspect. He seems a bit simple-minded. Once or twice I have caught him eyeing me in a most unnerving manner, but he has never said anything improper. He is good with the horses and the dogs."

Holmes frowned. "Why did Grimes not find Lily, if his duties include seeing after the stables?"

The lady looked disgusted. "He did not find her because he was still at his home, half-a-mile away, dead drunk. Charlie had given him a bottle of spirits for Christmas, and Grimes consumed the entire gift that night, at his cottage."

After a journey of another mile, the carriage halted, depositing us before high iron gates and a winter-bare yard. A tall man waited there, bundled in a heavy coat. With barely a nod to us, he gathered Miss Corbin into his arms.

"Aggie, thank God! I was so worried about you. Are these the gentlemen?"

As introductions were made, I appraised Mr. Charles Lewis. He was handsome, with thick blond hair and skin as fair and clear as a babe's. Distress had drawn untimely furrows into his brow, and sleeplessness left deep circles beneath his dark blue eyes, yet he still radiated an almost preternatural male beauty. It was clear to me where the English Lily had acquired her famed looks.

But it was also clear that he was uncomfortably familiar with his sister-in-law. His left hand stayed clamped to her waist until she awkwardly pulled free of him.

"It would be best for me to see where the tragedy occurred," Holmes said. "Miss Corbin may direct us, and then we will return to speak to the family, if you will gather them."

Mr. Lewis nodded and led us up the short, gravel-strewn lane to his residence. The house itself was large and unaesthetic, with multiple additions that distorted its Regency framework. It was beginning to show need of repair. I counted five broken or boarded up windows in the façade alone. Mr. Lewis went inside while Miss Corbin lead us to the rear of the dwelling, pointing out the stables, the carriage house, a privy, a few tool sheds, and a much-neglected greenhouse. We entered the stables, which were large enough for six horses. I noted the name "*Trickster*" painted on the nearest, empty paddock.

"If only I had been called in sooner," Holmes muttered. "Lestrade would never have been such a fool as to ignore me." He shook his head. "I assume the horse has been slaughtered?"

Miss Corbin had paused at the door. "No, Charlie gave Trickster to a passing peddler. Charlie has too soft a heart to hurt any creature, even in vengeance."

Holmes stepped inside the stall. All the straw had been removed, the cobbled stones on the floor swept clean. Still, he inspected the area with his usual intensity, and I heard him give a small gasp of breath.

"Ah – this is intriguing."

"What have you found?"

Holmes had taken out a penknife and was gently prizing an object from between the stones. He rested it in the palm of his hand. It was a tiny bit of glass, as blue as the sky.

"How on earth did you find that?"

"I was looking for it," my friend said. He rose and addressed Miss Corbin. "Where is Lily's Christmas gift?"

The lady folded her hands across her face.

"Oh, would that I knew, Mr. Holmes! I thought of it, as the undertaker was placing Lily in her coffin. She seemed so lonesome, and I wanted to tuck the doll in her arms. But I couldn't find it! I looked everywhere, I enlisted the maid to help me, but there was no trace of it in the house. I thought perhaps Norris taken it, as a remembrance of his little sister, but it wasn't in his room. Why do you ask?"

Holmes didn't answer. Instead, he leaned against the stable door, his eyes roaming over the house, the outbuildings, and the yard. Grimes came out of the carriage house, leading the big gray mare that had pulled our vehicle.

"Watson, will you and Miss Corbin assemble the family in the parlor and give me a few moments alone with this fellow?"

We nodded, but just as our client stepped toward the pathway, Holmes caught my sleeve, delaying me a moment and whispering in my ear.

"Observe them closely, Watson. Use all of your physician's talents. I may have need of your knowledge."

Though I confess this order confused me, it wasn't my duty to question it. I followed Miss Corbin into the home, grateful for her guidance, as the structure was a virtual labyrinth with many connecting rooms and darkened passageways. At last we reached the parlor, where the bereaved members of the Lewis family had assembled, along with their black-clad housekeeper and maid.

Before I could attempt any observational dissection of the assembly, I had to settle my nerves against the oppressiveness of the chamber. A sickly yellow light was provided by a few tallow candles – whether as a sign of mourning or thriftiness, I was uncertain. The illumination threw weird shadows around a room that had once been the showcase of a hunter. Great trophies of long-dead beasts cluttered the walls, their eyes wide and their frightful maws agape. Bear and zebra skin rugs, worn and greasy with age, were scattered across the floor. I had the impression that something vicious and stealthy might be lurking behind the heavy velvet curtains.

Miss Corbin spoke softly, and I tore my gaze away from the creatures on the wall, refocusing all my mental acuity on the family. I did my best to study them without staring, nodding politely and offering my condolences as introductions were made. The two domestics – a grey-haired mother and a slight, doe-eyed girl – appeared frightened out of their wits, holding hands as they kept to a corner. Mr. Lewis sat in an overstuffed chair, his head drooping, the picture of helplessness. Master Norris ignored my greeting, remaining sprawled before the fireplace, arranging his toy soldiers in battle formations, his legs swinging up and down idly, as if nothing could break his concentration on the mayhem about to erupt in his imaginary war. Only Mrs. Lewis, who sat in a high-backed chair opposite her husband, reacted to my presence with vigor.

"The writer of those awful stories? Charlie, you said the detective would come to ask us questions, not this hack! You'll not be putting our good name in the street, do you understand me, sir? We will speak only to the best journals!"

She was a large woman in every sense, her body filling up the heavy chair in which she sat, her voice so deep and booming that even the heads on the wall seemed to shake. I noted that the servants cowered deeper in their corner as Mrs. Lewis shook a meaty fist at me.

"Do you understand me, sir? We have suffered enough! The inspector made it clear – it was Lily's own foolishness that got her killed. She was becoming a wicked child!"

"Amanda," her husband whispered. "Please."

"No! My sister – " Here Mrs. Lewis pointed to our client. " – seems to think that I did it! Don't deny it, Aggie! You've been giving me the evil eye from the moment we found her. Maybe you hope I will be arrested, and hanged, so that you can have Charlie! You have always wanted him!"

"Amanda, hush," Miss Corbin ordered, her face turning scarlet with humiliation.

"Indeed, such recriminations serve no purpose," a soothing voice said. We all turned, and found Sherlock Holmes standing just inside the doorway. Knowing my friend's ability to move with the stealth of a ghost, I wondered how long he had been privy to the conversation. He stepped forward, nodding to the parties, before dismissing the housekeeper and the maid, asking them to make some tea.

"Who are you to give orders in my house?" Mrs. Lewis demanded. Her multiple chins were still quivering as Holmes drew closer.

"Your servants would feel much better with some task to occupy their hands and minds, and what I have to say is for the family circle only."

Mr. Lewis raised his head. "Have you found the truth?"

Holmes removed his gloves and stretched his hands out to the fire, as if he were merely a guest making himself at home. "Miss Lily was very spirited – children of that nature do frequently meet with tragic accidents. There have been many cases where a lad has been struck by a train, or drowned in a millpond, because one of his little friends dared him to test his courage. But when this occurs, there is often a tribe of children involved, as there must be witnesses to the feat of daring. That, we must agree, is not the case here."

Mrs. Lewis shook her head. "What are you implying, then? That one of us did it?"

"Madame, you would qualify as a likely suspect," Holmes stated, with such blandness that I admit I was taken aback. At first the lady did not seem to understand his words, but as Holmes continued to speak, her face drained of all color, and she began to clutch at her throat, as if the heavy black beads she wore were strangling her. "Lily's death occurred on the same night that you learned the truth – that your daughter was no longer a valuable commodity, for she had balked at your schemes to make her more attractive. At six, she was no longer a toddling child who could be easily controlled. You assumed she was insured – thus your words to your husband about 'another way to get money'. He had not yet informed you that he had also been swindled as to such funding."

"How – my God, how could you know that? Charlie! Charlie, did you tell him? Sir, I swear, I never meant I would harm Lily – I only meant – "

"What, Amanda?" her husband snapped. "What else could you have meant by those words? Do not deny you said them."

Holmes shook his head. "Please, there is no need for further quarreling. It brings us no closer to Lily's killer."

"Then what does?" Miss Corbin asked, her voice quivering with emotion.

Holmes didn't answer. His gaze was locked to the soldiers on the floor before young Norris.

"A fine set of figures," Holmes said.

The youngster, who had ignored the outbursts all around him, only shrugged. Holmes knelt, rubbing his chin as he surveyed the layout of the toys.

"I see you have chosen to recreate the Battle of Waterloo – but you appear to have Napoleon winning. That is rather unpatriotic of you, Master Norris! Let us correct this error."

Quick as a wink, Holmes flicked the figure of the French emperor towards the fire. The boy let out a shout and lunged forward, snatching the tiny statue back just before it rolled into the flames.

"You leave my soldiers alone!"

"Haven't you learned the old law of justice, an eye for an eye and a tooth for a tooth?"

Holmes grabbed a company of toy soldiers and then rose out of the lad's reach. It would be the work of a moment to toss the playthings into the fireplace. Both parents and I watched in horror. Miss Corbin rushed forward, but I threw out an arm, holding her back.

"You understand me, I take it?" Holmes asked the boy, who was making futile grabs at his arms. "I will not destroy them if you tell us the truth about Lily's doll."

There was a rasping sound behind us. I turned and saw Grimes standing in the doorway. He held a burlap bag in his hands.

"I found it, sir. Just where you reckoned it would be."

Master Norris stared at the handyman and then gave a cry. He ran to his father and buried his face in the folds of his coat. Mrs. Lewis drew sideways, her mourning jewelry clattering. Holmes motioned the handyman inside, signaling for him to place the bag on the floor. As Holmes opened it wide, we were all repulsed by a horrible smell, as from an open sewer. Holmes took down one of the candles from the mantel, allowing its illumination to reveal the sack's contents.

"It had to be flung somewhere," Holmes said. "If it remained at the scene, everyone would know why Lily had climbed into the stall."

Inside the sack, smeared with filth, was the pitiful remains of a porcelain doll. Its dress was torn, its limbs coated in muck, and half its head broken, so that it looked up at us with only one blue eye.

"There was no reason for Lily to venture into the horse's stall in the middle of a cold night unless she was carried or lured there. It was clearly impossible for any outsider to have gained entrance to the property with the gates locked and the mastiffs on guard. Therefore, Lily was either carried or lured by someone in the house. The lack of any injury, except the fatal one, and the fact that no hue-and-cry was raised by the child herself, works against the theory that she was snatched or dragged from her bed. Therefore, she went willingly – but why?"

Holmes lifted his head. All the family members were pale. The very room seemed to be holding its breath.

"Mr. Lewis had no cause to harm his own daughter. While Mrs. Lewis might, for an instant, have imagined that Lily's insurance would have saved them from financial ruin, it is unlikely that she could have conjured such a plan in so short of a time – or have led Lily from her bedroom without having been heard, especially as her last action toward her daughter was to punish her cruelly. Lily would have been fearful of her mother. She would have fretted or whined or cried out in alarm, and this – along with the tread of an adult and a child on the stairs – would have been heard."

Mrs. Lewis slumped in her chair.

"Neither Miss Corbin nor the servants had any reason to harm the girl. That left only one person."

Mr. Lewis forced his boy to turn around and face us all.

"And here, we are in a new realm," Holmes continued. "One of evil intent, based upon the most immature of motives."

Norris stared back at the circle. His dull eyes suddenly seemed to blaze, and his high-pitched voice cracked with fury.

"It wasn't right!" the boy snapped. "Lily got to go places, to ride on trains and ships, to meet famous people – I had to stay here like a convict! She got a pretty doll, all I got were these!"

He kicked the soldiers, sending an entire battalion into the fireplace. With a sound like an angry cat, he broke away and bolted for the door. Holmes told Grimes to run after him, to see that he did not harm himself.

Mr. Lewis moved to his wife, who had begun to sob. He dropped to his knees, gathering her into his arms.

My friend picked one of the soldiers, examining it in detail as he spoke.

"If it gives you consolation, I do not believe Norris intended to kill his sister. After I leave, you may see how well my version of events fits with his confession. He was angry and resentful that his sister, who always seemed to be favored over him, received a nicer gift for Christmas. He decided to deprive her of it. He crept into her bedroom when all were asleep. As he slipped it from her arms, she awoke, but made no protest – perhaps he warned her to say nothing, lest her mother return to punish her. From Lily's perspective, she had been unjustly dealt with only hours before, and so she followed without raising any alarm. The dogs knew the children and did not react. Norris was aware that the handyman was away, and that no one would hear them in the stables. He threw the doll at Trickster's hooves, taunting Lily to fetch it. She was terrified of the stallion, and this gave Norris pleasure – to think she would have to watch her plaything's inevitable destruction.

"But he didn't anticipate Lily's resolve, her growing courage, or her love for the doll. She entered the horse's stall. She was perhaps struck down at that very instant by the dumb animal. Seeing what he had caused, and not wishing to be blamed, Norris calmed the horse, let himself inside, and snatched up the doll. He took the toy, and all the shattered bits of it he could find – except for one small piece – then stuffed them down the through the seat of the privy in the yard, knowing it very unlikely that should anyone search for the item, they would look there."

"My God," Mr. Lewis cried, "we have raised a monster!"

Holmes returned the toy soldier to the decimated ranks. "No normal lad could witness such a thing and so calmly think of his own self-preservation. I fear that your boy is unbalanced, and will require professional care – an alienist of the first caliber. Perhaps Dr. Watson can recommend a specialist." My friend's face was grimmer and sadder than I could ever recall seeing it. "I am truly sorry to have brought such grief and horror to your home, but your daughter's memory deserved the truth. I leave the rest to your discretion."

And now, all these years later, I look back on elegantly scripted lines:

> *I never wrote to you again, once I had received your promise not to publish the case, and I think it only fair to tell you what occurred after Mr. Holmes gave his verdict. Norris confessed all, and grew less emotional with each retelling, as if he could not understand the suffering he had inflicted. He was sent away to an institution in Scotland, but they could make no progress with him, and he died of consumption just before his nineteenth birthday. My sister died of heart failure only weeks after her son was sent away. Charlie proposed to me at her funeral, an action I found so offensive that I fled from England for many years, making my residence in America. A fortnight ago, I learned that Charlie had passed. Therefore, I revoke the pledge I extracted from you. Perhaps, if you tell the story, the world will recall Lily's innocence and remember her fondly.*

* * * * *

In this memorable year '95 a curious and incongruous succession of cases had engaged his attention, ranging from his famous investigation of the sudden death of Cardinal Tosca – an inquiry which was carried out by him at the express desire of his Holiness the Pope – down to his arrest of Wilson, the notorious canary-trainer, which removed a plague-spot from the East End of London. Close on the heels of these two famous cases came the tragedy of Woodman's Lee, and the very obscure circumstances which surrounded the death of Captain Peter Carey.

– Dr. John H. Watson
"The Adventure of Black Peter"

The Murdered Millionaire
by Kevin P. Thornton

After

"Read the first line again please, Watson."

I obliged.

"*My brother is missing, and I would like you to find him.*"

Holmes drew on his pipe and stretched back into the armchair. He had been of a languid disposition these last few days. He was visiting me for a few days in London at my Queen Anne Street residence. Prior to that, two hectic weeks had allowed him to see off a "matter of international intrigue" of such secrecy he had not spoken of it at all. Consequently, his current relaxed manner served only to disgruntle me. I was used to our moods being the other way round, and as a result the world seemed slightly discombobulated. In retrospect, I realized that I was overreacting. Holmes was never one to gloat, but my fragile self-esteem imagined every raised eyebrow of his to be a message of victory, every stretched arm or leg to be a pointed gesture at me and my uselessness in his investigations.

In addition, he had asked me to find my notes on one of his unfinished cases, which had required a trip to the bank and the concomitant paperwork such appointments involve. My dispatch box, stored in the vaults at Cox and Company for heaven alone knows what reason, save that I valued my literary output more than gold, was also not organized in any systematic way, and it had taken me nearly two hours to find the document in question.

When I returned to my friend I was hot, dusty, tired, and marginally miffed. That Holmes was in one of his rare states of torpor seemed to be the final insult to cap the day, and my testiness would have been obvious even to the most oblivious Whitechapel navvy near the end of a payday splurge.

I was about to continue reading when Holmes said, "I'm sorry I can tell you nothing of my recent adventures. You know I trust you more than anyone in the world, and I would tell you all if I could. I may be able to one day. But know this my dear friend, just like our adventure for the King of Bohemia some years ago, this too required the utmost secrecy involving people of similar station, though much closer to home."

The weight of his words eventually sank in. "You mean . . . ." I was unable to enunciate my thought, lest I break Holmes's wall of covertness.

"Precisely. You understand then, my friend, that if I gave my word to Him, I cannot break that vow, not even for you."

"Of course. I understand. I'm sorry if I have seemed a little out of sorts. You don't deserve my foulness of temper."

"It is understandable. Every time we think smallpox is beaten, it comes back again and takes hundreds of thousands of lives."

"Millions worldwide this time if the reports are true," I said. "Against which the four patients I lost must seem almost inconsequential."

"Yet they are not," said Holmes. "One of the reasons you are ideally suited to your profession is you care deeply about your patients. To lose one is an affront to your abilities and it is, I suggest, the most likely reason you are out of sorts."

"I think you're right, and your observation is an excellent transition to the subject at hand. You are also passionate about your professional standing and measure such by your successes. Why then did you ask me to find my notes on one of your more spectacular failures?"

It is rare when I catch my friend Sherlock Holmes off guard. At my words, he sprung to his feet and stepped towards me, pointing. "It was no such thing," he said. "We were asked to investigate more than a month after the event in question, there was no extant evidence and the trail, such as it was, had gone cold." He glared at me as if I had strangled a puppy. Then he realized what I was up to. He pulled up, sat down again, and inclined his head in acknowledgement. "Well played, Watson. Well played indeed."

"Now," he said, "if you could review your notes, as sparse as they are, on what little we know, I will tell you why this is important."

"Very well. My storytelling style as you know, is to write as if in conversation. This is my recollection of the events of the disappearance of James Phillimore . . . ."

Before

"My brother is missing, and I would like you to find him."

Miss Phyllis Phillimore, the lady who sat in the visitor's chair at 221b Baker Street on that January morning, was prim, but she did not seem proper. Indeed, there was a hint of impropriety about her, as if she wore borrowed clothes and acted as another.

"What part of the East End are you from, Miss Phillimore?"

The lady rose in the chair and stretched herself to her full sitting height, impressive though not intimidating. "I am not from there. At least not anymore. I left there as soon as I could, and I'm not going back to Shoreditch. It was a hard place, Mister Holmes, hard on body and soul.

My brother rescued me from there, and now I need you to rescue him from whatever has befallen him."

"Then pray start at the beginning of your tale," said Holmes.

"My brother and I grew up in an orphanage. We have no notion of who our parents are, nor do we care. We had each other and that was enough. It was tough, Mister Holmes, let me tell you. An orphanage is a hard place to grow up, but I had James to look after me, and he had me to do the same.

"You wouldn't think from looking at us that we were brother and sister. James is the exact opposite of me – tall, fair-haired and handsome. Lord, he was always beautiful, even growing up. Anyways, all we have is the story they told us. We were both left abandoned on the steps of the church next door, with a note that said '*Please look after my babies.*' That makes us brother and sister as far as I'm concerned."

"Indeed," said Holmes. "As fascinating as all this is, I'm sure there is a relevant point due any time soon, is there not."

"It's important for you to know that although James and I had a difficult childhood, we are still family. James was five and I was three when we were left there, and normally that's too old to be adopted. Rich folk want babies, not older children, and we didn't help ourselves by insisting on sticking together. You'd think we'd have no say, but I can't tell you the times one of us was put up for adoption, except we was hiding when they came to inspect us. We weren't going to be split, so we were stuck at the orphanage, resigned to our fate."

"Until?" said Holmes.

"Until James was adopted. They took him away before I could stop them."

"How old was he?"

"He was fifteen, Mister Holmes. Long past any age for a likely adoption. In all the time I was there, eleven years until I ran away at fourteen, I never once saw anyone older than ten get taken by a family. Nobody wants a boy who's grown up like that. If you're there that long, it's nothing but the street for you when you leave. You've no skills, no education, no one to turn to. You go from having a roof over your head and three squares a day to nothing, without even a by-your-leave. So when they came and took him I was sad, but I was also happy for him. He had a chance, you see – a chance to get out from under."

"And how did you make out?" I asked, and I could see Holmes wince.

"How do you think sir?" she said. "I left less than a year later. Fourteen years old and on the streets. I'll tell you how I made out, Doctor Watson. I did what I had to in order to survive. I will save your delicate sensibilities the details of the ten years of my life from leaving the orphanage until last year. I am here, I am alive and well, and I am stronger than ever."

There was a silence as her words rang through the room.

"Madam," I said. "I meant no aspersion on you or your character. Please forgive me."

"I concur," said Holmes. "Now can we get to the part where your brother tracks you down, please?"

"I have said nothing of that," said Miss Phillimore.

"And yet you wish us to find your brother who was missing from your life for over a decade. This would suggest that you found each other as a precursor to losing him again. It is not a difficult conjecture that you were busy enough surviving in the East End so as not to be able to hunt for your brother. Ergo, he went away, made good, found you, and rescued you from the squalor of Shoreditch."

Miss Phyllis Phillimore seemed deflated, like an after-dinner speaker whose punchlines have been shouted from the audience.

"That is indeed what happened. James was always very smart, and the couple who adopted him were scientists and educators. James was a test case for a theory they had hypothesized, that even the most forlorn and lost child can be rescued with intense education and nutrition."

"And it worked?" I asked.

"I think so," she said. "All I can tell you is when he found me he was the same old James, my big brother, but he was different. He spoke and dressed like a toff. He took me to his home in Chiswick, out on the edge of London. It was a fine old place, a mansion."

"So he had done well," said Holmes.

"Well, he must have, mustn't he?" said Miss Phillimore. "At first it was wonderful. We caught up on what had happened to us. He learnt quickly with his guardians, displaying the intelligence I always knew he had, catching up on all the studies he'd never had a chance at before. He went to University and graduated, and then he started his own company and made a fortune." She giggled suddenly as if she had heard a joke.

"What was his business?" I asked.

"He didn't want to tell me at first, but I wheedled it out of him. He invented a clasp for fastening ladies' undergarments. It is far better than all the old ones, and as he had the patent both here and overseas, he was fair rolling in it."

"A clasp?" I said.

"Fascinating," said Holmes. "Build a better mousetrap and the world will beat a path to your door."

"'Ere, that's what James said just before he disappeared. Where did you 'ear that?"

"It was in *The Economist*," said Holmes. "An American wrote it. He was in favour of economic innovation. Emerson, I think, was his name."

"Anyways, we had a fine old time of it for a while. He took me shopping and bought me fine clothes and shoes, wined and dined me, and introduced me to all his friends. It was nice for a while, Mister Holmes." She paused, as if selecting her words with care. "But I didn't fit in. He'd had eleven years to become this hoity-toity person. Weekends with the Duke of Whoever and the Earl of Whatchamacallit, theatre down the Drury Lane, racing at Ascot. It wasn't my world, Mister Holmes, no matter how hard he tried to make me fit. So I packed me bags and told him I was off."

"And he was unhappy," said Holmes.

"He wouldn't let me leave, even though it was for the best. We argued for nigh on two days before we came to a compromise. He bought me my own place in Belgravia and settled an investment account on me. That was about nine months ago."

"That is very nice," murmured Holmes standing up. "However I have other clients to see. Perhaps you could come back at another time when you are prepared to get to the salient facts of you brother's disappearance."

"Hold your horses, Mister Holmes, I'm getting there. We settled into a routine, James and I. He had a key to my apartment. Sometime when he was late in town he would stay over and we would break our fast together the next morning. Other times I would visit him at his house in Chiswick on days when he had no visitors that would be surprised by his coarse little sister. It was an easy enough trip. The underground goes all the way out there now and he would be waiting for me at the station. It was nice to have him back, and I was enjoying the good life he had given me – having money, dressing up, learning to be a proper little lady. Then James was robbed and beaten up in Blackfriars one night, and everything changed again."

"A-ha!" said Holmes. "Take your time please, Miss Phillimore, and tell me everything you know of this attack, even the most inconsequential detail."

"Well that's the hardest part, Mister Holmes. There isn't a lot to tell. James claimed to have seen nothing, and the only other witness was a cab driver waiting on the rank. He said that three or four men attacked James and beat him about the head. The cabbie ran to help, shouting and screaming at the attackers. This seemed to have chased them off."

"The cab driver seems to have been a hero," I said.

"Quite," said Holmes. "Pray continue, Miss Phillimore."

"Anyways, the noise 'e made roused the beat bobby, who came running. Between them they put my brother in the cab and took him to

Barts, where they roused a doctor to treat him. That may have saved his life. In addition to his head injuries he'd also been stabbed."

"Did he ever tell you why he'd been in Blackfriars?" said Holmes.

"I'm sure I never asked," said Miss Phillimore. "What does it matter?"

"Everything matters," said Holmes, "or else nothing matters." Miss Phillimore gave Holmes a look I had seen before from his clients. It was puzzled and faintly distasteful, as if Holmes had missed the point and paid attention to the wrong part of the tale. It was his talent to perceive the slightest anomaly, and his clumsiness not to recognize how insensitive he sometimes seemed. As if reading my mind he drew back a little.

"My apologies, Miss Phillimore. Sometimes I focus on the minutiae of a case too deeply. Rest assured, I'm glad your brother was well treated. St. Bartholomew's Hospital is a fine establishment. Doctor Watson himself has served there. Whoever decided to take him there did him a favour and probably saved his life."

"I think that's what my brother thought," said Miss Phillimore. "In the aftermath of attack, he was very fearful, as if he was due another beating. I told him it was just happenstance, he'd been in the wrong place at the wrong time, but he didn't seem to believe me. He was also very grateful to his two saviours. He tried to reward the policeman, but he wouldn't take any money – said it wouldn't be right. I know he bought the cab driver his own rig, complete with two horses. And he took them out with him, back to Chiswick."

"What do you mean?" I said.

"My brother's home really was at the edge of London. He had a hundred acres of land behind the house that he leased to a farmer, and his home stood at the end of a short lane leading off the main road. And when I say lane, it was more of a close, not more than a stretch of lane with a wider bit at the end so you could turn a horse and carriage 'round and about. Everything down the close was his, including all the surrounding land, and the only other homes down there, two cottages, one on either side of his mansion. The house had once belonged to a Marquis or some such, and he'd built the cottages for his spinster aunts to prevent them from driving him mad in the main house, so the story goes."

Holmes began to look impatient. I frowned at him. Thankfully Miss Phillimore didn't notice and she continued.

"He gave the one cottage to the policeman and his wife, and the other to the cabdriver. There was a barn behind that one that he let the cabbie use, and he kept his brand new rig and horses back there."

"Do you remember the names of the two men, said Holmes.

"The constable was called Andrew Horsman, and the cab driver had a foreign-sounding name: Vincent Coetzee. He was from the colonies somewhere."

"Hmm," said Holmes. "Coetzee. It could be Dutch, depending on the spelling, but if he's a colonial, he is likely from the southern part of Africa, the Cape Colony perhaps or the Transvaal. Maybe even German South West Africa."

"That was very kind of your brother," I said. "Housing in London is not cheap. The two men must have appreciated the gesture."

"They did, I'm sure, but James also had his reasons. He were right scared, and I think he wanted them two out there as some form of protection. Mind you, as neighbours they're pretty useful to have – one to keep the place safe, and the other to take you wherever you wish to go. They didn't stop him going missing, though."

I heard Holmes suppress a sigh, as if to say "At last!"

"James was beaten up some six months back, during the summer. He left hospital, persuaded his rescuers to move out to his place, and seemed to get back to normal, slowly. Then he disappeared."

"When did that happen?" said Holmes.

"About four weeks ago?" said Miss Phillimore, but she whispered her answer, as if she knew she had done wrong.

Holmes, surprisingly, was calm. "Madam, you make it difficult for me to help. Whatever evidence existed has doubtless disappeared. You say your brother is missing. How do you know?

"Because he went back into his house and was never seen again."

After

"And that's all you have?" said Holmes.

"I'm afraid so. I remember her story of how he disappeared was devoid of details. There was no reason to believe any harm had come to him, and quite frankly if he wanted to disappear, he was a grown man with no responsibilities. Yet there was that part of the story that caused me to keep my notes and hope that one day you would find a solution."

"That he went into his house and was never seen again? I can see why that might have excited you, Watson, with your love of a locked room or an impossible crime. To me that was the least interesting part. Had we been invited to investigate immediately after his disappearance, the manner of how it was done would have been of some benefit in tracking him down. As it was. Miss Phyllis Phillimore wanted us to find her brother. I was unable to follow such a cold trail and then she seemed to lose interest."

"What do you think happened to him?"

"I don't think anything, as I don't have enough information. I can tell you that he is either alive or dead. If dead, what is the point in searching for his corpse, and if alive he is somewhere, likely not wishing to be found. In any event the client, despite her initial enthusiasm, never returned, and my attempts to reach out to her were rebuffed." He shrugged. "It isn't unusual for people to decide not to pursue my services."

"Then for heaven's sake, why did you ask me to retrieve my notes? Did you wish to test your memory against my own?"

"In a manner of speaking, yes. That is exactly what I wanted to do, and I found that your recollections are similar to my own, if a little more colloquial. No, the real reason I asked you to do so was to refresh your own mind. I received a letter from retired Inspector Andrew Horsman, asking if he could visit me, to discuss the case of the missing James Phillimore. He was the police constable who helped save Phillimore's life."

As if on a stage managers cue, there was the sound of the door knocker, and Holmes said, "Splendid. I believe he is here."

Retired Inspector Horsman – "Call me Andy" – was built like the rugby forward he had once been. Red of hair and face, he betrayed his Somerset background by his accent, still noticeable even after a lifetime as a London policeman. He sounded like the Pirate King from a Gilbert and Sullivan operetta, and I half expected him to burst into a rousing chorus of "*Oh, Better Far to Live and Die*".

He didn't, but his reason for visiting was just as stirring.

"I was told by Miss Phyllis Phillimore, way back when James Phillimore disappeared, that due to the failure of the Metropolitan Police in trying to find her brother, she'd intended to consult you. I warned her that it was too little too late, and that she would be wasting both your time and her money, begging your pardon, sir, but she wouldn't listen."

"No apologies are necessary, Inspector. You told her the truth, and I didn't feel that I had earned any right to a fee from her, given how little we could do."

"Thank you. In any event, due to the personal nature of this crime – if indeed a crime it was – I have never been able to let it go. There is a saying around Scotland Yard that when a man retired, he took with him his failures and left behind his successes. I have never been able to let the disappearance of James Phillimore alone, and I was hoping, now that I have discovered new information, to lay it all out for you and see what you think."

"I am delighted you thought of me," said Holmes. "Both Watson and I are eager to hear of your further investigations."

"Thank you. As I recall, Miss Phillimore came and presented her case to you about four weeks after Mister Phillimore's appearance. The circumstances were as follows: After the attack on Mister Phillimore, I had gratefully accepted his offer of accommodation on his estate in Chiswick. In return, I patrolled his land and kept him and his household safe. In truth, Mister Holmes, I felt my work unnecessary. Phillimore was convinced he would be attacked again, and no amount of reasoned debate would change his mind. It was as if he knew who his attackers were, despite his constant denials. I tried to persuade him he had been unfortunate, set about by a gang of ne'er-do-wells. His response was to pay me in kind to protect him. Sadly I was not able to do so, and he has been missing all these years."

"When he was attacked down Blackfriars way, was he robbed?" asked Holmes.

"No, he was not," said Horsman, "and that was a sticking point. I concluded at first that the cab driver, Vincent Coetzee, was upon them quick enough to have prevented robbery, but I later had questions about that. Neither Phillimore nor Coetzee could state with any certainty how many attackers there were. In Phillimore's case, it was because the first blow stunned him. With Coetzee, he said it was because it was dark, with poor lighting, and he was far enough away that it wasn't possible to see. I believed both of them, and I went and looked at the cab rank where Coetzee was waiting, and measured from there to where Phillimore was attacked. It was more than fifty yards. Even if Coetzee had reacted to the first sound, by the time he'd climbed down from the cab and run towards the attack, it would have taken him at least ten seconds to get to Phillimore. He said he was shouting as he ran and the assailants fled, but . . . ." Here he paused, and Holmes helped him out.

"But your question is, 'If there were multiple assailants and they had Phillimore helpless, why was he not robbed?' It takes less than a second to empty a man's jacket pockets, steal his fob and tiepin, and maybe even take his signet ring. The attackers had ample time, yet did none of this, so you think robbery may not have been the motive."

"That is precisely the problem, Mister Holmes. The man that Coetzee and I helped that night was someone I came to know as a kind and selfless man. Yes he was rich, but in the time I knew him, from his beating to his disappearance, I like to think I became his friend. We would talk most evenings at his request. When I came home, I would do my walk-around, then stop at the door to reassure him. Many's the time he invited me in for a drink, Mister Holmes, and though I am not a frequent tippler, he had only the best whisky from the Highlands, and a wee dram every now and then was a special event. He was a fine man with a delightful sense of humour."

"I wish we had met," said Holmes.

"You would have liked him. He was highly intelligent, but he never once talked down to me. I do not wish to believe he lied to the police about his assault, but I also do not believe it was a normal robbery gone wrong. Yet I did not want to doubt him. You see, when I became his friend and protector, I was a lowly constable. I don't know if he had words with anyone, but I do know he belonged to the same club as the Commissioner of Police, and within a month of our friendship I was a Sergeant. Given my lack of education, such a promotion was unprecedented.

"Come, come, Inspector," said Holmes, "You attained higher rank without his help. Surely it is possible you earned your way yourself."

"The first rung is the hardest to climb, Mister Holmes. I'll admit I was a good copper, and once I was a Sergeant I worked hard and proved myself. My promotion to Inspector was all my own work, but James Phillimore gave me the start I needed, and I owe him."

"What of the cab driver?"

"Vince was a nice-enough fellow, amiable and charming. He too benefitted from his friendship with Phillimore, who presented him with his own cab instead of him having to rent one. He also had not one but two horses, a luxury in the cabbing world, and had he been of a mind, he could have made good money."

"Had he been of a mind to?" queried Holmes.

"It is my belief that Mister Coetzee had other things on his mind rather than cabbing. He had one definite job every day, and that was to pick up Phillimore every morning and to bring him back every evening. Other than that, I don't believe he worked too hard."

"Do you have evidence to support this theory," said Holmes.

Horsman paused, gathering his thoughts. "I grew up on a farm outside of Taunton, in Somerset, along the road to Exeter. I know horses, and if Coetzee had worked hard as a cabbie all day, he should have come back at night with a tired horse. Neither of Coetzee's horses ever looked tired."

"So what is your theory then, Inspector Horsman?" said Holmes. I was surprised. His opinion of the constabulary had never been very high, but he had taken to the retired policeman. There was something about his simple way of explaining things that inspired confidence.

"I'm not sure," said the policeman. "Maybe Phillimore had him on retainer. I know they became very friendly and that Coetzee would dine at the main house some nights of every week. It could also be that Coetzee wasn't that ambitious. His needs were few. He owned his cab and his horse. He lived, as me, rent free. Not everyone is driven, Mister Holmes. It could be as simple as that."

"Very well," said Holmes. "Let us step forward to the day he disappeared."

"That morning was in early December and there had been a fresh dusting of snow on the ground. It was Coetzee's habit to go to the barn at about eight of the morning, harness up his hansom cab, and ride out into the close to wait for Phillimore. I had noticed in the last week that instead of letting the horse stand, he had taken to walking it and the cab in a circle around the close. I assumed this was because of the cold weather.

"Now I had just come off a week of night shifts and was about to get ready for bed when I heard a knock on the door. It was Coetzee."

"Something's amiss," he said. "James came out to meet me, said he had left his umbrella behind, and went back to fetch it. He hasn't come back out, and I am worried something is wrong. Please come with me."

"How could you refuse?" said Holmes.

"How indeed?" said Horsman. "I went with him back to the walkway to Phillimore's door. 'Look,' said Coetzee. 'There are his footprints. Out and back, right to my carriage.' What he said was true. There was the one set of footprints out and the other back. We followed them in. Phillimore's door was unlocked, which was most unusual. He always locked it behind him and I had encouraged such behavior as a way of assuaging his fears of another attack. We both went in and did a quick search of all the ground floor rooms. As I did so I looked out of the windows on each side. Next we checked upstairs, and finally the basement. There was no sign of Phillimore.

"He must still be here," I said to Coetzee. "Do you ride down to the village and bring back as many police as are available at the station. We must make a thorough search of the house."

"What did you think at the time" said Holmes.

"I thought that as it was an old house, there may be a bolt hole somewhere or a tunnel. I didn't know why he would be there, given he had just popped back in for an umbrella, and there were two of them in the stand by the front door, but I knew he must still be in the house."

"How so?" I asked.

"As we had searched from room to room, I also looked outside at the surrounds of the house. There were no other footprints whatsoever. The only person who had left and then re-entered the house was James Phillimore."

Holmes laughed in delight. "Watson, here is your impossible crime! Very well done, by the way, Inspector Horsman. You conducted exactly the investigation you were supposed to. I'll save you some time. When you did a thorough search you found nothing. No priest holes, bolt holes, tunnels, hidden rooms, or secret attics. You came to the conclusion that the only place James Phillimore could be was in the house, yet he was not in the house. Am I right?"

"You are, Mister Holmes."

"How many days did it take for the cab driver, Mister Vincent Coetzee, to disappear?"

Inspector Horsman looked shocked. "We never let that information be known. He didn't come back. How could you possibly know?"

"What other solution is there? Mister Coetzee did as you asked. He went to the police station, gave them your message, and then kept on going. At first you thought it was because he was scared he'd be blamed for Phillimore's disappearance, but you have since had darker suspicions, have you not? Tell me, Inspector, what new information did you receive that brought you to my door?"

"I found the hansom cab. It was operating on the far side of London, and I saw it by pure chance."

"How did you know it was the same one?"

"I knew Coetzee's carriage well. I'd had occasion to use his services, and when I stepped into this cab with my wife after a day out with her cousin at Victoria Park, I knew it. It still had the same license, and when I asked the driver about it, he had the temerity to tell me that he really was the licensee, Vincent Coetzee."

"Ha!" said Holmes. "Pray tell, what did you do with this imposter?"

"I may be retired, Mister Holmes, but I still have a reputation in the police. We swung by the nearest police station and I borrowed a cell for a chat with the fake Mister Coetzee. Once I explained to him that I had been looking for him for some years to help with a murder enquiry, he was ready to tell me anything I wanted. The way he told it, he found the cab abandoned at Waterloo Station, the same day both Phillimore and Coetzee went missing."

"And you concluded?" said Holmes.

"I suspected that Coetzee caught the boat train to Southampton, took a berth on the first ship he could find, and sailed away, back to wherever he was from."

"You have most of the parts," said Holmes. "You just need to connect them all. Tell me Inspector, where is Miss Phyllis Phillimore now. Do you know?"

"Only that she sold up and left London shortly after her brother disappeared."

"Interesting," said Holmes. "I have only a few more questions. The place where Phillimore was assaulted down in Blackfriars. Were there any clubs or social drinking places in the area?"

"Not that I know of," said Horsman. "There were rumours of a Molly house down there once upon a time, but I cannot say so for sure."

"Inspector," asked Holmes, "you were on the force long enough to have come across Molly bashing, did you not? Those times when drunken young aristocrats decide they're going to clean up a den of iniquity used by other drunken aristocrats? They wait outside and pound on an unfortunate victim until he is near dead."

"I have heard of them, and I have seen them," said Horsman, and his countenance grew more and more grim. "Is that what you think happened here?"

"It is possible. One more question. If you were to find a cab driver hanging around one of these houses, what would you think?"

"I would think one of two things," said the inspector. "Either he was part of the gang that beat up such people, which I do not believe, or . . . ." Suddenly he seemed to be at a loss for words.

"Or he chose such a rank to ply his trade," said Holmes, "because he was of a similar disposition."

Horsman sat back and mulled over what Holmes had said. He lent back as well, waiting for the inspector to follow the facts. "It fits," said Horsman. "It explains why he wasn't robbed. That wasn't their intention. They just wanted to teach him a lesson. It also explains why he expected another attack. He probably knew some of his attackers – those toffs all go to the same places. You can understand why he wanted to get away. But why such an elaborate plan? Why set up his disappearance in such a way?"

"What are you two talking about?" I said. "I'm used to losing sight of Holmes's deductions until he takes the trouble to explain them to me, but now there are two of you talking around me. I'm aware that a Molly house is a place where men who are interested in other men meet. Molly bashing is when men who don't like men who like men decide to take the law into their own hands and do harm to the men who like men, and maybe their men as well. But where are Phillimore and Coetzee?"

Holmes looked at me as a proud owner at Crufts and I nearly growled at him. "Well, Watson," he said, "Horsman and I believe, but cannot prove, that Phillimore's inclinations were thus, as were Coetzee's, and although they met in a troublesome manner, they became close and resolved to escape a society that permits such vindictiveness, perhaps back to whence Coetzee was from."

"Oh," I said, "you mean that Phillimore and Coetzee were homosexual?"

"Yes, that is what I mean."

"And you think Phyllis Phillimore waited until they settled somewhere more forgiving of their inclinations before going to join them."

"I do," said Holmes. "My subsequent researches showed that before Phillimore disappeared, he had transferred ownership of his property to his sister, Phyllis. Possibly she didn't know that yet when she sought my services, but at some time afterward – after receiving a message from her brother – she knew that she could sell out and join him."

The inspector nodded. "My wife and I retained ownership of our little cottage, while the rest of the property was sold around us."

"Sadly," said Holmes to me, "given the current political climate, I don't think you'll be writing the end of this story anytime soon."

"Where do you think they have gone?" said Horsman.

"Africa is still wild," said Holmes. "It would be easy enough for them to hide, especially if they have money, which they do. I imagine Mister Coetzee had some ideas on that."

"It's a shame," I said, "that they felt they had to run away."

"The real shame is that they were persecuted at all," said Holmes.

He pulled out his pipe.

"Holmes, what are you doing? This is not finished yet."

"Well there is no case, no mystery, nothing for us to do. I don't wish to find Phillimore for my own gratification. In this case, knowing that I could is enough. Why, what bothers you?

"What bothers me? You are ignoring the entire crux of the matter – the locked room mystery, or in this case the snowed-in-house mystery. How did Phillimore go back into the house and disappear?"

"You haven't worked it out? Horsman?"

"I have not, Mister Holmes," said the inspector.

"Nor I," I said. "I know you enjoy these moments – mayhap too much sometimes. Will you please put us out of our misery?"

Taking pity on us, Holmes relented.

"While this is conjecture, what I am about to tell you fits the facts as they are. I suspect a concatenation of events triggered James Phillimore's desire to disappear. The attack on his person scared him. He is a man of logic and engineering – an inventor. He deals in the tangible, and to have to face such hatred merely because of the way he chose to live his life was heart-wrenching, even terrifying. I believe the attack was the catalyst for his desire to disappear. The way he chose to do so was mischievous.

"Phillimore couldn't tell anyone what he planned to do, save his fellow escapee. Not even Miss Phyllis." He paused to light his pipe. "Watson, what do you need for an impossible crime?"

"You need both aspects," I said. "The crime, and the impossibility of the crime."

"No," said Holmes. "You need the *perception* of both, not necessarily the reality. In this case, no crime has been committed, and the event that occurred is clearly not impossible because it did happen. Therefore let us deconstruct it. Coetzee went and fetched his cab to pick up Phillimore. Of late he had been circling round the close while waiting. Inspector Horsman here ascribed this to the most logical reason. It was cold and he was allowing the horse to keep warm. But what if Coetzee was establishing a pattern, so that anyone seeing multiple tracks from horse and cab would not deem it odd."

"I would ask to what eventuality," I said, "but I suspect if I keep quiet you will put us out of our misery all the quicker. Pray continue."

"Coetzee claims to be waiting for Phillimore to come out. When he does, and then returns for his umbrella, he does not reappear. So what does Coetzee do? He calls Horsman to come and help him look for Phillimore. Why did he just not walk into Phillimore's house and look for him? It wasn't yet a mystery, merely a delayed umbrella search. Why did Coetzee need you, Mister Horsman?"

"Because he played me for a fool," said Horsman. "He needed me to sell the idea that Phillimore had disappeared, so he called me to come and see for myself. He led me to the footprints leading out to the cab, then the ones leading back into the house."

"The footprints that ended at the tracks of the horse and cab," said Holmes. "Yes, he needed you, Inspector, to make it all believable." He drew on his pipe, reflecting for a moment.

"Watson, Inspector, there were two other parts of the trick. Do you see them?" He stopped as if a teacher waiting for the brightest student to pre-empt him. Horsman and I were with the dunces in the back row and said nary a word.

"He needed *snow*," said Holmes. "An early fresh dusting so that a newly promoted, keen Sergeant would see the one set of footprints coming out of the front door, and another set going back in. The morning he disappeared was ripe for his invention. All the snow around the rest of the house was pristine, no footprints, no means by which Phillimore could be seen to have escaped. Such an observation may have been questioned by the local constabulary, but when it was given by one of their own there was no doubt, and the search for the secret passage was conducted with full vigour."

"Do you mean," said Horsman, "that he planned it all, even down to giving me the cottage so I would be there to do his bidding unwittingly the day he chose to run away?"

"I do not," said Holmes. "By all accounts Phillimore was a good man. He had done right by his sister and his two saviours, but he still feared for his life. If as we surmise, he knew his attackers and they were from the same social circle, then he also knew he would never truly be safe. The way he chose to live is illegal, and any amount of trouble could have been caused. Witness Oscar Wilde and his misfortunes. I suspect he made his plans around his circumstances, and had you not been living next door, he would have come up with another manner to escape. I think he liked you, Inspector, and was grateful to you, but he felt he couldn't stay in England. He wanted to disappear in as mysterious a manner as possible because that would delight him, so he used you, but I don't believe there was any malice involved, merely mischief."

"But what of the footprints?" I asked. "I agree he could have walked out the house and kept on walking, the tracks of the cab would have hidden his footprints. But he didn't, he walked out, then he went back in, then he disappeared. Without an explanation for that none of the rest of your tale makes sense."

"My dear Watson, I can think of at least five ways that particular misdirection could have been created. The easiest way, and the most likely, is that Phillimore had been overnighting in Coetzee's cottage, waiting for a snowy morning. The next morning when Coetzee arrives with the carriage as usual, James Phillimore was either hiding in the carriage, or perhaps he'd already started walking back to the city, knowing that Coetzee would be by soon to pick him up. The footprints that the inspector was led to believe were the disappearing James Phillimore were actually Coetzee's. There were two sets of footprints, one coming and one going. It was just the order of their creation that differed. Coetzee walked to the door, unlocked it, and then walked back to the road. The rest was illusion."

"How long have you known?" I said.

"I never knew," said Holmes. "I suspected, which is an entirely different matter. Had Miss Phyllis Phillimore been more insistent, I would have checked the passenger lists on outward bound ships, but she never asked."

"What are we to do?"

"We do nothing. We three know what happened. Phillimore made his escape and with any luck is living a good life on the African plains. I hope his sister is happily married and has surrounded her brother with a brood of nieces and nephews, and that they all live happily ever after."

Holmes was right. It was tragic that Phillimore felt he had to escape, but that was hardly his fault and he had done no real harm. Inspector Andy Horsman got up to leave. "I still miss them," he said. "Vince Coetzee was a good man, and James Phillimore was the kindest soul God ever created." Then he laughed. "By 'eck though, didn't he give me the run around all these years, trying to find out what happened to him! Well, I hope he's happy, him and Vince." He made for the door and then turned back to face us.

"There was one thing I forgot to mention," said Horsman. "The couple who adopted James Phillimore – well, they weren't exactly a couple, leastways not as I'd know it. They were both men, educators right enough, living together for many years quietly in the countryside. I found out when I was looking into Phillimore's background, trying to find if it had anything to do with his disappearance."

"Yet you never mentioned it to anyone?" I said.

"I might have," said Horsman, "but they knew nothing, and I saw no need to embroil them in a scandal." He stopped at the door, hat in hand. "Was I wrong, Mister Holmes? Did their life choices change James Phillimore in any way? Would he have been, well, *different* had he not been taken into their household?"

"Yes," said Holmes. "He would have been an intelligent yet unfulfilled street urchin. They gave him a home, an education, and a start in life. I suspect that all the choices he made were of his own free will. The only difference we all could have made would have been to create a society where he and Vince Coetzee could have lived freely and safely. Sadly, that is still a long way off."

> *Somewhere in the vaults of the bank of Cox and Co., at Charing Cross, there is a travel-worn and battered tin dispatch-box with my name, John H. Watson, M.D., Late Indian Army, painted upon the lid. It is crammed with papers, nearly all of which are records of cases to illustrate the curious problems which Mr. Sherlock Holmes had at various times to examine. Some, and not the least interesting, were complete failures, and as such will hardly bear narrating, since no final explanation is forthcoming. A problem without a solution may interest the student, but can hardly fail to annoy the casual reader. Among these unfinished tales is that of Mr. James Phillimore, who, stepping back into his own house to get his umbrella, was never more seen in this world.*
>
> – Dr. John H. Watson
> "The Problem of Thor Bridge"

Another Case of Identity
by Thomas A. Burns, Jr.

Since our auspicious meeting in 1881, I have accompanied my friend, Mr. Sherlock Holmes, during his investigations of hundreds of cases, only a small number of which I have chosen to chronicle, and only a fraction of those have eventually been published. There are many reasons why my narrative of a particular case may never become part of the public record. A case might be too politically sensitive, such as the mission that Holmes had carried out for the Royal Family of Holland, or that matter of supreme importance to the French government. Some of our adventures are frankly too sordid to conform to current publication standards – the repulsive story of the red leech comes to mind in this regard. Publication of the record of a particular case might serve to bring unwanted publicity to innocents, or spark a libel suit. For example, the affair of the Abbey School, in which the Duke of Greyminster was so deeply involved. Sometimes I find myself in disagreement with my literary agent about the public appeal of a tale, and, hard to believe as it may be, a few of my stories have been refused outright by a publisher: "The Adventure of the Middle-aged Bachelor and the two Loquacious Women" falls into the latter category. And finally, there are stories for which the world is simply not, nor may ever be prepared, such as "The Adventure of the Giant Rat of Sumatra".

Holmes, of course, is the final arbiter of whether the record of a given case may be published. I have been known to argue with him if he said no, but as his historiographer, I must always honour his wishes. However, I feel that some of his exploits are worth recording even though they may reside in my battered tin dispatch box for the rest of my days. So far, Holmes has refused to allow the publication of an account of the death of Reginald Balfour. When I asked him for a reason, he said, "There is another who shares complicity in this affair, Watson, and I'd rather he not be aware of what I know of it at the present time."

So it was that Holmes and I found ourselves in Baker Street on Monday morning, 11 May, 1896, yet another dry and sunny day. Over Mrs. Hudson's excellent breakfast of coffee and kippers, I was perusing *The Daily Mail*, a brand new paper which had just begun publication the previous week.

"Good Lord, Holmes!" I remarked. "Yorkshire set a record for the County Championship by accumulating an innings total of eight-hundred-eighty-seven against Warwickshire last Friday! Remarkable, what?"

I knew Holmes found my comments about sporting events tedious, but frankly, I was hoping that the minor annoyance might prompt him into speaking, of which he had done quite little for several days. He sprawled on the sofa in his mouse-grey gown, the pipe full of yesterday's dottles between his lips, in a brown study since wrapping up his last case – he didn't find the missing child in time. He did manage to prove that the lad's absence wasn't the result of kidnapping, as his parents feared, but that provided them cold comfort at best.

A tap at the door, then our landlady entered, partially closing it behind her. "You must get up, Mr. Holmes. You have a distinguished visitor."

"Send him away, woman!" Holmes exploded. "I am of no use to anyone!"

"It is the Duke of Brownley, sir, and I am afraid that he will not be put off. Oh my! He has followed me upstairs . . . ."

The door sprang open and a white-haired gentlemen burst into our rooms. Tall and stylish in full morning dress, he had a disconsolate expression and pallid complexion – an obvious indication that he was overwrought. Having heard Holmes's last comment, he said, "If you are as useless as that idiot Hopkins, then I am truly a woe-begotten wretch. I have just lost my only son, sir, and I suspect foul play. Will you not agree to hear me out?"

The phrase "lost my only son" apparently gained Holmes's attention. He sat up, smoothed his disarranged hair, and replied, "I must apologise, your Grace, for my state of dress. I wasn't expecting visitors."

"Nonsense, man!" the Duke ejaculated. "How else should you be dressed at this hour, in your own home?"

I said, "Mrs. Hudson, take the Duke's hat and stick. Sit down your Grace, and let me pour you some of this excellent coffee. Will you take a bit of breakfast? It may calm your nerves."

"I thank you for your kind offer, sir," the Duke answered, taking the high-backed chair, "but I am much too distraught to take refreshment."

"Some whisky, then? I think we can excuse the early hour."

The Duke acquiesced, and I poured him a tot of Holmes's best single malt, then a cup of coffee for the detective. The Duke tasted the whisky and I saw a little colour come back into his cheeks.

Now, sir," said Holmes, "tell us your sad tale. And omit no detail, however unimportant it may seem."

The Duke began, "I am Fitzhugh Balfour, the Duke of Brownley. My son, Reginald, arrived at Brownley Manor, my estate, on the night of Friday, the eighth of May, 1896, just before bedtime. He was sweating heavily, complaining of nausea and abdominal pain. He collapsed in the vestibule, saying, "She has poisoned me!"

Holmes interrupted. "Do you have any idea of whom he spoke, your Grace?"

The Duke looked annoyed at the inquiry. "No sir, I don't, or I would have mentioned it."

"Sorry. Pray continue your most interesting narrative."

"Reggie was put to bed in his old room with his former governess, Roberta, to watch over him. The only further words he uttered before he passed away during a seizure early on Saturday morning were 'Dr. Warren, No. 29, Harley Street'. We sent a wire to this Dr. Warren forthwith, summoning him to Brownley Manor, but received a note in return that the telegram couldn't be delivered because the doctor wasn't in residence."

"What time was the wire sent?" asked Holmes.

Again, the Duke scowled. "I sent the page to the telegraph office in the village before sunrise. He had to knock the operator out of bed to have him send it."

"And I take it that your son was under the care of this Doctor Warren?" Holmes asked.

"If he was, I didn't know of it," said the Duke. "These constant inquiries of yours are distracting, Mr. Holmes."

"I apologise, your Grace, but the truth often lurks in the most inconsequential of things."

"Rather," said the Duke. He took a sip of whisky, then continued, "Later that morning, we notified Scotland Yard. An Inspector Stanley Hopkins came to Brownley Manor, but after I told him what had transpired, he said only that he would look into it, but he saw no evidence that Reggie's death was not simply due to illness."

"Was there anything other than your son's earlier statement that suggested to you that the inspector was incorrect?" I asked the Duke.

"Poppycock!" he snarled. "Boy was a top oarsman for Westminster – never sick a day in his life!"

"Tell me more about Reginald," said Holmes. "What sort of chap was he? Did he have a position? What were his interests? Who were his friends?"

"He didn't require a position," the Duke said in a condescending tone. "I gave him an ample allowance. Does no harm for a fellow to take a few years after University, decide his course in life."

Wouldn't it be grand, I thought, if all of us had that opportunity.

"So what were his diversions?" asked Holmes.

"He resided at the townhouse in Cavendish Square. Spent a lot of time at his club. The Nonpareil." A tony gaming club.

Holmes asked, "And how were his debts?"

Now the Duke's expression became extremely frosty. "I'm sure I don't take your meaning, Mr. Holmes. I informed Reggie some time ago that if he was going to play at cards, he must absolutely manage any losses from his allowance. He never gave me any indication that he wasn't doing so."

"With whom did he play cards?"

"I neither know nor care."

"How about female friends?" Holmes inquired. "Enemies?"

"He hasn't got any of either!" the Duke exploded. "Mr. Holmes! I came to consult you because that fool Hopkins gave me the distinct impression that Scotland Yard is going to sweep Reggie's death under the rug. Now will you take this assignment or will you not?"

"Again, I must beg your pardon, Duke," said Holmes in a deferential tone. "I will aid you to the best of my meagre abilities. If your son was poisoned, there must be a reason that someone would do that. I must ask such questions in order to ascertain one. Where is Reggie's body now?"

"Hopkins sent a wagon to take Reggie to the mortuary at St. Bartholomew's Hospital for examination later on Saturday morning. I wasn't happy about that, but I suppose it was necessary to get this mess sorted. He said that he would inform me when the body would be released for burial."

"I shall consult the medical examiner at Barts, then pay a visit to you at Brownley Manor later this morning," Holmes told the Duke. "I shall want to speak to this Roberta, and to your page."

"I shall see that they are available," answered his Grace.

"Then, of course, I must visit the Nonpareil, and also try to locate the elusive Dr. Warren. After that, we shall see." Holmes regarded the Duke with a sympathetic expression. "Your Grace, you must prepare yourself for the possibility that you son did in fact die from a disease."

"If you tell me that you have good evidence that Reggie's claim that he was poisoned was unfounded after a thorough investigation, I will accept your word," the Duke said. "You do come highly recommended, Mr. Holmes. And it would be a comfort to know that he didn't die from foul play."

I could sense the immense grief beneath the Duke's matter-of-fact tone. I have dealt with parents who lost children on many occasions, but have never become accustomed to it. I think I would cease practicing if I did.

After his Grace had departed, Holmes turned to me. "If you have nothing better to occupy yourself today, Watson, I would much appreciate your company. Your medical expertise might prove invaluable in this case."

"It does appear that the young man expired because of some fatal malady," I said.

"Yes," said Holmes, "but mark you what I have said about theorizing in the absence of data. Let us give the Duke his money's worth, even if this be merely a low tragedy."

Holmes rang for the page and dispatched him to find a cab whilst we changed into morning dress – we were going to call on a duke later this day. The ride to Smithfield was protracted, as there was considerable congestion on Oxford Street, so it was nearly eleven before we debarked in front of Barts. Holmes led the way to the mortuary, where he was well-known, so it wasn't long before we were gazing at the corpse of the unfortunate Reggie Balfour. The boy looked serene in death, and much younger than his twenty-five years. Dr. Eames, the medical examiner, was in attendance.

"Have you formed an opinion about the cause of death?" Holmes asked the doctor.

"I found marked haemorrhage in the mucosal membranes of the gastrointestinal system, which was consistent with what I was told of the patient's complaints, and which could be indicative of any number of conditions," the medical examiner said. "I also found systemic organ damage."

"Then he could have been poisoned?" Holmes asked.

"Yes, but the signs aren't definitive," said Eames. "Enteric fever, food poisoning, or other intestinal maladies will also exhibit such signs."

"But those things aren't uniformly fatal," I said, "and if they are, suffering may be protracted before death occurs." I knew this first-hand from my own battle with enteric fever after Maiwand.

"That's correct," said the doctor.

"There have been no other reports of such diseases in the City?" Holmes asked.

"Now that you mention it, I had one other with similar signs." Eames replied.

"Whom?"

"He was a scullion, employed at the Criterion." Holmes and I occasionally dined at this Piccadilly restaurant.

"Most curious," Holmes observed. "No other cases linked there?" I knew what Holmes was considering – food poisoning.

"No," Eames said. "It seemed to be an isolated incident,"

There was no point in conducting my own examination after a full autopsy had been carried out, so we repaired back to our cab, giving the driver an order to go to Charing Cross Station, where we boarded a train for the village of Brownley.

We crossed the Thames and had a fine view of Battersea Park to the west and then a pleasant ride to Brownley, about half-an-hour south of London.

On arrival, we were informed by the ticket agent that Brownley Manor was approximately half-a-mile from the station, along the one long street that comprised the greatest part of the town. No cabs were in evidence, but it was a fine sunny day, so we decided to walk to the Duke's estate. It was peaceful to be here after the hustle-and-bustle of the capital, yet the poignant reason for our visit weighed heavily on my mind.

After passing out of the village proper, we came to a side road shaded by overarching oaks, which the ticket agent had told us was the approach to the manor. As we emerged from the leafy tunnel, the scent of spring flowers hung heavy in the air, and the bulk of the manor house reared up before us – a three-storey red brick mansion with stone dressings, which dated from the late eighteenth century. It featured tall arched windows on the ground floor flanking a gabled entry on either side, a slate roof lined with dormers, and four fine brick chimneys spaced equally along its length – a residence fit for a duke, indeed. We proceeded up a short brick stairway between meticulously trimmed rectangular yew hedges, and a heavy oaken door with gleaming brass fittings swung silently open at our approach.

"Obviously, someone at the station called ahead of our arrival," Holmes muttered.

A liveried butler took Holmes's card and conducted us to a sitting room with lofty, painted ceilings and a majestic brick fireplace. In only a few minutes, the Duke entered.

"What have you ascertained so far?" he asked Holmes in a brusque tone.

Holmes informed him of the medical examiner's findings. He asked, "Now that you've had time to reflect, are you sure you have no idea of the identity of the woman to whom your son referred?'

"None whatsoever," averred the Duke. "If Reggie was keeping company with a woman, he didn't see fit to share that information with me."

"I wonder if you have a recent photograph of your son that I might borrow for a while," Holmes asked.

"No sir," said the Duke. "If I want pictures of family members, I'll commission a portrait,"

Holmes spent a fruitless half-hour interrogating the page and Roberta the former governess, but got no further clarity regarding the cause of the unfortunate Reggie's demise.

"I suppose our next step is to return to London and attempt to speak with this Doctor Warren," Holmes said dejectedly. I dearly hoped that this case wasn't doomed to become another failure, following so closely on the heels of the affair of the missing boy the previous week.

The Duke hadn't seen fit to offer us luncheon, so I was famished by the time we returned to the railway station. I prevailed upon Holmes to allow me to procure box meals from an adjacent public house. As I have observed in other accounts of Holmes's adventures, he is wont to go without sustenance for days when on a case, especially when things aren't going well. I was determined not to allow this during this investigation.

Once back in London, we secured a cab outside Victoria Station and Holmes directed the driver to Dr. Warren's Harley Street office. We found the following note tacked to the locked front door:

> *Dr. Malachy Warren has been called away on urgent business* (it ran) *and the date of his return is undetermined at this time. The following physicians and surgeons have indicated that they will see Dr. Warren's patients who have urgent needs:*
>
> *Dr. Moore Agar – 6 Harley Street*
> *Dr. Arthur Ainstree – 35 Harley Street*
> *Mr. Ronald Atkinson, Surgeon – St. Mary's Hosp.*

"So, it seems that Dr. Warren has decamped for the duration," observed Holmes. "I wonder what the good doctor is so fearful of?"

We returned to Baker Street. While changing from our morning dress to less-formal attire, Holmes dispatched a wire to Stanley Hopkins at Scotland Yard, asking the inspector to join us for dinner. Mrs. Hudson was a bit miffed at the short notice, but finally allowed that she could stretch the menu to accommodate another diner.

Holmes's motives for involving Hopkins became clear at the table. Over a fine meal of boiled gigot of mutton with neeps and tatties, he assured the young policeman that he had no desire to step on his toes.

"By George," said Hopkins, "after all the assistance you've given to me, Mr. Holmes, and seeking no credit for yourself, I shouldn't care if you'd tread on them with hobnails. But I must tell you that I haven't been able to find any evidence that the poor chap didn't die of a sudden illness."

"Nor have we, sir, but I've promised the Duke that we'd leave no stone unturned. That is why I'd like you to accompany us to the Nonpareil Club this evening. As we aren't members, we'll need your badge to gain admittance."

"And what do you hope to discover there?"

"I want to talk to Reginald Balfour's mates to see if a motive for his alleged murder can be ascertained," said Holmes. "Also, the Duke tells me that he has no knowledge of his son's female friends. It's difficult to believe that a gentleman of that age doesn't have any."

Because a hansom cab is a bit of a tight squeeze for three large men, Holmes hired a brougham for the trip to Pall Mall. St. James's Street is a broad thoroughfare wide enough to accommodate carriages three abreast, and lined with fine Georgian townhouses that house some of London's most exclusive clubs, including the Thatched House Club, the Conservative Club, Boodle's, the Devonshire Club, and of course, the Nonpareil Card Club. After Hopkins displayed his badge, we were met in the foyer by the night manager, a Mr. Edwin Newsome, who conducted us to his office. On the way, we passed through a corridor, one wall of which was lined with framed drawings and photographs.

"Your members, I presume," Holmes said to Newsome.

"Yes," he replied. "This display represents a venerable tradition of the Nonpareil. Upon acceptance, a new member sits for his photograph, which will be displayed here in perpetuity, along with his coat of arms or family crest."

"Ordered by date of admittance, I see," observed Holmes.

"Of course. That way, we don't have to rearrange everything when a new member is admitted."

Holmes abruptly froze, staring intently at one of the photos. I came up behind him to see which one interested him so. It was a double picture with a comely young man above, with a high forehead and aquiline features, looking off into the distance instead of at the camera, as if he was uncomfortable having his picture made. Beneath was a family crest done in red and white. A brass plaque on the bottom of the frame noted:

Dr. Malachy Warren, b. 1847, member 1882

"Fascinating," said Holmes.

"What?" I said. "That he's been a member for fourteen years?"

He turned to look at me disbelievingly. "You don't see it?"

"See what?" I said, perplexed.

"Never mind." He turned and followed Newsome into his office. Typical.

After Holmes had informed the manager of the reason for our visit, Newsome said, "Of course, Mr. Holmes. Mr. Balfour's loss was a blow to all of us. I'm sure his comrades would be glad to speak with you about him."

"With whom did he spend most of his time?" Holmes asked.

"Mr. Balfour was very fond of whist," the manager said. "He was part of a regular foursome that comprised Mr. Bertie Greene, Mr. Rupert Bennington-Smythe, and Count Negretto Sylvius."

I could see Holmes's head twitch at that last name. "Which was Balfour's partner?" Holmes asked.

"Mr. Greene," said Newsome.

"I should like to speak with each of them," said Holmes. "Greene first, then Bennington-Smythe, and Count Sylvius, last, if he doesn't mind."

A few moments later, Newsome ushered Bertie Greene into the office, then departed. Greene was a young chap about Reggie Balfour's age. He had curly brown hair and broad features, and he was dressed in a grey-plaid towncoat that hung loosely on his scrawny frame, black trousers with a white shirt, and black tie. He appeared somewhat nervous in the presence of Holmes and a Scotland Yard inspector – Holmes's name had become quite well-known by then since I'd begun chronicling his cases.

"Sit down, Mr. Greene," Holmes said. "You have nothing to fear from us. We're simply looking into Mr. Balfour's last days at his father's request."

Greene seemed insulted by Holmes's remarks. "I'm not afraid," he said. "Just discommoded. We were having a rubber, and I was winning."

"For a change?" Holmes asked.

Greene suddenly looked guilty. "Well, yes," he said. "How did you know?"

"If I had a tailor who cut a bespoke towncoat that poorly, I should certainly hold him accountable," said Holmes. "I assume you had it made in better times, and haven't had it altered due to lack of funds. Just how much do you owe Bennington-Smythe and Sylvius?"

"Two-hundred-thirty-eight pounds and five shillings," Greene answered. "And I don't owe Bennington-Smythe anything. The Count takes care of that part of it."

Holmes took his gold cigarette case from an inner pocket and flipped it open, extracted one, and held it out to Greene. His hand trembled as he reached for one. "Take two," Holmes told him. Then, "The Count is graciously allowing you to make payments to him? With interest, I suppose?"

"He doesn't charge me any," Greene said. "He advances me the coin so I can keep playing, and when I win, like I am tonight, he deducts it from what I owe him."

"What a generous fellow!" said Holmes. "But I'll wager that you must make regular payments as well, correct? Weekly?"

"Once a month. He says it's good for my character, and it keeps me from getting into him too deeply."

"And it also keeps you at fighting weight," Holmes observed. "He's looking out for your well-being, the Count."

"He says that he likes to play whist," Greene said. "If he won all the time and didn't give a fellow a break, no one would play with him."

"And that would be a tragedy, indeed," finished Holmes. "I think I've learned all that I need to know from you, Mr. Greene. I also think we can dispense with an interview of Mr. Bennington-Smythe. Would you please ask the Count if he would be so kind to grace us with his presence?"

Once again Greene regarded Holmes fearfully, as if he wondered if he'd told too much. "You won't – "

"Run along, Mr. Greene," Holmes said. "A piece of advice. Mortgage all that you own, impose upon your family and friends if you must, but get yourself out from under the Count's thumb, and don't get back underneath it again. You won't regret it. That's all."

Greene turned and slinked out of the door. When he'd gone, I asked Holmes, "And just who is this Count Sylvius? A peer?"

"He has a reputation as a big-game hunter. But he's a womanizer, a cad, and an all-round rotter," Holmes said. "He's been within the spectrum of my awareness for some years now. And his title, if real at all, is certainly not British. Possibly Italian. Now that I'm cognisant that he's involved in this affair, I certainly suspect foul play in young Balfour's death."

"I agree, Mr. Holmes," said Hopkins. "The Yard has had rumours of this Count Sylvius, but nothing actionable, as yet."

"He prefers to have others do his dirty work," Holmes said. A tap on the door. "But hush, gentlemen. Here he is now."

The office door opened and the Count entered. He was a huge, dark-skinned fellow of southern-Italian aspect, dressed in the Continental fashion in tails with velvet lapels, white waistcoat, and black tie. He wore a great black moustache under a large beaky nose and sported a monocle that he probably didn't need, dangling on his chest. He favoured us with a thin-lipped smile as he made a little bow, then he stepped straight up to Holmes and extended his hand.

"I am so pleased to make your acquaintance, Mr. Holmes." His voice had just a hint of an Italian accent. "I have heard much of you, even in Rome."

Holmes seemed not to see the proffered hand. He motioned to the chair that Greene had just quitted. "I have heard much of you as well, Count."

The Count favoured us with an oily smile as he sat. "I hope it was all flattering."

"Hardly," Holmes said. "I am here to discuss with you anything that you might know of the demise of young Reginald Balfour. I am told you played cards with him."

"Yes, that is true. Such a pity. Reggie was a fine young man."

"I assume he owed you money?"

"On the contrary, Mr. Holmes, Reggie and I were square. He paid his debts to me in a regular manner."

"The Duke must provide him a generous allowance."

"Yes, that must be so."

"I wonder if you could tell me of Reggie's other acquaintances. Female friends, perhaps?"

"Not to my knowledge. Reggie seemed entirely dedicated to whist. He even talked about playing professionally one day, although I must say, I don't think that he possessed the necessary acumen."

Holmes reached again for his cigarette case, but the Count stopped him. "Please," he said, extracting his own black-and-gold case from his jacket, "you must try one of mine. Balkan Sobranies. The Latakia gives them quite a unique flavour."

"I prefer my Virginias," said Holmes, offering his case to Hopkins and myself. Neither of us took one. The Count produced a cigarette holder and fixed his cigarette to the end, and then pulled out a lighter. Holmes did allow the Count to give him a light. "Do you know whether Reggie had much to do with Dr. Malachy Warren?" he inquired.

The Count assumed a peculiar grin. "Oh, I would say that the two of them were certainly acquainted, but I couldn't tell you the nature of their assignation." It seemed to me that he was implying something more, but I couldn't fathom what.

"So they kept regular company?" Holmes pressed.

"I'm sure I don't know," replied the Count.

Holmes paused, considering, then asked, "And what is your relationship with the good doctor?"

The Count's grin blossomed into a broad smile. "We speak to each other on occasion, Mr. Holmes, as fellow club members will do. That was the extent of it."

I couldn't help but feel that the fellow was lying through his teeth, but I couldn't imagine why.

"Is that all, Mr. Holmes?" the Count asked. "My partners are anxiously waiting for me, so that we may resume our game."

"Yes, Count, that will be all. You'll hear from me if we need to resume our conversation."

“I look forward to that hour,” the Count said. He rose, touched his right forefinger to his eyebrow in a mock salute to the three of us, and then departed.

“There goes a very dangerous man,” said Hopkins.

“Indubitably,” Holmes agreed. “Only God knows the sins he’s responsible for, although I am aware of a few.”

“Care to share them with Scotland Yard?” asked the inspector.

“When I have evidence, certainly,” replied Holmes.

“Do you think he’s responsible for Reggie’s death?” I asked Holmes.

“Leaving aside for the moment the question of means,” began Holmes, “I can discern no motive for Count Sylvius to want Reggie out of the way. The boy was a golden goose for him, and apparently, much more assiduous in paying his debts than the hapless Greene, if the Count is to be believed.”

“So where do we go from here?” I asked.

“Baker Street,” replied Holmes. “I must be off early in the morning.”

“To do what?” I asked.

“To locate the evanescent Dr. Warren.”

We went to find Newsome to thank him for his accommodation. “No thanks necessary,” the club manager averred. “I only hope you can shed some light on Reggie’s tragic demise.”

“By the way,” said Holmes, “would it be possible for me to borrow Reggie’s photo from the corridor? I assure you, it will be returned.”

“By all means,” said Newsome.

When we arrived back at our digs, the bells of St. Marylebone’s were just chiming ten. Holmes went straight to bed after knocking up the page and sending him off with a wire, but I, knowing that sleep would be a rare commodity this night, poured a stiff brandy and sat in my chair to muse over this puzzling case – if even a crime had been done! We had no evidence that poor Balfour’s death was anything other than natural. Holmes now seemed convinced that the minatory Count Sylvius was somehow involved, but the man seemed to simply have no reason to want Reggie out of the way. After a bit, I could feel the Cognac doing its work, so I made my way upstairs to bed.

True to his word, Holmes was absent when I came downstairs at eight-forty-five. The morning papers were on the table, so I rang for coffee and breakfast. I reached for *The Daily Mail*, but spied an open book beneath it – a copy of *Who’s Who*. I perused the page that presented itself and found the following entry:

> *WARREN, Malachy Bernas, MD Univ. of Edinburgh 1871; F.R.C.P. (Lond.) 1886: 74th Regt of Foot, India, 1871; HM*

66th, Afghanistan, 1879: Returned to England 1881, entered private practice: Address 29 Harley Street, W

It wasn't unusual for a doctor to be transferred from the regiment that he had originally joined, according to the needs of the service. If Warren was with the 66th in 1879, he was likely at Maiwand in 1880! I strained to remember. After that disastrous battle and my wounding, I met many doctors in the course of my treatment. Was Dr. Warren one of them? I tried to summon up his features from the photograph at the club last evening.

It was near eleven when Holmes returned. "I have had an interesting morning, Watson," he said. "I see that you have had a chance to review Dr. Warren's *Who's Who* entry. Do you remember at all meeting him during or after Maiwand?"

"Yes," I replied. "I do seem to remember encountering a young man who looked like him, who helped care for me during that awful bout with enteric fever. He was unusually solicitous of my comfort – army doctors can be a cold lot." A pause. "I found it interesting that the entry contains no information about Warren's life before he entered medical school."

"It contains only that which Warren wanted," said Holmes. "The information was gleaned from a questionnaire provided by the good doctor himself." Holmes should know, having his own entry in *Who's Who*.

"I spent a fruitful morning at the War Office in Cumberland House," he continued. "With a bit of prodding from brother Mycroft, they were able to tell me why a healthy army doctor was returned so abruptly to England in 1881." He smiled, making me wait for it, then, "Doctor Warren was denied promotion due to excessive gambling – or more likely, because he owed the wrong people and had trouble paying."

"And yet he joins a gaming club after he returns to London," I observed. "He doesn't seem to have the best judgment, does he?"

"No, he doesn't," agreed Holmes. "What would you say to a little stroll over to Harley Street after lunch?"

After an excellent luncheon of fresh fish provided by our landlady, Holmes and I set out for Harley Street, just a few blocks east. It was glorious spring day, with a slight breeze from the northeast clearing away much of the objectionable street scents. If Warren still hadn't returned to his office, I resolved to ask Holmes if he cared to take in nearby Regent's Park. When we approached No. 29, I was gratified to see that the notice was still on the door. Holmes stopped in front of the steps and gave a low whistle. A ragamuffin suddenly appeared from a nearby stairwell leading to a basement.

"All quiet, Sam?" asked Holmes.

"Yessir. Nobody's come in or out."

Holmes fished in his pocket for a crown, which he flipped to the lad. "Good job. The surveillance is over. See that you pay the others."

As the boy ran off, Holmes brought out a ring of keys. It only required three or four tries before he had the door open and beckoned me inside. Passers-by on Harley Street paid us no mind – we could have been a pair of residents entering our home.

Holmes closed the door and I inhaled the familiar scents of a doctor's office – hints of iodine and carbolic mingled with lemon wax. We were in a hallway tiled in a black-and-white motif, with closed doors right, left and to the rear, and a broad, polished staircase rising to the first floor.

I regarded Holmes questioningly. "How is it that you have Warren's keys?"

He favoured me with a deprecating smile. "I observed Warren's locks the last time we were here," he said, "and earlier this morning, I visited a locksmith whom I once rescued from the dock. He was kind enough to provide me with a set of skeleton keys.

"These would be Warren's examining rooms, surgery, and office," Holmes continued, "with the living quarters upstairs. I think it more likely that clews to the doctor's present whereabouts will be found in the latter location."

We ascended the stairs, and Holmes had to ply his skeleton keys once more to unlock the door at the apex. As we passed through it, an odour of tobacco and food with an underlying sweetness of flowers or perfume wafted out from the rooms beyond. We entered a large salon that featured painted azure walls with vertical white stencilling in a diamonded pattern, ivory-upholstered furniture, and a marble fireplace. Three broad windows curtained in blue-and-white looked out over Harley Street. Holmes went straight to his work, opening drawers and cabinets, presumably searching for anything that might give an indication of where Warren might be.

"Why don't you look about in the other rooms?" Holmes said, indicating a doorway across from the one to the stairs.

I opened it and found myself in a hallway, again with doors left and right, and a staircase to the second floor at the end. I opened a door to a bedroom that was decidedly masculine, done in dark wood and leather and smelling of sweat and whisky. A second door led to a larger bedroom decorated with a feminine flair – again in blue-and-white, with lace doilies and throws covering white-painted furnishings with gold trim. A vanity topped with a mirrored triptych occupied one wall with a large white wardrobe on another. I opened the latter and found a dozen men's suits hanging in a row. In the bottom were several pair of men's shoes and boots, and a cardboard box. I picked it up. Southall's towels? The drawers of a nearby bureau contained yet more haberdashery. I was beginning to come to an unsettling conclusion.

I went back to the salon where I found Holmes at the liquor cabinet, holding a bottle of amber liquid up to the light streaming in through the windows.

"Holmes," I said, "I believe that Dr. Warren is a woman! And there is a man living here as well." I told him about the bedrooms that I found.

"Yes," replied Holmes. "I realized that as soon as I saw her picture at the Nonpareil Club. The absence of an Adam's apple is quite diagnostic. Come here and look at this."

I approached and he turned the bottle that he was holding so I could see the red-and-white label.

Craigshall
Single Malt Scotch Whisky
Made with Meticulous Care in our Lowlands Distillery
Aged in Oak 16 Years

Beneath the words, a familiar family crest was displayed – the same as the one beneath Warren's picture at the club!

"Now I think I have a good notion of where Dr. Warren might be," Holmes said.

"There's another floor above us," I pointed out.

"Yes," he replied. "We might as well take a look for thoroughness' sake."

Once again Holmes had to use his keys on the door at the top of the stairs. Pushing it open, we entered an attic room with a low ceiling, dark because insufficient light was admitted through the narrow stained glass windows. A sweet solvent aroma, not unlike that which pervaded our rooms in Baker Street on occasion, tickled my nostrils. Sure enough, in the low light I could see the silhouettes of flasks, condensers, and other chemical laboratory equipment, occupying two long tables in the centre of the room.

"Apparently Dr. Warren and I share an avocation," said Holmes.

Holmes approached a desk in a corner, while I surveyed the chemical equipment. Due to my long association with Holmes, I was able to ascertain that the equipment necessary to carry out an extraction has been erected on one bench. I found a beaker half-full of dried beans, tan mottled with brown, and an open notebook nearby. I picked up the latter, hoping to find out what the experimenter had been doing.

I raised my voice. "Holmes? Are you familiar with a process known as a 'Stillmark extraction'?"

"Watson," Holmes voice was low, and cold as ice. "Put that book on the bench, and get away from there. We must leave immediately."

I did as he asked. As I approached him, I could see that his face was livid, and he had an expression that I'd seldom seen on his countenance. Fear.

"Holmes, what's the matter? What's got you spooked?"

"Lectins, Watson. Lectins. Lectins. Stillmark carried out an aqueous extraction of the castor bean in 1888, and isolated an extremely toxic product. I fear that we might have become exposed to it here."

He ushered me out of the door and down the stairs, continuing all the way to the ground floor and out on to Harley Street, where he began walking south at a brisk pace. I had to trot to keep up.

"Holmes! Where are you going? Why such a hurry?"

"To the Argyll Baths off Regent Street," he said.

After entering the baths, we went into the dressing room to disrobe, and Holmes told the attendant, "Please do not touch these garments. Bring a laundry sack so that we may place them inside, then have them burned. We will eschew the warm room and go directly to the bathing pool."

Once at the pool, Holmes said, "Immerse yourself, Watson, and scrub every inch of you. Your life depends on your cleanliness."

When we were bathed to his satisfaction, I asked if we might go to one of the warm rooms to dry off, as I was chilled to the bone from the cold bath, and my shoulder was throbbing.

"No, Watson, in this case I think it better for our pores to remain shut. The next day or two will tell us whether we left Warren's laboratory in time."

That was the last he would say on the matter. He sent a wire to Baker Street for fresh clothes.

Afghanistan had taught me the futility of agonising over that which about I could do nothing. I resolved to put the possibility of exposure to the back of my mind and hope for the best.

We were back in Baker Street just before supper time. Holmes dispatched a pair of wires, one to Hopkins and the other to the Scottish Records Office in Edinburgh.

"Prepare yourself for an excursion," he said to me. "The Flying Scotsman leaves Charing Cross at ten a.m. tomorrow."

"And why, pray tell, are we going to Scotland?" I asked.

"To beard the lioness in her den."

Given Holmes's comments of yesterday, I was grateful to see the light of day on Wednesday morning. I had asked him once more about the substance to which we might have been exposed, and he said, "Don't fret about it, Watson. If we've received a lethal dose, there's nothing anyone can do. Best not to waste one's life worrying about losing it."

Holmes indicated that our trip to Scotland would only consume a day or two, so I packed a single valise, and carried my Norfolk jacket and my hat in case of chilly the weather up north. We boarded the Flying Scotsman and were whisked away precisely on time for the nine-hour trip – the fastest way to Scotland from London. Upon our arrival in the Scottish capital, we booked a room at the Royal Hotel, where a package from the Records Office awaited Holmes. After perusing the contents, he arranged for a carriage to take us south in the morning.

Under other circumstances, our morning ride would have been delightful. The Lowlands south of Edinburgh is a sprawling, sparsely forested, verdant land of cultivated fields and sheep pastures, impossibly green during the early spring lambing season. A Scot myself, even though I had no more family there and hadn't been back in quite some time, I felt a vague yearning for the land of my birth. I suppose that is natural.

After approximately two hours, we entered the village of Craigshall, whose narrow streets and grey stone buildings evoked an earlier, simpler time. The air was redolent with peat smoke, likely the product of our destination, a towering granite castle on a lofty hill above the town. After passing through tall wrought-iron gates, we made not for the castle which housed the distillery, but instead for a gabled cottage of stone and white-painted clapboard, cozily nestled into a hollow at the base of the hill.

We disembarked from the carriage and Holmes bade the driver to wait. Then led the way along a stone path, up to a stout wooden door rimmed with beds in which purple crocuses and yellow narcissus bloomed. He rapped sharply on the door with his stick. After a moment, it was opened by a white-haired gentleman in a black jacket, white shirt, bow tie, and tartan kilt.

Holmes held out his card. "I wish to speak with Miss Minerva Warrender," he said.

"She's expectin' ye, Mr. Holmes."

We entered into a well-appointed sitting room, but the doctor wasn't there. The butler led the way toward the rear of the house and into another, larger room with an oval dining table of dark wood flanking a grey stone fireplace, in which ashes still smouldered against the morning chill. Miss Warrender, still in male attire – jacket, waistcoat, and trousers – sat at the far end. She had a cigarette in a holder in her mouth, and she reached up and removed it with a slender hand when she saw us. A large gold ring clinked against the cut glass ashtray as she laid it down.

"Thank ye, Alasdair," she said. Her voice was a strong contralto with a slight Scottish burr, which could have belonged to a man or a woman.

"Welcome tae my home, gentlemen. Please be seated. May I offer you some refreshment?"

"Given the reason of our visit, we politely decline," said Holmes.

"I understand. But be assured that I would nae pollute the noble elixir of which my family was so justly proud with a noxious substance. Bring the Century Cask, Alasdair."

The butler nodded almost imperceptibly, then vanished. Holmes addressed Miss Warrender. "I thought you might return with us to Edinburgh, where you would surrender yourself to the police for the murders of James Blackfriar, a scullion, and Reginald Balfour, the Duke of Brownley's only son."

"I am mightily sorry about the scullion, Mr. Holmes. His death was quite unintentional."

"It happened because you had the unutterably poor judgment to poison Mr. Balfour in a restaurant. Surely you knew the risk with a toxin so potent."

"I did nae think Reggie would be daft enough to accept a drink from me in my home," she said. "So I suggested the Criterion as a suitable neutral ground to discuss our arrangement." She looked down at the table top. "Reggie did nae finish his wine," she said.

"And the scullion's colleagues informed me that boy was in the habit of draining the dregs before washing the wine glasses," Holmes replied. "It was likely the only way in which he would ever sample a vintage so fine."

Miss Warrender still studied the tabletop. "As I said, I regret that. It was unintentional."

"You also put your neighbours and others at risk when you isolated such a deadly poison in your laboratory," Holmes chided.

"Please g'ie me some credit for professional competence, Mr. Holmes. I planned to remain in that house after Reggie Balfour was eliminated, as I thought that would be the end o' my worries. Alasdair and I scrubbed the laboratory thoroughly when the procedure was finished."

She looked up suddenly, staring Holmes right in the eyes. "But I'm nae sorry for Reggie. He would hae bled me dry before he ruined me."

"He discovered your secret," Holmes said.

"Yes. I do nae know how he did. Previously at the club, he never gave any indication that anything was amiss, yet he came to me one evening and revealed that he knew all."

I turned at a slight disturbance behind me. Alasdair had entered, bearing a large silver tray that held a small cask with a spigot on the end, and four balloon glasses. He carried it past Holmes and I and set it on the table beside Miss Warrender.

"Gentlemen, I assure ye that this cask has nae been breached except for that tap, in over a hundred years," she said. She picked up one of the snifters and held it under the spigot, opening the valve and letting the liquid inside trickle down the side of the glass. A sweet, peaty aroma suffused the room, causing my mouth to water. She closed the tap and swirled the umber liquid around in the glass, where it coated the inside like a syrup.

She offered the snifter to Alasdair, who accepted it with one of his miniscule bows.

"Are ye sure, gentlemen? Ye'll hae only this chance to sample a single malt so auld and fine as this one."

I turned to the detective. "What was it you said to me yesterday, Holmes? Best not to waste one's life fretting about losing it?"

"A touch, Watson, a distinct touch!" To the doctor: "I am certain that you wouldn't poison your faithful old retainer, Miss Warrender. Go ahead. Pour two for us."

After the glasses had been distributed, smelt, sipped, and enjoyed, Miss Warrender said, "Mr. Holmes, will ye not hear my sad tale before ye bear me away to Edinburgh and the dock?"

"It will make no difference to your fate, Madam, but you are free to tell it whilst we enjoy this fine brew."

"I was born in this very house," she began, "one of twins. The other was my brother, Malachy. Our da had him tabbed to take over the family business, but one day, when we were eight, ma fell ill and we despaired of her life. The village doctor was called, and after many days labour, he saved her. After that, nothing would do but for Malachy to become a doctor. That boy was the apple of his father's eye, so he was prepared for the university at Edinburgh. For me, a suitable match would be found when I came of age."

She paused for a sip of the noble old whisky, then resumed her tale.

"All was well in Craig's Hall until that terrible autumn of '64. A plague of fever tore through the Lowlands, and when it was done, Da, Mum, and Malachy were among its victims. Only Alasdair and I remained. It was then I decided that I'd nae become a shepherd's wife. If my brother could nae realize his dream of becoming a doctor, I would do it for him. He and da had already started the process for admittance to Edinburgh. Malachy and I looked very much alike – peas in a pod, Mum used to call us – so it was nae great feat to dress as him, and finish the examinations. I went up to Edinburgh in his place in '67 and never looked back.

"After matriculating, I joined the army. An army doctor has much more privacy than most, so it wasn't too difficult to keep up the deception unless someone saw me disrobed, of which I was very careful. I would hae made the army my life, but I became close to a fellow officer and foolishly told him my secret. He agreed to keep it only if I would agree to leave the service."

"Your docket at the War Department says you were denied promotion due to excessive gambling," Holmes told her.

"Well, it had to say something if the actual reason was nae given. But my discharge turned out to be a blessing. I went into private practise, specializing in women's medicine, and I was very successful. Even though my patients were nae aware of my true sex, they seemed to find in me a kindred spirit. In a surprisingly short time, I was able to purchase the Harley Street practise that I have now.

"I brought Alasdair down to serve me after I returned to England, and we led a peaceful and fulfilling life. I loved my work, found diversion at my club, and did all of the things as a man that, as a lowly woman, I would never have been allowed to do."

"And Reggie Balfour would have ruined all that for you," said Holmes.

"Yes," she agreed. "When he first came to me, it was money he wanted. Reggie was an uncommonly poor whist player and had racked up considerable debt at the club. But money was something I had much of, due to the success of my practise and the annual stipend I received from the distillery. But then Reggie demanded that which I was unwilling to give to him."

"Of course he did," said Holmes.

"Oh, I am an adult, Mr. Holmes, and a woman does have needs. If it would have been but once, I could have borne it, but it was again, and again, and he finally demanded things to which nae man has any right. So, I determined to be rid of him."

"You mention needs. I take it you had other gentlemen friends from time to time?" asked Holmes.

"Yes, Mr. Holmes, I did. What of it?"

"I mean only that one of them may have been the source of Reggie's information about you."

"I cannae imagine that. I was very careful whom I told, and I did so only after long acquaintance. None of them would betray me!"

"Not even Count Sylvius?"

Now Miss Warrender wore an expression like that of a deer ringed by a pack of hounds. "Not Negretto. Especially not Negretto. He even talked of taking me back to his homeland if I ever tired of my vocation, where we could live openly as man and wife. Why would he do such a thing?"

"Because Reggie owed the Count money that he couldn't pay. It would amuse one such as him to have that money come from you – by proxy as it were."

"He would never!" she uttered. Her tone told us she didn't believe her own words.

"He would, and he did, Miss Warrender," Holmes said, not unkindly.

She sat quietly for a moment, contemplating the amber liquid in the glass before her. Then she placed her hand above it, squeezing the ring on her right hand with the fingers of her left. The top of the ring popped open and something within fell into the glass.

"No!" I cried, and sprang to my feet, but before I could stop her, she drained the glass and hurled it into the fireplace, where it shattered into a million shards. On the contrary, Holmes sat quietly, a melancholy expression on his face.

"I regret to tell you that I will nae be accompanying you to Edinburgh after all, Mr. Holmes. Surely you would nae deny a poor woman's request to spend her last hours in her ancestral home?"

Several days later, we found ourselves back in London. We paid the Duke of Brownley a visit earlier that day, at which time Holmes had told the nobleman that it was clear that his son had died of a sudden illness. True to his word, the Duke didn't demur. Holmes accepted his fee from the Duke, but on the way back to Baker Street, we stopped by a church in the East End, where he folded the fifty-pound notes, one by one, and stuffed them into the poor box.

"No good could come from informing the Duke that his son was a blaggard, Watson, and I had no proof but a dead woman's word. His father was much more apt to accept the lie that I told him and take comfort in it, but I surely have no wish to profit from it."

As a courtesy, Holmes asked Hopkins to come for dinner at Baker Street, to provide him the details of Reginald Balfour's murder.

"A sad tale, Mr. Holmes," Hopkins said when Holmes had done, "but a cautionary one. It's never a good thing for one to try to become something they are not."

"But indeed, my dear Hopkins, one may never know truly what one is, until one becomes."

"Now a woman must know that she is a woman, and a man that he is a man," Hopkins replied. "Everyone must know their place."

"Must they?" asked Holmes. "Difficulty arises when one is denied that which they desire because of arbitrary societal strictures. Miss Warrender wished to become a physician to honour her beloved brother's memory, but as a woman at the time, she wasn't allowed to do that.

Currently we have a school of medicine for women here in London, where Miss Warrender may well have been able to realize her life's purpose, had it existed but a few years earlier."

"That doesn't excuse her for wanton murder, though," said Hopkins.

"Doesn't it?" asked Holmes. "True, she would have had to have been held to account for the death of the innocent, an unfortunate accident arising from poor judgment. But her judgment had undoubtedly deteriorated due to the indignities that a scoundrel inflicted on her, indignities that no one should have to bear. I could argue that she killed Reginald Balfour in self-defence."

"I have a question," I said. "How did you know that Count Sylvius and Miss Warrender had been lovers?"

"Based on the Count's demeanour at our interview, I thought it likely," Holmes said. "Of course, I had no proof, but Miss Warrender confirmed it." Holmes turned the spigot on a familiar cask that sat on the sideboard behind him, which the lady had given him in gratitude for honouring her last request, and allowed a dram to drizzle into his glass. Swirling it round, he said, "Count Sylvius will pay someday, for what he has done to an essentially good woman. I can promise you that, Watson."

> *"It's all here, Count. The real facts as to the death of old Mrs. Harold, who left you the Blymer estate, which you so rapidly gambled away."*
>
> *"You are dreaming!'"*
>
> *"And the complete life history of Miss Minnie Warrender."*
>
> *"Tut! You will make nothing of that!"*
>
> *"Plenty more here, Count . . . ."*
>
> – Sherlock Holmes and Count Negretto Sylvius
> "The Adventure of the Mazarin Stone"

The Case of Indelible Evidence
by Dick Gillman

It was a bright morning in the final days of July 1896 that I descended the stairs from my bedroom. The enticing smell of kippers encouraged me to hurry on downwards. As I entered our sitting room, I could see from the ruinous display of scattered cutlery and a carelessly tossed, fine damask napkin that Holmes had already breakfasted.

As I reached for the bell-cord to advise Mrs. Hudson that I was now ready, I couldn't help but remark, somewhat testily, "It appears that some malevolent flying creature has annoyed you at breakfast. Indeed, sufficiently so that you felt compelled to take up arms against it and to engage it in mortal combat!"

Other than a brusque rustle of the broadsheet that hid him from my view, and an increase in the volume of blue smoke that rose steadily from behind it, there was no response to my jibe. I was, of course, used to Holmes's cavalier attitude to the proprieties of mealtimes but, in truth, I couldn't help but shake my head and express a heavy sigh.

Within minutes, my own breakfast appeared and, having been served by Mrs. Hudson, I tucked into a fine pair of Arbroath smokies. This was followed by coffee, buttered toast, and a generous portion of coarsely-cut Seville marmalade.

It was as I sat back, replete, and dabbing my lips with my napkin, that I noticed that Mrs. Hudson had brought up, on my breakfast tray, the small silver salver that was used to convey our mail from the hallway below. Curiously, there appeared to be upon it two identical envelopes, each in the same hand – one addressed to Holmes and the other to me.

Still feeling the need to elicit a response from my companion, I determined to offer him a challenge that I knew he would be unable to resist.

"I see that in the post we are both in receipt of identical envelopes. I would suggest, then, that the contents are also identical." I paused for a moment, allowing the fly to drift a little further downstream. "Assuming that I'm correct, I will wager you a florin that you are unable to determine what is contained within by simply examining the envelope."

On hearing this, the newspaper was slowly lowered and a thin smile was now to be seen upon Holmes's lips. "I fear that it would be unfair of me to accept, Watson . . . but if you insist . . . ."

I tossed the envelope addressed to Holmes over to my friend who caught it dextrously and, as he did so, I noted a twinkle in his eye as he began his observations.

Holmes pursed his lips before he began thus: "Let us see. The envelope is not of common commercial stock and, while gummed, it is of middling quality." Holmes turned it over in his fingers before continuing, "The postmark is of yesterday's date, and the letter appears to have been posted in Paddington."

I looked at my own envelope and then nodded silently in agreement. As I waited expectantly for more, Holmes held the envelope to his nose before then holding it aloft, viewing it against the light from the window that overlooked Baker Street.

Seeming satisfied with his observations, Holmes smiled and then lifted his forefinger towards me. "But there is much more. Within the envelope there is a stiff card which, I would suggest, is an invitation – and from its scent, to an event with literary connections." I raised an eyebrow at this as he continued, "Indeed, I believe it to be from Sir Thomas Clayton."

Holmes again held the envelope up to his nose and then furrowed his brow, as if considering the information that he had gleaned. After a few moments, he then once more raised it towards the light before announcing, "Yes, yes! It is an invitation to a gathering of notables at his house at . . . at 42 Gloucester Gardens on – yes, I believe it to be the twenty-fifth of this month!"

I looked at my friend with an expression of incredulity and utter disbelief! Taking up my own envelope, I tried, as best as I could, to examine it in a similar fashion to that which I had observed.

I blinked, perplexed, as I could detect nothing of what he had suggested. Looking towards my friend, I noted that he sat calmly and then inclined his head slightly as he extended his hand in a gesture that was clearly meant as an invitation for me to open my own envelope to verify his revelations.

Tearing it roughly, I found that it did indeed contain an invitation. My mouth fell open as I read the detail of the fine, copperplate script written upon it. This was a request that I attend a *soirée* hosted by Sir Thomas Clayton at his Gloucester Gardens home on the precise day identified by Holmes! "That . . . that is impossible! You couldn't possibly . . . ." I spluttered.

Holmes raised an eyebrow, remaining silent as he drew upon his pipe, before then laughing heartily. "Impossible? I hardly think so when the invitations are in response to a telegram that I penned to Sir Thomas, asking if we both might attend the affair!"

I sat back in my chair, stunned, before joining Holmes in a bout of hearty laughter. Once calmed, Holmes withdrew his pipe from his lips and then pointed the stem in my direction, chastening me by saying, "Never suggest that what you have observed is impossible, until you have considered and then discounted all other possibilities."

I pursed my lips and then nodded before asking, "What is your interest in this *soirée*? I haven't previously noticed your particular concern in matters literary?"

Holmes drew deeply upon his briar before replying, his voice now most serious. "It isn't only the reason for this gathering that interests me, but the attendees . . . and one in particular." Holmes now furrowed his brow, saying, "A certain Mister Henry Staunton, to be precise."

I frowned as I pressed my lips together in thought. The name Henry Staunton meant nothing to me. "Is he known to you as a villain?" I asked.

Holmes slowly shook his head. "No, but he has been present, on at least two previous occasions, when there has been an unexplained death soon after a social gathering akin to that to be hosted by Sir Thomas."

"You consider that he is an assassin?" I asked.

Holmes again drew strongly upon his pipe and then slowly released a thin blue stream of smoke towards our already almond-coloured ceiling before replying. "It is pure conjecture. Nothing more. However, there are to be present at Gloucester Gardens some gentlemen whose death, were it to occur, would be of particular concern to Her Majesty's Government."

I considered this for a moment before suggesting, "I take it, then, that our attendance is at the behest of Mycroft."

Holmes didn't respond. His face was without expression as he raised his newspaper and was once more hidden from my view.

Nothing further was said that day regarding the *soirée* and, for the two days prior to the twenty-fifth, Holmes was to be seen busying himself by poring over newspaper clippings from our collection. What information he gleaned from his research he didn't share.

For my part, I read a little from my June copy of *The Lancet*, and was intrigued by an article by Sir D'Arcy Power on the medical history of Samuel Pepys and how it related to his ocular complaints.

It was during this period of relative calm that I had the opportunity to record something of Holmes's previous case. I recall that it was on the afternoon of the party, while I was sitting at the dining table and engrossed in my jottings, that Holmes casually strolled over to the table and, to my surprise, plucked my pen from my hand.

I frowned and hardly had the words "Have a care!" passed my lips when several large drops of ink dripped from the nib of the pen in his grasp, landing squarely upon the open pages of my notebook.

Seeming to be oblivious to the result of his actions, Holmes announced, "Forgive my impertinence, but I had failed to observe that you had invested in one of Mr. Conklin's pens. I see that the primitive eye-dropper filling technique has been superseded by way of this small, crescent-shaped lever in the body of the pen which, I presume . . . . "

Holmes paused as he then proceeded to unscrew the nib section from the pen body to reveal the small, rubber bladder which contained the remaining ink. Thankfully, further spillage was averted as I carefully, yet firmly, removed the item from his grasp.

I began to re-assemble the pen, replying rather curtly, "Yes. I have had this for some months now." Dabbing at my ink-soiled notebook with a little blotting paper, I continued, "As you have so clearly demonstrated, rotating the cylindrical guard section and then depressing the lever compresses the ink bladder and, once released, creates a small vacuum to draw up ink into the pen from one's inkwell."

Holmes had now returned to his armchair and, seemingly satisfied as to the mechanics of my pen, remarked, "Rarely is there something new and novel. One often finds that a 'new' invention is simply a refinement of an existing design." Holmes wagged the stem of his pipe in my direction as he added, "This pen being a fine example. The inclusion of an internal ink reservoir, a quill within a quill, so to speak, has been envisaged since the seventeenth century."

Holmes then paused, his voice changing perceptibly. "However, I believe that this evening that we will truly see a demonstration of something unique."

I frowned and looked across at him, hoping that he would say more. However, it wasn't to be, as I observed that he had now drawn his knees up close to his chest and, with eyes half-closed, had settled back in his chair and withdrawn from the world.

It was at a little before seven o'clock that we readied ourselves for our outing. A light evening meal had been prepared by Mrs. Hudson with the promise of a fine supper of cold cuts to be enjoyed on our return. Dressed in our summer-weight coats and on donning our hats, we were soon down the stairs and out into Baker Street.

Despite Holmes energetically waving his cane above his head, cabs seemed to be intent on busily bustling about their business with little regard to my friend. Indeed, it took several minutes before Holmes could manage to secure one.

Shouting out our destination to the driver, we clambered aboard before Holmes rapped loudly upon the roof of the cab to indicate that we were safely installed. With the crack of the driver's whip and a sudden lurch, we were off.

As we proceeded on our way, I found that I was still curious as to why the evening might be so novel that it intrigued Holmes. Turning to him, I asked, "Tell me, what might I expect to observe this evening?"

Holmes smiled. "I hope that we will meet two pioneers in the field of science and optics who will keep us thoroughly entertained." Holmes paused briefly before asking, "Does the name Lumière mean anything to you?"

I thought for a moment while quietly saying the name over and over to myself, hoping to illuminate some clouded memory. "French!" I cried out. "There are two of them . . . brothers . . . and they can make a series of still pictures move!"

Holmes beamed and slapped his knee, shouting, "Bravo, Watson! Yes, they are here, visiting London to photograph various venues to broaden their moving picture catalogue. I believe it is their intent to advertise their wares, and both entertain and educate the public."

I was about to enquire further of the Lumière brothers' methods of capturing images when there was a cry of "Whoa!" from our driver, causing the cab to slide to rather an abrupt halt at our destination.

Dismounting, Holmes turned to me, eyes a-twinkle, asking, "Would you be so kind as to settle half your wager?" pointing a gloved finger towards the expectantly waiting cab driver. Smiling, I nodded and reached into my trouser pocket for a few coins. On taking a shilling, I tossed it up to the cabbie, who deftly caught it and was then swiftly on his way.

Looking around me, I saw that Gloucester Gardens was a wide street divided along its length by a granite-edged, central strip of grass. This was punctuated by the occasional plane tree and was partly surrounded by black-painted, iron railings. The properties on both sides of the road appeared to be mirror images of one another. Tall, four-storied and white-painted Georgian town houses were arranged so that each one appeared to gaze, haughtily, into the windows of its opposite neighbour.

Having regard to the boldly painted black house numbers that adorned the left-hand column of each house's porchway, it took us but a moment to find and then mount the steps of Number 42.

Holmes reached out a gloved hand and pulled strongly on the brass bell-knob. Within moments, the heavy, black-painted front-door opened and a smartly dressed servant nodded a greeting. Taking our invitations, he then led the way into the hallway of this most impressive house.

It was lit by a fine crystal chandelier and, as we approached a large, high-ceilinged and oak-panelled reception room, my thoughts turned towards our host. As I recalled, Sir Thomas was an industrialist – a person known to me as a frequent benefactor of Barts by way of his generous donations.

My further deliberations were interrupted by Holmes's stopping, a little abruptly, as he was greeted by Sir Thomas himself. "Ah, good evening, Holmes. After your telegram, your brother advised me, somewhat casually and over a rather fine glass of vintage port, of your interest in our guests. I understand that it isn't just our French visitors who might hold your attention this evening."

Holmes smiled thinly. "Indeed, Sir Thomas. While I'm looking forward to being entertained by your guests, I'm sure that there is another person who will vie for my attention." On hearing this, our host's expression turned to one of not exactly puzzlement, but rather of interest.

Holmes turned slightly in my direction in order to introduce me, and Sir Thomas stepped forward and reached out his hand, saying, "Doctor Watson, isn't it? I believe that we've met before, at Barts."

I smiled and nodded as I took his hand. "Yes, but I'm very much surprised that you remember me, Sir Thomas. I was presented to you but briefly."

Sir Thomas smiled in reply. "Ah, Doctor. While I'm afraid that some of my faculties may have dimmed, my memory for names and faces remains remarkably intact." I bowed my head briefly and smiled as he continued, "Please, gentlemen, allow me to introduce you to our honoured guests, Messieurs Louis and Auguste Lumière."

Before us stood two gentlemen, dressed in clearly Continental-styled evening wear of smart, high buttoned jackets over stiff, white-collared shirts with thin, ribbon-like bow ties. Each man, while not a mirror image of his brother, carried a strong familial resemblance. They were both rather portly with round, open faces, topped with masses of dark curls, and each sported a fine moustache.

It was evident that they had been listening and understood our conversation with Sir Thomas as, when they shook our hands, they addressed us each by name. I so much wanted to converse with them, but a gentle tug at my sleeve meant that I would have to postpone that pleasure until later in the evening.

With a nod to Sir Thomas and the Lumière brothers, Holmes took my elbow and steered me towards one of the side-tables upon which were several ice buckets in which bottles of fine Krug champagne were chilling.

Catching the eye and raising a forefinger towards one of the waiters, Holmes nodded towards me and then watched as two glasses of the Krug were poured. Handing one to me, Holmes appeared to sip nonchalantly at his drink while his eyes seemed to be riveted upon a gentleman some ten feet or so away. For my part, I moved to stand a little to one side of my friend so that I could also observe this fellow without drawing any attention to myself.

The gentleman in question, while similarly dressed to those around him, had a much trimmer physique. He was a wiry fellow of average height with somewhat gaunt, chiselled features and deep-set eyes. His hair was black, turning to grey and worn in what I thought to be unfashionably long waves that gleamed from the addition of pomade. From Holmes's interest, I took this person to be Henry Staunton.

As Staunton reached into his inside pocket and withdrew from it a silver cigar case, I noticed Holmes stiffen slightly. Puzzled at what he had observed, I leant closer. "What is it?" I whispered. Holmes looked grim and gave the merest single shake of the head to silence me. I understood that I would have to wait to question him further.

Once more taking my elbow, he guided me towards a small raised dais located at the back of the room. Here was an intriguing oblong wooden box with a protruding brass telescope-like lens that faced forwards, into the room. A smaller wooden box was mounted above the wooden body, while a brass cranking handle protruded from the long side. This device was, I observed, mounted upon a large, sturdy tripod which provided it with ample stability.

I walked around the dais and then turned to Holmes, asking, "Is this the Lumières' camera?"

Holmes pursed his lips before replying. "That is indeed one of its functions – but it is also a self-contained, miniature darkroom, and a means of projecting the image captured on the developed, flexible film onto a suitable screen."

I must admit that I was eager to learn more, and regarded the device with renewed interest. However, further investigation was denied as Sir Thomas had taken up a champagne glass from one of the side-tables and tapped loudly upon it to request silence. Only as he did this, and the assembled gentlemen turned to face him, was I able to fully observe the assembled guests. Holmes, however, appeared nonchalant, having previously, it seems, taken in all with but a single glance.

The assembled guests numbered perhaps twenty and, almost to a man, to be of middle years and dressed in the attire of important city gentlemen. Henry Staunton, I observed, had placed himself on the edge of this group.

Looking around me, I noted that there wasn't a familiar face amongst them. Turning to my friend, I asked, "Do you recognise any of these gentlemen?"

Holmes nodded slightly. "There are three here whom I've had the pleasure of meeting. The tall, military fellow is Colonel Sir David Blunt, and beside him is Mr. William Walcott, the eminent Egyptologist." I glanced at each one as casually as I could, following Holmes's gaze. He then continued. "The gentleman resting his hand on the end of the table is

Sir George Gormley, an important industrialist." As he finished speaking, a loud rap from the front of the room interrupted the hubbub of conversation.

Once Sir Thomas had gained everyone's attention, he announced, "Gentlemen, we are now quorate. Please, be seated." Holmes and I moved towards the rear of four rows of chairs and sat expectantly. Once all were in position and settled, Sir Thomas continued, "You have all had the pleasure of meeting our much-valued French guests, and I would now like to allow M. Auguste Lumière to address you."

I glanced towards Holmes, who seemed to be unmoved by this announcement and simply looked on expectantly as Auguste Lumière nodded to our host and then stepped forward.

In a clear but distinctly accented voice, Auguste Lumière began thus: "Gentlemen, we plan this evening to show you four of our moving films. They are but a small sample from our extensive catalogue which we hope, very soon, to expand to over one-thousand films." Lumière paused briefly as a hubbub of whispered comments and some brief applause emanated from the guests. Smiling, he then continued, "I hope that my selection will entertain you and that you will find them, err . . . enjoyable. The first location that you will see might be familiar to you, gentlemen, as we were permitted to film at the famous London Zoo."

To a further small round of applause, Auguste Lumière sat down. At a signal from our host, the lights dimmed and, to the sound of a whirring mechanism, a sudden, crisp, monochromatic image of a caged lion appeared on the wall before us and danced before our eyes. Almost as one, a collective gasp was heard from the assembled gentlemen. Indeed, one fellow had to be pulled back down into his seat as he had stood up, seemingly in disbelief and readiness to flee!

I sat transfixed as the image of the lion paced back and forth across its cage, dabbing out a paw towards a keeper who seemed to taunt it with pieces of meat. Alas, the sequence lasted perhaps a little less than a minute but it seemed as though I had held my breath for the whole time.

"Wonderful!" I cried out as the lights returned. I turned to look at Holmes to see if he had enjoyed the spectacle as much as I . . . but his attention seemed to have been caught once more by something else.

He turned towards me, saying, "Yes, quite so, Watson." But it was clear from his distant expression that his thoughts were elsewhere.

I turned round slightly in my seat, looking towards the dais. Louis Lumière was, I noted, busy with the contents of the small wooden box on top of the projector. It was then that I suddenly realised that this was a magazine holding the exposed film which was being threaded into the projector for the next performance.

With a signal from Sir Thomas, the lights were again dimmed. The second film was quite different, although it was equally enthralling. The camera, it would seem, had been placed at the very edge of a railway station platform. Here, it had filmed a French steam locomotive which was destined to move steadily towards the audience before passing unnervingly close. This appeared so real that some gentlemen seemed to be making ready to leap to safety.

At the end of this film, the lights returned and Sir Thomas announced that there was to be a short interlude. As I rose from my seat, I noticed that the waiters had already poured glasses of champagne which were set out on silver trays and to which guests served themselves.

As Holmes and I stood waiting to take another glass, there was a strangled cry from a fellow barely some six feet away from me. As he turned towards me, I could see blood pouring from his mouth. Shouts and cries were heard as bodies surged forward, forming a veritable scrum, to try and view what was occurring.

For my part, and with the forceful assistance of Holmes who pulled the peering bodies of onlookers out of my path, I forced my way forward, shouting, "Have a care! Give me room! I am a doctor. Out of my way!"

While Holmes's continued to deter further onlookers, I grasped the arm of my bloodied patient, quickly sitting him down. Looking within his blood-filled mouth, I could see that there was a fearsome gash in the fellow's tongue. Looking to Holmes, I hurriedly announced, "This will require stitching . . . and quickly! Given the hour, he needs to be taken to a hospital at once."

Holmes seemed to pause only for a second or two before declaring, "St Mary's, Praed Street." I nodded, once more benefitting from my friend's encyclopaedic knowledge of the geography of our metropolis.

Sir Thomas now appeared at my side, giving me a worried look as I valiantly sought to reduce the flow of blood with a clean handkerchief.

Seeing that the evening was now lost, Sir Thomas summoned one of his household to assist me while he began to shepherd his guests in readiness to escort them from the room.

For my part, I advised my patient to press firmly against the wound as best he could, and I instructed the footman to take the patient to a cab, giving him the address of St Mary's hospital.

It was as I straightened up from my ministrations that I noticed Holmes bend down towards the floor, retrieving a small item. Quickly wrapping whatever he had found within his own handkerchief, he then placed it carefully in his pocket before looking around. Suddenly, he leapt up onto the seat of a chair, looking towards the file of gentlemen being directed to leave the room.

Then his expression became as riven granite. I gave him a questioning look to which he replied, "He isn't there! He isn't amongst them!" The import of this was lost on me. While I understood that he was referring to Henry Staunton, the importance of his absence from the room left me a little mystified.

Holmes added gravely, "Something most serious has occurred here. What it is, I'm unsure . . . but we must return to Baker Street immediately and wait." I frowned and then looked towards my friend, but found that he was already charging in the direction of the door.

Making my way as best I could out into Gloucester Gardens, I found Holmes signalling to attract the attention of the driver of an approaching cab. Having done so and, on bundling me aboard, Holmes rapped loudly upon the cab roof before we lurched off at a good pace.

As we travelled, I began to run through my mind the events of the evening. As I did so, I happened to look down and found that both my shirt and waistcoat had absorbed a good deal of my patient's blood. "It was a terrible thing to happen to that fellow, Holmes. He was most unfortunate."

Holmes now turned to me. "Unfortunate? It was a deliberate, callous act which, I believe, could have happened to any one of us."

I could barely believe what I was hearing and, in truth, I shivered uncontrollably at the thought of suffering the same fate. "Deliberate?"

Holmes, still angered, held up a gloved hand before saying, "All in good time, for I have an experiment to conduct."

Despite my protestations, Holmes would say no more and, on arrival at Baker Street, he hurried off towards the domain of Mrs. Hudson rather than climbing the stairs to our rooms.

I changed my clothing and returned to the sitting room. Some minutes passed and I had already settled into my armchair when Holmes's familiar footsteps could be heard upon the stairs. Pushing the door open with his elbow, Holmes now approached with what appeared to be a bottle of champagne and two glasses.

Pursing my lips, I chided my friend, saying, "I'm surprised that you think it appropriate to celebrate this evening's work."

Holmes turned towards me, his eyes cold. "It is only a celebration of discovery. I take no delight in seeing a man so ruthlessly maimed."

Opening the champagne, he turned his back to me while, at the same time dipping his hand into his jacket pocket before proceeding to pour two generous glasses of the bubbling refreshment.

With a face lacking expression, Holmes now proffered a glass of champagne. "Here, Watson. This is my experiment." Still puzzled, I took the glass from him.

Turning slightly, he took up his own glass and, as he did so, I noticed that he now held his cane in his other hand.

Bemused and wondering as to what might be the nature of his experiment, I looked carefully at the glass in my hand. All appeared to be as one might expect. With a nod in my direction, Holmes then raised his glass in a toast, "Sir William Hamilton!" Having said this, he looking expectantly towards me.

I must confess that the name meant nothing to me, but out of respect for my friend, I responded, "Sir William Hamilton!" and raised my glass.

It was when the glass was a mere six inches from me lips that Holmes's cane lanced forward and rested solidly upon my forearm, preventing me from drinking. Such was the pressure that I was obliged to lower my glass.

Holmes removed his cane and then stepped forward, plucking the glass from my grasp. "Forgive me, old friend. I wouldn't let you suffer the same fate as your recent patient."

I blinked and looked on in horror as I saw Holmes dip his fingers into my glass of champagne and remove from it an inch-long, razor-sharp shard of glass.

"Great Heavens! But there was nothing there. I swear, nothing but champagne!"

Holmes slowly shook his head. "Not so, Watson. The subject of the toast was the clue. Sir William Hamilton was an expert in the field of optics, especially in the study of refraction of light."

Suddenly, I recalled an article that I had been reading in *The Lancet*, and now I understood why I had been unable to observe the sliver of glass hidden within the champagne.

Holmes observed my sudden change of expression, my moment of enlightenment, saying, "Yes. The champagne and the glass have identical optical properties – the same refractive index."

Holmes paused and then swirled his glass slightly, releasing a small maelstrom of bubbles within the straw-coloured liquid. "Once the sliver of glass is placed within the champagne, it becomes invisible. The rising bubbles also help to hide any distortion caused by its sharp edges which might otherwise be noticed."

I was still puzzled, asking, "You said that any one of the gentlemen present could have taken the glass . . . and . . . and you believe that the fragment of glass was placed in the champagne deliberately?" Holmes nodded. I then continued, "But for what purpose? Surely if it was a deliberate act, then my patient was the intended victim?"

Holmes walked over to his leather armchair and began to fill his favourite briar from the Persian slipper that served as his tobacco pouch.

"As you say, it depends on the intent. In this case, I believe it was to be solely a distraction. A gruesome, cruel distraction that held everyone's attention . . . everyone, but for one man!"

"Staunton!" I blurted out.

Holmes nodded as he struck a Vesta on the fender and hovered the flame above the filled pipe-bowl. Drawing strongly upon his now well-lit pipe, he continued, "What concerns me is his purpose. I fear that we have yet to discover who might be the true victim of this evening's charade."

On hearing this I frowned, and then remembered that Holmes had indicated that we must wait . . . but for what purpose?

It was some half-an-hour later, when Holmes and I had finished our last pipe of the evening and I was readying myself to retire, that the bell in the hallway below rang with a good deal of vigour. I took out my pocketwatch to consult it and, seeing that it was now almost ten o'clock, I rose from my chair and hurried down the stairs towards the front door.

As I did so, I spied a crack of light from the opening door of Mrs. Hudson's rooms and I waved her away with a soft, "I can take care of it."

Upon opening the front door, I found myself face-to-face with a government messenger. The poor fellow was nervous and short of breath, as he could barely pant, "Letter . . . a letter . . . for Mr. . . . Mr. Holmes, sir."

I smiled, nodded, and then took it from his shaking hand before wishing him a "Good-night". As I closed the door and began to climb the stairs, I noticed that the envelope had been sealed with not one, but two, wax seals. This was indeed concerning. On previous occasions, this occurrence had indicated that the envelope had originated from Mycroft Holmes, and its contents were of grave importance.

As I approached our sitting room door, I observed that Holmes had already crossed the room and was at the threshold, eager to take the envelope from my grasp. Having done so, he turned and then plucked from his desk his fine Italian stiletto, a memento from the Cagliari Affair, and deftly sliced open the envelope in a single movement.

Throwing the envelope carelessly to one side, Holmes swiftly read the contents of the single sheet of paper within before roughly tossing it in my direction. "Damn the man!" he exploded.

He then began to pace back and forth across the room for almost half-a-minute before finally throwing himself into his armchair, declaring, "It is my error. I should have been more watchful!"

I frowned on hearing this and then straightened the letter before reading aloud from it:

Sherlock,

Sir George Gormley died this evening. He was taken ill in his carriage, a short while after leaving Gloucester Gardens, passing before reaching his home. I have arranged for his body to be taken to the mortuary of The Heart Hospital in Westmoreland Street. As you are aware, it is but a short distance from Baker Street and, by taking him there, I trust it will add a little respectability as to the cause of death.

The letter was simply signed, *Mycroft*.

Having read this over again to myself, I looked towards Holmes, who now sat with his knees pulled up tightly to his chest, his face drained of colour. Seeing my friend's demeanour, I was reluctant to ask, "Do you truly believe this to be the work of Staunton?"

Holmes was silent for perhaps half-a-minute before nodding slowly and replying, "Sir George Gormley was the chairman of one of this country's largest family-run armaments companies. His murder will hamper development and manufacture of much-needed munitions for many months." Holmes paused before continuing, "His death is indeed a heavy blow for the nation – as were the previous deaths that occurred when Staunton was involved."

"And you're sure that it's Staunton?"

"Suffice it to say that he's well-known to Mycroft for past sins. We are satisfied that his mere presence makes his responsibility for the murders almost certain."

I pursed my lips and then tapped the letter with my forefinger while asking, "Murdered . . . it appears from this that Mycroft is also questioning the cause of death. But *how* was he murdered?"

Holmes now gazed, unseeing, towards some place far in the distance before answering. "I'm unsure, but I believe it was carried out before our very eyes, in that melee of distraction that occurred this evening."

Holmes then fell silent, retreating from the world, saying no more. Wishing "Good-night" to my unhearing and unseeing friend, I slowly made my way up the stairs to my bedroom.

It was the following morning at breakfast, as I reached for my second slice of toast, that a sharp tap on my shoulder and the words, "Come along, Watson. Sir George awaits." brought the previous evening's events flooding back.

Rising from the table, I found that I had some difficulty putting on my outer garments as I held on, manfully, to the last vestige of my breakfast.

Once out in Baker Street, a hansom was quickly found. Within minutes, we pulled up outside an imposing, rounded building whose white marble-clad façade proudly announced it to be "*The Heart Hospital*".

Dismounting from the cab, Holmes once more tilted his head to one side and looked in my direction. It took me a moment to realise its purpose before reaching into my pocket and taking from it a shilling. Tossing the coin up to the cabby, I announced, "I trust that this is the end of my indebtedness?" Smiling, Holmes gave a single nod before touching his hat with his cane in a confirmatory salute.

Climbing the few curved, marble steps and passing through the impressive entrance doors, we swiftly located a uniformed commissionaire, who directed us towards a discreetly labelled flight of stairs which led directly to the hospital mortuary.

Following the arrowed signage, I wasn't surprised to find a constable on duty outside the mortuary doors. With a smart salute to Holmes, who raised his cane in return, the constable opened one of a pair of the heavy double doors, allowing us to enter.

It would appear that our visit was expected as, on entering a short hallway, a mortuary attendant approached, saying, "This way, Mr. Holmes. You will find Sir George on Slab 3."

The hospital had been built relatively recently and, looking around me, the mortuary was modern and well-lit by electric lamps. Moving past two occupied slabs, we approached the third, scrupulously clean white ceramic. The corpse was covered completely by a freshly-laundered mortuary sheet, which Holmes carefully removed with some reverence.

Before us lay a man of middle years. At first glance, he seemed to be simply resting peacefully, like the marble carving of a medieval knight upon the lid of his tomb. His body seemed muscular and, as I walked around it, I could see no gross evidence of disease or his having been attacked.

Holmes, methodical as ever, began at the feet. He then steadily made his way upwards toward the head, using his glass, as and when required. He paid particular attention to the mouth and the eyes.

Taking a pace back, Holmes stood, deep in thought. Then turning towards me, he suggested, "Be a good fellow and assist me. I wish to turn Sir George onto his side."

I nodded and took the hip while Holmes grasped the shoulder. He gave a nod and together we slowly and respectfully rotated the body by ninety degrees. I supported him while Holmes again painstakingly examined the corpse. It was as I watched, that he suddenly froze, stopping at a point on the back a few inches above the pelvis and close to the spine.

Holmes frowned and then leaned forward, peering intently through his glass.

Turning to me and holding Sir George's shoulder, he proffered his glass, asking, "What do you make of that?" He pointed to a small, barely visible mark on the flesh of the back.

Peering at it with the lens, it seemed to be a tiny, curved incision. It was almost as if someone had pressed very hard upon Sir George's back with their fingernail. Puzzled, I returned the glass, commenting, "I'm unsure . . . but it's certainly not a wound that would take a man's life."

I looked towards my friend who, on hearing my reply, raised an eyebrow but didn't respond further. Holmes turned towards the mortuary attendant and beckoned him to approach, asking "I would like to have a small syringe and piece of gauze, if you would be so kind."

Within a few moments, the attendant returned and, on taking the syringe, Holmes inserted the needle into the wound. From it he withdrew a small sample of dark liquid which he then dispensed onto the gauze. Holmes then offered up the gauze to his nose and, at once, an expression of recognition passed across his face.

Holmes then held out the pad of gauze to me and I followed his action. The liquid, while only a minute volume, gave off the very slightest odour, something akin to that of tar. I gave Holmes a querying look. In response, he gestured to me and together we carefully turned Sir George's body to lie once more on its back. Replacing the mortuary sheet and, without a further word, he moved to one side where Sir George's clothes had been neatly stacked.

While all the clothes were present, I was intrigued when Holmes chose only to examine Sir George's coat, waistcoat, and then finally, his shirt. Each time, he held the garment towards the light before replacing it.

Seeming satisfied, and with a nod to the mortuary attendant, Holmes strode towards the exit with me trailing in his wake.

It wasn't until we were inside a cab and returning to Baker Street that he spoke. "I understand that some of the more fanciful detectives that adorn the pages of the ubiquitous *Penny Dreadful*, are in the habit of identifying a poison simply by its odour." I raised an eyebrow and then, after reflecting for a moment, slowly nodded in agreement. Holmes then continued. "While this is rarely correct, raw curare is the exception." I looked at my friend and realized that he was referring to the tar-like smell that I too had detected. "Of course, in its purest form, it is quite odourless . . . and never blue."

I frowned on hearing this, and then recalled that the dark patch on the gauze did indeed have something of a blue tinge to it. To me, the significance of this wasn't immediately understood and I sat silently, considering its import for the rest of the journey.

It was only after our return to Baker Street and while enjoying a light lunch of honey-roasted, sliced ham, freshly baked bread, and a modicum of accompanying salad, that I felt able to ask Holmes about the attack on Sir George. "Tell me – what do you believe was the weapon that was used?"

Holmes had retired from the dining table to his armchair, and was now drawing steadily upon his pipe. Removing the stem from his lips, he pointed it in my direction as he replied, "Why, it's identical to the one that you carry . . . but I doubt that it's chambered with the same ammunition."

My brow furrowed on hearing this, thinking only of my service revolver and how one like it couldn't possibly be responsible for Sir George's death. At this, I raised an eyebrow. "I think that on this occasion you may be in error," I replied, rather tartly.

Holmes's face bore a thin, wry smile as he replied, "Ah, I think not! What do you have, almost hidden from view, tucked within your jacket?"

Throwing open my jacket, I declared, "No weapon at all. Did you suspect, perhaps, a shoulder holster and a Webley?"

At this, Holmes suddenly roared with laughter and slapped the arm of his chair. Seeing my confusion, he tempered his laughter and became more serious as he declared, "No, it is what is within your inside pocket – that is the weapon that is identical to the one I saw in Staunton's jacket as he reached for his cigar case."

I looked again at my jacket and suddenly realized to what he was referring and plucked my fountain pen from my pocket. Holmes nodded, saying, "Yes, Henry Staunton is also the owner of one of Mr. Conklin's pens . . . and, to my sorrow, I have seen, but not recognised, a similar injury to that inflicted upon Sir George before." Holmes paused, saying in all seriousness, "Perhaps now you understand the relevance of the tiny, crescent-shaped, wound?"

"You've seen something similar before? When?"

Holmes drew strongly on this pipe before replying. "Some weeks ago, I was called upon to examine the body of one of Staunton's previous victims – a fellow who had been attacked in Oxford Street. Unfortunately, it was some days after the death and the body was corrupt. I was unable to take a sample from it. The wound, however, was identical in all respects but I failed to understand its significance."

On hearing this, I slumped back in my chair. My thoughts whirled as I spoke aloud. "The . . . the nib, and the pen was filled with a mixture of blue-black ink and raw curare. If he were to be searched, no weapon would be found . . . and the pen would function as expected!"

Holmes nodded slowly, drawing steadily upon his briar. However, as my mind cleared, I was now troubled, and asked, "Surely Sir George would have felt the sharp nib being inserted?"

Holmes blew out a cloud of smoke before asking, "Tell me what you know of the sensitivity to touch of the various areas of the body."

I thought for a few moments and then realised the reason for Holmes's request. "Of course. The back is deemed to be the least sensitive area. In the rough and tumble of the mêlée, a small puncture wound might, indeed, have felt like a blow to the back and have been ignored."

Holmes again slowly nodded. "Indeed. The time before paralysis occurs when curare is injected into muscle tissue – rather than directly into the blood stream – would be, perhaps, between fifteen and twenty-five minutes. Such a delay may well have removed any suspicion that the murder had occurred in Gloucester Gardens."

I frowned, then asked, "Then how are we to catch this fellow? It appears that he has covered his tracks well."

I looked towards Holmes, who was now gazing, unseeing, into the far distance. His eyes were half-closed and he drew languidly upon his pipe. After perhaps five minutes had passed, he spoke. "I have an inkling of an idea, and a telegram to Mycroft is in order." Now animated, he arose from his chair and, reaching for the telegram pad, he quickly dashed off a few lines before ringing for Billy the Page.

I was indeed curious as to his intentions, but Holmes would say nothing more that evening. It was the following morning, a little after breakfast, before the ringing of the bell in the hallway below and Mrs. Hudson's steady tread upon the stairs brought us news from Mycroft. On being handed the telegram, Holmes roughly tore open the envelope before devouring the contents, crying aloud, "Ha! Mycroft is in agreement! The game is truly afoot, Watson!"

I blinked as I hadn't the merest notion as to what he intended. Looking up from my copy of *The Times*, I enquired, "Please be so good as to enlighten me."

Holmes took his pipe from his lips. "What if it were to be made known, publicly, that the Oxford Street killer had been observed in the act of murdering his victim?"

I felt my eyes widen as I asked, "Is this true?"

Holmes slowly shook his head. "Unfortunately not. However, there could be planted a seed of doubt and, once sown, Staunton isn't a man who would allow it to flourish."

Holmes became more serious. "Our evening in Gloucester Gardens wasn't without benefit. It revealed to the assembled guests how the events in the world around us could be captured. An undeniable record, preserved for posterity . . . and perhaps, the courts."

I considered this for a moment before asking, "Tell me, how did the previous murders occur?"

Holmes now rose from his chair and began to pace across the room. "They were carried out in broad daylight. The first victim was shopping with his wife when, on a busy pavement, he was seemingly assaulted from behind in a similar manner to that of Sir George. The second was very similar."

Holmes suddenly paused in his pacing and turned to face me. "Imagine now what Staunton might be driven to do if he thought that the Lumière brothers had, inadvertently, captured his attack in Oxford Street while filming a famous London location for their library?"

My pipe almost fell from my mouth on hearing this. Blinking, I managed to stammer, "Well, I would imagine that he would do all that he could to destroy the evidence."

Holmes nodded slowly. "Yes. You mirror my thoughts exactly. But how are we to sow this seed of doubt and draw him to us?"

Holmes returned to his armchair and once more took up his briar. He sat for several minutes, drawing slowly upon it before suddenly rising from his chair and then heading down the stairs towards Baker Street without a further word.

It wasn't until a little after lunchtime that Holmes returned with a small, round package grasped firmly in his hand. I could see from his smug expression that he had achieved his purpose. "You look pleased indeed," I said. "Have you been successful in your planting?"

"I believe that I have. It did take a little persuasion from Mycroft with the editor of one of *The Evening Standard* and the cooperation of the Lumière brothers, but I believe that our story will be irresistible to Staunton." I gave Holmes a questioning look, but he would say no more on the subject other than, "I think you may find the early edition of *The Evening Standard* of interest."

I must admit I was intrigued, and by late afternoon I was champing at the bit, waiting for the sound of the newsboy in the street below crying, "*Evening Standard!*" At his very first shout, I went down the stairs and thrust a few coppers into the lad's hand before almost tearing a copy of the newspaper from his grasp and returning, post-haste, to our rooms.

To my great surprise, there was an item on the front page – a headline that read, "*Sherlock Holmes Seeks Evidence From the Famous French Film-making Brothers*.' My eyes widened as I went on to read aloud, "*Holmes revealed that a moving picture, taken by the Lumière brothers, is almost certain to have captured the likeness of the person responsible for the recent Oxford Street murder.*"

I looked towards Holmes, who was drawing contentedly upon his pipe with something of a wolfish grin upon his face. I continued reading, "*Mr. Holmes told* The Evening Standard *that the Lumière brothers had been present in Oxford Street at exactly the time of the attack. The film, now in Mr. Holmes's possession, is as yet unseen, but he intends to examine it this evening in his Baker Street rooms before then passing it on to Scotland Yard.*"

My eyes opened wide on reading this. "You intend to bring Staunton here?"

Holmes nodded slowly. "Indeed. I'm sure that he will call on some pretext and endeavour to steal or destroy the evidence."

I frowned, asking, "Surely then, he is aware that he is under suspicion?"

Holmes again nodded. "Indeed, but it hasn't caused him to stay his hand. He has already been interviewed by Lestrade, as have the other guests, but he was able to provide an alibi for the date and time in question for the first murder."

A few minutes later, the bell in the hallway below rang and on hearing this, Holmes strode quickly towards the door of our sitting room. Listening intently, he descended only to return carrying a tripod and a familiar oblong wooden box.

I blinked in surprise on seeing the Lumière's device, which Holmes quickly assembled and placed on its tripod, a little distance in front of the fireplace. Still unsure of my friend's intentions, I asked, "Do you intend to use that?"

Holmes shook his head, saying, "No. It is purely window-dressing – something to add a little authenticity to the scene. The Lumière brothers have been most generous and lent it to me for this little charade." Turning to his desk, Holmes now retrieved the package that he had brought to our rooms earlier. From it, he withdrew a round, metal canister which I knew contained the film. This he then placed, strategically, on top of the famous Lumière projector.

I remained silent for a few minutes, but then I could hold my tongue no longer. "Do you not consider this to be a most dangerous venture? What is to prevent this man, a known killer, from simply stealing the film and disposing of us in the process?"

Holmes had lit his pipe and, as he drew upon it slowly, it was clear from his expression that he'd given this matter some considerable thought. "I don't believe that this is his intention. The man is clearly capable of killing, but he will only do so if threatened or if there is an element of reward." Holmes paused for a moment before continuing. "Neither do I believe that he will take the risk of leaving Baker Street with the evidence on his person in case this is a trap . . . but precautions are in place."

I considered this for a moment, but then was unsure how Staunton might achieve the destruction of the film. I was indeed surprised, but enlightened, when Holmes descended to the kitchen and returned with a pail of water which he placed behind the coal scuttle.

It was perhaps some ten minutes later when again the bell in the hallway below rang, followed by the familiar tread of Mrs. Hudson and that of one other on the stairs to our rooms. Holmes was immediately alert and aquiver, like some ever-eager spaniel.

After a gentle tap on our sitting room door, Mrs. Hudson entered, together with the figure I knew to be Staunton. "Mr. Holmes, this is Mr. Carstairs, a gentleman of the press from *The Daily Mail*."

On hearing this, I tried to remain as expressionless as I could and watched as Holmes, with a querying expression upon his face, approached Staunton. Extending his hand, Holmes asked, "Mr. Carstairs? I believe I saw you at Sir Thomas' *soirée* in Gloucester Gardens recently."

Staunton smiled. "Indeed, I was there at the request of my editor, Mr. Holmes. It was unfortunate that the evening concluded so prematurely." Holmes nodded and Staunton continued. "Please excuse the lateness of the hour, but my editor was keen for me to be present while you reviewed this most important evidence."

Looking around him, Staunton then moved towards the fireplace and the Lumière brothers' projector. Reaching out, he plucked the film canister from the projector, asking, "Is this the film in question?"

Holmes nodded, his voice now taking on a warning tone. "Yes . . . but I would ask you to be most careful, Mr. Carstairs. It is the original, and there is no other copy."

Staunton nodded and, as I watched, a sly smile momentarily crossed his face before he said, "I was most intrigued as to how the motion of the pictures was achieved, Mr. Holmes." Opening the canister of film, he unwound about twelve inches of it before moving towards the gaslight beside our fireplace, seemingly to examine better the individual pictures.

Holmes moved slightly towards Staunton, saying, "Have a care, Mr. Carstairs, for it is quite delicate." Staunton nodded, but didn't seem to heed Holmes's warning and moved even closer.

Suddenly, without the film even touching the gas flame, there was an intense flash of ignition and instantly Staunton seemed totally enveloped in a furious flame. With an anguished scream, the torch-like figure seemed to dance before us, his clothes alight and his greased, pomaded hair adding fuel to the fire. Holmes raced forward, reaching to take up the pail of water from its resting place and partly dowsing the still-screaming Staunton.

Such was the fierceness of the blaze that both the remaining film and Staunton's clothes weren't fully extinguished by Holmes's action. On seeing this, I swiftly removed my jacket and bundled the screaming man to the floor, seeking to smother the engulfing flames.

While trying to starve the flames of oxygen, I looked up towards Staunton's blackened and blistered face, noting that he had been most grievously burned. Carefully, I removed my jacket from his torso and observed that, mercifully, he'd now lost consciousness.

Holmes reached for the bell cord and almost tore it from its fixing as he pulled heavily upon it. Even as he did so, Mrs. Hudson rushed into our rooms. On seeing the unconscious and charred figure of Staunton, she clapped a hand to her mouth and then reached out her other hand to the door frame to steady herself.

Leaving Holmes to comfort Mrs. Hudson and to watch over the stricken Staunton, I raced downstairs and out into Baker Street to hail a cab. Fortunately, within half-a-minute or so, I was able to obtain a four-wheeler which I directed to our doorway. Back upstairs, I found Holmes supporting the now semi-conscious and whimpering Staunton. Avoiding the raw flesh as much as I was able, I assisted in half-carrying the fellow down the stairs.

As carefully as we could, we lifted the now conscious and sobbing Staunton into the cab. On tossing a shilling to the driver, I shouted to take us to the nearest hospital. "At the gallop!" The cabbie touched his hat and with a crack of his whip, the cab set off at a fearsome pace. There was nothing further that we could do and, as I looked towards Holmes beside me, I saw that his face was grey and filled with anger.

Several hours later, as we slowly made our way back to our rooms, I spotted a familiar figure crossing Baker Street with two constables in his wake. I intercepted Inspector Lestrade before he could speak to Holmes and quickly told him what had occurred. On hearing this, the inspector rubbed his chin and frowned, saying, "There's a turn-up! I expected him to do a runner, as Mr. Holmes said might happen – but not this."

I briefly nodded and the three of us slowly made our way back to 221b, leaving the two constables outside. On closing the door, I ushered Lestrade towards the sofa. Holmes, however, immediately began to pace, his fists tight balls of white marble. "It was my fault. In my haste to gather evidence against this fellow, I failed to fully recognise the danger in my plan."

I frowned, saying, "I noticed the pail of water and understood its significance . . . but had you not considered the flammability of the film?"

Holmes paused in his pacing and then threw himself into his armchair. "Indeed, I had. However, I was unaware that confinement within the canister had the effect of concentrating any inflammable vapours."

I thought back to the moment when Staunton had approached the gaslight. The film had, indeed, not touched the flame, but had ignited merely by being in its proximity.

Lestrade looked concerned and was about to speak. I lifted my hand and pointed my finger in his direction while I slowly shook my head, knowing that this was the wisest course of action. On seeing this, Lestrade pursed his lips. Taking his pocket watch from his waistcoat and, on noting the time, he nodded his head, saying, "I'll nip down to the hospital and be in touch, Doctor."

At this Lestrade left, and as I watched, Holmes drew up his legs and then closed his eyes. I knew that he would most likely be silent for the remainder of the evening and continue to blame himself for some considerable time.

The following morning, there was little change in him. The arrival of a telegram from Lestrade advising us that Staunton had survived the night and was expected to live, despite his horrific burns, did little to dispel Holmes' despair.

Fearing that Holmes might seek release from his anguish by resorting to the syringe, I sought to ease matters, saying, "You had all in place. We were ready to pounce, should Staunton flee with the film, and you had the water, should he seek to destroy the film in the gas flame."

Holmes's expression was cold as he turned and looked towards me, replying bitterly, "But it wasn't enough. My knowledge was incomplete and I can but only blame myself."

I opened my mouth to argue with Holmes, but on seeing that I was about to speak, He held up his hand, its palm facing me. "I care not a fig for the man himself, but my failure to control the situation doesn't sit well with me."

While I felt that my friend was without blame, I understood that he had to face and overcome his own doubts.

It took several days for Holmes to return to his old self, and only then did I venture to raise the matter again. As we sat, enjoying the first pipe of the day, I asked, "Tell me, have you come to terms with the fate of Staunton?"

Holmes blew out a thin stream of blue smoke towards the ceiling, saying, without emotion, "Yes. I'm relieved that his reign has ended, and he will, undoubtedly, receive his just deserts through the courts." As he said this, he reached into his jacket pocket and removed from it a fountain pen. Using this, he began to jot something in his notebook.

On seeing this, I raised an eyebrow, asking "Is that not a Conklin?"

Holmes nodded slowly and, with a wry smile, replied, "*Fas est ab hoste doceri*, Watson, which, as you will know, means *One should learn even from one's enemies.*"

> *When our visitor was silent Holmes stretched out his hand and took down letter "S" of his commonplace book. For once he dug in vain into that mine of varied information.*
>
> *"There is Arthur H. Staunton, the rising young forger," said he, "and there was Henry Staunton, whom I helped to hang . . . ."*
>
> – Sherlock Holmes
> "The Missing Three-Quarter"

The Adventure of Parsley and Butter
by Jayantika Ganguly

On a hot summer day in the year 1897, I found an unusually excited Holmes at the breakfast table.

"Ah, Watson, you are finally awake," he said as soon as I entered the room. "Quickly, partake of your breakfast. We need to hurry!" He pushed the eggs towards me, urging me to eat.

"Is something the matter?"

Holmes chuckled wryly. "I would very much like it if you accompanied me to meet the patriarch of the Abernetty family."

I blinked, surprised. Lord Emery, QC, was known to be one of the finest barristers in the country. It was rumoured that he often advised the Queen herself. His courtroom tales had recently been chronicled by his young assistant, much as I did for Holmes. I'd read a few. They were very well-written. Even Holmes had praised the author, much to my surprise. He had mellowed since his return to London three years earlier, but his harsh criticism of my writings, and his accusations that I embellished, romanticised, and dramatized the actual events and neglected his deductive methodology, were clearly embedded in my memory. I had idly speculated whether Holmes would approve of this young assistant – I believe that his name was Jones – narrating his adventures instead of myself. I confess that I couldn't resist a small flash of irritation at the thought.

I reminded myself that such uncharitable considerations were unbecoming on such a bright morning and focused on Holmes. I spotted a letter in his hand. Even from a distance, I could clearly recognise that the paper stock was expensive.

"Did Lord Emery write to you?" I asked curiously. Ordinary folks certainly couldn't afford that type of paper.

Holmes smiled slightly. "I see that you have successfully assimilated my methods, my dear Doctor," he teased. "He did, indeed."

I raised an eyebrow enquiringly.

"From his epistle, it appears Lord Emery fears for his life," Holmes said calmly.

"Surely not!" I cried.

Holmes shrugged nonchalantly. "I'm as surprised as you. However, he insists that I make haste and visit him, lest the culprit succeed in his efforts."

"Could the letter be a forgery?"

Holmes laughed and shook his head. "Why? To lure us there, only to quickly discover the deception? To what purpose? In any case, the handwriting certainly matches what we know of the great patriarch of the Abernetty family," he told me. "The strokes are bold and decisive." He handed the letter to me.

He was correct, as usual. The handwriting was powerful – even I could see that, having read Holmes's monograph on the subject. The paper was exquisite and gold-lined, and the ink was a rich, smooth black that I'd never seen before. The letter read:

Saffron Garden
London

Dear Mr. Sherlock Holmes,

I am in great need of your assistance and request you to kindly visit me at my London residence immediately. My apologies for the short notice, but this matter is of the utmost urgency.

Peculiar occurrences over the last three days have forced me to conclude that there exists a threat to my person, and that this imminent danger is in close proximity to myself. There have been three clear attempts upon my life during this period, and two additional incidents which may or may not have been so.

While I intend to proceed with great caution until your arrival, I remain unsure when this murderous hand may strike again. As such, I have instructed my coachman to wait for you and bring you over at the earliest. I assure you that any inconvenience caused to you by my unreasonable request shall be duly compensated.

Yours sincerely,
Albert Abernetty
Lord Emery, QC

I looked at Holmes, horrified. "How long has the coachman been waiting? Why didn't you wake me immediately?"

Holmes chuckled. "How kind of you to be so concerned. Rest assured – it has been less than an hour."

I abandoned the rest of my meal and grabbed my coat. "We need to leave," I commented.

Two minutes later, we were being driven to Lord Emery in his luxurious coach. I was somewhat anxious, but Holmes didn't appear to be particularly bothered. When I asked him why, he simply shook his head.

"It must be an extraordinarily incompetent murderer who not only fails to kill an old man five times, but even fails to intimidate him," he told me. "You saw the letter. Would you say it was written by a gentleman over seventy who fears for his life?"

I frowned at him. "Do you mean to say that the contents are false?"

"No. All I'm saying is that Lord Emery's steady handwriting doesn't indicate even the slightest hint of anxiety."

"Possibly he possesses nerves of steel, like yourself," I retorted. "He's a very accomplished man. He couldn't possibly have achieved such heights if he had a nervous disposition."

"Perhaps," Holmes said absently.

The carriage slowed down. I parted the window curtain and peered outside. The light made my eyes water, and the heat of the hot summer day was stifling. We were at the gates of a beautiful estate.

As soon as we stepped out of the coach, a fresh-faced youth stepped forward and grabbed our hands.

"Oh, thank heavens that you're here, Mr. Holmes! Dr. Watson!" he cried excitedly in a high-pitched voice. "Uncle Albert has been waiting for you!"

"Calm down, Jones," a gruff voice said, and a handsome gentleman – perhaps around forty years of age – appeared behind him.

"But Cousin Howard . . . " Jones whined pitifully.

I stared at the youth in shock. I had heard that Jones was young, but this boy could hardly be more than fourteen or fifteen – even his voice hadn't yet broken. This *child* was Jones the assistant who wrote so well that even Holmes praised him?

I looked down at the pale hands that were still gripping mine tightly. Even the boy's hands were soft. What formidable talent at such a young age!

The older gentleman stepped forward and shook hands with us. "Howard Abernetty," he introduced himself. "I am the elder son. Edward, my brother, is with my father in the study." He narrowed his eyes at Holmes. "I hope you're as good as your brother Mycroft claims you to be, Mr. Sherlock Holmes."

Indignant, I opened my mouth to argue, but Jones spoke instead. "Don't insult him!" Jones snapped at his much-older cousin. "He's as good at his work as Uncle Albert is at his. It isn't something that a mediocre person such as yourself will ever understand."

Howard's face distorted with rage and he raised his hand, as if to slap the boy.

"I'll tell Uncle Albert if you dare to hit me again," Jones warned cheerfully.

"You . . . you *mongrel*!" Howard spat angrily and stormed away.

"Sorry about him," Jones told us as he led us towards the house. "He's been insufferable since I arrived. He's simply jealous that I inherited Uncle Albert's brains while he is so stupid. Edward is slightly better, but he doesn't like me, either. You see, I'm much cleverer than both of them." He looked quite smug.

I smiled warmly at the boy. I couldn't help it. "Holmes and I enjoy and admire your writings very much, Mr. Jones," I told him. "To be honest, I had expected you to be much older."

Holmes, on the other hand, eyed the boy curiously. "Just how old are you, Mr. Jones?"

"Sixteen this fall," Jones replied. "And I admire both of you very much, too!" He then asked shyly, "Would you both mind signing a copy of *The Strand* for me?"

I admit that I was quite flattered and agreed easily. Then I asked Jones about his future plans.

"Uncle Albert is sending me to Oxford to study law, just like he himself did!" He grinned brightly. "You see, that's also why my cousins hate me. Uncle Albert didn't let either of them study law. He said that they were too stupid – just like their mother." He lowered his voice conspiratorially. "Aunt Francine isn't so bad, though. She recognized immediately that I was actually Uncle Albert's illegitimate child when I first arrived here. I really don't know why Howard and Edward are such idiots – it took them so much longer. If they didn't look like Uncle Albert and Aunt Francine, I would think that they were adopted, or someone else's children."

I was startled into silence.

Jones burst out laughing. "Oh, don't be so shocked, Dr. Watson," he said. "Plenty of noblemen have affairs outside their marriage. In fact, it's probably more common than not among the British upper class! It's just that they don't speak of it. You see, my *Maman* brought me up to speak my mind in Montreal, and I've yet to learn the British way of keeping my mouth shut. I don't really mind, though. It's funny to watch the reactions that I get."

I glanced at Holmes, but he looked as impassive as ever.

By this time we were inside the house. I cleared my throat and asked the shockingly candid boy, "What about these attacks on Lord Emery?"

Jones smiled and allowed the blatant change of topic. "No one is trying to kill Uncle Albert," he said confidently. "Uncle Albert just keeps interrupting the poor fellow's attempts to murder someone else."

I was rendered speechless yet again.

"I hope that Howard is the intended victim," Jones said viciously. "He is horrible. He nearly killed me once. Who shoots at their long-lost younger brother as soon as their father announces that his estate will be split equally among all of his children?"

"It's more common than you would imagine," Holmes said drily.

Jones huffed. "I don't even need Uncle Albert's money. *Maman* and *Grand- père* left me a lot more than what I would get from Uncle Albert. I didn't even want to be here. I was happy in Montreal," His bright blue eyes dimmed. "I was sent to England two years ago when *Maman* died because she wanted me to know my father if she passed away before I reached adulthood. Uncle Albert said that he would raise me until I was an adult, and then he made me his assistant. Of course, he realised immediately how clever I was, and decided that I should follow in his footsteps."

"My dear child," a soft voice said, coming up behind us. "If you have finished narrating your life story to Mr. Holmes and Dr. Watson, I would like to apprise them of the matter at hand." A distinguished old gentleman stood before us, his sharp blue eyes – the same as Jones – fixed upon Holmes. Beside him stood a younger man, who was introduced to us as Edward, the second son.

"I apologise on behalf of my youngest," Lord Emery said sombrely. "I'm very grateful for your prompt arrival, Mr. Holmes. I would very much like to put this dreadful matter behind us as soon as possible."

Jones rolled his eyes. "Uncle Albert, you know that no one is trying to kill you."

"There have been six attempts on Father's life," Edward Abernetty said grimly. "While you were wasting Mr. Holmes's time just now, Father's tea has been poisoned. Fortunately, I realised that the fragrance was different from his usual tea."

Jones smirked. "This must be the most bumbling idiot of a murderer in the history of all murderers," he said. "Don't you think so, Uncle Albert?"

Lord Emery smiled sadly. "I wish you would call me Father and let me officially acknowledge you."

"Over my dead body!" The loud shout drew our attention. Howard Abernetty had returned. He glared at us, his face flushed with anger.

"Calm down, Howard," Jones said, mimicking the exact tone Howard had used earlier when we met at the gates.

It only served to enrage the man further.

Holmes stepped forward and asked loudly, "May I see a sample of the poisoned tea?"

"I threw it away," Edward replied. "It was poisoned, Mr. Holmes."

"Who brewed it?"

"I did," Jones spoke up. "I'm the one who usually brews Uncle Albert's tea."

"Did you feel that the tea was different when you prepared it?" Holmes asked the young boy.

Jones shook his head. "It was the same as ever. I brewed it and put the tray on the desk. Then I heard you arriving and left it there."

"So the tea was left unattended?" I asked.

Jones shook his head. "Edward came in before I left."

Holmes turned back to Edward. "Did you leave the tea unattended at any point?"

The man hesitated for a moment, then shook his head.

"And you realized that it was poisoned because it smelled somehow different?" Holmes enquired. His eyes gleamed. "How so?"

"It smelled strange – it just wasn't right – and I felt unwell as soon as I had a sip," Edward replied.

"You took a drink of it?" I asked. "What were your symptoms?"

"My throat burned. I felt dizzy."

"And then you threw it away," said Holmes.

"I was afraid that someone else would accidentally drink it, so I disposed of it immediately."

Destroying evidence so carelessly – no wonder Jones said they were stupid, I thought uncharitably.

"Yes, because there is no place in this entire manor where a small sample of poisoned tea could be saved for investigation," Jones remarked sarcastically.

"There are children in the house," Edward replied with gritted teeth.

Jones laughed. "Oh, you mean Michael and Meredith? Certainly they are little children," he said sarcastically. "A whole year younger than me!" he explained to us. "Thankfully, they are much nicer than both of you – at least there are *some* people in the family who don't resent my existence."

"Shut up, you pernicious ingrate!" Howard roared, rushing at Jones.

Holmes moved swiftly and blocked him.

Lord Emery sighed. "Mr. Holmes, Dr. Watson – I apologise for the unsightly behaviour of my children. Please excuse their conduct. Now, if you would be so kind as to accompany me to my study . . . ."

"Certainly," Holmes said.

"Thank you," Lord Emery said. He turned to his three sons. "Abner, Edward, Howard – come along."

I suddenly realized that Jones never revealed his first name in print. Somehow the name "Abner" didn't suit him.

Lord Emery led us to a large study filled with legal tomes. In fact, it would be more appropriate to call it a library rather than a study.

Once we were all seated, Lord Emery said, "Before I speak of the events of the past three days, let me give you a brief background of my family. My wife Francine and I married each other because our families willed it. However, we've always has an amicable relationship, and she bore me two sons, Howard and Edward. Francine has been in Italy since March, visiting her sister. She prefers living there, and I suspect that she will keep extending her visit until long after I'm gone." He made the comment without a hint of sadness or regret – it was simply a fact to be recorded.

"Howard is my oldest child, and will inherit the title upon my death. He has two children – Michael and Meredith, the twins. His wife Mary passed away several years ago.

"Edward, my second son, is engaged to Elizabeth, Lord Ridgewood's daughter. They will marry next spring. As for my youngest, Abner – I had no idea that he existed until I received a posthumous letter from his mother. While Francine and I have been largely faithful to each other over the years, Amber's mother was a notable exception. She was a remarkable lady – half my age but twice as bright. We met on a ship, and it was a brief affair. I didn't know that she was already carrying my child when we disembarked. We didn't keep in touch, although we had shared our addresses. Hence, I was shocked when I received a missive from her attorneys in Montreal two years ago, along with a letter from her. She told me about our child, and requested me to take care of Abner in her stead.

"As you've seen, there is animosity amongst my children. However, I love all three of them, and wish for them to have happy, successful lives. To this end, I have changed my will, leaving instructions that my personal assets are to be divided into three equal shares, which each child getting one. Howard, of course, will additionally inherit the title and the accompanying estates, and Edward will inherit the estates that came to the marriage from Francine's side. Abner has been learning everything that there is to know about my legal practice, working there on a daily basis, and he will continue to do so even after my death, until he knows it inside out. He will inherit the practice – as well as retaining his mother's inheritance, of course."

Howard leapt up from his seat, interrupting Lord Emery. "This is absurd! Father, you can't leave a third of your assets to this bastard! And Michael is supposed to inherit your practice – he has spent much more time preparing for it, unlike this . . . this – !" He gestured toward Abner Jones. "Besides, how do you even know that this Jones is your son? For all we know, his mother could have – "

Jones sprang from his chair, took a couple of quick steps, and executed a right hook almost as well as Holmes would have done.

Howard howled in pain, his nose dripping blood.

"Dare you say one more word against my *Maman*," Jones hissed menacingly. "And I will – "

"Enough!" Lord Emery snapped. "Sit down, both of you."

The youngest and oldest sons sat down sullenly. They looked quite similar – their Abernetty heredity was dominant and clear.

"Tell us of these attempted murders," said Holmes.

"What happened in the last three days?" I added.

Lord Emery shot us a grateful look. "Abner and I are in the habit of taking a walk in the gardens in the morning. The day before yesterday, as we were walking down our usual path, a particularly large limb suddenly gave a mighty crack and plunged to earth, nearly on top of us. It almost crushed us to death. If not for Abner's superb reflexes, we would have been seriously – perhaps even fatally – injured. We examined it and found that it had been nearly sawed through. More telling was that a rope was still looped around it, leading off into the dense trees. Clearly someone had waited until we passed underneath and then gave it a pull, breaking it loose. Then whomever it was fled through the trees before we could identify him.

"It was a clumsy set-up," Jones said. "There was ample time for us to save ourselves."

"You are young and spry, my child," Lord Emery said, smiling indulgently. "You sometimes run ahead," he pointed out, "and I'm left alone, walking by myself. Had you not been there, my old bones would have been unable to react in time."

Jones frowned. "We always walk together in the morning. Had I not been there, you would not have been there." Jones' frown deepened and he glanced at Holmes. "It was someone familiar with our route and our schedule," he added.

"I'm afraid so," Lord Emery nodded. He looked at Holmes and continued. "The second incident happened a few hours later. I'm not certain if it was purely by accident, or if it was purposefully done, since it's rare now for me to go upstairs. I slipped at the top of the steps and nearly fell to my death. Upon examination, I found that the carpet there was askew."

"Surely that was an accident," Howard said. "No one could know that you would suddenly decide to go digging around upstairs."

Lord Emery nodded noncommittally. "The third incident happened just before dinner that night," he said. "Abner and I were discussing one of his manuscripts when a snake suddenly appeared – he noticed it on the floor, making its way in my direction. My brave Abner reacted immediately – he caught it and threw it out of the open window." He looked straight at us. "I've lived in this house for over seventy years now – all my life – and I have never seen a snake in the vicinity, let alone inside the house."

"And I'm certain," added Jones, "that it was king cobra – highly poisonous!"

Edward looked shocked and glanced accusingly at Jones. "I was not told that it was a cobra! And you simply threw it out of the window? Do you mean to say that there is currently a highly poisonous snake wandering unbridled on our grounds?"

"Unless the perpetrator picked it up," Jones said carelessly. "Don't worry too much, though. Snakes, unlike humans, hardly attack unless provoked."

"Why didn't you just kill it?" Edward growled. Then he stood, as if he intended to go searching for it. "It would have been safer for everyone!"

"Why would I kill it?" Jones asked innocently.

"Enough, Edward," Lord Emery said tiredly.

I glanced toward Holmes to see if, like me, he doubted that the snake was an actual cobra. He seemed curiously disinterested – allowing the story to be told without asking any questions or following up on this or that statement. Had he perhaps already seen something that I had missed?

"My apologies, Mr. Holmes, Dr. Watson," continued Lord Emery. "There were two more incidents yesterday. Howard and I were sitting in the garden, discussing college options for the twins, when someone fired a gun at us from the same stand of trees where the rope was pulled the day before. Fortunately, Howard somehow realised what was happening and pushed us down just in time. Of course an inspection of the woods revealed nothing – they join a larger patch of forest that stretches onto the neighbouring property, and escape that way would be quite easy."

"Did you find evidence of the shot in the garden?" asked Holmes. "Did the bullet hit near you?"

"No," said the old man. "We never thought to look." He appeared to be rather embarrassed.

"Then, yesterday evening," he continued, "Abner and I had gone into town, and we were both attacked by a thug while we were waiting for our carriage outside my club. He charged toward us, a club raised high over his head, and Abner rendered him unconscious with one blow – he's a rather skilful fighter, you see, despite his size, something that he learned growing up in Canada – and the club manager called the police, but before they could arrive, the man twisted away from the doorman who held him and escaped into the night. I'm unsure if we were specifically targeted, or if the thug was simply looking for individuals who appeared to be wealthy. However, the man's actions seemed set on pure violence – for him to choose such a public spot for his attack seems indicative that it was meant for me. And then today, we had the poisoned tea."

He turned to Holmes. "What do you make of it?"

Holmes was perfectly calm as he replied, "Lord Emery, I suspect that these attacks, such as they are, can be easily explained, and that you aren't the target."

Lord Emery nodded and sighed unhappily. "It has occurred to me that Abner could be the one in danger."

"But Howard and I faced attacks, too," Edward interjected.

"How were you attacked?" countered Jones. "You took a sip of tea. It wasn't even your tea."

Just then, a piercing scream broke through the air. All of us rushed out of the study. We were met in the hall at the front door by a butler and a sobbing maid, who immediately led us to the rear of the house.

"It's Lady Meredith," the maid wailed piteously, while the butler charged ahead silently. "She . . . in the kitchen. She . . . ."

Howard's face lost all colour as he ran desperately ahead of us. Holmes followed him in a flash, a look of surprise on his face. Clearly he hadn't expected this. I hurried along as well, Jones keeping up with me.

We found Howard struggling in Holmes's grasp at the kitchen door. As soon as he saw Jones and me, Holmes thrust the elder brother towards us and went ahead into the kitchen.

I helped restrained Howard until Lord Emery and Edward appeared. Then, handing him into their care, I joined Holmes, where a young girl lay face down on the floor in a pool of blood, a knife protruding from her back.

Howard let out a cry like a wounded animal, struggling to be released. "Meredith!" he cried. "My Meredith!"

"Watson, be careful," said Holmes in a low tone. "Don't disturb the debris."

I saw what he meant – there had apparently been a struggle. Several dishes were broken, having been swept from the counter to the floor. There was quite a mess near the girl, and as I was uncertain what Holmes could see there – footprints perhaps – I heeded his advice and approached the victim carefully.

I dropped to my knees beside her, making a quick examination. Then I nearly cried out in surprise. It was only when Holmes shot me a warning look and a quick shake of the head that I reigned in my shock. He nodded, having seen the same thing.

I glanced back toward the door, where Howard continued to try and reach us. Lord Emery looked devastated, and Jones appeared to be on the verge of tears. I remembered him saying that the twins had been friendly to him.

Holmes's cold voice cut through the air. "She'll be fine," he declared.

"It is as he says," I told the family. "The young lady will be fine."

They looked quite relieved, and Howard nearly slumped in his brother's arms. "Thank God, thank God," he murmured. And then, his agitation returning, "But why is she just lying there? Get her up!" At that he broke free from those restraining him and dropped to his knees beside his daughter, is eyes fixed on the knife and the blood, and reaching out tentatively to touch her hair.

I wiped my sleeve across my brow. The kitchen was extremely hot – much warmer than what would be expected on that hot summer day. Glancing at a nearby table, I saw several loaves of bread, as well as a number of pastries and cakes – apparently recently baked and now cooling.

"Meredith never comes to the kitchen," Jones muttered. "Why would she – ?"

"If I may ask an extraneous question," Holmes said, rising and directing his eyes to Lord Emery. "Is it usually Jones who brews the tea when you entertain guests in your study?"

Lord Emery sighed and nodded. "And if not for the poisoned tea earlier this morning, Abner would have indeed visited the kitchen after your arrival to make another pot."

"Then if someone was waiting to ambush Jones in the kitchen and stabbed Meredith instead, he couldn't have gone very far!" Edward exclaimed. "We must find him! We must search the grounds!"

"There is no need for you to depart so quickly," Holmes said. "The culprit is still in the room."

"How can you possibly know that?" Edward demanded.

"By the depth to which the parsley has sunk into the butter," Holmes replied enigmatically.

His words drew our attention to the large slab of butter on the floor near the young lady's head, a part of the debris that Holmes has warned me not to disturb. Some of it was on her hair. A mess of chopped parsley leaves were scattered over and around it.

"What do you mean?" Edward asked.

"Wouldn't you say that this is a rather hot day?" Holmes asked pleasantly.

"It certainly is," Jones grumbled. "Especially in here."

"And as a result, the fallen butter is melting." He glanced toward the door. "Is the maid who screamed out there?"

She was, and the butler brought her in, where she looked in horror at the girl lying on the floor.

"Did you see the attack?" Holmes asked. The girl didn't answer, and the butler had to shake her gently by the arm.

"No sir, I didn't."

"So you found her lying here?"

"I did."

"And you immediately screamed."

She nodded.

"How long could she have been lying here before you discovered her?"

"At least five minutes. I had helped the cook set out the baking, and then, when she left to go to market, I went to another part of the house. It was no more than five minutes. When I came back, I found Lady Meredith. She . . . she . . . ." At that point the girl broke down crying, and was led out by the butler.

"Five minutes," said Holmes. "That's quite a while in such a hot room. But notice how the parsley has barely even begun to sink into the butter – it has hardly spread. From the time that we heard the maid's scream until now, assuming the assault on Lady Meredith was discovered immediately, then the herb should surely have sunk further on such a hot day, and in such an artificially hot room."

For several moments, all eyes were focussed on the butter. Even as we watched, we could see how fast the butter continued to soften, with the parsley sinking with it in front of our eyes. If the butter had indeed been on the floor for much longer before we heard the scream, the parsley should have already sunk and spread much farther by now. Holmes was right, as usual.

"But what does this damned parsley and butter have to do with my daughter?" Howard cried angrily.

"Don't you see?" answered Holmes. "If the attack had occurred as soon as the maid left, the butter would have been melting for five minutes, and it would have collapsed and spread over a wider area. But it had only started to melt when we arrived – which was right *after* the scream. Thus, it only fell to the floor – or was more likely placed upon the floor – and started to melt just *before* the scream. But if the attack had happened that late in the five-minute period, why did the maid not encounter the attacker? The back door there is shut and the bolt is pushed from the inside. The windows are open, but there is no sign that anyone went out that way. The attacker would have had to pass the maid – and he did not. But that isn't the most important factor here, for you see – "

"None of this makes any sense," said Howard, kneeling beside his daughter. "Meredith needs treatment. This doctor here is doing nothing for her. I'm taking her out of here now!"

Holmes stepped forward to block him. "There is no need," he said. "Your daughter is completely unharmed. There is no wound."

Howard stared at Holmes with an open mouth.

"I would suspect that this is pig's blood, likely from the block of meat there on the kitchen slab." Holmes pointed at a corner.

Suddenly, the young lady on the floor coughed, and made a most unconvincing attempt to seem as if she were returning to consciousness. "Daddy?" she said in a small voice. "Uncle Eddie? May I get up now? My legs hurt." Then the supposedly injured girl on the floor raised her head.

Silence reigned for a few moments, and then Jones burst out laughing. It was not a happy sound.

"You may," Holmes told the girl. "You may also instruct your brother to stop hiding in the cupboard."

Lady Meredith sat up gingerly and announced, "Michael, you heard the man. You can come out now."

A cupboard door opened slowly and a young man of about fourteen stepped out.

"Michael, you boor, you got butter and herbs and blood all over my hair!" the girl complained. "It will take *centuries* to get them off!"

"Howard. Edward." Lord Emery asked, his voice a low, angry growl. "What is the meaning of this?"

Howard looked astonished, his gaze going back and forth between his children and his brother. Clearly his grief at the sight of his supposedly injured daughter had been real, and he hadn't been included in the planning of this patently false drama. For the girl's injuries had been entirely staged – there was no wound, just a broken knife pushed through a tear in the girl's dress, and then bound with some kind of bandage to stand upright as if plunged into her back.

Holmes glanced at Edward. "Jones said that you were stupid," he stated baldly. The middle son opened his mouth to angrily reply, but Holmes continued. "What did you hope to accomplish with this foolishness? Did you think that neither Doctor Watson nor I would examine the wound, and would instead simply accept that the girl had been attacked? That a detective wouldn't look for clues, or that a doctor wouldn't offer treatment?"

Edward tried to speak, but it was more of a stammer. "We . . . the children and I had talked about doing something, but I never thought that they would . . . When I realized that father hadn't simply summoned a detective, but instead Sherlock Holmes – "

"We just want Jones gone," Michael said quietly. "Grandfather, ever since Jones arrived, you pay no attention to anyone else. It's as if you've forgotten that we even exist."

Jones smiled bitterly. "So both of you orchestrated this elaborate ruse to make it seem as if I was in danger – that someone had tried to kill me, but stabbed the wrong person? You haven't done a very good job, have you?"

"We weren't trying to *kill* you," Meredith said. "We just wanted to frighten you into leaving – so that you'd think that it was too dangerous to stay."

"I see," Jones said. His eyes were dull. "I should have known better when the two of you pretended to be friendly."

The twins squirmed uncomfortably.

"Look, Jones, it isn't that we dislike you personally," Michael muttered. "If you weren't Grandfather's illegitimate son, we could have been mates, but – "

"But I threaten to reduce your meagrely inheritance," Jones continued for him.

"And it isn't meagrely," Meredith said. "You have no idea how much it is worth."

Jones laughed. "I could buy and sell the lot of you." Then he looked at Holmes. "I'm sorry to have bothered you with all of this, Mr. Holmes."

Holmes shook his head. "This situation is like a boil, and it needs to be lanced. To have so many supposed attempts occurs so closely to one another – in the matter of just a very few days – and yet with none of them being successful, almost cried out that they are being staged – in this case, for the purpose of driving you away, Master Jones. I didn't even need to investigate fully to reach my conclusion.

"The attempt to pull down the limb does sound legitimate on the face of it. I have no doubt that I could find relevant evidence as to who is responsible if I visited the scene, but what purpose would that serve, except to confirm which of these brothers – Howard or Edward – sawed the limb and placed the rope."

Both brothers began to flare with anger, but they were immediately silenced as their father raised a hand, saying, "Continue, Mr. Holmes."

"The idea that the carpet had been fixed to trip you, Lord Emery, is quite unlikely. As you said, you rarely go upstairs, and such an event was dangerous to everyone. The conspirators could have just as easily killed one of the servants. If they had planned such a thing, they could warn each other to stay off the steps, but they couldn't do the same for the staff. And they didn't want you dead – not yet, anyway. After all, the will leaving a third of your estate to Abner was still in force. For the present, they just wanted their younger brother removed from the picture. After he was gone, they could work together to have him removed from the will – with or without your consent.

"The snake may or may not have been introduced into the house as a supposed threat – it's possible that a snake could have found its way in, in spite of having never done so in the previous seventy years. But young Jones's enthusiastic identification of the serpent as a king cobra seems rather more like youthful exaggeration than truth. And I could see Edward's surprise upon hearing it identified as such. The odds are that he might be the one to confirm that a snake was intentionally brought into the house – and thus he would know for certain that it wasn't a cobra.

"The gunshot may or may not have been real. Abner wasn't there, so there's no reason to think that it was an actual attempt to scare him away. It could have been Edward, firing a shot in order to seem to threaten your life, Lord Emery, or it might have simply been a poacher. Which is it, gentlemen?"

The two older sons shook their head. Howard looked honestly puzzled. "There were no plans to shoot at me. I think that it really was a poacher – but it seemed too useful an occurrence not to use, happening just when it did."

Holmes nodded. "I suspect with more certainty that the thug who attacked you both at your club was hired by your sons. One would hope that he had instructions to simply scare young Abner, and not to actually assault him, causing an injury. In any case, the lad adequately defended himself, and the man was able to flee after being caught – much to the relief of your other two sons, Lord Emery, since it's certain he would have implicated them when questioned.

"Then there was the tea," Holmes continued. "A patently false story, concocted on the fly by Edward so that they could claim yet another murderous attempt. And then this . . . ." He gestured toward the girl in the dress covered in blood, parsley, and butter. "Pathetic," he concluded.

Jones turned to Lord Emery. "Uncle Albert, I wish to return to Montreal immediately. I have no need of your inheritance – my own funds are much greater than anything that you can offer – and I never want to see anyone from this tragic family ever again." He walked away, his thin, young back looking heavily burdened.

"Abner, wait!" Lord Emery called. Jones stopped but didn't turn around.

"Father, let him go," Edward said gently. "No one wants him here, not even the staff."

"Is this what all of you wish?" Lord Emery asked quietly, looking intently at Howard and Edward, and his two grandchildren.

"Yes," came their unanimous response.

Lord Emery sighed. "Perhaps I expected too much . . . I had hoped at least the children would be kind to another child who had grown up without a father and lost a mother recently." He looked toward his grandchildren with a kind of sad disgust. They at least had enough decency to look a bit ashamed. Then he turned away from his family and walked to Jones, a weary old man. He put his arm around the boy's shoulders. "I will write a letter today. I release my claim on everything – all of it. The title, the estate, the money. Abner and I will both leave for Canada immediately, and you'll never see either of us again. You can do as you please."

"Grandfather! That is not what we – " Michael began, but Lord Emery turned abruptly and held up a hand to silence him.

"Michael and Meredith, what you did to Amber is cruel and unforgivable. I hadn't expected such duplicity from you," he said grimly. He turned to his legitimate sons. "As for you two, I had neither expected your avarice to be so great, nor such viciousness towards a mere child. Goodbye."

"But Father?" Edward cried. "What about Mother?"

"She can live the rest of her life as she pleases. She can consider herself a widow if she wishes. We were never close – it was never a true marriage in the sense of a loving union of two souls. In any case, we all know the truth – that she has no plans to return. And at my age, death is only a few years away. Better to spend it without her." Lord Emery's eyes then flashed angrily. "In fact, since this household is so adept at enacting elaborate ruses, why not simply announce to the world that the old man is in fact dead? I'm certain you can come up with an adequate explanation. It will also save me the trouble of writing a letter." He gestured toward the mess on the floor. "You were so skilful at faking an injury that I have no doubts about your ability to come up with a simulacrum of my dead body to bury in the family crypt."

And then, amidst the bewildered gazes of his family, Lord Emery turned, laid his hand back on Jones's shoulder, and walked away, holding tightly. With a last glance at the stunned and fractured group – the two elder brothers, and the grandchildren, one in a torn and stained dress – Holmes and I followed.

Outside, Holmes suggested that Lord Emery and Jones join us in Baker Street, where further arrangements for their departure could be arranged. The father and son agreed listlessly, indicating that there was nothing in the house that they wished to retrieve.

Later in the afternoon, after an excellent lunch supplied by Mrs. Hudson, the four of us sat down to discuss.

"There is a ship leaving for Canada the day after tomorrow," Holmes said.

"We'll be on it," Jones said. "I'll purchase the tickets." He glanced at Lord Emery and hesitated. Then he asked quietly, "Are you sure you want to do this? You're a great and important man here. No one will know you in Montreal. *Maman* never revealed your identity to anyone except *Grand-père* and our attorney. Do you really want to leave everything behind just for me?"

Lord Emery smiled softly. "Abner, would you support your penniless father for the remainder of his life?"

Jones grinned brightly. "Yes, Father."

Lord Emery's elderly face lit up and he suddenly looked twenty years younger. "It's a pity about Oxford, though," he muttered.

Jones shrugged. "It hardly matters. I wouldn't be able to practice anyway."

That surprised me. "Why?" I asked.

"A disability," Jones replied, laughing. "Mr. Holmes has already figured it out, correct?"

Holmes nodded.

"I'm a girl, Dr. Watson," Jones told me. "Although I've become very good at pretending to be a boy."

I was flabbergasted. "But . . . but why would you . . . ?"

"I needed to change my identity when I came to England," Jones replied. "You see, Dr. Watson, Abner Jones is not my real name. My name is Ursula Amber Le Chevalier."

I was shocked speechless once again. It was hard to believe that young Jones was actually one of the most famous heiresses in the world! No wonder he – she – didn't care about her father's inheritance.

Arrangements for their departure were made swiftly, and they left for Canada.

The Abernetty family did manage to pass off their patriarch's disappearance as his death – I was incensed when I read the funeral announcement in the newspaper, but Holmes was quite amused.

A few months later, we received a letter from Montreal, signed by a Mr. A. Jones. After that, such a delivery has become a regular occurrence. Holmes and I also kept an eye out for the adventures of the famous Le Chevalier heiress. She sent us a portrait of herself upon her eighteenth birthday – she had grown up into an ethereal beauty. Seeing it, I imagined there would be a veritable army of young men pursuing her.

"Perhaps we could visit them," I suggested, feeling vaguely like a troubled father with a lovely but mischievous child. Mary and I had dreamed of having a beautiful daughter of our own . . . unfortunately, that wasn't meant to be.

However, I could sympathise with Lord Emery.

To my surprise, Holmes didn't reject the suggestion outright, and merely said, "Perhaps."

We did end up attending her wedding a few years later. Lord Emery, who had taken on the name Albert Jones, looked rather healthy and happy for his age. Clearly, his daughter was taking good care of him.

> *"You will remember, Watson, how the dreadful business of the Abernetty family was first brought to my notice by the depth which the parsley had sunk into the butter upon a hot day."*
>
> – Sherlock Holmes
> "The Adventure of the Six Napoleons"

The Adventure of the Nile Traveler
by John Davis

My friend Sherlock Holmes is nothing if not as complicated as the Gordian Knot. Indeed, he's a system of mental layers through which one must travel, painstakingly and level by level, and only then can one discern his bottomless depth of thought. One need only recall a strange case which occurred during his three years away from London, when he carried out unexplained Crown business for his mysterious brother Mycroft. (I should add that Holmes also performed humanitarian deeds in relation to this which were later revealed as Homeric in scope.)

It was a peaceful afternoon, and I was seated in my chair near the fireplace of 221b Baker Street, reading the morning's *Times*, when Holmes entered, carrying a package.

"Good day," I said. "I see that you've been by the post. A message from abroad?"

"Not at all. I've received a gift beyond measure." With that intriguing comment, he unwrapped a framed *carte de visite* of General Charles George Gordon, CB, late of the siege of Khartoum, where he was killed during the Mahdi uprising against the Egyptian-Ottoman government, and known to all as both a fine soldier and also a pious Christian.

Looking closer, I could see that the small photograph had been signed by the man himself, strangely autographed, "*M. May our just efforts prevail, d.v. Charles George Gordon, your friend.*" Holmes took this unexpected gift and gave it pride of place on the mantel, while carefully removing his framed drawing of the odd, human-flesh-colored Olm, an aquatic salamander known to exist only in Slovenian caves. Gordon was posed in his Ottoman *fez*, the habiliment of the empire for which he served in Egypt as a military governor on loan from Great Britain. He was dressed exactly as he appeared in my larger framed print hanging on the wall next to the fireplace. Yet in the photograph, the man seemed utterly lost in a distant reverie. What could he have been contemplating?

Might I digress a moment to comment yet again on Holmes's perplexing nature? I daresay that he never seemed to be moved by those emotions known to the common run of mankind. His was a world of reason, thoughtful deduction, and then action on those evolved principles. Yet with the Gordon print, he seemed perhaps wistful, indeed longing, for something about which I could not speculate. Such a mood hovered over us that afternoon.

As I was considering it, Holmes unexpectedly shot a question at me. "Are you free?

I raised an eyebrow, and he pointed toward the newspaper in my hand, continuing, "A criminal is showing his face to the public – it's there in *The Times*. It's time to act."

"Then act we must," I concurred, completely mystified, but folding the newspaper and reaching for my coat.

"I'll explain in our cab," said Holmes.

"During those first months when I was believed to I be dead," Holmes related as I listened, certain that this would eventually connect to why we were making our way across London, "and rusticating in the Far East, Mycroft would occasionally send me instructions. Upon completion of one of his tasks, I was next advised to go to Cairo, and there to contact our British Legation to the Khedive of Egypt. I did so, and was welcomed with great professionalism by our dedicated civil servants abroad. They provided me with a letter, inside a large envelope with the royal signet upon it. Imagine my astonishment when it advised me to travel up the hotly contested Nile and into the lands previously conquered by the Mahdi – indeed to their capital outside the ruined city of Khartoum where the great massacre had taken place. I was to meet their current leader, the Khalifa, and to present the letter."

"It seems rather arch to expect you to travel all that way simply to deliver something that any officer of the government could do, does it not?"

"Quite," he responded. "Of course, there was a perfectly understandable reason that I was so selected. Mycroft had also sent another more-personal envelope and message, also handed to me by our Legation, which he'd written so that I alone should understand it. Of course, its meaning was known only to me, for it was in code. Mycroft and I worked it out when we were mere youths. While other boys were climbing trees and swimming in ponds, we created a variation on the Metternich Code of 1847 – an improvement which we should one day offer the British government."

I smiled. "You leave me speechless."

"I deciphered the message before leaving on the long journey southward toward Khartoum. It was keyed to a memorized phrase by Friedrich Schiller, taken from his fifteenth – or was it fourteenth? – letter, '*On the Aesthetic Education of Man*'. The phrase is this: '. . . *man only plays when in the full meaning of the word he is a man, and he is only completely a man when he plays*'. I discovered that I had not only an official government reason for being there, but also another chillingly odd private mission to accomplish. He wanted to me to – well, I anticipate my story."

Without bothering to further explain how a coded message could be derived from Schiller's random quote, he continued. "We plowed our way up the Nile in the steamboat *Ballon Pasha.* I'd been allowed safe passage due to the kindly intervention of a former acquaintance, Sir Richard Burton's former dragoman, Ali Budak. His expansive skills in the ways of the varied tribes along that river's flood are well known. I'd met Burton and Budak several years before the former's death, while attending a presentation that he gave at the Diogenes Club on his recent translation of *The 1,001 Arabian Nights.* Our mutual interests in things ethnological, anthropological, scientific, and philological matched one another excellently. Would that there were more like them in the world! Though neither Burton nor I were religious adherents, we nevertheless spent a valuable evening discussing the merits of the Mohammedan, Animist, and Coptic Orthodox faiths and their practices prevalent in the regions explored by Burton – which would prove to be useful as my trip to Egypt continued."

Holmes then described his visit to the Mahdi's successor, the Khalifa, Abdallahi ibn Muhammad, who governed in Omdurman, across the Nile from Khartoum. "Omdurman was made the capital of his newly created state. Upon presenting the official message to the Khedive, I withdrew so that he could discuss the response to the royal interrogative with his compatriots. While waiting, I spent valuable time touring the former government house in Khartoum, across the river. It had been from here that Gordon directed his men during the siege. I saw where he had watched the Nile slowly falling, knowing that the absence of its protection would allow the Mahdi's warriors to attack him at Khartoum's weakest point. I observed where Gordon walked each day and evening. Did you know that he once drew a bead in his daily journal to represent what a bullet flying at one's head looked like? I visited his personal rooms, where he prayed for divine intervention, while plotting human ones.

"Lastly, I sought out the grain warehouse, kept nearby and under careful watch during the latter phase of starvation during the siege. No one guarded the place now, a sort of peace having fallen upon the region. Indeed, the granary was empty. This delighted me, for in the second coded letter, I had been instructed by Mycroft to specifically examine each room of this storage facility, to measure its floorboards, and to note anything unusual. Indeed, I quickly found a trap-door in the wooden floor in a small room to one side of the granary, some six-by-six feet in area. It fit what

Mycroft had described, and I knew that I'd hit upon the solution to Mycroft's inquiry. Discovering a set of discreetly hidden hinges along one wall, I discerned that the door made up the entire square floor. The hinges were covered in dust, certainly from the grain that had been stored there during the siege. When the chaos of the battle was over, the room had been emptied, and afterwards no one had bothered with it any longer. As I lifted the wooden floor by the hinges, I was indeed taken aback!"

"What was it?" I asked. "What was under the floor?"

"Watson, patience! All will be revealed. But for now, I see that we have arrived at our destination."

Our hansom pulled to a stop in front of the Royal Crown Theatre in Oxendon Street at Coventry Street, just west of Leicester Square. We were directly across from the Civil Service Cooperative Society, which was already dark for the day. As we stepped to the ground, I recalled that the theatre was currently performing a run of Shakespeare's plays. As if reading my thoughts, Holmes said, "All of the plays scheduled for this week deal with Italy. The man we seek is an actor – as well as Italian linguist who wears a unique hat and has a distinct limp."

"You are miles ahead of me," I replied.

"Oh yes, and he's a master forger as well. He has fashion sense, can act remarkably well, and can simulate Egyptian Arabic sufficient to convince others that he is from the place."

He looked around is if searching for someone, remarking, "You know, Watson, Shakespeare appeals to me when he features masters of disguise. Consider Iago in *Othello*, who betrays the man who trusts him. Or how about Julius Caesar, betrayed by Brutus such that Caesar cries out in disbelief '*Et tu, Brute!*' when he discovers his seeming friend is a traitorous cad. Ah, but there is Lestrade."

Walking our way was the Scotland Yard inspector. He seemed perturbed.

"Mr. Holmes, I received a wire from the Foreign Office to interrupt my dinner for another of your adventures. What is it? I hope you know how irritating this is."

"Doubtless you've brought the good humor that I've come to expect, Lestrade," Holmes purred. "Your wisdom on the machinations of the criminal mind being legendary, I'd hoped to assist you once again in the arrest of another such foul felon. In fact, this one is an actor."

"An actor?" repeated Lestrade.

"Precisely. But the theater is due to empty in just a few minutes, and we're standing in exactly the wrong place to lay our hands on him. It isn't the galleys that we wish to observe, but the actors' entrance around back. Allow me to describe the man in order make an arrest."

He did so as we proceeded to the stage door, which let out onto an alley that led through to Whitcomb Court. Besides mentioning the man's hat and limp, he also provided a name which was unknown to me. Lestrade indicated that he'd been told how to identify the man in the wire that he'd received. We had just arrived at the stage door, where the inspector was prepared to pepper Holmes with further questions, when a dapper fellow of swarthy complexion, wearing an oversized top hat and well-appointed Savile Row clothing, and with a distinctive but well-controlled limp, emerged from the building.

With a glance toward Holmes for confirmation, Lestrade stepped forward. "Halt – I arrest you in the name of the Queen!" he announced.

Clearly shaken, the culprit responded in his native tongue. "*Di cosa stai parlando? Cos'è questo oltraggio*!" Then catching himself, he quickly composed his demeanor and cried out, "What is the meaning of this outrage?"

Reading from a piece of paper, Lestrade responded, stating,"Mr. Roberto D'Giorgio, alias Artie Thompson, alias Roberto Turay, you are hereby arrested for your activities both here, abroad, and in America."

"I've never been so insulted!" D'Giorgio exploded. "I have never acted in America! Never *been* to America! I demand recompense! I demand that you all be arrested for false arrest! For lies! For lies and false arrest!" In spite of his protests, he was led to a prisoner wagon waiting on a nearby street, where he was then handcuffed and placed inside.

Standing on the street, Lestrade looked warily at Holmes. "I assume that you will explain why I received orders to arrest this man."

"All will be revealed," answered Holmes. We then joined Lestrade in a waiting growler and followed the prisoner's conveyance south, around the pereimeter of Trafalgar Square, and so on to Scotland Yard.

D'Giorgio in custody was nothing if not outrageous. He screamed for justice. He demanded the heads of Lestrade, Holmes, and your narrator. He howled that his royal patrons would see to his release, and that such a foul insult to the British stage would rock the theatrical world. All in all, he played the part of the injured party magnificently.

"When I get out of here, I'll use all my wealth to bring down the entire Scotland Yard!" wailed D'Giorgio as he was placed in a chair in one of the Yard's interview rooms.

"Sadly, you will find that the wealth you've stolen is now nowhere to be had," Holmes intoned. "The story of the massive golden cross that you acquired is known."

"I'm sure I don't know what you are talking about, Mr. Sherlock Holmes," sneered the actor. "You can't arrest someone for stealing something they don't have, never had, and never heard of."

"Spare yourself the theatrics," sighed Holmes. "Your lies are being transribed for the court, and your antics don't impress me. Likewise for Inspector Lestrade there behind you, who seems bored with the whole proceeding and doubtless wishes to simply have you tried and convicted. We are not impressed. I assure you that honesty with us can only help you. There are others who seek to try you for crimes when Britain is finished with you, and I hear that the tender mercies of American justice are rough and ready, while those of Egyptian jails are positively medieval. If we don't find you to be a willing and indeed utterly honest prisoner, then we have a duty to release you to those foreign legal arrangements."

Silently, D'Giorgio – or Thompson or Turay – pondered. As if to encourage him, Holmes began to speak.

"Let me tell you a story," he said, going through the tedious motions of lighting his pipe. I glanced at Lestrade, expecting him to exhibit impatience, but he was quite alert, his glance moving evenly between Holmes and the prisoner.

"As I was discussing with Watson earlier this evening, I was in Cairo five years ago, and had an interesting conversation there with the Patriarch of the Coptic Church."

I might have imagined it, but D'Giorgio's eyes seemed to widen the slightest bit, and he sat just a little more still and wary. Lestrade cocked his head with interest.

"The Patriarch then told me a tale that I'll now recount," Holmes said, his pipe now lit to his satisfaction, "initially to my utter disbelief. It was a narrative so bold and brash that I'd have thought it fantasy, had it not come from one so esteemed and somber. It seems that in late 1884, not quite fourteen years ago, a man appeared one day in the Town of the Eleven Churches, in Ethiopia. You may remember that Italy sought this region when trying to expand its own power. Although brought on a stave-supported carriage by four hearty men, the man of whom I speak, riding inside the cupola, was dressed in the scratchy, coarse garb of a simple monk. He convinced the people that he'd come on pilgrimage to pay homage to the memory of St. Lalibela, who was responsible for the building of the eleven churches, and that he wanted to pray at each one of them. Although the man arrived wearing a simple monk's cowl and garment, upon entering the first church, he whisked those off to reveal underneath the magnificent liturgical robes of a high clergyman of the Orthodox faith.

"The people were astonished to watch as he bowed low and seemed lost in deep prayer at each of the eleven temples that he visited throughout those distant Ethiopian mountains. At last he came to the *Beta Giyorgise* Church, where the famed thirteenth-century Cross of St. Lalibela was kept. It hung behind the *iconostasis*, a solid, decorated wooden partition which separates the holy practices of the Orthodox service from the assembled pilgrims. When the door is opened to this secluded area, reserved only for the clergy, the Cross in all its glory was visible to the people in the church hall.

"On this, the last day of our mysterious clergyman's visit, he asked if he could pray at the foot of the cross. He also asked, however, that the tiny permanent population of this remote village – for such it is despite the notoriety that it receives as a pilgrimage destination – pray with him. This touching request required all of them to assemble in the church hall. The monk, carried by the four bearers of the sedan chair upon which he had arrived, was brought through the church hall to the solid wooden curtain. The monk's carriage, with him inside, was then placed before the sacred doorway. The door was opened and his palanquin was slid through. There the monk made it clear that he dare not alight until his foot touched only the hidden holy ground beyond the door. When it closed behind him, he was heard to begin reciting barely audible prayers. His servants then withdrew to the rear of the church, disappearing into the gloom. The monk had asked that all the candles be extinguished by his servants, and that the assembled pray with him for two hours in absolute silence and in total darkness, the better to emulate Jesus in the tomb. He remained behind the closed partition where the grand cross hung, and the assembled parishioners knelt in front, praying.

"Two hours passed. Utter silence reigned. Suddenly, a sharp cry went up! 'Help me! Help!' cried the monk. Soon his four servants appeared out of the gloom and raced through the door and into the sanctuary. There lay our monk, complete in his liturgical finery, a gash pouring blood across his head's crown, and more blood pouring from his sandaled foot. His servants cried, 'Bar the doors! Help us carry him to safety!' Pilgrims and townsfolk scattered this way and that, searching for a criminal who had beat the monk bloody. The monk was unceremoniously rolled onto his sedan chair and hustled out of the temple. Town sentinels ran up to the top of the stone structure to see who had gotten away with the deed. It was only some minutes later, when the candles were again lit, that someone saw to their shock that the Cross of St. Lalibela had been stolen!

"Hours later, after somewhat primitive medical treatment had been proffered to the stunned monk, his sorrowful expedition, which had arrived in such spiritual expectation, filed away in tangible grief. The sedan's carrying staves were manhandled by his once hearty but now-sad bearers, the very picture of sorrow beyond imagination."

Holmes fell silent for a moment, and I remarked, "I can't imagine that anyone in that remote habitation could have skills to solve this crime. My guess is that superstition took hold."

"Regrettably, yes. It was noised about the town that deviltry of some strange kind was in play – for anyone who made the complete eleven-church pilgrimage was sure to bring about the revenge of the Evil One."

"Nonsense," I replied. "There's no such thing as magic, or deviltry, or what have you. All a lot of gimcrackery."

"My thoughts as well. It was at that point in the story that the Patriarch told me perhaps his most astounding revelation. It caused all of the searching for the criminal responsible for the theft of the Great Cross of St. Lalibela to come to an end. A few days after the theft, a letter arrived, addressed to the senior priest of the eleven churches. It read:

To My Brothers and Sisters in Faith,

You were recently visited by a monk attempting to emulate our holy St. Lalibela, a man of pure conscience and holy faith. His hope was to visit all of your churches as one would in Jerusalem, as a simple pilgrim. He wished to follow the guidance of the holy saint who created them for this purpose. Our pilgrim visited, and was impressed by the piety of your entire flock.

Sadly, our enemy the Devil cannot be gainsaid. He has counter-attacked. He did so upon this monk's visit to the final church. He caused the Holy Cross of St. Lalibela to fall upon the monk's head, and further one arm of the cross to almost crush the monk's toe. Yet Our Lord will not be mocked, and He saved our monk. In fact, now I must tell you that in fact I *was the monk whose life was saved. For this I thank Him, and ask you to cease your searches for the cross, as it is a small price to pay for my salvation.*

Your Patriarch of Alexandria
Near Cairo, Egypt

The Patriarch added, "That letter to the senior priest was signed by me." Then, seeing my frown, he added. "It was *signed* by me, but it was *not* my signature, nor have I ever been to the eleven churches in my life. It was a complete fraud."

Holmes turned his gaze back to D'Giorgio. "One of your four colleagues who deceived the poor but pious inhabitants of the Town of the Eleven Churches revealed this story to agents of the British government. It was from him that we learned of the entire scheme, and also from him that we discovered you to be the guiding light behind the charade."

"Who said this?" growled D'Giorgio. "Which one? He is a liar! A scoundrel!"

"His name is irrelevant. As you can see, with this witness you are well and truly caught. He told us who you are, what you did, and where you could now be found – living in England and employed as an actor at the Prince of Wales Theatre. From those small facts, the rest of your history was easily determined – both here in England, where you have committed a number of previously undetected crimes, and elsewhere. The knowledge of what you did in Ethiopia is a powerful bargaining chip for our Foreign Office, and you're about to be ground between some mighty stones. Your cooperation now will go a long way toward earning a little forgiveness."

D'Giorgio's mind was visibly racing as he pondered his options. Finally, as if a string inside him had been cut, he sagged a bit and began to speak, confirming and elaborating upon the tale shared by Holmes.

"My four colleagues and I, pretending to be the injured Patriarch and his servants, left the eleven churches in the direction of the Nile. Once we were some days and distance away from the eleven churches, I composed the letter in the Patriarch's hand that you quoted. Since the eleven churches' residents didn't know what the Patriarch looked like, neither would they know his handwriting – or so we reasoned. Our purpose was to call off the hunt, and to let us make clean our getaway.

"As you might have surmised, we'd secreted the cross in the base of my palenquin. After I had been 'praying' for quite a while, my men slipped into the sacred space by way of a curtained doorway. They operated in practiced precision by removing the cross from the chain by which it hung over the altar. This we'd already practiced over and over again long before we ever departed for the Red Sea and Ethiopia. My associates were able to accomplish this feat rapidly, in pure darkness. Remove the cross, slide it into its wooden pouch upon which I was carried, and no one the wiser. It had never left the sanctuary during the hubbub which resulted when I called out in genuine horror at the crushing of my toe.

"For you see, things did not go as planned. I truly was in great pain, for in spite of our practice, one of the men lost his grip, and the cross fell first upon my head, causing the gash. I was able to stymie the urge to make a noise in this instance. Yet the cross slipped their hands again, and one of the arms crushed my small toe. I could not help it – I cried out! Fearing this would bring all to my rescue and ruin our long-prepared scheme, my men worked all the harder, swifter, and with great precision. In the short moment between my scream and the appearance of the first congregant with a candle, they'd accomplished the deed: The cross was completely hidden within my palenquin, and my men had slipped away.

"What follows astounds even me," he continued. "We left without suspicion and marched night and day across the desert. A day or so after our departure I dispatched my letter – supposedly from the Patriarch – to the unknowing victims via a wandering mendicant, who asked a significant fee. In time, we reached a tributary of the Nile and commissioned a boat to take us to Khartoum, where the Egyptian government held sway. Upon arrival there, we were escorted through the gates where we found lodging. Then, to our utter horror, we learned that we'd arrived to find the place surrounded by maddened tribesmen of the Mahdi uprising. We and our treasure were locked in the city. What to do?

"Once again, I donned my Patriarch's raiment and approached the British military governor, General Gordon. I proposed that he give us passage out on one of the last steam vessels he'd be sending down to Cairo. As you know, his mission was to evacuate all of the European and Egyptian population, and then return along with them. He was told by his government to leave the city to the Mahdi, because the British parliament under Gladstone wanted nothing to do with another war abroad."

"Quite." I unconsciously muttered.

"So we found ourselves treated royally by the unwitting Gordon, whose piety exposed my own falsity. He gave us what preferments he could offer in the doomed city – better lodging and food. But now, rather than pretend to be a regular merchant who could disappear into the crowd, I was forced to maintain my pretense of being the Patriarch of the Copts.

"Perhaps you already know, but I hadn't fooled General Gordon. One evening during the siege, he began to ask me questions of faith, about which I knew nothing. I hoped that I'd deceived him by clever but vague answers, but while we sat discussing the finer points of comparative religion, he stopped in mid-sentence, saying, 'Since I don't know your real name, I hope you'll be kind enough to tell me why you're conducting this elaborate deception?' I was stunned. He sat, silent as a cat, awaiting my answer. I protested my innocence and announced my total confusion about why he'd think such an imposture even possible. Gordon then stated, 'My first guess was that you were a Mahdi spy. I immediately spotted your complete lack of religious knowledge. I saw your references to things theological were totally fabricated nonsense. All this revealed you to be a fraud. But what kind of fraud? Surely the Mahdi, himself religious, although a vain and self-righteousness man, would have insured that his own spy would know enough to protect himself. You did not. So I collected several days of your discussions by secretly listening in to you and your mates, through the ear of a loyal houseboy whom I courteously loaned to you."

D'Giorgio then said, "I was crestfallen to learn this. He'd employed a spy to find us out. He even knew about the treasure. He knew everything. I confessed my guilt and exposed the entire plot, from our trip across Ethiopia from the Red Sea, to our arrival in Khartoum.

"And then, do you know what happened? I confess that I was shocked. He first advised me that with the complete collapse of law in Khartoum, he had absolute power of life and death. I shuddered to guess his next statement. But he continued, saying, 'I will have you and your conspirators held under guard. Then, with the relief of Khartoum, which I believe is only a mere week or so away, you shall be tried by a proper Crown Court, or extradicted to your home country. I am not God, nor do I have time to play judge with a common criminal.'"

"Remarkable man, Gordon," expostulated Holmes. "Continue."

"In the chaos following the attack by the Mahdi's army on Khartoum, we were set free in the mayhem when his warriors broke into the prison. We fled in five directions. I counted myself as lucky, for the Mahdist attackers believed us to be their fellow warriors – after all, we were held prisoner by Gordon and his Egyptian soldiers. I didn't want to spend an extra minute in the apocalyptic scene that Khartoum had become. We surrepticiously made our way out of Khartoum and back to Cairo, where we resumed our previous lives. I knew that the treasure was still in Khartoum, but I thanked providence to have been delivered from a fate worse than death. I resolved to go back and recover the treasure some day, once I had money enough to steal it again."

"Where had you hidden it?" Holmes inquired.

D'Giorgio rubbed his jaw. "I didn't hide it. I don't know where it is. Gordon's men took it from the palenquin upon our arrest, and unless the Mahdi himself discovered it, it remains hidden wherever Gordon put it." A rueful look came across his face. "Perhaps I needn't have confessed. If you have no cross, you have no evidence, except for the the story of one of the other men. I was a fool."

"Your confession to having stolen from the eleven churches is sufficient to cause you to spend your life in jail," Holmes said, "but once you came to our attention and the other bits of your past were discovered, the question of your involvement in the theft of the cross becomes less important. Presumably, since you've told all that you're willing to tell, your cell won't be in England. Do you prefer the kindness of penitentiary life in America? Or would you choose Egypt? Or dare I add Ethiopia?"

"Why does the theft of the cross really matter? Stealing from a backward region and a primitive people means nothing!"

"By your crime, you stole a device which could secure peace in a conflicted region of the world where three empires – ours, the French, and the Ottoman – contend for power. You have no idea what claims were shattered by your actions, including Italian and Ethiopian claims, when you made off with the historical proof of authority in the region."

Having apparently heard the part of the story which interested him, Holmes stood, relinquishing the remanining questioning to Lestrade. We were later told that over the course of the next few days, D'Giorgio admitted all, surrendering his reluctance to relate the complete extent of his crimes. He poured out details of a nefarious life not only in British regions, but across the globe. He narrated conspiracies carried out under the guise of Artie Thompson, and criminal activies of Signor Roberto Turay, and of course the illegal scenarios performed by the Italian actor D'Giorgio.

We returned to Baker Street where Mrs. Hudson brought tea. Holmes seemed strangely distant.

"Is there something wrong?" I asked.

"Once again, Watson, you are attentive beyond all imagination. You're right about my preoccupation, as usual. You see, I cannot but be puzzled by the the actions of Gordon toward D'Giorgio. He let D'Giorgio's crimes pass. Gordon preferred D'Giorgio be tried by a possible future civilized court once the siege ended, rather than by autocratic will, the latter of which he could easily have imposed. I'm indebted to my brother Mycroft who saw to it that we knew this."

I nodded. "I understand that it is by way of your brother that you were notified of D'Giorgio's presence here in London, leading to his arrest. I recall from what you told me earlier today that is was Mycroft who sent you to Khartoum, which is where you learned of the Patriarch's curious story . . . ." I left the statement hanging, letting him continue his story from before.

"As I was saying, I opened the secret door in the floor of the storeroom – "

" – To find the stolen cross," I finished for him.

He nodded. "Quite. It had been hidden there by Gordon during the siege, with the secret trapdoor covered by grain. I'm sure that he expected it to be recovered in a few days, never knowing what was about to happen.

“Gordon sent dispatches down the Nile to the embassy in Cairo right up to the very end – first by steamer, and when the Nile River level fell, overland by secret camel-driving messenger. In one of the last of them, he told Mycroft of the hidden cross, and approximately where it was hidden. It was that which motivated Mycroft to send me to Khartoum, with the diplomatic mission only so much distraction.

“And of course you knew this when you interviewed D’Giorgio, using it to get him to reveal how the theft was accomplished.”

“It is an odd truism that criminals want their deeds to be known. In short, they want to confess so the world knows of their cleverness. Whether they confess out of a strange sort of guilt, or pleasure, such as where they show the police how they fooled them, they want the world to know none-the-less. D’Giorgio was a miscreant, but an incredibly adept one. The object of his theft, had he ever been able to recover it, would have kept him wealthy beyond all measure had he succeeded. Once exposed, he wanted to at least be seen as a success in my eyes, causing me, his nemesis, to admit his skills. I find approaching interviews with this in mind often brings about a confession. Really, we had nothing on D’Giorgio that he couldn’t have denied, and had he remained the outraged actor, we’d have been hard-pressed to convict him.”

“But the cross,” I said, returning to the main object of Holmes’s story. “You did recover it, I assume.”

“I did. I had to bide my time, and after discovering it, two days of waiting turned to four. Never one to waste time, I sought out Burton’s former dragoman, Ali Budak, now representing himself as a merchant from Turkmenistan.

“I identified myself to find myself warmly remembered, and I explained to Budak that I required the efforts of some six hearty, trustworthy men. They were to perform a disappearing act which could only be done by someone as enterprising Burton’s legendary friend and helper. He was equal to the test.”

Warming to his tale, Holmes continued. “I described the cross’s dimensions, and sketched out a specialized container that he should have made. Then, treasure could be extracted from its secret place, hidden within a sleeve of wood, and carried to the river port.

“Few know that the Mahdi’s successors have no allies,” Holmes said, seemingly changing subjects. I knew, however, that this was related to his narrative. “They are surrounded by colonial powers in Africa, and have tribal enemies on all sides. Driven by a fanatical belief, however, the Mahdi’s followers set upon the idea to create their own power without allies. The Khalifa has employed shipbuilders to manufacture his own river steamers, and copper smiths to fashion a bullet factory. You'll recall that they'd captured weapons aplenty from the defeated Egyptian foes."

"It was in all the papers at the time."

"Yes. So my friend Budak was able to fashion a wooden case for the treasure in the granary, and then have his men transport it to the harbor's ship construction works. Claiming that it was a piece of a new steamship's flooring, specially reinforced to support a captured Krupp cannon and all the better to shoot their enemies, they helped affix it to the deck of the steamship *Mahdi*, even then being prepared for combat, and nearly ready for launch."

"One of the Khalifa's own ships?" I said with a smile.

Holmes nodded. "There was no other way to get something out of the country then, than to hide it in plain sight. Once it was safely installed, I felt that I could relax, though only slightly. I resumed the pretense of being in Khartoum on a diplomatic mission, visiting different sites of interest and waiting for a reply from their government.

"Eventually I received the response from the Khalifa's government to our Britannic Majesty's Governmental inquiry. I knew not the details, nor did I care, but I then proceeded to return downstream to Cairo. Meanwhile Budak, together with his confederates, kept watch as the *Mahdi* launched and sailed downstream to the sea.

"I arrived in Cairo, and from there proceeded, on Mycroft's instructions, to the lodgings of the Patriarch of the Coptic Orthodox Church, where I learned the story which I related earlier at Scotland Yard. He's a remarkably modest, pious, and kind man, Watson – very informed and progressive. I'm not familiar with his faith, other than that information provided by Burton, but it sufficed to allow me to spend a worthwhile visit with him to the satisfaction of my requirement from Mycroft."

"I understand that Mycroft had received word from Gordon as to the location of the hidden cross, but what further need was there to communicate with the Patriarch?"

"He is responsible for all Coptic Christians throughout the world. He establishes their dogma, together with his liturgical advisors. It was he who told me the remarkable story of the Cross of St. Lalibela. What I learned was that the saint was in fact also a king, Gebre Meskel Lalibela, who lived seven-hundred years or so ago in what is now Ethiopia. A pious, almost monkish man, he sought to make a living testimony to his faith by commissioning the eleven churches – doing so because access to the Holy Land of Palestine was cut off because of the Crusades. These churches were to be locations of pilgrimage, so that the reverent could visit a holy place in lieu of those that were currently embattled. What's utterly beyond belief, Watson, is that each of these churches was hewn from the living rock! Each was built from the top down, hewn through gigantic pieces of stone."

"Amazing!" I exclaimed.

"What's more amazing is what they did next," submitted Holmes, almost conspiratorially. "The faithful of the eleven churches have always been privy to many of the secrets of Africa. As we now know, there are vast reserves of gold and other resources buried deep inland, for one must travel through savannah, jungle, mountain, and prairie to reach these magnificent riches. These Ethiopian Coptic Christians know of this vast, hidden African treasure. They've always sought it out not to enrich themselves, but to pay honor to God. They created the Cross of St. Lalibela, which is a golden masterwork, using these materials. It is replete with diamonds, jewels beyond compare, and artwork – such carvings as never before seen are engraved upon the solid gold cross."

I began to understand. "Mycroft learned of the stolen cross from Gordon. You were able to recover it and present it to the Patriarch – the *true* Patriarch, and not the false second one portrayed by D'Giorgio – earning the good-will of the Coptic Church, along with the possibility of knowledge of some of the locations of Africa's hidden riches.

Holmes nodded, pleased at my understanding.

"And you did recover the cross, I presume?"

"I did. When the *Mahdi* reached Cairo, the Patriarch's agents talked their way aboard and did some supposedly urgent repair work on the deck, replacing that section which held the hidden cross. Once it was back in his possession, and it was verified to be the real object, the Patriarch had it sent by special transit from Egypt through the Suez Canal, and then taken overland back to the Town of the Eleven Churches, where it was met with cheering and prayer."

"But that should cause you satisfaction. Instead, you seem rather pensive."

He glanced toward the mantel and the small photograph of Gordon that had arrived that morning. "I'm really not reflecting on that so much as on Gordon. Here was a man, facing death itself, who believed that proper English rule of law should prevail over autocratic will. Thus he remanded D'Giorgio to prison. There D'Giorgio was to await trial once the besieged city was liberated by a British force, even then underway to relieve Khartoum. Or so Gordon believed. As we all know, they didn't arrive in time, D'Giorgio escaped, and Gordon was killed.

"And yet, there was more to this tale. Gordon could well have cared less about the cross, since his own earthly end was in the offing. He could have justly executed D'Giorgio, for he had the power to do so. Instead, he saw the cross as the manifestation of a people's piety, and protected it. He sent word to Mycroft, and in a way he guarded it even after his own life came to an end, protecting something for other people who were not even his own co-religionists. Why does a man do that? I find little reason for doing so."

"Perhaps reason is not part of the equation in this case."

"Indeed. Perhaps not, Watson. Perhaps something else . . . ."

So ended the curious case of the two Patriarchs. Some months later, the Emperor of Ethiopia sent Holmes a "finder's fee" of a princely sum in thanks for his efforts in restoring a prize which helped him claim his rights to a region disputed by European powers. Holmes, as might be recalled, sent a large donation thereafter to his friend, the Patriarch, in Egypt, to help pay for a school to educate young students in the rule of law. Seeing that Holmes's mind was troubled upon the subject, I never asked who sent him the photograph of General Gordon, late of Khartoum, although Gordon's written message on it, addressed to "*M*", strongly indicated that it had come by way of Mycroft Holmes. In any case, it remained prominently displayed on our lodging's mantelpiece ever after. Gordon was perhaps the only person whose motives could not be fairly perceived by that master of reason, Sherlock Holmes.

"You know that I am preoccupied with this case of the two Coptic Patriarchs, which should come to a head to-day."

– Sherlock Holmes
"The Adventure of the Retired Colourman"

"I then passed through Persia, looked in at Mecca, and paid a short but interesting visit to the Khalifa at Khartoum, the results of which I have communicated to the Foreign Office."

– Sherlock Holmes
"The Empty House"

The Curious Case of the Crusader's Cross
by DJ Tyrer

The curious case of the two Coptic Patriarchs was one in which I was to play but a minor role, and one that the full details of which my good friend, Sherlock Holmes, requested I keep from my pen for some years out of respect for the wishes of those involved, but which I'm now at liberty to recount.

It all began as I arrived at 221b Baker Street to see the boy-in-buttons showing a smartly-dressed but out-of-breath man in through the door.

Entering, I found that my friend was in his usual seat, pipe in hand, smoke wreathing his head as if it were a halo, and the man was before him, his hat in his hands, toying with it as if in a state of nerves or embarrassment

"Ah, Watson," exclaimed Holmes, jabbing towards me with his pipe, "your timing is perfect. Allow me to introduce the banker, Mr. Threadneedle."

He started at his name. "You know me, sir?"

"Indeed."

The man gave a nervous chuckle. "It seems everything I've heard about your capabilities is true, Mr. Holmes."

Holmes gave a snort.

"You are a leading member of the Roman Catholic community in this city, are you not, sir?"

The man gave a quick nod, his expression still somewhat perplexed.

"It would not be in error to say so."

"I've seen your photograph – and, a name such as yours is much more memorable than a Smith or a Brown, and especially suited to your line of work." Holmes shook his head. "There is really no trick, beyond a good memory."

"Indeed, indeed," muttered Threadneedle, although he sounded less-than-convinced.

"But, I digress. You have come here on some urgent business – I can deduce that much from your lack of puff. Be seated and tell us all about your problem. This," he gestured at me, "is my good friend, Dr. John Watson, and you may speak freely before him."

Mr. Threadneedle nodded at me and sat down. I did likewise. After a moment's rest to comport himself, he began to speak.

"You are quite right that I'm a man of some importance amongst those of us in this city who profess adherence to the Bishop of Rome. As a man of both means and connections, it frequently falls upon me to help organise and finance undertakings of importance. At the same time, I'm also a man of discretion, and that is why I have come to you, Mr. Holmes."

Holmes nodded and our guest continued, wringing his hands in a nervous fashion.

"It began just over a month ago. You may not be aware, but, amongst the Copts – that is that section of the Egyptian people who profess Christianity rather than Mohammedanism – there are a number who, despite the differences of language and liturgical rite, are Catholics in union with Rome, in addition to those who follow the Coptic Orthodox Church."

Holmes nodded again, as if this were all common knowledge.

"Well, a few years ago," continued Threadneedle, "the Pope re-established the Coptic Catholic Patriarchate, which, as you may guess, proved quite the reinvigoration for the community out there. But while there was an Apostolic Vicar in place, there was no reigning Patriarch."

I gave a cough at this point and the man looked at me with an apologetic expression.

"I am sorry, Dr. Watson, this must all seem quite arcane to you, but it is a necessary foundation upon which to build my explanation for the evil that has befallen us, for, you see, just over a month ago, the newly-appointed Patriarch arrived in London seeking support and funds for the restoration of the faith in Egypt and new missionary endeavours in the Soudan, Abyssinia, and other benighted corners of the Dark Continent."

"But, why did he come here?" I asked. "Surely, Rome would be a better destination."

Threadneedle nodded. "Of course, that is where he said he had come from, having been but newly anointed Patriarch by His Holiness, but given England's influence in his homeland, it was natural that he would come here seeking support."

"You said 'where he said he had come from'," I observed, and Holmes gave me an approving nod that was followed by a forlorn one from our guest.

"Yes. It had been expected that the Apostolic Vicar, Cyrillus Macaire, would receive the Pope's blessing, but the new Patriarch was a man by the name of Demetrius of whom we had no intelligence, save a letter of introduction from the Pope himself. A symbol of faith in which, it would prove, our trust was misplaced."

He sighed. "As you can imagine, our desire to assist such an endeavour was bolstered by the presence of a man of such importance in our midst, and I was chosen to head the fundraising drive. In addition, through my own initiative, I was able to obtain a small gold cross from a family of honour and antiquity, whose name I shall leave unsaid, for they have played no further part in this embarrassing saga and do not deserve to have their reputation blemished in any manner. This cross was said to have been brought back by a crusader ancestor of theirs from Alexandria, the city of St. Mark and the original seat of the Coptic Patriarchate, and seemed a fitting gift to bestow upon the holy endeavour.

"I also paid for the Patriarch's suite in one of the best hotels in the city, as befitted his rank.

"Alas, to my shame, blinded as I was by the Papal letter and the self-importance garnered from the role to which I found myself elected by my peers, I did nothing to confirm the man's words or identity before handing over the cross and a substantial sum of money."

Threadneedle sighed once more, then resumed speaking, his voice running faster and faster as he approached the disaster that overcame him.

"Imagine my shock when, just a few days ago, the Apostolic Vicar, Cyrillus Macaire, arrived in London with the news that he had been newly appointed to the rank of Patriarch!"

"The first Patriarch was a fraud?" I exclaimed and the man practically wailed his acknowledgement of the fact.

"It is so!" he sobbed.

"Two Patriarchs?" murmured Holmes and the banker nodded.

"Yes, one real and one false."

"And, of course, the false one had absconded with all that you had given him," I said.

"He had, leaving nothing behind save the hotel bill and the letter he claimed to have received from the Pope."

"You have this letter?" Holmes asked.

"Yes." Threadneedle pulled a crumpled missive from his jacket pocket and thrust it at Holmes, saying, "Take it."

Holmes smoothed it out a little and glanced at it for no more than a moment, then set it aside and told the man to continue, saying, "You went to Scotland Yard, of course?"

"I would have done so immediately," Threadneedle said, his tone still agitated, "but His Beatitude, possessing a calmer disposition than my own, bade me keep silent about the crime. You see, none of the fundraising we undertook, as luck would have it, actually used the false Patriarch's name. Aside from a few of us, all equally embarrassed at ourselves for falling for such a ruse, nobody knew that there had ever been anyone else besides His Beatitude, Cyrillus Macaire. If we made what happened public, our community would be shaken and we would surely be made into figures of fun, and the Patriarch's good work would likely be undermined before it even got underway.

"It is his wish that we finish off the fundraising without any fuss. He departs for Egypt in a week, and then the entire episode can be forgotten about."

He paused, then nodded to himself.

"No, he was quite right not to involve the police."

"And, yet," I said, unable to help myself, "you are here."

"That may be," Holmes said drily, "because this is 221b Baker Street and not Scotland Yard, Watson."

"Indeed," said the banker. "I was quite ready to go along with His Beatitude's wishes, until, just this morning, I'm certain that I spotted the false Patriarch walking along the Kensington Road with a woman. Although his mode of dress had changed – he wore a regular suit – I recognised him nonetheless, for his wild and bushy eyebrows and deep-set eyes are quite distinctive. I realised, then, that he might perpetrate some new fraud upon unsuspecting victims and that, while I could not allow my faith to be brought into ridicule, I could not allow him to wander free, and so I made way here as swiftly as I could.

"That is why I have come to you, Mr. Holmes. Although few details are known, it is whispered that you have helped out His Holiness and many others of high standing and done so discreetly. I'm certain I can trust you to bring this man to some kind of justice without it bringing embarrassment upon the church."

Holmes nodded, slowly, and sucked deeply upon his pipe before answering.

"You can rely upon me, sir. Already some avenues of investigation present themselves to me. I believe I can prevent further fraud and, with a little luck, may even be able to retrieve what has been stolen from you already."

"You do?" exclaimed Threadneedle, leaning towards Holmes like an eager child.

"Indeed, I do. And you shall have my utmost discretion."

The man pumped his hand. "Thank you! Thank you!"

Then he rose, and Holmes called for the page to show him out, telling the lad to return promptly.

When they were gone, I looked at Holmes, who was reaching for pen and paper.

"So, what do you make of it all?"

Holmes wrote a short message, and then said, "I believe we're up against a foe of surprising cunning, given the somewhat lacklustre nature of his tools." He gestured vaguely to where the supposedly-Papal letter lay. "Not the best paper, but I dare say that anyone told it was written by His Holiness is more interested in the content than the form. It is easy for the lazy eye to see what is expected to be there rather than to see what is really there – and the greater the audacity in a ruse, the greater its chance of success."

"So you're saying that, had this villain come pretending to be a simple missionary, he would have been more likely found out?"

"Precisely, Watson. By choosing the more-elaborate lie, not only was there a greater chance of success, but greater reward. Ah, and speaking of reward – "

The boy had just returned from showing Mr. Threadneedle out.

" – there is a shilling in it if you can take this message to the telegraph office and see it is sent immediately."

Holmes passed the note he had been writing to the lad, who nodded and was off in a flash.

Holmes merely gave me a thin and mysterious smile.

"All shall be revealed at the appropriate time. Now," he rose and grabbed his coat, "let us go and find a crusader's cross . . . ."

We headed out into a light summer drizzle and I whistled for a hansom.

Amongst Holmes's copious knowledge is that of every disreputable pawnshop and criminal middleman in London. I asked him how he could be certain it had been disposed of.

"My primary reason for suspecting it has already been sold," said Holmes as we bounced along a cobbled street, "is that the first Patriarch came asking for money and Mr. Threadneedle said the obtaining of the cross was done on his own initiative. Of course, it is no great task to persuade someone into doing something they believe is their own idea, but I'm inclined to accept that the cross was not part of the original plan."

"And he wished to make an immediate sale,' I suggested, "in case he was sought?"

"Indeed. Those who donate funds are unlikely to keep a record of the banknotes they used, but an ancient cross is something that can easily be traced back to its original owner, necessitating its prompt disposal. Thus, it's highly likely that it's already in the hands of some unscrupulous fellow."

The hansom clattered to a halt and we descended from it and approached our first destination.

I hadn't paid much attention to our journey, having been caught up in our conversation, and was a little disconcerted to discover that the shop we stood outside wasn't the insalubrious establishment or back-alley dealer I had imagined would be our destination, but a fine-looking place with the words *Edmont – Antiquities* emblazoned above the entrance.

"Holmes?"

He chuckled as he led the way to the door.

"It may be that the unprincipled fellow who took the cross disposed of it in some slum, but, given the effort he put into his charade, it's quite possible he did his research and sought out someone better placed to provide him with a good price."

The bell above the door jangled as we entered the veritable cavern of delights filled with all manner of old and wondrous things.

"Don't let appearances fool you," said Holmes as he peered at a grotesque taxidermic construction reminiscent of the notorious Feejee Mermaid of yesteryear. "Edmont is as corrupt as his ilk comes, a son of the rookeries, not his current haunts. But he has knowledge and contacts and that is all a man of his sort needs to prosper."

There was a sound of movement to the rear of the shop and Holmes dashed forwards, between the crowded shelves.

"Ah, there you are," he cried and I caught up with him a moment later to find he had the proprietor of the shop by the collar.

"Mr. Holmes, please!" said the man, his eyes wide behind a pair of pince-nez glasses. "You have no reason to manhandle me so."

Although smartly dressed and with a golden chain running across his chest to his pocket watch, his thin, pockmarked features struck me as too coarse and furtive for a man of quality.

"Do I not?" Holmes asked him. "Is it not so that I need merely reach out my hand to touch any number of stolen items and misplaced pieces of treasure trove?"

"Lies . . . ." muttered the man as Holmes continued to hold his collar tight.

Holmes chuckled. "You may drop the pretence, Edmont. We haven't come to catalogue your misdemeanours. I am interested in one thing and one thing only: A medieval cross that would have come into your possession within the last month. I am willing to wager you have it, or else know where it is to be found."

The man glanced about, as if seeking an escape route, but there was none and, with a sigh, he said, "I don't have it, Mr. Holmes, honest I don't."

Then, he looked up at Holmes with a sly expression. "But I do believe I can help you obtain it – for the right remuneration, of course."

"Of course. You remain true to your nature."

The man looked at Holmes expectantly.

"Tell me what you know," said Holmes, "and I will reward you as I see fit."

With a grunt, the man said, "You drive a hard bargain. Very well. I've seen the cross you seek. Byzantine, from the Levant, perhaps. I am merely acting as an intermediary, putting the seller in touch with an interested party for a modest fee."

"You know who is selling it?"

"He will return here this very evening, at seven, Mr. Holmes."

"Then we shall be here." Holmes passed him a banknote. "I doubt this will make up for your lost finder's fee . . . ."

Edmont snorted. "It barely covers the cost of a new collar to replace the one you have mangled," he said, but tucked it into his waistcoat pocket, nonetheless.

Holmes smiled. "A step closer, Watson. Come." And we left the shop.

"Watson, I want you to keep an eye on our friend, Mr. Edmont. I'm certain he's telling the truth in general terms, but he's far from an honest person. It may be that he lied about the time or will attempt to warn the criminal. I want you to watch his shop. Keep note of who enters and leaves. You remember Threadneedle's description of the false Patriarch? Good. Watch for him in particular. Should Edmont leave, follow him – discreetly."

"But what if either of them makes use of the back entrance to the shop?" I asked.

Gesturing towards the mouth of an alleyway beside the shop, Holmes said, "That leads to the side door. Anyone wishing to enter or leave that way will still be visible to you.

"I shall return before seven," he concluded.

"You can rely on me," I told him. "But what do you plan to do?"

"I intend to seek spiritual counsel," Holmes replied gnomically.

As he hailed a passing hansom, I went a little way down the street and ensconced myself in a nearby coffee house, where I could avail myself of refreshments while simultaneously being able to see the front of Edmont's shop.

My own afternoon was of no consequence, for Edmont did not leave and he only received one customer, a pretty-looking young woman who left with a small package tied up in brown paper and string. Of the villainous imposter, there was no sign.

Only later would Holmes explain his mission to me in any detail.

Holmes returned about six-thirty with an air of purpose, and I sensed there was satisfaction in his stride as he approached me on the street corner.

I told him of my uneventful observations and he nodded with satisfaction.

"Then soon we shall have him. Indeed, it may be hubris, but I believe I'm very close to solving this particular mystery."

Of course, even for one of such marvellous faculties as he, there is indeed a risk of the proverbial pride coming before a fall. Not that the blame wholly lay with him, for I can only curse my own foolishness and unobservant surveillance for what came to pass.

"We shall wait for our quarry inside, I think," said Holmes and we returned to the well-stocked shop.

Edmont smiled an unctuous grin at us as the bell jangled to announce our entrance.

"Ah, Mr. Holmes, delighted to see you again. Punctual as ever. But, alas, you are too late."

"What?"

"Yes, it seems that the fellow you are hunting lacks your reliability, or perhaps he was in more of a hurry to offload the cross – who can say?"

"But he never – "

I may have said something intemperate at that point as the truth struck me.

"The woman!" Threadneedle had mentioned a female companion, but it had never occurred to me that the dastard might send her instead.

"The cross?" said Holmes in as soft a tone as one might use to enquire over a spoon misplaced in the cutlery drawer..

"I refused it, naturally," Edmont said with a smirk. "No point in paying for goods that I would have to hand over to you. As far as I knew, you planned to nab whoever had the cross – either in my place of business," he shook his head, as if shocked at such an imposition, "or upon their leaving and take it from them. I wasn't under the impression I was supposed to retrieve the cross myself. Or were you planning to reimburse me for the outlay?"

Edmont shrugged. "What else could I have done, Mr. Holmes? Miss Keel was most unhappy – yes, she was – but what was I to do?"

"You know her name?" Holmes asked him.

"I do, but nothing more. This is not a game in which one wishes too much to be known of oneself by the other."

Holmes looked him square in the face, and I knew that Holmes believed him. Lying was too great a risk – and the truth allowed the man a chance to crow.

At that time, my fingers were taut upon the head of my cane with anger, but now I can allow myself a bitter chuckle at our predicament: The old cross had played us in the most-artfully cross manner possible . . . .

Although my temper was fraying, more so at myself than at the tricky fellow, Holmes remained as stoic as ever. To him, a reversal in fortunes such as this was less a disaster than an opportunity to reanalyse the situation, correct misapprehensions, and draw up fresh battle plans.

"Come, Watson, we need detain Mr. Edmont no longer."

As we turned to go, he cast a look at the man and added, "But should you prove to come into possession of that cross without informing me immediately . . . ."

Holmes left the threat dangling.

"Of course not, Mr. Holmes . . . ." he called after us as we exited and sought a hansom.

"So the woman is involved," said Holmes as we settled ourselves into the cab's seats. "It was always a possibility, of course, but when one is speaking of Catholic clergymen, even ones who are not the genuine article, it is easy to overlook the potential of a woman to play a part."

"But not as easy," I told him, ruefully, "as to overlook her when she is standing right before you."

"True, Watson, very true." Holmes barked a laugh, but I could see his mind was preoccupied, not mirthful.

"Could you describe her?" he asked after a moment's silence.

"Not in any detail. I paid very little heed to her."

He raised an eyebrow at that, but made no comment, instead saying, "I perhaps erred in concentrating upon other avenues of enquiry – " Singularly failing to explain what those avenues were. " – when my focus should have been upon what we knew for certain. Still, I see no reason why we shouldn't run the blackguard down soon."

Unfortunately, as the days passed, it seemed that we might never do so.

Whether Edmont had told the woman that we were on the case or whether his sudden refusal to do business had spooked her partner in crime, it seemed that they had decided not to pursue the sale of the cross any further, as we surveyed all the potential points of sale of which Holmes was aware with no luck. Nor was there are word from his contacts on the streets and in the gutters of our great but tainted city. Nobody could claim to have seen the man, or to have heard of anyone seeking to sell an antique cross.

The mysterious Miss Keel was a cipher, the name yielding nothing among the ruffians we questioned. As for the man we knew as "Demetrius", it seemed unlikely that was his real name. Like a mirage, they might seem tantalisingly near one moment, but always proved elusive.

Either the villain and his lady were lying low, wary of our pursuit, or they had fled London altogether; and though Holmes approached each potential new lead or contact with all due energy, our ongoing stagnation on the case did nothing for his mood, which had taken on a definite melancholy aspect.

"Still," he said to me, "there remains one stone I have yet to turn over."

He said nothing of what his thoughts dwelt upon, but I recalled him, back when it all began, having sent the page out to take a telegram. Holmes had said nothing of a reply and I guessed that, when it came, the answer would either open up the case to him or seal it off completely.

I could only hope it would come soon and bear positive news.

Holmes was in a melancholy and philosophic mood when I came down the next morning, passing a rather pathetic-looking man as I entered. That, of course, was the notorious Josiah Amberley, referred to in the press as the instigator of "The Haven Horror", and whose undoing I have previously recorded in "The Retired Colourman".

Mr. Amberley had sought Holmes's assistance concerning a tale of a missing wife and savings.

"What will you do about it?" I asked.

The response startled me a little: "Well, the immediate question, my dear Watson, happens to be, 'What will *you* do about it?' – If you would be good enough to understudy me. You know that I am preoccupied with this case of the two Coptic Patriarchs, which should come to a head today."

This last fact was news to me, but I saw that there was a telegram on the table beside his seat and realised that whatever information he had been seeking had come to him at last and looked set to resolve the case in some manner.

But my curiosity as to the contents of the telegram was not to be assuaged, for Holmes continued, saying, "I really have not time to go out to Lewisham, and yet evidence taken on the spot has a special value. The old fellow was quite insistent that I should go, but I explained my difficulty. He is prepared to meet a representative."

"By all means," I answered. "I confess, I don't see that I can be of much service, but I am willing to do my best."

So it was that, on that summer afternoon, I set forth to Lewisham, while Holmes pursued his own lead, little knowing that even as there would be small discussion of that curious case, the one I was embarking upon would, within a week, be the eager debate of all England – much, I am sure, to the relief of Mr. Threadneedle, given what followed.

It was late that evening before I returned to Baker Street and gave an account of my mission. Holmes lay with his gaunt figure stretched in his deep chair, his pipe curling forth slow wreaths of acrid tobacco, while his eyelids drooped over his eyes so lazily that he might almost have been asleep, were it not that at any halt or questionable passage of my narrative they half lifted, and two grey eyes, as bright and keen as rapiers, transfixing me with their searching glare.

Holmes seemed especially severe as I described my visit to Lewisham and all that I had uncovered, which seemed to be but a fraction of what he expected and, indeed, perhaps not as much as he himself already had thanks to the telephone and the help of Scotland Yard. His words and tone seemed to imply he had already reached a conclusion concerning the case – one that would lead to an extraordinary revelation when, eventually, I returned to Lewisham with him by my side.

But, as I finished narrating my investigation, Holmes surprised me by telling me, in a more tender tone than previously, "Well, leave it there, Watson. Let us escape from this weary workaday world by the side door of music. Carina sings tonight at the Albert Hall, and we still have time to dress, dine, and enjoy."

Now, Sherlock Holmes is seldom a sentimental fellow, but he can appreciate beauty as finely as any man, and I have known him to find the distraction of art a means of refreshing his mind, readying it to return to a problem with renewed vigour. Thus it was that I assumed his suggestion represented nothing more than such a revitalization prior to his tackling the new case and that the one involving the false Patriarch must have been resolved, one way or another.

But, over a most-enjoyable meal, Holmes revealed that there was more to his proposition than mere relaxation, and that it involved the resolution that had been so long in coming. At last, he revealed to me his own suspicions and activities.

"I dare say you shall be annoyed with me, my dear Watson, for I must admit that I solved the case of the two Coptic Patriarchs before Mr. Threadneedle ever left the room."

"What on earth can you mean?" I asked him. "If you solved it within the first five minutes, whatever purpose was there in our tramping all over London and achieving nothing?"

"Yes, I had the answer from the very beginning, but I had no proof – and, without proof, I could not be certain that my suspicions were correct. Certainly not to do more than I did. Yet, tonight, we shall finally bring the miscreants to justice."

"I'm afraid I really don't understand," I said.

"It is quite simple. It was the audacity of the venture, combined with the fact that the appointment of a new Coptic Catholic Patriarch occurred with so little fanfare."

"I don't follow."

"Don't you? This is, after all, the case of the two Coptic Patriarchs."

"Wait, you don't mean to say – ?"

"Yes, Watson. *Neither* of our erstwhile Patriarchs was the genuine article. Indeed, while there are steps underway to appoint the Apostolic Vicar, Cyrillus Macaire, to just such a position, they have not yet come to fruition."

"So, the second Patriarch . . . ?"

"Was *not* Cyrillus Macaire, at all, but a *second* impostor." Holmes smiled wolfishly, as if he had his prey's scent in his nostrils. "The plan might almost be called genius. Caught up in their fervour, Threadneedle and his co-religionists fell prey to a rather simplistic ploy, believing this 'Demetrius' was the newly-minted Patriarch. But, it was a ploy that might have been seen through if allowed to play out too long. Thus, 'Cyrillus Macaire' arrived with the announcement that *he* was the new Patriarch."

I nodded, slowly. "Embarrassed and focussed upon the first one, I can see they wouldn't even think to suspect that he wasn't who he said he was, especially as he bore the name of the man they expected to see appointed."

"Precisely, Watson. A simple, but effective, means of redirecting one's attention elsewhere, like a performance of legerdemain.

"The second Patriarch, understandably, cautioned against involving the Yard or allowing the story into the newspapers, thus keeping his co-conspirator safe – or, so he thought. Of course, sooner or later, the ruse would be revealed, but they would be long gone and safe from whatever investigation might follow."

"But how did you know?"

"As I said, I was struck by the audacity of the first crime and allowed myself to wonder if an even more audacious one was planned. Then, I considered that neither Mr. Threadneedle, nor myself, were aware of the appointment of a new Patriarch. Could it be that 'Cyrillus Macaire' was not whom he claimed to be? It seemed almost too marvellous to be true, and yet, I couldn't rule it out.

"Hence the telegram I had the page deliver that morning. It was to His Holiness, the Pope, asking as to the status of the Apostolic Vicar."

"So while you waited for a reply, you sought to retrieve the cross?"

"Exactly. And you know how we fared in that endeavour."

"But, where did you go to when you said you were going to 'seek spiritual counsel'?"

Holmes chuckled. "Where do you think? I went to visit the second Patriarch.

"Of course, I couldn't confront him directly, nor did I know what the real Cyrillus Macaire looks like well enough to be certain whether or not he was the man himself. But I was able to assess him and certainly left feeling more certain than before that he was not the man he claimed to be.

"I trailed him, hoping he might lead me to his co-conspirator or, at least, provide some solid evidence of his guilt, but while he never saw me following him, neither did I see anything that I could use."

"And then, you returned to find the cross had slipped through our fingers."

"Yes. The woman, of course, was, as she still is, the key, but without a detailed description, there was nothing we could do to chase her down and, I must be honest, I began to wonder if my preoccupation with the second Patriarch was nothing but a will-o'-the-wisp, distracting me from the real criminal. Had I been a fool? It seemed as if I had and that the villain had made his escape while my attention was focussed elsewhere."

"But you hadn't had a reply to your telegram," I said. "I take it that was what arrived today?"

"That is correct. An answer to my query to the Holy See was the last possible lead that remained, and it confirmed what I had known all along and never should have doubted: That there were two fake Patriarchs."

"No wonder you had no desire to travel to Lewisham!"

"Indeed, not. With you taking my place, I went to the hotel where the second Patriarch was living off the goodwill of Mr. Threadneedle, accompanied by our employer, and confronted him."

"Whatever happened?"

"I was perhaps precipitate in my actions, for the man was in no mood, upon being exposed as a fraud, to be detained without a struggle. He had with him a silver-topped ebony walking stick with which he proved remarkably proficient. Mr. Threadneedle took a blow to the head that rendered him temporarily out of action and it was only thanks to my skill in singlestick fighting that allowed me to fend off his blows with my cane and land one or two in return. I daresay I shall have some bright bruises upon my arms in the coming days – but, he shall shine the worse!"

Holmes smiled again. "He ran for it and escaped my pursuit, but in his hurry, he not only left behind bundles of cash, but also an advertising bill for tonight's performance."

"Which is why we're going there?" I asked and he nodded.

"But," I continued, "how can you be certain that he will be there? After all, he may have been intending to be entertained upon our employer's account and now be on his way out of the country?"

"Oh, he is almost certainly readying himself to depart England, but he hasn't left yet."

"But, how can you be certain?"

"The woman, Watson, the woman! It was quite simple to deduce that the woman who slipped by you and whom Mr. Threadneedle saw in the street with the man he identified as 'Demetrius' might be singing at the Albert Hall."

"Carina?"

He nodded. "Not her real name, of course."

"'*Beautiful lady*'," I translated.

"Indeed, she is."

"You have seen her."

"From afar. I watched as she rehearsed, hoping to see her co-conspirators, but with no luck. I suspect they will come to her, or she to them, after the performance."

"But you're certain that she is the woman?" I asked, knowing that he surely was, but wondering how he could be so positive.

Holmes didn't answer, but glanced at his pocket watch, rose from the table, and said, "Come, it is time."

As a hansom conveyed us to the Albert Hall, Holmes finished his explanation.

"It was her name that answers your question," Holmes said, leaving me feeling even less certain than before. "You see, '*Carina*' also means '*keel*'. Offstage, she is known as Miss Audrey Keel."

The woman from Edmont's store.

"We were looking for her in all the wrong places, Watson. Not in the gutter, but the world of refinement."

"But how can you be certain they will come to her?"

"Further enquiries among some of her fellow artistes revealed that her brother was one-half of a pair specializing in legerdemain – the art of distraction."

"The Two Patriarchs . . . ."

"Exactly. Her brother and his partner, whom I am told she is quite friendly with, are regular attendees backstage – always one, if not both. They will not abandon her – and, I doubt they guess that I have made the connection. After all, what is an advertising bill?"

"What indeed?" I echoed, acknowledging that I hadn't earlier seen the connection.

"We shall enjoy a convivial evening's entertainment, and then, under the guise of going to pay our respects to the performer, seek to intercept her two partners in crime. And if they aren't there, we shall follow her to wherever they lair."

It was a sound plan.

Miss Keel – *Carina* – was even more delightful to look upon than I remembered from my brief glimpse of her in the street days before, and her singing exceptional, I quite enjoyed the show. However, I did feel an odd sense of embarrassment or guilt at watching her, knowing that she was little more than the tethered goat we were using to capture our real prey.

"Sheer sentimentality," said Holmes when I revealed the thought to him, and I could scarcely argue the point.

As soon as the concert drew to a close, we left our seats and moved with alacrity through the throng, threading our way through to the backstage area, and thence to the dressing rooms.

"Carina's room," Holmes asked a stagehand and the man pointed and said, "Third door on the left."

"Thank you, my man. Come on, Watson, not a moment to spare."

Then, before we had gone more than a few steps, he cried, "There! Don't let them get away!"

I was in no mood to. The two men – the two Patriarchs – had just exited Carina's dressing room, with the songstress in tow. I recognised the one, a heavyset man with bushy eyebrows and deep-set eyes, from Threadneedle's description. The other man was a little taller and thinner with a glowering expression.

The two men raised their walking sticks and came at us down the narrow corridor.

"A rematch, eh?" snapped Holmes, raising his own cane and fending off their blows.

I wielded mine, also, striking the heavyset man in the knee and forcing him into a pained crouch, from which position I was able to seize him and force him into submission.

With a series of precisely-controlled blows, Holmes forced the other man back and sent the stick spinning from his hand.

Carina – Audrey Keel – gave a scream as a blow to the stomach sent her brother slumping against the wall, the fight knocked out of him.

With the perfect manners of a gentleman, Holmes greeted her and introduced himself.

"An admirer," he said, "but alas, also your hunter."

"We are here about the fraud your brother and lover have perpetrated, Miss Keel," I told her, as I maintained my grip on the struggling man.

Her face paled and a hand flew to her mouth.

"Your Beatitude," said Holmes, with a mock bow to the woman's brother. "Or, should I say, Mr. Keel."

The man groaned and muttered darkly at us.

"Oh, Mr. Holmes!" gasped Miss Keel. "Please, they meant no harm!"

Holmes laughed, mirthlessly.

"No harm, Miss Keel? They may not be footpads, but they have caused great harm to those who thought they were doing good. Your brother and his partner are villains, without a doubt."

"They just wanted a better life than that which fate has so far allocated them."

"A wish everyone in this city likely shares, my dear, but not one that justifies such base deceit. However . . . ." Holmes left the word hanging.

"However?" she asked, eyes wide and glistening. I must confess the sight of her stabbed at my heart.

"However, despite everything that has happened, my employer wants recent events to remain out of the public's knowledge. If the stolen money, or as much of it as is practicable, were to be returned, then he might consider the sound beating they have received sufficient punishment and allow the matter to rest there."

"Of course," she said, relief flooding her voice. "It is in our lodging house. I will show you forthwith and pledge things will remain there."

"Oh, and – " Holmes added, " – there was also the matter of a certain antique cross."

Miss Keel nodded. "Yes, I have it on me, here." She produced it and handed it over to him.

Holmes took it and gently kissed her hand.

"Thank you, my dear. Now, if you will lead us to your lodgings, so that we might retrieve the money and be on our way . . . ."

"This way. A carriage is waiting."

Holmes smiled as he pulled her brother to his feet.

"Oh, and Carina, if I may call you so, please leave the tawdry world of criminality behind for, I believe, you have a bright future ahead of you upon the stage – one much to be preferred to a life behind bars. For," he added in an ominous tone, "should I discover you – or they – " He nodded to the two men. " – have returned to your ignominious ways, I shall not hesitate to hand you over to the full weight of the law."

She paled and assured him that they never would.

And that is how we resolved the curious case of the two Coptic Patriarchs – two Patriarchs who never were. The money and cross were returned, and the subsequent events in Lewisham ensured no attention was paid to any of it by the newspapermen. Within a year, Cyrillus Macaire was, indeed, raised to the Patriarchate and, I believe, received a substantial donation through the offices of Mr. Threadneedle. As for Miss Keel, many are surely aware of the success of the singer Carina upon the stage –

success that, it would seem, has kept her brother and lover from returning to a life of crime.

> *"You know that I am preoccupied with this case of the two Coptic Patriarchs, which should come to a head to-day."*
>
> – Sherlock Holmes
> "The Adventure of the Retired Colourman"

An Act of Faith
by Harry DeMaio

Chapter I

My relationships over time with Sherlock Holmes have been many and varied. Friend, companion, supporter, associate detective, amanuensis, protector, healer, and occasionally, surrogate. Witness the following dialogue as we discussed an impending case:

"Would you be good enough to understudy me? You know that I am preoccupied with this case of the two Coptic Patriarchs, which should come to a head today."

In fact, I did not know. I was totally unaware of his involvement with two religious leaders. Holmes tends to believe that by osmosis or some such process, I keep current with all of his activities, thoughts, opinions, and conclusions – Watson, the alter ego. Of course, I agreed to be his stand-in in the case we refer to as "The Adventure of the Retired Colourman", but my curiosity nagged at me. What of these Coptic Patriarchs?

I have learned, however, that Holmes keeps his own counsel until he is prepared to "reveal all". Obviously, as far as the Patriarchs were concerned, he hadn't yet reached that stage, in spite of his comments to the contrary. Any queries on my part would be deflected. He assumes my knowledge, but will not contribute to it until he is ready. As I have often done in the past, I suppressed my inquisitiveness and waited. This time it didn't take long.

During an evening lull in our mutual schedules, we were sitting in our respective chairs, inhaling and sipping a sumptuous cognac. Holmes's pipe had gone out and he impatiently rattled through the daily papers. I was scanning yet another medical journal.

"What twaddle!" he grumbled. "Your literary agent goes too far, Watson. A full page advertisement for the Spiritualist Society sponsored by Conan Doyle and several of his associates. What total nonsense."

"It may not all be nonsense, Holmes. You know, it occurs to me that after all the time we have been together, I still know nothing of your religious beliefs."

"Nor do I, Watson, nor do I."

"Surely, you have some thoughts on the subject. I follow the Anglican tradition but not very devoutly. What about you?"

"Let's just say I am an agnostic. I am a man of science. Hard facts, observable data, logical progressions. I have little patience for the ineffable."

"Don't you wonder how the world came about?"

"All right, call me a Deist. Some intelligence kicked off the universe, but then left us all on our own to muddle along. No ongoing intervention. No further involvement or intercession by an omniscient and loving being. How else to explain the hash this world is in? Wars, oppression, sickness, accidents, natural and unnatural disasters, hatred, abounding crime."

"Let me remind you that those criminals and sicknesses have allowed you and me to make a substantial living."

"I am well aware of it, and highly uncomfortable."

"I find it very strange that someone who professes to be godless has been so frequently involved with religion and institutions of belief. Recall your work for the Vatican, your time in Tibet, your services to the Archbishop of Canterbury, the Jewish community, Hinduism, Buddhism, Islam, and most recently the Coptic Orthodox Church."

"In matters of fact, not matters of faith."

I thought I saw my opportunity. Had I caught him in an expansive mood? "Just what was involved in the case of the two Coptic Patriarchs. You never told me. Was the outcome successful?"

"As successful as such things can be."

"Enlighten me!"

"To what extent are you familiar with the Coptic Orthodox Church?" he asked.

"Not at all."

"Then a few facts to provide background: The Coptic language is an outgrowth of ancient Egyptian, using Greek letters. It differs from Arabic and is still in general use throughout churches in Egypt, Africa, and other countries. Incidentally, there is a small Coptic community here in England that shares a Presbyterian church building.

"The Coptic Church is one of several Orthodox Christian rites and traces its origins to St. Mark, close to two-thousand years ago. It is officially known as the Coptic Orthodox Church of Alexandria, although today it is based in Cairo. It is not to be confused with the Greek Orthodox Church. Estimates differ on the population of the Church, but it numbers in the hundreds of thousands, mostly in Egypt.

"The Church is led by a Patriarch who is also known as a Pope. The current Pope is Cyril V, the one-hundred-twelfth person to hold that title. He was born in 1831. He rose to the Patriarchate from his position as Abbot of a large monastery. He took office in 1874. It's interesting to note that the Coptic Church had its origins in monastic life and is heavily populated to this day by influential monks and monasteries. Thereby hangs our case."

Chapter II

I was almost sorry I had introduced the subject, but my curiosity was still not assuaged. "Fine," I said, "You've identified the current official Patriarch. Who is the other?"

"As you may have suspected, a monastic usurper to the throne who adopted the name Pope Mark IX."

"Shouldn't that sort of issue be settled in an ecclesiastical court?"

"Oh, the issue was settled. The usurper is dead. Murdered here in London."

"Murdered? Here? How? When? By whom?" I could guess why.

"Gently, Watson, gently! All will be revealed."

"Holmes, don't condescend. It's irritating."

"Sorry, old chap. Let me give you some more data. The victim was an abbot from a major monastery school outside Alexandria who specialized in ecumenical relations. His name, incidentally, was indeed Mark or Makarios. A Greek and a graduate of Oxford, he wrote and published several treatises in which he proposed a consolidation of the Orthodox Churches – not just in Africa but worldwide. He developed a significant following among the concerned clergy and among international church authorities. Needless to say, none of this sat very well with Pope Cyril or the Islamic Egyptian authorities who felt threatened by the prospect of an enlarged Christian base."

"A-ha! So members of the Egyptian government assassinated him."

"So some thought. Scotland Yard and Mycroft were both of the same opinion, although Cyril was also a viable candidate for inflicting death. There was even a suggestion that the Roman Church might have had a hand in it. There was no shortage of theories. You know my feelings about theories. There was an extreme shortage of facts."

"What was he doing in London? Orthodox Churches are not major players in England."

"He had been invited as a guest speaker at an Ecumenical Conference sponsored by the Anglican Church. The Archbishop of Canterbury presided, and there was a veritable parade of international academic, religious, social. and governmental luminaries in attendance. Even the press paid attention. Mark was a star attraction by himself, and the little-known Coptic Church was a source of curiosity, especially when it became apparent that a Patriarchal coup was in progress."

"So how was his speech received?"

"He never got a chance to give it. On the morning of the second day, when he was scheduled to speak, one of the two monks who were with him as his assistants went up to the room where he was staying at the Archbishop's palace and discovered his fully-dressed body spread-eagled on the floor. His notes were scattered about and the table next to the bed was tumbled over. In shock, Josephus, the monk, immediately called for help. A vestryman happened to be in the immediate vicinity, and he in turn summoned the Archbishop's physician. The doctor, after a cursory examination, declared the Patriarch dead. There were no apparent signs of violence. Needless to say, this was kept out of the newspapers"

"The Archbishop of Canterbury had already left for the conference and was only informed of the death after he finished his introductory remarks for the morning. Greatly upset, he discovered to his chagrin that the vestryman had also notified the police. Mumbling some remarks to the audience that the next speaker was unfortunately discommoded, he rushed from the hall and back to the palace in time to meet Inspector Gregson arriving from the Yard. Suspicious and plodding by nature, Gregson was reluctant to accept any immediate diagnosis of natural causes, especially when he learned of the political intrigue that surrounded the Patriarch's visit. The body was transported quickly to the morgue and put through a thorough analysis. The verdict: Injected cyanide poisoning.

"Josephus and his monastic companion, Malachi, were subjected to intense questioning by the police, but they both proved to be intensely devoted to pseudo-Pope from their early days in the hermitage. That in itself did not absolve them of potential guilt, but Gregson was inclined to look elsewhere."

I listened to all of this and two thoughts crossed my mind: How did Mycroft Holmes become involved, and why did Sherlock Holmes take up the case? The answer to Question One was simple: The event showed signs of turning into an international incident and the Foreign Office, Home Office, and Scotland Yard were at full alert. Mycroft's attention in his true role of the British government was a given. Question Two took a little more explanation.

Holmes continued. "The morning after the Patriarch's demise, I was sitting here reading the descriptions of his death in the press when Mrs. Hudson tapped on the door and approached. She apologized but said there was tall, foreign gentleman in clerical garb who wished to see me most urgently. You, Watson, were out tending to the sick, the halt, and the lame.

"I bade my visitor be seated and forbore my usual identification parlor games. He was, as Mrs. Hudson observed, foreign, dark of visage, bearded, and intense. His wardrobe bore clerical characteristics, but unlike those one would normally see on English or European members of the cloth. He introduced himself as Father Nicholas Pendarius, Apostolic Vicar of the Coptic Orthodox Church of Alexandria, Egypt. I learned that he was essentially the Executive Officer and Chief Trouble Shooter for Pope Cyril V. He was in my rooms at the Patriarch's direction.

"The Pope was sorely distressed at the death of Patriarch Mark. On the one hand, he was relieved that the competition offered by Mark had come to an end. However, suspicion was growing rampant that his demise had been engineered by the minions of the Coptic Pope. This was patently untrue and intolerable to His Holiness. He and Father Pendarius had little confidence that the English police would find the true culprits and bring the issue to a satisfactory conclusion.

"It is little known that Pope Cyril and the Roman Pontiff are in frequent communication. The Vatican, he said, had been well served by me in the past and the Patriarch of Alexandria (in Cairo) was strongly advised to seek out my assistance. Father Pendarius, who was already in London as an observer of the Ecumenical Conference (and of Patriarch Mark) was commissioned to make this happen.

"I told the priest that Scotland Yard and the Home Office believed they had the situation well in hand. They would be unhappy if I were to interfere. I didn't mention Mycroft by name. I would take on the commission only if Pope Cyril could be identified as my client. Pendarius was reluctant but we finally agreed that he would act as my official patron on behalf of the Church and His Holiness. We would maintain daily contact. He would be staying on in London at the Archbishop's palace till the matter was solved, or at least closed.

"The Conference had already come to an unproductive conclusion with prayerful declarations of intent, but no concrete plans for action.

"When the cleric had left, I sent a message to Gregson and described the situation. Since he and the Yard had made no significant progress, he acquiesced to my involvement. I agreed to meet him in his office and review what scant evidence the police had uncovered. 'Scant' was the appropriate descriptor. The Morgue Director had uncovered a small wound caused by a hypodermic needle. He confirmed to the inspector that this was how the cyanide had been injected. The needle and vial of cyanide haven't been discovered.

"Gregson had collected the papers that had been scattered about Patriarch Mark's Spartan room. They turned out to be the text of the speech he was to deliver but never did. I asked to borrow the text and the inspector reluctantly agreed. It turned out the speech was a composite of the several treatises Patriarch Mark had issued on the subject of joining the various Orthodox Churches into a Universal Apostolic Christian Ministry.

"Gregson had insisted that the two monk-assistants remain in London. Plans were being put in place to return the Patriarch's body to Alexandria, and when it was released they could accompany it. A list of conference attendees had been assembled, and those who had not left the country were being questioned, so far with few results. The Anglican Prelate was mortified that some of his learned and reverend invitees were falling under suspicion, but he protested in vain."

"I left Gregson to his queries and sought out my brother. I met him in the Stranger's Room of the Diogenes Club. Mycroft was his usual semi-mobile self, but intensely sharp and intellectually acute as usual."

Chapter III

"As I told you, Watson, Her Majesty's government was not well and truly pleased with the situation on several counts:

"First, at the best of times, Egypt is an extremely sensitive environment. From 1882, under the Veiled Protectorate and Granville Doctrine, the small but effective British Army of Occupation has controlled Cairo, Alexandria, and surrounding areas. Essentially, the British Foreign Office *is* the Egyptian Government. Mycroft fully expects any number of explosive events to happen as discontent builds.

"Second, Islam and the Coptic Church are constantly at odds and there have been several near fatal incidents lately.

"Third, the Eastern Orthodox Churches trace their existence back close to two-thousand years. The Anglican Church has a great regard and concern for the safety and integrity of these institutions and their leadership.

"Finally, the murderous demise of a Coptic Patriarch within the precincts of London is bound to raise protests on a local, national, and international basis. Where were the vaunted security processes of the British Home Office? What was the role of the Foreign Office? Both the Prime Minister and the Queen have initiated queries and issued apologies on behalf of Her Majesty's government. Mycroft did not need any of this."

I looked at Holmes. "What," I asked, "was Mycroft's reaction to your involvement?"

"He was especially interested in the attitude of Pope Cyril V and the followers of Patriarch Mark. Was there a clash building there in which the Empire might unwillingly become involved? Who was this Father Pendarius? What was my obligation to this client?

"Yes, who is this Father Pendarius?"

"An excellent question. One I asked Mycroft to vigorously pursue, Watson. He is in contact with Lord Cromer, the Egyptian Consul-General and his office is investigating our clerical friend."

Holmes admitted that this case was not as easily wrapped up as he supposed when he asked me to be his surrogate in another adventure. The next morning, he invited Father Pendarius to join both of us at Baker Street to compare notes. The mysterious priest arrived and I was duly introduced.

Mrs. Hudson was awed by the priest and unbidden, brought in a plentiful supply of tea, scones, and other nourishment. Pendarius disappointed her by saying a fulsome thanks but he did not partake of English delicacies. I, on the other hand, did, and tucked in mightily.

The priest reported that as a member of the conference and Pope Cyril's deputy, he had been vigorously but respectfully questioned by Inspector Gregson. Nothing much came of it, although there was a lingering suspicion of the Pope's involvement – the very circumstance that Holmes had been commissioned to allay. Holmes mentioned the text of the Patriarch's speech, which he had reviewed. Pendarius said he was familiar with the treatises upon which the speech was based, but he had not seen the speech itself. On another subject, the poisonous needle was still missing – likely destroyed. Pendarius raised the question of how thoroughly the two monk-assistants had been questioned. He was suspicious of them, in spite of their sworn fealty to Patriarch Mark. We agreed to meet again tomorrow, or earlier if circumstances justified it.

When he had left, Holmes turned to me and asked, "What does your intuition say, Doctor?"

I confessed to a bothersome feeling of unrest. "You may simply accuse me of prejudice, but there is something about him that I find disturbing. Have you heard back from Mycroft?"

"Not yet. I'm hoping that he can cut through the usual bureaucratic nonsense and use his relationship with the Consul-General to our advantage. I also asked him to gather as much as he could about Pope Cyril. It's clear that the Patriarch Mark IX constituted a clear and present danger to the current Coptic hierarchy, beginning at the very top. My previous experiences with religious leaders have convinced me that they are as dangerous as many of the most despotic secular authorities."

"A very cynical – "

" – But highly justified opinion, my dear Watson. Recall the episode of Cardinal Tosca."

I held my peace. The morning progressed and Holmes turned his attention to several other cases that were on his agenda. I went about a foreshortened visitation schedule of some of my more seriously ill patients.

Later in the day, Inspector Gregson called by unannounced to tell us that Scotland Yard was releasing the body for a return trip to Alexandria. It was to be accompanied by a military guard and of course, the two monk assistants. The coffin would be turned over to the British Army of Occupation upon arrival. They would ensure that the rites of burial were strictly observed and that mourning did not disintegrate into demonstrations. At the moment, Patriarch Mark's followers were headless, but that condition would not last long. Already, there were several contenders who sought to fill his place. A stream of monastics were jockeying for positions. Meanwhile in Cairo, Cyril V and his hierarchy were bracing for potential repercussions. The Coptic situation was indeed volatile.

Chapter IV

In the early evening, Holmes, Gregson, and I were summoned by Mycroft Holmes. Father Pendarius was also invited, but we were told by the staff at the Anglican Archbishop's Palace that he was nowhere to be found and that his room had been emptied. Clearly suspicious! Mycroft, in his usual fashion, would shed no light on our requests for information until we were ensconced once again in the Diogenes Stranger's Room.

Sherlock Holmes was not the only brother gifted with a sense of the dramatic. When we had each selected a snifter and poured a measure of excellent cognac, Mycroft cleared his throat and announced, "Gentlemen, we have been duped. I have been in contact with Colonel Bradstreet of British Intelligence in Cairo. Father Nicholas Pendarius does indeed exist and is the Pope's Executive Officer, but he is short, portly, and in his early sixties with a flowing grey beard. He lives with His Holiness in the Patriarchal Palace at Saint Mark's Coptic Orthodox Cathedral. He has not left Cairo in the last six months. Our now-missing friend is no doubt a cleverly disguised fraud. We don't know where he is or what he currently looks like."

"Do we know who he is?" Gregson asked. "Why did he contact you, Mr. Holmes, and secure your services?"

"Bradstreet's best estimate is that he is a paid assassin who goes by the name of Ali, but there are several other possibilities. As to your other question, we believe he was engaging in a strategic coverup to deflect any possible suspicion away from him. If you need a disguise, who better to have on your side than Sherlock Holmes? Which brings me to the next topic.

"The Foreign Office, Egyptian Consul-General, and the Occupation Army Intelligence Department all fear for the continued welfare of Pope

Cyril. So, too, does the authentic Father Pendarius. Sherlock, they want you to pursue this Ali – or whomever he is. Take him out of commission, and find out who the master plotter is who triggered Patriarch Mark's death. The consensus is that the assassin's work is not yet finished. How soon can you leave for Cairo?"

Holmes snorted. "Aren't we being a bit presumptuous? You and the government (who may be the same thing) wish to tear me away from my practice and current obligations to deal with an unsubstantiated suspicion. I'm certain there are native detectives in Egypt who are as well or better suited for the assignment. They also have the advantage of familiarity."

"Likely true, but none have the confidence of Her Majesty and her Prime Minister, both of whom strongly wish to avoid any religious disturbance in Egypt. If you wish, I can have the Prime Minister relay his desires."

I intervened. "Has anyone approached His Holiness on this matter?"

Mycroft replied, "Pope Cyril has been made aware of the situation by the real Father Pendarius and has shown concern for the stability of the Church, but not much for his own personal welfare. He is aging and may have a somewhat fatalistic view of the whole affair – a fatalism that is unshared by his hierarchy. He is quite popular with them – especially since he has consistently resisted secular government interference in the affairs of the Church. That resistance, however, hasn't made him as popular with the politicians, both British and Egyptian."

Gregson spoke up. "That may be a good reason for assassination."

Mycroft gave Gregson a cold, piercing stare. "That is not how Her Majesty's government behaves."

Holmes turned to me and asked, "Watson, are you of a mind to look upon the Sphinx?"

"Give me time to settle my affairs."

He turned to his brother and said. "I'm reluctant, but you can tell the Prime Minister that he need not stir."

It turned out that we would be accompanied on our voyage by the casket containing the remains of Patriarch Mark IX. A military guard, as well as his monastic retinue, would also be in attendance. Once in Egypt, an elaborate funeral would be carried out at Saint Mark's Coptic Orthodox Cathedral as directed by the Pope. His political sense, no doubt, was in play.

Chapter V

Egypt

Our shipboard journey was largely uneventful. Nevertheless, I kept checking the passengers and crew on the outside chance that our adversary Ali might also be on board, No such luck. As Holmes pointed out, it was unlikely I would even recognize him since he would certainly be heavily disguised. If, as we supposed, he had returned to Egypt, he'd probably taken an earlier voyage.

We landed at the bustling port of Alexandria and promptly secured a *felucca* to sail south to Cairo on the north-flowing Nile. We took rooms at the Shepheard's Hotel, long famed for its luxurious accommodations, as well as being a highly popular watering hole for the British occupiers. In spite of my many journeys, I'm not a good sailor, perhaps a holdover from my overseas tour of duty with the Army. In any event, I welcomed being on dry land and seized the opportunity for a good night's sleep for the first time in several days. We had an appointment for breakfast with Colonel Bradstreet of British Intelligence.

Bradstreet was a martial archetype right out of the pages of *The Army Times*. From his glistening shoes to his bristling moustache, spit-and-polish prevailed. One could almost cut ones' self on the creases of his uniform trousers. Even his swagger stick gleamed. Both Holmes and I were still suffering from the effects of our African sea trek and presented a rather sorry visual alternative to this military paragon. He was accompanied by an equally resplendent subaltern, Lieutenant Symonds. They took up places at our table and sat with precise military posture. I wondered what their version of "At ease!" would be like. I was not to find out.

"Mr. Holmes, Doctor Watson, welcome to Cairo. Deuced irritating, this assassination of the Coptic hierarch. Our plates are already full with threats and pressures. The Sudanese are at it again and Ethiopia is another hotbed. We're a small unit and ill-equipped to deal with ecclesiastic intrigues. By the way, this isn't our first encounter with the infamous Ali."

Holmes interrupted. "You are convinced that Ali is our culprit?"

Symonds responded. "Oh yes, this one has his handprints all over it. Cyanide is one of his favorite tools. Actually more of a woman's weapon, but who knows with the Sayeedi. They'll do anything."

Clearly the lieutenant's prejudices were showing.

Bradstreet continued, "You should also know that a new Patriarch has been chosen to replace the deceased Mark IX. His name is Eusebius and he is a monastic firebrand. He, too, supports the idea of combining the several Orthodox sects in Egypt and the Mediterranean.

"The funeral is scheduled for tomorrow at ten at the Cathedral here in Cairo. Eusebius will celebrate the Divine Liturgy, a quite elaborate ceremony with many participants. The Pope will preside. The Consul-General has elected not to attend. We will be in attendance, representing the British government. By we, I include you two."

Holmes replied, "We shall be there. In the meantime, we would like to meet with the true Father Pendarius. We can also examine the Cathedral at the same time." He turned to Symonds. "Can that be arranged?"

The lieutenant wasn't going to renege in front of his commander, even though it was apparent he wasn't pleased with the assignment. This whole affair was quite distasteful to him. "I'll see to it."

We finished a hearty Shepheard's breakfast and retired to our rooms to improve our presentability. A bit later, we were told that Father Pendarius had invited Holmes and me to lunch at the Patriarchal Palace. Symonds would accompany us. At eleven-thirty he arrived, resplendent in uniform in a newly developed armored motor-car, a Daimler Phoenix. So much for a subtle entrance. Clearly the Army of Occupation took their image quite seriously. Fortunately, the ride to the Azbakeya district was a short one. The Palace entrance was close to the Cathedral's center. The lieutenant left the car in a prominent spot, British Army markings clearly visible.

A monk greeted us and bade us follow him to a private room where Father Pendarius awaited us. He was just as Mycroft described – short, portly, and in his early sixties with a flowing grey beard – a total contrast to the pretender we encountered in London.

"God's blessings on you, gentlemen. Welcome! I am Father Nicholas Pendarius, Apostolic Vicar of the Coptic Orthodox Church of Alexandria, although we are based here in Cairo. That is always a source of confusion to non-members of our Church. You might characterize me as His Holiness' Executive Officer."

We introduced ourselves.

"I understand that you have travelled all the way from London to investigate the tragic murder of Patriarch Mark IX. A shameful thing. Pope Cyril and the Patriarch did not always see eye to eye, but we all serve the same Lord and profess the same faith. I stand ready to assist in any way I can, but first let me introduce you to some Coptic hospitality. Brother Athanasios, you may serve lunch."

We were provided with a salad and wonderful lamb dish which I was hard pressed to further identify, along with a splendid wine which also escaped my oenological skills. Father Pendarius took the time to relate some of the history of the Coptic faith, much of which I was now familiar with. He spoke glowingly of Pope Cyril and the reforms and enhancements he had already made and was still introducing. Clearly, he was highly dedicated to His Holiness.

Holmes asked him to describe the next day's ceremonies. We were told that a session of mourning would be carried out this evening to be followed tomorrow by the Divine Liturgy. Patriarch Eusebius, Mark's successor, would be the celebrant, assisted by a corps of bishops and priests. Pendarius would be one of them. The Pope would preside from his sacerdotal throne.

The liturgy begins with the vestiture of the celebrant who then chooses the bread and wine to be used in the main ritual. A traditional offertory and consecration follows and concludes with a distribution of communion to the participants. Hymns in Coptic and Egyptian would be chanted throughout. A short homily by Eusebius and brief comments by His Holiness. The coffin, which had occupied the lower altar, would then be removed by ecclesiastical pall bearers and transported to a final burial site in Alexandria. All told, an impressive ceremony.

The priest offered a tour of the Cathedral, which Holmes eagerly accepted. Over time, the Churches have been destroyed, razed, and rebuilt several times, both in Alexandria and Cairo. The current version is endowed with beautiful vaulted ceilings, an extensive array of altars (side and central) and a large seating area for the faithful. Murals of saints adorn the walls and ceilings. Holmes took a short walking tour of the sacristies where preparation for the rituals take place.

Finally, Father Pendarius pled pressure of business – attendance on the Pope and preparation for the funeral services – and left us by the Cathedral entrance. I had to control my laughter as Symonds struggled to start the Daimler in front of a gathering crowd.

Chapter VI

Later in the evening after dinner, Colonel Bradstreet rejoined us to discuss tomorrow's proceedings. The British Army would be on display both in and outside the venue. It was hoped that there would be no demonstrations, but the Consul-General wanted to take no chances. "These Egyptians can be quite emotional, don't you know."

We were assigned to places in one of the forward pews while soldiers were to take up positions none too subtly by all of the doors. Credentials were to be checked. That alone might trigger disturbances. Neither Holmes nor I were particularly comfortable with this show of British Occupation. We invited Bradshaw to join us in a whisky in one of the Shepheard's bars, which he gladly accepted, and proceeded to regale us with a litany of problems he and his organization faced daily. "A policeman's lot is not a happy one."

Wonder of wonders, Holmes shared his thinking and plans with us. He is not usually so forthcoming. He was convinced that Ali would stage another attack. What wasn't clear was who the target would be. Could it be the Pope, presiding on his throne? Or might it be Eusebius, the current usurper following in Mark IX's footsteps?

"Flexibility is the watchword, gentlemen. I propose to intercept our adversary. Unfortunately, he knows me, so I'll have to change my appearance: A bearded, grey-haired cleric in a sea of bearded, grey-haired clerics."

He withdrew and left me to my thoughts.

Next morning, we stood in the hotel lobby awaiting Bradstreet and Symonds. True to his word, Holmes looked the part of a Coptic priest in a dark cassock and headpiece. A substantial beard shrouded his lower face. The Daimler Phoenix pulled up with the subaltern at the wheel and Bradstreet in the rear, both militarily resplendent. Holmes carried a medium sized satchel and joined Bradstreet in the back seat. I sat up front with the driver. A group of horse-drawn wagons transporting the Cathedral guardians had left earlier. Once again, the trip to the Church was short, but we were hampered by a large crowd descending on the property. It was clear that there would be intense interest in the Liturgy and the coffin, which had been brought in and surrounded by guards and clergy. Bishops, priests, monks, and several Patriarchs milled about in the sanctuary. The Pope would arrive at the last minute accompanied by Pendarius, a bishop or two, and several server monks.

The choir began a lengthy series of dirges and chants and the congregation began to settle in. The liturgical participants headed for the sacristies to don their robes except for Eusebius. He would publicly take on his vestments as the first step prior to the Liturgy. The Pope arrived.

Bradstreet looked around and stared at me. "Where is Holmes?" he mouthed. I shrugged. The Colonel was much annoyed. He was about to send Symonds on a search mission but changed his mind as the event began. A procession emerged from the sacristies and formed at the foot of the high altar. Eusebius, clad in a plain cassock, came last and moved to the center of the group. Two tall monks wearing long surplices advanced on him carrying ornate vestments. As the first monk approached the Patriarch, he was set upon by his companion and thrown to the ground. A glass and metal object clattered to the floor.

The second monk, Holmes, grabbed the hypodermic needle while holding on to his adversary. Two soldiers rushed to his assistance. The true

Pendarius, two bishops, and several soldiers formed a protective cordon around the Pope. Bradstreet ran up to the altar and roughly put handcuffs on the monk. "Ali-ben-Gaza, you are under arrest for the attempted murder of Patriarch Eusebius the First. Come along quietly."

It was indeed our London pretender. Holmes handed over the hypodermic and stepped away.

Chaos briefly ruled. Pope Cyril rose from his throne and looked over the congregation as Ali was dragged out. He said, "We are here to honor the memory of one of God's dearly beloved servants. Let us duly proceed with that sacred mission." He nodded at Eusebius, who had regained his composure. Holmes was still standing by the patriarch. He picked up the vestments and handed them to a bishop. They proceeded with the vesting ceremony and the Divine Liturgy began.

Bradstreet and Symonds took Ali into custody in the Daimler, leaving Holmes and me stranded at the Church. When we finally found a cab to take us back to the hotel, he shed his disguise and we descended upon the bar. Even though it was still midday, we felt the need for a calming libation. We'd had enough stimulation already. I mentioned that before we left Cairo, I would like to travel to Giza and look on the Sphinx and the Pyramids. Holmes said that we would, but that he had one more task to carry out before we could do that.

Bradstreet came by, thanked Holmes and me, and confirmed that the assassin was indeed Ali, in spite of his changed appearance. True to the traditions of his sordid profession, he refused to talk, but the Colonel was convinced it was just a matter of time before he confessed fully.

Epilogue

The Egyptian sun had risen fully on another heat-filled day and, after finishing breakfast, Holmes and I took another cab back to the Patriarchal Palace. Unannounced, we asked to speak with Father Pendarius. We were told that he was with His Holiness but could see us shortly. When he did arrive, he said that Pope Cyril wished to speak with us and would we come with him right away. We entered the surprisingly sparse papal apartment, bowed, and kissed the Pope's ring. He gestured for us to be seated, reached into a drawer, and drew out a pair of silver crosses which he blessed and then passed on to each of us.

"I cannot tell you how grateful I am for ridding us of this terrible scourge. Has he admitted to his crimes?"

"No, Your Holiness. I suspect that he will not."

"Do you have any suspicions as to what his motivations were?"

"Greed. He was acting for someone who was willing to pay dearly for his services."

"Who is that person?"

"I'm sorry, Your Holiness, but it would only be idle speculation on my part."

"I hope the British police will adequately deal with him."

"They can be most severe with murderers."

"You are probably aware that Mark, and now Eusebius, have been at philosophical odds with me for quite some time, but I did not wish them harm."

"We are sure that is the case."

"Well, let me wish you Godspeed on your journey home, and thank you both once again for your service to the Lord."

"Farewell, your Holiness."

As we walked away from the Papal Offices, Father Pendarius paused and stared at us.

"You know, don't you?"

"That you hired Ali?" I replied, "We strongly suspected."

"What do you plan to do?"

Holmes replied, "The question is – what do you plan to do?"

"I could not let them destroy the Coptic Church."

"Then we hope you have not destroyed yourself."

"You know that I am preoccupied with this case of the two Coptic Patriarchs, which should come to a head to-day."

– Sherlock Holmes
"The Adventure of the Retired Colourman"

The Adventure of the Conk-Singleton Forgery
by Arthur Hall

Once more searching amongst my notes recording the extraordinary adventures of my friend Mr. Sherlock Holmes at the request of my publisher, I have discovered a case so far untold to the general public. On approaching him, I was given grudging permission to relate it to the best of my recollection.

He had, in fact, given the matter some thought before the affair I later entitled "The Six Napoleons" was brought to our attention by Inspector Lestrade and, when that was settled, Holmes lost no time in resorting to a study of the letter which we had previously received.

"The writer was rather vague, Watson. I have learned from *Burke's Peerage* that Mr. Edward Conk-Singleton is the only son of Lord Andersley, and deduced from his mention of forgery that he has been defrauded in some way, but that is all." He paused for an instant, and then added, "Apart, that is, from my surprise at his use of such poor quality writing-paper and envelope, which suggests that he is no longer as prosperous as formerly."

I placed my empty coffee cup to one side with my used plate. "Have you now replied to him?"

"I did so when Lestrade presented us with the affair that we concluded yesterday, informing Mr. Conk-Singleton that I would give his problem my attention at the first opportunity. Now that I'm able to do so, I have sent him a telegram. There has been no reply, so I presume that he has agreed with my suggestion that he should visit us in about – " He took out his pocket-watch and glanced at it. " – ten minutes from now."

Holmes immediately called for Mrs. Hudson, who appeared promptly to take away the remains of our breakfasts. I sought out my notebook and ensured that my pencil was sharp, wondering whether our visitor would conform to the aristocratic image that I had formed in my mind.

We had settled in our chairs and almost finished our first cigarettes of the day when the doorbell rang and our landlady answered. Holmes and I exchanged puzzled glances as we overheard her tone, which was remarkably similar to that reserved for Wiggins and the Baker Street Irregulars.

"He is five minutes late," Holmes observed.

For a moment there was silence, save for the rattle of a passing four-wheeler outside. Then I heard a heavy tread upon the stairs. Holmes and I turned towards the door as it opened to admit our client, who was immediately announced in disapproving tones by Mrs. Hudson.

Holmes stared at the man in silence for an instant, as our landlady retreated.

"Mr. Conk-Singleton," he said, rising. "Do come in and make yourself comfortable. I am Sherlock Holmes, and this is Doctor John Watson, whose assistance I have found to be invaluable and in whom you may confide as you would in me."

After we had shaken hands, I studied the fellow as he seated himself. He was of average height and the exact opposite of the sort of man I had expected. His hair and beard were over-long, not tended for some time and, together with his worn pea-coat, this gave him a Bohemian look.

"Before we begin," Holmes said, "allow me to call for some tea, or coffee if you prefer."

Our visitor held up a hand. "No, not for me, thank you, Mr. Holmes. I am anxious to lay the facts of my case before you and return to my work."

"That would be the portrait or landscape you are in the midst of creating. Very well then, let us proceed."

Mr. Conk-Singleton regarded Holmes with an astonished stare. "How could you know that? What do you know of me?"

"Only what my works of reference tell me – that you are the son of Lord Andersley."

"I would rather be known for my art than for my heritage. How did you conclude that I'm an artist? Has my father been here?"

This was evidently a matter of concern to him, for red patches had appeared on both his cheeks.

Holmes smiled faintly, and kept his voice to an even tone.

"I have never had the pleasure of making your father's acquaintance. As for my identification of your profession, when I see that your fingernails – and indeed, your boots – are stained with paint of various colours and that you have – forgive me – adopted the appearance of one who lives an unorthodox existence, what else am I to deduce?"

"Oh yes, I see. It was quite simple, really."

Holmes scowled, as I had known him do before when, as he saw it, his skills had been belittled.

"A further observation would be, perhaps, that your father has likely disinherited you, and there is no mystery about that also. The effect that the mention of his name produced told me of your anger or disapproval of him, and your apparel would undoubtedly be of finer quality had he been kindly disposed to your chosen way of living."

A parade of expressions crossed our client's face, and for some moments I expected him to explode into a rage. As it was he became suddenly much calmer, and when he next spoke it was in a quite normal manner.

"I see that your reputation is well earned, Mr. Holmes."

"Perhaps you could describe to us the nature of your difficulty," I said, with my notebook ready, to break the short silence that had ensued.

"Your letter mentioned forgery, I think," Holmes reminded him.

Our client nodded. "I have been puzzled by it, these five weeks past. It is a strange situation, and I can see no purpose or reason in it."

"Pray begin at the beginning," Holmes leaned forward in his chair, "omitting not the smallest detail."

"It has been almost a year now," Mr. Conk-Singleton reflected, "since I was obliged to leave my father's house, I stayed for short periods with various friends, and eventually secured accommodation in Stepney, and found myself an attic studio in nearby Bethnal Green. For some months I was able to support myself by painting miniature portraits, usually of the children of clients met through acquaintances or in taverns frequented by local artists, actors, and the like. All was proceeding well, although I had to miss a meal or two, until the day I was approached by a woman called Marie Dubois."

"She visited you at your studio?" asked Holmes.

"She did. One afternoon I turned from my easel to find her standing there. I was quite surprised, as I'm used to complete privacy as I work, but she closed the door after her and said at once that she wished to commission me to paint her portrait."

"Did she indicate that she had been recommended?"

Our client shook his head. "Now that you mention it, Mr. Holmes, I recall that she avoided answering when I asked how she knew of me. I suppose I had become excited at the prospect that I was becoming well-known."

"Undoubtedly. Did you then begin this venture?"

"I agreed immediately. She came to me three times weekly until the painting attained its present state, which is near completion."

"You will have no difficulty then, in describing her?"

"None whatsoever. She is of above-average height, I would say, with a rather dark complexion and very black hair. She has a French way of speaking our language of course, but I quickly became used to it, although I do not speak that tongue and we were able to converse quite easily. I learned that she is originally from Marseilles, but now lives in Paris and is in England to visit a number of friends."

"What subsequently occurred to cause you to be discontented with this situation?"

"It was about seven weeks ago that I finished her image on the canvas and began on the background," he said after taking a moment for recollection. "She had described to me a scene of surrounding trees and a forest fence, and seemed pleased with my interpretation of her wishes.

"I should mention here perhaps that when I first occupied the studio it was in a filthy condition, and I was obliged to clean it thoroughly. Also, if I say it myself, I am meticulous in clearing up at the end of each day, so it was strange indeed that I should arrive one morning to find paint drops spilled upon the floorboards and one of my easels moved out of place. At first I thought it was my own absent-mindedness, but when this occurred subsequently, I knew that someone was gaining entry overnight."

Holmes interest deepened suddenly. I recognised the glitter in his eyes from of old.

"Did these signs appear randomly, or immediately after painting a particular person?"

"That is what I was about to say, Mr. Holmes – the indications were present only after the visits of Miss Dubois."

"Did you mention them to her?"

"No, as I did not see how she could be concerned."

"Doubtless you remained in your studio overnight subsequently, to get to the truth of the matter."

"Of course, I began to do this. With the lights extinguished I forced myself to stay awake until dawn following the day of her next departure, but to no avail."

"Did you inform the lady of your intention to keep watch?"

"Not that I recall, but it is possible that I may have mentioned it."

Holmes considered for a moment. "Did her behaviour subsequently change?"

"It did, for it was then that she began to miss appointments. When next I saw her I asked, in an indirect manner, why her attendances had become irregular, rather than according to the thrice weekly arrangement we had formerly, and she replied that this was because only the background scene of the portrait was still unfinished and that did not require her presence. She now called in, she said, only to view the progress of the painting, so that she could anticipate its delivery."

"Have these night visits continued since then?" I asked, when I saw that Holmes had paused for reflection.

"They have, Doctor, but now I have no way of knowing when to expect them."

"And you have found no alteration to your work?"

"None."

Holmes abandoned his brief reverie. "Mr. Conk-Singleton, have you, yourself, formed any theory which could explain these happenings?"

Our client nodded vigorously. "The misplaced easel and the spots of paint can mean only one thing. Someone is gaining entry to my studio and copying my work! I cannot speculate as to why because, God knows, I am far from famous, but this unfinished portrait is being forged progressively. I would like you gentlemen to keep a closer watch on my studio, nightly if possible, since there are two of you, and apprehend the culprit. Until now I have not approached the official force because I felt that my case would be taken lightly, but if we were able to present the forger to them, then they could hardly fail to proceed."

"Quite so," Holmes confirmed. "Your letter indicated that your studio is in Bethnel Green."

"It is. At 37 Kirkfield Road."

"How would you describe it?"

"It is one long room only, with a window overlooking the street and a large skylight at the opposite end. There is one room below, which was occupied by the late owner, and both premises are accessible only by the single staircase."

"Excellent. And, of course, you were able to see no indications of forced entry following the night visits?"

"That puzzled me also, but there were none."

"Have there been any other unusual occurrences, either in your building or nearby, since you were approached with the commission to portray Miss Dubois on canvas?"

"Only the suicide of the owner who lived below, Mr. Abel Leech. But this could have no connection, surely."

Holmes straightened himself in his chair, his face impassive. "That has yet to be established, I think. As far as you know, was the official force satisfied that Mr. Leech's death was by his own hand?"

"I was interviewed, because of the close proximity of my studio to the dead man's rooms, by Inspector Gregson of Scotland Yard. He seemed certain that the circumstances were as they appeared."

"How did Mr. Leech bring about his own demise?"

"I was told that he hanged himself in his sitting room."

"Well," said Holmes as he rose from his chair, "you have certainly brought a curious situation to our attention, Mr. Conk-Singleton. Tell me, are you returning to your studio now?"

"Not for several hours. I have to visit a friend concerning another matter."

"You would have no objection, then, to our visiting Mr. Leech's rooms in your absence?"

Our client looked totally surprised. "Of course not, but I cannot see how that will advance your investigation. Also, I am unsure as to how to obtain the key."

"Pray have no concern on those scores, but I think it would be just as well if you prolonged the completion of your work for the moment. I think that I can promise you that you will hear from us before very long. And now, sir, I will bid you good day. Doctor Watson will show you out."

As often happens, our client appeared bewildered at this rather sudden dismissal, but I was able to reassure him concerning Holmes's methods as we descended the stairs.

"A somewhat peculiar fellow," Holmes said as I returned to our sitting room.

"I knew it, the instant I saw him."

"And what, pray, did you base your assessment upon?"

I glanced at him with surprise. "Really, Holmes – you of all people. Is it not obvious from his apparel? Brown boots in town? That is unconventional enough, I would have thought, but combined with dark grey trousers?"

A smile crept across Holmes's face. "As I have long maintained, Watson, we will make a detective out of you yet."

We arrived in Kirkfield Road shortly before mid-day. The hansom left us a short distance away at Holmes's request, and I realised that he wished our visit to pass unobserved as far as possible.

The building where Mr. Conk-Singleton employed his creative talents was not impressive. Like most of those adjacent to it, maintenance had been sadly neglected. As we approached, we saw that a money-lender plied his trade from next door, while a rather shabby pie-shop operated at the opposite side. Holmes pushed open a long-unpainted door and we stepped in to be confronted by a gloomy staircase. There were but two doors, one on our immediate left and one at the top of the stairs. Clearly, these premises had once been part of a much larger house, perhaps even connected to those now occupied by the money-lender.

The stairs were dusty and the walls peeling with the remains of dull olive-green paint. The fragrance from the pie-shop was not appealing. Holmes wrinkled his nose with distaste and produced his pick-lock, which quickly gained us entrance to Mr. Leech's rooms.

"Stay near the door for a moment, Watson. I see that Gregson and company and any number of others have probably ruined any chance there might have been of learning anything, but it is as well to be certain. The carpet has been replaced and the furniture put in order against the wall." He took a measuring tape from his pocket and ascertained the height of one of the three identical chairs. "The table is of sufficient weight to require several men to move it. Mr. Leech must, therefore, have stood upon a chair with the noose around his neck. Although the rope has been removed, the place of its attachment to the ceiling is obvious, since the heavy gas chandelier was taken down and, as you see, stored over there in the corner. The additional accommodation appears to consist of a tiny kitchen and a single bedroom, where I expect to find the final clue to confirm my theory. We will expand our search, I think."

The kitchen yielded nothing of interest. We entered the rather drab bedroom then, and Holmes looked around carefully before opening the wardrobe. He withdrew a threadbare suit and spread it upon the bed, measuring it while I watched.

"There is nothing more to be gained from remaining here. I now know what took place."

"What occurred here?"

"Mr. Abel Leech was murdered."

"Are you certain?" I asked, feeling foolish the moment the words left my mouth.

"Quite certain."

He said no more until we had left the rooms and re-locked the door. "Now, let us see what the studio will reveal to us."

We ascended the dull staircase and entered Mr. Conk-Singleton's studio, gaining admittance in the same manner. It was indeed as he had described it, with a window overlooking the street and a skylight situated at the opposite end of a long room. It didn't surprise me that the fellow was untidy in his habits, with brushes and blank canvases scattered indiscriminately, or that his cleaning of the place fell far short of his claim. Holmes spent a moment in absolute stillness, his eyes taking in every detail of the chamber. They came to rest on an easel bearing the portrait of a strikingly handsome woman, presumably she who had commissioned it.

"There, Watson – the paint splashes on the floor near the easel. Do you see? Notice that the colours are as used on the portrait, plus one that is different." He gazed at the painting for a little while before turning his attention to the bare floorboards near the door. "Here we have part of a footprint in the fine layer of dust. If our client wears the same boots when working here as he did in Baker Street, then there has indeed been an intruder, since this impression is of a quite different style." At that he proceeded to walk all around the room, but if he saw anything more of significance he didn't share it.

"Very well," he said at last. "We will now return to Baker Street to discover what Mrs. Hudson has in store for us. When luncheon is over, I think a visit to Scotland Yard will be in order."

I enjoyed my roast lamb with mint sauce immensely, but Holmes ate with indifference. This came as no surprise to me, as I knew that he thought of little else when occupied with a case. The instant that I pushed my empty dessert plate away, he leapt to his feet.

"I you have no objection, Watson, I think we will forego coffee. I'm anxious to find Gregson at his office, so the sooner we get to the Yard the better it will be."

"As you say." I rose from my seat and took up my hat and coat. He did likewise and in minutes we stood in Baker Street, his stick raised to summon a passing hansom.

On the way I tried several times to extract from him an explanation as to whatever he had concluded at 37 Kirkfield Road, but he wouldn't be drawn.

"A little patience, old fellow, and you and Gregson shall know all that I've discovered," was his only utterance before he began to silently observe the passing scene. We were fortunate to find that Inspector Gregson had returned only hours before from a burglary case in Mayfair.

The Scotland Yard man shook his flaxen head. "As I recall, Mr. Holmes, my investigation revealed that this Mr. Abel Leech had a most melancholy disposition, and so it came as no surprise to the few who knew him that he took his own life."

"I took careful measurements of his approximate height, by means of his clothing, plus the height of the chair that he would have been obliged to stand upon. Allowing for the height of the room, I estimate the length of rope required to hang this man to be no more than four feet."

Gregson reached across his desk to a stack of files that were presumably awaiting removal.

"It was, in fact, less than three," he said after quickly consulting the contents."

"Then the unfortunate Mr. Leech would have had to levitate, or jump into the air, in order to place the noose around his neck."

There was silence for a moment, and nothing except a murmur of conversation from the long corridor could be heard.

"I appear to be in error." Gregson's pallor was more bloodless even than usual. "You have seldom been wrong in your assistance in the past, Mr. Holmes, so I will re-open the investigation. Can you, perhaps, suggest a motive for this crime?"

"My current client is the occupier of the studio above the rooms of Mr. Leech. He has asked me to confirm his suspicions that an intruder has several times entered the studio with the intention of copying his work. I have yet to reach my conclusions, because I believe that there is far more involved here, but of one thing I am certain: Mr. Leech was killed to ensure his silence. It is probable that he observed the forger either arriving or leaving, and this tells me at once that more is involved than is at first apparent."

"Is the painting likely to be valuable, then?"

"Not at all. My client, Mr. Conk-Singleton, is something of an amateur artist who barely supports himself on his earnings, and the portrait has been specially commissioned by a woman presently visiting here from France."

"All of which has no connection to the murder of Mr. Leech" Gregson ventured, "unless your theory concerning the intruder is correct."

"Quite so. Doubtless things will become clearer as my investigation proceeds."

"I wish you well with it, Mr. Holmes. As I've said, the death of Abel Leech is now the subject of a murder enquiry, and I trust that you will share with us any information you unearth that could be of help. We'll pursue this until the truth becomes clear for, as you know, the files here at the Yard are never closed beforehand."

We returned to Baker Street with Holmes in a sombre mood. He said little as we spent two hours smoking in our sitting room before dinner, adopting a contemplative pose as I buried myself in the mid-day edition of *The Standard.* It was after we had eaten and I had poured the last cup from the coffee-pot that he stood up abruptly, gesturing that I should remain seated.

"Remain where you are, Watson. Enjoy the rest of your coffee. As for me, it is unlikely that I will be returning until late, so pray tell Mrs. Hudson that I will need nothing further."

"But Holmes!" I exclaimed as he put on his coat. "Where are you going? If I can be of service, I will be glad to accompany you."

"I am about to return to Kirkfield Road, in order to observe Mr. Conk-Singleton's studio until the early hours. If my suppositions are correct, our intruder will favour us with a further visit within the next few days. This will most likely happen when our client has left for his lodgings, but I cannot be sure. For tonight, I think it best that you stay here to receive any message that Gregson may send, although that doesn't preclude my having need of your assistance subsequently."

Before I could protest, Holmes had turned swiftly away, and I heard him descend the stairs before the door was closed noisily. I moved to the window to see which direction he took, but he procured a hansom immediately and was gone.

I saw nothing of Holmes until the following morning. At breakfast he informed me that his vigil had been cold but uneventful.

"I found a deep doorway almost opposite Mr. Conk-Singleton's studio. I knew that my concealment was adequate when he left his premises and passed within a few feet of me, quite unaware of my presence. From then on, apart from the regular appearance of a constable on his beat and two men so sodden with drink that they were unable to walk straight, I saw no one. I think, Watson, that I must spend another night or two in this manner before the forger of our client's work appears."

And so it proved to be. I spent the next three days reading accumulated medical journals that required my attention. As Holmes's nightly departure was immediately after dinner, I saw little of him during this time. I assumed that his watchfulness had been so far unrewarded, since he had mentioned nothing of it. Indeed, he had said very little at all.

Finally, I could stand the suspense no longer.

"Has there been any progress at Kirkfield Road?" I enquired as we finished our cheese-and-potato pie on the fourth evening.

"That was an excellent dinner," he said with unusual appreciation. "As for your question, the answer is that our adversaries must be becoming increasingly concerned about the delay in the portrait's completion. Every night that passes is therefore more likely than the last to produce a visit from our mysterious forger or Miss Dubois, or perhaps both of them. But I see that you are anxious for the thrill of the game, old friend. Very well, if it is convenient we will keep watch together tonight."

Holmes's anticipation was soon proven correct. We had stood, he in his ear-flapped travelling cap and ulster, in the doorway for some time when our client locked the premises and walked swiftly away. I heard a distant church clock chime the hour of nine o'clock when an unaccompanied woman appeared and was able to gain entry to the building at once. In the silence we heard her footfalls upon the stairs before the faint light of a candle shone from above.

"Evidently she, too, is proficient with locks," Holmes whispered. "Also she is living nearby, since no hansom or four-wheeler delivered her. Probably she took lodgings that are situated conveniently."

"We could enter the building now," I suggested. "She cannot escape."

"Indeed, there is no way that she could, but my intention is to follow her when she leaves. I wish to know the meaning of this portrait-copying, and why it was necessary to end a man's life to conceal the identities of the intruders. When I give this affair into Gregson's hands, it must not be incomplete."

"Holmes – the light has been extinguished!"

No sooner had the faint echo of my words died away than the woman reappeared. After locking the door she set off in the direction from which she had approached, and Holmes and I followed in the shadows. As the streets were empty, she apparently thought it unnecessary to ascertain that she walked them alone, for she turned her head not once as she crossed into a dark alley that took her into another thoroughfare from which she turned a corner before ascending the steps of an old house behind metal railings.

We stopped at the corner, using its concealment to observe her destination.

"Meredith Row," Holmes said quietly. "I have been here before."

When the woman had entered and the door had closed we approached the building, and I have no doubt that Holmes would have followed her directly, had not an indistinct figure emerged from behind a cluster of bushes growing in the front garden of a house across the street.

We both were still at once, and my hand closed upon my service revolver in my pocket.

"Good evening, Mr. Sherlock Holmes and Doctor Watson," The figure advanced, taking on the shape of a man as it stood briefly under a streetlamp. The voice was level and without inflexion or accent.

"Who are you, sir?" I enquired.

He took one step closer. "My name is Garside. My employer is your brother, on whose orders I have been maintaining a watch on this house. He anticipated that our paths would cross before long, and requests that you visit him in his office tomorrow morning. If you give your name to the attendant, you will be admitted at once."

"By what other name do you know my brother?" Holmes asked.

"His Christian name is 'Mycroft'." In the poor light, I saw the man smile. "Yes, I am genuine, Mr. Holmes."

Holmes nodded. "Good night then, Mr. Garside."

"Goodnight, gentlemen," he replied as we left.

We were in Whitehall before nine the next morning. Holmes had surprised me by making no reference to our encounter with Mr. Garside, other than to affirm my availability to accompany him.

"Doubtless we will kept waiting until my brother finds a spare moment," he remarked as we approached the building.

"Holmes, I'm at a loss to understand the connection between Mycroft and this woman, Marie Dubois."

"It isn't yet clear to me, but I have my suspicions. I do hope that we are about to learn something useful, rather than simply to be told not to interfere in some other affair in which she may be involved."

Holmes was wrong, at least, in his prediction of Mycroft's behaviour. The door was opened before us by a stern-looking man in a morning-suit.

"Good morning, gentlemen," he said. "You are expected. Please follow me." Before either of us could say a word, he strode away at a smart pace.

Holmes and I exchanged glances and complied, allowing ourselves to be led down dimly-lit corridors past busts and statues of former members of government. Near a junction with a much wider passage our guide came to an abrupt halt, knocking sharply on a door of panelled oak. On hearing an acknowledgement from within, he bowed and stood aside for us to enter.

The door closed behind us as the elder Holmes rose from behind a large and ornate desk. I barely had time to take in the tall windows and portrait-lined walls of the cavernous room before he spread his arms in greeting and gestured for us to each take a well-upholstered chair.

"Sherlock," he beamed, "and Doctor Watson. How glad I am to see that you found your way here. I told Garside, only yesterday, that it would not be long before our paths crossed."

As he offered us tea, which we both declined, I noticed that Mycroft had changed little since I saw him last. A little more portly, perhaps, and a few more grey hairs around his temples. His manner was exactly as I remembered.

"It is good to see you, Mycroft," Holmes replied, "but I am at a loss to understand why we are here."

"Ah, but of course you would be wondering, dear boy. Let me enlighten you immediately. My people have been watching that house in Kirkfield Road for some little time now, and when you were seen entering I knew at once that the artist fellow who works on the top floor had engaged you. What I need to know is in what capacity, exactly, and whether your activities will in any way interfere with an operation in progress conducted by Her Majesty's Government."

Holmes shrugged his shoulders. "All I can tell you is that the artist, Mr. Conk-Singleton, is having difficulty with an unknown intruder who is apparently copying a portrait on which he is currently working. I am to identify the forger, and my client will prosecute him. As to why this is taking place and by whom, these things I have yet to discover."

"I believe I can assist you with the answers to both those questions, and then you will see the wider application and importance of this. I can, of course, depend upon the absolute discretion of both you gentlemen?"

There followed a stony silence that lasted for but a few moments. Mycroft had asked us this question before, in this very room, with the same result. Holmes sat, statue-like, staring at his brother angrily.

"Yes, of course," Mycroft said then. I thought I saw a trace of embarrassment in his expression, but it could have been a trick of the light that filtered through the half-closed curtains. He leaned forward in his chair, as if wary of being overheard. "About two months ago, one of our clerks, Smith-Harrison, was discovered to have abused his position. He had apparently fallen into that old trap, gambling, and owed a great deal of money to a gaming house in the capital. In order to obtain the necessary funds for repayment, he divulged certain information to a woman who had approached him. We know not how this came to be, as yet. This was Margaret de la Roche, who you know as Marie Dubois. It was she that you were following last night."

"She is some sort of French agent?" I ventured.

"Precisely, Doctor, but not of their government. She is freelance and works internationally, and for the highest bidder. We have been aware for some time of a secret consortium of French arms manufacturers whose objective is to create an immense increase in their profits by initiating a war between their country and ours. Fortunately we have the situation monitored by a group of our people who have slowly infiltrated the inner circle of these rogue industrialists and will inform us as soon as their plan reaches critical proportions. We will then relay the information to Paris, and their government will hopefully put paid to the scheme."

The concept of men so inured to the sacredness of human life that they would destroy so much of it for no other purpose than to increase their own wealth appalled me, but I said nothing.

Holmes's face betrayed none of his feelings on the matter.

"Are we to know the nature of the stolen information," he asked.

Mycroft nodded. "A certain phrase was established, in order that our agents would be able to recognise each other, since they were sent out at different times. We are aware that Smith-Harrison divulged this to Mademoiselle de la Roche, or Dubois if you prefer – not that it will do him any good, since he has been dealt with and the money impounded."

"Why, I wonder, did this woman not immediately depart for France with the information, or pass it to an accomplice?"

"This woman is no amateur, Sherlock," Mycroft explained. "She has become conscious of our observation of her movements. Garside, or one of his colleagues, would report immediately any attempt to travel or to receive visitors who might convey what she has learned elsewhere. My people or Scotland Yard would act at once. In fact, this would have occurred before now, had not my superiors insisted that we stay our hands until we become certain that she is acting alone."

Holmes bowed his head in concentration. "I believe that she has already devised a method of sending this information to her employers," he said. "For why would such a woman as you describe choose a time when she was under close scrutiny by her adversaries to commission a virtually unknown artist to paint her portrait? I think it unlikely that Mr. Conk-Singleton is aware of it, but he is, in effect, the vehicle that she intends to use to complete her task."

"Something hidden in the portrait, then?" Mycroft enquired.

"Undoubtedly."

"But why are they, whoever they are, copying the picture in our client's studio?" I queried. "Or could it be that he is in error with that assumption?"

Mycroft gave a satisfied smile. "When there are two identical objects, or people for that matter, involved in such circumstances as these, the intention is invariably to substitute one for the other at some point in the proceedings. Would you not agree, Sherlock?"

"I had already reached that conclusion," Holmes confirmed. "It follows that the two portraits are not identical, but have been made to *seem* so, since the exercise is otherwise pointless. If we may be permitted to pursue our investigation unhindered, Mycroft, I think we may be able to settle this matter to our mutual satisfaction."

The elder Holmes leaned back in his chair and laced his fingers across his ample stomach. "It will do no harm, I suppose, to have a second line of enquiry into this affair. But take care, Sherlock, not to undermine in any way the progress of the official investigation. If you succeed in causing this woman, and any accomplice she may have, to be open to arrest, you will see that I am informed immediately, won't you?"

Our hansom was almost back at Baker Street when Holmes emerged from a silent reverie to direct the driver to halt near a Post Office.

"Have you telegraphed Inspector Gregson?" I asked him as he returned from a short absence.

He called for the cabby to drive on. "No, but we will have a visitor, likely this afternoon if it is convenient for him, to ascertain whether our surmise is correct, or if our client's portrait has been subjected to alteration."

"You wish to be certain that it is the forgery that contains the information, rather than the original?"

"Precisely. As I have mentioned before, Watson, one must be sure of the facts before attempting to build upon them."

It was, in fact, a good two hours after we had consumed a luncheon of roast beef with Yorkshire pudding and smoked several pipes that our doorbell rang.

"Ah, McMasters!" Holmes exclaimed, as Mrs. Hudson showed a small, shrew-like man in a top hat and rather worn suit into our sitting room.

"Always glad to be of service, Mr. Holmes," our visitor subserviently assured us.

After introducing me, Holmes explained: "McMasters was once the most successful art thief in the capital. When I finally secured his arrest, I discovered several extenuating circumstances which I will not elaborate upon now, but suffice it to say that my testimony caused the judge to take a more lenient view than he may have done otherwise."

"And very grateful for that I am too, sir," Mr. McMasters affirmed. "I now have a shop where I obtain and sell paintings legally, which brings in less money but leaves me without any fear of the law."

"I am very glad to hear of your redemption," I commented.

"Oh yes, it was that all right. And now, Mr. Holmes, how may I assist you today?"

"If you would be so kind as to accompany us to Bethnal Green, there is a portrait that I would like you to inspect. I would be obliged if you would reveal any irregularities or singular features to us."

"That should cause me no great difficulty, sir."

"Capital. It should not take long, I think."

"We do not know if Mr. Conk-Singleton will be in his studio, Holmes," I reminded him when we had procured a four-wheeler.

"If he was there earlier, then he will remain until we arrive," Holmes said as we turned a sharp corner. "I dispatched a telegram to him at the same time as I did so to McMasters."

I said little during the journey, listening instead to the conversation between Holmes and Mr. McMasters. I gathered that their connection was from the period shortly after my marriage, when I paid fewer visits to Baker Street for some time.

We alighted in Kirkfield Road and I paid the driver. The building appeared deserted, but I glanced up and saw our client, clad in a paint-stained smock, move past the window. Holmes opened the door and we took the stairs in single file. The door to the studio was flung open and Mr. Conk-Singleton looked down on us.

"Welcome, gentlemen. I trust you have made some advance in your investigation, Mr. Holmes?"

"You can be quite certain that we are entering the final chapters of it. Allow me to introduce Mr. McMasters, whom you will find to have much in common with yourself."

He went on to make the introduction and to explain the purpose of McMasters' presence.

Our client looked annoyed at first, and I supposed this was because he thought himself capable of detecting any alteration to his own work, but the advantage of a fresh pair of knowledgeable eyes must have occurred to him, for he led us further into the studio to where the portrait stood in near-completion.

"Please take care. You will observe that some of the paint is not yet dry."

Mr. McMasters gave him a quick glare of disgust, no doubt because such an elementary warning was unnecessary, and proceeded to turn his head this way and that while making little noises of approval and satisfaction. This continued while we watched in silence for about ten minutes, until he turned to us, smiling as he addressed Holmes.

"You need have no fears here, Mr. Holmes. The brush strokes are clear and consistent, the colours without variation. I would stake my reputation – no, my *life* – that no other hand save that of the artist has laid a brush to that canvas."

"Excellent. My thanks to you, McMasters. Perhaps you would care to accompany Doctor Watson downstairs, where he will call you a hansom to return you to your shop."

When this was done, I returned to the studio to find Holmes reporting to Mr. Conk-Singleton.

"I'm certain therefore," he said, "that a similar examination, applied to the forgery, will reveal to us the purpose of all this."

Our client nodded his head. "But how will we acquire the copy?"

"Is the genuine portrait now completed?"

"I have delayed finishing it, as you previously suggested, but this has become increasingly difficult as I worked upon it. As it is now, I could give it the final touches within an hour."

Holmes let his eyes wander around the room, looking thoughtful. I knew from of old that his mind was racing.

"Very well," he said at last. "The time has come to lay the hidden aspects of this case bare. Have you received any indication as to Miss Dubois' next visit?"

"Not at all. As I mentioned before, she now appears unannounced."

"Indeed. If you will follow my instructions exactly, I believe we can settle this soon."

"I will do as you direct, Mr. Holmes. I now have other commissions that I am anxious to begin to fulfil."

"Capital. When Miss Dubois next appears, I want you to confirm to her that the portrait is complete. Tell her also that it has not turned out as well as you hoped and you are disappointed. Accordingly, say that you intend to destroy it the following morning, and that she owes you nothing. I anticipate that she will be outraged of course, will entreat you to reconsider, and perhaps offer you an increased payment. If you wish to discover the truth of all this you must stand firm, because everything is dependent upon her leaving here without the portrait. The only other thing you must do is to wire me immediately before returning to your lodgings, to wait there until I send for you."

Mr. Conk-Singleton had looked dejected at the mention of the destruction of his work, but now his face brightened. "This I will do, whenever Miss Dubois chooses to make her final visit."

"We will be waiting to hear from you. Come, Watson. I see that a hansom has discharged its fare across the street."

The next five days occupied Holmes with a case that I have recorded and entitled "The Adventure of the Bishop's Nightmare", and which has been consigned to my dispatch box at Cox and Company until such time as Holmes consents to its release. I took little part in it because of several medical emergencies which confronted me in the meantime, but Holmes narrated the details at its conclusion. At the end of this time we were before a roaring fire in our sitting room, enjoying our after-dinner pipes, when the doorbell rang and Mrs. Hudson laid a yellow envelope before Holmes.

He tore the contents free of their covering and his expression lightened at once.

"At last! Watson, it is the expected wire from Mr. Conk-Singleton. By the time we reach his studio it will be fully dark, which will aid our purpose." He smiled. "It will be satisfying to reflect that I have solved two cases in one day."

At Holmes's direction, the cabby left us some distance from 37 Kirkfield Road. We stood, concealed by shadows, for fully five minutes before he was sure that the building was unobserved.

"I want to be certain," he explained, "not only that Garside or another of Mycroft's people are not nearby – they are probably be concentrating still on Meredith Row – but also that Miss Dubois and her associates haven't become suspicious. I've seen to it that Gregson has been informed, and I suppose that I'm duty-bound to disclose the outcome of this to my brother if all goes well."

At that we approached the building and gained entranced by his use of his pick-lock. I closed the door behind us with a faint echo and we ascended the stairs with care.

"No lights, Watson. We cannot risk even a candle," he whispered. "I trust you have your service revolver?"

"My hand is upon it at this moment," I replied quietly as we opened the door.

In the darkness the studio looked enormous. It was lit faintly by the light from the window and skylights, and the atmosphere was thick with the smell of paint and spirit. The raucous laughter of some passers-by reached us from the street and occasional hansoms or landaus were heard briefly, but otherwise we waited in silence.

Gradually the activity outside dwindled before ceasing altogether. Now only the distant chimes of the church clock broke into our separate thoughts. We had stood, unmoving, for almost three hours, when I felt Holmes grip my arm and lean close.

"They are here," he whispered. "Make no sound and remain still until they're within our grasp."

Then I heard what his keen ears had already discerned – a scrabbling and scratching as the lock to the outer door was turned, far more clumsily than when Holmes had opened it previously. There was an audible curse in a foreign language, and then cautious footfalls on the stairs.

The door opened to admit two figures, their shapes indistinct in the darkness. From the quick exchange in French, too fast for me to follow, although Holmes doubtless understood, it became apparent that they were a man and a woman. For a moment all was still, and then the man lit an oil lamp in the same instant that Holmes stepped sideways, barring their retreat.

"Good evening, Miss Dubois – or should I say *Mademoiselle de la Roche*?" They froze instantly, appearing shocked by our presence. "And you sir are, I think, Monsieur Jules Claudell, who is wanted by the French police for art theft and forgery."

The man recovered himself quickly, and placed the lamp on a side-table.

"And who are you, sir? An agent of the English police, I imagine."

His speech was so heavily accented that I found it hard to understand. Holmes, however, had no such difficulty.

"Not at all. My name is Sherlock Holmes."

"That name means nothing to me."

"Possibly not, but I see from the change in your companion's expression that she recognises it."

Miss Dubois launched into a tirade of rapid French and Monsieur Claudell inclined his head to listen. She was evidently explaining to him with whom they were dealing, for he brushed his hand across his short beard in a nervous gesture.

"So, but we are caught, all the same." He reached slowly into the case he carried, and I produced my service revolver at once.

"Thank you, Watson," Holmes responded. "I would be obliged, Monsieur Claudell, if you would refrain from extracting that paint-knife from your bag. I'm sure you are as adept at throwing it as you would be if it were a weapon designed for that purpose, and I have no desire to be used as a pin-cushion."

The Frenchman dropped the bag to the floor.

"What do you want with us?" Miss Dubois asked in an affronted manner. "We have committed no crime that you can prove, and you have no authority to detain us."

Holmes raised his eyebrows. "If you do not consider art forgery a crime, possibly because neither the artist nor his work are famous, you will certainly acknowledge that murder falls within that description. As for my authority, it is no more than that of an ordinary law-abiding citizen, but I think it's time that we summoned the official force regarding these matters. Watson, pray be so kind as to pass me your revolver."

I did this cautiously, since this action provided our prisoners with a momentary opportunity to gain the upper hand. They made no such attempt however, and Holmes pointed the weapon in their direction as he reached into his pocket without averting his eyes.

"Here is a police whistle, Watson. I would be obliged if you would go down into the street and use it. Unless I'm much mistaken, I believe that you will find that Inspector Gregson and one or two constables are close at hand."

I complied instantly, and reflected that Holmes must have warned Gregson of the anticipated situation, since he and two uniformed police officers appeared almost at once from the shadows further along the street. In the studio, nothing further had occurred.

"Ah, Gregson!" Holmes exclaimed. "These are the two I mentioned in my wire. Whether one or both of them murdered Mr. Abel Leech I am uncertain, but you will doubtless be able to ascertain the truth of it when they are in custody."

"Thank you, Mr. Holmes," the Scotland Yard man replied as he looked the prisoners over. "It will be good to close the file on this matter. It never sits well with me to leave loose ends." He gestured to one of his companions. "Take them out, Noakes."

The constables had almost reached the door with their charges, when Holmes turned suddenly, as if he had recalled an unsettled aspect of the case.

"One moment!" He addressed the prisoners once more, after retrieving Monsieur Claudell's portrait from the bag which lay at his feet. "Presumably you intended to effect the exchange tonight. Perhaps you would care to explain the purpose, or the significance, of the second portrait – " He glanced at the picture displayed on the easel. " – for it is very nearly identical. Come, it cannot matter to you now. Why did you, Miss Dubois, not simply take Mr. Conk-Singleton's work for Monsieur Claudell to alter, before returning to your masters in France?"

She related Holmes's words to her companion, who replied only with a crafty smile, before replying.

"That is for you to discover, Mr. Holmes, if you can."

Gregson glanced through the window. "The transportation that I ordered has arrived, I see. These two will be in the cells within the hour, and we'll see if they are so flippant then. We'll leave you now, gentlemen, with our thanks once again."

We watched from the window as the police coach, with the prisoners safely manacled inside, began its journey back to the Yard. Holmes secured the premises and we walked to the end of the street before we were fortunate enough to encounter a passing landau.

Shortly afterwards we were back in our lodgings, enjoying a glass of brandy before retiring. After removing both portraits from Monsieur Claudell's bag, which we had brought with us, Holmes placed them on the hearth, side by side.

"As you see, Watson, it is only a detail in the background that is different." With a long finger he indicated a group of trees, which differed slightly on the forgery. "You will recall that Mycroft mentioned that Miss Dubois had induced one of his staff to divulge a recognition signal to her, in exchange for payment, so we must proceed with the assumption that it is that which is hidden somewhere here. But I perceive that you are weary, old fellow. I suggest that you retreat to your room, while I attempt to make some sense of this, and allow yourself a good night's rest. No, do not concern yourself regarding me. I'm no stranger to remaining awake until morning, as you know, and I'm quite determined that the solution to this little puzzle will not elude me. Good night, and I hope to be able to throw some light upon this at breakfast."

Surprisingly, I slept well and did not dream at all. I came down rather late to our sitting room to find Holmes in fine form, looking as alert as ever and about to begin his consumption of a plate of bacon and eggs. He immediately called for Mrs. Hudson to serve me similarly.

"You look amazingly unaffected by the loss of a night's sleep, if I may say so."

"That, my dear Watson, is because I slept almost as long as yourself."

"Ah, you were too tired, after all, to attempt to decipher whatever is hidden in the picture. A wise decision. Things always seem easier when you confront them with a mind that is fresh."

He laughed shortly. "You misunderstand me, old fellow. Pah! The puzzle was a simple one, after all. I tried several numerical ciphers with which I'm familiar, based on the number of trees painted in the background of the forgery and the irregularity of their spacing, but it was not until the fifth application that I finally discovered the key. After that I went to my bed and slept, only about an hour after you had retired."

"You never cease to amaze me, " I said truthfully. "The only thing that I'm still not clear about is your question to Miss Dubois, of early this morning. Why did they need to involve Mr. Conk-Singleton at all? Why did she not allow Monsieur Claudell to paint the picture from the outset? Or, as you put it then, why didn't she take the finished portrait to Monsieur Claudell to be altered after Mr. Conk-Singleton had completed it?"

"That had already occurred to me," he glanced at his pocket watch. "I therefore wired Gregson a little earlier, requesting that he ask those two beauties the same question. It may be that they have become more amenable by this time. Ah, I hear the doorbell now, and Mrs. Hudson has delayed bringing our coffee while she answers. I shall be surprised if she doesn't bring us a telegram in a few minutes."

He was, of course, correct. Our good landlady brought in a pot of steaming coffee and laid a yellow envelope before him. While I poured for us both he extracted the form and glanced over its contents.

"There is no mystery here, Watson," he said with an air of disappointment as he placed the message within my reach.

I read it and understood at once. Both Miss Dubois and Monsieur Claudell were aware that they were under observation by Mycroft's people. They were both notorious in their own fields of subterfuge, and so this was nothing new to them. Had they attempted to dispatch the portrait, by any medium, to France, it would have been immediately intercepted. They resolved therefore to involve Mr. Conk-Singleton, and on completion of his work they would make the substitution without his knowledge before Miss Dubois requested him to effect the picture's transportation, no doubt giving some excuse as to why she was unable to do this personally. There was indeed no mystery.

Holmes's mood had changed. He appeared suddenly downcast, frowning as he regarded his untouched coffee.

"I congratulate you," I said lightly. "Again you have succeeded where Scotland Yard failed."

"But I have derived little satisfaction from it." He glanced toward the window. "It seems certain that it will rain soon, Watson, but I feel that a brisk walk would be beneficial. Bring your umbrella, and who knows? By the time we return a more interesting problem may well have presented itself."

> *"Put the pearl in the safe, Watson," said he, "and get out the papers of the Conk-Singleton forgery case . . . ."*
>
> – Sherlock Holmes
> "The Adventure of the Six Napoleons"

A Simple Matter
by Susan Knight

"I say, Holmes," I remarked over breakfast, while reading the morning paper, "Lord Giles is getting married. I took him to be a confirmed bachelor."

Holmes leaned back, shaking his head. "Another good man lost," he said.

I had to laugh, even though my friend's negative view of the state of matrimony inevitably brought back memories of the blissfully happy but all too few years I spent with dearest Mary, long since deceased, alas. If Holmes was insensitive to my pain, I had to forgive him, and even pity him – he who had never experienced the joy of loving a fine woman and being loved by her. Nevertheless, I could not let his words go unchallenged.

"Can you not accept," I asked, "that for many men, a good marriage is a rock on which to build a fulfilled life? Many eminent men, you know, owe a great deal to their wives."

"My dear Watson," he replied, "what a rosy-tinted world you live in. Who can say how much more those men might have achieved without the distractions of family, the increasing demands of their frivolous, small-minded wives, of their noisy brood of children? No, I will not have it. Mark my words, Lord Giles is lost."

Despite the forcefulness of his assertion, I noticed that he was at the same time absentmindedly fingering the gold sovereign that hung from his watch chain. The same sovereign which had been gifted to him so many years before by a woman. By *the* woman, in fact – Irene Adler, for whom I suspected, although never dared to say as much, he still carried a torch. In the photograph that Holmes begged from the King of Bohemia in payment for services rendered, and which he still kept by him, intelligence shines from her eyes. But what eyes they are! What formidable beauty! No, despite the fact that "admiration" was how he termed his feelings for one of the few people who had ever got the better of him, methinks the gentleman doth protest a little too much.

Meanwhile, Holmes was opening a letter which had arrived by the morning post. He started to peruse it, a smile curling his lips. "Well now, Watson," he said, "we are to have a visitor shortly. Mr. Fairdale Hobbs. A most interesting young man, and the very exemplar of the merits of the single life."

"You know him, then?"

"Indeed. Our paths first crossed at the British Museum reading room. We wished to consult the very same volume on Nubian written texts – an astonishing coincidence, since the book had not been requested, so the librarian informed us, since 1863."

"He is a scholar, then."

"Precisely. Your perspicacity never fails to amaze me."

I decided to ignore the jibe.

"So which of you got the book?" I asked.

"The young man was polite enough to allow me to study it first. He was in any case working his way through several other tomes on Coptic and Egyptian writing systems."

"Fascinating," I commented drily.

"You would be surprised, Watson, at how truly engrossing the subject is. But I wonder why Mr. Hobbs wishes to visit me here. I hardly think it is to discuss hieroglyphs."

We did not have to wait long to discover the matter. It was less than half-an-hour later that Mrs. Hudson showed the young man up to our rooms. Mr. Fairdale Hobbs was over average height by a considerable few inches and, perhaps because of that, or perhaps because he spent much of his time hunched over books, he had developed something of a stoop. It was evident that he paid scant attention to his dress, for his suit was ill-fitting and worn at the cuffs, his shoes scuffed, and his hat, which he had removed from his head, decidedly rusty. Prematurely balding, poorly shaved, and wearing thick horn-rimmed spectacles, the unfortunate young man, a perfect specimen of an absent-minded professor, was far from presenting a handsome aspect. Despite this, there was something pleasing about him, a gentleness of mien, even though at that moment some strong emotion was clearly agitating him.

Holmes introduced me as a friend and colleague whose discretion was as impeccable as his own.

"Now, Mr. Hobbs," he went on, "pray tell what has brought you to me. Your letter provides little information, although your erratic orthography indicates a state of distracted anxiety."

"Oh Mr. Holmes," the young man said, in a voice that was deep and low, "You are correct. I am consumed with anxiety. It's quite dreadful to think what has happened to the poor girl. I am quite beside myself. Whatever can be done?"

He paced up and down, wringing his hands.

"Please be seated and try to collect yourself," Holmes said, with more patience than usual when faced with such a haphazard report. "You must explain more cogently, you know. Who is this 'she' of whom you speak, and what have you to do with her?"

Hobbs threw himself into the nearest chair which happened to have today's newspaper lying on it. I started to protest, but Holmes gave a warning shake of his head.

"Sally," Hobbs exclaimed, covering his eyes. "Dearest Sally."

"Sally who?"

The young man frowned. "I . . . I . . . It will come to me. If I ever knew it. I am not sure, you know, that I did."

I saw Holmes's patience starting to ebb away.

"Very well," he said. "Just tell me how you came to meet this Sally."

"Oh, at the Museum," Hobbs replied. "Just like yourself, Mr. Holmes."

"I see. In the Reading Room, was it? Over Nubian manuscripts?"

Hobbs actually emitted a hysterical little chuckle.

"Goodness no. I cannot imagine Sally there. Not at all. No, we met in the Egyptian Hall. She was contemplating the mummies, do you see." His expression softened at the memory. "She asked me about them."

"She spoke first, then?"

"I think maybe she took me for one of the attendants. I myself, of course, would never presume to address a young lady not of my acquaintance under such circumstances. Indeed, I had not noticed her to be there at all, because, you see, I was engrossed in trying to decipher a piece of papyrus in one of the cases. It seemed to be some sort of a love song, dating, I believe, from the Eighteenth Dynasty. Most absorbing, do you see."

He looked up at us, blinking.

"Yes, yes. Pray proceed."

"Well, I quite jumped when she spoke to me. She even had to repeat herself . . . You know, Mr. Holmes, she was so open and so truly interested in the subject. And yet at the same time so innocent. She could not believe that actual bodies lay swathed within the painted wooden cases, and thought that I was teasing her. I started to explain that they were indeed coffins, which quite shocked her. 'Are they not rotten and stinking?' she asked." He shook his head, smiling. "Ah, the sweet innocence of her."

"Yes, yes," said Holmes, a trifle testily.

"So then of course, I had to describe to her the way the ancients embalmed the bodies after removing the inner organs, placing a hook in the nose to draw out the brains, and so on."

"I am sure she enjoyed that," I said, intending irony.

"Indeed she did, Dr. Watson. She was enthralled, and even invited me to join her in the tea room, so that I could expatiate further on the subject."

"Rather forward of the young person, did you not think?" Holmes remarked.

"My fault for the way I am describing it, Mr. Holmes. If only you had been there, you would have seen how sweetly open she was."

"Hmm," said Holmes, frowning.

They had, it seemed, passed a pleasant half-hour over tea.

"She took such great delight in cream cakes," said Hobbs. "I cannot eat cream, you know, for it upsets my digestion, but it was quite charming to watch her consume so many. Not greedily, but so very delicately."

"At your expense?"

"Well of course. I could not ask a young lady to pay."

They had made an arrangement to meet again at the museum for the following day.

"She told me – or at least I thought she told me – that she worked in a florist shop nearby, and was free every lunchtime. She loved, she said, to spend that hour in the museum. Except that most of the time she was ignorant of that which she was viewing, and it was then that she expressed the wish to have me with her every day, because I explained things so well." A dreamy look crossed his face, and he sighed.

"And then?" Holmes tone, I noticed was getting sharper with each reminiscence from the young gentleman.

"So that was how we started meeting regularly. At first we spoke of ancient Egypt, progressing to the Sumerians and ancient Babylonians, you know. Then, one day . . . Oh, Mr. Holmes, one day when I was explaining cuneiform script to her, she took my hand in one of hers and placed the dear little forefinger of the other on my lips. 'Enough,' she whispered. 'Enough, Fairdale.' And then she told me that she had fallen in love with me. Me of all men. I could not believe it."

Neither, by his expression, could Holmes.

"I know it was forward of her, but after all, Mr. Holmes, she is a simple, unlettered little thing. When I asked whatever could she see in me – for I am not a vain man and am fully aware that my physical attributes are not generally pleasing to the opposite sex – she told me that she loved me for my mind and my great kindness. And then . . . oh I tremble to recount it, she placed my hand on her beating heart."

"In the British Museum?" I asked. "Surely not."

"Oh, did I not say? No, we were taking a stroll around Russell Square at the time – under the trees, you know. How very pretty she looked in the sunlight with her little fair curls."

Holmes leant back, groaning.

"These details are all very touching, Mr. Hobbs, but perhaps you can summarise quickly, and tell me what has befallen Sally."

"You also think something has happened to her, then, Mr. Holmes?"

"Well, my dear fellow, I presumed as much, since your first words on entering here were to that effect, were they not?"

"Yes, indeed. You are right. I am sorry . . . It was the note, do you see."

"The note? What note?"

"Somehow Sally and I had come to an understanding. I'm not quite sure how it happened, it was all so quick, and in truth, she is not the wife I should ever have envisaged for myself, and yet, when I think about it, how could I do better than a sweet-hearted young woman who would look after me? That's what she said: That I needed looking after, and that she would be the one to do it. I was deeply, deeply moved by her sweet words. We went and bought a ring for her finger right then. A little sapphire, to match her lovely blue eyes."

Holmes cleared his throat meaningfully.

"Yes, yes, the point. Well then for several days after that, I waited for her in our usual place by the Elgin marbles, but she didn't come. I waited and waited, and eventually started to worry. What if she were sick? What if – Oh God! – she had regretted her words of love and was even now avoiding me? I had to know, yet I did not have an address for her."

"You did not even know her last name," I pointed out.

"Well . . . I am sure I have that written down somewhere. Anyway, since she had told me that she worked in a florist's shop, I visited all such premises in the surrounds of the museum, but to no avail. No Sally to be found in any of them." He shook his head in puzzlement. "I must have got it wrong, do you see. It mustn't have been a florist after all."

"What then?"

"Well, on the fourth day, I found not my Sally but another young woman altogether standing by the statuary. She was in a state of extreme agitation. To my amazement, she asked if I were Mr. Fairdale Hobbs, and when I said that I was, she exclaimed 'Thank God!' and told me that she was Sally's sister, Iris."

"Excuse me, had you heard tell of this young person before?" asked Holmes.

"No, but then Sally and I did not talk of such things."

Only of mummification, cuneiform scripts, and love, I thought.

"Iris thrust a letter into my hand, saying it had been pushed through her letter-box that very morning. Mr. Holmes, Dr. Watson, what a terrible thing! What a terrible terrible thing!"

"Mr. Hobbs," Holmes said, "you must explain."

"I can do better. Here is the same missive."

He thrust it at Holmes who, having read it, passed it to me.

It was indeed shocking, as well as ill-written in a blocky print, with many atrocious spelling mistakes:

> *To hum it may kinsirn*
>
> *If ye wish to see yor Sal agin put a hunnerd ginnys in a cloth bag an leeve it unner the big Dook statue in Russell Square at midnite on Wedsday . . . or she wil be soled to wite slavvers. Ye ave bin wornd.*
>
> *A frend*

"Extraordinary!" said Holmes. "Quite extraordinary."

"Indeed. I can tell you now, gentlemen, I near fainted away at the news. My darling Sally in the hands of white slavers! It was unimaginable. Iris had to support me to a nearby bench, where I tried to recover my wits. I was trembling all over, do you see. The horror of it!" His voice was breaking with emotion, though he managed to continue his narrative after a moment collecting himself. "Iris herself, a simple shop girl like her sister, was, of course, in no position to pay such a large ransom and, both their parents being dead, there was no hope to be had there. Iris told me how Sally had confided our love to her, and now expressed the hope that I could help out in some way. Oh, Mr. Holmes, Dr. Watson, the poor girl was distraught. As, indeed, was I, like I said. Trembling uncontrollably. I thought I would faint away . . . Even now . . . ."

"I trust you told her that you have no intention of paying this preposterous sum, Mr. Hobbs."

"My goodness, sir, I have paid it already. Of course I have. I would pay anything to save my dear Sally from such a terrible fate. How can you possibly think otherwise?"

Holmes was about to reply, but the young man continued. "I have some savings, you know, so was able to raise the money. I took it to the appointed place – with some difficulty since the Square was closed and I had to clamber over the railings, fearing at every moment to be apprehended by a member of the constabulary. But I succeeded and left it as instructed. Oh dear, oh dear . . . ."

The poor boy collapsed in floods of tears, his whole long body shaking. Even Holmes was taken aback.

"A glass of brandy there, Watson," he said. "Quick, man!"

"No, no, no," cried Hobbs. "I never touch spirituous liqueur. Perhaps a glass of water."

I poured some from a carafe on the side table and gave it into his trembling hand.

Holmes shook his head.

"Oh foolish, foolish young man. Let me guess. Sally has not returned."

"She has not."

"I am afraid she played you for a fool, Mr. Hobbs. So now, I suppose, you wish to employ me to recover your money."

Mr. Hobbs reared up.

"Not at all! What is money, after all, compared to love? To love, Mr. Holmes!" He gave us a challenging look and, though his words were naïve, the sincerity of them could not but inspire respect. In me at least. "No, I wish you to find Sally, to save her. I can pay you for your time, of course. Whatever it takes – " He struck an attitude. " – though it ruin me."

Holmes paused. He joined his hands together at the fingertips and pressed these to his lips, considering.

"Mr. Holmes," the young man cried. "You are my only hope. I know it looks to you as if Sally has made a fool of me, and yet if you met her, if you met her sister who is quite beside herself, I am sure you would change your mind. Pray speak to Iris, at least. She is to meet me as usual at twelve noon by the Marbles."

"Well," the reply came at last, "there are certainly elements of your story that intrigue. Let us go with you then to meet this sister, this Iris. After that, perhaps I will take on the case. However, Mr. Hobbs, if I do so, you must be prepared for the worst."

"That Sally has already been ruined? That I can accept, you know, for it would not be her fault, poor innocent child that she is. I would take her to my heart all the more willingly."

Was there no end to his heroics? Clearly this was a young man who had lived too exclusively in the company of books, the sort that deal in idealistic romance and self-sacrifice.

"No," Holmes said, "I rather meant that you must be prepared to accept that she is a cold-hearted fraud who has hoodwinked you, Mr. Fairdale Hobbs. That she has extorted money from you under false pretences, taking advantage of your generous and credulous nature."

"Ha!" the young man replied, "all I can say to that, Mr. Sherlock Holmes, is that you yourself must be prepared for once to be wrong."

Holmes simply smiled and shook his head.

The three of us thereupon took a cab to the British Museum, Holmes muttering to me that he would not be surprised if this Iris failed to turn up also, being most probably in league with the sister.

"They have his money. What more do they want?"

My friend, however, was mistaken in this respect, at least, for the girl was indeed standing as arranged by Lord Elgin's fine marble statuary, waiting for Hobbs. She looked most surprised to see that he was accompanied by myself and Holmes, but was not one whit dismayed, even though she recognised the name of the great detective. Indeed, she seemed pleased that we were there – a point, I felt, very much in her favour.

In fact, the impression the sister gave was altogether a positive one, being a neat little body, with smooth dark hair, lively brown eyes, and an olive complexion, as if she hailed from a place under the Mediterranean sun rather than from beneath the habitual foggy skies of London. A charming dimple appeared in one cheek when she smiled, which sadly, just then, was infrequently.

"Any news," she cried to our companion.

He shook his head. "None on your side either then, I assume?" he replied.

"None."

She tried then unsuccessfully to control her emotions, weeping into an already sodden handkerchief, and curious heads started turning our way. Holmes, ever discomforted by the sight of a woman in distress, suggested that we might repair to a quieter place to discuss the matter.

"I should like, indeed," he said, "to see where exactly you left the bag of money, Mr. Hobbs. In Russell Square, I believe it was."

We walked through the museum to the rear exit, hurrying past ancient Greeks and Romans frozen in heroic poses, past Grecian urns such as those described by the poet Keats, past the colossal carved column drum from the Temple of Artemis at Ephesos, not pausing for a moment to study these wonders. To have such a resource on my doorstep and not avail of it reflects sadly upon me. When dear Mary was alive, indeed, we were in the habit of frequenting museums and galleries quite regularly. I vowed, as we rushed past, that in her memory I must soon return at some more propitious time.

By now we had reached that doorway at the back of the building which provides egress into the Square. This is, for those not acquainted with the space, a large and pleasant garden park extending northwards to Woburn Place, with winding gravel paths between green lawns and flower beds, gracefully planted trees providing shade to those resting on the benches beneath them. The statue we sought soon came into view, for it was most imposing. Carved into the plinth were words identifying the subject as the fifth Duke of Bedford, Francis Russell, who gave the Square his name. The Duke was depicted with his hand on a plough and surrounded by sheep for some reason, I presumed symbolically, for he was assuredly neither a farm labourer nor a shepherd.

"This is where you left the money?" asked Holmes.

"Yes, indeed. Tucked up there in behind that cherub."

It was lucky, I thought, that Hobbs was so tall, for a man or woman of normal stature would have difficulty reaching so far. Holmes, tall himself, examined the place.

"Long gone, of course," he said, but continued to search the spot with some interest.

"Why here, I wonder?"

"This is where we plighted our troth," Hobbs replied with emotion.

"But how were the kidnappers to know that?"

The young man paused for thought.

"They must have forced the information out of Sally. Oh God! The poor poor girl!"

"Calm yourself, man."

"Can you help us, Mr. Holmes?" Iris asked. She looked so appealing, those brown eyes overflowing with tears, that I was sure even he was not cold-hearted enough to refuse.

"I confess there are elements here that pique my interest," the detective replied. "Yes, indeed, I have little doubt that I will find your Sally for you, and quite soon."

They were both full of gratitude, of course, though I wondered quite how Holmes intended to achieve this conjuring trick.

"Watson," he said, waving his hand in a vague direction, "perhaps you and Mr. Hobbs could comb the surrounding area in case the villains have left something incriminating behind them."

I glanced in some surprise at my friend. It was unusual indeed for him to assign such a search to myself or others, since he would ever doubt our ability to perform the task with sufficient assiduity. However, I understood that perhaps he wished to speak to Iris in private, asking questions the answers to which he might not wish Hobbs to hear. I duly led the young man out of earshot. We poked, fruitlessly enough among the bushes, finding only an empty bottle of porter, the remains of a pot of jellied eels, pages torn from an *Illustrated London News*, and a lady's glove which Iris said did not belong to Sally.

I asked nothing further of my companion regarding the matter until the two of us were back in Baker Street.

"Well?" I said finally. "Did the charming little sister turn your head after all?"

"Such a remark, Watson," Holmes replied, sighing, "is beneath even you."

"What then? It seems a hopeless case."

"Not at all. It is a very simple matter."

"I can see no clues as to the thing at all. Can you really think Sally is in the hands of white slavers?"

Holmes laughed.

"Look at the note again, Watson. Does it not already tell you much about the case?"

He handed it to me and I studied it closely, even turning it over, without discovering any more from it than I had already observed.

"The paper is rough, the writer barely literate. It speaks of low-life villains to me. More than that . . . ." I shook my head.

"I am afraid you have been led, Watson, as the author intended, up the garden path. The spelling of most of the words, it is true, is comically bad. And yet '*Russell Square*' and '*statue*', not the simplest of words, are correctly inscribed."

"Whoever penned it might have copied the name . . . ."

"That will not do, Watson. No, the writer is as literate as you or me. He, or perhaps she, wanted there to be no confusion as to where the money should be left, which is why those particular words are correctly spelt. That raises another point: The note was delivered to Iris, and yet it is clearly intended for Mr. Hobbs, a man with more money than sense, a man who knows Russell Square intimately. He lodges nearby, you know. In Great Orme Street, I believe he told us. Moreover, he has a sentimental attachment to the place and especially to the site of the statue where the money was to be left."

I could not argue.

"So poor Hobbs is indeed the victim of a trick," I said. "But I can hardly believe Iris to be involved. Unless she is an actress akin to Sarah Bernhardt, her worries for her sister seem genuine."

"Ah, that is another issue. You say 'sister', and yet when I quizzed her on the subject it turns out that they are not blood relations. Sally's mother married Iris's father, the two parents having been widowed and both girls already fully grown. I suspected as much when Hobbs described his *amour* as fair-haired with blue eyes, while Iris, as you saw, is dark with brown eyes. It can happen that way in families, of course – my brother Mycroft and myself, for example, being of very different physical types – but it is quite unusual."

"Yes, I see."

"You very astutely removed Hobbs from the scene," Holmes continued, "no doubt realising that I had questions for the girl. They were related to her sister's supposed work in a florist's shop. You will remember that Hobbs told us how he'd searched all around the museum for such places, but none knew of a Sally."

I nodded.

"Iris was able to inform me that it is *she* who works in such an establishment, while her stepsister is a dancer in vaudeville. Indeed, Iris, a sensible enough girl, had already visited the theatre, only to learn that Sally had not put in an appearance there for several days."

"But why would Sally lie about her place of work?"

"I suspect the theatre in question has a dubious reputation. Indeed, Iris suggested as much without actually saying it. It is in Soho, you see."

A notorious part of the city, and yet not-far-removed from the Museum.

"So Sally might have become mixed up with a crowd of low-lifes after all. Perhaps they indeed, knowing she had become close to a man of means, abducted her."

"Perhaps," he replied, and chuckled. "We'll see."

The following day Holmes rather surprised me by expressing his intention of visiting the British Museum to pursue his interrupted studies of Nubian texts.

"What of the case?" I asked.

"Oh, that can wait," came the terse response.

Since I had pressing medical duties to attend to, our paths hardly crossed again for several days. Either he or I were gone in the early hours, and either he or I returned late.

It was not until the fifth day that we both returned for supper, he rubbing his hands and looking extremely pleased with himself.

"Your studies are going well," I remarked.

"Yes, indeed. It is all most satisfactory." He paused. "I know you have been busy, Watson, but are you by any chance free tomorrow?"

"I can be," I replied. "I think Colonel Lennox's gout might await my ministrations for a day or two more."

"Capital."

He did not explain further, but chuckled frequently to himself over the course of the evening, the which I admit I found somewhat irritating. However, Mrs. Hudson's fine mutton stew, and the warming glass of grog afterwards, put me in a better humour, and I was soon dozing off over my copy of *The Lancet*, able to ignore the occasional guffaw from the direction of the other armchair.

It was over breakfast the next morning, after I had presumed to ask at last what was the pressing matter that required my attendance that day, that Holmes made his astounding announcement.

"I wish you to come and meet my betrothed," he said.

I dropped the teaspoon I was using to decapitate my boiled egg.

"Good heavens, Holmes!" I replied, "You jest of course."

"Not a bit. I have taken to heart your words praising the condition of matrimony and have decided at last to take that giant leap into the darkness myself."

The wicked smile with which he accompanied his words led me to conclude that he was indeed joking, but that there was an ulterior motive at issue. I decided to play along.

"I shall be delighted to meet the lady," I replied solemnly.

"Excellent. I have invited our new friends Mr. Hobbs and Miss Iris Goodhart to join us as well. But now I must go and get ready. One must look one's best, you know, when one is courting."

And with a wink and another chuckle, he was off, only to return some time later, looking not at all dandified, but rather down at heel and dusty, and inexplicably sporting thick glasses.

"Not a word, Watson," he said, observing my face. "Let us go."

So it was that, just before noon, we arrived once more at the British Museum, where we found the other two awaiting us out front, wondering expressions on their faces.

"Watson," said Holmes, "not to terrify the young person with strangers, I plan to go on ahead. Please be so good as to accompany our friends here to the Hotel Russell and wait there for perhaps fifteen minutes."

"You will join us?"

"No. Then I should like you to take a turn in the Square, making for the statue we all know so well."

It was very strange, but I recognised that keen gaze. The chase was on and I began to have an inkling of the matter.

The Hotel Russell, only very recently completed, is a truly splendid building at the side of the Square. Its massive façade is of terracotta stone with arches and turrets and sculptures around its many scores of windows. Both my companions were in awe, and indeed young Iris looked almost afraid to enter through its imposing door, held open for us as it was by a uniformed attendant with a superior expression on his face. Inside we found it even more impressive, a lobby of Carrera marble of all hues, from pillars in charcoal grey to golden walls and paler ceiling, while the floor sported in mosaics a flaming sun encircled by the signs of the zodiac, the whole place illuminated by a huge chandelier dripping crystal.

"Oh my!" exclaimed Iris.

We found a bench upholstered in gold velvet and sat upon it to wait out the fifteen minutes. My companions at first displayed a degree of unease, especially whenever one of the attendants passed by, fearing no doubt we would be asked what business we had there. When no such occurred, Hobbs at least relaxed somewhat and started to quiz me.

"I am most puzzled, Dr. Watson, as to what is afoot. Has Mr. Holmes given up the search for my Sally entirely because his own heart has been captured by another? It is hardly professional, sir."

"It is heartless," Iris said, "if it is so. Why should we be witness to his great happiness, when we remain bereft?"

"I do not think you need worry," I replied. "Mr. Holmes is a consummate professional. If he has invited you here, it is assuredly not to crow over you, but for a deeper purpose. However, he has not yet confided the matter to me, so I cannot enlighten you further."

The fifteen minutes being up, we left the hotel, I pressing a coin into the doorman's hand, since it seemed expected. He curled his lips in acknowledgement, and I wondered, as I have done many times before, at the arrogance of lackeys of all sorts who seem to feel they are in some way superior to those they are supposed to serve. That is by the way, however – simply an observation by one whom Holmes considers utterly lacking in that ability.

We crossed the busy thoroughfare and entered the Gardens. Approaching the statue, we soon perceived ahead of us a couple walking sedately arm-in-arm, one of whom I recognised as my friend and colleague Sherlock Holmes. The other appeared from the back to be a very young lady. She was wearing a jade green dress and jacket, her fair curls surmounted by a bonnet embellished with ribbons. At that moment, the pair turned around.

Hobbs started in astonishment.

"It cannot be!" he said.

"Good heavens!" exclaimed Iris.

"Here are my friends now," Holmes remarked jovially to his partner, "come to congratulate us on our happiness."

The young person had turned pale. She tried to wriggle away from Holmes, but he had her held tight.

"Don't be shy, my dear Sally," he urged.

"Bert!" she called out.

A youth suddenly appeared from behind the statue, stocky and with the damaged face of a pugilist. He made to attack Holmes, but the latter, being well versed in martial arts himself, and nimbler on his feet to boot, was soon able to overpower his slower, heavier opponent, and held him fast in an armlock. Meanwhile the girl had tried to run off, but I was able to catch her easily enough, for no woman can run fast in a long skirt, no matter how she tries.

Hobbs had slumped down on to the plinth of the statue, Iris beside him trying to comfort him, for his eyes were at last opened to the duplicity of the woman he loved.

"I almost wish," he muttered, "that you had not found her, Mr. Holmes, so that I could guard within my heart the pure unsullied image of her."

"Now, now, Hobbs," Holmes said. "Pull yourself together, man. You are not the first and will not be the last to succumb to a woman's wiles."

"How could you be so cruel, Sally?" cried Iris.

Her stepsister made no reply.

"Easily enough for one-hundred guineas, I suppose," replied Holmes. "As well as whatever sum they hoped to squeeze from me, or any other poor dupe who fell for her pretty face and flattering words."

Sally was trying to look remorseful. "I really cared for you, Fairdale," she murmured, blinking long lashes over those truly very blue eyes. "But you know, life is hard – and anyway Bert made me."

The young man in question then let forth a torrent of words not suitable for recording here, though the tenor was that it was all her idea.

"She said there was lots of boobs like Hobbsy here in that there museum," he concluded. "Noses in books, never had a woman. We could make a killing. That's what she said."

Hobbs looked as if he could make a killing right then, and Bert would be the victim.

"Right," said Holmes. "That's that then. A simple enough matter after all, as I informed you, Watson . . . So now let's get this pair of masterminds off to the nearest police station."

"That would be Holborn, I think," I said.

Hobbs, however, demurred. He was for letting them go – or rather, for letting Sally go.

"I should not like to see her in prison," he said.

"We can give you back your money, Fairdale," Sally said, with hope in her voice. "Well, most of it. Can't we, Bert?"

The young man gave a sullen nod.

"And your ring, too," she continued, reaching into her reticule and pulling out a pawnbroker's note.

Hobbs gazed at it aghast. Then shook his head.

"Mr. Hobbs," said Holmes, "I would most strongly advise against letting them loose. What would stop them from carrying on their wicked game?"

"Oh no, Sherrinford, I wouldn't do that. I have learnt my lesson," said Sally, weeping little pearly tears. "I have, Sherrinford, really I have."

"Sherrinford?" I asked.

"The name she knows me by," Holmes replied.

Back in Baker Street, over an evil-smelling pipe, Holmes said, "You know, Watson, I am utterly disgusted that, after all my efforts, Hobbs insisted on letting the miscreants go free."

"Let us hope," I said, "that you have put enough fear into them that they will not try that trick on anyone else."

"Of course," he went on, "it was obvious to me from the start that it was all a crude ruse to fleece the unwitting. White slavers, indeed. Only someone quite unworldly would be taken in by that."

"Scholars, you mean?"

"Precisely. Certain scholars, at least." He took a satisfied puff.

"But how did you know where to find her?"

"Oh that was simplicity itself. I reckoned that if they succeeded once, so easily, they would try again. I took to hanging around various galleries of the museum, gazing intently at the various exhibits. My disguise as a single-minded scholar was rather convincing, was it not?" He smiled and I nodded, as I was expected to do. "It was in the Horology Department that I was eventually approached by a young woman who resembled the description of Sally given to me by Hobbs."

"Horology?" I asked.

"Yes. Luckily I am well versed in the workings of astrolabes, orreries, marine chronometers, and the like, and was able to explain them convincingly to Sally – though even if I had spoken nonsense, I doubt she would have been any the wiser. She is a foolish girl, though admittedly with a kind of animal charm. But you know, Watson, she did not even bother to change her name."

"Was she not fearful of bumping into Hobbs?"

"She knew, I think, that he would not wander from his established path, his interests being extremely narrow and confined to the ancient Middle East. It was a risk, of course, but I think the game diverted her as much as the result."

"The game?"

"Fixing to catch some poor impressionable dope in her net. 'Sherrinford' fitted the bill perfectly, a man obsessed with clocks and watches, and, though shabby, with a wallet packed with bankers' notes. I can concur with Hobbs that the young lady certainly enjoys her cream teas."

"And Bert?"

"I thought there had to be a confederate somewhere. You were right, Watson, about that at least. A low-life from the theatre – a doorman, I believe. Someone who comes heavy on anyone trying to take unpaid liberties with the young dancers. Something of a bonehead, too, whom she charmed into assisting her scheme."

"He composed the note, then?"

"More likely she did, for I doubt that Bert can even write his own name. You must have noticed how the letter was written, the words printed out, presumably to disguise her feminine hand."

"So she was the instigator, then?"

"Most certainly. Unluckily for her, Hobbs knew to call upon me, or she might have got away with it." He inhaled deeply on his pipe. "So Watson, can you now bring yourself to admit that I am right?"

"You are often right," I replied. "But in what specifically?"

I do not think he liked that "often", for he sniffed. "Always right" would be more to his taste.

"You must surely agree with me at last, as to the bad influence on men of all classes of the female sex. Mr. Fairdale Hobbs is much better off without his Sally."

That was indubitably so. However, some three months later we received an invitation to attend the nuptials of Mr. Fairdale Hobbs and Miss Iris Goodhart.

"That is capital news!" I said. "She is a lovely girl – sensible, as you yourself allowed. I am sure she will make him happy."

But Holmes only sighed, and cast the card from him.

"Another good man lost," he said.

"You arranged an affair for a lodger of mine last year," she said. "Mr. Fairdale Hobbs."

"Ah, yes – a simple matter."

"But he would never cease talking of it – your kindness, sir, and the way in which you brought light into the darkness. I remembered his words when I was in doubt and darkness myself.

– Mrs. Warren and Sherlock Holmes
"The Adventure of the Red Circle"

The Hammerford Will Business
by David Marcum

The unexpected rain was sluicing along the gutters like streams diverted into mill races. Although I'd carried my umbrella when I left the night before, I was unprepared for the sheer volume of the suddenly intense downpour, and thus my footwear was insufficient. And yet, I'm uncertain as to what could have been considered proper in those conditions – stream waders perhaps? In any case, my cab deposited me as close as possible to the edge of the kerb, but the running water rising around the otherwise-steady old horse's legs unnerved him, and the driver was unable to hold the hansom entirely steady. It was no surprise when my step down landed me one-footed in the temporary brook before I could propel myself onward.

I didn't blame the cabbie, for he was having his own problems steadying the horse. With my payment and a tip, and a nod to him besides – for I knew the fellow from quite a ways back – I crossed to the door of 221 Baker Street and let myself inside.

I carried with me news of the War, fresh in the latest edition of *The Times*. Apparently a few days before, De Wet was forced over the Orange River with the loss of his guns and convoy. I marveled yet again how this modern world was constantly being made smaller as events from the other side of the globe could be known within days, or even hours, of their occurrence.

I left my umbrella standing near the door to dry and climbed the stairs, past the landing outside the sitting room and the usually-closed-and-locked door to Holmes's bedroom (the regular access being from the sitting room), and so on to my own room, one flight higher. There I changed clothes, glad to be warm and dry once again, and thus refreshed, I went back down. From the landing, I called to Mrs. Hudson for fresh coffee and a bit of breakfast, while also intending to have a restorative whisky in me before it arrived. I hadn't been to bed the previous night.

I opened the door to find Holmes standing by the fireplace, his back to me as he faced the window, holding up a document to the watery gray light. "Good morning, Watson," he said. "But not so pleasant, I fear. How is your patient?"

"Mrs. Effler will live to complain another day," I said. I glanced toward the sideboard and decided that it was perhaps a bit too early in the day after all to seek comfort from the whisky bottle. I wondered if my poor late brother had ever had such thoughts before deciding that it was always the exact right time for a wee dram, and then maybe just one more . . . .

As I reached my chair, Holmes spun and held out the piece of paper. His other hand held a small envelope. "What do you make of this?"

He handed it to me, but after twenty years of this, I recognized that I was still being tested, and although I took the small folded sheet, I extended my other hand for the envelope as well. He smiled and gave it to me.

Having it proved to be singularly useless, for neither envelope nor note provided a great deal of information. The note was about five-inches square, folded over once and creased firmly down the center. The paper was of good quality, cream-colored and thick, with a high linen content. Setting it aside for a moment, I considered the envelope, addressed with Holmes's name and nothing else. No return address, no stamp, and no stains or smears. I could find no traces of finger-marks, or revealing telltale smudges of cobbler's wax, beef tallow, or soot from the smokestack of a west-bound Norwegian collier. It had been handled carefully before delivery. However, I did see one now-dried water spot – a stray raindrop, no doubt – that had slightly distorted the otherwise uniform smoothness of the envelope's surface. I looked up.

"The water stain – from when it was exposed to the elements for the scant moment between being removed from a pocket, perhaps, and then pushed through our letter-slot, probably not all that long ago?"

"That is my surmise as well. Mrs. Hudson found and brought it up just before you arrived."

Turning my attention to the letter, I held it up, and then the envelope beside it. The same paper, but there was some sort of watermark on the letter that didn't appear on the envelope, and I didn't recognize it. No doubt Holmes could tell me its significance. The note had a simple message, written in a bold right hand with black ink. The letters themselves were firm and economical, carefully blotted, with none rising too high above its neighbors or showing great loops or losses of control, indicating some sort of free spirit. I had the sense that the author was a man.

Stay out of Sir George Lewis's business.
Don't go to Hammerford.

I turned it over once again, but saw nothing else of interest. "The watermark?" I asked.

"Cramwells of Bond Street." He nodded toward one of his reference books, which I saw was lying open on his chair. It contained examples of trade symbols from various industries, and had been heavily annotated over the years as Holmes added hundreds of other entries that he didn't want to keep in his brain-attic. "Cramwells maintains an exclusive clientele – *very* exclusive. Was the author careless? The watermark could have been trimmed away – we've seen that sort of thing done before. Does this person not realize that there is a clue to be tracked through this paper, or does he simply not care? Does he want to be found? I'll set some inquiries in motion."

"And in the meantime," I said, glancing toward the rain running down the tall windows overlooking Baker Street, my dismayed expectations clearly visible on my face, "I foresee a trip to Hammerford."

"You *fear* it, you mean," Holmes replied with a smile. "And why not? Our decks are clear for once, Mrs. Effler and her little matter of blackmail notwithstanding, and contrary to the words, this note is almost an invitation to involve ourselves in London's latest nine-day wonder. The author might as well have waved a flag or lit a signal fire. But for now, warm yourself and enjoy your coffee. Nap if you can. Before we head out Richmond-way, I want to familiarize myself a bit further with the matter."

Taking back the note and envelope, he tucked them into his pocket and then retreated to his bedroom, even as Mrs. Hudson arrived with my coffee – and much more to my liking, a mound of hot comestibles that would serve to restore me after my trying night.

Within a few minutes, both Holmes and the food were gone, though in different directions, and I sorted through several stacks of old newspapers to see about assembling a cogent and linear narrative of the recent events that had been occurring in connection with Sir George Lewis's estate along the Thames, near the Royal Botanic Gardens. I suspected that having a thorough knowledge of the case – or as much so as one could glean from an overenthusiastic press – would prove to be useful.

Sir George Lewis was a man in his middle-forties who was known for wealth that he didn't earn, and a dissipated lifestyle that had aged him and destroyed his health before his time. He had inherited a number of highly successful paper mills scattered around the north of England, and he was fortunate to have good and experienced managers who took the responsibility of running them quite serious – not for the benefit of the absent owner, but rather to care for the many employees whose livelihood depended upon them. Sometimes whole villages and towns were contrived completely around the running of the mills, and if they had been poorly supervised, all there would have suffered.

Despite his documented failures of character, Sir George was at least smart enough to leave things alone, letting others be the caretakers of what he didn't understand, and complacently collecting the regular income. He was a well-known figure in London circles and had been for years, since his early-twenties, long before he'd inherited the fortune conferred upon him by the sudden and unexpected death of his father. He had never married, but had steadily been associated with a number of actresses and heiresses, and other women of undocumented pedigrees, both home-grown and otherwise. Gradually the wild life he'd led for so many years had seemed to pall for him, and one heard less and less of his antics as he'd presumably withdrawn to Hammerford, his family's estate west of London.

The place itself, as some of the newspapers looking to provide a deeper and more compelling story revealed, had a rather strange history, in that it had been standing there for over four-hundred years in some form or another. Under the current owner, its upkeep had been substantially neglected, and it was reported that except for the small parts of the house in which Sir George and a few servants functionally lived, most of the old pile was long closed-up and empty.

At some point in the past, Sir George had dithered back-and-forth about how accessible he wished for his estate to be. When construction for a new Kew Bridge was proposed, to replace the old one not far upstream from the estate, the gentleman had lobbied to have the entire road shifted so that the crossing would be closer to Hammerford – presumably to provide quicker means for him to cross the river. However, it was uncertain why he actually wished for this, as he generally only traveled in one direction – to London – and the Kew Garden Station was quite close to Hammerford, just a short carriage ride to the southwest on the same side of the river. Nevertheless, he'd been quite in the news a year or so earlier for his Quixotic attempt to relocate the ancient bridge, leading to one late-night burning in effigy of his figure before he seemed to abandon his efforts.

Nothing of note had been heard from him in the two years since – until the sudden and unexpected arrival of a man who claimed to be his brother.

That fellow purported to be Ambrose Lewis, the supposedly long-deceased older sibling of Sir George. He'd first arrived in London a couple of months before, after having been reported to have died nearly two decades earlier. His appearance, just after the New Year in that bleak late-winter, was like a circus coming to town, and to a capital worn-out by tedious and depressing news from the Boer War, it was as if someone had set fire to a paraffin-soaked torch. This man, who may or may not have been who he claimed, cut quite a figure. He was tall – several inches over six feet – and broad. He projected a hearty vitality, compared with the rather caved-in, weary, and slumped Sir George. The man's weathered face was covered by countless lines, crossing themselves in horizontal and vertical cuts, as if he'd squinted into bright sunshine for so long that his skin was leathered. He wore his hair – a noticeable red – long and down to his shoulders, combed but straight.

But his clothing was what one noticed first, and then it was what one noticed the most – in a style like something from the seventeenth century, but in garish and unmatching colors, particularly a rusty-shaded orange that did nothing to complement the odd shade of his hair. He was big but not fat, and his doublet – for he wore one of those – fit him well. He always had a long crimson silk sash tied around his throat, and the rumor, first printed in a newspaper or magazine article that I couldn't locate, was that it was a reminder of some lost love – a story that fired the public's imagination and grew with each new profile in the press. He was loud and had a braying laugh, making him the center of attention wherever he went, and the public took to him with a huge fascination the likes of which hadn't been seen in quite a while.

Holmes and I had both run across the man once, as he was entering Simpsons while we departed. He had four or five forgettable little sycophants trailing around him, gnat-like and guffawing at whatever it was that he'd just said. By then the man had been mentioned in a number of newspapers, and both Holmes and I knew of him and recognized him instantly. We'd stepped aside and then made some passing remark between us about having finally seen the famed Ambrose Lewis, but hadn't discussed him any further. A few weeks later, I had some business in Mayfair, delivering a document related to one of Holmes's investigations, and I saw the same fellow leaving a very fine home, and that time he was alone. While still the most noticeable figure in the street that day, he was subdued, looking thoughtful as he pulled the building's door quietly shut behind him and stepped across the short distance to a waiting carriage. He was away almost before I'd had time to recognize him.

He seemed to have such a prosaic name – Ambrose Lewis – to be associated with such a big and theatrical personality. But the story of his return was even stranger than his appearance.

As I read through the press accounts from a couple of months earlier when he'd first burst on the London scene like an exploding shell, I saw that I'd correctly recalled the essentials. Ambrose Lewis – if this was he – had been Sir George Lewis's older brother, and had died – or so it was believed – in a boating accident in 1882, nearly twenty years earlier. He, his younger brother George, and a third man, Richard Nason, had been on Ambrose's yacht off Margate, having sailed down the Thames from

London a day or so before, with no other purpose than to make the trip. There had been a sudden squall, the craft had lurched, and Ambrose was washed overboard and away toward the open sea before he could be saved.

Their father, Sir Edward Lewis, had been heartbroken and had died within the month, leaving the younger George as the rather surprised new heir. The younger surviving brother had then proceeded to spend the next two decades as described, which was no surprise to anyone who had known him before the tragedy. And now, completely without warning, the supposedly dead older brother had returned. As might be expected, Sir George was contesting his claim.

Apparently the prodigal son did look a great deal as one would have expected a nineteen-years-older Ambrose to appear, if one forgave the time and weathering that had been troweled on since then. But those who had known Ambrose in the olden days – and it turned out that there weren't many, as he'd apparently been as friendless and introspective in those days as his brother was wild – claimed to be uncertain, as it was hard to precisely focus upon and define the man underneath the lurid costume. Certainly Ambrose of old had never clothed himself in such costumes, and while he'd had red hair, it had been kept short and conservative. The newly returned Ambrose refused to meet with any of his old acquaintances. Some said that it was because he was an imposter who feared discovery, while others speculated that he was simply waiting to do so when his case to regain his inheritance as the elder son had been legitimately established – but in fact he had made no effort to begin any legal proceedings to establish himself as the rightful heir. Instead, he made frequent appearances here and there around London, without prior announcement and always causing a sensation – seen to be seen, a celebrity who was guaranteed to enliven interest in whatever event he attended, but with no other apparent purpose to his return. And it was driving his brother, Sir George, to distraction.

The press began pestering Sir George as soon as his apparent brother announced himself, and when they found that he refused to give direct answers, they filled the long inches of their newspaper columns with ever-spiraling speculations. And so it would have continued and possibly died away if Ambrose hadn't touched off the next fuse and escalated the narrative to the next level.

When pressed, he had previously refused to say where he'd been during those long years. But finally, when a number of reporters were in his presence, he unexpectedly told a most-unique tale. Comparing himself to that famed long-ago vanisher Rip Van Winkle, who had fallen asleep and awakened twenty years later, Ambrose stated that he'd never actually been on the yacht where he was presumed to have been lost and drowned. Instead, he averred that one day he'd walked along the grounds behind

Hammerford and had decided to lay down under the famed and massive ancient willow on the banks of the Thames, well back from the shore. Underneath, he'd been hidden from everyone. There he had fallen asleep, only to awaken there in the same spot, now in 1901, nineteen years since he had vanished. He found himself strangely garbed and far older than he would have liked, having skipped over the last two decades. At that point, when pressed for further details, especially as to why his brother had told a different story, he had stopped, refusing to elaborate. Everything he left unsaid – all the empty space in his story – was like a license to pour coal oil on a fire for the members of the press, especially the disreputable ones, who generated reams of speculation of greater or lesser ridiculousness.

But Ambrose Lewis must have awakened with money, because he immediately set himself up at the Langham in high style on the day of his reappearance, and proceeded to fund a number of fancy suppers and gatherings nearly every night. Anyone with sense knew that this story couldn't be true – clearly he was using it as a distraction to avoid truly answering the question – but nevertheless the press loved it, and they were inspired to new heights in their creative conjectures about the mystery that was Ambrose Lewis.

After studying the newspapers, I felt that I recalled the essentials of the affair, although it seemed nothing more than an attempt to pester Sir George, with the recent tale of having slept through the past couple of decades being some part toward making a run on the estate. Ambrose, being the older child, would have been the heir, and if this curiously theatrical fellow really was him, then I supposed that he had a legitimate claim – although it was peculiar that he was so far making no effort to establish it.

I ceased my pondering at that point when I nearly fell asleep, having been up all night. I was just beginning to dream, something about a great willow with evil intentions who sang passers-by into a trance before opening a gap in his trunk and swallowing them. It was at that point that I was startled awake, realizing that only moments had passed. Mrs. Hudson was carrying in several items for lunch, apologizing when she realized that she had awakened me. I assured her that I had barely been asleep. I didn't add that I would have preferred the sleep to the food.

Afterwards, I drank several more cups of coffee to stay awake, and was therefore relatively alert when Holmes returned in mid-afternoon and asked if I was free to run with him down to Hammerford. He mentioned it casually, as if he had wondered whether I was interested in joining him for a walk along Baker Street to Mrs. Brett's coffee shop at Portland Mansions, and his tone was the same when he added that I ought to bring my gun – a comment that was quite unnecessary, as I'd learned nearly half-my-life ago that being friends with Sherlock Holmes meant that I should only step out of doors when I was armed.

On the rattling train from Baker Street Station, we settled in for the nine-mile ride to Kew, and as no one was sitting nearby, Holmes was able to inform me, despite the noise, of his activities earlier in the day.

"I knew Ambrose Lewis once," he began, much to my surprise. "We're about the same age," he continued. "As you might recall, I attended a day school in Kennington for a short period of time, and Ambrose was there as well. Our paths never really crossed – I'm not sure that we said two words to one another the entire time that I was there. As I recall, he was a sizable lad, quiet and even-tempered, and never any trouble. Looking back, I find it curious that someone of his background would have studied there, but I heard something about his father having some unusual ideas concerning the raising of his sons. Perhaps planting Ambrose for a while amongst the 'common folk' was supposed to teach him something.

"In any case, my first stop this morning was to see if Mycroft had any insights. I found him in his office, his desk completely clear, and yet one could almost imagine it stacked deep across the entire surface with complex and interrelated documents that only he could see. He seemed a little too unsurprised about the note warning me away from this business, which is telling in and of itself, but he also recalled that I had known Ambrose Lewis in school, and he asked that I make a full investigation of the situation.

"'It's of national interest, you see,' he explained. 'As you know, paper is sometimes used in the manufacture of high-explosive munitions. The Hammerford mills have contracted with His Majesty's Government to supply highly specialized paper for some of our weaponry, and some of their factories have now been re-tooled to do this exclusively. I would suspect that within the next decade or so, when the upcoming war with Germany can simply no longer be avoided, the Hammerford mills will turn their efforts exclusively toward the national defense. Thus, it's in our interest to keep a close eye on whatever is happening within the Lewis family, and any possible claims under the Hammerford Will.'"

I raised my eyebrows and Holmes nodded. "My reaction as well. He mentioned it as if I should have heard of it – like casually mentioning the *Codex Gigas.*"

I didn't interrupt to remind Holmes that – until the previous November when we had been tasked to recover it – neither of us had ever before heard of the *Codex Gigas.*

"I expected that I'd need to make a tedious effort to get a look at this infamous will, but fortunately – and suspiciously – Mycroft recalled the particulars. Essentially, Sir Edward Lewis, the father of Ambrose and George, had incorrectly fancied himself something of legal expert, and he stubbornly insisted – against the strong advice of his own advisors – on wording the document in his own atypical way. Thus, the Hammerford Estate itself was entailed to the oldest surviving male heir, while the factories and family fortune, as built solely through Sir Edward's efforts, would remain separate. In the end, it wasn't so unusual an arrangement, but legal experts say that the wording is fraught with peril for the way that verification of who is and isn't an heir might be interpreted. Therefore, accurate identification that the newly arrived and overly flamboyant Ambrose Lewis is who he claims might be of paramount importance, especially to the Government in connection with the factory contracts.

"'Be my eyes and ears, Sherlock,' Mycroft intoned. 'I have my own thoughts on the matter, but I'm not inclined to rush around and shepherd this thing to a successful conclusion.'"

"Which leads me," I interjected, "to theorize as to the origin of the note you received this morning."

"Indeed. Who better than Mycroft to know that telling me not to interest myself in a matter will instead tempt me to look, when otherwise I would have ignored it."

I'd hoped to hear more about Holmes's further investigations that morning, but a pair of chattering couples who had been walking to-and-fro through the train as we traveled chose that moment to sit near us, and we remained in silence through the rest of the journey. The train arrived at the Kew Garden Station and we disembarked with the surging crowd. I was surprised to see so many families apparently intending to visit the Botanic Garden. It was still cold, and even though the early March rains had stopped for a little while, there was a rawness to the air.

We stepped out of the handsome station and into a tidy square which opened to the north. The rains of earlier in the day seemed to have passed for the moment. Pausing to get our bearings, we became something of a stone in the stream as various little groups gathered and worked their way around us, heading toward the Gardens. I happened to glance to our right, where a solid-looking pub built from the same brick as the station was located, and saw that a young lad seemed to have his attention focused on us with singular intensity. Then, almost immediately, he hopped down from the barrel where he'd been perched and scampered into the tavern.

"I saw him," murmured Holmes, even though he hadn't seemed to be looking in that direction. "I suspect that he was waiting for us, and is now off to inform someone that we've arrived."

I smiled. "You made it easy for him," I said. "Your insistence upon wearing your Inverness and fore-and-aft cap in both city and countryside tend to make you quite recognizable."

"As I've explained before," Holmes replied good-naturedly, "I could not care less about the dictates of fashion. Furthermore, I wish to be prepared for any eventuality, and should I be called upon later this afternoon to track a fugitive along the river-bank, I'd much rather be dressed this way than in some City-suitable clothing that will make Sir George feel happy because I wore a coat and hat and shiny shoes that please his aesthetics. I'm not a theater critic – I'm a consulting detective, and I dress like one, the same as any professional that wears the clothing of his trade. And besides," he said, shrugging the Inverness tighter, "it's a cold day, and this coat and hat are very warm old friends, quite fitting for my requirements in every way."

He looked around and seemed to see something that satisfied him. "And I should also mention that people now *expect* to see me garbed thusly, thanks to those stories that you printed during my time out of the country, and courtesy of the illustrations by Mr. Paget. Therefore, when they expect to see someone in a deerstalker hat, they won't see me during those times when I've removed it and chosen instead to appear differently – unlike our friend over there, who refuses to give up on wearing those dark spectacles."

I followed his glance and saw, across the square, our old acquaintance Barker, the private detective from the Surrey-side of the Thames. Holmes often affectionately referred to him as his "hated rival", but in truth they had worked closely together on a number of cases, always successfully, and Holmes was ever-willing to admit that there was more than enough work in London to support any number of private investigators.

I had only met Barker officially for the first time two or three years before, when I'd run across him while he separately investigated the disappearance of a Lewisham doctor – a case that tragically intersected with Holmes's own queries into a vanished wife. I have no idea how long Holmes had known Barker before I first encountered him during that affair, but clearly they were already long acquainted. It was only after the case of the Lewisham disappearances, in July of '98, that I realized that I'd actually seen Barker once before, specifically on the evening of 5 April, 1894, the very day that Holmes revealed to me that he hadn't perished at the Reichenbach Falls three years before that.

I had been ignorant of Holmes's survival, or the fact that he was back in London, prepared to capture a deadly killer who had been of high importance in the late Professor Moriarty's organization. Having maintained my interest in the various crimes of the day, I'd walked over to a house where a puzzling murder had recently occurred, enjoying the early spring evening, and glad to be out and about after a long day in my surgery. I'd joined the crowd in front of the house for a short time, listening to the various speculations that arose – including one by a tall man in colored glasses. While I hadn't known him at that time in any way, having never been introduced to him by Holmes, I recalled in hindsight that the man was Barker. After being around him several further times during the last couple of years, I realized that he always wore the tinted spectacles, although a reason had never been revealed. I wondered how, as a detective, he could function while maintaining a very noted feature of his appearance that was so recognizable. And that question arose once again when I saw Barker standing there across the square, making no effort to avoid being seen. He nodded to both of us, touched a finger to the brim of his bowler, and then turned and started walking briskly to the northeast.

Holmes anticipated my question. "I arranged for friend Barker to join us. He has his own task to carry out, and I expect that we shall see him presently. Now, shall we arrange transportation to Hammerford?"

We engaged a rackety-looking hansom and set off across the still-wet roadway. It wasn't far, but there were several abrupt turns as we worked our way back and forth, always northeast toward the river. I was surprised to see that our route took us alongside a brick manufactory, and then the sprawling drainage works which processed sewage from along this area of the southern shore for deposit into the Thames. I mentioned it to the driver.

"That's right, sir," he growled. "Hammerford has been here for four-hundred years, and all of this grew up around it – despite what the Lewis family did over the years to try and stop it. Right over that way is the rail line and the bridge, and there to the other direction is the sewage works. Sometimes the stink of it hangs like fog over the river around here. I don't know how they stand it at the old house – except I've heard that they don't have a choice – Sir George isn't allowed to leave. Something to do with the conditions of the will set up by old Sir Edward requires that Sir George stay there. Oh, he can go up to London sometimes, and he desperately wants to move there permanent-like, and when he was younger he would get away for a little while, but the inheritance ties him to the house – to have the money, he has to live in the house, and the lawyers are very strict about it. They say that's why he tried to get the new bridge moved – so that it would be built where the house is. If it had to be torn down, he'd be free."

His comments made me even more curious about this perplexing Hammerford Will. Surely a man of wealth, such as Sir George, could have turned his resources into breaking it, or at least overturning whatever specific language required him to stay here in this otherwise unpleasant location.

And yet, when we first turned at the gate and down the long sloping drive to the old house, I could see that there was some dark charm to it. The entrance was at a place the driver called "Gipsy Corner", and it became apparent as it spread in front of us that Hammerford was a wide and low-slung manor, made of stone that had blackened through the centuries. The drive itself ran down a gentle hill that followed the natural grade toward the river, but then it angled back up, as the house itself was built on a low rise. This plateau was essentially the same area as the structure, and I wondered if it had existed naturally that way all those many years ago, and that the house had been constructed to specifically fit onto it, or if the earth to form the rise had first been brought in, a massive effort, to raise the house's proposed location above the flood plain.

Behind the house was the Thames, flowing placid at this point, with the far shore a couple-of-hundred feet away. There was the expected amount of traffic making its way up and downstream – at least what could be seen through a substantial line of willows stretching along the riverbank. One of them, a noble giant fully twice as tall as the others, rivaled the house in terms of what drew one's attention. I wondered if it was older than the building, and felt that this must surely be the tree where Ambrose Lewis claimed to have slept away nearly twenty years. Looking at it, one could almost believe that it did truly possess some ancient powers where something like that might occur.

As we approached the front door, it became more apparent that the building was in a state of long-term neglect. The drive curved so that we ran alongside the building for a moment, allowing use to see the moss-covered stones, cracked and crumbling mortar, and window panes that appeared to have rotted in places. Additionally, there was cracked or missing glass in a number of the windows. Only the glass in the windows from a few rooms along the right side of the building near the central front door appeared to be in good repair. The front steps sagged in several places, and one was out of alignment, revealing a dark space underneath through a wide triangular opening. I suspected, based on the slight muddy line leading across the stones to the hole, that it made a tidy little home under there for some wild creature.

I was a bit dismayed when Holmes paid the cabbie and freed him to return to the station, but I assumed that he had an alternate way in mind for our own escape from the place. There was no bell, so Holmes lifted the heavy and discolored knocker hanging in the center of the oak door – which itself seemed to be in good condition – and announced our arrival.

The door was answered by a sour old man, stooped more by bitterness than his actual years. It rolled off of him in waves, and somehow in those very first moments, he seemed to epitomize the mean spirit of the ancient house, as if the former would never die while the latter stood, and vice-versa.

Our names meant nothing to him, and without comment he turned and walked away, implying that we were to follow. Our destination proved to be the very first door encountered on the right of the vast and damp-smelling hall. The old servant threw it open, stepped aside for us to pass, and then when we had done so, he reached and pulled it shut with nary an introduction.

While the room was in much better shape than the outer building would have implied, with rows of books on the shelves, a large fireplace throwing out welcome heat, and various tasteful artworks resting on fine tables scattered throughout, our attention was pulled toward a fat man draped across a divan near the front window. An open book was dropped on the floor beside him, and he glared at us while declaiming in a querulous voice, "I saw you coming!" He gestured a pale hand toward one of the tall front windows, which revealed a view back toward the gate and the curiously named "Gipsy Corner". As I looked that way, a carriage was halfway down the drive, coming toward the house, but apparently Sir George hadn't noticed it. The sole occupant was quite recognizable.

My attention was turned back to the room when Sir George whined petulantly, "We do not entertain visitors!"

Having seen him before in years past, I knew that this was Sir George Lewis, although he looked much worse than the last time I'd encountered him, over ten years before, outside of the Haymarket Theatre when my late wife Mary and I had managed to obtain tickets for a very popular play. At the time, we'd been making out way through the crowd toward the theatre entrance when several ushers had abruptly blocked our passage, along with that of a number of other resentful patrons, so that Sir George would be allowed to cross from carriage to entrance without hindrance, or being required to interact with the proletariats. It had mattered little to me at the time, but I confess that I hadn't liked him then, and I liked him less now.

"Who are you?" he whined in a voice that sounded much older than his years. With a shock, I realized that the man sprawled out in front of us was over half-a-decade younger than myself. I felt a small sense of self-satisfaction at my own efforts to stay healthy and fit when compared to this debauched wreckage displayed before me.

"I am Sherlock Holmes, and this is Doctor John Watson. We received a note this morning regarding your situation here at Hammerford."

"My *situation*?" the man snarled. "What *situation* is that? My father's will, perhaps, that requires me to live year after year in this fetid pile, interminably disturbed by the sounds of the passing trains on the one side, and the stench of Kew's sewage on the other? Or can it be that some impostor has arrived in London, pretending to be my older brother? Or is there some other business beyond that of which I haven't even yet comprehended to make my life a further living hell?"

Whatever Holmes's response might have been was interrupted by a loud and forceful pounding. I realized that I was hearing what the knocker on the front door sounded like from within. I wanted to tell Holmes who I'd seen through the window, as he hadn't been standing in a position to observe it for himself, in order to give him some warning if needed, but I realized that it might be better to let things play out. Even if Holmes were momentarily surprised, he would quickly adapt to the changing situation. I did manage to catch his eye and let him know that something interesting was about to happen.

We three paused, as if waiting to see whether we would be interrupted before continuing. We heard the front door open, the sound of an abrupt and muted conversation, and then, after a few seconds, there was a soft knock on the door from the hall. The door opened to reveal a pudgy man in his twenties who stepped in and, with a small cough, said, "Umm, Sir George? Mr. Ambrose – that is, the man claiming to be your brother – he is *here*!"

I glanced at Holmes, who had a sudden sparkle in his eye. It was the same expression that a boy would have if he was in a front-row seat at the Maskelyne Theatre, leaning forward in hot anticipation to see the latest magical illusion. He found this entertaining, I realized. And then I further realized that I did as well.

Turning back to the door, I saw the young man pushed aside by the tall figure of Ambrose Lewis – should that be his real name. It had been he that I'd seen on the carriage coming down the drive.

Ambrose Lewis was dressed as I would have expected, in his well-known theatrical and dated habiliments. I wouldn't have been surprised if he'd had entered the room while sweeping a cavalier hat with proud feather from his head, but he had no hat at all, just a dirty old wooden box in both hands, about a foot-square on each side. The young man who had introduced him, looking somehow familiar, pushed the door shut and stood just inside near Ambrose, while keeping his eyes locked on the box.

"Well," boomed the tall man, "we meet again, George! I'll bet you never expected it – at least, not on this side of the Gates of Hell!"

Due to the odd costume, I expected him to hold forth with dated phrases peppered with "Thee" and "Thou", but instead he simply spoke typical English, although his accent has some strange ring to it. I suddenly recognized it – I'd heard the same from Britishers who had spent years living in France. Was that were Ambrose had been since his supposed death?

Sir George tried to push himself deeper into the divan. "You aren't Ambrose!" he squeaked. "How could you let him in, Philip?"

"I didn't have much choice," replied the young man. "I was near the door when Tyers answered it, and he just pushed his way inside. He seemed to know where he was going – this room – so I jumped in front long enough to knock first."

"You've heard that I was back," said the tall man, as if the others hadn't spoken. "We're you surprised? I went to sleep under the Great Willow nineteen years ago, and now here I am, reawakened, and ready to take control of my fortune. Have you kept it safe for me, George?"

"It isn't yours!" snarled the fat man, pushing himself somewhat upright with sudden energy. "You're dead! I saw you die!"

"Is that what you believed?" said Ambrose in a quieter tone. There was danger there now. "You and Richard Nason both claimed that, didn't you?"

Sir George simply nodded, and Ambrose continued. "But Richard can't confirm your story – that I fell from our yacht off Margate – because he died too, didn't he? Not long after me, from what I've learned. But he wants to tell his story, nonetheless. Let's see what Richard has to say!"

With that, he lifted the lid of the wooden box and shook it violently toward Sir George, causing its contents to tumble out. It contained a skull, which hit the thick rug and then rolled over and over before resting within a foot or two of where Sir George cowered, his legs now pulled up and arms tight around him as if to ward off any touch from the thing. It somehow settled upright, facing toward Sir George, its grinning teeth giving it a foxy expression. Sir George gave a keening whine.

"Can you hear him, George?" asked Ambrose. "I can. He accuses you, George. He knows the truth – that there was no accident on the yacht, as you claimed. That instead you and Richard leapt upon me while I napped under the Great Willow, cutting my throat, killing your own brother to gain the inheritance that you had so long desired, but were prevented from having while I lived due to the excessive complications of father's Hammerford Will. You buried me there, in a shallow grave, and then went out to sea, only to return and claim that I'd died there instead."

Sir George was shaking his head, his eyes shut, a constant whimper escaping his drooling lips. I didn't like the look of his color.

Meanwhile, Philip, the young man, was looking back and forth between Sir George and Ambrose, as if trying to make sense of what he was hearing. Seeing the vexed look upon his face suddenly revealed to me why he looked familiar – he was the spitting image of a younger Sir George himself.

Ambrose dropped the box and stepped forward toward his cringing brother, nudging the skull with his toe. "Can you hear him, George? He speaks the truth. You killed me George – killed me and buried me beside the river, never to be found again. And yet, here I am."

He reached up then and tugged at the long crimson silk sash tied around his throat. Sir George watched in the same way that an animal will freeze before a swaying cobra. The knot loosened and the scarf was pulled away, revealing Ambrose Lewis's bare throat. I have seen many wounds, so I wasn't forced to look away, but it was terrible to behold.

The skin was red and raw, in spite of apparently having been cut nearly twenty years before. The edges were puckered and gaping, as if the flesh underneath had managed to heal on its own, while the severing of the epidermis had never been properly closed or sutured, and instead allowed to remain open like parted lips, a kiss of death, while healing in that state forever.

Ambrose glanced our way. "I remember you, Sherlock Holmes. And this would be Doctor Watson. You see the wound. You no doubt perceive it correctly – it wasn't properly treated at the time, and when I finally located a physician, it was too late. The edges of the cut had already died – necrotized, the doctor said, and infected by the soil from my grave – and after the dead skin was trimmed back, there wasn't enough slack in the remaining flesh of my throat to pull the wound shut for sewing."

He looked back at his brother. "Look upon it, George. See what killing me did. And now I have returned, because you refused to answer my simple requests for help, when it would have cost you *nothing*!"

Sir George wouldn't look toward the big man, but he shook his head, and his whine resolved into an intelligible question.

"Requests for help? I don't know what you mean." He seemed genuinely puzzled.

Ambrose was suddenly taken aback. It seemed as if what had previously occurred had been according to some plan up to this moment, but George's simple statement of ignorance had popped it off the track.

"Are you saying that you didn't receive my letters?"

"Letters?" Sir George looked at him then. "Of course not. Do you think I would have been able to ignore them? You're dead. I thought you were dead . . . ."

"So do you acknowledge, then, that this man is your brother?" asked Holmes, his calm voice jarring as it intruded into the tight drama being played out by the two other men.

George's eyes widened then, as if suddenly realizing what such an admission might mean – what a loss it would be to him financially, and worse, that it would apparently be an admission to the old crime of attempted murder."

"Nonsense," he snarled, apparently deciding to stick to his earlier story. "My brother died when he fell from the yacht. We couldn't reach him."

"I see," said Holmes. "Then there's one way to verify it," he added, "beyond the obvious physical similarities between your brother as he was described nearly twenty years ago and this man here." He looked at the oddly-costumed character before him. "The tattoo of the two-headed tiger."

Ambrose looked puzzled, but only for the briefest of moments. Then, with a grin that showed what he must have looked like when he was young, he removed his coat and pulled up the sleeve of his billowy shirt, revealing a marking on his forearm. It wasn't pretty, and the inks had blurred and blended over the intervening years as disfigurements of that sort and age will, but the two-headed tiger could clearly be seen."

"It is an old tattoo," Holmes remarked. "It hasn't been recently applied by smearing and blue-ing the inks, as if you had tried to make it appear to have been received years ago."

Ambrose nodded. "A friend and I obtained them while at university. When I . . . when I left England, and I believed that my old life was gone forever, I was grateful for the everlasting reminder."

"And you should be grateful now as well," added Holmes. "When doing my research about you today, I happened to run across this fact, which seemed to be the easiest way to verify that you are who you say."

I noticed that while this had been going on, the young man, Philip, had been edging his way toward the door to the hall. With a couple of steps, I positioned myself in front of him, putting my back against the exit even as I pulled my gun. "I don't believe that we're ready for you to leave yet."

The young man snarled and then looked behind him, as if considering whether to dash toward one of the tall windows and toss himself through. And yet he was clearly a coward, and I could actually see the notion of flight drain away from him.

"What is this about, Philip?" called Sir George, levering himself upright and sliding toward the edge of the divan, while keeping his feet well away from the grinning skull. "What does he mean about letters?" Then he glanced at Holmes. "Philip is my secretary. He would know about letters."

"And he is your son as well," added Holmes. Sir George gave a start, and Holmes added, "It's no secret, if one knows where to ask. There is a fellow that passes his days in a St. James's Street club, collecting facts just like this and making a living from knowing where to sell these secrets. He confirmed yours to me only a few hours ago."

"What's this about?" repeated Sir George to the young man, now considerably more forceful.

Philip looked around, from his father – as was clearly evident – to the window, and then toward the door (and me) before doing so again. Clearly he had no inclination to speak.

"Perhaps," said Holmes, "you could tell us about the letters from your perspective, Sir Ambrose."

The tall man started, and then gave a rueful shake of the head. "'Sir Ambrose'. I guess if I'm back, then that title must be acknowledged, in spite of how little I want such an anchor around my neck." He looked at the seated fat man. "Sorry about that, George. I never wanted to be Sir Ambrose. I don't want it now. Father's will trapped both of us, but if you'd only talked to me, instead of trying to kill me, we probably could have worked something out after he died. But in the end, I was happy for you to be shackled with that burden instead of me, because of what you did to achieve it."

He seemed to settle into himself for a minute while he prepared his mind to speak, and then I could see that he wasn't the foppish character at all, but simply a middle-aged man, solid and capable, yet suddenly weary, and seemingly glad to be at the end of some long and unpleasant task.

"After my brother thought that he'd killed me – " He stopped suddenly with a shake of his head. "No, I must back up a bit. You should know that our father, George's and mine, was not a good man. He was demanding, and cruel, and it was clear that he never liked either of us. But he was enthralled with his family name, and the history and longevity of his house, both figurative and literal, and the idea of the Lewis dynasty, stretching back into the forgotten past and forward just as far. He became much worse when we were small, after our mother died. Somehow the idea that death could reach into his own abode only made him much more interested in his legacy. That's when he likely began making up all the requirements and *sine qua non* that he eventually put into that cursed will.

"He didn't like us, either of us, but we were his sons and he was forced to use what he had – that being me, the eldest who was expected to carry on what he had built.

"But I wasn't suited for it. I didn't want it, and I never cared for the family history or the industries that our father had built, or any of the responsibility. And yet, I was prepared to shoulder it. George, on the other hand, seemed to crave all of that, and would have gladly taken it on, but there was simply no way. I was the eldest, and upon me it would settle. It was how our father saw the world, and it was the way that it was meant to be.

"When we were both young men, father contrived that terrible Hammerford Will. He knew that I was unhappy with what he'd planned for me, and he hoped to tie me up – to strangle me – in such a way with his restrictions and conditions and codicils that I could never shirk away from my destiny. And I was prepared to do it, seeing no other path.

"But it seems that George considered a way out for me that I'd never considered on my own – my death. If I'd had the idea myself, I would have done it – fake an accident and vanish to live another life. And that's very near what actually happened, except that it occurred to George instead of me and, with the help of his wily and always-smiling friend Richard Nason, he decided to carry out the deed for real." He gestured to the horrible old wound across his throat. Sir George, however, continued to look at the curious skull still watching him from the floor.

"I was napping one day underneath the Great Willow, as I often did when trying to forget what faced me, when George and Richard approached. Thinking nothing of it, I lazily remained on the ground, completely unprepared, when Richard suddenly sprang, hitting me on the head. Thank heavens I was unconscious when they actually slit my throat, and once again thanks that whichever one did it was ignorant of the proper method. They sliced the skin, no doubt producing a certain amount of convincing blood, but praise be they missed the important blood vessels.

"If I'd been awake, I probably would have kept fighting, and they would have had no choice but to inflict further wounds, eventually actually killing me. But I was unconscious, and they thought that they'd finished me, so they were left with a body. I assume that they chose to bury me there under the tree for several reasons. No one but me ever went there, and when the willow branches were full, nothing could be seen from outside – it was like being in a vaulted room. Likely they didn't want to be seen carrying me somewhere else for burial, and just tossing me into the river would have produced a murdered corpse – leading the authorities right back to George, who had the only motive. Better to hide me right there and say that I'd died elsewhere in a completely different and accidental manner, without a body.

"As I said, I had no awareness of any of this. I awoke hours later in darkness, wracked with terrible pain, and weight upon me. They had buried me in a shallow grave, and if I'd really been dead, I have no doubt that animals would have eventually pulled me up, revealing my murder in spite of their amateur efforts and precautions. In any case, when they tumbled me into whatever hole they'd managed to excavate amongst the willow roots, my body had folded in such a way as to leave a void-like cavity between my knees and my face – an open space with air. Otherwise I would have probably suffocated. There must have also been an opening of sorts between this cavity and the surface, just large enough for the exchange of air, for I'd been able to breathe for several hours.

"I began to thrash about, and before long I'd uncovered myself. I remembered the attack, but was still shocked to find the wound on my throat. My first impulse was to lurch toward the house and seek assistance, but then, I began to fear what would happen if I met George or Richard Nason – they would quickly finish the job, and I was too weak to defend myself. While I considered this, another idea occurred to me – a really brilliant notion – whereupon I realized that this was a blessing in disguise. They had killed me, freeing me from the terrible life that had been laid upon me by our father. Rather than go back and willingly bind myself to that again, I would instead remain free. I was intelligent – I would find a way to support myself. I had no interest in either Hammerford or the industry that supported it, and there was nothing in either Kew or London to tie me down – no sweetheart, and no sentimentality. No, I would slip away and start a new life, and shake the dust of this place from my feet forever.

"There's no need to examine the next nineteen years in great detail. I found medical treatment from a doctor of dubious reputation who might have done better by me physically, but at least he asked no questions. I had adequate money in my pockets – I suppose that George and Richard had been too shaken to search them and take it, or perhaps they simply had no need of it. I made the crossing to France, discovered a place that I liked, and settled in, breaking all ties with my past life. I obtained work, supported myself, and in the meantime found a way to do something that I enjoyed for a living instead of simply earning my meat and cheese. I met a woman who saw beyond my scar – which I've otherwise kept hidden for years – although with something much less noticeable than this hideous kerchief. We had a child, and another and another. It was as perfect a life as I could have wished for.

"But then the worm in the bud presented itself, as they always do, one way or another. One of my daughters needs surgery. It isn't a life-threatening matter, so there's no urgency, but it's more than we can afford. There was someone who would help us with the money, but my wife, who knew my curious history, began to insist that I obtain what was really mine – at least a portion of it – in order to use it for the purpose of caring for my family and giving us some greater security. Eventually, after much discussion and convincing on her part and reluctance on mine, I agreed and wrote a letter to my brother."

He then looked directly at George, who somehow found it within himself to look back. "You didn't answer," continued Ambrose, "so I wrote another. And then two more. Four in all. There was never any acknowledgement. I was discrete – I just told you that I was still alive, without going into details, and I expected that you would at least write back, if only to deny it." He looked toward Philip, who still seemed poised as if to bolt toward some safe place that didn't exist. "Now I guess that I understand why I never heard anything. You hid the letters, didn't you? Or destroyed them."

The young man turned his head, and Ambrose looked back toward Holmes. "Our father, by way of his Hammerford Will, was quite specific in how he wanted the estate to be passed on. Legitimacy of the heirs was of secondary concern as long as there *is* an heir. He was afraid that I might not have a son, at least through legal wedlock, so he included language whereupon a documented bastard can inherit the estate as well." Looking back at Philip, he added, "I learned enough about George before I arrived to know that he has no heir by marriage, so you must be the other alternative. I can see by your appearance and your behavior that you're certainly George's son. It must have been awful for you to open those letters and learn that the true heir still lived."

At that point, there was a confident knock upon the door behind me. I suspected who it was, and stepped aside to open it. I was correct. With a grin, Barker stepped into the room with a nod. In his hand were several small bottles.

"Just like you said, Mr. Holmes. The only hard part was finding which room was his." Barker nodded his head toward Philip. "He thought that he was being clever, but they never are." He handed the bottles to me.

I saw that they were all slightly different in size, shape, and color, and all had been prepared at different chemists. But the labels were all the same, identifying their contents: *Digitalis.* All had relatively recent dates, and all were more than half-empty.

I looked at Philip, realizing that I didn't know his last name yet. "Have you been using these on your father? It's a wonder that he isn't dead already."

Philip started to speak, no doubt some angry denial, but then he slammed his mouth shut, turning to look at the fat man on the divan. I glanced toward Holmes. "How did you know? To have Barker look for them? And what he would find?"

"As part of my inquiries this morning, I wanted to verify the condition of your health, Mr. Lewis." He spoke to the younger brother, and his pointed use of "Mister" instead of "Sir" didn't pass unnoticed. "My brother Mycroft, who has had his eye on this situation already, provided me with the names of your physicians. I have some past acquaintance with one of them, Dr. Moore Agar of No. 6 Harley Street, and he was willing to give me a short *précis* of your condition, along with the fact that you are frequently dissatisfied that a simple prescription cannot be written to absolve you of a lifetime of bodily sins. He knew of at least two other doctors whom you had also visited in search of some miraculous restoration, and one of them knew a fourth. As they were all located near one another, and each was willing to give me a recommendation to speak with the next on my list, I quickly learned that each of them had diagnosed you with rather obvious heart problems, chief among your other complaints, and had prescribed digitalis.

"A check of their records revealed which chemists had filled the prescriptions, and that the recent dates, along with subsequent requested refills as signed by Mr. Philip Ellington here, meant that quite a bit of digitalis was being used in this house – far too much than can be safely prescribed during that amount of time. With what I learned about Mr. Ellington's identity, and his connection to a claim on the family fortune through the tangled Hammerford Will should you die, it became fairly obvious that a plot was in motion to kill you.

"But was this scheme somehow related to the curious arrival two months ago of that over-the-top figure who claimed to be your brother, but who never did anything toward regaining the estate except find ways to titillate the press? It seemed unlikely, although I didn't entirely discount it. Yet, I continued to gather enough facts until I thought that I had a tenuous understanding of what was happening here, and then Dr. Watson and I came down to see for ourselves.

"I had alerted Barker to join us, with instructions to gain entry to the house and check on the prescribed medicine. When he saw us arrive at the station, he went ahead to await our entry at the front of the house, which would serve as a distraction for him to go in by the back way. But when Watson and I left the station, we also noticed a lad who was obviously watching for our arrival in Kew. He ran into the pub to tell someone – that would be you, Sir Ambrose. As soon as Watson and I departed by way of a cab for this house, you immediately followed. How long had you been down here, waiting for us to show up?"

Sir Ambrose smiled. "Most of the day. I knew that things were set in motion for you to become involved, as we wanted you as an independent witness when my plans culminated – when I revealed myself to George."

"We?" I asked.

Ambrose swallowed, considering whether to answer. Then, "The man . . . my friend who also has a double-headed tiger tattoo. When I left England after my supposed death, I cut all ties with the past – even with my friend. He spent the years since thinking that I was dead. But when I needed help, and George wouldn't acknowledge my letters or offer any assistance, I didn't know where else to turn. It was then that I thought of my friend.

"I slipped back to England – not as you see me now. This outlandish costume and ridiculous disguise – " And here he reached up and pulled off a wig, revealing a mostly-bald head with short-cropped reddish-gray hair underneath. " – was all his idea. The rest of it was, too. He has a streak of theatricality about him when he handles certain affairs, and he somehow he talked me into this. He felt that George – and the public – needed to be led along by way of this dramatic idiocy, to being somehow on my side when the cracking blow was struck. They needed to have a satisfying end to the story when my claim was finally pressed, so that I will be accepted, and that an interesting presentation in the press would work perfectly. He came up with the costume and the parties, and then I came back to London, intending that it should all apply pressure to George. I wrote two more letters to him – and once again they were ignored." He glanced at Philip Ellington before continuing.

"I was becoming impatient after two months of nothing moving forward – Would any reasonable man wish to continue prancing around for that long in these trappings? – and I argued with my friend, thinking that his enthusiasm for concocting some grand and convoluted game had blinded him to the fact that George was too stubborn to budge. Of course, in the meantime, to my friend's credit, we've also been laying proper legal groundwork for me to resume control of the estate, which I believe has passed completely unnoticed." George seemed to wither a bit at this statement. "So if nothing else," continued Ambrose, "this whole business with the disguise has been a successful decoy from what my friend has managed to accomplish in the shadows. He informs me that all is ready. He is rather influential, and he knows a great many important people. One of these, apparently, is your brother, Mr. Holmes."

Ambrose shifted his feet, looking now toward Holmes instead of his defeated brother. "It was your brother's idea to have my friend write you that note this morning. He said that you can sometimes be 'willful', as he put it, and that if he 'commanded' you to involve yourself, you'd likely refuse. So my friend sent you a note rudely demanding that you stay out of this business and not to come to Hammerford. And then, based on your brother's advice and his knowledge of what you would then do, I came directly down here this morning, soon after you would have received it, because it was certain that you would be along sometime later today to help wrap things up."

Holmes smiled. "My brother exaggerates. I would have been proud to assist, command or no, if either he or you – or your friend – had asked it of me. Although," he added, nodding toward the skull on the rug, "I'm not sure that I would have counseled toward the use of that stage prop there."

"Prop?" asked Ambrose, with a smile. "They both thought that it would put a scare into George. How did you know that it isn't real?"

"Oh, it's real enough," said Holmes. "But it isn't the skull of Richard Nason, whom I verified had died not long after your supposed passing in 1882. Apparently he was drunk and fell down a well on his country estate."

Holmes spoke to George Lewis. "Curiously, you were there that night, and it wasn't that long at all after he helped you cut your brother's throat. It turned out rather amazingly lucky for you that the only witness to how you acquired the family fortune died so quickly. From the little I've learned of this Richard Nason, his help wouldn't have come cheap, and someone like that would have likely bled you dry with the knowledge of what you had done. I usually have a great deal of sympathy for those who are the victims of blackmailers, but it adds a curious twist if the reason that a man is being blackmailed in the first place is because he himself has committed a murder – or at least believes that he has done so." He added, "That is one possibility to consider."

George Lewis started with slack wet lips, his pale face looking as fearful at what Holmes seemed to know about the fate of Nason as he had when first seeing the skull staring up at him.

Looking back at Ambrose Lewis, Holmes said, "I'm sure that Watson immediately noticed as soon as I did that the skull you tossed at your brother couldn't be that of Richard Nason."

I nodded. "It's too clean, and more importantly, the jaw remained fixed in place in that death-grin even as it rolled over the floor. It's clearly a medical artifact, likely one cleaned, preserved, and wired into place for use by medical students."

Sir Ambrose nodded. "My friend found it for me. It was his idea to confront George with it. Another straw with the purpose of breaking the camel's back."

He took a couple of steps toward the skull and leaned over to pick it up. As he bent down, his brother George had apparently had enough, and he pulled back both feet, rolling onto his back on the divan and then kicking out toward his brother's unprotected head.

But Holmes had anticipated it, and was there even as the force of the man's legs was released. Holmes stepped in and dipped, coming up between the two brothers and catching both of George's ankles to deflect them upwards, and in doing so, lifting and rolling George in the opposite direction by directing his own force against him. The divan tipped over backward and, with a heavy thump, the obese figure tumbled and spilled onto the floor. He stayed there, lying on his fat stomach with his face buried in the rug and both arms sheltering his head. He began to weep, and then wail, kicking his legs and sobbing like a spoiled child having a fit.

The rest of us watched him with varying emotions – Barker with obvious amusement, Sir Ambrose with pity, and the man's son Philip with undisguised disgust. Over the sounds of it all, Holmes said, "Shall we summon the police?"

Ambrose shook his head. "There are worse punishments for him. We've broken the will – somewhat. George gets to keep the title – and good riddance. It will die with him. And he can stay here in the house with a small allowance – enough to maintain it at its current level of . . . comfort. Both of those, from my perspective, are punishment enough – a life sentence. Of course, he's free to move away whenever he wants, but the allowance ends if he does, and I don't suppose he can find any other way to support himself."

He looked toward his illegitimate nephew. "The same for this one. If he wants to stay here, on a salary to care for his father, he can. There's no need for him to murder George now, since there's nothing for him to inherit. But I suspect, if he has the same stunted character of his father, that he'll walk out right now and never be heard from again. Isn't that right?"

Ambrose said this in a quiet voice, without warmth of righteous anger or any other indication of how he felt. It was a strong voice, however, and commanding, and I realized that whatever he'd done during his other life in France must have been successful, based on seeing how he carried himself in that moment. And with that level of character at his command, I was certain that the family business, which he was acquiring without any desire to have it, would be well-served.

Philip Ellington didn't need any time at all to consider his response. With a sneer, but thankfully without a speech or a simple goodbye or even a backwards glance at his puling father, he wormed his way around Barker and slipped through the door. Soon after he was gone, after having gathered whatever possessions he could carry from his own room, and probably also taking a number of unknown valuables stolen from George Lewis.

Barker, having made sure that his services were no longer required, also departed. I had the sense that he intended to keep his eye on where Philip Ellington landed, just to be certain . . . .

"I've initiated inquiries into the death of Richard Nason, as well as your father," said Holmes when they had left. "Both of them dying so soon after your supposed murder, and each death serving to benefit this pathetic specimen – " He nodded toward the sobbing figure by the overturned divan. " – is quite suspicious."

Ambrose Lewis shook his head. "I wish that you wouldn't take it any further," he said quietly. "Nothing would be served at this point. Nason had no family, and I feel no need to avenge my father. If he was murdered, he brought it upon himself. No, I meant what I said. George being hanged would only release him from the peculiar punishment of remaining here at Hammerford."

Holmes shrugged, and I agreed.

We left George Lewis sniveling on the floor of his curious prison, with an indifferent Tyers watching from the door to the hallway. I asked Sir Ambrose if he wished to look around the old house before leaving, but he adamantly did not. However, when we reached the broken front steps, he did indicate that he wouldn't mind walking down to the river, to the old willow where he had "died", as he put it, before being resurrected into a new and better life.

As we rounded the house and pushed through the tall uncut grass, still wet from the morning's rains and dead in that late winter before spring's expected arrival, he told us a bit about his life in France – his beloved wife and family, and the vineyard where he'd labored for so many years, and how it was finally starting to achieve noted success. But he didn't have time to tell us much else before we found ourselves standing beside the great tree, a behemoth that had surely reigned there for centuries, quite possibly longer than the house itself, its roots forced deep into the rich and moist soil beside the river.

Ambrose paused then, even as Holmes had walked to one side, looking for a thin spot in the densely hanging fronds through which we could pass underneath the canopy. I could see into the shadowed chamber beyond, darkly dappled, with illuminated spots here and there across the mostly bare ground broken by exposed gnarled roots. I wondered if the shallow grave where the man beside me had been laid would still be obvious, or if it had been smoothed over by two decades of high waters and occasional floods.

"I . . . I cannot go in," said Ambrose.

I looked toward him and Holmes, having heard it as well, stopped looking for an entrance and walked back the few steps to join us.

"I thought that I wanted to see it," said the big man, "but now I do not. I fear to be even this close. What if . . . what if the last nineteen years have been nothing but a dream – the last tortured vision of my oxygen-starved brain as I either bleed to death or suffocate from the soil shoveled on top of me? If I return to that spot, if I stand there once again, on that place which was my grave, it may all be revealed – that none of this is real. That my wonderful life since that moment is nothing but an illusion. My wife, my children – what if they've never truly existed? What if they and everything I love were to vanish? What if . . . ?" His voice broke, and a tear tracked down his wrinkled face.

I expected Holmes to be disgusted – to comment that the fears expressed by the man with the terrible wound across his throat were irrelevant and illogical, and that he need not fall back from facing what he had just expressed. But even after knowing Holmes for so long, I still sometimes seemed to forget what a great heart is hidden underneath that cold and logical exterior he has constructed, and which he tries to convince both himself and others is his true self. Of course, he has fooled none of us who know him better.

Instead of negating Ambrose Lewis's concerns, Holmes laid a hand on the man's arm and pulled him back into motion toward the house. "There is nothing here to see. That man did die. Go and live *your* life. Leave the arrangements for regaining the estate to your friend and my brother, and to Watson and me, and return to your family." Ambrose nodded, and his tears of fear changed to those of relief. If this were a dream that he'd had at his death, it didn't have to end.

While we'd returned to the station, Holmes holding the reins of the carriage in which Ambrose had journeyed out to Hammerford, the man, still dressed in the bizarre clothing, told us of the hardships that he, someone normally quite reticent, had endured over the last couple of months while playing the part of a larger-than-life character in as full a view as an actor on a brightly lit stage. Shaking his head with a rueful laugh, he said, "I think that my friend arranged this more to punish me for letting him believe that I was dead for all these years than to actually force George's hand."

Later on the train, as we were making the short trip back to London, Ambrose Lewis had fallen into an exhausted sleep, and I considered that statement while looking at the snoring man seated across from us. Softly I asked, "Who do you think that his friend is – this fellow who managed these curious 'negotiations' in relation to Sir George and the Hammerford Will?"

"Oh, there's no mystery in that," Holmes replied in equally low tones. "Once I perceived that Mycroft had a larger part in things than he let on, a few inquiries revealed that it could be no other than his crony Sir James Damery, of Mayfair."

"What?" I said. "Colonel James Damery, the Royal Family's 'fixer'?"

"That's him."

"He lives in Mayfair, you say?" I named an address and Holmes nodded, raising an eyebrow. I explained how I'd seen Ambrose Lewis coming out of a Mayfair house – that house – a month or so earlier.

"That clinches it, then," said Holmes. "Sir James – or 'Colonel Damery' as he's likely known around your club – has a reputation for frankness, and his large, bluff, honest personality and laughing Irish eyes all serve him well when he's arranging this or that affair, or cleaning up any number of messes that regularly end up at his door."

I frowned. "I'm not so sure about the 'frankness' if he was willing to involve you without simply asking for your consent in his bizarre scheme."

"Oh, don't blame him too much for that. That was Mycroft's hand. As Ambrose indicated, they apparently wanted a pair of uninvolved witnesses for whatever comes next – legal decisions concerning the transfer of ownership of the various mills, announcements in the press that Ambrose Lewis has returned, and so on – and we, having seen it play out, will be able to give our honest independent testimony. The story will be accepted, Ambrose will take over the industry which has generated such interest within the government, and then the story will sink away like a rotting log hooked by a fishing line, pulled up from where it's been hidden for years, shiny and slick and visible in the sunlight for a brief moment, and then cut loose to settle back again, once more forgotten and obscure."

"Setting aside your vivid metaphor," I countered, "I might have a word with Sir James when next we meet."

"I wouldn't," said Holmes. "No harm was done, and I suspect that we may encounter him again, and if he should have another interesting little matter in which I might assist, I'd hate for him to reconsider and postpone meeting with us, based on the mistaken idea that I didn't appreciate this experience."

My feelings on the topic weren't yet quite so sanguine, but my response was interrupted by a rattle of heavy rain hitting the window of the train carriage. My thoughts turned to the sleeping man across from us, and how I felt responsible for getting him back to the Langham, where he'd invited us to dine with him. I imagined walking with him across the lobby, with everyone turning to stare, and I hoped that he'd brought some normal clothes from France, as I didn't fancy being part of the last act of the frenzy that had trailed after Ambrose Lewis for the past two months.

The next couple of weeks played out to great enthusiasm in the press as Ambrose Lewis was confirmed to be the long-lost older brother. Then, as Holmes predicted, the public quickly lost interest when the colorful version of Ambrose dropped from sight, and it was doubtful that anyone even recognized him as he carried out his necessary daily affairs dressed as any other businessman. The last flicker of interest from the press flared and died a few weeks later when that old wreck of a house, Hammerford, burned one night. George Lewis perished in the fire, but no one else was endangered, as he was now living there alone. No servants remained, not even the sour Tyers who had met us at the door at the start of our visit. The house was gone, and only the great willow remained to give that segment of the riverbank any significance.

But that was still in the future when we joined Ambrose Lewis for dinner the night we returned from Kew. Fortunately no one recognized the conservatively dressed man who had so recently had been featured in every day's periodicals. However, Holmes could not remain as anonymous, and it was no surprise when our meal was unexpectedly intruded-upon by a young fellow in his twenties. He had seen us from across the room and realized that only Holmes could help him. It seemed that his new wife had recently been arrested for being found unconscious in a newly discovered tunnel beneath the vaults of the Capital and Counties Bank. Bullion had been stolen, and she had no knowledge of how she'd ended up there, or who had cut a Cyrillic *M* into the back of her right hand. Inspector Athelney Jones was in charge of the case, and the young fellow was lucky not to be in custody along with his bride. Before the night had finished, we – including Ambrose Lewis – were prowling along Brick Lane in Whitechapel, trying to locate an elusive two-fingered Levantine who was rumored to know the truth of the matter.

Eventually I would catch up on my sleep, but not that night.

"Do you know anything of this man [Sir James] Damery?"

"Only that this name is a household word in society."

"Well, I can tell you a little more than that. He has rather a reputation for arranging delicate matters which are to be kept out of the papers. You may remember his negotiations with Sir George Lewis over the Hammerford Will case. He is a man of the world with a natural turn for diplomacy . . . ."

– Sherlock Holmes and Doctor John H. Watson
"The Adventure of the Illustrious Client"

The Adventure of Mr. Fairdale Hobbs
by Arthur Hall

During the years when I lived in Baker Street with my friend, the consulting detective Mr. Sherlock Holmes, I was privileged to share many extraordinary adventures with him, as he would often honour me by requesting my assistance.

There were, of course, occasional similarities between the cases – that is to say that one bank robbery was much like another. Yet I was always able, when given permission to publish an account of the circumstances at a much later date, to discern some distinguishing feature which qualified the tale as unique.

"I fear, Watson, that we must postpone further discussion of my early cases until another time. I believe I heard the doorbell just now and Mrs. Hudson has admitted someone." My friend sat up straight in his chair as we prepared to fill our pipes after dinner early one evening.

"You have already said that you have no appointments, Holmes."

"Indeed I did, and I expected none, but this fellow whose tread on the stairs is so heavy may have brought us something interesting. Besides, I have two cases on hand that will doubtless come to fruition before the end of the month, but nothing that requires my immediate attention."

This abrupt alteration to the evening caused me only momentary surprise. I had long become accustomed to my friend's Bohemian character, and his sudden changes of mood and intentions. We put away our pipes and waited in silence for the few seconds that passed before our landlady opened the door to usher in a middle-aged man of average height, dressed in a worn but well-pressed tweed suit.

"Good evening, Mr. Holmes and Doctor Watson," he said without waiting to be announced. "It is good to make your acquaintances, sirs."

"And you, sir." I responded.

Holmes glanced towards the door, having realised that Mrs. Hudson was hovering. "Would you care for tea, Mr. Hobbs?"

"No thank you, sir. If you don't mind, I would rather tell you what brings me here."

Holmes waited until Mrs. Hudson had withdrawn, then gestured that our visitor should sit. "I think you will find the basket chair the most comfortable."

"I hope you will pardon this intrusion, gentlemen," Mr. Hobbs replied. "I was sent to London only this afternoon, and so hadn't enough time to make an appointment, since the nearest Post Office is further away than the railway station."

Holmes nodded. "Further away from where, pray?"

"Why, from where I live and work these days, sir. That is Gaunt Manor, in Cambridgeshire. The nearest village Willadale, is almost five miles away."

"Gaunt Manor?" I asked. "Sounds rather picturesque."

He nodded. "I'm employed there. I do just about everything to keep the place going except tend the horses. Our stable-lad, Joel, does that."

"And in whose service are you now?" Holmes asked. "The owner of Gaunt Manor, I presume."

"That's right, sir. Mrs. Rosemary Prescott. I found her crying when I reported for duty this morning and, having no one else to talk to I suppose, she confessed the reason for her distress to me. We have, you see, become rather closer over the last few years than is usual between mistress and servant. Sometimes I find myself looking upon her as the daughter I never had. As soon as I grasped her problem, I remembered how I'd once heard of you, and suggested that she seek your guidance, but she said only that she would consider the situation. I gathered that she was reluctant to involve anyone else, for she is something of a recluse, but I was summoned just after mid-day and given leave to consult you."

"I thank you for the recommendation, Mr. Hobbs," Holmes acknowledged. "Mrs. Prescott is a young woman, then?"

"She is indeed, but widowed less than two years ago. Mr. Carlton was killed after falling off a horse. Struck by a low-hanging branch, no more than half-a-mile from home."

"But you already worked at Gaunt Manor while he lived?"

"For some years now, Mr. Holmes." He scratched his head, thoughtfully. "The truth is, I can't remember how many. I'm getting forgetful these days."

"This lady then has become reclusive since her husband's death. Has she no children?"

"Oh yes, didn't I mention Alice? She must be fifteen years old, by now. Shortly after her father died, she pleaded with her mother to be allowed to join a convent. This didn't surprise Mrs. Prescott a great deal, for Alice has been very religious since early childhood. Permission was refused at first – Mrs. Prescott was still grieving, of course – but when her daughter told of her own sadness at the loss of her father, she relented. I think what decided the matter was Alice's insistence that to eventually join the Sisterhood was the only way she would ever again know peace."

Holmes sat up in his chair. "Is it this young lady who is causing such anguish to her mother?"

"Not herself, but this will explain." Mr. Hobbs reached into his pocket and extracted a folded sheet of paper which he handed to my friend, who read the contents with a grim expression.

Mrs. Rosemary Prescott,

This is to inform you that your daughter, Alice, has been taken away from the protection of the Sisterhood of Golgotha. You can be assured that she will be cared for, and will come to no harm, until mid-day of this coming Sunday, by which time you will have paid the sum of two-thousand pounds for her safe return.

I must impress upon you that the money must be brought to a place about which you will be advised, and by no one other than yourself. Your appearance is known to us and you will be met for the exchange. The substitution of an emissary will be viewed with the greatest suspicion and considered as a breach of faith so you must not, in any circumstances, consider such a course of action.

You are urged also not to attempt to consult the official police force regarding this matter. Failure to comply with this restriction will result in the loss of your chance to be reunited with your daughter, and her permanent disappearance.

For now, kindly take no action until you hear from us.

"It is unsigned." Holmes placed the letter upon a side-table, his brows knitted in deep thought.

"Can you make anything of it, sir?" Mr. Hobbs asked eagerly.

"One or two trivial facts only. That the kidnappers, or at least one of them, aren't of the lower classes is evident from the educated phrases used here. Also, the paper is of fine quality, which suggests that they aren't poor. That there are more than one is obvious from the use of the words '*us*' and '*we*', unless this is a device employed to mislead us. The two points which immediately engage my interest are the stipulation that Mrs. Prescott herself should deliver the ransom, and the importance placed upon this. Also, I'm wondering about the means that these abductors could have employed to remove the girl from the convent. By any chance, has the envelope which must have enclosed this letter been retained?"

"I believe that Mrs. Prescott, in her anguish, tore it to shreds."

“This occurs all too often and it is a pity, for the envelope invariably reveals something of the sender. But wait! I’m taking it that this letter arrived by post. Is that, in fact, the case?”

Mr. Hobbs shook his head. “I picked up the pieces from where Mrs. Prescott had dropped them and, as far as I could tell, only her name had been written. There appeared to be other mark at all.”

“So the message was delivered by hand, which tells us that the writer, or whoever brought it, isn’t far off. Did it not occur to you, Mr. Hobbs, to immediately send a telegram to this convent in order to ascertain the circumstances of the girl’s withdrawal from there?”

“I could not, sir. That place is situated in the Orkney Islands, to the north of Scotland.”

“Where exactly, pray?”

“I believe it is near Skara Brae, but there is no wire service there and the order would not accept any communication in any case, for one of their strictest rules is that of isolation.”

“I see.” Holmes rested his chin on his steepled fingers and considered all that he had heard. After a few moments of silence had passed he rose to his feet. “Very well, Mr. Hobbs, you may tell your employer that I am already at work on her case. Today is Wednesday, so we have three clear days before the kidnappers will carry out their threat. I would be obliged if you would convey these recommendations to Mrs. Prescott: Firstly, she can expect the instructions for payment to include a meeting quite near to the local village or the surrounding area, and she must on no account venture forth from her home until this is arranged. If she intends to withdraw the ransom from a bank or elsewhere, she must send you with a letter of authority. I take it that she has complied with their demands, and not notified the official force?”

“It was all that I could do to convince her to involve you, Mr. Holmes. She was all for simply paying the money.”

“Hopefully that will not be necessary, but perhaps it would be as well to have the sum available. Pray tell the lady that she will hear from me shortly, and request that she retain at all costs the contents of the kidnapper’s next communication.”

“I will convey your words to her, immediately upon my return.”

“Capital. Now, if you have nothing else to tell me of this unfortunate affair, I will bid you good-day.”

Mr. Hobbs considered for a moment before, having thought of nothing further, becoming effusive with his thanks. I escorted him to the front door, where I looked along the gaslit street, silent at this hour. A hansom appeared suddenly and he summoned it as it passed. In an instant, he was gone.

Holmes had written a telegram, putting down his pen as I entered the room.

"To Lestrade?" I ventured.

"No, Watson. For now I think it best to keep Scotland Yard out of this. If their involvement became somehow known to the kidnappers, they might carry out their threat. I don't think so, but we cannot afford the risk."

"To whom is the telegram addressed, then?"

"To Barker, the private enquiry agent. You know that I have used him occasionally, since that affair of the Retired Colourman, as you called it. If the page-boy is still here, I'm afraid I must incur his displeasure for disturbing him at this hour."

"You are sending Barker to Cambridge?"

Holmes smiled. "I'm sending Barker to the Orkney Isles. But now, dear fellow, I do believe that sleep would be advisable. After breakfast we should both pack a bag. It is you and I who will depart on an excursion to Cambridge."

When I presented myself for breakfast, I discovered that Holmes had written and dispatched another wire.

"To Willadale," he explained, "to ensure that we have somewhere to lay our heads tonight."

"You don't think to stay at Gaunt Manor, to be on hand when anything further occurs?"

"That would be most unwise."

I nodded. "You have already made some progress, then?"

"It would be more accurate to say that I have come to understand that things aren't the way they appear in this affair. But come, let us waste no time in consuming our breakfasts, for my *Bradshaw* tells me that our train to Cambridge leaves in little more than an hour. I believe I hear Mrs. Hudson on the stairs already."

And so we ate more quickly than usual, refraining from calling for a second pot of coffee. We spoke little, but as we rose from the table Holmes turned to me.

"Your bag is packed, I take it?"

"Since before I retired, last night."

"And your revolver?"

"With me, as always."

He reached for his hat and coat. "Excellent. Stout fellow."

The hurried journey through the East End of London to Bishopsgate Station was passed mostly in silence. The hansom left us before we boarded the train with minutes to spare, and my only memory until we reached our destination is of our conversation that referred to a recent case of abduction concerning the young Lord Saltire and his father, the Duke of Holdernesse.

"No, Watson," my friend assured me, "I don't expect this business to turn out in the same fashion. Some of the features are quite different."

"You believe then that this unfortunate girl will be murdered by her kidnappers?"

"I have every reason to doubt that. However, it is by no means impossible, unless I've made a grave error of judgement. There is little point in theorizing at this stage. We must be patient while events play themselves out before us."

Beyond that, he would say nothing of his expectations. We arrived at Cambridge within a couple of hours, and Holmes consulted the local time-table, announcing that we had only fifteen minutes to wait. The train that took us down the branch line was a small and uncomfortable conveyance, but we sound found ourselves carrying our bags along the platform of the tiny Willadale Station.

The elderly man who waited with his cart near the station exit struck me as a very honest fellow.

"Of course I know The Crossed Swords, sir. I've lived here all my life and I can tell you that the rooms are clean and the food plentiful and good. It's not worth me taking you, though. You just walk to the end of the lane before you turn left. You can't miss it then."

"Our thanks to you," Holmes replied. "You would, I think, know everyone hereabouts, since you have always lived locally?"

"That be true, sir. There can't be many that I'm not acquainted with."

"Perhaps then, you can tell me where I am likely to find a young fellow who once worked for a friend of mine. His name is Joel, a stable lad – although I must confess to forgetting his other name."

The old fellow took off his cap and scratched his grey head. "Ah," he remembered after a moment, "You must mean Joel Crabber. Well, he's still a stable lad, or so I hear, at a place called Gaunt Manor, some distance along the road that meets this one at the crossroads back there. Thinking about it, I'd say you're in luck, because Joel comes to the village every Friday morning to buy horse feed. If you were to wait near the corn merchants shop, just down the road from the Crossed Swords and opposite the police station, you're bound to run into him at about ten o'clock tomorrow."

Holmes thanked the man again, and gave him a half-sovereign for his trouble. The inn proved to be as the fellow had described and, after unpacking our few things in our rooms, we spent an hour smoking together in a comfortable lounge.

"Why are you interested in the stable lad?" I enquired when we had settled ourselves. "According to Mr. Hobbs, he plays no part in this business."

"He hardly mentioned him, it is true." My friend blew out a cloud of pungent smoke. "But if you recall the letter from the kidnappers, it displays certain familiarities. The title of the religious order, for instance, and the daughter's name, is known to them."

"You mean that they were informed by someone working at, or in some way close to, Gaunt Manor?"

"Indeed. They had to have a local agent, who may or may not be concerned with the abduction. You will recall that Mr. Hobbs remarked that Joel was the only servant, besides himself."

"He also stated that Mrs. Prescott is something of a recluse, remaining in her home since her husband's death. Why, then, would the kidnappers insist that she should deliver the ransom personally?"

"I believe I may be able to throw some light upon that shortly. I've told the landlord that I expect a telegram either this evening or tomorrow. Unless he has changed his methods considerably, Barker will have obtained the information that I requested by then. But look, old fellow, some of the other guests are already making their way to the dining room. I suggest that we do likewise and continue our conversation over dinner."

But there was no word from Barker at dinner, nor at breakfast the following morning. It wasn't yet ten o'clock when Holmes and I took up a position near the police station, a place where we appeared to be discussing the sartorial examples in the tailor's shop window while, in reality, we closely observed the arriving customers at the corn merchants.

Three carts presented themselves, all containing a driver and passenger. Then a trap with a single occupant came to a halt near the entrance.

Holmes shook his head. "Too old. Joel has been described or confirmed as a young fellow, by both Mr. Hobbs and our friend at the station."

I looked up and down the street, where an occasional hansom and four-wheeler made an appearance, but saw nothing of interest.

"It is now twenty minutes past the hour," I saw from my pocket-watch. "Perhaps he will come on a different day."

"No, Watson," Holmes pointed to the end of the street, where a cart was driven at speed past the inn. "Unless I am much mistaken, here is our stable lad. He is late today, I think."

We waited until the boy had hurriedly entered the shop and emerged, about ten minutes later, with another fellow helping to load several heavy sacks onto his cart. When that was finished the helper disappeared back into the shop and the lad took up the reins. As we walked past, Holmes held the horse's head.

The lad was about to voice his objections, but Holmes was quicker.

"Not yet, Master Crabber," he said. "I wish to speak to you."

The boy's glare was hostile. "I don't know you! Who are you?"

"My name is Sherlock Holmes. I am a consulting detective from London. It has come to my notice that you are involved in a conspiracy to extort money from your employer."

The boy took on a furtive look at once, and I knew that Holmes's identification was correct. "Who says so, then?"

"The evidence is quite clear. I confess to being at a loss to imagine how you thought you would remain unpunished, now that your accomplice has confessed. You were instrumental in putting Mrs. Prescott's daughter in mortal danger. It is well known that kidnappers invariably murder their victims, so as to prevent them from identifying them to the police. At the very least, you will be charged as an accessory."

"But he swore Alice would come to no harm, if I told him where she is living!" Crabber's face was now full of alarm. "I swear, Mr. Holmes, I never knew there would be murder. Oh, my God!" He put his hands to his face and wept, all defiance gone. "What can I do?"

"If you are truthful with me, I will do what I can for you," Holmes said more calmly. "We believe that your co-conspirator has given us a false name. If you tell us who he truly is, and where he has been hiding, it will go well with you."

"He is Mr. Grenville Prescott!" the lad wailed.

"A relation of your employer?"

"Her brother-in-law. The younger brother of her deceased husband."

"I presume he paid you for your services?"

Crabber averted his eyes. "He gave me five pounds."

"He pays well, indeed. Where is he now?"

"I had to visit him, to tell him about Alice. He rents a cottage in Little Bursford. The address is Number 2 Pear Tree Grove."

My friend nodded. "How far is that from here?"

"You turn left at the end of this street." The lad pointed past the library, to where we could see the entrance to a wide lane. "If you go straight for a mile-and-a-half, you'll be there."

"I'm obliged to you for your frankness," Holmes said. "You must tell no one of our conversation and, as I have already promised, I will convey a favourable impression of you because you didn't fully realise the likely consequences of your actions."

"Thank you, sir."

"But you must swear to never again be tempted by the lure of easy profit. Such arrangements are almost always rooted in dishonesty."

Crabber lowered his head, ashamed of his small part in this. "Yes, I swear."

"Then we will bid you good-day."

"You certainly put fear into that ruffian, Holmes," I remarked when we had walked well out of earshot.

"A little too much, perhaps. I deplore his betrayal of his employer, but I cannot believe that he's the criminal type."

"Is that why you promised to speak for him?"

He shrugged his shoulders. "His only crime, after all, was to tell this man Grenville Prescott where his niece is living. As much could have transpired during normal conversation. Nevertheless, we have done some good here. Crabber will not easily stray down the wrong road, I think."

"Were you surprised to learn that the kidnapper is the late Mr. Prescott's brother?"

"Not entirely. One of the suppositions that I had formed about this case was that a relation of some sort might be involved. You see, if Mrs. Prescott is a recluse, seeing no one, then it's likely that her tormenter is someone close. Who else does a friendless woman have but her family?"

He said little else then as we walked around that charming village until the hour for luncheon arrived. My thoughts were occupied with theories of my own, and wondering if we were to enlist the aid of the local force to arrest this man Grenville Prescott. I also reflected that Holmes's leniency with the stable boy had revealed a glimpse of the compassionate heart that beats within the breast of the man who was known, to almost all that he had ever encountered, as the calculating reasoner whose emotions could be likened to the workings of a machine.

"I presume we will be visiting Little Bursford this afternoon?" I ventured as we concluded our luncheon with cups of strong coffee.

"Your presumption is correct. I must ask the landlord if he knows anyone from whom we can hire a trap for a couple of hours. Our business should take no longer than that."

At just that moment the fellow appeared. He was a portly man of about fifty, red-faced and smiling.

"The telegram you were expecting, Mr. Holmes."

My friend took it from the tray. "My thanks to you, landlord. I wonder, are you aware of anyone who could let us have a trap for an hour or two?"

"I can think of several, sir, but none of them are nearby. You might be better, if you don't mind using such a conveyance, to borrow the cart that we use for deliveries of one kind or another. You'll find the horse grazing in the field at the back of the inn, and the cart is kept in the yard."

"Many thanks, once again," Holmes said as the man took our used cups and departed. He tore open the envelope eagerly.

"Did the wire reveal anything?" I asked before he could rise.

He nodded. "Barker has found exactly what I had begun to suspect."

He paused as the noise from the surrounding tables increased. A man who looked like a local farmer had amused his companions by drinking a pint of ale in a single swallow.

I looked at Holmes expectantly but he said nothing more, instead sliding the telegram towards me.

It contained a single sentence: *All is well with the Sisterhood of Golgotha.*

"What does this mean?" I asked in astonishment.

"Simply that there has been no kidnapping after all. There is something deeper here, I think."

We accepted the landlord's offer and were soon on our way in his cart, pulled by a lively young colt who accepted the control of the reins reluctantly. Crabber hadn't misinformed us, for the distance to Little Bursford was indeed no more than a mile-and-a-half. We emerged from a wide and leafy lane, with fields on either side, to be confronted with a village of small thatched cottages with an ancient church at the distant end of the central street. We had no difficulty in finding Pear Tree Grove, since the sign near the village green had been newly painted. Number 2 was identical to several other dwellings, except the door-knocker was shaped like a tiger's head and had been polished to a fine gloss.

Holmes rapped on the door but once with his stick, as I tethered the horse to the fence at the edge of the field that faced the house. The door opened at once to reveal a tall thin man of ghostly white pallor.

"Come in, gentlemen," he said at once. "I have been expecting you."

We entered and were bidden to sit. The man held up a half-empty whisky bottle, but we both declined.

"How is it that you knew we would come, Mr. Prescott," I enquired.

He let his gaze roam around the room, taking in the brass warming pans and oak beams as if searching for words. "We have heard of the exploits of Mr. Holmes, even here, and of your recording of them, Doctor. As for your presence in my temporary home, I knew because word travels very quickly about new arrivals in the villages. From the moment I heard your name, I knew my game was up."

"Did you really intend to kill your sister-in-law?" Holmes asked.

I looked at him sharply, for this hadn't been mentioned until now.

"I would have done, had my plan succeeded and she had delivered the ransom, believing that her daughter had been abducted. Since my brother's death, she has hardly ventured from Gaunt Manor, but I knew this would entice her. However," Mr. Prescott held up a quivering hand, "the burden of guilt that I would assume has already had its effect upon me. I cannot sleep, and my meals have been replaced by whisky."

"Clearly you are no murderer, but how did this situation arise? If there is a dispute of some sort between you, could you not have visited her and come to some arrangement?"

Our host shook his head in despair. "I will acquaint you with the full facts, and then you will understand."

He turned to a writing-desk in the corner of the room. From a drawer he took a single sheet of paper and handed it to Holmes. My friend cast his eyes over it quickly.

"Your brother is the author of this?" he enquired.

"He sent it to me in London, shortly before his death. That is why I came to live here."

"To wreak vengeance?"

"How else could I act, in the circumstances?"

"Is there proof of this – elsewhere perhaps?"

Mr. Prescott lowered himself into a chair, his head bowed. "In Willadale there is the firm of solicitors, Warren, Candale, and Monk. They represented my brother for many years, and he wrote an identical account in their office in front of witnesses. As for the document you hold in your hand, you may retain it if you wish."

Holmes nodded his head. "Very well, Mr. Prescott. I will take this document, and we will certainly pay this concern a visit. As for you, if you have spoken truthfully, you have committed no crime except to make threats by means of the letter you delivered to your sister-in-law, and when truth prevails, your actions will attract no punishment. I recommend that you return to London to resume your life there, with the assurance that justice will be done without any risk to your freedom."

We left him then, unmistakeably grieving but somehow, I felt, surrounded by an air of relief.

Holmes said little as we drove back to Willadale. He appeared deep in thought, but I was confused by this latest development. Finally, before our journey was even half over, I could restrain myself no longer.

"I had thought, Holmes, that Mr. Prescott would be arrested for the attempted kidnapping of his niece. What has transpired to absolve him?"

"All will become clear to you, Watson, when we visit Gaunt Manor tomorrow morning. We'll go directly there after consulting Warren, Candale, and Monk, in Willadale."

He would say nothing more, avoiding all my subsequent attempts to procure enlightenment in favour of an extensive lecture about the connection of Oliver Cromwell to the Cambridge area. This he insisted upon continuing throughout dinner, and I confess to being somewhat relieved when we retired to the lounge with our pipes. During the evening we consumed two glasses of a fine old brandy that the landlord recommended and Holmes, at last changing the subject of his discourse, revealed to me the details of a case which took place before our association. At some future time I hope for this to be published, with his permission, probably under the title "The Adventure of the Broken Chalice".

Next morning, his eagerness for breakfast to be over was obvious.

"Come, Watson, finish your toast and coffee and we will proceed. I have already ascertained from the landlord that the offices of Warren, Candale, and Monk are situated near the undertaker's premises in Catherine Street."

We presented ourselves as a young clerk opened the doors to begin the business of the day. In answer to our enquiries, he informed us that Mr. Monk had recently passed away and Mr. Warren was away at present. He would seek however, an audience with Mr. Candale, provided that no appointments for this time had already been arranged.

We were summoned after about ten minutes to a rather soberly furnished office that smelled strongly of wood polish. Mr. Candale was a tall, thin gentleman who was well into his old age. His body was angular, his movements stiff, and his dress funereal.

"Good morning, gentlemen," he gave a slight bow and bade us be seated, before settling himself behind the massive desk that took up much of the room. "Pray tell me how I can assist you."

My friend introduced us, explaining that we were in the village in the course of an enquiry. "I have been given a document, sir, and it is imperative that I confirm it as genuine."

"What does the document contain?"

"It is an account of events that occurred shortly before the death of one of your clients, Mr. Carlton Prescott, written in his own hand. It is his brother, Mr. Grenville Prescott, who has sent us to you because a similar account was written here in front of witnesses."

Mr. Candale rubbed his chin. "I remember the occasion well, for I, myself, was among the witnesses. The signatures were only to confirm that it was the hand of Mr. Carlton Prescott that wrote the account. What the contents were I don't know, and neither do the others who signed, since the document was immediately sealed and consigned to our safe at the writer's request, where it has remained ever since."

"I would be obliged," said Holmes, "if you would retrieve it for comparison with the account that I have here. It is crucial that I ascertain that the author is the same."

"I can vouch for the version that we have retained, of course."

"As for the other, I have the word of Mr. Grenville Prescott."

Mr. Candale's expression became more serious. "If you will furnish me with written authority from him, I will produce that which was left with us."

"Mr. Prescott has given us no such thing, but I will request that he attends personally within the next few days, for the purposes of confirmation."

"I am sorry, gentlemen," the solicitor got to his feet awkwardly, "but I cannot accede to such a request without some form of authority. If you can obtain this I will be glad to oblige, but for now I will wish you both good day."

Holmes stood and I saw the steely glint of determination in his eyes. "Sir, I should tell you that to delay might well permit a murderer to escape justice. It would be a more speedy solution to wire Scotland Yard, with a view to obtaining reassurance as to my discretion."

Then began a long contemplative silence, during which Mr. Candale became even more solemn.

"Very well," he said at last. "In view of the fact that you are a consulting detective – oh yes, I have heard of your work assisting Scotland Yard, Mr. Holmes – and the circumstances that you describe, I will retrieve the document that was left in our care. After all, as you have said, all that you require is to ascertain that the two accounts were written by the same hand."

"Precisely," Holmes confirmed with a scowl on his face. Any reference to him as an assistant to the official force, to which he had so many times presented a completed case in advance of their own investigations, was certain to produce this effect. "I'm obliged to you, Mr. Candale."

Later that morning we found ourselves, having again prevailed upon the landlord for the hire of his cart, handing the conveyance to a very subdued Joel in the courtyard of Gaunt Manor.

I must confess that the first thought to enter my head as the place came into sight was that it fully deserved its title. It was a structure of grey stone, covered in moss in many places, comprising of a short central corridor or gallery which led from either end to decaying wings with tall windows.

"Hardly an attractive place," I remarked as we walked across uneven flagstones with weeds sprouting between them.

"Late Tudor or early Stuart, I would think. That design was quite common during those periods. But look – that rather warped door is opening, and I see Mr. Fairdale Hobbs is waiting to greet us. He is innocent, but I don't think he will come well out of this. I fear we may have to forego luncheon, Watson, for I don't expect our business here to be over quickly."

Our client could hardly contain himself. As we reached the top of the steps, he emerged and confronted us expectantly.

"Have you made progress, Mr. Holmes?" he asked as soon as he had greeted us.

"I have. All is now clear to me."

Relief swept over Mr. Hobbs' face. "Then Alice will be returned?"

"Alice was never absent, nor was she at any time in danger."

"I am afraid I don't understand."

"If Mrs. Prescott permits you to remain as we interview her, you will quickly comprehend the true nature of the situation. You presented these circumstances to us as a tragedy, and I will tell you that the truth of them is indeed a tragedy. If you would conduct us into your employer's presence, I would be obliged."

Mr. Hobbs could have had no conception as to what Holmes was about to reveal, but he sensed that the news wouldn't be pleasant. As he led us into a long corridor, I saw that his countenance had become visibly grey.

We were shown into a room with much overstuffed furniture. A woman lay draped across a chaise-longue near the tall open windows with her back to us. She rose and turned to face us as we approached.

"Mr. Sherlock Holmes and Doctor Watson," Mr. Hobbs announced.

She smiled and nodded. "The gentlemen we engaged to rescue my daughter, of course. I take it that you have succeeded?"

Mrs. Prescott possessed considerable beauty, although well past the first flush of her youth. In a costume of dark green, her shoulder-length hair shone in the light from the windows, and I saw that she had preserved her figure well. It wasn't until the wariness of her expression and the wildness of her eyes were noticed that she could be perceived as a woman somewhat deranged.

"On that score, madam, you need have no fear. Your daughter was never kidnapped, nor was she in any sort of danger."

"But," she began, aghast, "the letter? The threats?"

"All with a single purpose – to cause you to leave this house."

"For what reason? I don't understand this."

"It was a device to provide an opportunity for your murder."

All colour left her face, and Mr. Hobbs, who had remained without seeking her permission, drew nearer to her.

"Who would contemplate such a thing?" she asked in a whisper.

"I'm sure that you already know the answer to that, unless you have other enemies. It is your brother-in-law, Mr. Grenville Prescott."

"Grenville? I haven't seen him since my husband's death."

"That is hardly surprising. Having killed his brother, it would be truly strange if he had friendly intentions toward you."

"What can you mean by that?" But her face had changed to that of a furtive animal. She was ready to defend herself, but knew the battle was already lost.

"There was no riding accident. You struck your husband with some sort of bludgeon, probably a fallen branch, and successfully maintained the deceit."

She collected herself quickly, her voice harsher now. "Why would I do such a thing? Carlton and I were close and had much affection for each other. I loved him!"

"I believe that you did," Holmes affirmed, "and, sadly, that was why you took his life. You had for some time suspected him of conducting regular assignations with a woman living in Little Bursford, and I suspect that the strain of this growing resentment became too much for you. When you could tolerate it no longer, you murdered him."

"Carlton was secretive about some things," she said, and at that moment tears began to flow, signalling her capitulation. "He wouldn't talk of it, and I couldn't bear to share him."

"Neither did you," Holmes said in a voice that was almost kindly. "It is true that he visited a woman, but it was the sister of a fallen army comrade who is blind. He helped her, as he had sworn to do, with food and a nurse to ensure her welfare."

"That is why you described these events as a true tragedy," Mr. Hobbs realised then.

"Indeed. Your husband was disturbed by your worsening behaviour," my friend continued to Mrs. Prescott, "and came to realise that you had become irrational. It is clear from his writings that he expected some sort of attack, but probably not a murderous one."

The room was silent for several moments, the only sounds were the cries of the captive peacocks that I could see caged among the colourful flowers of the garden.

"So this was to be Grenville's revenge?" Mrs. Prescott burst out suddenly. "But how could he have known of how things lay between Carlton and myself? How did you discover all this, Mr. Holmes?"

Holmes took the letter from his pocket. "As I have stated, your husband sensed impending conflict between you. He wrote a full account of his fears, which he left with his brother. Another copy was left with his solicitor. I have compared them, and there is no question but that they were written by the same hand."

"If only Mr. and Mrs. Prescott had talked about the situation, this would never have come about," I observed. "He would have been alive to this day."

"All men and women have their secrets," Holmes replied. "Sometimes for the most extraordinary and unnecessary reasons. Mr. Hobbs, may I prevail upon you to ride to Willadale and inform the constable there of what you have witnessed this morning? Watson and I will remain with Mrs. Prescott until you return."

During his absence, she sat staring into the far distance, tearful but not speaking. I considered that Mrs. Prescott was more likely to end her days in an asylum than at the end of a hangman's rope, and I couldn't help but pity her. Very little conversation between Holmes and myself ensued, until Mr. Hobbs returned in the company of Constable Hutchins, who led his prisoner away after acquainting himself with the circumstances.

"The daughter will doubtless be cared for by the Sisters of Golgotha," Holmes said as we were about to leave. He turned then to regard Mr. Fairdale Hobbs, who stood, an uncertain and dejected figure, near the door. "I see, Mr. Hobbs, that you are saddened by your altered circumstances. You are now without employment – indeed without a roof over your head since Gaunt Manor will certainly be sold and the proceeds invested for the benefit of Alice Prescott. It may have crossed your mind that none of this would have arisen had you not consulted me in Baker Street. Nevertheless, you have the satisfaction of knowing that you were instrumental in causing justice to be done where the need wasn't previously perceived. I tell you not to concern yourself about your situation or your lodgings. In the course of my work I have acquired many whom I can call upon for assistance and support, and I wouldn't be at all surprised to hear that your difficulties are settled before this day is out."

> *"You arranged an affair for a lodger of mine last year," she said. "Mr. Fairdale Hobbs."*
>
> *"Ah, yes – a simple matter."*
>
> *"But he would never cease talking of it – your kindness, sir, and the way in which you brought light into the darkness. I remembered his words when I was in doubt and darkness myself.*
>
> – Mrs. Warren and Sherlock Holmes
> "The Adventure of the Red Circle"

The Adventure of the Abergavenny Murder
by Craig Stephen Copland

Royston Giles Tamblyn III paid a visit to 221b Baker Street without an appointment on the morning of Saturday, 4 May 1901. He was a handsome young fellow with flawless pale skin, well-combed hair that was blond-on-its-way-to-brown, and straight, gleaming teeth. He was dressed in a blazer and flannels, a creaseless white shirt, and an expertly tied old-school tie. In his polished boots, had I bent over to inspect them, I could have seen my reflection.

When he sat down, he gave a small tug upwards on his trousers to keep the material from stretching over the kneecaps, and he exuded the confident manners that come with excellent breeding and demanding schoolmasters.

When told by Holmes to state his case, he succinctly told us that in the middle of the night, two nights ago, he had been walking in Regent's Park and had witnessed a murder.

"Did you indeed?" asked Holmes. "And did you report it to the police?"

"I did. They refused to believe me."

"What about your family members? You must have told them."

"I did. They also refused to believe me."

I was, I must admit, not at all surprised to hear about the reactions of either the police or his family, and I knew that Holmes would be of the same mind.

The reason, of course, was that Royston Giles Tamblyn III was twelve years old and had already acquired something of a reputation in certain circles of London.

The previous autumn, *The Strand* had hosted a contest for schoolboys and schoolgirls to write an original mystery story. A panel of judges, of which I was one, was given the submissions to read and assess. The names of the authors were removed so that we didn't know who had written which story, nor whether it was by a boy or a girl. The magazine, however, neglected to limit the number of entries any young writer could submit, with the result that some industrious scholars sent in two or more.

When the results were revealed, Master Royston Giles Tamblyn III took first, second, and third places. His stories were, frankly, brilliant. The characters were singularly colorful, his twists of plots deceptive and thus delightful, his settings overflowing with imaginative details, and his grasp of English vocabulary and grammar at a level that the editors of *The Strand* would have been thrilled to see coming from much older writers who preferred to serve their commas spliced and their infinitives split.

I had expected that Holmes would respond by curtly assuring the lad that he would look into the matter and send him on his way.

He did not do that.

Instead, he carried out a rather intense interrogation and questioned the boy for half-an-hour.

"Where did this happen?" asked Holmes.

"In Regent's Park."

"Where in the Park? Be precise."

"In the northwest corner, twenty yards southwest of the intersection of Avenue Road and the Outer Circle."

"When?"

"Twenty-two minutes past midnight."

"What were you doing out in Regent's Park past midnight?"

"Taking my dog for a walk."

"Twelve-year-old dog owners do not take dogs for walks after midnight. What were you doing there?"

Holmes can be quite intimidating when he wants to, and I expected the young fellow to become hesitant, if not cower. He did neither. He paused, as if ordering his words, and replied calmly.

"Sir, I am an author. As Dr. Watson will tell you, the best place to find characters and plots is by observing people in real life. There are many events that take place in our parks late at night that I secretly observe and record. They become material for my stories. I walk through the Park several nights a week. It has been quite useful."

"Do your parents permit this?"

"My parents are currently in Rangoon in Burma. My father is employed by the Foreign Office and serves as the Military Attaché in that post. I live with my grandparents."

"And they let you wander out at that hour?"

"They are elderly and retire at half-ten. I leave and return silently without disturbing them."

"Do you? Very well, describe what you observed. Be concise and precise."

"I had spent the previous hour walking my dog around the circumference of the Park, and – "

"What are your dog's breed and name?"

"He is a border collie, and I call him Berky. It is short for Berkshires. My grandmother named him. That was my grandfather's regiment. Dr.

Watson will confirm that they fought with distinction during the Second Afghan War."

Holmes glanced at me, and I nodded. I was seconded to the 66th Regiment, the Berkshires, during the Battle of Maiwand. I wouldn't have called our defeat and desperate retreat distinguished, but if that is what the lad wanted to believe, I wasn't about to correct him.

"Keep going," said Holmes.

"We had almost returned to the Avenue Road entrance to the Park when I saw a man approaching us. He was still some distance away and hadn't seen us. I stepped into the copse of trees beside the path so I could observe him. As he was passing the road, a man jumped – "

"Stop. Describe the man you observed – the victim."

"Yes, sir. He was on the tall side, almost as tall as you, sir. Broad-shouldered. Not at all portly. The night was cool, and he was wearing a peacoat and a workman's hat and walking smartly."

"His age?"

"Getting on a bit. About the age of you and Dr. Watson."

"His shoes and trousers?"

"Dark. His boots were polished. Military style. I could see a glint of moonlight reflecting in them as he approached."

"Did you see his face?"

"Not clearly, sir. His cap put a shadow on the upper part. He had a full beard but neatly trimmed."

"Did he cry out? Call for help?"

"No, sir. It all happened too quickly. He said something, but I cannot say for certain what it was."

"Then say what you think it might have been."

"It sounded like *sic semper tyrannis,* but it is possible I'm letting my imagination take over. I cannot be certain, sir. And it is possible that it was the assailant who said that. I couldn't tell, and I don't want to mislead you, Mr. Holmes."

"You are doing quite well so far, young man. Now then, the assailant. Describe him."

"Shorter. A smaller man. Wiry. But he moved like a cat. He sprang out from behind the trees, and within a second, was in front of the victim. He was wearing a trench coat, but it was open, and he had one arm tucked behind his back. He leapt in front of the victim, and, as he did so, he pulled his hand out, and he had a sword concealed. It happened in a flash. I only saw the sword for a second, and he stuck it up and into the other man."

"What do you mean 'up and into'? Explain."

"Yes, Mr. Holmes. As I said, the victim was wearing a peacoat, and it came down to just below his waist. The tip of the sword entered below the hem of the coat and was pushed up and into the body."

"From that angle and point of entry," said Holmes, "it would have penetrated the abdomen and, with enough force, have come out the other side of the body. Did you see it do that? Or did the back of the coat suddenly extend outward?"

"No, sir. It was a curved sword. Like a Scimitar."

"A Scimitar? Are you familiar with the categories of swords? If so, what type of Scimitar?"

"Either a Talwar or a Shamshir. If I had to say, then I would say a Shamshir."

Holmes paused and stared at the boy.

"What school do you attend, young man?"

"St. John's Wood Grammar School, sir."

"I'm certain that instruction in the various types of Scimitars isn't on the curriculum of your school. Pray tell, how is it that you can tell a Talwar from a Shamshir in the middle of the night?"

"From my grandfather, sir. He's an old army man and, like many of his fellow soldiers, he collected things from the places he served all over the world. His house is crammed with old pistols, swords, caps, badges, cheap paintings, and the like. He brought home some swords from the Subcontinent and has them on the wall. Between them, there is a print showing all the different types of Scimitars. I have read it over many times and memorized it."

"Have you now? Quite a singular interest. Very well, then. What happened after the attack?"

"The victim fell first to his knees and then flat on his face. The attacker moved quickly. He sheathed his sword and then leaned down and rolled the victim over on to his back, then lifted him from his shoulders, then put his hands under the armpits, and dragged him along Avenue Road to Albert Road. I followed him, taking care not to be seen. When he got to the St. James Terrace, there was a cab waiting. He lifted the body into the back of the cab, and they sped off."

"How do you know it was a cab?"

"It had a plate on the back."

"What was the PCO number?"

"Two six nine five two."

Again, Holmes paused his questions. This time he leaned back, took out his pipe, slowly lit it, and took a languorous draft.

A minute passed with nothing being said. I could see that Master Royston was becoming uncomfortable and, succumbing to the awkward atmosphere, he said something.

"Have I presented you with a three-pipe problem, Mr. Holmes?"

Holmes didn't answer and, looking utterly annoyed, glared at the boy.

"I'm sorry, sir. I'm so sorry. But I have read all of Dr. Watson's accounts of your adventures, and you described a case that way. I was concerned that I had presented you with a bizarre situation."

"You did not. So, get up and take us there."

"To the scene of the crime, sir?"

"Yes, of course."

There is something in the constitution of all twelve-year-old boys that renders them unable to conceal unexpected joy. Master Royston's face lit up like an electric bulb. He appeared to be thrilled to bits to have Sherlock Holmes demand that he assist him in solving a crime – and not just any crime.

A murder.

It is only a block from 221b Baker Street to the Outer Circle of the Regent's Park and, once there, we turned left and walked quickly north along the circumference path to the place where the lad claimed the incident had taken place. He was somewhat excited and ran ahead, permitting me to challenge Holmes.

"Do you truly believe his story? He has a reputation for a marvelous imagination."

"Of that, I am aware. However, his demeanor has an air of sincerity. His knowledge of the details he observed is beyond those given by most of the clients who come to me as addled adults. And, if nothing else, it is a pleasant morning for a walk. Therefore, let us see what we can see."

It took a brisk fifteen minutes to follow the Outer Circle to Avenue Road. Master Royston stopped there and gestured to the center of the path.

"It was here," he said.

Holmes and I stopped and gazed at the ground. As far as I could tell, there was nothing to indicate that anything, let alone a murder, had taken place there. But Holmes dropped to his knees and took out his glass. Methodically, he turned over stone pebbles. He kept this up for a full ten minutes, moving inch by inch along the path. I moved away, stood beside the boy, and leaned in to whisper to him, but he spoke first.

"It's quite all right, Dr. Watson. I know that detective work has to be slow and careful. It is a capital mistake to hurry an investigation."

Holmes stopped his grazing. He leaned down close to the ground, then straightened up, took an envelope out of his suit pocket, and began to drop pebbles into it.

"It's too early to tell," he said. "But there is a possibility that the stain on these stones is blood. Now then, young man, show me where you were hiding."

"Right here, sir. Behind this tree," Royston said as he began to walk to the spot he had indicated.

"*Stop!*" shouted Holmes, and both the boy and I froze in our tracks.

"You are about to trample evidence!" said Holmes. "If you want to be a detective, start acting like one!"

"Sorry, sir. Sorry, sorry," said Royston as he jumped back and away.

Holmes moved into the copse of trees and approached the designated place from the far side. Once again, he dropped to his knees and took out his glass. He didn't take long and returned to where the two of us were standing.

"Are you wearing the same shoes?" he asked.

"Yes, sir."

"Lift up your left shoe and show me the sole."

The lad did as ordered.

"That is good. Now, put your finger on your leg at the height of the top of your dog's nose. I assume it has a familiar place for pushing into you. All dogs do."

"Here, sir."

"Excellent. Now, show me the route where the assailant dragged the body out of the Park, and for goodness sake, keep to the edge of the roadway, not the portion along which it was dragged."

We walked up the extension of Avenue Road that leads into the Park. It had a macadam surface, and there was nothing that resembled a set of footprints, but, in three places, Holmes stopped and examined what appeared to be scuff marks that could have been left by a pair of heels as a body was dragged, face-up, out to Albert Street.

Once there, he stopped and lit a cigarette. After a few puffs in silence, he turned to Royston.

"Your account is credible. It appears that some untoward event took place here, and I shall accept your case. I commend you for your excellent skills in observation. I shall proceed with my investigation accordingly. Now, kindly go back home to your grandparents. Good day."

"Oh, Mr. Holmes, sir. Can I come with you? I so want to learn how you do detective work. All I know is from what I've read of your adventures. I could take notes and get whatever you needed. Please, sir. Please?"

"No."

"But sir – "

"No. You show considerable promise for a boy your age. However, I have never taken on an apprentice and am not about to start. I have enough to deal with trying to keep Dr. Watson from getting overly excited. Go home. I will call upon you when you're needed."

The boy was crestfallen, but there was no doubting Holmes's command. As he turned to walk north on Avenue Road, Holmes called out to him.

"One more question."

The lad skipped back to us.

"Yes, sir? What, sir?"

"Your dog was with you all the time, was it not?"

"Oh, yes, sir. He comes with me every time I go out."

"Did it not bark on seeing a man being stabbed to death."

"Oh, no sir. He is a very obedient dog. I spent hours training him since he was a pup. I told him to be silent, and he obeyed."

"Good. Now, be on your way."

"Where to next?" I asked.

"To find the body and identify the victim."

"So, you believe the lad?"

"No conclusion can be certain at this stage, but the probabilities are leaning in that direction."

"Fine. Then how in the world are you going to find a body that was taken away in a cab two nights ago?"

"If you had a body in a cab in the middle of the night and wished to dispose of it quickly, where would you get rid of it?"

"I would toss it in the Thames. All sorts of bodies end up there."

"Brilliant, Watson. With no traffic, it is no more than fifteen minutes from here to the Waterloo Bridge. Therefore, let us hail a cab ourselves and proceed to Tower Bridge."

"Tower? But you said – "

"My dear Watson, the tossing, if it happened, took place thirty-six hours ago. The Thames flows downstream to the sea. Bodies are constantly being pulled out of Dead Man's Hole. There is a good chance that we shall find our man in the Tower Bridge Mortuary."

Hydrologists can explain it to you, for I cannot. The confluence of the river currents in the Thames and the tidal currents coming and going from the Estuary has created a backwater pool adjacent to the north tower of Tower Bridge. In that spot, detritus of all sorts, including an endless stream of bodies, collects and has to be cleaned out daily. Knowing of the need, the architects of our recently-opened magnificent Tower Bridge, in their wisdom, put a mortuary in the base of the north tower. It can be accessed through one of the arches in the foundation and then down a narrow staircase to rooms where rows of concrete slabs have been built to accommodate the bodies that are hauled out of Dead Man's Hole. If the morticians and police can identify the deceased, the next of kin are notified and instructed to come and claim the body and arrange for a proper funeral. Those that remain unclaimed are sent out to the Potter's Field sections of one of the Magnificent Seven – the seven great public cemeteries that were established sixty years ago in the far suburbs of London.

It was early afternoon of the same Saturday when Holmes and I exited our cab at the north tower and descended to the mortuary.

"Good day, sirs," said the resident mortician. "I'll wager you're just dying to come and see what we have here."

We forced a chuckle for the benefit of a man whose service to the public had to be appreciated but never envied. Holmes gave him the detailed description that Royston Tamblyn had provided earlier, and confirmed that we were conducting an investigation and not looking for a missing loved one. And no, we didn't have a name for the chap we were looking for.

The mortician flashed a wide grin in response.

"Right-oh, there, my good fellows. The bloke you're looking for just paid us a visit an hour ago. Must say, he's a very grave man. But still fresh, and hadn't yet offered his face and fingers to the turtles. Follow me."

He led us to one of the many sheet-covered corpses in a room where the fetid atmosphere was enough to render even a veteran doctor nauseous.

"This the chap you're looking for?" he said as he pulled back the sheet, exposing the head and upper body. "Fits your description to a *T*, I'd say. He didn't have no wallet or papers on him, so no telling who he is. We'll have our artist man do a sketch of him to circulate out to the shops and stations. We call him our Grim Sketcher, but his true name is Frankie. Amazing talent, he has. Can take a face that mostly gone and draw how he must have looked when alive. He can help you identify this fellow, and that's for right sure."

"That will not be necessary," said Holmes. "I know this man. His name is Clive Abergavenny – Colonel Clive Abergavenny, to be precise. He lives on Mackennel Street by Regent's Park. If he has any family, you should be able to find them by paying a visit to his home."

At Holmes's request, the mortician removed the sheet, exposing the entire body of the dead man. His clothing, still soaking wet, was as described by our twelve-year-old client. So, also, were the height and shape of the man, and his closely trimmed beard.

On escaping the dank, unpleasant depths of the tower, we emerged into the glorious sunshine of a spring morning along the north bank of the Thames. I took several deep gasps of the fresh air to clear my lungs and turned to Holmes.

"You knew that fellow?"

"I knew of him. He is quite well-off and owns a substantial house. He is a retired officer from the Royal Marines and has a reputation as an unpleasant, nasty-tempered man. His wife and family left him years ago and, to the best of my knowledge, he lives alone. Beyond that, I know nothing."

"Are you going to take on the case and find out who did him in?"

"Not yet. We shall go now to Scotland Yard and file a report. Lestrade will initiate his investigation. If he comes up empty-handed after a fortnight, he will call me in. As the only description we have of the assailant is of a wiry fellow wearing a trench-coat, who may or may not quote Latin phrases, Lestrade will have little to go on. Therefore, I expect to hear from him."

A short cab ride took us to the Embankment and the headquarters of Scotland Yard. It being a Saturday afternoon, Inspector Lestrade wasn't on duty, but we gave a full report to the desk officer. Holmes made a point of speaking favorably of the actions of Royston Tamblyn and, not being able to resist giving the Yard a none-too-subtle poke, reminded them of their failure to believe his first report, and directed them to consult the boy if they needed additional help.

"Do try to enjoy the remainder of the weekend, my dear Watson," said Holmes. "The murder of this Abergavenny fellow will have to wait until I receive the call for assistance. Meanwhile, my hands are full with the case of the Ferrers Documents, and I must spend the next few days puttering around burned-out tenements in the East End."

I did enjoy the rest of the weekend, and the next few days. The weather was pleasant, and the English do not tend to visit the doctor during the summertime. I didn't see much of Holmes during that period. He was out early and late with his own tasks, and I was staying busy Barts. I was surprised one Friday when I was stopped by a breathless boy in one of the hallways.

"He told me," the lad gasped, "that I had to get this to you before you departed for the day. He was quite insistent."

I gave the young chap a shilling for the cost and an extra one to make up for what I was quite sure had been a less-than-pleasant send-off from Sherlock Holmes.

I opened the envelope and read:

Imperative you come home at once. Disaster at Scotland Yard.

I arrived at Baker Street and saw Holmes standing on the sidewalk, pacing. He hopped up and into the cab.

"Ah, Watson. Thank you. I knew I could count on you. Are you unencumbered now for the day?"

"I can be, if you will tell me what this is all about."

He handed me a letter marked with the emblem of Scotland Yard.

"This just arrived."

It ran:

Dear Mr. Sherlock Holmes:

The Metropolitan Police express their thanks and appreciation to Mr. Sherlock Holmes for his excellent service in the case of the murder of Colonel Clive Abergavenny. Based on the information you so generously provided to us, we have been able to identify the perpetrator and make an arrest. Mr. Royston Tamblyn, the twelve-year-old boy to whom you directed us, was taken into custody this morning and, in keeping with the laws pertaining to juvenile justice, charged with the murder of Colonel Abergavenny. He will be held in a juvenile detention house until his trial.

Scotland Yard could not have solved this case so quickly without your help, and we again express our thanks.

Yours sincerely,
G. Lestrade

"What?" I gasped. "That is preposterous. How could they have – " I was unable to find words to express my outrage.

"By acting with their usual incompetence and taking the easiest route available, instead of conducting a thorough investigation. We shall try to straighten them out and get the boy back home. It was a foolish mistake on my part to have given them his name."

On pulling into Scotland Yard, we leapt from the cab and stormed into the building.

“We are here,” said Holmes, “to meet with Inspector Lestrade. We must see him immediately.”

The young constable behind the desk smiled.

“Good day, Mr. Holmes, and you as well, Dr. Watson. Inspector Lestrade told me that you would come charging in here, and here you are. You know your way to his office, so please, go ahead and enjoy your visit.”

Holmes muttered a few words that I shall not repeat as we made our way down the corridor to Lestrade’s office.

“Lestrade!” said Holmes. “What is the meaning of this?”

He smacked the letter down on Lestrade’s desk.

“This is absurd! How can you be so lazy and incompetent to arrest a child and fail to do even a rudimentary investigation? How?”

Lestrade leaned back in his swivel chair and beamed a smug smile.

“And a good day to you as well, Mr. Holmes. Do take a seat and let me explain to you what happens when my men do the slow, plodding, methodical police work that you disparage as being so *unimaginative.* Would you like an explanation?”

Holmes sat down one of the hardback chairs that had been put in place facing the desk. He perched himself on the front edge and assumed the posture of one who had a ramrod affixed to his spine.

“Yes, you know I would.”

“Would you now? Good, then let me explain. Or shall I have them bring in a cup of tea first?”

“No to the tea. Yes, to your explanation.”

“You thought that this Colonel Abergavenny fellow was a stranger to the Tamblyn family, didn’t you? Well, it didn’t take my men long to discern that he was no such thing. He was well-known to them. And not only that, but there was bad blood between them. Very bad blood. It all began with the boy’s father, Captain Royston Giles Tamblyn the Second.”

“Have you contacted him?” said Holmes. “Under the laws pertaining to juvenile justice, you are required to do so. You cannot interrogate a child without the presence of his parents.”

“Is that so? Well now, we would have contacted the father, but it turns out to be rather difficult to do so.”

“Why is that? He works out of the High Commission in Burma. They have a telegraph service that connects them to Whitehall.”

“Is that so? Well now, if he were to be in Rangoon, we might just do that, but seeing as he is six feet under the ground in the Norwood Cemetery, it is more than somewhat difficult.”

“He’s dead?”

"That is the usual condition of those who are six feet under the ground."

Holmes wasn't expecting to hear that. For a moment, he said nothing but then carried on.

"What about his mother?"

"The mother who remarried and moved to Rangoon? We are attempting to contact her as we speak, but she assigned custody to his grandparents, so we have let them know. Happy to explain all this to you, Mr. Holmes. Of course, these are matters that unimaginative police slogging turns up. You might try it sometime. Elementary, as you are wont to say."

"I would like to speak to him. Please give me the address of where he is being held."

"I'm terribly sorry, but I cannot do that. Under the laws for juvenile delinquents, that information is confidential and cannot be released to people who have no legal or familial connection to him."

"He is my client and contracted for my services."

"I'm afraid that won't do. Under British law, a child of twelve cannot enter into a legally binding contract."

Holmes gave me a look, and I took my cue.

"I am," I said, "Royston Tamblyn's personal physician. Under the same law, I have the right to see him, examine him for his health, and confirm that he is safe and being kept in sanitary conditions."

Lestrade gave me a bit of an eyeball.

"Dr. Watson, you and your friend Sherlock Holmes may just be too clever by half. However, I will accept your declaration, but I will have it confirmed by the boy himself before releasing his whereabouts. I can let you know by Monday."

"Before we go," said Holmes, "is it permissible for you to tell us more about the past relationship between Colonel Abergavenny and the Tamblyn family?"

"No. It is not. I'm bound to protect all those dear little rompers who transgress the law and cannot disclose confidential information about our investigation. Not even in cases of murder, and not even to you, Mr. Sherlock Holmes. So, gentlemen, allow me to bid you a fine weekend. I plan to have the same. Good day."

Holmes strode out of the Scotland Yard building, across the Victoria Embankment, and stopped on the wide pavement adjacent to the Thames seawall. He lit a cigarette, took several puffs, threw it down, and crushed it under his heel.

"Holmes," I said, "there is no point in being angry with Lestrade. He is only following what the law demands. Legal reforms to protect juveniles taken into custody were passed for good reason. You surely don't want the Press knowing all the details of any case involving a child charged with murder. They would be all over the matter like flies to manure."

"You are right, of course, Watson. But arresting the boy is nonsense. How could he have possibly have killed a grown man, a military veteran, dragged his body to some vehicle, and then disposed of it in the Thames? It is impossible."

"I agree, but there is something going on that the boy didn't tell us. We can find out on Monday. I suspect he will be smart enough to confirm that I'm his physician when asked."

"I would rather not wait until Monday."

"You have no alternative."

"No?"

"No."

"Yes. I do. If I cannot talk to the boy, I can talk to his grandparents. Come, Watson. We shall pay a call to an elderly couple up in St. John's Wood."

Mr. and Mrs. Royston Tamblyn welcomed us into their modest home and sat us down in their parlor over a cup of tea and biscuits. The old fellow was tall and thin, and everything about him proclaimed a history in Her Majesty's military forces. Even as his body, now seventy-five years old at least, had begun to stoop ever so slightly, he held his head erect and his shoulders back.

He greeted me with a warm handshake and then said something that surprised me.

"We have met before, Dr. Watson."

I wracked my brain, but for the life of me couldn't remember ever having seen this man.

"I'm awfully sorry," I sputtered, "but I'm afraid I don't recall. Are you sure, sir? I do believe I wouldn't forget having had the pleasure of being introduced to you."

"I'm sure. And it wasn't a pleasure. . . for either of us. I fought with the Berkshires."

"You were in . . . in Maiwand?"

"I was. It was not our finest hour, was it, Doctor?"

A flood of images, all horrible, swept across my mind. The carnage of a lost battle, the dead and injured young men with limbs torn off and faces shattered, the sickening smell of death all came back to me. And then I remembered him. A tall major had raced out into the heat of the battle to rescue a man who had fallen and couldn't walk or even crawl. Under fire, the major and I picked him up and carried him to my hospital tent, taking one in the back of his leg as he did so. I dressed his wound and he departed, returning to the front that was about to be forced into an ignominious retreat. It was the only time he and I encountered each other, but neither of would ever forget any aspect of that dreadful day.

"Major Tamblyn," I said, "it is a pleasure now, if not then, to meet you again. I remember your courage with great respect."

"As I do yours, Doctor. The last I heard, you took a Jezail in the shoulder and were carried out in poor shape. I assumed that when my grandson brought copies of *The Strand* home to read that it was the same Doctor Watson who had written all those wonderful stories about Sherlock Holmes."

There is a bond between men who fought and suffered together that is as strong as that between brothers. I felt a profound affinity to this old soldier and would have happily spent the next hour sharing a bottle of whisky and swapping stories from our past. But Holmes wasn't prepared to let that happen.

"It is concerning your grandson that we are here," he said. "We need to talk about him."

Holmes launched into a summary of Royston's visit, our investigation of the scene of the crime, and our recent trip to Scotland Yard.

The old couple seemed deeply upset and somewhat confused over what had taken place the day before when the police arrived with a warrant, searched their home, and interrogated their grandson. They did acknowledge that they knew where he was now being held, but implored Holmes not to ask them to divulge the location, as the police had made it clear that the law demanded they adhere to the strict demands for confidentiality. Consequences of failing to do so, they had been told, would be dire.

"I understand your situation," said Holmes, "and will not attempt to have you tell me any information that you have been forbidden to divulge. However, if I am to of any use to your grandson, I need your help in understanding what took place last week."

"If we can help our grandson," said the old soldier, "we will do anything we can. What do you need to know?"

"What happened to his father?"

Mr. Tamblyn started to respond, but his lower lip began to tremble, and it was obvious that he was having great difficulty voicing an answer. He gave a glance to his wife; one of those pleading glances that pass between married couples and says *I cannot do this . . . Darling . . . please, carry on.* She nodded back to him and took over.

"Answering such a question," she said, "is difficult for us, but if it has to be done, then we have to do it. Our son," she said, " – well, his full name is Royston Giles Tamblyn the Second, but we called him Big Roy, and our grandson was Little Roy. My husband was Old Roy . . . but that isn't what you need to know, is it? Big Roy served in the Royal Marines and had been promoted to Major. He married a beautiful woman, our daughter-in-law, Emily, who bore him two perfect children, a son and a daughter. They had a pleasant home in Kent, and it seemed as if they had a charmed life. That all came to a horrible end four years ago. Are you familiar with the incident that the Press called 'The Benin Massacre'?"

"Only vaguely," said Holmes. "I do not make it a practice to concern myself with overseas skirmishes."

Holmes may not have known much about it, but I did. As one who had served Her Majesty overseas, I regularly stayed abreast of conflicts that took place throughout the Empire.

The Kingdom of Benin was an independent city-state in the south-western part of what later became known as Nigeria. In late 1896, as part of a local trade dispute, the King of Benin ordered an embargo on the export of palm oil. Nearby British merchants, finding their income severely diminished, cried foul and called for some arm-twisting negotiations to force the Kingdom to relent.

An Expedition was organized, made up of two-hundred-and-fifty African mercenaries, thinly disguised as porters and drummers, and a cluster of British officers. Their ostensible purpose was to enter into trade negotiations, but their true purpose was to remove the King of Benin and replace him with a council of locals who were friendly to British merchants.

Somebody tipped off the King, and he sent a squad of his men south to ambush the British party. Our fellows were caught unawares and decimated, with only two British officers surviving. A Punitive Expedition was then quickly assembled, made up of over a thousand Marines and several hundred other warriors. They marched on Benin and laid it waste, burning most of the homes and buildings, demolishing the city walls, shooting and bayoneting anyone who opposed them, and looting anything and everything of value. Stories of needless killings and unspeakable atrocities filtered back to London.

The jingoists cheered on the news, thrilled to know that Great Britain taught those heathen natives a lesson they would never forget. Others, more inclined to pacifism, decried the barbaric taking of innocent lives, the unvarnished greed, and the exploitation of the native people. Speeches were made in both Houses of Parliament condemning the slaughter, but the events in the Cape Province soon overtook news from a minor city-state, and the incident in Benin City vanished off the pages of the newspapers.

"I'm familiar with it," I said. "It was a most unfortunate event. Was your son a member of the Marines who stormed the city?"

"He was," said Mrs. Tamblyn, "and so was Colonel Abergavenny. Roy observed that the Colonel not only allowed his men to commit atrocities – he encouraged them. He also absconded with a wagon-load of plunder – gold, bronze statuary, ivory carvings, pieces of textile art – that was worth a fortune and was arranging to sell it for his personal profit.

"Roy confronted him and demanded that he turn his loot over to Admiral Rawson immediately, or he would report against him. Colonel Abergavenny promised to do so, but that evil, treacherous man immediately filed a false accusation against Roy, claiming that it was he, in exchange for several hundred pounds worth of gold, who tipped off the King about the earlier advancing party that was massacred. He bribed two local officials to say that they had received the information and paid him, and planted a few gold coins in Roy's duffel. A court-martial was ordered. Military justice, as you know, Doctor, is swift and harsh. He was tried and found guilty within three days and hanged on the fourth."

"But what about his fellow officers and the Marines who served under him?" I protested. "Surely, they must have stood up for him."

"They were already on their way back to their ship and out to sea. They didn't hear about the verdict and sentence for several weeks. They were enraged, as we all were, but there was nothing any of us could do about it."

"Nothing," said Holmes, "except wait for an appropriate opportunity and execute him, which your grandson happened to be present to observe."

"That is what we believe must have happened, sir," said the elderly lady. "And may God judge us, but no one is sad to see that monster dead. Someone did what had to be done. Forgive me, if I confess, we were all thankful."

"It is not my role to judge or forgive," said Holmes. "But that doesn't explain why Scotland Yard charged your grandchild with the murder."

"When they searched our home, they examined one of the swords my husband had brought back from India, a Scimitar. It was mounted over there, beside the hearth," she said, gesturing to a now bare stretch of wall.

"There was a dark stain on the hilt that they said might be blood. Curiously, they said they would send it to the police lab and subject it to the Sherlock Holmes test."

I detected a faint trace of a wince on the face of my chemically-talented friend.

"That proves next to nothing," said Holmes.

"No, but then they searched his room. Right out on his desk, they found a story he had written only a few days earlier. It was disguised only superficially – set in France – but it described in quite terrifying detail the way a boy stalked the traitor who had betrayed the boy's father and killed him. The details exactly matched the death of Colonel Abergavenny. It was all they needed."

Holmes stood up and began to pace, shaking his head. "Absurd. If writers are to be judged on the crimes they describe, our Dr. Watson would have been hanged, sent to prison, and exiled many times over."

"That is what we felt, Mr. Holmes. But they took Little Roy away and charged him all the same."

"And are you, madam," said Holmes, "willing to swear in a court of law that your grandson couldn't have committed murder?"

"On the Bible, on my eternal soul."

"And you, sir?" he asked, turning to the old soldier.

"I would. So, please, Mr. Holmes. You are now our only hope. Please do whatever you have to do to find out what truly happened and spare our grandson. We aren't wealthy people, but we will cover whatever fee you might see fit to charge, and – "

"There will be no charge, my good man. I will leave no stone unturned to return your grandson to your care. But please, forgive me for asking, what has been told to his mother. Has she abandoned her son?"

"Oh, not at all, sir," said the grandmother. "She writes to him every week, sometimes twice. And he writes to her. But when her husband was hanged, she was destitute. A widow of a soldier convicted of treason receives no pension. We offered to look after her and the children, but doing so was beyond our means. We agreed that she should do whatever had to be done to find another husband. It wasn't easy, her being the wife of a hanged traitor. But she met a decent man, a cousin of mine, much older, a fellow working as a military attaché with the Foreign Office who was posted to Burma. We sent her a telegram telling her what had happened, and she wrote back that she and her daughter would book passage to England on the first available ship. But she will be lucky if she is home in time for the trial."

Holmes hadn't stopped pacing from one side of the parlor to the other, but now he did and looked at the distraught couple.

"Pray, send a wire to the mother assuring her that I will do everything within my power to make sure that her son is freed to return to the love and safety of his family."

"Oh, Mr. Holmes," began Mrs. Tamblyn. "How can we – "

"Enough. This is what I do. My hope is that I have been able to impart at least a small portion of peace of mind to you in the midst of your turmoil. And now we must bid you good day. We have considerable work to do."

I bade the couple goodbye and told them that I would say a prayer that they might hold up under these devastating circumstances. The officer of the Berkshires was stone-faced, peaked, and said nothing. His wife, clutching his arm, looked me in the eye.

"When you were in the hospital tent in Maiwand, Doctor, and when one of the men who was a dear friend of yours died in front of you, did you stop and grieve for a week?"

"No," I said. "I couldn't. There were others to tend to."

"Of course not, Doctor. You had no choice. You had a job to do and you carried on and did what had to be done. We have to do the same."

Out on the pavement in front of the Tamblyn house, Holmes lit a cigarette and pondered for a moment.

"Watson, my deeply felt thanks for coming to my side so readily. You have a gift of conveying kindness and compassion that I fear I lack. And your picking up my cue to claim to be Royston's personal physician was very clever. You must let me know straight away when you are granted permission to see him. I suspect that Lestrade will not allow me to accompany you, and I must prepare you to ask all the questions that I would if I were to be there. And now, finally, allow me to bid you an enjoyable evening or what is left of it. I have work to do, including tracking down that cab number, and I shall be waiting to hear from you."

I didn't see him for the rest of the weekend, but on Monday evening, a note arrived, marked with the crest of Scotland Yard. It ran:

> *To: Dr. J. Watson*
> *From: Inspector G. Lestrade*
> *Regarding: Visit to Master Royston Giles Tamblyn III*
>
> *The juvenile named above has confirmed that you are his personal physician, and therefore an appointment has been arranged for Wednesday morning at this address*
>
> [For the reasons noted below, I have removed the address from my account.]
>
> *The location of the homes where juveniles are kept in custody is highly confidential. Revealing it is a criminal offense.*
>
> *Although it is a severe breach of protocol, this invitation is extended to Mr. Sherlock Holmes, and he has been granted permission to accompany you. Kindly inform him that the*

granting of this permission was given over the objections of Scotland Yard, but at the insistence of those who supervise the boys in the home. As a condition of his being granted permission, he is expected to give a talk to the boys about the perils of a life of crime. I'm sure he will not object to doing so.

Holmes met me at one of London's stations at seven on Wednesday morning. We took a train to a village on the outskirts of the great city and continued on foot for a while to a large manor house, surrounded by four or five acres of lawns and woodlands, all enclosed by a substantial brick wall. I learned later that it is one of over one-hundred houses, reformatories, and schools of industry that the government has either built or purchased over the past several decades to accommodate children and youth who have either committed criminal acts or are considered to be at risk if left in the situation in which they had been living.

A guard met us at the gate and checked our names off the list he held on his clipboard.

"Welcome, Mr. Holmes and Dr. Watson," he said. "The lads will be thrilled to see you. Young Tamblyn is waiting for you. If you look, you can see him standing there on the porch."

Up ahead, I didn't observe a boy standing. I saw one running toward us. He didn't stop running until he had collided with Holmes and thrown his arms around him. Then he jumped over to me and did likewise, giving me a tight, affectionate hug. His face was beaming.

"Oh, oh . . . I'm so happy you came. Thank you. Come, let me show you where I live. The other boys – some of them didn't believe me when I said you were coming, but the headmistress said you were – well, they can't wait to meet Sherlock Holmes and Dr. Watson. There's thirty of us living here, and we are just as rum a lot as you will ever find."

We followed him through the study hall, where twenty-nine sets of eyeballs followed us from our entrance to exit. I could hear the name of Sherlock Holmes being whispered as we passed, and once or twice, my own name.

"Master Royston," said Holmes. "I'm not here to be paraded like a prize heifer. Kindly lead us to a place where we can speak in confidence."

"Oh, yes, of course, sir. But it would never do. I would be thought awfully selfish if I kept you all to myself. I had to let my chums see you as well."

"Fine. We have been seen. Now, we need to talk."

He found us a small sitting room that had only enough chairs for the three of us and, as I could tell that Holmes wasn't in the mood for levity,

I took the initiative to start the conversation. After all, I was his personal physician, and Holmes was the add-on."

"Master Royston, you are much too cheerful for a boy in custody who is facing a charge of murder. What is the reason for your happy disposition?"

"Oh, Doctor Watson. This place is a dream come true. You would be so envious. Every boy has a story to tell, and they are all beyond belief. I couldn't imagine the bizarre twists and circumstances that brought them here. I shall have scores of stories to write and submit to contests as soon as I get out of here. It has been great fun."

"I noticed that some of the boys here are older and bigger than you are, and some have a bit of a nasty look to them. Are they not bullying you and giving you beatings?"

"Oh, no, not at all."

"Why not?"

"Well, the first reason is that I told them that I had contracted with Sherlock Holmes to work on my case. At first, some of them didn't believe me, but it was on Sunday that the Headmistress, Mrs. Ratchet – some of the boys mispronounce it in a vulgar way that I'm sure you can guess – announced that you would be coming to visit us because I was your client. Oh, the boys were so envious of me, and they all asked how they could get to be your clients as well."

"I hope," said Holmes, "you didn't tell them. But that hardly seems to me a reason to keep you safe from any unwanted aggression in a place like this."

"Oh no, that isn't the only reason. Did you know that in here – and it is the same for every prison I've been told – that there is a pecking order? Very firm class distinctions. And it all depends on what you were charged with. At the bottom are the petty thieves. You know, those who stole candy and shoes and such from shopkeepers. And just up from them are the boys who were charged with assault, beating up another lad rather badly. Of course, they move up a notch if they gave a beating to a schoolmaster – one of them was in the middle of getting caning, and he grabbed the cane out of his headmaster's hand and gave him a terrific beating with it."

"I suggest," said Holmes, "that he need not apply to Oxford. They take a dim view of such behavior regardless of how justly it is warranted. Go on."

"Well, if you were recruited to be a member of a gang of thieves who were adult men and who break into the homes of toff families . . . well, that is worth something. And almost at the top are those boys who were part of gangs who carried pistols and helped rob banks. They are the truly frightening ones. And then there is me."

"You?"

"I'm the only one here who has been charged with murder! And not just any old murder like poisoning. Oh no. My charge said that I had met my victim face to face and run him through with a sword, and it was all to defend the honor of my father. Oh my, Mr. Holmes. You wouldn't believe the points that put on my card. They couldn't wait to show me respect. Much more than I could ever hope for at St. John's Grammar School. Every day at lunch and supper, one of the boys offers me his dessert just to show his respect. It's all quite the adventure. I'm in no hurry for my trial to come and have to go back to my old life. Except, of course, I know it is upsetting to my grandparents, but they came to visit right after you met with them, and they told me that you were helping us. That relieved them wonderfully, Mr. Holmes. Thank you."

"You're welcome. Now then, enough of your being king of the castle in a temporary home for juveniles. Why did you lie to me?"

"Lie?"

"Yes. Lie. You know what I mean. Why did you lie to me about your father?"

The beaming smile vanished from his young face. He stopped looking at us and dropped his gaze to the carpet. I watched as he clenched his fist and, for a minute, I was afraid he was going to break into tears. But he got control of himself and spoke slowly and quietly.

"I know that my father was innocent. I know that he was betrayed and framed by a treacherous, evil monster. But that wasn't the verdict of the court-martial. According to the law, my father was a traitor who betrayed the Empire, who betrayed the Queen. Because of him, they said, many fine men died in an ambush. I don't want anyone to know that. So I made up a story. It wasn't all false. My step-father is where I said he was. But my true father was hanged. It's the story I tell to everyone who asks. I don't expect you to understand, Mr. Holmes. But that was why."

Holmes's face softened, and, as much as he is capable of doing so, he allowed a look of compassion to come over him.

"I do understand, and I don't condemn you. But why then did you lie about Colonel Abergavenny. He was no stranger to you. You knew who he was. It was no accident that you happened to run into him on that path at that time of night. The truth, please, Roy."

"The truth, sir, is that I was spying on him."

"Why?"

"I have read many mystery stories, sir, especially the ones Dr. Watson writes about your adventures. I'd learned that successful detectives had to be stealthy and patient. They watch a criminal in silence, and sometimes it takes many hours, or days. But they wait until they see him carrying out a crime, or they overhear him talking about it. They build evidence carefully, evidence that will stand up in court. And then they trap him. Well, I knew that Colonel Abergavenny was a criminal. I knew that he had smuggled back all the loot he stole in Benin. He was too careful to conduct criminal negotiations inside his house. His staff might have overheard, and they weren't at all loyal to him. So he met men outside his home, on the paths of Regent's Park, after midnight. I got close enough to hear some of what they were saying. They were talking about smuggling arms, and gold, and opium, and mollies and dollies, whatever they are, and how much was going to be paid. And I wrote it all down in my notebooks, and all I needed were a few more details, and I could have brought it all to Scotland Yard, but then one of his many enemies got to him first and killed the villain before I could turn him in."

"And the story you wrote? Scotland Yard believes that it was an account of how you carried out the killing."

"Oh, no, sir. Not really. It was how I imagined a son might avenge the death of his father. But I set it in Paris, and the boy was sixteen, and the treachery took place in Côte d'Ivoire, not Benin City."

"And the murder was done with a Scimitar after midnight."

"That was a coincidence. I thought it was a good way to kill a villain, and yes, I imagined myself doing in the Colonel just like that, being silent and all. I guess someone came to the same conclusion as I did."

I had been with Holmes too many times ever to think that he believed in coincidence when it came to crime. But the boy seemed sincere and, I had to admit, I might have come up with a similar way to murder someone, were I given to writing fiction.

Holmes was ready to depart when I had to give him a reminder.

"Don't forget. You have to give a talk to the boys."

He gave a puff of exasperation. "Fine, then let's get on with it."

All of the inmates of the home assembled in the study hall and gave a cheer and applause when the headmistress introduced me and Sherlock Holmes.

In fulfilling his requirement to tell the boys a morally uplifting story, Holmes recounted to them the true – he claimed – account of the band of six delinquent boys who broke into the home of the old Egyptian and stole all his most precious possessions. They bound him but otherwise did him no physical harm. Yet, in anguish at what was happening to him, his heart stopped, and he died, but not before screaming a curse upon the boys.

The boys were not as clever as they thought they were, and were soon apprehended, tried, and sent to a reformatory, one very much like the one we were all now sitting in. In truth, it might have this very one, as the location of these places are kept secret.

Everything went along with no problems until the first anniversary of the death of the old Egyptian. That night, at midnight, a horrible, blood-curdling scream was heard from somewhere in the building, but no one knew exactly where. The following morning, one of the thieves was found in the garden. He was dead. His face was contorted in terror. He had been disemboweled, and his intestines were strewn on the ground around him.

On the second anniversary of the theft, a second scream from nowhere was heard. In the morning, the next boy was found in the study hall. He had been tied up and hanged, but not choked to death. He had slowly bled to death after his feet had been cut off.

The third year, the third boy died. He was found in the lavatory, still sitting on the loo but impaled – beginning in the you-know-where.

The fourth boy, exactly a year later, was found sitting at a desk in the study hall, but facing his head, which had been removed, placed on the desk, and was looking back at him.

On the fifth anniversary . . . .

Holmes stopped and looked at his watch.

"Dear me . . . the fifth anniversary is today. Nothing has happened yet. Do be careful and let me know if you hear anything at midnight tonight. Good day, boys."

As I looked out over the thirty lads, I saw a sea of pale young faces, every one ashen and horror-stricken.

On the train on the way back into London, I took him to task.

"Holmes, that was downright horrid of you. You left those boys – "

"Less likely to re-offend. Precisely."

I let that one go, as I had other questions for him. After a pause of five minutes, I asked him the first.

"What did you learn over the past two days? Anything of interest?"

"I made inquiries about Colonel Abergavenny. It turns out that he was indeed a nasty piece of work. My contacts in Scotland Yard confirmed that he was suspected not only of smuggling, but of arranging beatings of any competitors, or even of having them murdered."

"Good heavens. He must have had a slew of enemies."

"He did. And I couldn't find a single person who mourned his 'tragic' passing."

We both retreated into silence until we approached the station, and then I remembered the other thing I wanted to know.

"Did you track down the cab number."

"I did. It is licensed to a Mr. Rory Hamilton. He lives in Fitzrovia, and I paid him a visit."

"Yes?"

"He claims that on the night in question, it was his turn to host a card party of his friends. There were eight of them altogether at his place, and they all played whist until after one o'clock in the morning. His wife was also present, and she confirmed that she was with him all evening. On top of that, he gave me the names of all of the players, and showed me the scorecard. He recounted all the hands he'd won and lost and what his wife served for midnight meal. His alibi was watertight."

"What about the cab number then? Did Royston get it wrong."

"No. Mr. Hamilton doesn't own the cab. He leases it. In the evening, it's returned to a common yard along with a hundred others. It could be let out at night to another driver, and it isn't unknown for someone to hitch a horse and borrow the cab for a night without paying the fee."

"Gypsy cabs?"

"Precisely."

"And these other chaps, his friends. Just the usual rum lot."

"Yes, with one thing in common."

"And that was?"

"They were all former Royal Marines."

I gasped. "And did they, by chance, all happen to be part of the Benin Expedition?"

"Every one of them."

When we disembarked at the station, Holmes caught my arm as I was about to walk to the exit.

"Please wait a minute until the crowds have cleared. I need you to help with a small experiment."

Two minutes later, all the other passengers having cleared away from the train, he turned his back to me.

"My dear Watson. Please place your hands under my arms. I'm going to fall back into them, and you are going to drag me to the line of cabs."

"Holmes, that must be a hundred yards from here."

"Precisely. Now grab. Here I come."

He fell back, and I struggled to keep him from hitting the platform. Then I started to walk backward, dragging his inert body. I hadn't gone more than twenty yards before I stopped, my heart pounding dangerously. I let Holmes fall to the ground, holding up his torso and head with the leg I planted firmly behind him. After a minute to catch my breath, I started up again, and had to stop after another twenty yards.

"It's no use, Holmes. I'm too old for this type of task."

He scrambled back to his feet.

"Precisely. And a twelve-year-old is too young. Thank you."

A notice arrived in the post, addressed to me, later that week, announcing the date of the trial of Royston Tamblyn. It was a full six weeks away. Holmes took note of it, with a sigh of relief.

"Time is always of the essence, and I remain retained on the matter of the Ferrers Documents. These few weeks will give me adequate hours and days to work with the barrister assigned to Royston and assemble the case."

"Will you be able to discern the true killer by then?"

"One thing at a time, Watson. It isn't immediately necessary that I solve the case and bring the true murderer to justice, only that I find enough evidence to convince a judge that there is more than enough reasonable doubt as to Royston's guilt. That is all we need for the trial. I'll be busy doing a thorough job on that. We cannot afford to have our evidence diminished or disallowed."

"Permit me to remind you that you told the grandparents that you wouldn't be charging a fee."

"I am not exactly a poor man, Watson."

He set out to pull all the evidence together, but was unexpectedly taken off the case by the arrival at Baker Street of Dr. Thorneycroft Huxtable, the founder of the Priory School. At his insistence, we traveled north to his school, where we undertook the adventure I have already put to account in a story published in *The Strand.* Fortunately, that case took up less than a week, and we were back in London.

Over the next few weeks, I continued to see little of Holmes. He did invite me twice to come as his guest for dinner at Simpson's, as he was looking for ways to spend the enormous financial reward that we had secured from Lord Holdernesse, but he revealed little about the current state of his work on the trial of Royston Tamblyn.

"His barrister and I are getting along swimmingly," was all that he deigned to tell me.

When the date of the trial was almost upon us, he took me out one more time and, on that occasion, was somewhat more loquacious.

"One must never allow oneself to be overconfident," he said. "However, we are feeling quite sure of ourselves. My diligent sleuthing has turned up ten witnesses to whom we have issued subpoenas and who are all prepared to testify under oath that they had heard rumors of plots against the life of Colonel Clive Abergavenny. Two of them will even go so far as to admit that they had been invited to participate in such plots and, had it not been for the murder that did take place, the Colonel would have surely died from another's hand. He was deeply involved in smuggling contraband goods into England and had a reputation of not honoring his debts. Such a practice doesn't go over well in the underworld of criminals. And you should see what he was smuggling. I've provided the barrister with twenty-seven eight-by-ten silver gelatined photographs of gold bars, paintings, bricks of opium, guns and ammunition, and young men and women – all of which he had illegally imported."

"Will that be enough?" I asked.

"It most certainly should be. And if not, the barrister is prepared to ask the judge to let him drag his body three-hundred feet through the courthouse and stuff it into a cab. And you, my friend, know how difficult that will be."

"And not to throw it in the Thames?"

That brought a chuckle from him. "I fear not, even if doing so were well deserved."

"Excellent, Holmes. I look forward to it."

The courthouse in which juvenile criminals were tried was well-removed from the courts of law in a location that was a highly-guarded secret. The Press were not notified and were blessedly absent from anywhere in the vicinity on the morning of the trial. I arrived early and helped Holmes unload two cases of evidence that he placed under the long table allotted to the defense. The file containing the twenty-seven eight-by-ten silver gelatined photographs was carefully placed on top of a case.

We had no sooner completed that task when the Crown Prosecutor, flanked by two young assistants, entered and placed their boxes of evidence under their table. In keeping with the confidentiality provided to juveniles, no one from the general public was allowed to enter. About ten minutes before the scheduled start of the trial, a wigged and gowned barrister entered, accompanied by a young assistant and Master Royston Giles Tamblyn III. Royston was dressed in the same blazer, white shirt, and school tie as he had been on the morning we had met him back in early May. His complexion had acquired a mild tan, rendering him the picture of youthful health and innocence.

Holmes and I were seated two rows back from the defendant, and I leaned over to him and whispered.

"Who is his barrister?"

"His name is Terence Boston. He was highly recommended."

The row in front of us was filled by Royston's grandparents and an attractive woman in her thirties who bore a distinct family resemblance to the young defendant.

"Is that his mother?" I whispered.

"It is. She arrived three days ago. The boy was beyond thrilled to see her."

"She will be relieved when the case against him is thrown out," I said.

Holmes might have responded, but the court official appeared, and we rose. The judge, Justice Robert Bayford OBC KC, then entered, climbed up to the dais, and took his place behind the bench. We were seated and then subjected to a lengthy lecture concerning the special provisions of a juvenile court, the most obvious one being the absence of a jury of one's peers.

"What's he like?" I whispered to Holmes.

"Stern, but fair to those boys he doesn't consider criminal, merely stupid, a condition of most males under the age of twenty-five. But he is very harsh on those shown to be bad to the marrow of their bones."

In a sonorous-bordering-on-pompous voice, the judge continued. Once the talk was over, he looked first at the Crown and then the barrister and asked if they were prepared. Both of them, in strong, confident voices, declared that they were.

The judge then looked directly at the defendant. He named him and stated the charge against him, noting how very serious the charge was.

Next, he asked for the plea of the defendant to the charge. Mr. Terence Boston, cleared his throat, adjusted his robe, and pushed back his chair in preparation for standing to answer.

He did not get to.

Royston Tamblyn stood up and, in a loud, clear voice, stated. "Guilty as charged Your Honor, and I'm prepared to make a full confession."

For a second, the room gasped and fell silent.

"*Roy! No!*" shrieked his mother from behind him as she attempted to lean forward, grasp the folds of his blazer, and force him back down into his chair. Her reach exceeded her grasp.

The barrister was now on his feet. "Your Honor, I am terribly sorry, please ignore my client's – "

"Be quiet and sit down, Mr. Boston," ordered the judge. "I will hear what your client has to say, and then I will decide whether it is permissible or not. If you have something to say, young man, you will do so from the witness box. Come up here and take your place beside me."

Royston edged his way from behind the defense desk, as he did so, his mother again stood and tried to grasp him. He leaned away from her but smiled warmly.

"It is quite all right, Mum. Please relax. I love you." And he walked up to the front of the room.

Again, the barrister attempted to interrupt.

"Your Honor – "

Down came the judge's gavel.

"Mr. Boston, be seated and don't interrupt again."

The barrister turned around to face Holmes. They gave each other one of those shrugs with palms facing up that one offers when utterly befuddled.

As Royston entered the witness box, a court official came toward him, holding a Bible.

"That isn't required," said the judge. "Under English law, anyone of any age may testify. Those under fourteen years of age aren't to be sworn in and cannot, therefore, be charged with perjury if they fail to tell the truth."

He then turned toward Royston and glowered down at him.

"Nevertheless, young man, you are expected to tell the truth and nothing but the truth. Do you understand?"

"Yes, Your Honor."

"And you will do so?"

"Yes, Your Honor."

"Very well, then, proceed."

"I have written it out, so I will be sure not to make a mistake. May I read my confession, Your Honor?"

From the inside pocket of his blazer, he extracted a sheet of folded paper.

"You may. Now, say what you have to say."

With only the occasional glance at his prepared speech, Royston looked at the judge and told his story.

"As I look back on my short life, Your Honor, I ask myself, *what could have happened that would lead me to do the evil deed I have done?* I believe that it all goes back to when I was nine years old and I read every one of the wonderful stories by Mr. G.A. Henty, who told me about boys who were facing terrifying situations but who acted courageously, even risking their lives, to do what they believed was the right and proper thing to do. I wanted to be like one of those boys. In April of this year, I got it into my mind that I would do just that. I would be a boy that acted with courage, even if my own life might end. But as a result of the horrible events connected to the death of my father, my mind was utterly twisted, and the courageous act I undertook, avenging my father's death, was the wrong choice. I took another man's life, for which I am now deeply and truly sorry."

He went on, replete with quite polished assonance, alliteration, and creative metaphors, to describe the false accusations against his father and the woeful miscarriage of justice that ended with his being hanged. Then came a minute-by-minute description of the night of Thursday, 2nd May, 1901, when he removed a Scimitar from his grandfather's wall, borrowed – without permission – a cab from the compound, and hid out in Regent's

Park, where he knew Colonel Abergavenny would soon appear. He surprised the Colonel and ran him through, killing him on the spot. Alone, he huffed and puffed and dragged the body back to the cab, drove to Waterloo Bridge, tossed the body into the Thames, returned the cab, and snuck back into his bedroom by three o'clock in the morning. His grandparents suspected nothing.

It was while he was in detention, he claimed, that one morning at Chapel, the Chaplain has preached from the text in the *Book of Numbers,* where God had said, "*Behold, ye have sinned against the Lord, and be sure your sin will find you out.*"

"Those words," said Royston, "touched my heart, and I knew that I had to confess my sin. Since that day, I have resolved in my heart to tell the truth, no matter the cost. I will accept whatever the law decides as my punishment, and I am determined to never again wander from the path of righteousness until the day I die. In conclusion, Your Honor, I confess that I murdered Colonel Abergavenny and that I, Royston Giles Tamblyn, acted alone."

He laid his paper down on the edge of the box and looked up at the judge.

The courtroom was silent. Everyone present had, I was sure, stopped breathing. The barrister pushed his chair back and looked as if he were about to stand and say something, but a sharp downward-pointing finger from the judge froze him in place.

An entire long, stunned minute passed. Justice Bayford glared first at Royston and then at the notes he had made as he listened to the polished oration.

"Young man," the judge finally said, "it is undeniable that you are of sound mind, and that you understand what took place. I can see and hear your remorse for your dreadful action, and I have no doubt that you will never re-offend. Neither the law nor society would be served by sending you away for years to come. Nevertheless, murder is murder. It is that most heinous crime on the books, and it cannot go unpunished. I have no choice but to sentence you to a period of time in a reformatory, but I will designate that it be one that houses a school of industry so that your time isn't wasted. Your sentence is for six years, with the provision that it be shortened to four years if your behavior so warrants."

He brought down his gavel and announced, "Officers, please escort the prisoner out of the courtroom. This case has been concluded. Those present will leave the courtroom."

A bailiff took Royston by the arm and led him out of the box and toward the exit. As he was about to pass us, Holmes stood and stepped in front of him, blocking his way. Doing so was a serious breach of courtroom behavior, and I quickly jumped up beside him and tried to pull him back. He would not budge, and Royston was forced to stop, his face only inches from Holmes's.

"You lied in a court of law," whispered Holmes, his face white with anger.

Royston, inaudibly, mouthed an answer, "I know. I'm sorry, Mr. Holmes."

"Why?" demanded Holmes.

Again, the mouthed answer, "I had to."

"Why?"

His answer, this time, could be heard. "Ask me in four years."

"*Move aside!*" bellowed the bailiff. "It is forbidden to block the movement of the prisoner. Move aside, sir. *Now!*"

Holmes stepped aside, and those present in the room followed the bailiff out in much the same fashion as one does at the end of a funeral. Royston was led into a waiting police wagon, and the small group of us watched in silence as it drove off.

I turned to see Royston's mother, pale and trembling, and being supported by her mother-in-law. The old soldier stood and watched impassively at the vacant stretch of road where the police wagon had disappeared from sight.

I introduced myself to the distraught mother and spoke to her and Mrs. Tamblyn.

"I will continue to serve as his official physician. If there is anything I can do to be of assistance to you, do not hesitate let me know."

His mother looked up at me and managed to get out a halting, "Thank you."

His grandmother, struggling to support her daughter-in-law, said, "Thank you, Doctor. You are a good man. We appreciate your care for Little Roy. But we shall carry on. We have no choice. We have to."

Holmes had already begun to walk away from the courthouse, and I hurried to catch up with him. He was leaning forward, marching quickly with his fists clenched. I knew that he was in no mood for any conversation, and I kept pace with him for three blocks.

Then his pace abruptly slowed. And then he stopped. I looked at him, and the anger had passed from his face. He was looking off to the distance at nothing in particular.

"Of course," he said, but not to me. "Yes, of course."

"Of course, what?" I said.

"Oh . . . yes, Watson. Why of course . . . yes, of course . . . of course it is nearing lunchtime. Simpson's trolleys of ham and beef will be ready.

If we change our direction, we should be there as they open the doors. What say, old friend? Another treat courtesy of the Duke of Holdernesse?"

He didn't wait for me to answer and started walking toward the Strand.

At the insistence of Sherlock Holmes, I didn't write an account of the Abergavenny murder following the trial.

"Unresolved cases aren't to be shared with the public," was the only reason he would give me.

I did receive a notice from the government office responsible for juvenile justice, confirming that, as the boy's physician, I was requested to pay quarterly visits to the reformatory where he was incarcerated. However, I was to understand that it was forbidden for me to inquire about anything other than his health when conducting my examinations.

For the next two years, I traveled north every three months to a location I'm not at liberty to disclose and checked up on Royston Giles Tamblyn III. He was invariably healthy, growing like a weed, and in good spirits. At the end of those first two years, another notice came informing me that a contract had been let to a local doctor to look after all of the boys and that my services would no longer be required.

During my examinations, I had been desperate to talk to Royston about the case, but, as it was a violation of regulations to do so, I refrained. I did, however, have access to his records and noted that once a fortnight, his mother and younger sister visited him. Both Mr. and Mrs. Tamblyn, his grandparents, did as well, once a month. That changed toward the end of the second year, and it was only his grandmother who visited. The old soldier's health, I heard, was failing, and such excursions were now beyond his ability to enjoy.

What struck me as curious was the record, once a month, of a visit by another adult male – a different one each time. I made a note of their names and, when I returned to Baker Street, looked into the file box where my notes and those of Holmes were stored. One by one, the names corresponded with those who had been playing cards together the night of the murder.

During the first week of September of 1905, I spent several days at Holmes's retirement home on the Sussex Downs. At the end of the third day, we were relaxing with a late-afternoon brandy and catching up on the newspapers.

"Watson," he said to me without removing the paper from in from of him, "would you mind joining me the morning after next?"

"On Saturday? Yes, I can easily arrange to be free. What for?"

"A funeral. To be more precise, only for the internment, as the service is private. It will require a journey up to Norwood. Can you fit that in?"

"I can, but for whom?"

"Your comrade-in-arms, Old Roy Tamblyn. He passed away yesterday."

I would have no objection to paying my respects to anyone who fought alongside me at Maiwand, but the request from Holmes was highly unusual.

"Holmes, we have known scores of old soldiers who have died and were buried. You never went to any of their funerals. Why this one?"

"Because the grandson was released from custody two weeks ago. He will be there."

"Holmes, it will be his grandfather's funeral. You cannot possibly be planning to accost him and tear a strip off him for what he did at the trial. That . . . that is inhuman."

"Who says I'm angry with him?"

On the Saturday morning, we caught an early train to Norwood and walked the six blocks back north to the monumental cemetery. The Tamblyn plot was along the north access road, and we arrived twenty minutes before the scheduled service. A grave had been freshly dug immediately adjacent to a modest headstone that bore the name of Major Roy Giles Tamblyn II.

A cluster of older fellows and some my age had already assembled. They had the unmistakable look of military veterans, and I joined up with them and exchanged banter as to where and when we had served. Two had been with me at Maiwand. We shook hands, adding a friendly left hand to clasp the upper right arm of a comrade.

The motorized hearse and the limousine from the funeral home arrived, and I retreated from the graveside and joined Holmes, standing well back from the service.

The family emerged from the long black motorcar. The grandmother led the way, using a cane but walking on her own. She was followed by the mother we had met at the trial and a pretty adolescent girl. Behind them was a young man, wearing a formal frock coat and top hat. He was as tall as Holmes and strikingly handsome. Four years in reformatory hadn't been unkind to Little Roy.

Behind all of them was a man of about my age. He had a gentle if somewhat chubby face and looked every bit the former foreign officer and kindly step-father that I assumed he was.

Eight pallbearers lifted the casket from the hearse and carried it to the graveside. All eight were strapping men whose names, I was quite sure, I could recall from seeing them written in a record book.

The service was brief and conducted by a priest, as given in *The Book of Common Prayer*. Once it was over, the pallbearers and the veterans stood and waited and, one by one, came up to the widow and her daughter-in-law and paid their respects. However, Royston Giles Tamblyn III broke away and walked over to Holmes and me.

"Good morning, Mr. Holmes, Dr. Watson. I am so glad you came. I was hoping to see you here."

He extended his hand to both of us.

"Why did you lie?" said Holmes.

"I had to. I had no choice."

"It was your grandfather who killed him, wasn't it?"

"It was. And was it my dog?"

"It was."

"I knew it. I knew it," he said, shaking his head. "The minute those words were out of my mouth, I knew I had made a stupid mistake. I had read 'Silver Blaze'. I knew you would deduce that the attacker was known to Berky."

"As was Colonel Abergavenny," said Holmes.

"Oh, yes. Berky and I had been running into him along the paths for weeks before. He had no idea who I was, but he was quite fond of dogs and would stop and bend over and pat Berky. When he did that on that night, it allowed Grandfather to step out from behind the tree and execute him. Grandfather knew how to kill a man silently with a Scimitar."

"And you had to take the blame because, as a juvenile, you couldn't be hanged."

"Yes. That was the plan. We knew that if Scotland Yard couldn't solve the crime, they would bring in Sherlock Holmes, and he would. All of them were committed to executing the Colonel, but any one of them, even my grandfather, would have been sent to the gallows. As a twelve-year-old, the most I would face would be six or seven years in reformatory."

"And so you planted the evidence that led to your arrest."

"First, we sent an anonymous note to Scotland Yard claiming to be from a school mate saying that I had boasted about avenging my father's death. Then I pricked my finger and put some blood on the Scimitar, and I dashed off that story about the murder in Paris."

"And then you asked me to help defend you."

"Well, yes, of course. We couldn't have you working for Scotland Yard or the Crown. That would never do. It would ruin everything. We had to have all your time before the trial consumed with building a case to defend me."

"How very clever. And the cab? Rory Hamilton drove it to Albert Drive and helped you and your grandfather dispose of the body."

"He did. His wife played his hand at the card game and made him memorize all the hands played and what was eaten and what the other seven men who served under my father chatted about."

"And these eight men . . . they let you spend four years of your life in custody. Yet you bear them no grudge."

"Oh, no. A fair arrangement was agreed. Each of them would sacrifice a portion of their monthly income for the next four years. It was paid into a fund, and I will use it to go to Sandhurst starting next year. My juvenile record will be expunged, but there was no possibility of a scholarship. I will have to pay the full fees. But there is enough now for my entire time there. Five years from now, I will join the Royal Marines."

"And you all conspired to make this happen? Who was the mastermind? Hamilton? Your grandfather? You? Who?"

"On no, Mr. Holmes. We all just did what we were told. We were informed in no uncertain terms that there was a job to be done. It had to be done. So, we all had to do what we had to do, and carry on."

"You mean . . . by your – ?"

"Yes, Mr. Holmes."

"My colleague, Dr. Watson, could tell you that we are very busy at present. I am retained in this case of the Ferrers Documents, and the Abergavenny murder is coming up for trial. Only a very important issue could call me from London at present."

– Sherlock Holmes
"The Adventure of the Priory School"

The Chinese Puzzle Box
by Gayle Lange Puhl

Our newest client was ushered into our sitting room at 221b Baker Street on a sunny afternoon in May. Fairdale Hobbs was a sturdy young man not yet forty, with a head of greying brown curls and hazel eyes. Dressed in a quiet brown suit, he sat on our sofa and told Holmes his problem.

"I'm a solicitor at the large London firm of Taylor, Twynnings, and Todd," he said. "Due to illness, I was raised by my mother's sister. She found I had some intelligence and encouraged me to make something of myself. I saw other boys apprenticed out to blacksmiths and printers. I wanted something more. I had to work hard for my education, but I finally passed the bar in Durham. I came down to London six years ago at the invitation of my present firm. I currently have rooms at Mrs. Warren's boarding house in Great Orme Street, near the British Museum. I handle mostly estates, trusts, and the drafting and execution of wills.

"One of the clients to whom I was assigned two years ago was Peter Bonne. He died last week of natural causes at the age of nearly eighty, and his family has gathered at his rooms in Syder Street, also near the Museum. Tomorrow is the funeral.

"Peter Bonne was a real adventurer, the kind of explorer of which books are written. He made his money in South African gold mines and invested it in factories and forests in England and the United States. As a result, for the second half of his life he was able to travel the world and indulge his love of the odd and bizarre. He traveled to over forty countries. He was a four-time past president of the Imperial Explorers Club based here in London. I had only been in his house a few times before he died, but it was a fine big set of rooms, filled with strange souvenirs of his adventures.

"His health wasn't good. Knocking about the African back countries, drinking brackish water when there was nothing else available, or slipping down Amazonian rivers accompanied only by native bearers and deadly mosquitoes took a toll on his body. He used to spend hours telling me of his travels, including the many months he spent in hospitals during those years. He did everything from climbing mountains to mixing in a few civil wars, but through it all his spirits never flagged, and he continued to collect all sorts of artifacts, which he had shipped back to London.

"Your client sounds as if he was an interesting man," said Sherlock Holmes. "However, I fail to see where my services come in."

"A month before he died, Mr. Bonne had this Chinese puzzle box delivered to my flat. With it came a note, which stated that he had written a will. The note said the puzzle box held the key to the will's hiding place, and he entrusted me to handle his affairs after he was gone.

"I hurried over to see him at once, but he had suffered an attack of apoplexy the night before, after he had posted the box, and was then unable to speak. I reassured him I would see to everything. Only last week did he pass away.

"Mr. Holmes, I've tried my best during the past few weeks to open the box and extract the aforementioned key. I can't. I've totally failed. I'm hoping that you can figure out the mystery of the box. Peter Bonne's relatives expect the reading of the will to take place soon after the funeral. Any long delay will surely upset them, and they can be a vocal bunch."

Holmes reached out and took the puzzle box from Hobbs. Even from where I was sitting, I could tell that it was a beautiful thing. The box was heavily lacquered in a bright Imperial yellow. Images of the Chinese calendar – oxen, roosters, dragons, tigers, and other creatures – were deeply incised in the wood in no particular order, so that it appeared they were frolicking across its surface. There were lines traced behind the figures, looking as if all the beasts had escaped from their cages. The entire effect was quite charming and very Oriental.

Holmes weighed the box in his hand and turned it over and around, examining the figures closely. He held it to his ear and shook it. There was a faint rattle. He pulled out his magnifying lens from the pocket of his dressing gown and peered closely at each side of the box. Replacing the lens, he held the box in both hands for several minutes, his fingers poking and pulling at the carvings on each side. Nothing happened.

"Mr. Hobbs, I thank you for this very unusual problem. Please tell me, did Mr. Bonne make a habit of collecting puzzle boxes during his travels?"

"No. He had several collections by the time he stopped traveling, notably primitive African tribal stools, pre-Columbian prehistoric clay vessels and figurines, rare mounted birds from all over the world, and ceremonial religious costumes from the Far East. There might be a shrunken head or two, or a Japanese sword here and there, but I never noticed any puzzle boxes until I received this one in the mail."

"Since his death, you have found no other such boxes in his house?"

"That is correct! But he had a very large home and it's filled with many odd things. There might be more amidst all the clutter."

"Tell me of his heirs."

"I don't think his was a close family, but he did speak of them. Lucius Whitehall, one of his nephews, is the oldest, and the son of a brewer. He claims to suffer from a number of illnesses, none of which impede his enjoyment of that which he really likes – eating at the best restaurants and indulging in wines. He claims some sort of injury from his school days and seldom exercises. He keeps a man, Brixton, who waits upon him hand and foot.

"Mr. Bonne had a niece named Elizabeth. Her father was in the City and indulged her until his death. She turned out to be a beautiful woman, but undeniably wild. She moved to Paris right after her father's funeral. Family stories, according to Mr. Bonne, linked her to at least three husbands and innumerable lovers. After the last husband's death, she took back her maiden name. She returned to London only last week with a dreadful reputation. She told me upon her arrival at Syder Street that she had left both a baron and a count threatening suicide in France. I fear that she isn't to be trusted around any of my male friends, although she has already demanded that I introduce her to my entire circle, including the married ones.

"Walter Bonne, the other nephew, sulks about the place, picking fights with everyone, and ordering the servants about with terrible oaths. I have spoken to him about his temper, but he sneers at me for being what he calls 'the hired help'. He lives in a cottage on the coast and complains about the price of everything. He sells his excess produce from his garden for cash and, according to Mr. Peter Bonne, managed to get an invitation from him to spend the winter months in Syder Street each year. That is when the price of coal goes up, Mr. Bonne said. Mr. Bonne never minded, but the servants hated it because his nephew would never leave as much as a half-farthing as a tip.

"Have any of these people mentioned an interest in Chinese puzzle boxes?"

"No."

"You say Peter Bonne's funeral is tomorrow and the reading of the will set for as soon as possible."

"Yes. That is, if it's is discovered by then."

"Do his relatives know that it hasn't been found?"

"Yes. I told each upon their arrival."

"So much depends upon the puzzle box and its contents."

"Exactly. Can you help me, Mr. Holmes? I fear that the entire matter is darkness to me."

Holmes's long, sensitive fingers ran along the top of the yellow box. "I shall take your case, Mr. Hobbs," he said. "For now, go back to Syder Street. Perhaps you would like to make another search for more puzzle boxes or the will. It might be hidden among all those interesting artifacts your client has stored in his house. Enlist his heirs in the search. It could only help, if only for purposes of elimination. Return here tomorrow after the funeral and we shall see what kind of progress has been made."

"His relatives, being told the will is yet to be found, have already been ransacking the place since each has arrived."

"Good. Let them continue doing so."

Mr. Fairdale Hobbs left with many expressions of thanks. Holmes returned to his armchair and stared at the puzzle box for half-an-hour. I busied myself with my notes and a medical paper in *The Lancet* until I saw he was fingering the box again.

Holmes took it into his bedroom but didn't shut the door. He sat at his table for some time, alternately consulting books from his bookshelf and trying to open the box. After an hour of this, he came back out and wrapped the box in a bit of brown paper.

"Fancy a drive to Soho, Watson? It's a fine afternoon."

"Soho?"

"Yes. I want to show this box to an old friend of mine, Ling Tan. He keeps a small apothecary in Bright Street and has an interest in Chinese puzzle boxes. We met years ago when I was working on a case involving a missing necklace. Before your time, I believe."

Of course I wanted to accompany my friend on such an errand. My watch said that it hadn't yet reached four o'clock when we stepped out of the hackney in front of Ling Tan's shop. The area of Soho in which we found ourselves in was tough and dirty. The shop that Holmes was looking for was a hole-in-the-wall place, with a single window decorated with jars and boxes labeled in symbols I couldn't read. Inside, as the tinny bell sounded with our entrance, I saw a short counter lined with containers of all sizes. Behind it was a wall consisting of what seemed to be hundreds of little drawers, from the baseboard to the ceiling. Each carried a paper slip indicating the contents. Again, I could identify nothing, as all the writings were in what I felt was surely Chinese. There was an odd aroma in the air, like musk and spices. Between the counter and the little drawers stood a young man, not more than twenty, dressed in drab Chinese garb. He greeted us in English, smiling and nodding, his palms pressed together. Holmes stepped forward.

To my surprise, Holmes spoke to the clerk in a foreign language that he later confirmed to me was Mandarin. The clerk bowed low and disappeared behind a curtain in one corner. A moment later he pulled it open and waved us inside. A short corridor led us to a parlor occupied by a wizened old Chinese man, decked out in a blue silk robe and round cap topped with a black button. He was sitting in an armchair placed by a small fireplace. On the floor was a luxurious rug, and the walls were hung with rich tapestries and silken cloths. There was an atmosphere of burning incense. The young man pulled out a couple of carved chairs and a matching table, and then left us. Holmes greeted the old man in Chinese and apparently introduced me, as I picked out the name "Watson". We sat at the old man's gesture.

Soon the young man returned with a tea service on an ancient wooden tray. The old man gestured again and the young man served us the tea using small round cups without handles. I took a sip, as did Holmes. It was delicious.

Holmes set the wrapped box on the table. He carefully removed the paper and spoke a few words. Ling Tan leaned forward and examined the box.

He looked to me to be nearly a hundred years old. Though seated, he appeared to be of medium height with a noticeable belly. His hands were veined in blue and his fingers were thin with prominent knuckles. A grey queue hung down his back. His fingernails were long and well-kept, and on one finger he wore a ring engraved with yet another Chinese symbol.

Holmes and I sat silently as the old man examined the box. After several minutes, he called out and the young man appeared. Exchanging a few words, he left and came back with two rolls of yellowed paper, bound with red silk string with tassels on their ends. Ling Tan carefully unrolled them, consulted the contents, and then gave them back to the young man.

Again the clerk left. Ling Tan picked up the box and made a rapid series of moves over its surface. The top and sides moved and expanded. In what seemed like an instant the box yielded up its contents: A sheet of foolscap folded many times and a tarnished brass key.

Ling Tan presented them to Holmes, who then gave them to me. Then Holmes motioned for the old man to show him how he had opened the box. After a few demonstrations, Holmes replicated the movements, successfully opening and closing the puzzle box himself. The two men exchanged some more words, we rose and bowed to him, and a minute later we were out on the street in the May twilight, searching for a cab.

Back at 221b Baker Street, I handed over the mysterious contents of the box. He stretched out in his chair by the fire lit earlier by Mrs. Hudson and examined the key.

"It's small, as you have noticed. Flat handle, round shank, and a simple design to manipulate the lock. The handle carries a design but no words or letters. Too small to be a door key, but it might be a watch key, yet I doubt it. No company name is engraved on it, and there's no indication to what kind of lock it was made for. Let's see the paper.

"Here is a half-sheet of foolscap, torn at the bottom. There are words on it in blue ink, written in a florid fashion. Here. Read it aloud."

I took the paper from Holmes's hand and smoothed it out over my knee. It was much creased from being folded, but the paper was in excellent condition with no tears or yellowing.

From the welcoming door to the stairs bereft
My personal gifts have been left.
A final adventure I give to mine
To find that which is hidden fine.
Discover that which spoke to me
To learn what treasures I gifted thee.

I looked at my friend in amazement. "How extraordinary! What can it mean?"

Holmes rubbed his hands together and looked very pleased. "A challenge! A treasure hunt! I like Peter Bonne. I wish I could have met him. Instead of writing a conventional will and leaving it somewhere obvious like a desk drawer, he hid the clue to its whereabouts in a Chinese puzzle box and dared his solicitor to find it. Excellent! However, by the mantelpiece clock it's getting late, and there is nothing more that we can do tonight. Might I suggest a short walk to the Athens Restaurant on Grosvenor Street? They specialize in moussaka, and the wine is not to be questioned."

Mr. Hobbs arrived the next day just after lunch. Dressed somberly in a dark suit and with a black armband on his sleeve, he sat in a suitable mourning attitude on the sofa, turning his hat in his fingers. He reported no progress in the search for the will at his late client's house.

"It was a nice funeral," he said. "A good turnout of Peter Bonne's old friends – some from the British Museum – a delegation from the Imperial Explorers Club led by their current president, Sir Benjamin Frye, and of course the relatives and me. He was interred in Highgate Cemetery this morning and a lunch was provided at the club. His heirs went back to the apartment afterwards, and I came right here."

Holmes brought forth the Chinese puzzle box and, under Mr. Hobbs' fascinated gaze, opened it and extracted the key and paper. He handed both to our client.

Fairdale Hobbs peered at the key and admitted he had never seen it before. He was equally confused by the poem and handed it back to Holmes with a frown.

"Other than saying the will is somewhere in his house, this writing says nothing helpful," he declared. "What can it mean, Mr. Holmes?"

"Did Peter Bonne collect pocket watches or timepieces of any sort?"

"I don't think so. He carried a fine gold watch, much battered and dented from his travels. There is a clock in the parlor and another in his study, but he never mentioned anything unusual about them."

"Are their keys accounted for?"

"Yes. The watch key was found on his chain, and the winding clocks had keys laid right next to them."

"I think it's time for us to see Peter Bonne's place for ourselves, Mr. Hobbs," said my friend. "Come along, Watson. Mr. Hobbs, I'm eager to visit such a house."

Syder Street was a quiet avenue near Bloomsbury, lined with staid redbrick terrace houses, each nearly identical to the next. Peter Bonne's home was situated in the middle of the block. A course of curtains were drawn in mourning, and there was a black wreath on the communal front door. We entered, climbed the stairs to the landing, and knocked. A sturdy young maid opened the door and greeted Mr. Hobbs.

"Hello, Mr. Hobbs. Sir Benjamin Frye just left. He came soon after the others returned to pay his respects. He seemed sorry to miss you, sir. Mr. Case came with him, but they left together."

"Thank you, Dimmy," said our client. She took our hats and led us to a large parlor.

It was a handsome room, panelled in dark oak, with an Adams-style fireplace, and a marble mantelpiece. There were multiple armchairs and low tables with a round table in the center, draped in an embroidered cloth and supporting a shiny gramophone next to a plush-covered photograph album. There a woman stood before a mahogany highboy, opening each compartment and searching through it. On the sofa by the fireplace, a large, heavy man in a smoking jacket and impeccable trousers reclined, a drink in his hand, and watching the woman with suspicion.

"I wouldn't put it past you, Elizabeth, to find that will and pocket it so that the rest of us get nothing. I heard that the third husband didn't leave you much money."

"You are a horrible person, Lucius. You are hard up yourself. Is that last year's smoking jacket? Besides, my second husband left me plenty, so there is no need for you to worry."

The man on the sofa looked as if he was about to respond when we appeared in the doorway. At the sight of Mr. Crawford, the woman stopped what she had been doing, hurried up to him, and fingered his lapel. "Have you found it?" she breathed. "Have you found the will?"

"We are one step closer, Miss Mowbray," said our client. He placed the puzzle box on the center table. "Mr. Holmes and Dr. Watson, this is Miss Elizabeth Mowbray and one of her cousins, Lucius Whitehall." The man slowly raised himself from the cushions, shook our hands, and then dropped back down as if the task had been exhausting. He didn't look well, and with his white face and thinning hair, I estimated his age at forty years, although in his state of health he appeared older.

Elizabeth Mowbray may have come back from Paris with a reputation, but it must have taken a while to develop it. She was just past thirty-eight, I estimated, and her blonde hair hadn't been blonde all her life. Tiny lines had begun to form around her eyes and lips that no amount of paint or powder could conceal. Her neck was long and still graceful, but the faintest of jowls were forming, and she was dressed in a black afternoon frock ten years too young for her figure.

Suddenly there was a crash from a nearby room. We heard a yell of anger and a pounding of footsteps in the hall outside. An athletic man in his early thirties, wearing a rumpled dark suit with a mourning band on the sleeve, burst into the room and confronted Fairdale Hobbs.

"One of those stupid maids put that vase in the wrong spot and now it's broken!" he yelled not two feet away from Hobbs' face. "I'm not taking responsibility for it, do you hear me!! Have you found that will yet? Uncle Peter was an idiot for hiding it like he did! Who are these men?" He stepped back and glared at Holmes and me as if he thought we had come to pocket the silver.

"Mr. Sherlock Holmes and Dr. Watson, this is Walter Bonne," said our client, making every effort to hold his temper. The angry man obviously felt no similar restraint.

"A-ha! The great Sherlock Holmes! Hobbs told us he had gone to you with that ridiculous box. I would have just smashed the thing and gotten the will out of it that way, but Hobbs said that I couldn't for 'legal reasons'. Ha! Now the old man is planted and it's time to divvy up the goods. Where is the will?" He looked eagerly from one to the other of us as if ready to snatch the document out of the hand that held it and read it on the spot.

"Do you think you're mentioned in Peter Bonne's will?" asked Holmes.

"Of course I am," snorted Bonne. "I'm the only one to carry the family name, and that should count for something, I think. Uncle Peter was proud about the family – traced it back to some officer under William the Conqueror. Wouldn't be surprised if he left me this place and all his money. You others can have the junk inside. I've got no use for stuffed birds and African tribal stools. Give me the ducats, man, and I'll be happy."

"Walter, that is a terrible thing to say!" cried Elizabeth. "Uncle Peter was always fond of me when I was a child, and I'm sure that he wouldn't have forgotten me. I used to sit on his lap in my ruffled dresses and listen to those long boring stories he told about the jungle and those horrible natives he was always nattering on about! I'm sure I earned a place in his will – and a good place too. After all," she continued, turning to me and providing a devastating smile that gave me a flash of what she must have looked like when she was twenty, "Do I look like the kind of woman to be left alone and defenseless in this big, bad world?"

"Alone and defenseless? You?" drawled Lucius Whitehall from his comfortable place on the sofa. "Lizzy, you could be thrown into the deepest jungle in South America and within ten minutes you would be made queen of the local tribe and decked out in all the riches available for miles around. Not to mention the local men. Why, you would have your pick and the rest to fight over your favors."

Miss Mowbray made a move as if to scratch his eyes out but stopped herself. "What makes you think that Uncle Peter left *you* anything? All you've ever done is drink his single malt and eat everything put in front of you and ask for seconds. He knew that if he left you any money, it would go straight to the local restaurants and wine sellers."

"I believe in living well, I admit. Uncle Peter did what he wanted with his money. Why shouldn't I do the same . . . with his money?"

Fairdale Hobbs stepped forward. "I have put the problem of locating the will into the hands of Mr. Sherlock Holmes," he announced. "He has uncovered the solution to the puzzle box. He found a key and a paper. Mr. Holmes?"

Holmes held up the small key. All eyes turned to the metal object.

"I believe this key turns the lock that conceals the will. The poem included in the box with it was written to guide us to the will. The next step is to discover the lock that this key fits."

Walter Bonne took the paper that Holmes held out to him and impatiently read it aloud.

"'*From the welcoming door*' . . . '*gifted thee*' . . . this babbling makes no sense!" he exclaimed. "This entire place has been searched. All the papers in the library have been sifted through. There is no sign of a will. I think the old man's mind was gone and he forgot where he put it. This Chinese puzzle box was some kind of deranged joke that he played on us all."

Holmes smiled. "You say the flat has been searched. Mr. Hobbs. How many rooms are there in this house?"

"Six, plus the servants' quarters."

"How many servants are there?"

"Two, both women. Sarah Nightingale, the head housemaid, and Dimmy Walsh, under her. Mr. Peter Bonne had his major meals delivered, so he had a very simple kitchen set up in the back for breakfasts and teas and such."

"Don't forget Brixton," said Lucius Whitehall. "He's my man, and has been here a week. I pay him a healthy wage, but dash me if I know why. He is lazy and ineffective, and I have to yell at him to get him to move. Dashed if I know why I keep him on."

"Why do you, dear Lucius?" murmured Miss Mowbray sweetly. "We all have wondered that." Whitehall shot her a murderous glance.

Holmes continued as if nothing had happened. "Then we have three servants, the three of you, Mr. Hobbs, and Watson, and me. Mr. Hobbs, please ring for the servants, please."

Our client yanked a bell pull by the fireplace and in a few minutes the two women and Whitehall's man Brixton were lined up on the carpet. Sarah Nightingale was an active woman of middle years. Dimmy Walsh was the younger maid who had met us when we arrived.

Brixton was a wiry man of under medium height, not yet in his mid-twenties. He was dark-haired, horse-faced, and dressed in neat livery. He looked from one to the other of us, his intelligent eyes sparkling but giving nothing away, He ducked his head to his master, but with an insolent air. Holmes explained the circumstances of the missing will.

"I need more information about Peter Bonne. Miss Nightingale: How long did you work for him?"

"I was hired the first day he walked into this house, Mr. Holmes. It was ten years ago. He took me on as a second housemaid, but six years later Ophelia Quincy left and I got her job."

"How many servants did Mr. Bonne keep?"

"There was a staff of five regulars, sir. Miss Quincy was the housekeeper. She had her own room where she also kept the accounts. I shared a room with the other maid, but she soon quit because of all the dusting and polishing. There are a lot of things in this flat to keep clean, you see. After she left, Mr. Bonne went through a series of maids, but they never lasted long. There was also Mr. Bonne's friend, MacIntyre, who ran errands and did the heavy lifting. A series of hall boys were hired over the years to clean boots and lay the fires and such.

"Back then Mr. Bonne used to host meetings of the Imperial Explorers Club. He wrote articles for the newspapers and magazines. He would have important travelers come and speak and stay, sometimes for a week. He invited people from the universities to dinners and then led them around the house, telling stories of the things he'd found. He needed a full staff to keep the flat presentable."

"Then why are the staff so few now?"

"A few years ago he began to show his age, sir. MacIntyre, who had been on some of his travels with him, died. Mr. Bonne sort of lost heart. He stopped hosting the Explorer Club meetings here, and would instead leave the house to attend them. He complained of pain in his fingers when he tried to write. He began turning down invitations. He was defeated for the Imperial Explorers Club presidency by Sir Benjamin Frye. It got harder for him to get in and out of bed and move around. Gradually he closed off part of the flat and let most of the staff go – all with good references and two months' wages. Mr. Bonne was always a kind, generous man.

"It was just me until he couldn't navigate anymore, and then he hired Dimmy to help me get him around and care for him. He had lost a lot of weight by then." The other maid nodded, her eyes as round as saucers and her hands grasped in front of her.

"What rooms did he close off?"

"All he really used toward the end were his study, the library, and his bedroom. There they are, just across the hall. He had us shut down the dining room and the second bedroom, except for when Mr. Walter Bonne visited."

"What about the staff quarters?"

"Bless your soul, sir, he never went there in all the years that I worked for him. Dimmy had the first maid's room and I had the housekeeper's room, next to the kitchen, but Mr. MacIntyre's room was shut down years ago. We opened that room for Miss Mowbray. There was another small maid's bedroom and the servant's hall. We gave the small bedroom to Brixton, There is also a coal cupboard on the back landing that leads both downstairs and up to the other flats."

"I understand that Mr. Walter Bonne has stayed here each winter. Where does he sleep?"

"I had the second bedroom, across the hall from Uncle Peter's," interrupted Bonne. "And why shouldn't I? I was family, after all, and the only one to visit him. While Lucius was spending his winters in Egyptian fleshpots and Elizabeth was cavorting in the South of France with her European royalty, I was here, listening to Uncle Peter rambling on about Japanese idols and South American pots. I ought to get his entire estate just for the verbal torture I had to endure."

"Do you have that bedroom now?"

"No, I do not. After I got word of his death, I came straight up to London, had the linens changed on Uncle Peter's bed, and moved in. The second bedroom is good enough for Lucius, I guess. It's right next to the dining room, his natural habitat. Besides, I got here first."

"My room is full of taxidermied birds," shuddered Miss Mowbray.

"I spend most of my time here," said Whitehall. "It has a good fire, more light, and it's furnished with a very nice sofa."

"It appears that the only rooms to which Peter Bonne had easy access in his final months were those across the hall. That does simplify matters."

Holmes paced back and forth for a few minutes while the rest of us waited. Finally, he turned on his heel and faced us. He pulled out the small key from his pocket and held it out.

"We are looking for a lock that will fit this key. Here, have a good look at it. Now, the lock could be on a box or a piece of furniture. It could be on a drawer or a panel in the wall. Peter Bonne was restricted in his movements during his last year of life, and since he sent the Chinese puzzle box to Mr. Hobbs only a month ago, I believe he wrote out his will shortly before that. Mr. Bonne was a man of the world and knew a holographic will, properly phrased and witnessed, would be valid in court. Did he ever ask you to witness him signing a paper, Miss Nightingale? Miss Walsh?"

"Once, after lunch, when I came up for the tray, he asked me to get Dimmy, and he scratched something with a pen, then told us to put our names under his," said the housekeeper. "He never told us what it was, and he had a sheet of paper over it, except for the part for our names."

"When was that?" asked Fairdale Hobbs eagerly.

"I remember that was the Wednesday before he had his stroke, poor man."

"Miss Walsh, do you remember that?" asked Holmes. The maid blushed as all eyes fixed on her.

"Yes, sir. I remember because he had me put a package downstairs for the postman the next morning and he had never asked me to post any package before that."

"Was it about this size?" Holmes inquired. He measured out a space with his hands.

"Yes."

"That would have been the Chinese puzzle box," said Holmes. "Was that the morning of the night he had his attack of apoplexy?"

"Yes, sir," replied the maid. "It was a great shock to both of us. Miss Nightingale found him."

"Yes, sir," said the housekeeper. "It was after dinner. He fell out of bed. I heard the thud and found him on the carpet. Dimmy went to the doctor but he couldn't help. Doctor Gooden said we should just make him comfortable. Poor man couldn't say a word. Never did again, I believe. Mr. Hobbs came the next morning. Sir Benjamin came after that, and Professor Tyler from the British Museum, and even Mr. Case, from the Avian Society. He had always been interested in Mr. Bonne's bird collection."

"The vultures began to gather," muttered Lucius Whitehall.

"That is not fair, Mr. Whitehall," protested our client. "Those men were all friends of long standing to Mr. Bonne. They came from common courtesy and genuine concern, I am sure. Sir Benjamin was very upset. He insisted on sitting next to Mr. Bone's bed for over an hour when I was there once, and left only when the doctor turned us out so Mr. Bonne could get some rest."

"Miss Mowbray, I've been told by Mr. Hobbs that you and your cousins have been searching these rooms ever since you were informed that the will was missing. I now propose a more systematic search. The maids can return to their rooms. If nothing is found in the flat, it may become necessary to search their bedrooms and possessions. I hesitate to suggest that, but this matter is too important to take half measures. I trust there would be no objections?"

The women slowly shook their heads. Clearly they weren't happy with the request, but under the circumstances couldn't protest. Holmes sent them to their rooms to make ready for the search.

But Brixton lingered, refused to leave and spoke up sharply, his country accent shrill and loud. "I don't likes it! Me things are me own, and I resents being suspected in this business. Mr. Whitehall, I works for you. Must I allow this?"

Lucius Whitehall dropped his eyes before his valet. "I feel I must protest, Mr. Holmes. Brixton has been in my employ for nearly a year now, and has always given satisfaction. I don't think a search of his belongings or his person is needed."

Elizabeth Mowbray stared at her cousin in surprise. "How can you say that, Lucius? You called him lazy this morning! I for one want him searched, right here and now. He has a slinking, furtive air about him, and I wouldn't trust him further than I could throw the coal scuttle."

"I agree with Elizabeth," said Walter Bonne. "He has been hanging about my door the last few days, snooping and prying. I found him in my room yesterday, with no good explanation, going through that big wardrobe of Uncle Peter's. He said he was looking for a fresh tie for you and he had stumbled into the wrong room. I sent him out with a flea in his ear and a hand at his collar. I say strip him to his smalls."

Brixton was still turned to his master. "You can't allow this, Mr. Whitehall! You knows what might happen!"

Holmes looked down at the fat man, who was peering back from the sofa, and asked mildly, "What would happen, Mr. Whitehall? It's clear that Mr. Brixton has a hold over you. Your tremblings and agitated breath are matched only by his own, save for the level of fear you've demonstrated in his presence. Since he walked in this room, I've noticed his clenched hands and hard glances toward you. For some reason you're afraid of him, and he feels triumphant towards you. I think it's a secret shared by you both, yet he holds the upper hand in your relationship."

He spun around to Brixton. "What is it?" he asked. "Or must we have the police in?"

The valet turned on his employer. "If that happens, I tells what I knows, Mr. High-and-Mighty Whitehall!"

Lucius Whitehall's face went white. "Shut up, Brixton! I've paid you well – !"

"If I am to go into th' nick, you will finds yourself in trouble! Let me tell 'em! This here great gentleman be nothing more than an *imposter*. He's no better than me! Why, I am better than he ever was, 'cause at least me parents was married!"

All eyes swung over to Lucius Whitehall, who gave a large sob and buried his face in his thick hands. The little valet stood triumphant, one hand pointing at his employer.

"I was born north of Seven Dials," Brixton explained, "and me father never made much as a news agent. Me mother had th' four of us and had to work as a seamstress until her eyes give out. I was the oldest. When I was big enough, I left to go out and earn me own living. I scraped by doin' this and that until I was taken on by Mr. Whitehall here as his valet. He got me at cheap wages and considered it a good bargain.

"Bein' a smart lad, I snoops about his things, lookin' for something small an' valuable I could pawn. What I finds is a paper, carefully tucked away at the bottom of an old trunk."

"Thief!" came the cry from the sofa. "Scoundrel!"

"Aye, I admits I was lookin' out for the main chance, and when I finds it I keeps it. I finds a letter, addressed to his dad from his mother. She was in France and she was askin' for details on the location where his *real* mother was stayin' in Whitechapel. The baby was due any day, ya see, and they had made arrangements to pick it up as soon as it was born. The wife couldn't have children, it seems, and they paid a lot of money to the girl's father for the child.

"Rich people did that sort of thing back then – buy some baby an' pretend it was blood. When it becomes known that the son of the house is some doxy's bastard, it causes a scandal. When I confronted Whitehall with the paper, he tries to snatch it back, then offers to pay me. He don't want to go to the police, ya see, because then it would all come out and he's afraid all his fine friends would scorn him. His folks didn't want anyone to know his dad and ma couldn't have kids for the shame of it, so they never took out any papers on him. He spends all these years passing himself off as one of the Whitehalls of Middlesex, and him no better than a gutter rat. All his friends in his clubs would have a good giggle, wouldn't they, smoking fine cigars and playing billiards with a man with no legal rights to an honest name. His dad could be a murderer for all they knows.

He'd be thrown out of every club in London. It would drag his folks' name through the mud. Used to talk all the time about his 'illustrious ancestors' and his 'family tree'. I sets what I thinks is a reasonable raise in me wages and took the paper in for safekeeping."

"I haven't had a good night's sleep since," moaned Whitehall. "He grew more insolent, more defiant. When I began to get complaints from the housemaids, I dismissed all the servants and took on a daily. I made sure she was the ugliest woman I could find."

I happened to glance at Miss Mowbray and Bonne. I could see from their expressions that the news of Whitehall's parentage, and his suddenly tenuous connection to a claim upon the estate, was something that they wished to explore and exploit. But before they could comment, Holmes spoke.

"Well, I can see my original plan cannot work," he said. "Mr. Hobbs, I suggest you and Mr. Bonne escort Mr. Brixton to the back and lock him in the coal cupboard. Then our search can commence. We will decide what to do with him later."

The modified plan was put into effect. The maids were surprised when the search started with their rooms, but stood by as their things were quickly examined. It took no more than a visual glance to discover if there was any lock that could accommodate the key. None were found in the women's rooms. Brixton's room was also gone through, carried out under the sound of the valet pounding on the larder door and demanding to be released. The maids were told he was a thief and were suitably horrified. They quickly agreed not to let him out of the locked door.

The servants' hall was searched. There was a frisson of excitement when a small box on the table yielded to the key, but it turned out to be just Dimmy Walsh's sewing box, filled with nothing but spools of thread and a tiny silver pair of scissors. Holmes brought out his magnifying lens, but no secret compartment or concealed space was found. Miss Walsh explained that that lock never had worked well and now appeared to be completely broken. Holmes grunted, but moved on to the rest of the apartment.

The guest bedrooms were examined. Nothing was found, although I thought that the collection of taxidermied birds in Miss Mowbray's room was magnificent. It was no wonder that Mr. Case of the Avian Society had expressed such interest in it. She had turned up her nose at the colorful fowl until Mr. Hobbs mentioned what the birds might bring at auction. I actually saw her pat a Greater Arctic Tern as she exited the room before me.

The dining room had many built-in drawers for napery, silverware, and china, but eventually every drawer was unlocked by Miss Nightingale's set of household keys and no will was found.

Holmes concentrated his attention on Peter Bonne's own rooms. He took over the search in the study, the library, and his bedroom, where Bonne had spent most of his time in the months before his attack of apoplexy. The bedroom was carefully examined. It was notable for the African tribal stools and the walls draped with Japanese silks. In the study, Holmes started with the carriage clock on the mantelpiece, but the little key didn't fit and the clock's own key was easily found. All of us must have shifted and examined two-hundred items collected from his adventures displayed there. The library was thoroughly searched from the contents of the tall bookcases to the upholstery of the leather chairs. No source for the lock that fitted the key was found.

As Mr. Hobbs, the heirs, and Holmes and I gathered in the parlor, the last room to be searched, Holmes held up his hand. "Watson, do you notice anything?"

I listened. "I can't hear Brixton yelling," I said.

"Perhaps the fool can't be heard from here," growled Walter Bonne. "Or maybe he got tired and quit."

"I'm going to check," said Holmes and all of us clattered down the corridor after him. The housekeeper's room and the servants' hall were empty and silent. A muffled moan drew us to the valet's temporary prison. Mr. Bonne found the coal cupboard's key, which had been left in the lock, but was now dropped down a couple of steps on the back stairs. Holmes unlocked the door.

A quick look in the cupboard disclosed the female servants, smudged in black dust and each bound by their own aprons and gagged with their own caps, lying on the coal-covered floor.

"He jumped us, sir," said Sarah Nightingale. She was trembling, not from fear, but from rage. "He slid a piece of paper under the door and dislodged the key that Mr. Hobbs had left in the latch. It landed on the paper and he drew it in and unlocked the door. He bragged about it the whole time he was threatening us and tying us up. He'd grabbed a knife that I had in the kitchen for fixing tea. Swore he would slit our throats if we tried to cry for help or run. A black-hearted villain, sir, that man! Scared us both, sir, and after we were locked in, we couldn't make enough noise to draw your attention."

Holmes drew me to one side as the others comforted the women and sent them to recover in the servants' hall with a pot of coffee from the stove and a tin of biscuits from the kitchen shelf.

"I am a prize blockhead, Watson," he said. "I never thought to search Brixton before we locked him up. He must have been carrying that letter around with him all the time, knowing that if Whitehall ever found it, all his power over his employer would disappear."

Holmes walked the few feet down the hallway to the back tradesmen's entrance. "Yes, this door is unlocked and our prize is long gone. Look, just a set of steps up and down and no footmarks in sight. No way to tell which way he went. Well, I must inform the others, but this episode will not burnish my reputation when you include it in your memoirs."

Voices were raised when Holmes reported the results of his investigation. Mr. Hobbs took all the blame for leaving the key in the lock, and Mr. Bonne was very energetic in his condemnation of both Mr. Hobbs and Brixton. Mr. Whitehall, surprisingly enough, took the news in the calmest manner of all.

"It's all right, Mr. Holmes. I looked over the coal after the women were freed and found this, trampled into the pile." He held out a dirty piece of paper. There were words written on it in a feminine hand. "It's Mother's letter, the one Brixton had found. He must have left it behind in all the confusion. Now I have it back and no one will have another chance to blackmail me again."

He strode over to the coal stove and thrust it into the flames lit for the kettle. There was a small flash of red and orange, and in seconds the paper was ashes, vigorously ground into oblivion by the poker.

"What is to stop Brixton from going to the newspapers and blurting your secret all over town?" asked Miss Mowbray.

"He has no paper with which to back up his claim," said Holmes. "In telling the story, he would have to confess to the theft of Mr. Whitehall's property and to the crime of blackmail. I think he would find himself in more trouble than it was worth. Doubtless the man has a criminal past."

"But *we* know your secret," said Elizabeth Mowbray slyly. "What is to stop one of us from spreading your origin story all over London?"

"You have no proof," Whitehall replied. He seemed to have regained his courage and his composure after the dark revelation. "You never read the letter, and all that you heard from Brixton were allegations. I would go on the stand and deny everything. I could easily find which of you would try such a thing, and neither you nor Walter have backgrounds so pure that damage couldn't be done to your own reputations. Mr. Hobbs cannot profit from such a disclosure, and Mr. Holmes and Doctor Watson are known as honourable men."

Walter Bonne growled. "I guess I won't talk, Lucius. God knows I have enough skeletons in my closet that I don't want you setting detectives on my track. Elizabeth is known for her dalliances, but I have heard one or two other things that might keep any reputable man in society from proposing lawful wedlock to her."

Miss Mowbray bit her lip in frustration and angrily led the way down the hallway to the parlor.

It was a large room, with the afore-mentioned fireplace against one wall and two tall broad windows to the left, overlooking the street. There was a sofa, several armchairs, a round table in the center of the room bearing a crank Berliner gramophone displaying its graceful horn, and shelves of artifacts and old books. The large highboy with many drawers that Miss Mowbray had been examining when we first arrived stood between the windows. The floor was covered in an odd woven rush carpet with a geometric pattern on it – a prize, no doubt, from one of Peter Bonne's many travels. The windows were draped in heavy velvet cloth over Irish lace. An upright piano stood against the right wall. Strange plants and cacti filled every corner. On a shelf high on the right over the piano sat a taxidermied Great Horned Owl. It may have been only my fancy, but its eyes seemed to follow me everywhere I went in the room.

Altogether it was a comfortable space, with just enough alien decor to remind a visitor that its owner had been an unusual man.

Holmes divided the room into four parts and the rest of them began to search. Every drawer was tried, every Burmese statuette was moved, every sheet of paper was read to ensure it wasn't the will of Peter Bonne.

While the heirs and Mr. Hobbs were busy, Holmes conducted his own examination. First he eliminated the mantel clock by finding its own key. Then he paced off the room's length and breadth. He pulled out his magnifying lens and his measuring tape and went over every inch of the fireplace and the mantelpiece. He paid special attention to the coal scuttle, the hearth rug, and the bricks underneath. He called for a short ladder from the kitchen and climbed up it at certain points to examine the crown molding that ran around the room just under the ceiling. He asked me to help move the table from the middle of the room and he lifted the carpet to view the floor underneath. Nothing was found. The carpet was put down again, and the table replaced.

One by one the others finished their areas and stopped. Lucius Whitehall resumed his place upon the sofa, staring dreamily at the ceiling, no doubt quietly celebrating the destruction of the letter that had held him in bondage to his former valet.

Elizabeth Mowbray sat in an armchair, her fingers picking at the material of her dress and her eyes darting about, as if she still searched for the will from her seat. Once she got up abruptly, ran across the room, and rummaged through the piano bench again, leaving a welter of sheet music in her wake. She failed to find the will and slunk back to her chair.

Walter Bonne looked the longest, even poking into places in the room others had searched before. It was as if he couldn't admit defeat. Finally he roared in frustration, threw a heavy book through which he'd been thumbing onto the floor, and turned on us all.

"Curse him! Why did he have to make such a job of it? Uncle Peter was always the most contrary and irritating man I ever met. I could give you all sorts of crazy examples. Remember when we were younger and he had us here that time for Christmas? He hid our presents all over the place and it took two days to finally find them. Turns out he was moving them from place to place, so whenever we thought we had searched a room, he would sneak them in when we weren't looking and we would have to look again. They always were found in the most obvious places – pinned to the curtains, for instance – so it seemed to us we were going mad not to have seen them before. When we finally came back with the packages, he laid back in his armchair and roared with laughter!

"'That will teach you,' he said, 'that nothing in life is easy. I had to brave murderous natives and horrible conditions for my first gold mine, and I worked hard to bring back everything in this house. I had a lot of fun doing it, but I had a lot of pain too. Remember, "God doesn't give with both hands".'"

"He always had to be clever," snorted Mr. Bonne. "Clever, clever Uncle Peter!"

"His gift to me that year was a lovely mirrored compact set in gold," said Miss Mowbray.

"I got a retractable ivory and gold toothpick," Mr. Whitehall said.

"Mine was an old Spanish doubloon," responded Walter Bonne.

The cousins sat silently a few moments, their thoughts far away from the present situation.

I looked at Holmes. He was standing by the fireplace, his lens held motionless in one hand as he stared at Walter Bonne. The expression on his pale face was as one transfixed. As he regained his composure his eyes roamed around the parlour as he slowly put his magnifying lens in his coat pocket. I stepped up next to him and heard him murmur "*Dieu ne donne pas des deux mains*." Then he declared, "I believe I have solved the location of the missing will."

The announcement galvanized the three heirs, and Mr. Fairdale Hobbs as well. There was a rush of movement and Holmes waved everyone back to their seats, myself included. He took up a prominent position on the hearth rug. The final denouement of a case before a rapt audience had always been Holmes's favorite part of his avocation.

Whenever possible he would play it to the hilt. His sense of the dramatic required it, and he had a very great sense of the dramatic. Now his pale face was alight with excitement. He thrust one hand under his coattails and raised the other in the air. His profile, seen from where I sat, was as still and sharp as a hatchet's edge. His black hair, tousled from the day's search, was ruffled over his forehead, and his steely grey eyes swept over the group.

He indicated the puzzle box, which had been placed on the center table by Mr. Hobbs when we had arrived hours before, and placed next to it the foolscap containing the poem and the little key he had shown us before.

"These are the three major clues Peter Bonne left to the discovery of his will," he began. "A Chinese puzzle box, a poem, and a key. Now I was told by Mr. Hobbs, Peter Bonne's legal representative, there are no other Chinese puzzle boxes in this entire flat. Having spent the most of this day, along with you, searching this flat, I can attest to that."

The others and I nodded.

"Peter Bonne spent the second half of his life traveling the world, having adventures, and gathering up what caught his fancy. This flat contains some very fine collections of rare birds, African tribal stools, pre-Columbian pottery, and many other unusual and valuable things. But there is one major problem with collecting things, be they rare jewels or postcards: One can never collect them all.

"Every collection in the world is incomplete. Either one does not have the money, the space, the time, or the opportunity to gather up a totally complete collection of anything. When one may be assured, say, that he has gathered up the most thorough accumulation of butterflies on the planet, one report of a newly-discovered specimen found in the Himalayas would spoil it. It would no longer be complete."

"But Uncle Peter didn't collect butterflies," said Elizabeth Mowbray.

"No, he didn't. We found dozens of rare books, birds, sheet music for the piano, Japanese costumes, pottery, and many other unique and beautiful things. But we never found another Chinese puzzle box . . . and we never found any discs to be played on this gramophone."

Our eyes were now all trained on the gramophone on the table. A mahogany box supported a turntable connected to the big sound bell by a mechanism that included the playing needle. A steel crank with a wooden turned handle stuck out on one side to power it. There was a drawer built into the base, with a key sticking out of the lock.

"That drawer could hold the music discs," said Lucius Whitehall. "The key is right there. Did anyone open it and look for discs?"

"Let's do it now!" said Water Bonne, and he jumped up, grabbed the key, and turned it. The heirs and our client and I crowded around as the drawer was pulled open. There was a sigh as each of us realized the drawer was empty.

"No will," said Mr. Hobbs.

"More importantly, there are no discs," said Holmes. "What is the use of a gramophone with no discs to play upon it?"

"None," said our client.

"Mr. Hobbs, do you know when Mr. Bonne acquired this gramophone?" asked Holmes.

Fairdale Hobbs frowned. "It wasn't here last summer. I do remember noticing it on this table just after the New Year."

"So it was obtained only a few months ago," said Holmes "Yet it came with no music discs. I do not believe gramophones of this size usually come with a storage drawer. This instrument must have been a custom construction.

"The drawer wasn't the hiding place for the will," continued the detective. "The key to open the drawer was in plain sight. Yet the gramophone plays into this investigation somehow because there is nothing else that goes with it. The puzzle box is solitary and so is the gramophone. Plus, there is that one line in the poem. '*Discover that which spoke to me*.' A gramophone, through its discs, speaks.

"I have made a thorough study of the Chinese puzzle box. In fact, Watson and I even took it to an expert to discover its secrets. Let us now subject this gramophone to the same scrutiny. I run my fingers over the box. This panel in the back shifts to expose the works inside. That is obviously to allow any repairs needed. Nothing there. But, if I examine the machine closely with my lens . . . ah, what have we here?"

Holmes pointed to the base of the fluted metal horn that acted as an amplifier for the gramophone. It was connected to the mechanism that ended in the needle that drew the vibrations from the discs usually resting on the turntable. Just below the join where the bell and the sound chamber met was a tiny keyhole.

"Usually the horn and the sound chamber are fitted so tightly together that nothing is needed to hold them in place except for this armature which supports the weight of the horn," said Holmes. "This must have been especially-made. Ah!"

He turned the tiny puzzle box key in the lock and drew away the horn. Folded inside the sound chamber was a wad of paper completely filling the space. Mr. Fairdale Hobbs reached forward and prized the paper from its confinement. The others watched breathlessly.

He unfolded it. "It is the will. Written out in Peter Bonne's own hand and duly witnessed by Sarah Nightingale and Dimitria Walsh."

"What does it say?" exclaimed the cousins excitedly.

"I will have to take it back to my office and go over it carefully," said the solicitor. "I see other names mentioned as beneficiaries, such as the Avian Society, the Imperial Explorers Club, and even the British Museum, but from a first glance each of you are in it, with sizable inheritances mentioned."

Amid the general rejoicing, Holmes gathered his things and motioned to me. "I was gratified to be of help," he said to Mr. Fairdale Hobbs, shaking his hand.

"Thank you, Mr. Holmes," said our client. The other three heirs offered their thanks and extended handshakes to both of us. "Please, submit your bill to the estate and I will see that it is settled promptly."

"It could be settled right now, if you would indulge me," answered my friend. The quartet stared at the detective.

"What do you wish?" asked Elizabeth Mowbray.

"The Chinese puzzle box," replied Holmes. "If I could receive that it, would fully repay me for such small labour as I have done."

"The box is properly mine, as a gift from Peter Bonne," said Fairdale Hobbs. "If that is all you require, I cannot see any objection."

A few minutes later we were in a cab, the puzzle box resting on Holmes's knee, driving through the now dark streets. With a few words, Holmes diverted the cab to Soho and we soon arrived in front of Ling Tan's shop.

Holmes left me in the carriage and went into the shop. In less than a quarter-hour later he returned, climbed inside, and we were on our way to Baker Street. He no longer carried the box.

He saw my questioning glance and smiled. "I have repaid an old debt, my friend. Years ago, when I was very young and Ling Tan had just arrived in this country, he saved me from a dangerous situation. I won't give you any details, but I can assure you I was put into it by my own inexperience and overconfidence. I learned several lessons that night and I felt that I owed my continued existence to Ling Tan and his family."

"How does the Chinese puzzle box come into all that?" I asked.

"Back in China, when he was a boy, Ling Tan helped his grandfather create puzzle boxes. He recognized this as one of the last that his grandfather had made before his death. He told me that when we first brought it in. I have returned it to him and his family as a mark of respect. Now the debt between us has been settled. I am relieved that I am no longer beholden to the old man."

"Why is that, Holmes?" I wondered.

"Because, Watson, Ling Tan is the head of one of the biggest jewel smuggling operations in London, and the police have been on his track for years."

"You arranged an affair for a lodger of mine last year," she said. "Mr. Fairdale Hobbs."

"Ah, yes – a simple matter."

"But he would never cease talking of it – your kindness, sir, and the way in which you brought light into the darkness. I remembered his words when I was in doubt and darkness myself.

– Mrs. Warren and Sherlock Holmes
"The Adventure of the Red Circle"

The Adventure of the Refused Knighthood
by Craig Stephen Copland

Sherlock Holmes was not happy.

"No, Mrs. Hudson, I will not see her now. Send her away and tell her to come back later."

It was just past seven in the morning, and we were enjoying an early coffee on a pleasant Sunday in the first week of June 1902, when Mrs. Hudson interrupted us.

Our longsuffering landlady did not leave.

"She apologized for not having an appointment and will not give her name, but says that it is imperative that she speak with you."

"Good Lord," said Holmes. "What is the populace of London coming to? I said – "

"I heard what you said, and you might wish to reconsider, Mr. Holmes."

"For what reason? Is there something peculiar about her?"

"She is around thirty years of age, has a handsome face, is wearing a coat and scarf such as could be found in a rag-and-bone shop, and – "

"Tell her – "

"No, Mr. Holmes, I shan't. I shall tell her that you will be happy to see her straight away."

Holmes was momentarily silent and gave Mrs. Hudson and sideways look. A wisp of a smile crept across his face.

"And pray tell, why should I do that?"

"Her boots."

"Her boots, Mrs. Hudson?"

"Yes, Mr. Holmes, her boots. They cost more than you pay me in rent every month. Each of them."

Holmes leaned back in his chair and adjusted his dressing gown. "A young woman of means comes in disguise at an ungodly hour but will not give up her select footwear. This should prove interesting. Please, Mrs. Hudson, show her in."

The woman who appeared was stooped over like a frightened animal. I stood and gestured her to a seat on the sofa. As she walked toward it, her eyes kept darting around the room and, upon reaching her place, she sat looking toward us. Her face, although exceptionally well-formed, was pale, her eyes were reddened and puffy, and her mouth was drawn tight. Her whole body was trembling.

She removed the non-descript scarf from her head, exposing a disorganized mane of grey-and-black hair. I stole a glance at her boots and could see that Mrs. Hudson had described them accurately.

"Please, madam," said Holmes. "Will you take a cup of tea before we begin?"

"No . . . I mean, no thank you. Tea would not help me. What I need is . . . is a promise. I need a promise."

"Yes, go on."

"I have been told that Mr. Sherlock Holmes can be trusted never to betray what he is told in confidence. Is that true?"

"Madam, several thousand people have sat where you are now sitting during the past two decades. I have been told no end of astonishing things and have never betrayed the trust with which in good faith they were imparted to me. I assure you, I am not about to start doing so this morning."

"What if you refuse to take my case after I tell you something?"

"I may indeed refuse it. That matters not. Whatever is said truthfully by you to me and Dr. Watson will never be disclosed. On that, you have my word."

She appeared to relax, and her visible trembling subsided.

"Thank you, sir. What I am about to confess to you would destroy my marriage. It would shatter my husband's career. Neither he nor I would ever recover our reputations."

"You have my promise. Please state your case."

Instead of speaking, the woman raised her hands to her head and extracted a succession of hairpins. She lifted the mangy grey wig and set it on the sofa beside her, exposing perfectly coiffed blonde hair that been tightly curled, with every hair in place. She then took a handkerchief from her sleeve and wiped away the dark shadows from around her eyes.

I gasped.

The woman who now sat looking at us was none other than Lady Ethel Oakeley, the wife of Sir Hugh Oakeley, the Secretary of War in the current government. Prior to her marriage to the significantly older widower, she had become famous throughout England as the most promising actress in the West End. Her maiden name was then Ethel Terry, the niece of the renowned doyen of the theater, Dame Ellen Terry. The marriage of a glamorous actress to a senior Member of Parliament had filled the social pages of the press when it took place two years ago and could have given rise to a storm of rumors and scandals. But it soon became the consensus that the young woman had conducted herself with exceptional grace and elegance and had become a prized asset of the political class. She was the last person I would have expected to seek the help of Sherlock Holmes.

"I can see," she said, her voice unsteady, "that you recognize me. My problem will touch not only on my reputation and that of my husband. It has repercussions for the future of the British Empire and for the possibility of war throughout Europe."

"Given who you are," said Holmes, "and your husband's position, that does not surprise me. Kindly state your case. You will be treated with the utmost discretion."

"Thank you, Mr. Holmes," she said. "My situation has come about because . . . ."

Here she paused and began again to tremble. Her fists were clenched white, and her eyes tightly shut. When she opened them, tears appeared. She started several times to try to say something and halted. Finally, she took a deep breath and blurted it out.

"Because I killed a man."

She then sank her head into her hands and convulsed with sobs. Holmes waited again until she had recovered control of herself.

"Was the death an accident? In self-defense? In defense of your honor? What happened?"

"Oh, no. It was murder. I planned it an hour in advance before I shot him."

Holmes was not expecting to hear that.

"You what? When did this happen?"

"Last night. Just after midnight."

"Where?"

"At his home in St. John's Wood," she said, lifting her head from her hands.

Holmes was thoroughly nonplussed. Many women may have sat on the sofa across from him in years past, but none had confessed to premeditated murder. He extracted a cigarette from his case, lit it, and took a long, slow draft.

"You will have to be more specific, madam. No doubt there were actions and reactions that led to your shooting a man. You will need to start at the beginning of your state of affairs. Please try to be concise."

He looked directly at her, expecting her to begin her account. She surprised us by standing, walking over to Holmes, and picking his cigarette case up from the side table. She took out a cigarette, placed it in her mouth, and then, still shaking, leaned down toward Holmes. Her unspoken request was obvious. Holmes struck a Lucifer and held it up to her.

"Tobacco," she said, "is a much safer way to calm one's nerves than alcohol when confessing to murder."

"Indeed, it is," said Holmes. "Now, your story."

She sat back down on the sofa and took several drafts on her cigarette before launching into her account.

"When my marriage began, I entered a heavenly dream. Even if my husband was twenty-five years older than me, he was energetic and attentive, and our life was a continuous cycle of splendid parties, travel to the Continent, meetings with the best and brightest leaders of industry, the arts, and governments foreign and our own, and the theater every Wednesday evening. I felt as if I had died and gone to paradise. I did not miss my former life for a second . . . and then that all changed."

"When your husband was appointed to the Cabinet," said Holmes. "After which you hardly saw him at all. You became desperately lonely. Whereupon, you foolishly engaged in indiscretions which you now regret. Correct?"

"Well, why . . . yes. That is exactly what happened. How did you know?"

"It is a tale as old as time, madam. You are far from the first woman to sit where you're sitting and relate such a story. Granted, none who came before you had recently killed a man. Go on."

"To relieve my desolation, I offered to assist at a few charity events, particularly those associated with the arts and letters. It was at one of those events – a revealing of a wonderful new painting of Queen Alexandra at the Portrait Gallery – that I met him."

"And he was," said Holmes, "handsome, gallant, charming, and attentive. He engaged you in fascinating conversation and, whilst conducting himself like a perfect gentleman, nevertheless made it clear to you that he found you attractive. He admired you, and you were flattered. You enjoyed the attention. Correct?"

"Well, yes. That was what happened."

"And are you now telling me that when he threatened to expose your indiscretion and ruin your life unless you obeyed his every wish, you murdered him. Correct?"

"Yes . . . well, no. I did not exactly murder him. It would be more accurate to say that I executed him. There is a difference. That is why I have come for your help."

"His name."

"General Edmund Ludenberg."

My lower jaw dropped a full inch. The man she named had served with distinction under Kitchener in the Cape and was now a senior staff member at Sandhurst, respected and admired throughout Britain. He was considered London's most eligible bachelor, and was constantly in the social pages as he was accompanied to unending functions of the rich and shameless by a continually changing stream of beautiful women. One week, an elegant older widow was on his arm, and the next, a stunning young student who was still in her final year of studies at Oxford. That he had been shot dead by this woman sitting in front of me was beyond belief.

"Madam," said Holmes, "I have given you my promise of confidentiality, and I will not disclose what you have told me to the police. However, if what you have told me is true, then I expect that Scotland Yard will be able to connect you to his death. I cannot take your side to protect you. What is it you want from me? And what do you mean that you *executed him*?"

"I discovered that he was a villainous traitor to His Majesty. He was an agent of the German Kaiser. He was about to pass on secrets that would bring terrible consequences to the British Empire."

That was hard to believe. The man's reputation as a much-admired senior army officer was beyond reproach.

"Explain," said Holmes.

"During the few weeks . . . well . . . to be truthful, the three months that I enjoyed his friendship, he cajoled me with requests to help him advance his career."

"By requiring you to obtain secret information from your husband and pass it along to him?"

"Yes. That was what happened. At first, the requests seemed innocuous, but then they escalated. Three weeks ago . . . Are you familiar, Mr. Holmes, with the project known as the *Dreadnought*?"

"Of course. It has been extensively covered by the press."

"My husband had a complete set of the preliminary plans for the battleship in the safe in his office. I knew the combination, and when Sir Hugh recently visited America, I loaned them to General Ludenberg. He returned them a week later, and I put them back in the safe."

"During which time he copied them."

"I assume he did."

"And sent those plans to the Kaiser."

"At the time, I believed that he only wanted them for his own use. I now must assume he shared them with officials from the German Embassy. He is well-connected to the diplomats of many countries. I have come to suspect that they are all spies."

"If he indeed did so," said Holmes, "that was an act of high treason. But if the deed was already done, your shooting him was somewhat after the fact – a closing the barn door after the horses have bolted. Why kill him – or, if you insist, execute him?"

Again, the woman appeared to be sorely distressed. She started several times to speak and then stopped.

"There was something else," she stammered. "I cannot disclose to you exactly what it was except to say that it was of overwhelming importance. Something that could either guarantee peace in Europe for decades to come or lead to war. He was about to act in such a way as would lead Britain and our allies into war with the nations of the Triple Alliance."

"You will have to more forthcoming, my Lady. Otherwise, I will have no choice but to ask you to leave."

"Please, Mr. Holmes, if I were to reveal the details of this issue, I would be committing treason."

"Then you must at least convince me of its importance, as I am somewhat skeptical. There is nothing happening at the moment in world affairs that strikes me as having the possibility of the consequences that you are claiming."

"I can only speak in the vaguest terms, sir. You will have to draw your own conclusions."

"Then speak."

"You are aware that Great Britain is an ally of France?"

"Anyone who can read the newspapers is aware of that. Wherein is the great secret?"

"Yes, Mr. Holmes. Everyone knows that. What is . . . what is hoped for – dreamed of – is that a far more powerful *entente* could develop which would be so overwhelming it would render impossible any threat from the Kaiser and his alliance."

"Beyond France and possibly Russia?"

"I can say no more, Mr. Holmes."

Holmes and I looked at each other as the inevitable conclusion came to both of us.

"A formal alliance with America?" said Holmes.

"I cannot tell you."

"But you will not deny."

She was silent.

"And you casually disclosed details of this venture with your . . . your friend."

Again, she said nothing.

Holmes took another slow draft on his cigarette.

"Then tell me what happened last night."

"The general had dismissed his staff for the afternoon and evening. He does that every Saturday."

"Allowing you to visit without being identified."

She nodded and then continued whilst lowering her eyes and gazing at the carpet.

"I . . . I admitted myself to his house at our appointed time but, as often happens, he was delayed. I had over an hour by myself."

"During which," said Holmes, "you spied on him."

"I am a very curious person by nature. I inspected his desk and private files, and there I discovered confidential cables between him and high-ranking officials in the German government. I also saw the draft of the details of the *entente* to which I alluded a moment ago. With it, in his hand, were his suggestions for disrupting not only the future agreement, but for destroying the current negotiations with France."

"Whereupon you realized the enormity of your indiscretion."

She buried her head in her hands and uttered a muffled, "Yes."

"And then what?"

Her head remained sunk into her hands, but she spoke clearly. "When he returned, I confronted him. I begged him. He laughed at me. He threatened to expose me and destroy not only me but my husband. He demanded that I safeguard his secret – that I become a party to his villainy."

"Go on."

"I . . . I had no choice but to agree. Please do not humiliate me by asking me to describe what I did. I can only tell you that half-an-hour later, he had fallen into a deep sleep."

"Where did the gun come from?"

"I had found it in his desk. I had used guns before in the theater, except that all our cartridges were blank."

"And you shot him? In the head?"

She raised her head and looked at Holmes. "I did."

"And then?"

"I placed the gun in his hand. It was foolish of me, but I tried to make it look like a suicide. I took the papers I had discovered, pulled on my coat, and fled from the house. I ran into the park and walked around blindly for several hours. I came to my senses and lit a small fire and burned the papers. As soon as it was morning, I came directly to your door."

"And just what is it you expect me to do? I cannot mislead the police and allow them to accuse anyone else of murder."

"I know . . . I know. I have convinced myself that what I did was for the protection of the Empire, and that I had only acted as the executioner of a traitor. I thought that you could . . . maybe . . . investigate and discover the web of spies of which he was a part. Expose them. They would then become suspects, and the police would have no reason to think of me."

Her beautiful face was pale, strained, and taut. Tears were running down her cheeks.

"Please, Mr. Holmes, please. I am begging you to help me."

Holmes slowly stood and walked over to the bow window and gazed for a full minute into the morning light. He turned back to her and spoke from across the room.

"I cannot excuse or condone murder, madam, nor will I deliberately mislead the police. However, I shall investigate this web of spies you claim exists and, if I find your description to be credible, I shall expose them. The truth concerning what you did will come out. It always does. There is some reason to expect that in the context of what you say you did on behalf of the Empire, public opinion will gather behind you and the courts will be lenient. That is all I can offer."

"Thank you, sir. Thank you. I have to go now. My husband returns this morning from the Continent. But you will keep your promise not to tell anyone?"

"Madam, I will never perjure myself in a court of law nor to the police. I will promise only that I will not voluntarily disclose what you have told me."

He walked across the room and picked up the lady's coat and scarf. He handed her the scarf and assisted her with her coat. As she departed the room, she turned one last time to Holmes.

"I cannot thank you enough, Mr. Holmes. I knew you would help me."

Once she had gone, I went and found Mrs. Hudson and I returned to the sitting room bearing a fresh pot of coffee. I poured a cup for both of us and handed one to Holmes.

"Goodness, Holmes. In all these years, there has never been an interview like that. What are you going to do?"

He sipped on his coffee.

"Nothing."

"I beg your pardon? You cannot just ignore what she told you."

"Yes, my friend, I can, if I am certain that it did not happen."

"What? Holmes, the woman was visibly distraught. She wasn't trying to deceive you. Surely, you could see that. She had tears running down her face."

"There is nothing sooner dry as women's tears."

"She was utterly sincere."

"My dear Doctor, you are a man of medicine. I am merely a consulting detective. However, I have read enough to know that it is not unheard of for someone, for any number of reasons – and it occurs more often in women than in men – to believe that something took place which, in truth, never happened. The woman is delusional."

"Holmes, how can you possibly – "

"Her boots."

"What of them?"

"They were freshly polished, gleaming, without a speck of grass or mud on them. No one who spends hours walking through Regents Park emerges with boots that look like that, and furthermore. . . ."

"Yes. What?"

"Her coat and scarf."

"They were obviously used to disguise herself."

"And if they had been worn all night in a park and next to a fire, they would not bear the odor of having been purchased from a rag-and-bone shop and removed from a closet an hour earlier. And furthermore, her hair. No woman who has spent the hours before midnight in the intimate company of a man emerges with every hair in place and smelling like bath salts and perfume. She came to us directly from her own house and, for whatever cause, has convinced herself that last night she murdered General Ludenberg. I suspect that she has indeed been carrying on an indiscreet friendship with him, has become highly distressed over it, and may have had such a vivid dream that her poor mind became deranged. She believes what she did in her dream actually happened. But it did not."

"Are you sure you don't want to confirm that? Shouldn't we inquire about the general?"

"Unnecessary. A waste of my time. Thank you for the coffee."

He returned to sipping on his cup and reading the newspaper. I shook my head and returned to my coffee. The woman had been exceptionally believable, and I marveled at Holmes's ability to notice what I had completely failed to see.

After a half-hour and another cup of coffee, I turned to him.

"It is a glorious June morning. Might you fancy a brisk walk ourselves in Regents Park? We could both use the exercise and fresh air."

He put down his newspaper and nodded. "An excellent suggestion, my friend."

We walked down the stairs to Baker Street, stepped out on to the pavement, and got no farther.

"Mr. Holmes!" Inspector Lestrade shouted. "Get in. We need you!"

"And where, my good Inspector," said Holmes, "might you be taking us?"

"Henry Street. St. John's Wood. I have a general lying dead in his bed."

In a bedroom on the upper floor of a finely appointed terrace house in St. John's Wood lay the body of the formerly handsome and publicly feted General Edmund Ludenberg. The right side of his face was a bloodied mass, and the pillow and bedding beneath it were still damp with the copious amounts of blood that had flowed from his head.

"There he is, Holmes," said Lestrade. "What do you make of him?"

The corpse was lying supine on the left side of a double bed and wearing only a nightshirt. In his hand was a short-barrelled Webley Bulldog revolver. The bedding to the right of him was rumpled, and the pillow somewhat out of position.

"Doctor," said Holmes to me, "would you mind examining the general and noting your initial observations?"

"The appearance and temperature of the flesh," I said after touching the exposed lower portion one of the legs, "indicate that he has been dead at least six hours."

I bent over the body and, as I did not have my doctor's bag with me, used my penknife to scrape away the matted hair on the side of his cranium.

"He was hit on the right temple," I said. "However, there is no evidence of powder anywhere close to the wound. Whoever shot him did so from at least two or three feet away."

After a few more scrapes, I stepped back.

"Good heavens. He's been shot twice. There is a bullet wound in his cheek and another in the temple."

Holmes and Lestrade exchanged glances.

"One could assume," said Holmes, "that the first shot was not fatal. Hence the need for a second."

"And that," said Lestrade, "rather puts the lie to suicide. Not many chaps shoot themselves a second time from several feet away after missing the right spot the first time. Anything else, Doctor?"

I wasn't at all sure of myself. I had, like Holmes, been bound by a promise of confidentiality and couldn't make statements beyond what I could directly observe.

"Assuming that the shots were fired in quick succession," I said, "the death was instantaneous. The cause of death is undisputed. He appears to have been an otherwise healthy man. There is no odor of spirits anywhere around him, and we can assume that he was sober when he died."

"Was he asleep?" asked Lestrade.

"That cannot be determined."

"Fine, thank you, Doctor. What about you, Mr. Holmes? Anything to add? Might I point out the empty side of the bed and ask for your oh-so-scientific deductions?"

"You are referring, Inspector, to the rumpled nature of the bedding and pillow, the distinct odor of perfume – a select French one sold under the appropriate name of *Mon Péché* – and the several strands of light blonde hair. Someone, a female apparently, may have lain beside him prior to his death."

"Right. And whoever she was, she is now my primary suspect. I want you to drop whatever else you're doing and find her. You do know who this fellow is, right? He was privy to no end of official secrets. I'm not inclined to believe that he was murdered by any old jilted lover. She was most likely a glamorous foreign agent. You agree?"

"A definite possibility, Inspector. With your permission, I shall conduct an examination of the house."

"You're not likely to find anything. He lived alone. A confirmed bachelor, just like you. But go ahead if you want. His cooks, man-servant, maids, and the like are all confined to the house. We're holding them here until we have finished our examination of the premises. You can interrogate them to your heart's content, but we already did. None were here last night. They were given every Saturday afternoon and evening off."

Holmes gave a cursory glance to the bedroom and then turned and walked toward the door. I followed him, and we descended to the ground floor of the house.

"Watson," he said, "would you be so kind as to start an inspection of his office and library whilst I examine the other rooms?"

"What am I to look for?"

"Anything written in German."

I began with a quick look at the general's bookshelves. There were, indeed, several books in the German language: Plays by Schiller, Goethe's *Die Leiden des jungen Werthers,* several books by Nietzche, and a smattering of novels. Some of them had notes protruding from them, scribbled in German. The man was fluent in the language.

I found his appointment diary and was immediately impressed by the busyness of his life. Every fifteen minutes was accounted for. His evenings were either spent at his club or the theater, concert hall, ballet, or *soirée*, with the name of the lady who was to accompany him duly noted. Lady Oakeley's name was not amongst them. I gave the man credit for discretion.

In the past two months, he'd had several meetings either at the German Embassy or with officials of the German armed forces in his office at Sandhurst. I bent the corners of the pages where these had been listed to have them ready for Holmes.

An hour passed before he joined me in the library. I explained my findings to him and showed him the diary. For the next hour, he read through it and scribbled notes.

"Excellent, Watson. Fine work. We can go now. I'm feeling somewhat eleven o'clockish. What say we have a spot of tea and scones over on the High Street?"

We found an elegant tea room at the corner of St. John's Wood High Street and Wellington Place, where we enjoyed an excellent pot of Ceylon tea and fresh scones. Holmes sipped and nibbled in silence until I decided to engage him in conversation.

"Well now, Holmes, do you still believe the lady was deluded?"

"Not entirely."

"I must say, her story is quite congruent with what we observed this morning."

"In part."

"What do you mean by that?"

"The central components of her story are borne out by what took place in the general's house. Although the items I listed earlier – her boots, her hair, and her clothing – remain unexplained."

"Are you saying that she was lying? She certainly seemed to me to be telling nothing but the truth."

"Lying? No, not necessarily. Deluded, but only in part, is a tentative hypothesis."

He lapsed back into taciturn silence until we stepped into the morning sunshine of the High Street pavement.

"You did," he said, "suggest that a walk in the park would be a good idea. Are you still game?"

"I am."

"Excellent. Then let us do that. My only request is that you refrain from any attempts at conversation and leave me free to think."

We crossed over Park Road and entered the trail that led us along the edge of the canal. I thought Holmes was on his way to the Zoological Gardens, but he turned right at the Baptist College, and we cut across to the boating lake. As it was now late morning, it was busy with couples and families all rowing punts in a lake that was no more than four feet deep. It was an altogether pleasant outing, although Holmes continued to stroll in silence, his hands clasped behind his back and his shoulders leaning ever-so-slightly forward.

It had gone noon when we found ourselves back in Baker Street. As we approached 221b, I noticed Mrs. Hudson standing on the pavement outside our entry door. She was looking up and down the street, and when she saw us approaching, she began to run toward us.

"My dear," I shouted as she puffed her way to meet us. "Please. Stop running. What is it?"

"Mr. Holmes," she gasped. "you have visitors."

"Do I? By the look on your face, I suspect the king and the queen are sitting up in our parlor."

The poor woman was struggling to catch her breath.

"Mr. Holmes, your visitors are the next thing to them, and this is not something to make light of."

Holmes left Mrs. Hudson standing on the pavement and strode quickly to our door.

"Very well, then, let me see what they want. I shall tell them I'm busy with other matters and send them on their way."

I hurried along behind him, leaving a horrified Mrs. Hudson glaring at us.

Holmes and I ascended the stairs and entered the room together. And then I stopped, frozen in my tracks. Across from us stood two of the most important men in the British Empire: The Prime Minister and the Secretary of War. Both of them looked as if they were attending a funeral.

Lord Melborne, our bald and bearded Prime Minister, spoke first.

"I trust you gentlemen have enjoyed your leisurely walk in the park."

Holmes nodded and replied, "And I assume that if you know what we were doing during the past hour, you also know where we were earlier this morning, and *that* is the reason we are now honored by your visit."

"An excellent deduction," said Sir Hugh Oakeley, the Secretary of War. "And it for your renowned skills in such practices that brings us to you. Please, gentlemen, be seated."

The Prime Minister and the senior member of his cabinet sat down in the armchairs usually used by Holmes and me. I sat on the sofa while Holmes pulled a chair away from our breakfast table.

"Hugh," said his Lordship, "if you would not mind, please enlighten these fine fellows."

"Yes, Prime Minister," said the Secretary, who now turned to us and spoke in lowered tones.

"I returned this morning from the Continent to learn of the death of General Ludenberg. I was subsequently informed that Scotland Yard had requested the assistance of the famous detective, Mr. Sherlock Holmes, in investigating what appears to be a cold-blooded murder. I'm sure you appreciate the delicacy of this matter to His Majesty's Government."

"Yes, Mr. Secretary, I do," said Holmes. "The tragic loss of a highly respected general is always cause for concern."

"It is of particular concern," continued Sir Hugh, "when there is a possibility of a scandal attached to the event."

"A scandal, Mr. Secretary?"

"Yes, Mr. Holmes. You do not have to pretend innocence. You know perfectly well that General Ludenberg was famous for being a Lothario and was constantly accompanied by any number of trollops, music hall queens, widows, students, and duchesses both foreign and domestic."

The Prime Minister harrumphed.

"If you say so, Mr. Secretary," said Holmes, with the innocence of a cherub.

"The story that is being released to the Press is that what was clumsily staged as a suicide has been investigated by Scotland Yard and determined to have been a murder by a jilted lover. The 'hell hath no fury' line with which I am sure you are familiar."

"I am indeed, sir."

"And you are also aware that such news is utterly false."

"It is?"

"Mr. Holmes, kindly do not play the *naïf*. General Ludenberg was far too clever to allow himself to be such a pathetic victim. His Majesty's Government has irrefutable evidence that the general was working as a spy for Kaiser Wilhelm."

"I'm shocked . . . shocked. Can you tell me what that evidence was?"

"Our agents in Berlin learned that a complete copy, extensively detailed, of the preliminary plans for the design of the *HMS Dreadnought* was obtained by the German navy. We have traced the route by which they traveled back to General Ludenberg."

"How terribly distressing to hear."

"Bloody distressing," said the Prime Minister.

"Yes, it was," added the Secretary. "What we do not know is how he obtained them in the first place. We were prepared to, shall we say, *extract* him from his current position and encourage him to enlighten us when he ended up dead."

"How very inconsiderate of him."

"Quite so. We strongly suspect that the general was the leader of an entire network of spies who have embedded themselves in Whitehall and throughout His Majesty's armed forces. If we were to start an official investigation, the word would spread like wildfire through the web of traitors, and they would vanish like a puff of smoke. Therefore, upon hearing that Scotland Yard had already requested the assistance of Mr. Sherlock Holmes, we have decided to make use of your services as well."

"Have you now? Do you mind if I ask how?"

"Mr. Holmes, it will be reported that you will continue to work for Scotland Yard and that you have been charged with identifying who amongst General Luderberg's former paramours was most likely to have taken revenge upon him. Whilst doing so, your true mission will be to identify all of the spies who have been reporting to him and assisting him with his treasonous activities. In particular, you will identify who shot him and why. Is that clear, Mr. Holmes? Oh, and in case you are wondering, Mr. Holmes, we are not *asking* you."

I could see Holmes stiffen on that one. His Bohemian soul didn't take kindly to having people of any rank give him orders.

"And what if I refuse? I habitually decline cases that are tainted by politics."

"Oh, please, Mr. Holmes. We do not have time for that. But if you insist, then I shall respond with a question. Are you or are you not a loyal subject of His Majesty?"

"I am, and I am also a free citizen."

"Yes, of course. Very well, Mr. Holmes, the choice is yours. But do let me add that the British Empire is in need of your unique services, and we would hope that you would respond enthusiastically to such a request. The future of the Empire is at stake. What is now referred to as the *Pax Britannicus* is at risk. Furthermore, His Majesty is quite an enthusiastic supporter of yours, and we would not wish to disappoint him, would we, Mr. Holmes?"

The Secretary coolly stared at Holmes, who returned the look. It was apparent that this member of His Majesty's Cabinet did not ascend to his lofty position by being easily cowed. But, then again, neither did Holmes.

To my surprise, Holmes averted his gaze, stood, and walked over to the writing desk. From the narrow drawers at the top of the left pedestal, he took out two quires of paper of slightly different hues and extracted two sheets from each. He then picked up the pen and inkwell, walked back to the table, and placed the paper and ink in front of our visitors.

"Kindly affix your signatures to the bottom of these pages. Mr. Secretary, you may do so on the lighter colored pages. Your Lordship on the darker ones."

Neither of them moved.

"I beg your pardon," said the Secretary.

"Oh, I'm sorry," said Holmes. "Did I not make myself clear?"

"You cannot be seriously asking us to place our signatures on a blank piece of paper. You could write anything on them and make it look as if we had written it."

"Precisely. A few moments ago, you informed me that I had been dragooned into a matter in which the future of the Empire and world peace were at risk. If you now do not trust me with the relatively minor detail of creating misleading bait with which to snare your spies, then you cannot be seriously asking me to work for you, and there is no point in continuing this conversation."

The two of them looked at each other, and the Prime Minister shrugged, picked up the pen, and signed his two blank pages. His underling did likewise.

"Thank you, gentlemen," said Holmes. "I expect that I shall need a week to complete the task you have given me. Allow me to wish you a good day and whatever success you are capable of achieving."

"And when," asked Sir Hugh, "may we expect your first report?"

"Within one hour after I have finished preparing it."

The two distinguished visitors rose and departed. Once we heard the door on Baker Street close, Holmes began pacing back and forth from the bow window to the far end of the chemical table and back again.

"I have never . . . *that woman*!" he said, stopping at the window. "Do you suppose, Watson, that she knew exactly what she was doing when she requested my promise of confidentiality?"

"She was terribly distraught. That much, at least, was obvious. Beyond that, it is impossible to know what was going on in her mind. Or in any woman's mind on any day, distraught or otherwise."

"You're right. It's impossible and a waste of my time to try to understand, and there is nothing to be gained at the moment by exposing her. We have more pressing needs. Would you be so kind as to accompany me back to St. John's Wood?"

"You've changed your mind?"

"I change my mind when the facts change, my friend. What do you do?"

For reasons I wasn't sure of, Holmes first walked south to Marylebone and paid a short visit to his bank. Then he hailed a cab, and the two of us traveled the few blocks north to the St. John's Wood High Street. I sat on a bench and enjoyed the fresh air whilst he spent an hour in a stenographers' shop. When he emerged, he was smiling.

"It always takes much longer when I am forced to type letters myself rather than pay a skilled typist, but confidentiality is imperative. Come, Watson, back to the scene of the crime."

By now, the word of the murder of General Ludenberg had become news, and a crowd of curious neighbors and the Press had gathered on the street. The police had cordoned off the entrance but, on recognizing Sherlock Holmes, waved us forward. A reporter also knew who he was and shouted.

"Mr. Sherlock Holmes! Was it one of his lovers?"

Holmes turned back briefly. "The investigation is still in its early stages, but jealousy and revenge cannot be ruled out."

A cacophony of questions followed, all of which he ignored.

Once inside, he moved swiftly to the general's library, and I followed.

"Given the vertiginous heights from which I have received my orders," he said, "I assume that I'm now entitled to engage in burglary. Please stand guard at the door whilst I open the general's desk."

I watched as he knelt down beside of the large oak desk, took his lock-picking tools in his hands, and opened the drawer. He placed two envelopes inside, one of a lighter shade than the other. Then he closed the drawer and locked it before opening a larger, unlocked drawer on the pedestal and ferreting around until he found a ledger book. He glanced through it and laid it on the desk.

"Did you see his dispatch box anywhere?" he asked me.

"Not here. Perhaps in his bedroom?"

We made our way to the upper floor, where the door to the general's bedroom was guarded by a constable. On seeing Holmes, he moved aside.

"Good day, Mr. Holmes. The inspector told us that you would be coming around. Let me know if there is anything we can do to help you. It's still a bit of a mess in there, but they took the body away an hour ago. Nasty piece of work by some crazy woman, it seems."

"Thank you, Officer. I shall only be a minute, but I do wish to speak to the household staff after that. Are they still sequestered in the house?"

"All in the kitchen, sir. But the inspector questioned them earlier this morning. Not one of them was here last night. He'd given them the night off. All claim they knew nothing until they showed up here this morning."

"Ah, yes. But you know and I know that a man's staff always knows things, do they not?"

"Oh, right you are on that one, Mr. Holmes. Somebody always knows something."

Holmes gave the fellow a clap on the shoulder and we entered the bedroom. The bed and pillow were still covered in blood, but otherwise the room was in perfect order. I glanced around, hoping to see a military dispatch box, but there was none. The dresser was bare, as were the bedside tables and lampstands.

Holmes proceeded to the closet and emerged a minute later bearing a metal box, emblazoned by the coat of arms of the British Army. He set it on the bed and, using his tools, soon had it opened.

He then took two more envelopes from his suitcoat pocket, placed them in the box, slid it closed, and locked it. He returned it to wherever inside the closet he had found it.

"Task accomplished," he said. "Now, to the staff."

"What did you do?" I whispered once we were past the constable guarding the door.

"Nothing much. Only planted the final notes he had received from Downing Street and Westminster before his unfortunate demise."

"A-ha! You made them up, didn't you! What were they about?"

"Several items, both mundane and momentous. The most significant was about the second edition of the *Dreadnought* that is being secretly built down in the Docklands. Larger, faster, and much more heavily gunned than the first."

"It is? When did that start?"

"It didn't."

"But is it going to?"

He stopped, turned his head back toward me and rolled his eyes.

"No, my dear Watson. It does not exist. But I'm sure that the Kaiser will want to know all about it once he hears. Now, please be prepared to take notes."

As we approached the kitchen, we again passed a policeman guarding the door and, I assumed, making sure that the staff didn't leave the premises before being given permission by Scotland Yard. I could hear chatting and even low laughter coming from the assembled staff, but they all fell silent when Holmes and I entered and he stood in front of them, spreading his arms, palms facing up.

"Ladies and gentlemen," he said. "I assume that all of you know who I am, and please put yourselves at ease. There is no suspicion whatsoever resting on any one of you. It has been firmly established that none of you were present in this house when the terrible crime against General Ludenberg took place."

He smiled warmly at them, and they, in turn, smiled back.

"It is a widely known fact," he continued, "that when a household comes to a sudden end, as this one has, with no family remaining to carry on, the ones who innocently suffer are the staff. You have depended on General Ludenberg for your wages, and with his passing, it is fully understood that you will all have to start looking for new situations. I assure you that Scotland Yard is sympathetic to the predicament that has been so unfairly thrust upon you."

He now had their undivided attention. I counted eight of them altogether – five women and three men. Two of the women wore maids' uniforms, and two were dressed as cooks. One woman was far better dressed and most likely served as the general's private secretary. One of the men wore the uniform of a driver, the second was dressed as a gentleman's gentleman, and the third seemed to be a laborer. They were all looking intently at Sherlock Holmes.

"Scotland Yard," Holmes continued, "has empowered me to see that you are paid whatever wages you would have earned and to make sure that none of you are left in a tight spot to pay your rent or provide food for your families. Accordingly, you will receive your full wages not only to the end of this month, but will be paid in full through to the end of August."

The visible looks of relief and happiness spread across all of the faces. Murmurs of appreciation were heard and a few comments about how good Scotland Yard was to those who toiled in service.

"Unfortunately," said Holmes, "I have no record of your current rate of remuneration. We shall proceed, therefore, on a basis of trust. If so respected a man as General Ludenberg placed his confidence in your integrity whilst he was alive, his estate cannot question that confidence now that he is no longer with us. Therefore, I have no choice but to ask each of you to compute what your wage would be from the date of your last pay packet through to the end of the summer. You will confide that amount to me. I shall accept it as truthful, and that is the amount that you will receive. Is that agreeable?"

Eight heads nodded, and several mouths muttered their concurrence. Holmes carried on.

"As one's income is a private matter, we will not conduct the exercise publicly. Dr. Watson and I shall meet you individually in the library. The constable will call you in turn, you will sign for your pay, and then you will be free to leave and return to your homes and families. I trust that you'll be able to put this terrible day behind you and move on to much happier times in the future."

I followed him out of the kitchen and down the hall.

"Holmes," I said once we were out of earshot of the kitchen. "That ledger you found in the desk – did it not contain the rates of pay of all of the staff?"

"It did. And frankly, the general was a bit of a skinflint. He paid these good people at least fifteen percent below the going wage in London."

"Then what are you doing?"

"It will become self-explanatory by the time I have finished. Here, take this package. It has a large supply of banknotes and coins. You shall be the paymaster. Halloa! Constable! Would you please ask the younger cook to come to the library and speak with us?"

"You're not suspecting that any of the staff killed him, are you?" I asked.

"No, not in the least. None of them are murderers. Merely spies. To be fair, it may be only one of them. We shall dispose of the cooks first as they are the least likely."

"How do you know that?"

"The general was far too smart to pay regular visits himself to the agents of the Kaiser. Someone served as his messenger. Whomever did so was free not only to meet with him privately but also to travel across

London at irregular hours. Cooks are confined to the kitchen, the greengrocer, and the markets. They may make excellent trifle but make poor messengers."

The younger cook came in, quoted the wages owed to her, thanked us profusely and departed. The older one did likewise. After they were gone, I checked the amounts given against the household ledger and informed Holmes that both had inflated their wages by a few shillings.

"And so they should," he said. "They deserved more than they were being paid. Next on my list are the maids. In addition to my questions about their wages, I would appreciate it if you, my good friend, would ask them these questions."

He handed me a piece of paper with a few lines scribbled on it.

"Good heavens. These are quite personal."

"And you are a doctor. You ask women far more personal questions all the time. I do not."

The younger maid entered, a slender wisp of a girl with a pretty face that bordered on moonish. Holmes asked about her wages, and she answered. Then he gestured to me and stood and walked over to the window for a cigarette.

"My dear," I said, in my most doctorly voice, "your name is Molly Swidger, is it not?"

"I am, sir," she said and curtsied.

"Well then, Miss Molly, please excuse me if it is necessary that we ask you about more than your wages. Mr. Holmes is, as you know, investigating the most unfortunate death of General Ludenberg."

The poor thing blushed. "Oh, certainly, Doctor. You can ask anything you want, but I swear, I know nothing about it. It was a shock to all of us when we came to the house this morning, sir."

"Of course, my dear, we know that. And forgive me, but I must ask a question about the general's character and deportment. Can you tell me, in complete confidence, of course, and you may respond as you would to your own doctor, if at any time the general behaved toward you in a manner that would not be described, shall we say, as gentlemanly?"

"Not gentlemanly, doctor? What do you mean?"

"Well, not the way an employer should treat the young women on his staff."

"Oh, if you mean he used a few curse words now and again – well, yes, he did, and I suppose a gentleman should not do that, should he?"

"I was thinking more if he ever . . . well, you know . . . pinched your cheek or patted your bottom . . . or something like that."

The poor girl was horrified. "Ow, no sir! He never did nothing like that. Not ever. If he had, I would have run out of the house straight away.

How could you even think to ask a question like that, sir? If I have given you the impression that I might have put up with that, I am sorry. Please, tell me what I did to make you think like you did, and I shall stop acting that way immediately. I am a good girl, I am – "

With every clause in her run-on response, she was becoming more and more upset. I interrupted her, apologized profusely, reminded her that police and detectives had to ask certain questions of everybody, gave her the money, dismissed her . . . and glared at Holmes.

"She may," I said, somewhat indignantly, "have been of sterling priggishness, but she also was less than truthful concerning her wages."

"Ah, thank you, Watson. Now, the older maid is on her way. You do not have to ask her about pats to the *gluteus maximus*, only the question I have written down."

The senior maid did not strike me as likely to have needed to fend off any man. Had I been required to guess a name for the woman who entered, I might have offered up *Brunhilda,* and I concluded that any chap who might be so foolish as to pat her bottom did so at his peril

"Madam Tilly Skimpole, is it not?" asked Holmes.

"It is."

"And how long have you been in service with General Ludenberg?"

"Six years."

"And the wages owed to you through to the end of next month?"

The amount she quoted was three pounds in excess of what was in the ledger. Holmes thanked her and directed her to me. I decided on a different tact this time.

"Madam Skimpole, we all know that in six years as a maid, there is nothing that took place under this roof that could possibly have escaped your eye."

"Right. Nothing. What do you want to know?"

"What evidence have you observed that the general, shall we say, *entertained* women in the house in a way that could rise to a scandal?"

"Never."

"Never?"

"Do you not know the meaning of that word, Doctor? It means *not ever*. Not at all. Not in six years. Not once. Can I make it any clearer to you, Doctor?"

"No, you have been very clear. But it is our understanding that all of the staff were given Saturday afternoons and evenings off, and that the general had the house to himself. Is it possible that you might have missed seeing someone?"

"No, Doctor. Not ever. Never. A woman always knows when another woman has spent the night in her house."

"Ah, how true. We thank you, madam."

As soon as she had departed, Holmes looked over to me.

"Is that true, Watson? Do women always know that? I don't believe that even I, after a quarter-century as a detective, could make that claim with such complete certainty."

"The female of the human species has strange powers that even the most brilliant male mind will never comprehend . . . not ever. Never."

"If you say so. However, it does render Lady Oakeley much more astute and brilliant than I had been giving her credit for. But now, the final woman, Watson. His secretary cometh."

According to the ledger, General Ludenberg's private secretary was a Mrs. Violet Linkwater, and she now marched into the room. She walked past Holmes and me and across to the far end of the desk. She lifted a straight-backed chair and sat down facing us.

"Do be seated, Mr. Holmes," she said. "This is the chair in which I have sat for the past eleven years, and I will continue to do so."

"And so you should, Mrs. Linkwater. And would you mind telling us what wages are owed to you?"

The sum she quoted was exceptionally high, a veritable gentleman's income. I stifled a gasp, and Holmes could not avoid widening his eyes. Mrs. Linkwater was looking directly and him and said nothing.

Having learned years ago from Holmes that there are certain marks that identify all typists, I observed that this women's fingernails were shorter than was the style and that a slight line of wear appeared on the underside of the cuffs of her jacket. Her clothes were conservative but stylish and not at all inexpensive. Her skirt and jacket were navy, and her blouse appeared to be fine white Egyptian cotton, augmented by a large amber broach under her slender chin. I would have put her age around forty, although she bore no trace of the thickening torso that visits most women of that age.

Holmes had also concluded that this was a no-nonsense type of woman and carried on accordingly.

"Mrs. Linkwater, there are a few questions I need to ask you concerning General Ludenberg. They will take only a few minutes, and then you will be free to return to your home in time to have dinner ready for your husband and children."

"I do not have children, Mr. Holmes, and I do have a cook, and a maid."

"An impressive household, and thus I assume that your husband is somewhat older than you, a pensioner perhaps, or a veteran, and that you have chosen to work full-time for the general to supplement your household income."

"No, Mr. Holmes. I work because I want to. My husband is a doctor with a practice in Harley Street."

My brain lit up. Her husband, Doctor Leicester Linkwater, was a highly respected and generously paid orthopedic surgeon whom I had heard speak at a doctors' conference several years ago. He was already at the peak of his game and still had many years of practice ahead of him. The small flicker of Holmes's eyebrow told me that he also had heard of him.

"Ah, yes, of course. Now then, please help me understand your position. You were General Ludenberg's private secretary for what – ten years, you said?"

"I said eleven."

"Eleven, yes. Quite a long time. Please accept my condolences on his tragic death. It must have come as a great shock to you."

She gave a small shrug, and her face remained impassive.

"It did," she said. "However, there will be other opportunities. I will begin to look tomorrow. I am not worried."

"Yes, of course. Now then. In your role with the general, you typed all of his correspondence and filed all of his documents, did you not?"

"All of them."

"Including those that were confidential and contained information pertaining to His Majesty's Government?"

"Yes, and to Her Majesty's before the change in monarchs."

"And did anyone else have access to those letters and documents?"

"No. Only the general and me."

"Except, of course, for those that were written in foreign languages. A translator would be necessary for those."

"No, Mr. Holmes. None would be needed. I am perfectly capable of communicating in French, Spanish, German, and Italian. The Portuguese understand Spanish, the Dutch all speak German. The Russians not only speak French, they prefer to do so. No translator ever read any of General Ludenberg's communications."

"But you read all of it. Very well, then, given that the general has been murdered, I must ask you if there was anything in his recent correspondence that would lead you to believe that his life was in danger?"

"I cannot speak to that, Mr. Holmes. When I began my work for the general, I took an oath of confidentiality and secrecy, and I regret that I cannot breach my promise just because he is dead."

"Mrs. Linkwater, may I remind you that I am investigating a murder."

"And may I remind you, Mr. Holmes, that you have no authority in the matter. If I am ordered by the Courts in accordance with the laws of

England to divulge confidential information, I shall do so. Until that time, I cannot. Is there anything else you wish to ask me, sir?"

"No. Not at this time. Doctor Watson has your pay packet. Kindly give my regards to your husband."

The next member to visit the library was the general's driver. He was dressed in his livery uniform, a grey tunic with parallel rows of brass buttons and trousers adorned with a long black stripe down the outside of the leg. The fellow himself, a Mr. George Runcewell, was a young man, small in stature but bearing a well-formed face. He stood at the door, holding his cap in his hands until Holmes bade him enter.

The interview was brief. Holmes asked him to state the wages owed to him, and he gave an amount that was at least ten percent below what I would have expected, according to the ledger.

"That seems to me," said Holmes, "to be a rather paltry amount. Most drivers would earn more than that."

"General Ludenberg, sir, was always fair and decent to me. I would never dream of taking advantage of him whilst he was living nor of his estate now that he is no longer with us. I am an honest man, and I prefer to fall asleep each night with a clear conscience."

"A most noble and admirable practice," said Holmes, and he sent him on his way with his meager wage.

"My faith," I said, "in human nature has been redeemed. Good to see a young man who is not greedy in the least."

"Quite so," said Holmes. "I suspect that our next fellow may not be as agreeable to you."

Mr. Tom Pinch, the gardener, entered. He was dressed as a working man in clothes that needed laundered and shoes that bore the residue of a lifetime working in grass, leaves, and dirt.

"No, sir. I am not one of General Luderberg's household employees. I am an independent laborer, and I am master of my own time."

"And how much are you owed for your time?" asked Holmes.

"Fifteen pounds," the man said, somewhat more loudly than necessary. "That's what I'm owed. I had set aside the next six weeks to prepare his garden for the winter and have little chance of replacing those days with another customer."

I looked over at Holmes, assuming that he would challenge such an exorbitant amount, but he said nothing. Instead, he chatted pleasantly for a few minutes with the surly chap about the best shrubs and flowering trees to be used for attracting bees. Then he nodded in my direction, indicating that I should count out the full fifteen pounds and hand it over.

"Holmes," I said after the gardener had departed. "Have you taken leave of your senses? That was highway robbery. Five pounds at the most would have been fair. It does not take six weeks or more to turn over a small garden. I could have done it myself in a week."

"Then I shall call upon you when I retire to my gardens in Sussex."

"Holmes, please, the man is a blackguard."

"He may well be. His probity is not my concern. The final member of the staff, General Ludenberg's man-servant, is the only one left, is he not?"

A tall, severe man, attired in an immaculately starched morning suit, entered the library and stood still, hands clasped together behind his back.

"My name, gentlemen, is Herbert Rumplechook. I serve – or should I say I *served* – as General Ludenberg's valet, as well as having responsibilities for the overall management of his household."

"Indeed," said Holmes. "And all of the other members of the staff reported to you, did they?"

"With the exception of Mrs. Linkwater, yes. She reported directly to the general."

"And how many years have you held this position?"

"One year."

"Only a year?"

"That is what I said, sir."

"Who was here before you?"

"A Mr. Hiram Grewgious, who, for reasons to which I am not privy, departed somewhat suddenly just over a year ago and now resides, I am told, in America."

"A rather odd thing to happen," said Holmes.

"If you say so, sir."

"And after his departure, you became the supervisor of the rest of the staff."

"I did indeed say that, sir."

"And have you noticed any activity by any of them during the year of your tenure that might lead you to be suspicious of them."

"They had all been hired before I began my service, sir. If the general saw fit to have them in his house, it was not within my purview to question them. They were all quite an industrious lot."

"Excellent. Very well. Kindly state the wages owed to you, sign for them, and I wish you good fortune in your next situation."

"Thank you, sir. Your thoughtfulness is appreciated."

I counted out his remuneration and inserted it into his pay packet. Yet again, it was well in excess of what the ledger had indicated.

"A penny for your thoughts, Watson," said Holmes when we were alone in the library. He was pacing back and forth along the wall by the window.

"I wouldn't trust the gardener as far as I could throw him," I said.

"And neither would I. Therefore, we can cross him off the list of spies."

"I beg your pardon. What do you mean, 'cross him off'?"

"He was obviously not a trusted messenger of General Ludenberg. There was no love lost between them, and he doesn't give one iota of respect to the man's memory or his estate. Therefore, off the list."

"I suppose," I said, "that you didn't consider either the cooks or the maids to be suitable material for covert espionage."

"Did you?"

"No."

"Right, so off the list."

"And the valet was too recent an addition," I said.

"Precisely. Whatever spying has taken place started well before he arrived."

"Fine. Then no doubt, you are about to tell me that when you eliminate the impossible – "

"Precisely. There are only two remaining."

"I wouldn't have included the driver. He came across as scrupulously honest even to the point of being willing to forego a portion of the wage that was rightly owed to him."

"Indeed, he did. For that reason, he is my number one suspect."

"Come now, Holmes."

"Any man who goes out of his way to demonstrate how honest he is becomes a suspect. A case of 'me thinks the driver doth protest too much'. And did you happen to notice his left hand?"

"No, why?"

"He was wearing a wedding ring, and he is of the age to be the father to small children. No young man with a family can afford to lose a farthing from his wages, unless . . . ."

"Unless what?"

"Unless he has another source of income to supplement his daily earnings. It is likely, although not yet irrefutable, that the general and the Germans paid him handsomely to serve as an envoy."

"Then you have crossed off the private secretary, Mrs. Linkwater?"

"Not at all."

"Why not?" I said. "She surely doesn't need the money."

"True, but what *does* a woman like that need? Allow me to answer before you go off on an illogical tangent. She is a brilliant and industrious woman who has been working in her current role for over a decade. She likely knows of the general's treasonous activities, yet she persists in working for him. I suspect that what she needs is the thrill, the excitement, the engaging of her both her mind and animal spirits. She has become addicted to the warming of the blood that comes from working every day so close to danger."

"Rather reminds me of you, Holmes."

He paused and stared at me.

"I suppose, my friend, that you may be right. In the same way as I could have been a brilliant criminal, more diabolical than even Moriarty, Mrs. Linkwater could have been an excellent detective. Such a shame she chose the dark side."

"If she indeed did."

"Ah, yes. An excellent *caveat*, Watson. She may be merely enjoying the heat without stepping inside the fire."

"And what will you do now that you have reduced your list of probable assistant traitors to two?"

"I shall follow them myself, and I shall set my Irregulars upon them. Every move they make shall be observed and reported on."

"And then follow the ones with whom they meet?"

"Precisely. And follow whomever that individual meets, and bribe – pardon me, *reward* – the messenger boys they send to the post offices for disclosing the contents of every letter or telegram, and justifiably remunerate members of household staffs throughout London to inform on their masters and mistresses."

"Holmes, would you stoop to that? People in service are famous for protecting the confidentiality of their employers."

"It is possible to appeal to their higher ideals. You know, for King and Country and all that rot."

"Well, if you say so. Now, are we done here in St. John's Wood?"

"We have to make a short visit two blocks away."

"To Lady Oakeley? In broad daylight? Holmes, you promised."

"And I keep my promises."

It was a short walk to the house on Ordnance Hill, where Sir Hugh and Lady Oakeley lived. A maid opened the door for us, bade us wait in the vestibule, and went to call Her Ladyship. I could hear her voice coming from a room on the ground floor, and although I could not make out what she was saying, I heard the distinct peal of her laughter. A moment later, she appeared in the hallway with a look of horror and fear written across her face.

"Mr. Holmes . . . you gave me your word . . . you promised."

"I am not here to call upon you, my lady. I came to call for your husband, but as he is not at home and is most likely meeting in Downing Street as we speak, I took it upon myself to pay my respects to you."

"My husband? But why would you want to speak to him if not to betray me?"

"Because he is my client, along with the Prime Minister."

A look of utter confusion swept across her famously beautiful face.

"Your husband, my dear lady, and the Prime Minister paid me a visit just after the noon hour and demanded that I help them find whoever murdered General Ludenberg."

The poor woman gasped, stepped back from us, and sank into a chair.

"Dear God, no. Oh, dear God. I am undone. Now everything will come out."

"No," said Holmes, "it shall not. They confirmed to me your accusation of treason against the general, and I will carry out an investigation. Your identity will not be revealed at this time, and the web of spies will be exposed."

Her countenance changed from deathly pale to an almost imperceptible smile.

"Oh, thank you, Mr. Holmes. Thank you."

"There is one condition."

"Yes. Whatever you say. Anything. I will do it."

"You must tell me the truth about what took place last night."

"But I told you."

"What you told me was that you spent the rest of the night wandering through the park. You did not. Your boots betrayed you. They were shining, without a speck of dirt on them when you entered my house. You did not come to see me directly from hours walking in a park. What were you doing? The truth, madam."

A flicker of confusion crossed her face, but then she nodded. "Of course, my boots were polished. I was taught when I was still in my teens that a lady never goes anywhere without attending to her shoes or boots. The habit is as natural to me as breathing. I carry a small brush in my purse at all times and stopping to make sure that my footwear is respectable is as inconsequential as stopping to use the loo. I cannot even recall where I did so. Most likely I put my foot up on one of the raised garden beds . . . yes, now I remember, that was where – at the entrance to the park near York Terrace. That was where I stopped."

In my mind, I could picture the exact place, only a couple of blocks from 221b Baker Street. What she had said made perfect sense to me, if not to Holmes.

"And did you also," he said, "stand beside the garden bed and change your clothes? Or perhaps take a bath in the boating lake? And fix your hair in the public lavatory?"

Again, for a flickering instant, she appeared not to understand what he had said, but then she shook her head.

"Mr. Holmes, I had decided to come to you and beseech your help. I live in St. John's Wood and walk daily through my neighborhood. It would utterly commonplace for me to be seen and recognized without causing a whisper of question. What would have been inexplicable would be if I were recognized knocking on your door. I had to rush back to my house and change my coat and shawl for an old set I held onto from my days in the theater. I didn't bother to change my boots, as no man at any time of day can tell anything about a woman from her footwear, and women are not out and about at that hour. Surely you know that, Mr. Holmes."

"Your hair was perfectly coiffed. Don't tell me that you accomplished that feat whilst standing beside a garden bed."

"Of course not. Again, sir, since I was a young woman, I have never attended an appointment with anyone, great or common, without attending to my appearance. When I said I came directly to see you, I understood that to mean that I made myself presentable and then came to see you. I should have expected that you wouldn't understand that."

Now it was Holmes's turn to appear perplexed. He looked at me as if silently consulting my confirmation on the practices of the women of London. I shrugged and nodded.

"Then kindly," he said, "explain how the side of the bed adjacent to where the general was found had only been rumpled but not creased in the least. No one had lain there for more than a minute."

The woman blushed and turned her face to me.

"Dr. Watson, I implore you. You were a married man. Please answer that question for your bachelor friend."

I gave Holmes a look and saw that he was now blushing.

"Very well, madam," he said. "Kindly forgive my unwarranted intrusion into your home. I expect that I shall, to the satisfaction of both you and your husband, expose the web of spies before the next weekend. Good day, madam."

We hailed a cab and Holmes sat taciturn, brooding until we were back at Baker Street, where he turned to me.

"I will be fully engaged until Friday afternoon," he said, "but if you are free then to meet me, I would welcome your company."

"And what are you going to be up to between now and then?"

"Laying traps and catching spies."

The week passed without any new developments in the case that I was made aware of. The press was filled with titillating accounts of the death of General Ludenberg. Those newspapers with a more moralistic posture to their editorials invoked the warning that those who sowed the wind reaped the whirlwind. His death was lamented, but it merely reinforced the biblical truism about the wages of sin.

Those newspapers who considered themselves more enlightened and progressive were quick to cast the blame on the government's failure to reduce poverty in the East End, as it was a scientifically proven fact that only desperation to escape misery would lead a woman to engage in a liaison to which she must have been drawn by the allure of augmenting her income.

No reporter so far had even the vaguest hint that espionage and high treason might be involved.

I pondered these events in my mind on the Friday afternoon as I returned from my work back to 221b Baker Street. To my surprise, the front room was not plugged full of tobacco smoke, and Holmes was not ensconced in his armchair, puffing on his pipe. Instead, the entire chemistry table had been cleared and was now covered with a long piece of table paper. Holmes was leaning over it, holding a straight edge in one hand and a pencil in the other.

"Welcome, Watson!" he sang out as I entered. "You're just in time to observe the final touches to my masterpiece."

"It doesn't look much like a Rembrandt to me," I said. "More like an over-sized spider's web, with a few tasty morsels caught in it."

I was gazing at what resembled a schematic depiction of an inter-connected network of lines and nodes, with names and occasional small photographs pasted on at many of the points where the lines intersected.

"My spider's web exactly. Once you start to follow one spy, you end up finding an entire maze of strings that connect him to others – some more traitorous and others merely dupes – all over London."

"I can see Mr. George Runcewell here at the left edge," I said.

"Yes. Exactly where I began. I followed him, and within hours of Scotland Yard's letting the staff back depart the house, he returned, most likely went to the desk and the general's dispatch box, uncovered the false information that I had placed there, and then he made a beeline for a pub on Oxford Street. There, he just happened to run into a Mr. Hans von Bülow, who just happens to be the Second Secretary at the German Embassy. Bülow then hot-footed it back to his house and two hours later met with two other men, one of whom holds a high rank in the Royal Navy and one who is a lecturer at Cambridge, on loan from Heidelberg. The Navy man, at first light the following morning, hurries down to the docklands to inspect the secret site wherein the next edition of the *Dreadnought*, bigger and better, is being constructed."

"And finds nothing?"

"Exactly. He pays a visit to two other chaps in a pub a block away from Whitehall, and by Tuesday, the three of them have visited every dockyard in the south of England that is known to carry out the construction of ships of the line."

"And found nothing."

"Yes! But they keep on meeting with others who, in turn, meet with others. By this morning, I had over two score of Irregulars, their sisters, and even their mothers following men all over London. Our driver was only one of five men who have access to government secrets and who meet regularly with Mr. von Bülow."

"He's the lynchpin, is he? And are you going to report him?"

"I already have, two days ago. Now, I have just to put the finishing touches on my *pièce de résistance,* and I will personally deliver it to a certain address on Downing Street."

"Holmes, you look altogether pleased as punch."

"I am." In between his final lines and scribbles at the far-right end of the table, he stopped from time to time to rub his hands in unrestrained glee.

"What about his other paramours?"

"The man was an expert in the fine art of discretion. I chatted with a dozen women – every one of them charming, articulate, and quite lovely to look at – who had been seen on his arm in the past year. To a one of them, they all praised his gallantry, his wit, and his unfailing gentlemanly behavior."

"That seems odd. Why would he engage in an illicit liaison with Lady Oakeley whilst never crossing a gentlemanly line with any of the others?"

"Perhaps because she was the only one who was married to the Secretary of War."

"I suppose, yes, that makes sense. But," I added, "what about Mrs. Violet Linkwater, the secretary?"

"A blank. A cipher. Nothing."

"Holmes, she seemed anything but that."

"I had her followed around the clock. I met a dozen people who knew her, none of whom gave any hint of her ever having done anything untoward. She never returned to the general's house. She has spent the week in her own home, except for venturing out to the theater on Wednesday evening, something she is reported to have done weekly since her marriage to Dr. Linkwater."

He began slowly and carefully to roll up his masterpiece and, having done so, inserted it into a cardboard tube. He tucked it under his arm and turned to me.

"Coming, Watson? It isn't every day that we get to save the Empire."

He descended the stairs and exited on to the pavement of Baker Street.

"Holmes . . . ."

"What man? Speak up. We need to get there before five."

"Didn't Lady Oakeley also say something about attending the theater every Wednesday?"

He stared at me. "Yes . . . she did."

He closed his eyes for several seconds before speaking.

"It may be just a coincidence, but it bears looking into. We can stop off at a theater or two in the West End before going on to Number 10. I still have excellent contacts in the box offices."

I instructed the cab driver to take us through the West End, and we made quick stops at Covent Garden, the Royal Opera House, and the Lyceum Theatre. Each time, Holmes hopped out and ran to the box office. I made use of the time by buying a copy of *The Times* from a local newsboy.

After making his third visit, Holmes returned to the cab with a clouded countenance.

"I have been informed that Sir Hugh and Lady Ethel do indeed have a subscription at several theaters and attend on Wednesday evenings."

"And what about Dr. Linkwater and his wife?" I asked.

"They also have similar subscriptions, also for Wednesday evenings."

"It is quite possible," I said, "that they might encounter each other from time to time."

"No, Watson, it is not merely quite possible. It is inevitable. Their seats are adjacent to each other in the dress circle."

"The two women know each other?"

"More than that. They sit beside each other every Wednesday night and have for the past two years."

The cab was sitting idle. Holmes hadn't given the driver the request to take us to Downing Street. He was looking out the window and scowling.

"Holmes," I said, "you might want to take a look at this afternoon's newspaper."

I handed it to him. On the front page, a secondary headline announced:

German Diplomat Disappears

The brief article below stated that a Mr. Hans von Bülow, the Second Secretary at the German Embassy, had been reported missing. The report quoted the German Ambassador as saying, "Herr von *Bülow was a man of highly disciplined habits. You could set your watch by his actions. He has never missed a day of work in his life. We fear that something untoward has happened to him*."

Holmes put the paper down on the floor of the cab and shouted to the driver an address on Ordnance Hill in St. John's Wood.

"That woman," he said, "is playing me for a fool! There are now far too many pieces of data that do not fit into her story, and I am going to demand the truth."

The cab driver raced back north through central London, up to Marylebone, and from there to St. John's Wood. Holmes's eyes were closed for the entire journey, but his lips kept moving as if he were rehearsing the diatribe he was about to deliver.

As soon as we arrived at our destination, Holmes leapt from the cab and sprinted to the door. He banged his fist and smashed the knocker down repeatedly. A maid opened the door and appeared to be ready to tell him to restrain himself when he pushed past her and into the central hall.

"Lady Oakeley!" he bellowed. "Lady Oakeley, come here this instant."

The maid looked at him in horror and hurried into the interior of the house. A moment later, Lady Ethel Oakeley appeared, looking both shocked and angry.

"Good heavens, Mr. Holmes! What has come over you? There is no reason for such beastly behavior. I must ask you to leave this house immediately!"

"I will go nowhere until I am told the truth. You have handed me a pack of lies, and I will not stand for it!"

A desperate, pained look swept across her lovely face. "Mr. Holmes, please. I came to you to ask for your help and protection. And you respond by storming into my house and falsely accusing me of lying. How can you do this to me?"

"I am doing it, madam, because I abhor being lied to. My promise of confidentiality is null and void to people who do not tell me the truth."

"But it is the truth." She had paled, and her voice trembled.

"Why did you not tell me that General Ludenberg's private secretary was your theater mate? *She* told you about his treasonous acts, did she not?"

"What? . . . No, no. We are friendly to each other, but never talk about anything except what is on the stage."

"That is not what she told me."

Now the lady looked surprised.

"Then . . . then she must be trying to save her own skin. She never told me anything."

"And why did you not tell me that you shot General Ludenberg three times?"

"I . . . I was trembling. My hand was shaking. I was not sure I had killed him. The third shot hit his head."

"The general was drunk. The decanters of both his Claret and wine on his dresser were empty. Which did you drink?"

"The wine. I drank the wine. It was an excellent Port."

"A brilliant performance, Lady Oakeley, but it will not do. Only *two* shots were fired. There were no decanters of anything in the bedroom. You were never in the house, and your entire story is a confection. His appointment schedule left no time for you to spend Saturday evenings with him. I do not know what sort of game you're playing with me, but I have no use for it. Now, either stop your fabrications, or I shall disclose whatever you have told me, truth or not, to Scotland Yard, your husband, and the Press."

For what seemed an eternity, she stood in the middle of the vestibule, frozen, and stared at Holmes. Then her body appeared to relax, and a thin smile, more like a smirk, appeared on her face. She turned and faced back into the hallway.

"Hughie! Arthur!" she shouted into the interior of the house. "Can you please join us."

Holmes and I stared at each other. He looked as baffled as I was. Into the vestibule stepped the Prime Minister and the Secretary of War. They were greeted by Lady Oakeley.

"Hugh, darling. I gave it my best, but the script that you two gave me was horribly thin. I never had to *ad-lib* so much in my life."

"My dear," said her husband. "You were magnificent. Marvelous performance. Don't you agree, Prime Minister?"

Lord Melborne harrumphed. "Yes, splendid, splendid. Bravo. Ha, and what have we here?"

His Lordship walked to Holmes and pulled the cardboard tube from under his arm.

"What ho? This must be the report we had been told about. Come, let's take a look at it. We can roll it out in the dining room."

He turned abruptly, left the parlor, and walked toward the dining room. Sir Hugh and Lady Oakeley followed him, as did Holmes and I. Both of us were speechless.

The Prime Minister extracted Holmes's masterpiece and, using several pieces of silver as paperweights, laid the schematic diagram out on the table. From his waistcoat pocket, he took out his monocle and began to examine the links and nodes that Holmes had uncovered.

"A-ha! That scoundrel, Sir Desmond, in the Admiralty. I knew we should never have trusted him. And look here: Joe Murphy in the Coal Miners' Union. He's an anarchist if ever there was one."

"And here, Prime Minister," said Sir Hugh. "Commander D'arcy in the Mediterranean Fleet. How did we miss him? He has access to all sorts of goings-on of the Royal Navy."

For several minutes, the two of them went on like this, poring over Holmes's document.

"Shall we arrest all these scoundrels?" asked the Secretary of War.

"Oh, good heavens, no," said the Prime Minister. "Much better to keep them on and make sure that all they ever see is false information. That should put the wind up Kaiser Billy."

The Secretary guffawed. "Capital, yes, capital."

"Gentlemen!" Holmes shouted. "Enough! I demand an explanation."

The two politicians looked at each other.

"Did he say *demanded*?" asked the Secretary.

"Yes. *Demanded.* A bit impudent, don't you think?" answered his Lordship.

"Well, then, if Mr. Sherlock Holmes *demands* an explanation, I guess that we'd better give him one."

The Prime Minister harrumphed. "Bloody right. So then, Hugh, my boy, why don't you give Mr. Sherlock Holmes his explanation."

The Secretary of War turned to Holmes.

"My dear Mr. Holmes, we have read all about you for years. We knew your distaste for taking on anything that touched on politics, even if your dear brother asked you. But we also knew that you couldn't resist the pleas of a desperate woman, especially if she were young and beautiful. I suggested to his Lordship that my magnificent young wife with her brilliant skills as an actress would be just the ticket to allow us to gain your services. By doing so, we would avoid alerting our nest of spies that we were on to them, save His Majesty's Treasury a small fortune, and catch the lot of them. And you have done it!"

"And a jolly good job, I must say," added the Prime Minister. "And your idea, Hugh, about the alliance with America – brilliant. That hooked your fish, didn't it?"

"Yes, Prime Minister. Of course, it was you who came up with King Bertie being such an admirer of Sherlock Holmes. Very clever, indeed, Prime Minister."

Holmes's face had reddened, and I was certain that if I held a match to his skin, it would ignite.

"Who then is the murderer?" said Holmes.

"The murderer? Oh, please, Mr. Holmes. No one committed *murder*. Once we knew that Ludenberg was such a horrible traitor, we had to have him removed. He had already sent the plans for the *Dreadnought* to the Germans. High treason is a capital offense, and we have efficient ways of looking after such situations. Of course, we cannot discuss those with you."

"Prove what you are saying," said Holmes. "How did you know he was a traitor?"

"Oh, Mr. Holmes. Elementary. Mrs. Linkwater told Lady Oakeley about the *Dreadnought*, and she told Sir Hugh, and our agents in Berlin confirmed it. Really, awfully elementary."

"And what did you do to the German fellow? Did you have him removed as well?"

"Buhler? Their spymaster? Oh no, he has diplomatic immunity and is alive and well. Although he did manage to wake up and find himself on a slow boat to Mexico."

The Prime Minister chortled. "But we have to hand it to you, Holmes. You came through for the Empire. You did. Jolly good show. Worthy of an honor, I'd say. What say you, Hugh, my boy?"

"Oh, yes. An OBE? Or perhaps a CMG? The Order of the Bath?"

"Now, now, Hugh, mustn't be stingy. He deserves a knighthood."

"Oh, yes, Prime Minister, a knighthood, indeed. What do you say to that, Ethel, darling?"

"Indubitably," sang Lady Oakeley. She leapt onto a nearby chair and, standing in front of Holmes, raised her arms in a theatrical flourish, and lowered her imaginary sword to the shoulder of Sherlock Holmes.

"I dub thee, Sir Sherlock du Strand. Rise, Sir Sherlock!" she said, and then filled the room with her laughter. The two politicians joined in the merriment.

Holmes was about to burst a blood vessel.

"You can take your knighthood and – "

Even for Sherlock Holmes, who has never been known to kowtow to any toff, let alone a politician, his response was exceptionally disrespectful. The two men to whom it was directed stopped laughing. Then, with the arrogant insouciance that only those born to wealth and power can exhibit, they laughed again.

"I say there, Hugh, my boy, Mr. Sherlock Holmes does not want our knighthood."

"Pity. What do you think of that, Ethel, dearest?"

"Oh, yes, such a pity. I was so looking forward to reading lovely stories about Sir Sherlock Holmes."

I could tell that Holmes was about to unload a stream of invective upon them, and I grabbed his arm and forcibly pulled him away and out of the house. Once on the pavement, he stood in silence for a minute, then took out a cigarette, lit it, threw it to the pavement, and crushed it under his heel.

Sherlock Holmes was not happy.

"They will not get away with that."

"Now, Holmes. Come, my friend. It isn't all bad. After all, you did expose a web of spies that were a threat to the Empire. Please, don't do anything rash just to get even."

He lit another cigarette and this time took several long, slow drafts. His body relaxed and I detected a twinkle in his eye.

"Rash, Watson? No, I will not act rashly. However, I do believe that there is a national election in the offing, is there not? I wouldn't mind seeing those two and their ilk thoroughly thrashed and defenestrated."

"Holmes, you cannot rig a national election."

"No? Just watch me."

I remember the date very well, for it was in the same month that Holmes refused a knighthood for services which may perhaps some day be described.

– Dr. John H. Watson
"The Adventure of the Three Garridebs"

The Case of the Consulting Physician
by John Lawrence

This story was written by Dr. John Watson in 1927, some 25 years after the events recorded in the account occurred. It is published here for the first time. – J.L.

It hardly seemed possible, in mid-June of 1902, that more than two decades had passed since New Year's Day of 1881 when I had first met Sherlock Holmes and agreed to share rooms at 221b Baker Street in London. I had just returned then from the Battle at Maiwand following my shoulder injury at the Afghan campaign, when I was fortuitously introduced to Holmes by my medical school colleague Stamford. Now, on this particular morning, I watched Holmes as he undertook one of his periodic efforts to organize the clutter that overwhelmed our sitting room – just the latest attempt in all those years that I had known him.

Holmes was examining the souvenirs of dozens of cases and packing them into several wooden boxes. I sat in my old comfortable chair, ruminating about the years of our collaboration as my eyes ran across the many scientific journals and theses stacked on the bookshelves awaiting sorting.

"Yes, Watson, you are right," Holmes said. "I have been most fortunate to have a medical man as my compatriot and friend all these years."

I couldn't help but agree with him. "Yes, my thoughts exactly," I responded, but then stopped abruptly. "See here!" I cried. "Once again, this mischief of breaking into my thoughts and voicing my own opinions! There is a time not that long ago that you surely would have been burned at the stake as a witch for such deviltry!"

Holmes laughed heartily. "It is a trick that never seems to lose its impact on you, my friend," he responded.

"All right, tell me how you guessed my innermost thoughts," I insisted, regretting the use of the work "guessed" as soon as it emerged from my lips.

"You know that I never guess," Holmes remonstrated. He picked up his pipe and packed it with some of the shag tobacco he had crammed into the Persian slipper. Lighting his pipe, he blew a stream of blue smoke into the air, and a smile crossed his face.

"I could see that you were looking intently at my collection of medical articles and monographs," he began. "Naturally, consideration of medical matters led you to think of your own history as a physician and then the grave injury that nearly cost you your life in Afghanistan. Your hand involuntarily moved to clasp the injury and you even winced slightly, recalling the pain. But then you glanced in my direction and a smile crossed your face, suggesting to me a recognition that – however unpleasant the injury had been – by a strange fortune it had enabled us to meet and begin our long and productive partnership. At which point, I made my comment about my good fortune in having a medical man as my associate."

"It always seems very simple when you describe it thusly," I admitted.

Holmes continued puttering about the room, picking up a book or folder and dropping it into a box. He paused as he passed by a part of the wall pocked with several indentation and lingered briefly.

I couldn't help myself. "Yes, Holmes, Her Majesty Queen Victoria is deeply missed by her grieving subjects." Holmes turned to me with knowing smile on his face.

"Watson, you are a delight!" he cried.

"Well, I saw you pause as you passed the '*V*' which you had shot into the wall to honor the Sovereign," I explained, "and that must have led you to consider the great loss we all felt at her passing." Little more need be said about the death of the great queen, an inauspicious way for Great Britain to begin the new century. For the vast majority of Britons then living, she had been the only sovereign they had known. For nearly sixty-four years, from the age of steam engines through the rise of great powers and trading pacts, wars and the expansion of the Empire, Victoria had ruled: Dour, imperial, and always dressed in black as perpetual mourning for her late Albert.

"An incomparable loss," Holmes agreed. "Now, our unqualified loyalty must be pledged to Albert Edward," the son who had waited longer to inherit the crown than any Prince of Wales in British history.

"He will be challenged to live up to the legend that his mother became," I noted. The new king, who was widely known as "Bertie" but would rule as Edward VII, had led a spirited life as a young prince. As a result, his relations with his mother, a reserved, proper ruler, had been strained. Indeed, some believed Victoria had blamed a scandal involving the young Albert Edward for exposing his father to the typhus that had killed him. Rumors quoted the queen as having confessed, "I never can or shall look at him without a shudder." Like any mother, Victoria had worried about Bertie's many escapades and indiscretions that damaged his own reputation and drove the monarchy itself to the brink of public disapproval. Rumor had it that as Prince of Wales, he had engaged in sordid and immoral activities with a virtual galaxy of women, married and unmarried, of the highest social position and of no position at all, both before and since his marriage to Princess Alexandra of Denmark.

Although Victoria had departed this Earth in January 1901, the coronation of her successor had been delayed a year-and-a-half and now was scheduled for June 26th. All England – indeed, the entire British Empire and much of the rest of the world – awaited the grand event for which feverish planning had been underway since the late Queen's funeral. Since Holmes had provided assistance to the government (and perhaps the Royal Family as well) over the years, I fully anticipated he would be attending the festivities.

"I suspect his mother kept a tight grasp on life to spare the nation from Bertie's reign as long as she could," Holmes mused. "You know, of course, she would not even share the most confidential of state papers with him for fear his lack of discretion would lead him to misuse the information they contained."

"I had no idea," I responded. "After all, he is the most well-educated monarch in our history, at both Oxford and Cambridge."

"True, but as you are surely aware, there is a significant distinction between 'education' and 'wisdom'," he stated. "It remains to be seen how much of the latter King Edward VII will display."

Uncomfortable with questioning the intellect of the man who ruled the Empire, I elected to change the subject. "I presume you will be an honoured guest at the coronation?" I inquired.

"Not unless I wish to strong-arm my way into Westminster Abbey," Holmes replied. "I am amongst the millions of our countrymen without an invitation."

I was shocked by this oversight. "After your many services to the government?" I responded, but Holmes waved off my outrage.

"It is a minor issue, I assure you," he said, "if it is any issue at all. Neither the King's life nor my own is likely to much influenced by my attendance. I wish him well and would gratefully serve him at any time." He grew pensive for a moment, doubtless considering his ambivalence for the new monarch. "And for almost any purpose, I would think."

It was clear that I was far more indignant at the oversight than Holmes himself, which made what occurred next even more curious. As I was preparing to offer another opinion about the thanklessness of the royal family, there was a sudden knock on the door.

"Come in, Mrs. Hudson," Holmes called out.

Our landlady opened the door, holding a silver tray on which an envelope was resting.

"Excuse me, but I believe you need to see this letter without delay," she said, eyeing the disorganization of the room. "It is from Buckingham Palace!" – the London residence of none other than the King of whom we had just been speaking so unceremoniously.

Holmes strode to her and reached out for the envelope.

"Oh, no, Mr. Holmes!" she said, involuntarily pulling the tray away and looking in my direction. "It is for Dr. Watson!"

"Well," Holmes said, smiling, "it seems one of us has gained Royal attention!"

"For me?" I asked, reaching for the envelope. "Why, I cannot imagine what it might be."

I carried the thin, tan envelope over to the writing table and sat down. Both Holmes and Mrs. Hudson hovered, anxious to learn the reason for such a missive. I tore open the letter and began to read out loud the typewritten message:

> *Mr. Dear Dr. Watson,*
>
> *I am writing to you seeking a professional opinion on a most confidential matter.*

I looked upon and spoke to Mrs. Hudson. "If you do not mind, Mrs. Hudson, I am afraid I must ask for privacy, given the request of this correspondent," I said. "Medical information, you can understand."

Our housekeeper quickly gathered up her things and hurried from the room. After she had firmly closed the door, I resumed my reading.

> *Perhaps you are aware of my own standing as a physician and surgeon,* (the letter continued).

Here, I glanced at the signature, which read "*Frederick Treves*".

"Well, of course I am well aware of Dr. Treves!" I exclaimed to Holmes. "He is the author of *Surgically Applied Anatomy* and *A Student's Handbook of Surgical Operations*, both first rate texts." I could see that Holmes had no familiarity either with Treves or his publications. He moved to his medical reference book and quickly turned the pages until he found Treves' name.

"Quite a distinguished surgeon," Holmes declared. "He gained some notoriety treating that pathetically deformed man, Merrick, the one that they called 'The Elephant Man', and then became a surgeon to the late Queen. Quite a spectacular ascendency in the profession."

"Yes, and now he serves as one of the Serjeants Surgeons to His Majesty, the King," I added, continuing to read aloud:

> *A matter of some importance requires the greatest surgical adroitness. Unfortunately, the circumstances also happen to have grave political overtones and perhaps some intrigue. Such matters as these lie entirely outside my skills as a physician. It occurs to me that you, given your own professional training and your collaborations with Mr. Holmes, might be in a unique position to provide me the peace of mind and confidentiality I desperately require. I am therefore hopeful that you will be willing to receive me at 11 o'clock this morning at your Baker Street rooms.*
>
> *Sincerely yours,*
> *Frederick Treves*
> *Surgeon*

I turned to Holmes with what must have been a look of pure puzzlement on my face.

"What possible assistance might I provide to a physician as distinguished as Treves?" I wondered aloud.

Holmes came over and requested to be allowed a look at the letter, which I was only too pleased to hand to him.

"Well, quite impressive stationery," he said. "Heavy quality and expensive engraving." He peered closely at the text. "Typed on an Underwood, I have no doubt, likely a Number Two. I have, you know, been working on an article on the typescripts of various typing devices. Quite a good machine. Yes, this certainly bears the stamp of authenticity. But I think we need only wait briefly for a more complete explanation, as it is nearly eleven o'clock now and I hear a carriage outside that is likely to be delivering our visitor."

I went to the window and looked out. Indeed, a fine carriage was drawing up before the house. There was no heraldry on the door, indicating a desire to maintain the confidentiality of the occupant, but without question, he was a man of means and standing.

Holmes quickly straightened up the very worst of the clutter in the room as we heard footsteps on the stairs followed by a knock on the door, which opened to admit Mrs. Hudson.

"Dr. Treves," she announced. Holmes nodded his approval and she admitted our visitor and departed herself.

Our guest was a man of perhaps fifty or so, with thinning hair and a graying mustache. He was dressed in well-tailored clothes, including a cutaway jacket and waistcoat, and a pair of golden pince-nez glass was perched on his nose. He turned to be certain the door had been firmly closed behind Mrs. Hudson, and then walked towards Holmes and myself, extending his hand to me.

"I am pleased to make your acquaintance, Dr. Watson," he said. "I am Dr. Treves. I hope you have received my letter. Ah, yes, I see it in your hand, Mr. Holmes. A pleasure to meet you as well."

Holmes nodded, unaccustomed to being recognized second – although I must say that for once, I enjoyed being the object of a visitor's primary attention. "Please, Doctor, be seated," I offered. "Some tea?"

"No, nothing, thank you," he said. "I very much appreciate your agreeing to see me and request that you honour the necessity for absolute confidentiality." Holmes and I nodded our agreement. "As you know, the King's coronation is supposed to occur in just two weeks," he began.

"'Supposed to occur'?" Holmes interrupted.

"Yes, Mr. Holmes, it is on that point that I have come to consult with you this morning."

"Is there a problem with the health of a member of the Royal Family?" I asked.

Treves said nothing, but looked back and forth at Holmes and me, clearly straining to utter the words.

"It is the King himself," he declared in hushed tones. "He is ill, in great distress and, I fear, at tremendous risk of a catastrophic infection that, quite frankly, a man of his age and overall health – typhoid fever, a heavy smoker, more alcohol than is advisable – is extremely unlikely to survive."

His words fell like a thunderclap to my ears. Just the previous year, the Queen had succumbed at the age of 81. Now her successor, a generation younger, lay at death's door, if the learned physician was correct.

"What do you suspect?" I asked. "Peritonitis? Diverticulitis?"

"I am nearly certain of perityphlitis," he replied. Glancing at Holmes, he added, "A severe inflammation of the caecum, undoubtedly related to infection that could result in sepsis and – "

"I understand completely," I declared, turning to Holmes who had an uncharacteristically quizzical look on his face. "The King is almost certainly experiencing what is commonly referred to as 'appendicitis', a serious infection of the small appendage to the colon. But surely this is good news," I said to Treves. "You are widely regarded as the most knowledgeable surgeon in the successful treatment of patients with this diagnosis!"

The renowned physician's face turned gray. "Not expert enough to save my own daughter, Hetty" he said softly. "I lost her to this very disease a year-and-a-half ago. She was just eighteen years old."

The room was quiet for several moments, and then, Treves began to speak once again.

"I believe the medical course is clear," the doctor said. "I cannot, of course, guarantee the success of the outcome, but if we act swiftly, I believe we have a good chance to save the King. If there is delay, then I can make no assurances."

"Then why should there be any delay?" Holmes asked brusquely.

"Why, indeed," Treves repeated. "Absent drainage and irrigation of the belly, the King will not live to have the crown placed upon his head. Of that I am certain! Yet he is being obstinate, believing so radical an invasion is unnecessary. 'I have a coronation on hand,' he insisted to me."

"How did you respond to him?" I inquired.

"I told him, 'With the greatest respect, sir, it will be a funeral if you don't have the operation.'

"Unfortunately, there are those in the Court who appear to be encouraging his erroneous belief. They prefer more traditional approaches – liquids, rest, purgatives – but these will unquestionably result in the King's death, I have no doubt. Here is the chart the doctors have written on our patient for the past week," he said, handing a folder to me. "You can see the notations of the various attending physicians – each has their initials by their notes – and to a man they concur with the symptoms exactly as I have described them. And yet, they obstinately refuse to authorize the proper treatment."

I reviewed the charts for a few moments before handing them to Holmes, who studied them and handed them back to Treves.

"What role can I possibly play?" I asked. "I don't share the medical skills that you possess. Indeed, few do! Why should His Majesty give credence to anything I would say since he, however unwisely, doubts your advice?"

"It is true I am a Serjeants Surgeon to His Majesty, but I'm not the only one," Treves began. "For reasons unclear to me, there is disagreement that is unnecessarily threatening the King's life, in my opinion. You, sir, are universally well-regarded in medical circles, and you are far removed from the Royal Court," he continued. "You would bring a knowledgeable opinion free from the intrigue that influences every aspect of life at the palace."

"Even treating the health of the King?" asked Holmes.

"Oh, yes, Mr. Holmes," he replied. "But I fear something other than medical opinion might well be playing a role in this dispute, and that is where I thought you might assist while Dr. Watson and I attend to the King's medical crisis. You can see why. You are a pair of experts, each in your own right, are so invaluable to me in this matter."

Treves asked that we accompany him to Buckingham Palace at once, as the King's condition might weaken at any moment and put him beyond even his medical skills. Within an hour, we had arrived at the magnificent palace and been admitted. We quickly walked upstairs to the audience chamber on the second floor. "I expect we'll be visited by some of the other medical staff once they learn of our arrival," he said as we settled into comfortable chairs.

"Who are these other physicians?" Holmes asked.

"There are several who have attended the King for some time – in some cases decades," Treves replied. "Frankly, some are less skilled in surgery than one would like. Some haven't kept up on the latest medical journals. In my view, the King would be better served were the physicians attending to him of a higher quality, but he has his favorites."

As expected, we didn't wait long before several grave-looking men appeared in the doorway. They greeted Treves with varying degrees of enthusiasm and cast doubtful looks towards Holmes and myself.

"Gentlemen, I am pleased to introduce you to the distinguished physician, Dr. John Watson," he said, extending his arm in my direction. "You may have read some of his very fine articles on battlefield surgery which described new techniques for treating abdominal injuries while minimizing the chances for opportunistic infections."

I considered Treves' comments thoughtfully, as I have never published any such articles. While a surgeon in combat must be inventive when operating under inhospitable conditions, little of the surgeries I performed in Afghanistan had any applicability to the circumstances of a gravely ill King lying in his palace bed. Still, Treves' introduction brought forth murmurs of "Yes, of course," and "An honor for you to join us," and so I was not inclined to correct him about his misplaced representation of my innovative surgical techniques. Holmes, for the moment, went unintroduced as Treves and the other physicians began to discuss the patient's condition, and I was drawn into their circle to participate.

"Little change in condition, Treves," said an older man, clearly a senior member of the team. "Extreme abdominal sensitivity, fever, and a pronounced swelling in the lower right quadrant of the belly."

"All quite consistent with appendicitis," I noted. "And what treatments have been provided in the last eight hours?"

Here the physicians looked at each other and at Treves before a younger member of the medical team replied. "We are continuing with non-invasive treatment," he said. "Fluids, rest, purgatives, icing of the abdomen."

"But you have seen no improvement?" I asked.

"No, nothing to speak of," the young physician admitted. "Frankly, I'm concerned about the possibility of rupture and peritonitis if we don't see significant change fairly soon. These conditions can deteriorate quite rapidly, as you may know."

"I am well aware of the prognosis," Treves interjected. Certainly, everyone in the room knew of the loss of his daughter two years earlier from just such an infection, and the men all grew respectfully silent.

"Why has no drain inserted to determine whether a rupture has occurred and to remove fluids if it has?" I asked forthrightly.

Here there was some stirring amongst the physicians before the older gentleman again spoke up. "We think that very unwise," he responded, looking at Treves. "At least, most of us do. The technique is highly dangerous for a patient of the King's age and physical condition. The treatment may well be worse than the condition."

"With all due respect, Sir Jeffrey, the outcome of the current course will most certainly be worse than any other possible outcome, I assure you," Treves declared. "My surgical plan is well-established, as years of experience have proven."

"Treves, as we know, your methods are far from assured of success," Sir Jeffrey responded. The words seemed especially cruel given Treves' own reference to his late daughter. "I believe more traditional treatments will prove of great success if we but give them several days to take effect."

"If we wait several days," Treves responded, "we will be preparing for the coronation of a very different king, I assure you!"

He walked past his colleagues towards the door and bade me follow him down the hall into the King's bed chamber. The monarch was reclined in a large wooden bed, the bedclothes pulled up around his chest. His eyes were closed and his breathing seemed somewhat laboured. Nearby, Queen Alexandra sat with an expression of the greatest disquiet on her face, although she brightened slightly when she saw Treves enter the room.

"Your Majesty," Treves said, bowing slightly as he approached her. "May I present Dr. John Watson of London, whom I have asked to consult with us on the King's treatment?"

The Queen nodded towards us, and he and I bowed. "And may I present – " I began, looking for Holmes, but realizing he hadn't followed us into the sickroom. "Your Majesty, I will do everything I may to assure the full recovery of His Majesty. If you don't mind, I will conduct a brief examination."

The Queen discreetly walked to another part of the room while Treves and I removed some of the bedclothes covering the King's corpulent abdomen. The sight of his lower belly was certainly disturbing, to say the least. There was obvious swelling – even beyond its normal considerable girth – that was quite warm to the touch. The King groaned slightly when I applied gentle pressure. After a few additional moments of examination, I replaced the blanket over his prostrate figure and motioned Treves to join me outside the room.

"Treves, there is no question that this is a most serious case!" I began. "The inflammation extends considerably towards the umbilicus, which suggests infection. Water and rest will have no benefit whatsoever. Frankly, I cannot imagine why surgery hasn't been the unanimous recommendation of the medical staff."

"We have until the morning to make that decision, I have concluded, but after that, I fear it will be too late," he responded. "Let us return to your rooms with Holmes and determine how to proceed."

We walked back to collect Holmes, but he was nowhere to be seen. Treves called over one of the palace staff who was straightening up the room. "Have you seen the gentleman who arrived with us – the tall man in the overcoat?" he asked.

"Yes, sir," the response came. "He has departed already."

"Departed?" Treves said.

"Yes. After receiving a note, he asked for a carriage and he departed."

"What note?" I inquired.

"A note that arrived with instructions to be delivered to a '*Mr. Holmes*' who had just arrived at the palace," the man said. "I asked him whether that was his name, and he acknowledged it was, so I handed him the note. He opened and read it, and quickly left."

"Who gave you the note?" I asked.

"Dr. Jeffrey handed it to me," he replied. "He said, 'Here is an envelope I have found on the table over there,'" he explained, pointing to the far side of the room. "Attached to the envelope was a note asking that it be delivered to '*Mr. Holmes*'."

"How peculiar!" Treves said.

"I must leave right now and try to find him," I said.

"You don't suspect something evil is afoot, do you?" Terves asked.

"Holmes is more than able to defend himself," I assured him. "He is in pursuit."

"In pursuit?" Treves asked in a perplexed tone. "In pursuit of *what*?"

"I understand your confusion, Dr. Treves," I explained. "I spend much of my life asking the very same question. Holmes is on the scent, I have no doubt."

We rushed out of the palace to a waiting carriage and flew back to Baker Street, but he hadn't returned. It was drawing close to dinner time and I asked Treves to join me for a meal. We left word for Holmes with Mrs. Hudson and walked to one of our favorite restaurants a few blocks away.

"In my judgment, we can wait until morning to conduct the surgery, but no later," he repeated. "But for the disagreement amongst the physicians, I would recommend we initiate the procedure tonight."

"How will you proceed if the disagreement persists?" I inquired.

"I will have no alternative but to go to the Queen and explain to her that without surgical intervention, her husband is doomed," he answered. "Frankly, I'm hopeful that you and Mr. Holmes may be of assistance if that step is required."

"I presume the Queen is familiar with my extensive scholarship on treating abdominal wounds on the battlefield?" I asked with a smile.

We waited more than an hour, and finally, Holmes arrived and joined us at the table. Unlike Treves and myself, he had a jaunty air about him that seemed ill-suited to gravity of the situation. After ordering a dinner of hearty roasted beef and vegetables, he took a drink of his beer and sat back.

"Progress, Treves and Watson, progress!" he said with satisfaction.

"Holmes, one of the staff at Buckingham Palace said you received a note while we were examining the King," I said.

"Yes," he replied with satisfaction. "And here it is." He produced a piece of the Royal stationery much like the one Treves had used for his own note to us, but this message – obviously written with pencil in great haste – was barely legible and far more ominous.

> *Holmes –*
>
> *You have* no role *here.* Do not interfere *with medical business.* Leave immediately *or prepare to suffer* grave embarrassment.

Despite the abysmal penmanship, the author had taken care to emphasize certain words with great vigor. There was no signature. On the envelope was scrawled "*Sherlock Holmes*".

"I will never understand why some people insist upon providing me with clues!" Holmes said merrily. "I was perfectly content to remain in the library and await the report of your examination. Instead, I am presented with this most instructional message, the untangling of which consumed the entire remainder of the afternoon and some of the evening as well."

"And what can you tell me, Mr. Holmes?" Treves inquired.

"Oh, prepare to operate, Doctor," Holmes replied, "as early in the morning as you can."

"And the resistance from my colleagues?"

"I think you will find it has quite melted away," Holmes said with confidence.

I was up very early the next morning and, by arrangement, a carriage collected me at Baker Street at eight a.m. for the short ride to Buckingham Palace, where I was whisked through the guard house and shown up to the sickroom. The King remained in great distress but had been informed that there was no alternative to surgery and no time to delay. A nearby room had already been outfitted as a surgical theatre.

Treves led me into an adjoining room where we could speak privately. "I have been here half the night," Treves said upon greeting me. "I don't know by what magic Mr. Holmes achieved this complete reversal, but at nine o'clock last evening, I was sent a note that informed me of the unanimous agreement by the other physicians that the surgery should proceed at once. I'm deeply grateful to him, and to you for joining me in this operation."

"Join you?" I cried. I lowered my voice. "Treves, you know that I'm no surgeon of your skill!"

"You are a reliable partner," he said, placing his hand on my arm. "That is what I need right now, every bit as much as a surgical assistant." Quickly we changed into our surgical gowns. "Come, let us get to this business without delay!" Treves urged.

He disappeared into the sickroom, and then returned with a number of other gentlemen, some of whom I recognized from our earlier visit to the King's bedside. "Dr. Watson will be assisting me today with the surgery," he informed his colleagues, including Dr. Frederick Hewitt, who would serve as the anesthesiologist, Alfred Fripp, who had been the King's personal surgeon for several years, and Dr. Francis Laking, who had been treating the King for several days along with Treves.

"Watson, Watson," Hewitt muttered. "I seem to recall a John Watson when I was a medical student." Hewitt peered towards me but as his eyesight was extremely poor. He failed to recognize me and the conversation quickly moved to more immediate concerns.

Treves explained the procedure for every step of the operation. Shortly after noon, we gathered in the operating suite. A door opened and the King walked laboriously into the room, assisted by Dr. Jeffrey, greeting each of the physicians whom he recognized. He paused for a moment when he saw my unfamiliar face and stared at me closely.

"This is Dr. John Watson," Treves announced, "the renowned Army surgeon who has consented to assist me in this matter."

The King gave a sharp nod of his head. "Of course, of course," he said. "I am fortunate to have you, Doctor!"

With that, he hoisted himself onto the surgical table with some difficulty owing to his discomfort and his significant portliness. Dr. Hewitt spoke with the King to calm his evident nervousness and then began to administer the anesthesia to render him unconscious so the surgery could begin. Almost immediately, the King began to choke and his face turned purple as the other physicians watched in alarm. Hewitt was unperturbed and responded by grasping the King's beard and pulling it quite sharply. The King's jaw pulled forward, clearing his windpipe, and after a moment, he took a deep breath and his color returned to normal.

"An obstructive apnea," Hewitt explained, "undoubtedly due to the weight on his diaphragm." He examined the King's breathing again. "I think you should be alright to proceed now," he said to Treves, amid audible sighs of relief from the other physicians.

I moved to stand next to Treves as he exposed the King's very sizeable abdomen before liberally applying an antiseptic wash according to explicit directions provided by Dr. Lister, the pioneering surgeon. Treves picked up a scalpel and deftly began to cut into the inflamed portion of the lower abdomen as I administered sterilized cloths to staunch the bleeding.

"This is going to be slightly more complicated than the typical case," Treves said to me in an aside. He pulled apart the incision slightly to expose several inches of yellowish fat girdling the King's mid-section. "I would say there is four inches or more to cut through before we reach the abdominal wall!" Once he did so and inserted the rubber tubing, it quickly became clear that the King's appendix had indeed ruptured and the great swelling and pain he had been enduring was due to an abscess that had formed. I will spare the further graphic details of the surgery to readers whose tastes may not run to descriptions of abdominal drainage. Suffice it to say that the operation occurred not a moment too soon, as further reliance on the disproven treatments would surely have led to sepsis and certain death within days.

Within an hour-and-a-half, the surgery was complete. Treves had elected not to attempt to remove the appendix itself, which would have required a much larger wound and greatly expanded the possibility of infection. Instead, the abdomen had been drained and the wound packed with sterile gauze. A tube had been left in place to allow the drainage to continue. Now, it would simply require careful observation to ensure the infection dissipated and the wound healed cleanly.

"My congratulations, Treves," I declared as we pulled off our surgical gowns. "You have a deft and practiced hand in the operating theatre."

"Thank you, Watson," he responded. "I was fortunate to have your assistance today. There were several moments when your experience in cauterizing gave me great confidence."

The other physicians, having paused to look at Treves' handwork, now filed into the room and clapped him on the back. "Bravo!" and "Well done!" they called out as they filed past, nodding their heads to me in acknowledgement even though, I imagine, they fully recognized that the credit properly belonged to the colleague they had so recently maligned and dismissed.

"We will need to watch him carefully over the next several days, but I'm hopeful," Treves said. "I'll personally monitor the drainage and repacking of the wound periodically until I'm certain there is no evidence of further infection."

We washed our hands carefully before stepping back into the makeshift operating room to check on our patient. He remained snoring comfortably with no further signs of the apnea that had come close to ending the surgery before it had even begun.

"Come," Treves said, "let us go find Mr. Holmes and tell him of today's success."

After leaving explicit instructions as to his whereabouts with the nursing staff, Treves and I departed the palace.

A carriage ride returned us to Baker Street, where we were greeted by Mrs. Hudson who, like virtually everyone in our busy city, had no idea of the great danger from which their King had been rescued by the expert ministrations of my companion.

"Mr. Holmes is awaiting your arrival," she pleasantly said. "He was certain you would be arriving very soon." We climbed the familiar stairs and opened the door to reveal him sitting in his comfortable chair, smoking one of his favorite briars.

"Ah Watson. Treves," he said expectantly. "I presume from your demeanor that you achieved a successful outcome."

"Most definitely," I replied. Gesturing to my medical colleague, I added, "Treves is a skilled and fearless surgeon. There are not many men who might have been as decisive in cutting into the considerable abdomen of our King, but he did so without hesitation and with great dexterity."

"Thank you, Watson," the object of my comments replied. "It was an interesting case, and I was most fortunate to have your colleague assisting me." He made a little bow in my direction, to which I reciprocated. "And

I certainly want to acknowledge your own considerable contribution to the successful surgery, Holmes."

"*My* contribution?" Holmes responded. "Whatever do you mean? I was nowhere near the surgery, and good fortune I was not, for my skills with a scalpel and retractor are vastly inferior to Watson's prowess."

"Come, come, Holmes, I think you know what I mean," Treves replied. "Last evening, the King lay near death, and I was unable to secure the consensus amongst my fellow medical men to take the one action with a chance of saving his life. Several hours later, I'm summoned to the palace and ushered into the sickroom with instructions to prepare for surgery – orders I had been anxiously awaiting for two weeks. Surely there is a great deal to tell about how this fortunate change in circumstances came about."

Holmes regarded the physician and puffed on his pipe. "Well, why don't we just say, as did the Bard himself, '*All's well that ends well*'. I think you'll find the King most generous in his response to you for your services, and that your role as Sergeant Surgeon to the King remains most secure."

"Yes, yes, but how did all this come about?"

"As Watson will tell you, Doctor," Holmes replied. "I'm not always at liberty to discuss my methods, but I can assure you no further challenges to your authority. I have no doubt that the King will live as long and healthy a life as your ministrations enable him."

Treves clearly wasn't pleased with Holmes's unwillingness to share more information, but he was reconciled to honouring the detective's discretion. "Then I will thank you again, both of you, for your inestimable assistance," he said.

"And one more thing, if I may," said Holmes. "My name was not prominently mentioned in connection with this affair and I should prefer to keep it that way. Let the plaudits fall where they ought: On the medical men and their impressive skills."

"Of course, Mr. Holmes," Treves answered.

After we had heard him descend the stairs and close the front door, I turned to Holmes. "Come now, surely you cannot keep the answer to the mystery from me!" I implored.

"Well, we do have our secrets," he said smiling, "and some of those with respect to this case must remain secret even from you, Watson. Even from you."

Holmes sat in one of the comfortable chairs, lit his briar, and stretched out his long legs.

"In many ways, not a very remarkable story," he began, "except for affecting the survival of the King and the future of the monarchy.

"The key to the case, in my view, was that Dr. Treves alone served as the advocate for immediate surgery," Holmes said. "True, one might discount his fervent advocacy of such a course, given his specialization in appendix removal and his great sensitivity over having lost his own daughter. But I was struck by the reluctance of the other consulting physicians who seemed to dismiss Treves' greater experience in dealing with this particular condition."

"I must say I agree with you," I interjected. "While undoubtedly the King is anything but a fit physical specimen – those four inches or so of fat could lead to no other conclusion – I couldn't make sense of the resistance of the other physicians. Clearly, there was but one suitable course which was removal of the appendix or drainage of the abdomen!"

"Yes, precisely," Holmes answered. "There seemed to be no logical medical rationale for delay, particularly since the leading practitioner of appendectomies was standing by the King's bedside urging just such a course.

"I think you know my methods well enough to recognize why I began to reach a very dark conclusion," he continued. "What lay behind their opposition to the surgery? No alternative treatment was available and clearly, the regimen they followed had produced nothing but a worsening of the King's condition. Inaction, as you explained to me, could only ensure a rupture of the appendix, sepsis throughout the King's body, and certain death.

"Now assuming that no one wished the King ill, the only rationale seemed to me misplaced medical judgment. Perhaps the medical men were fearful that the chances of surgical success were so miniscule that they wished to avoid encouraging a procedure that could result in their incurring culpability for the King's death."

"Yes, that seems possible," I responded. "But these are distinguished physicians, men at the very top of the profession. Surely they could explain to the Queen and others that the King's condition left them no alternative but to undertake such a risky procedure."

"I agree," said Holmes. "If they were prepared to make that argument, who in England has sufficient credibility to dispute their recommendation? Which is why I rejected that explanation for their inaction."

"But what other explanation can there be?" I wondered aloud. "If they didn't believe their current treatments effective and they weren't reluctant to recommend a precarious procedure, what other motive might there be?"

"Ah, Watson, how many times have you heard me say when confronted with just such a conundrum, 'When you have eliminated the impossible – '"

"' – Whatever remains, however improbable, must be the truth'," I completed. "But what remains in this case?" I wracked my brain for whatever option remained that might explain the obstinance of the medical experts, with the exception of Treves. Suddenly, a black thought entered my mind.

"No, Holmes!" I cried. "You cannot be serious! It is impossible!"

"*Whatever* remains," Holmes replied, looking at me with the gravest expression I have ever seen on his face. "*Whatever*."

I sat back in my chair to fully comprehend the implications of my friend's deduction. Holmes was not inclined to idle speculation or fancy. If he believed what he was saying, he must not only be convinced of its accuracy, but also have corroborated his theory through his investigations.

"Who would have such a motivation?" I asked. "Who could possibly wish such an outcome?"

"Oh, that is the least problematical issue," Holmes said. "There are any number of influential people and powerful interests that Edward may have offended. It is always a sound rule to ask '*Cui bono?*' Who benefits should Edward never be coronated and the Crown passes instead to the Prince of Wales? '*Uneasy lies the head that wears a crown*' – yet another of Shakespeare's observations that might have some applicability in this affair.

"Clearly I lacked the time to investigate everyone with a grievance against the King, which might well be a lengthy list given his decades of – let us say – *rambunctious* behavior," Holmes said. "But I certainly could focus on those who, despite convincing testimony to the contrary, seemed adamant to deny the King his one chance for a recovery.

"And so, that is what I did. I spent much of yesterday deep in the newspaper records and other sources examining the backgrounds of the men who now hovered over our critically ill monarch, trying to find a cause that might explain their reticence in following Treves' persuasive diagnosis.

"Watson," he continued, "I cannot reveal the details of those inquiries, even to you – even if you promise me, as I am hoping you will, that the details of this story remain undisclosed for some time. Indeed, I think this a perfect example of a case that belongs in your box at Cox and Company, rather than in the pages of *The Strand* or any other publication.

"What I found was deeply disturbing, it goes without saying. One of the attending physicians – and here, Watson, I will not reveal the identity, even to you – possesses a motive against the King that he dared not reveal, but that unquestionably provided him more than a little rationale for denying Edward the only treatment that would save his life.

"Treves, it turns out, was not the only father to lose a cherished daughter, as it turns out. So did at least two of the other attending physicians treating the King, and another lost a son to disease in the army. I need not tell you that the loss of a child profoundly affects any parent beyond any anguish those of us without issue might imagine – the psychologists have been quite clear on this point.

"The connection of two of those lost children to Edward, or the Crown, seem tangential at best. One daughter died after an accident at the father's estate while he was attending to one of the King's earlier illnesses. He deeply blamed himself for being absent when his daughter desperately needed medical care, but the King certainly bore no plausible responsibility for the loss of the child.

"The second case, that of the son, might have produced a grievance against Edward since the son had been in military service to the Crown at the time of his death, the result of an attack in India."

"But surely no educated person would blame the monarch because a child dies in military service!" I responded. "Such decisions are made by the government, not the Crown!"

"I agree. The likelihood of seeking revenge for such a loss did not strike me as plausible either, and I dismissed that suspect as well. But the third case – ah, there seemed more promise, since the death of the daughter was shrouded in secrecy. It was only reported in *The Times* that she had taken ill quite suddenly and passed away, with no discussion of the details of her illness.

"However, *The Times* isn't the only source of news. I delved in the back issues of the penny weeklies that cover the seamier side of life in our city to see whether this particular death had occasioned any coverage."

"And did it?" I asked expectantly. "Did you find something?"

Holmes leaned forward in his chair, drawing his head close to mine and spoke in a hushed tone.

"Yes, Watson, I most certainly did find something," Holmes said. "Something so grievous and contemptible that it left no doubt in my mind that it was the answer to this entire case.

"The daughter was just nineteen years old and had a most independent nature. Although her father preferred that she engage in university study, she preferred to flirt with society and became engaged as a lady's assistant to Miss Alice Keppel."

"I have heard the salacious rumors about Miss Keppel and the King, of course," I said. Holmes looked at me with surprise. "Well, you aren't the only one who dabbles with the penny weeklies, you know!"

Alice Keppel was only half the King's age, but well-founded rumors had swirled around her indiscreet relationship to the King. It was said that she had become his mistress two or three years earlier and enjoyed an unusually close friendship with Edward, one that could hardly escape public attention, including that of the Queen who, for whatever reason, chose to overlook his improper behavior.

"This young woman accompanied Miss Keppel almost everywhere," Holmes continued, "and in doing so, she inevitably became known to the Prince. Despite the relationship with Miss Keppel, it appears the Prince had sufficient time and energy to also strike up a brief relationship with this young woman.

"Trouble quickly arose, rumor had it, when word of the Prince's unfaithfulness to his mistress, if that is an appropriate concept, the young lady was discharged from service. Shortly thereafter, the young lady became quite ill with a medical condition. Given her father's prominence and association with the Royal Family, she concealed the condition from him, seeking treatments from unreliable quacks whose ministrations were utterly ineffective."

I considered Holmes's story thus far and was naturally appalled. "How did you proceed?" I inquired.

"There was little I could do but confront the father directly with my findings," Holmes said, "and this I did last night in a surreptitious visit to his home in Mayfair. I sent a message to him early in the evening, explaining that I would be arriving at six o'clock and that it would be to his distinct advantage to see me. Frankly, I assumed that someone of his station would recognize that the arrival of Sherlock Holmes at his door was not something to be trifled with.

"I arrived promptly and used the heavy brass knocker to announce my arrival. I gave my name to the butler who answered the door, and was promptly escorted into the library. After a few moments, the door swung open and Doctor – well, let me not use names – entered the room and walked directly up to me. He conveyed an unmistakable attitude of superiority.

"'I am not used to visits from the police,' he haughtily declared.

"'That is just as well,' I replied, 'since the police might have a far more extensive list of questions if they, rather than I, were knocking at your door. However, I am a private consulting detective, with little interest in involving the police in the matter which brings me to your library this evening.'

"'I know of your reputation, of course,' he began. 'I would ask you to sit down, Mr. Holmes, but I first would like to know the explanation for your unsolicited arrival. What can a – what did you say, a *private consulting detective*? – possibly want from me? And on whose behalf are you consulting, if you don't mind my asking?'

"'Actually, I *do* mind,' I responded, settling into a comfortable chair beside the large fireplace and gesturing for the doctor to sit as well, an invitation which he ignored. I recognized the effrontery of my action, but I felt I held the upper hand in the conversation, and besides, I was offended by his aristocratic air.

"'I am here to insist that you discontinue your opposition to the King's surgery,' I boldly stated. 'I believe that you are well aware that Treves' surgical option alone can save the King's life, and yet you have rallied your colleagues, except for Treves, in opposition to an appendectomy. If you persist in your unreasonable opposition for simply another day, you surely know that England will soon conduct a funeral rather than a coronation.'

"I have seen men become distraught and agitated when I have confronted them with their misdeeds, Watson, but I must say I have never seen the kind of reaction my words elicited on this distinguished physician. I do believe that had he had a scalpel or other dangerous tool of his profession at hand, he would have assaulted me right there in his magnificent library.

"'Have you lost your mind?' he thundered. 'How *dare* you come to my home and make such unfounded and conspiratorial accusations against me! I do not care a whit for your reputation or connections. I shall summon the police and have you hauled off to the Old Bailey!'

"'I would counsel against such an action,' I replied.

"'And give me one reason why I should listen to a word that comes from your impertinent mouth!' he insisted.

"'Well, first, because I would have very little trouble connecting you to the threatening note left for me at the Palace, despite your crude attempt to disguise your handwriting, which I saw clearly displayed on the King's medical chart yesterday. You may not be aware of the papers I that I've written precisely on the topic of efforts to conceal one's telltale penmanship.

"'Second, because the memory of your daughter would be sullied if all of the details of this matter to be publicly discussed, as they surely would be, were I subjected to police examination.'

"He stopped moving towards the door and stood motionless. 'What do you know of my daughter?' he asked.

"'Doctor, I know nearly everything, and what I do not yet know for certain, I have no doubt I can hypothesize – though that is not in my nature – and you could confirm. For example, I know that your daughter, against your wishes, left your home to become an assistant to Miss Keppel, that through the arrangement she was introduced to Edward when he was still Prince Albert. I have no doubt that, as was the case with apparently innumerable other attractive young women, the Prince was able to entice her into sordid behavior.'

"'By now, the doctor's face had returned to its normal hue and his arrogant air had been utterly deflated. Instead his head hung and he reached to his eyes to wipe away tears.

"'Of course, it became worse,' I continued. 'She developed a condition quite common amongst those engaged in such indiscriminate behavior, a condition that she concealed from you, even though she must have known you were aware of the Prince's own case of this disease was under expert treatment. By the time her physical condition became serious enough to convince her of the fruitlessness of the treatments she was receiving, it was too late. She told you of her plight, and your examination revealed the infections had progressed too far. Within weeks, she had fallen gravely ill and – '

"'Stop!' he said, holding up his hand. 'Stop. I cannot relive the awfulness.' He turned to face me and the tears continued to stream down his cheeks. 'Yes, Mr. Holmes. Yes. She was terribly ill, far beyond treatment by the time she confessed her behavior to me. She refused to identify from whom she had contracted the infection, but given her position with Miss Keppel and my own knowledge of the Prince's medical condition, it was hardly a difficult diagnosis to make. Within weeks, she was gone.' His voice choked. 'And I was unable to do anything to help her, despite my degrees and diplomas. And I was unable to do anything in retribution against the person who had brought such a disgrace upon her and upon me as well.

"'But I am a professional physician, and my job is not to judge my patients,' he continued. 'I had a responsibility to the Prince, who shortly thereafter succeeded to the throne, and I could not allow my personal antagonism to mutate into thoughts of revenge, although I had innumerable opportunities to provide the King with something other than the medicines he required.

"'And then this new illness appeared several weeks ago, and something changed in my outlook,' he continued. 'Surely, I could never take any action to administer a dangerous drug to the Sovereign, but withholding medical assistance did not seem to me to fall into the same category.' His face grew grave as looked up at me and spoke. 'This . . . *man* – this egotistical, indulgent dilettante! He has left a trail of ruined women behind him like a dog abandons bones it has chewed and tired of, with no concern for his own immorality or their disgrace. He does not deserve to wear the Crown! And suddenly, because of my position and stature in the Court, I had a means to ensure that he never would.'

"He sat down at last into a chair and stared blankly ahead. 'Yes, I knew Treves was right,' he admitted. 'I knew an appendectomy was called for, or at least drainage of the abdomen. I knew that time was running out, that the appendix would burst and that afterwards, the chances of sepsis were beyond doubt. A man in that condition had virtually no chance of surviving such a turn of events.

"'The King himself had deep reservations about proceeding with an operation, even under the supervision of so skilled a surgeon as Treves. It wasn't difficult to alarm him sufficiently that he allowed me to continue a non-surgical course which I convinced him had a greater likelihood of success than an invasive procedure. Yes, I knew that my prognosis was flawed and that following my recommendations means that it would be George, not Edward, who will be coronated as King. I considered that outcome the appropriate one for the nation.'

Holmes completed this recitation and remained silent for a few moments.

"Even in my long career of exposure to the vilest criminals that the sewers of London have dredged up, I've never had the revulsion and loathing I felt for this celebrated medical professional," he said. "I could barely believe what was being confessed to me. But I also knew there was little time to act if we were to avoid precisely the outcome this medical malcontent desired.

"I walked to where he sat and handed him a piece of paper from the desk. 'You must send a note at once to Treves,' I instructed, 'informing him of the change in your opinion, and that the surgery must take place as early tomorrow as feasible.'

"Without a word, he rose to sit at desk, where he quickly wrote the note I had dictated. He summoned his butler and directed the letter be carried immediately to Treves, and that a confirmation of its receipt be brought back to him.

"'Now, we are going to the Palace, where you will inform the King and Queen of your change in opinion, and that they must prepare for tomorrow's procedure.'

"We were soon passing through the gates of Buckingham Palace and, upon entering, were escorted to the King's bedchamber where he lay moaning and only semi-conscious. In a few moments, Queen Alexandra arrived. Although I had little doubt the doctor would obey my precise instructions, I determined to remain in the room to be certain, which naturally necessitated an introduction.

"'Your Majesties, I have the honour to present to you Mr. Holmes,' he said.

“The King stirred, lifting his head slightly from the pillows and looking in my direction.

“‘Mycroft, is that you?’ he asked.

“‘No, Your Majesty,’ I replied, ‘Mycroft is my older brother. I know of his long service to the Foreign Ministry. I am his brother, Sherlock.’

“‘A physician?’ he responded.

“‘No,’ the doctor interjected, ‘but Mr. Holmes has made,’ he searched for the words, ‘invaluable contributions to our efforts on your behalf.’

“‘Ah, very well,’ replied Edward, resting his great head on the pillow again. ‘I shall knight you, too, as well as all these physicians who are endeavoring to save my life.’

“‘That is very kind of you, but let us focus first on your recovery,’ I replied. ‘I believe the doctor has some thoughts about the next course of treatment.’

“The doctor cleared his throat. ‘Yes, Your Majesties, we have determined that despite our best efforts, it will be necessary for Dr. Treves to conduct a surgery tomorrow to remove the infected appendix,’ he said. This remark was not well received by Edward or the Queen, but as it was coming from so authoritative a source, they offered no resistance. ‘I will be speaking with Dr. Treves later this evening to put all of the plans in place,’ he continued. ‘I think that by tomorrow evening this time, you will be feeling considerably better and assured of a healthy recovery.’

“We exchanged some comments all around and then took our leave of the sickroom. I told the doctor I would monitor each step of the process and would speak with Treves myself to ensure the directions were clearly conveyed. If there was any deviation from our agreement, I promised, my call would not be to him or to the palace, but to Scotland Yard.”

And that is precisely what transpired prior to the surgery taking place the next day just after noon. I was among the physicians who visited with the King the following day, and was surprised to find him alert, sitting up in his bed, reading the newspapers and, I am sorry to say, smoking a cigar. It was soon clear the treatment had been effective and within a couple of weeks, the drainage had ceased and the infection was gone. On 9th August, the King was formally crowned Edward VII, beginning what would be a tragically brief although surprisingly distinguished era in British history.

The King made good on his pledge of knighthoods for all of the physicians who participated in his successful treatment including, of course, Treves. One day in the summer, a visitor to Baker Street arrived in a carriage from the Palace and ascended the stairs to our rooms. He brought with him two oversized envelopes which we opened to reveal formal announcements from the King that he was conferring knighthoods on Holmes and myself in appreciation for our endeavors in saving his life.

After the courier had departed, Holmes sat at his desk and drafted a letter in his own hand, which I replicate here.

Your Majesty,

I am in receipt of your gracious announcement of your desire to confer upon me a knighthood in connection with my service to you during your recent illness. While I am grateful beyond words for your extreme kindness and recognition, such an honour as this is far beyond any contribution I could possibly have made in the successful outcome of your treatment, and I am unable in good conscience to accept your munificent gesture.

I hope that you appreciate both my gratefulness and my desire to ensure that knighthoods are reserved to those for whom public recognition is a benefit. In my occupation, however, such an acknowledgement might complicate certain activities I am called upon to perform. Therefore, with the greatest respect and wishes for a long reign, I choose to decline this generous offer.

With respect,
Sherlock Holmes

I fully understood Holmes's desire for anonymity and agreed a knighthood could complicate the conduct of the unconventional occupation he relished. Moreover, accepting such a recognition would invariably raise questions as to exactly what role he played in the King's treatment and recovery, and he had no desire for such speculation.

On my part, while a knighthood was certainly something to which most men aspire, I felt my own contributions to the successful treatment of Edward VII were similarly undeserving of so great an honour, and so I also declined. Besides, how could I subject Holmes to future collaborations with a knight of the realm at his side!

Alas, Edward's tenure proved all too short, lasting less than a decade before his many health problems proved too debilitating. And yet, considering the five decades he had waited to actually become King, his reign was not without some significant achievements that brought honour to his name and the nation.

As for the mysterious medical saboteur, his name remains unknown to me. While I certainly could have followed Holmes's clues (some of which I have not included in this account), I chose to honour his request that I not do so. Presumably the physician who conspired to cut short the brief reign of Edward VII was among those the King honored with a knighthood, and he may well have continued to provide medical care to the King and his successor for years to come.

The one physician I can be sure was not implicated in the dastardly plan was Treves himself, with whom I remained friendly for many years. Tragically, even incomprehensively, the celebrated surgeon himself died at the age of seventy as a result of a burst appendix.

> *I remember the date very well, for it was in the same month that Holmes refused a knighthood for services which may perhaps someday be described.*
>
> – Dr. John H. Watson
> "The Three Garridebs"

The Man from Deptford
by John Linwood Grant

Sherlock Holmes once spoke to me of an early case of his which was, in his words: "A story for which the world is not yet prepared." I trusted his judgement back then, just as I do now, years later – for he has read the following account, and bid me lock it far from sight. By the time these papers are unsealed, all those mentioned within will be at rest. My words will stand, but they will belong to history alone.

And that, I do believe, is where they are safer left . . . .

It was a rather dull autumn day in '02, just as I was abandoning a disappointing luncheon sandwich, when Mrs. Hudson came to the door of Holmes's rooms at Baker Street and announced we had an unexpected visitor. Not that unusual an event – nor especially inconvenient, given that we had concluded our meal – but she wore that careful expression which meant that our visitor might be one of some importance.

I had already half risen from my chair when she added, "It is Inspector Merivale, Mr. Holmes."

I resumed my place. Merivale. We had never met, but had I not endured enough talk of this bright young officer during the last few months? "Merivale shows great promise", and "My friend at the Yard, Merivale, consulted me the other day . . . ." Recently it seemed as if Holmes only acknowledged a single other investigative mind of any note, and I confess that this had grated on me. But though we are poor and mean creatures, at least the Lord gave us the ability to recognise it, and so I pushed my plate aside, and sought to make my expression one of welcome . . . .

It was as if I had been flung back in time, back to a certain chemical laboratory at my old friend Stamford's hospital. Lucius Merivale was tall and thin, with a pronounced brow, a sharp gaze, and a hawk-like nose. Any sense of meanness fled at the sight of him. Whether my friend saw it or not, had it not been for the unfashionably long blonde hair, surely Merivale was a younger Holmes!

Suppressing a chuckle at my observation, I stood, extending my hand.

He grasped it eagerly. "Dear me," he said. "To be in the presence of Dr. John Watson, as well as Mr. Holmes! A rare treat."

"You are too kind, Inspector," I said.

He refused my offer of a seat. "Mr. Holmes, sir, I am in a quandary, and there is not one man at Scotland Yard who will advise me."

"Pray continue." Holmes was tamping a rough-cut, oily mix into the bowl of his pipe, and I made the tactical move of going to the window and opening it to its fullest extent.

"It is the St. Pancras case."

"Is that not closed?" asked Holmes. "I demonstrated conclusively that Pimley must be the one who – "

"Oh, he is guilty, Mr. Holmes, he is guilty." Merivale paced in agitation. "But he has spoken in the cells, and said on whose commission he acted."

I swilled the tea-leaves around in the bottom my cup. "Even better then, surely?"

The inspector spun to give me a most melancholy look.

"He says . . . he says that The Man from Deptford instructed him."

Holmes stiffened. "A man from Deptford?"

"No. Dear me, sir no – he was quite clear. *The* Man from Deptford."

I understood neither the peculiar exactness with which Merivale spoke, nor the frown on my friend's face, a frown so deep it might have been carved there. Holmes did not respond at first, only turned the pipe-stem between his fingers.

At last he said: "That cannot be, Merivale. The man is playing you, or has some other motive . . . ."

"Is this one of your old cases, Holmes?" I asked.

"Later, old fellow. I must speak with Mycroft – and with your prisoner, Inspector."

"I can arrange access to the prisoner, Mr. Holmes, and give you the file on – "

Holmes waved one hand, dismissive. "I remember all the details, thank you. Had I but had this additional piece of knowledge, I might have acted sooner."

"Would it change Pimley's guilt?"

"No. But I would not have been sitting here, contemplating a lamb chop for supper. I might have been abroad in London Town, seeking news of a man I must never meet."

"What can I do to help, Holmes?" I asked.

"Help? You can – and must – do nothing."

And with that he swept from the room.

"Well, I'll be blowed!" I said.

The inspector looked at me and sought to speak. Failing to do so, he fled at Holmes's heels.

The Thames ran sluggish between tides that afternoon, a swathe of less-than-wholesome water which split the city. The sky was low, that steely grey which warns of rain. I had arrived at the Embankment a half-hour before the time proposed for a certain assignation, and settled on a bench, making a poor job of reading my newspaper. Each foraging pigeon, each passing pleasure boat or ferry, distracted me.

The St. Pancras case.

My friend had explained it in his usual succinct manner only a few days before. Ernst von Kleber, a German diplomat, had asked to view a painting kept in the vault of the Corfven Gallery, a portrait of one of his ancestors. Neither the diplomat nor the artist were deemed of any great importance, and the matter would have passed without note had not von Kleber been assaulted shortly after leaving the vault. A police constable, on his usual beat behind St. Pancras Station, tried to intervene, with the result that whilst the diplomat was wounded, the officer received a fatal stab wound.

Holmes analysed certain substances on a cap found at the scene, and proved that it belonged to one George Pimley, a picture framer who regularly worked for the gallery. Taken into custody, the man confessed, claiming that that he intended only robbery, not murder. A tragic affair – too many thieves these days were willing to use the knife. But what had this to do with Deptford, and why did Holmes and Merivale seem so distracted?

A figure almost as tall as Merrivale, but with his hair clipped short, his manner easy, approached my bench, and I tipped my hat, feeling like a character in one of my own stories.

He sat down. "Dr. Watson."

"Inspector Gregson."

Gregson arranged his large hands on his lap. "Bit unusual, being asked to meet you without your illustrious colleague."

"He will not see me. He is either away from his rooms, or cloistered with your Merivale."

The inspector raised his eyebrows. "Merivale? A sharp fellow. So has there been an argument between you?"

"Not an argument." I watched a deep-laden collier work its way against the current, boatmen turning small craft to avoid it. "There is something which Holmes feels he must keep to himself. Tell me, Gregson, what is Deptford to you?"

"A confounded nuisance. Prostitutes, drunken hands from the cattle-yards, and butchers with a temper. They say it was more orderly before the Royal Dock closed, but that was before my time."

"But if I said to you that I had spoken with 'The Man from Deptford'?"

I knew Gregson as a brave enough fellow. Why, then, did he flinch?

"Should you say such a thing, Doctor, I would not believe you. And I would then advise you to wrap those words in oilcloth and sink them in the river."

"That will not work with me, if Holmes is already involved."

He sighed. "It would be better if – "

"Please, Gregson."

"Very well. Do you by any chance recall the murder of Frederick Caille, the business magnate, and three other men, in the year of '86?"

I had to ponder. Apart from it being so long ago, that had been a year in which Holmes and I were involved in a number of difficult cases, and I was in some quandary as to the future of my medical career. But . . . .

"Wait a minute. Didn't Caille meet his end in the Deptford Victualling Yard? The man was garroted, I believe."

"In the Royal Victoria Yard, yes. Garroted at the hands of a certain man whom I will not name, whom I could not investigate, even if I wished to do so. And I do not."

Gregson rose and, taking my hand, shook it with unexpected warmth. "Mr. Holmes will do what he must, but you, Doctor – do not get involved, I pray you."

And with that extraordinary statement, he left me to the pigeons and the dull perfume of Father Thames.

Little wiser, I took a hansom to Baker Street, and there, after persuading Mrs. Hudson that I needed no more than a cup of tea, I turned to Holmes's files and clippings. To add to my unease, I could find no records pertaining to Frederick Caille's murder. That seemed unusual.

Gregson had indicated that one man was involved, and yes, I had some vague memory of newspaper stories at the time. An assassin, the headlines proclaimed at first, but that came to nothing, and it was eventually chalked up to either a gang or business rivals.

Holmes had shown little interest – but it was never his case, of course. Even my friend, with his keen mind, could not be involved in every murder across such a vast city as London. But what, so many years later, could be the connection to George Pimley and the St. Pancras case?

When Holmes himself returned to his rooms, he was distracted, flinging himself into his chair without word and reaching immediately for his pipe.

"It will not do," I said, as pungent smoke began to fug the air. "And you should know that it will not."

"Gregson did not talk, then?"

"How did you – "

"I know you too well, Watson. If frustrated, whom would you ask? Not Lestrade, nor Merivale, whom you hardly know. You would turn, in any matter of the Yard, to Gregson, and he, being a good enough fellow, would at least meet with you. What I could not determine was how much he would say."

"He offered nothing but Frederick Caille," I muttered, aggrieved.

"Ah, Caille. That was the beginning, though far from the end." He drew deep on his pipe, and the cloud which followed almost obscured his face. "Watson, I value no man above you, but you can be a terrier, unable to know when to let go."

"If there is danger – "

"There is either little danger – or there is all. That is my quandary. You heard Merivale speak of 'The Man from Deptford'. I find it hard to believe that such a man might be involved, and yet hard to understand why George Pimley would invoke that name. It may well be a ploy, to avoid the noose, to say that he was under such duress that he had no choice, on his own life. I do not think that it will spare him. But if it is not . . . ."

"Who is this mysterious other man?"

Holmes turned hooded eyes upon me. "You must not speak of him, other to myself or Merivale. Do you give me your word?"

"I . . . yes, I do."

"Very well. His name is Edwin Dry. He kills people, for coin."

"A common killer, then, when all is said and done."

"We are not so fortunate."

"But you seek him?"

"I do not. I avoid, where possible, any knowledge of his actions, and any involvement in the consequences of his work."

"Because . . . ." I hesitated, remembering Merivale's visit. "This is something to do with your brother Mycroft."

Holmes winced. "Mycroft is . . . aware of certain matters. It is my fervent hope that I shall never be a politician, Watson – there are such compromises to be made . . . ." He returned to his pipe. "There were no tears shed for Frederick Caille in Government circles. His business empire was corrupt. His industries provided substandard building materials, tainted foodstuffs, and all manner of other fraudulent goods. Ordinary people died as a result."

"If Caille was such a blackguard, did he not deserve a trial, and the due process of British justice?"

"He was challenged several times through the courts. All attempts failed. We both know that wealthy men have ways to deflect the sword of justice, do we not? But in the end, another means was found."

"Good Lord, Holmes – are you suggesting that the authorities sanctioned murder? That they paid for Caille to be . . . *removed*?"

“I am not,” he said fiercely. “Neither are you. This is precisely why I did not want you involved. To speculate in such a way is to be drawn into a world more treacherous than the worst stews in London.”

I tried to take in what he said. “Then you are forbidden to interfere if this Dry fellow is in play?”

“Forbidden?” He formed a thin smile. “I am advised. Requested. Encouraged to consider other more pressing business.”

“And this is such a situation?”

Holmes stretched out his long legs, templed his fingers, and appeared to sink deep into thought. I had almost wearied of an answer when he lifted his head again.

“My dear Watson, you have the knack, sometimes, of asking the most difficult questions. The truth is that I do not know. Mycroft does not know.”

“Then – ”

“I shall investigate this connection to the Pimley case – cautiously, with Merivale’s assistance.”

“And mine.”

“I cannot – ”

“And mine.” I held his gaze.

“Brave fellow,” was all he said, and for next hour or so we sat quiet, each in his own thoughts.

Merivale arrived soon after supper, agitated.

“The Commissioner has told me to let this go.” he said without preamble.

“Then tell him that you have.” Holmes rang for Mrs. Hudson, and requested a pot of coffee for three. “Let Pimley be taken down for his deeds at St. Pancras.”

“Did you see this picture framer, Holmes?” I asked.

“I did. He claimed that he met a man in a public house, an ‘ordinary looking cove’. Pimley was offered a drink, then another . . . and finally it was put to him that von Kleber would be at the gallery for some time, that the German carried marks in his wallet to the equivalent of five-hundred pounds. The stranger said he knew how to make such monies ‘disappear’, but was too well known to the local police to accost von Kleber himself. Any accomplice must be a man with no criminal record, and would receive half the sum for a simple robbery.

“Our man Pimley is a frequenter of the races, and even illicit cock fights. Heavily in debt, he agreed – and was advised to take a knife, merely to threaten. He was even supplied with von Kleber’s route back to his hotel, one which included several quiet streets behind St. Pancras.”

I eased my stiff leg and poured coffee for us.

"But the stabbings – "

"Pimley panicked at von Kleber's unexpected resistance," Merivale supplied. "And when a young constable heard the scuffle and joined them, our man was in a weeping panic. His blows were amateur, but his blade was very sharp."

"And what of 'Deptford' in all this?" I was still muddled.

Holmes stroked his chin. "Pimley's words when we were in his cell, apparently uttered by the one who recruited him: 'I would not welsh on this agreement if I were you, George. The Man from Deptford will not be crossed, if you get my meaning. This here's a growing game, and he has toolers, cracksmen, and more joining him every day.' And the stranger gave, as Pimley describes it, the coldest smile he had ever seen."

We drank our coffee, Merivale breaking up a biscuit with thin fingers but eating not a crumb of it.

"I don't suppose," I offered, "that with this von Kleber being a German, there was some – "

"No," said my two companions simultaneously. Merivale flushed. Holmes gestured him to speak.

"We looked into that at the Yard, Doctor. No suggestion of politics or espionage. Von Kleber had some minor trade responsibilities, and was of no real interest to either of our Governments. A place-filler. Nor, before you ask, is the portrait he examined of value or relevance. He had been told to take a sum of money to the bank, and thought he might go to the gallery on the way. Nothing more, nothing less." With his crisp explanation, he reminded me once more of my friend.

"I had considered that aspect, Watson," Holmes said to me, which I think was meant kindly.

"Yet," said Merivale, "this Deptford business, sir – from what you have told me, robbery plays no part in the assassin's work."

"None at all. What little is known – and I stress the word 'little' – has him as interested only in the dispatch of his targets."

"What is his *modus operandi*?" I asked, seeking again to take an equal part in the conversation.

Holmes snorted. "Oh, there you have the heart of it. Mycroft cannot even be precise as to which deaths we can attribute to Dry. A dozen are certain. He has been known to use knife, garrote, revolver – whatever was required. He leaves no fingerprints, no evidence of any value even to Sherlock Holmes."

"Perhaps this assassin doesn't really exist, as such" I mused. "Forgive me, Holmes, but your brother gives little away, and can be devilishly obtuse. Might not 'Edwin Dry' be a convenient term used when certain unpleasant course of action must be undertaken – by those in authority?"

"I once thought that possible myself – but sometimes I feel him, Watson. I feel him in the shadow of Christchurch, and by the Wapping docks – across the broad estuary, and in the most sordid of alleys . . . he is there, a dark-eyed Angel of Death."

Rarely had I heard my friend speak of any adversary in such fanciful terms.

"Why have you never even hinted of this man, in all our years together? I would have expected a passing mention, at least."

"Have I not? Do you recall our taking of Colonel Sebastian Moran, when I showed you the entry for him in my index of bibliographies?"

"I could hardly forget, Holmes. You had just returned – seemingly from the dead."

"And what had I written next to Moran's entry?"

It seemed an odd question, but that day was etched into my memory.

"Why you had written '*The second most dangerous man in London*', the first being of course Professor – "

"Let me stop you there, Watson. The good Professor was three years dead when I added that note of mine – hardly a danger any more. So to whom might I have been referring?"

"Good God."

"Precisely. However, Merivale is worried, and rightly so. I will consider this one investigation, in the hope that I am correct, that this is all deception. And to avoid the inspector here stumbling upon something which puts him on the same mortuary slab as von Kleber."

Merivale took this sentiment with apparent discomfort, but nodded.

"Thank you, Mr. Holmes."

Those days – those long days. Holmes used me and protected me in equal measure. I was sent, muffled and inconspicuous, to gather idle talk amongst some his underworld contacts, but never to speak directly of Deptford or explain myself. I was only to seek rumours of quiet recruitment to crime, of new strands being formed.

We met quietly at Holmes's chambers from time to time, and my friend amused himself by solving a couple of minor cases for Merivale, in order to free that worthy for more important matters. Cerebral assistance was the lot of Merivale, which irked me somewhat – though I did, I admit, come to agree that the inspector was certainly a cut above his colleagues.

It was an odd time, for though I had known my friend to disappear into the alleys and more sordid parts of the city for days on end, I was less used to such a game. I was a soldier far from his regiment, a scout sent into unknown territory. This was London, the proud and prosperous capital of an Empire, and yet my time with Holmes had shown me many dark places – the opium dens, the low taverns and squalid tenements . . . and my scouting was done always at night.

I was no master of disguise, but I borrowed clothes from my daily's husband, an affable fellow who worked as a jobbing gardener, and made myself less of a doctor, and more of a street-hawker or barrowman seeking a quiet pint of ale.

And I did have "native" help. A limping girl named Charlie, known to Holmes through his "Irregulars", guided me between doss house and workhouse. She vouched for me in certain doorways and in the alleys behind taverns. She was bright, eyes sharp beneath matted black hair, and more than once I tried to determine more about her – but she never took the bait. I would have said she was thirteen, fourteen years old.

"Hoxey's Rooms," she would say. "Coinin', an' the beast with two backs. Ma Hoxey'll slit yer for thruppence and yer boots."

Or "The Good Admiral. Lascars, false papers for Jack Tars, an' gin as would blind an helerphant."

I paid her for every outing, though my ready pocket made her suspicious of my wants. A hand meant friendly on her thin shoulders one night was taken as an advance, a response which shocked me. She saw this, and was almost a little girl for one brief moment.

"Sorry, Watson, ol' chap." she said, in a passable imitation of Holmes.

We smiled at each other, and after that the hunt went well.

On our fifth scouting mission, Charlie found me O'Leary's Men, on the edge of Deptford – as close as Holmes would have me go.

These were London Irish for the most part, an undoubted gang. From the girl's mouth, they were involved in every kind of minor crime that could be imagined, but avoided the Fenians or anything which might put blood on their hands.

Colm O'Leary looked me over as we sat in a public house off Creek Lane, the building itself an older remnant pressed between tar works and cheap boarding houses.

"And would I not be rolling you for your wallet and watch, Doctor, if Charlie girl here couldn't vouch for you? A risky business, asking what you does." He turned a greasy cap in big, oil-stained fingers. Had my friend been there, no doubt he could have told me precisely what the Irishman had been up to. "A man has to be careful these days."

I bought whisky for him and his immediate companions, and we sat beneath a sputtering gaslight, staring at each other.

"Sure, and do I not have a liking for your Mr. Holmes?" he said at last. "The Blessed Mary Herself would weep to see men set against each other as they are these days."

"In what way, Mr. O'Leary?"

"Colm, me boy, just Colm. And as for ways, why, were my own lads not pushed and pressed to leave me, not this last Sunday?"

I leaned in, forced the thin whisky down, and listened. By the broaching of a second bottle of spirits, O'Leary was in full flow . . . .

" . . . right under the nose of a sergeant, would you believe, Johnny-boy? And they say the Gully Bleeders must pay a handsome cut now, to this feller you seek – but never to him direct, mind. There's always one or three between."

He painted a damning picture of gangs and their deeds – rarely murder, as at St. Pancras, but threats and intimidation, beatings – and at the centre . . . .

"They're calling him 'The Man from Deptford'," said O'Leary. "But a goat can call itself a plough-horse, and still not turn a field." Laughed uproariously at his own wit, he slammed his glass on the table – and then gave me a dark, steady look.

"Johnny-boy, there was such a man. And for all I know, he's still with us. Edwin Dry, and surely was he not the death of any feller as met him?"

"But?"

The Irishman shook his head, slow and doleful.

"I have me doubts. Honest to God, would I be a-sitting here with a fine feller such as yourself, speaking such tattle, if I thought the Deptford Assassin was near me door?"

"An impostor, then? Can you give me a name?" I reached under my greatcoat, and drawing out five sovereigns, I placed them on the grimy table.

The gas seemed lower, the room cold. O'Leary and his companions had eyes only for the coins. Charlie was by the door, looking ready to run.

A hand twice the size of mine covered the sovereigns.

"Samuel Gethins," said O'Leary, his voice now deep and steady, as if the whisky had been water. "That's a name, whether false or not. And if it's known I told you so, you'll find a different greeting on my streets, Johnny-boy."

My delight at having something more than rumour to share with my friend was short-lived, for when I returned to 221b Baker Street in the early hours of the morning, Mrs. Hudson was already at the street door, her face pale and a hat placed crooked over her hairnet.

"Oh, Dr. Watson, what a blessing! I was just about to seek help. Mr. Holmes is injured."

I ran up the stairs, ignoring my aches, to burst into our old rooms. Merivale was there, dishevelled, with his hands in a bowl of bloody water

– as he saw me and lifted them out, it was obvious that he had sustained a long, shallow cut across the back of them. Holmes lay back in his chair, his face lined, but his eyes were open.

"What in God's name has happened?" I cried.

Holmes gave a tired smile. "Nothing too dramatic, old chap. Mrs. Hudson will over-react."

"So you say."

I went over to him, checking for injury and feeling his pulse. Unsteady, but not weak. He had a bruise at one temple, and his jacket was slashed across the shoulder – no blood, though.

"We came close," said Merivale, drying his hands and peering to see if the bleeding had stopped.

"I have iodine for that, and a dressing," I said, hunting out the old medical bag which I kept at Holmes's rooms for such situations.

"An ugly bravo with a knife." The inspector let me minister to him, and I was relieved to see that stitches would not be needed. "Caught me by luck."

Whilst the officer had the more obvious wound, my eye was still on Holmes.

"Were you knocked out, Holmes? Are you hurt elsewhere?"

My friend raised both long hands, seeking to pacify me.

"Watson, I have had far worse. A scuffle, at a public house in Rotherhithe. One of my questions must have hit a nerve."

Mrs. Hudson, now less anxious, brought hot tea and heavily-buttered toast, insisting that we all three partake, nor would she leave until we began to do so.

"I have a name," I said, more ravenous than I had thought.

"Gethins," said Holmes.

"Why, yes. But – "

"Oh, my dear fellow, no need to look so crestfallen. Quite the contrary. If that is the name you have unearthed, entirely separately from our own endeavours, then you have done excellent service, do you see? This is corroboration." He passed his cigarette case around, and between gulps of tea, recounted his exploits with the inspector.

It seemed that Merrivale had taken a more heavy-handed route than mine, with Holmes deliberately in his shadow. Fences and coiners, buck cabbies and cracksmen – all had been questioned, some against their will. They had heard rumours of gangs and spheres of influence, but nothing concrete.

And then last night, tracking down a prospective informant to Southwark, they had been lured east, and ended up behind a low place called The Queen's Head, to be set upon by four ruffians.

"They were powerful men, all armed," said Holmes, "but inexpert. My Baritsu and the inspector's cane were adequate to preserve us."

"But not adequate for complete success." Merrivale sounded, rueful. "They managed to flee, but in worse condition than you find us."

Holmes nodded. "However, I was able to pin Jackie Weng, not unknown in Limehouse, against a wall for a few vital seconds. And Jackie, though a heavy-fisted brute and a captain of thuggery, has less sense than my Persian slipper.

"'What is behind this, Jackie?' I demanded. 'That you work far from your patch, and risk assaulting Sherlock Holmes?'

"'I'll not talk,' he gasped. 'Gethins would kill me.'

"At that point, one of the others smote me across the head with his billy-club. Merivale surged forth, giving the man a crack in return with his cane, and they fled."

"Good heavens." I poured more tea, stewed though it was by now. I remembered Weng from the affair of Lord Saltersley's salver – the man was no more Chinese than was I, but by some trick of the physiognomy, or even long-lost ancestry, managed to pass himself off as such.

I recounted my own painstaking trail with the girl, Charlie, and how I had ended up with O'Leary's Men. Holmes clicked his tongue in annoyance and I asked what I had done wrong.

"You? Oh, my apologies, Watson. I was thinking of the girl – she has a fine mind, a brave spirit, and yet she will not be raised from the streets. I have twice found her a position, only to have her run."

Perhaps the last few nights had taught me more than I thought. For although I have been told that I am by nature somewhat conservative and conventional, I had watched the girl, and listened to her. That which might seem opportunity to us could easily be viewed as servitude by her . . . .

"Samuel Gethins," I said, trying to concentrate. Despite the excitement, I was bone-weary. I answered Holmes's every question, along with a few from Merivale, and for two hours we pooled our intelligence on the situation. The inspector added summaries of police reports, until at last we had a single tapestry.

"We have been here before, Holmes," I said, surveying the scribbles notes across the table.

"Not quite, my dear Watson," said he. "There is no Napoleon of Crime here, not even a de Grouchy or Massena." He smiled at the inspector's blank expression. "An old case, Merivale, long buried. But Watson's comment is apt. It appears to be true – someone in London seeks to pull together many gangs and small fraternities, many illicit ventures, to create an organisation of sorts, a network for the co-ordination of crime.

We see it, gentlemen, in its infancy – a child who reaches for its blocks, not yet fully conversant with its alphabet."

The inspector frowned. "And St. Pancras?"

"A block which fell by accident – and fortuitously for us, alerted us to the greater danger."

"This is the work of Edwin Dry?"

Holmes's lips took a sour turn. "Surely not. It is the work of one or more who steal Dry's reputation, and use it to compel those too impressionable or afraid to realise the absurdity of it all." His barked laugh was as bitter as his smile. "Why should the man who murdered Frederick Caille and his associates, who put an end to the White . . . well, never mind. It is a subterfuge. And a most risky subterfuge, at that."

I could barely keep my eyes open.

"Because this gang-master has drawn the attention of Sherlock Holmes?"

"No, Watson. Because if he is not careful, he may draw the attention of the true Deptford Assassin."

I slept until the early evening on Holmes's divan, awakened by the aroma of sausages, kidneys, and chops. Merivale was eating heartily. Holmes, who rarely ate when at the highpoint of a case, was poring over newspaper clippings and journals in the corner.

"Doctor – there is enough for half-a-dozen men here," said the inspector. I joined him, suddenly famished. As I finished my first plateful, Holmes lit his pipe, and sat back at the old chemistry table.

"Interesting. I do not, as I first supposed, believe Gethins to be an alias. There are mentions of a Scottish fence and general ne'er-do-well, Angus Gethins, in '77. He fell foul of Inspector Gally of Southwark. I thought the name vaguely familiar – it is not common. Our Samuel Gethins may be son or nephew to the man, though neither Angus nor the inspector are with us now. Angus is buried at Holy Trinity Church in Rotherhithe, a generous stone's throw from Deptford."

Merivale skewered half a sausage. "Where would we find Samuel? South of the river, clearly."

"As to that," said Holmes, "I have a theory, one which takes us back to Frederick Caille. Mycroft assures me that the case was still ascribed to the Deptford Assassin on the streets, long after 'educated' public opinion had moved on. A peculiarity, almost an amusing one, that only the highest and lowest in the land are certain of Edwin Dry's existence."

"Surely the papers – " I began.

"Watson, the papers are owned and edited by men, often men of more power than integrity. Do you think they consider their own lives so disposable that they would risk a professional killer's direct attention? Better to serve up other rumours, and name those who cannot hurt them."

I had been carrying one question for many days, and could no longer hold it in.

"Do you, too, fear him, Holmes?"

"I do not. Nor does my brother. But the man we speak of is . . . a force of nature. A fire set to clear the undergrowth – a bolt of lightning, directed by such rods as others erect. I am cautious, informed, and aware, which is what is needed. You and Merivale, however . . . ."

"You do not trust us, sir?" The inspector blinked.

"He looks to our welfare," I said before Holmes could answer. "Lest we – by accident – call down the tempest and perish by it."

Holmes gave a sharp laugh. "This becomes too fanciful, gentlemen. I should have known not to encourage Watson into metaphor or simile. Let us be plain – we deal with a bold impostor who toys with crime across our city, and it is surely our task to interrupt his plans before they mature."

"You spoke of a theory?"

"I did, Watson. First of all, see the map that Merivale and I have marked."

On the table where my friend usually conducted his noxious chemical experiments, they had pinned a map of central London, a map stuck with a bewildering array of further pins with coloured heads. The meaning of the colours eluded me, but I could see how the density increased as Deptford was approached, save for a broad area where not a single pin stood, close to the Thames."

"That blank, Watson, is the immediate vicinity of the Royal Victoria Victualling Yard. And I have made some enquiries. It so happens that the offices in which Caille and his fellows were killed are no longer in use – possibly this relates to the memories of what occurred there. The offices lie on the edge of the Yard, and are now only popular with rats and spiders. If Gethins seeks to bolster his imposture and his reputation, then where better to secrete himself?

"The Yard is home to hundreds of workmen and clerks coming and going, a flood of humanity easily used to cover comings and goings, and movement of purloined goods. Furthermore, it lies near streets which are almost rookeries, along with railway yards, manufacturing works, and warehouses. A moderately clever man could both hide himself there, and use its history to reinforce fear of 'The Man from Deptford'."

Over a period of two weeks, I had seen Merivale at the most peculiar hours, and yet had spoken to him little.

"What do you think, Inspector?"

He did not seem happy.

"When first I came to Mr. Holmes for advice on certain other cases, I sought a scientific mind, one which might advance the field of police investigations. And I found it. By God, I found it." He dipped his head to Holmes. "But this latest situation . . . I am unused to so much wild conjecture. Do we raid the Victualling Yard, with all the outcry that would cause? And the possibility that we chase a goose which is not there? Do we send word to Mr. Holmes's brother, or press the Commissioner on this matter? I confess I feel out of my depth."

"I often am with Holmes," I offered.

The two tall, lean men regarded each other. Some strange telepathy must have occurred, for both of them nodded almost imperceptibly at the same time.

"Your service revolver, I think, Watson. Sturdy boots and dark clothes. Tomorrow night we shall visit the Royal Victoria Victualling Yard at Deptford, and prove or disprove my theory."

Each scrawny cat, each dog that did not growl, but stayed silent in its alley. Each stumbling drunk and thin-shawled prostitute . . . I was being watched. We were being watched.

I couldn't shake the prickle of it as we slipped between street-lamps, picking the quietest lanes and narrowest routes to the Victualling Yard. My two companions seemed unaffected, but twice, thrice, I felt that I had a second shadow. Mug-hunters? O'Leary's Men? Agents of Samuel Gethins? I had no idea.

Holmes had explained that we must avoid the official entrance, where watchmen and late shift workers would be found, and we passed that by, going by a public house called The Evelyn Arms and north. Coming at the Yard from that direction, we made a little-used gate by a small wet-dock, left over from Navy days, which would be our entrance. From there we were to shadow the river, moving along the rear of warehouses and thus down to the block of disused offices in question.

I would have been little more surprised to see the Foreign Secretary than I was to find the girl, Charlie, waiting for us by the gate.

"Merely our lookout," he murmured, seeing my worried expression. "And our key."

At his nod, she clambered easily up the crumbling masonry, and slipped her thin body over the top of the wooden gate itself, which did not meet the arch in which it was set. No adult could have managed such a thing. Bolts grated, and the gate was open.

"A talented girl," said Holmes.

Inside, Charlie was admonished to stay where she was, concealed, and only to whistle a warning if she saw anyone come that way, blocking our planned route of exit.

"I have read certain files which I should not," said Merrivale, keeping his voice low. He was walking in a nervous crouch, turning his head from side to side. "They say that sixteen years ago, the assassin must have gone bold through the length of the Yard, have done his deed, and then strolled away. No one noticed him. No one ever seems to notice him."

"Three men are rather more obvious," murmured Holmes, "Keep to the shadows, behind that old sugar warehouse, and there are the offices we seek. You know the layout."

He had sketched it for us back in his rooms. A discrete side entrance led to corridors and rows of small offices for clerks, and finally the larger office of – once – an Assistant Victualling Officer. In the antechamber to that room, two bravos and a corrupt police constable in the magnate's pay had met their ends, whilst Caille himself had been killed just outside, apparently attempting to escape. Such events certainly gave the sprawling building an unwholesome feel.

Holmes's picks opened the side door easily – and as he eased it open an inch or two, I immediately saw two heavy-set ruffians at the end of this first corridor, a good thirty feet from where we waited and looking away from us.

We were armed, but could only fire *in extremis,* for the sound of shots would rouse the night shifts around the Yard and all manner of attention. We were, in many ways, common burglars. If Holmes and I might be able to bluster, Merivale, with no official case, would be in serious trouble – unless we found substantial evidence of illegal activities.

The men laughed, sharing a jug, and turned the corner, out of sight.

"Is this enough to draw in the official force?" I whispered. "There is clearly something amiss."

"And what if those are talleymen for one of the night shifts, warming their bellies, or two foremen with a quarter-hour free?" Holmes slid the door open further. "No, we must see more."

He was first inside, his bullseye lantern low, and went directly into the first of the cramped offices. We followed. A broken chair, dust, and the corpse of a rat long-dead. The following room, its door closed but not locked, was more to my friend's liking – baled tobacco and smaller crates of brandy – fine brandy if the labels were genuine.

"Contraband, surely, at least," I began. "It is a start – "

And there our venture was taken from our hands, for we heard a long, low whistle from outside – Charlie's agreed signal that were other men abroad.

Merrivale raised his cane and ran to the corridor, which proved a far worse move than crouching in cover and hoping to be overlooked. I heard shouts, a grunt of pain, and could see no course but to go after him . . . .

Jackie Weng was against the wall, winded, but the inspector was on his knees, a curved dagger in his shoulder.

"You scoundrel!" I lurched forward and felled Weng with a blow from my blackthorn stick. Other hands gripped my shoulders and then relented as Holmes tussled with a second ruffian who had assaulted me. His opponent was heavy and yet fast, giving Holmes a hard time, until a small figure leapt into the corridor and drove a pair of rusty scissors into the man's calf muscle.

"Charlie!" I gasped. "Alert the watch! Fetch the constabulary!"

She hesitated, but ran from the building.

And I was soon glad that I had driven her so, for a moment later the two men we had seen before came running around the corner from further within the building. One had a double-barrelled pistol held steady, the other a knife so long it was almost a bayonet.

"Hold!" The pistol-man, broad-cheeked and with a scarred lip, had his aim in on me.

Holmes stopped, as did I.

Merivale was bleeding but conscious. Jackie Weng was insensible, and the third man lay on the tiled floor, clutching his leg and moaning.

"Ben Maudsley." Holmes sighed. "I thought you still in Leeds Gaol."

"Out this last fortnight, Mr. Holmes, and onto a good one this time. I does work for The Man from Deptford now."

"Are you so sure?"

The scarred man shrugged. "Whatever name he uses, it suits me, if me cut is fair and dandy."

"You think your employer is the Deptford Assassin?" Holmes gave one of his harsh, barked laughs. "Oh, Maudsley, let the true Edwin Dry hear that proud claim, and you will have no throat by dawn."

"Ah, mebbe he's gorn, how does I know?" said Maudsley, though his voice was not so steady as before. "But enough prattle, you. I does have a proper master who will want to see such as you."

"Samuel Gethins."

"What he calls hi'self to such as us, who is close with him. He does know his business, that's what matters." He kicked the inspector, who fell on his side, unmoving. I made to help Merivale but the third man was up, limping, and drew my arms behind my back. The pistol did not waver.

"The police will be here any minute," said Holmes. "You may yet go down as dupes and thieves, not murderers."

Maudsley advanced. "They'll find ways to make me dance this time, so does I care? If they take me, I'll be the man as took down Mr. Sherlock Holmes, so – "

I confess it took me a second to understand what happened next. As bright blood gushed and sprayed the nearest whitewashed wall, some calmer part of me, always the medical man, observed its origin as Maudlsey's common carotid artery, a half-inch before that vessel forms its dependent internal and external branches . . . .

Then comprehension came – the hilt of a slender throwing knife stood proud from the man's neck. The pistol fell from his clutching hands, whilst his companion, white-faced, cursed and chose to slam past us, escaping out into the Yard. One ruffian only remained, and Holmes turned and drove his elbow into that man's face, crushing his nose and dropping him.

I stumbled to Merivale, who was breathing.

"A shoulder wound, Holmes," I said. "Shock and blood loss, but not fatal. What do we do?"

"We wait," he replied. "You saw that blade, sent silent and with deadly accuracy."

"Yes, but wait for what?"

My hands were trembling, shame to say, and I thought I heard a police whistle in the distance. I know that immediately after that there came a cry from further within the building, but Holmes's raised hand bid me stay. The cry was neither one of alarm, nor one of surprise.

It was a scream of terror.

When all was silent save for the inspector's laboured breathing, Holmes nodded at me.

"Now we go forward, and see how the game has played out."

This time we advanced with our revolvers ready, into the next corridor. We checked each room, I to the left, Holmes to the right, until I was faced with the main office. The double doors were wide open, the antechamber apparently empty . . . .

I was the first of us to reach Samuel Gethins, who had been so foolish as to present himself as "The Man from Deptford". His body was propped in plain sight behind an oaken desk which had once been of some quality, though now cobwebbed and wormed. Beyond the chair in which he sat, a broad window stood open to the night.

My examination was brief, and I had completed it before Holmes strode into the room.

"Dead, though still warm as life," I said. "One blow from an extremely sharp knife, directly into the heart from beneath. Instantly fatal."

"Much as I expected." Holmes peered at what might be a calling-card, positioned squarely on the desk. He picked the card up with finger and thumb, using his handkerchief, and examined it by his lantern.

"Common heavy stock, from any stationer, neither the cheapest nor the most expensive. Indian ink, perfect copperplate writing. Look, Watson – no indented letters, no stress on any particular word, no sign of emotion. It is from the man himself."

He turned the object so that I might read its face:

> *This man need concern you no more, Mr. Holmes. Why rouse the hangman, when I am to hand?*

"He is the Devil!" I said, caught between card and corpse as to which I found the most chilling.

"He is a criminal. But he is correct – our chase is done.

Holmes paid the body no attention, but padded around the edges of the room, his gaze darting everywhere.

"Footprints," he announced. "But what footprints! Light, featureless . . . ." He took forceps from his jacket, and picked up a miniscule scrap of something. "Layers of latex. Our assassin coats his boots with latex. A quiet step, and the option to peel away the latex afterwards. He will never be identified by his footwear, nor will the latex show any distinctive properties when analysed. I would posit that his clothing is constantly brushed, to leave no telltale fibres or – "

"Holmes, we must see to Merivale."

"Of course. And let the constabulary swarm here – their hobnailed boots can do no damage. There will be nothing else to be found."

Back in the first corridor, the inspector was breathing more easily. The flow of blood had ceased. I helped him to his feet, only paused by the realisation that the dagger had gone from Ben Maudsley's throat.

Jackie Weng had not regained consciousness, whilst the other ruffian slouched sullen, clutching his wounded leg. Our expressions silenced any comment from him.

We made the open, with the inspector propped between us, just as dawn began to finger the Yard. Coopers, butchers, and apprentices – turning up for their daily shift – stared at the three of us, but already the shrill of whistles possessed the Yard. Two night watchmen, then constables, and finally a police sergeant, came to us in swift succession, until we stood in a circle of interest. A doctor was called, and a police van. The watchmen dispersed the crowd, whilst the policemen were sent, at Merivale's gasped order, to secure the abandoned offices.

And I am sure that I saw a small, ragged figure in the crowd, a thin face with a smile upon it. We owed her at least a new pair of scissors . . . .

Merivale licked dry lips. "Gethins?"

"Dead," said Holmes.

As soon as we were sure that the inspector was in no danger, and would receive proper treatment, Holmes and I slipped away into the tangle of Deptford. It should not take long to find a cab to take us back to Baker Street without fuss or further questions.

We stood not far from The Evelyn Arms, watching labourers trickle out, readied for a long working day by sausages, bread, and beer.

"This business is closed, then," I said. "And the St. Pancras case as well."

"What?" Holmes jerked from reverie. "Ah, yes. It is, Watson. A criminal conspiracy revealed and broken. A form of justice done, I suppose."

"Dry . . . do you suppose that he has been watching us, all this time? Waiting to see what move we – you – made."

"I am certain of it."

"Yet his intervention saved our lives."

He gave an exasperated gasp. "Watson, you persist in misreading the world according to your own generous spirit. He had clearly decided that Ben Maudsley and Samuel Gethins were to be removed – if we had any relevance at all, it was that we provided a convenient opening, a distraction. Consider this – the ink on that card was not wet!"

"I don't . . . oh."

A plan long made, the outcome certain. That was a dark and sobering thought.

"What sort of mind could such a creature have? If he truly exists, his deeds are almost inconceivable. Surely – "

"Mind?" Holmes had the strangest look upon his long face. "A truly rational mind, a focused one. Logical above all else, never yielding to common emotion. Unaffected by the praise or condemnation of others, and determined only to achieve each goal he sets himself."

"Almost a Moriarty?"

"No." That came out sharp, instant. "Professor Moriarty was all too human. He had his convoluted plans, his wish for mastery – and his frustrations, his petty angers at being thwarted. This man . . . ."

His shoulders slumped, his face betraying that utter weariness which sometimes took him when a case was over, and I raised one arm high to signal the empty hansom cab which just then came trotting around the corner. But before we stepped into the cab, He looked to me and placed one hand on my arm.

"This Edwin Dry . . . ." He tightened his grip for a heartbeat before letting go. "Perhaps he is the monster I might have become, did I not have my Watson."

I could not bring myself to answer him, to argue either way.

The hansom rattled over cobbled streets, leaving Deptford and all it held behind us. The air smelled of tar and chimney smoke, of the great Thames and the dirt-strewn streets of London. But there would be kippers for breakfast at Baker Street, and hot tea, Mrs. Hudson's worried smile of welcome, and a chance to unlace my boots.

A small, comforting world, where no assassin trod . . . .

"In the St. Pancras case you may remember that a cap was found beside the dead policeman. The accused man denies that it is his. But he is a picture-frame maker who habitually handles glue."

"Is it one of your cases?"

"No; my friend, Merivale, of the Yard, asked me to look into the case . . . ."

– Sherlock Holmes and Dr. John H. Watson
"Shoscombe Old Place"

The Case of the Impossible Assassin
by Paula Hammond

A man's days are rarely his own – but a married man's are so filled with the pleasures of being friend, husband, provider, and protector, that the past few months had passed in a whirl. Work and home had become the steady metronome of my life, and so settled was I in this new rhythm that I had barely seen my dear friend, Sherlock Holmes. It was, then, with considerable surprise that I opened a telegram to find the following:

> *I travel tonight on the 7 p.m. boat train to Paris. If your wife can spare you for a fortnight, I am in urgent need of my Watson. Bring winter clothing, climbing boots, your revolver, and medical bag. A carriage is reserved.*

Holmes never writes when a telegram will serve and mysterious missives from him were nothing new. I stared at it a while, wondering what strange adventures it might foretell, before passing it across the breakfast table to my wife.

"What do you think?" she asked. "Will you go?"

I shook my head. "Why, my dear, anyone would think that you're tired of me already!"

"Why certainly!" she smiled, delighted at the joke. "How on earth is a woman supposed to get her new home just-so when her new husband is forever under her feet?"

"Well, you did say that you were thinking of inviting your mother to stay to help with the refurbishing. Perhaps I should leave you two to your machinations . . . ." I trailed off laughing.

For a while we sat in silence, until my dearest picked up the telegram again and said, in that thoughtful way of hers, "In earnest, I would not have you abandon your oldest friend in his time of need. Besides, there is still a lot to be done, and I did promise mother a visit once we were settled . . . Perhaps you should take up the offer?"

While I had absolute trust in Dr. Walker to handle the practice in my absence, I was reluctant to abandon my little slice of matrimonial bliss so soon. Hot chocolate was served while we batted the subject back and forth until slowly my reservations abated, and I began to feel that old, familiar thrill stirring in my heart.

Military life had made me a ready traveller and by 6:50 p.m. I was at the station, my old knapsack slung across one shoulder. Holmes had already secured our carriage and, minutes later, I was seated opposite him, exchanging heart-felt greetings.

Slowly, the great glass canopy of Charing Cross Station gave way to rows of sooty terraces and neat urban farms and, soon, we were steaming towards Dover – and adventures yet to come.

It had been a busy time for Holmes with the affair of the Abbey School, the case of poor Lance-Corporal Emsworth, and a commission from the Sultan of Turkey to occupy his finely-tuned mind. And it was of this final, and most mysterious affair, that he now began to speak.

"I must apologize, Watson, for the suddenness of my telegram," he said. "I've been keeping this pot warm for far too long and it has now reached the point where if I do not give it the attention it needs – and in person – the consequences may be catastrophic."

I regarded him – that languid pose, those cool grey eyes with their far-away look – and it seemed inconceivable that one racing towards a case with such weighty consequences could appear so calm. However I knew that, while Holmes could be quite the dramatist, he rarely used hyperbole.

I soon learned that it was to Constantinople we were bound – a journey of sixty-seven hours forty-six minutes from Paris Gare du Nord, according to *Bradshaw's*. London to Dover would take us two hours. Add another one-hour-twenty-five for the Channel crossing. Almost three days! I'd been looking forward to a restful journey, but now I was pleased that I'd thought to pack the back issues of *The British Medical Journal* that I'd been studiously ignoring since my honeymoon!

Holmes stretched out his long legs on the padded bench seat, his own traveling bag stashed behind his head as a makeshift pillow. I was less inclined to use the railway's upholstery in such a cavalier fashion, but made myself as comfortable as I could while Holmes told me what he knew of the case.

"You will no doubt have heard of the First Congress?" he began.

"Republicans, aren't they?" I hazarded, wishing I'd paid more attention to the political pages.

"Ostensibly a collection of liberals fighting for the return of Turkish parliamentary democracy. They held their first meeting in Paris last year."

"Intent on the over-throw of the crown?"

"Hardly. They simply want representation. They have a good-deal of public support too and, on Mycroft's urging, our own government has been discreetly encouraging dialogue between the two parties. Besides, the Sultan is hardly a model ruler."

"Oh? I thought he was considered quite the reformer?"

"He has done much good, but behind the scenes – ? There are rumors. Dark stuff. Mass disappearances. In some quarters he's referred to as 'The Scarlet Sultan' – although I emphasize that these are rumors. Even Mycroft's spiderish network has been unable to discern how much truth there is behind the accusations – and if true – how much the Sultan knows and how much can be laid at the feet of over-zealous panjandrums. One thing is certain: His secret police have too much influence, too little restraint, and the First Congress are in their sights."

"Dangerous?"

Holmes paused, clearly debating exactly how much he could reveal. "This is certainly a delicate situation. We will be working at the behest of the Sultan, and on the recommendation of the British ambassador. That affords us some surety. However, the Sultan's behaviour of late has been irrational. He fears revolution. Mycroft fears that both foreign and Turkish agents are muddying the waters, and manipulating the situation to their own advantage. My brother describes the situation as a primed powder-keg."

"And the *situation*?"

With one of his characteristic bursts of energy, Holmes swung his legs off the seat and bolted upright, his eyes sparkling with that dry glitter which materialized whenever his intellect was challenged.

"Watson!" he said, leaning forwards, his voice a tense whisper. "In all my years investigating the strange and seemingly unfathomable, I have never heard the like! Two of the Sultan's closest advisors – dead – and in circumstances that make the word 'bizarre' seem too commonplace!

"Let me lay it out for you, if I may? I've been so long alone with my thoughts that your clarity and common-sense are much-needed."

I accepted the complement with keen pleasure and I set myself to pay particular attention.

"The commission landed at my door two weeks ago, while I was busy on the Emsworth case. I managed to beg seven day's grace from Dodd to make what plans I could, though I knew I would be unable to travel to Constantinople before today. However, I haven't been idle and here, Watson, we have luck on our side. It seems that detective 'fiction' –" He coughed out the phrase. " – is all the rage in Constantinople. Their chief Investigating Officer, Detective Münif, is an ardent fan of your writing and a devoted student of my techniques. I have been provided with the most complete case notes – and every assistance – but clarity still eludes me.

“The victims had been on a hunting trip on the slopes of Mount Kartepe, which lies to the east of Constantinople. The region is mostly thick forest – ancient hazelnut, oak, and chestnut – with one small village perched precariously on side of the mountain. Locally the area’s known as the Snow Hills, but the weather this year has been so unpredictable that heavy snowstorms have travelled as far as the metropolis. The men were therefore well-prepared for and – indeed – expecting the worst. But when their bodies were found, they were stark naked!

“Münif has been thorough, meticulously measuring, cataloguing, and recording everything before allowing the bodies to be removed. He has also provided me with photographs of the scene, and the tale these tell is most remarkable.

“Footprints suggest that the victims set off from camp at a veritable sprint, clearly barefooted, but wearing undershirts – cotton fibers were found snagged on the undergrowth. Crushed and broken foliage attests to the fact that they ran desperately, frantically, seemingly without purpose or plan. One of them looks to have fallen down a steep incline, grasping at the earth, pulling up handfuls of frozen grass to slow his descent as he tumbled. Another clearly collided with a tree during his flight – blood on the trunk at head height indicates the severity of the impact. Yet according to locals, the moon was full, and the men knew the terrain well enough to be aware of its dangers.

“Later, the two re-grouped and doubled-back, returning to the tent, one helping support his injured companion. Perhaps they felt the danger had passed and hoped to return to their shelter? If so, they were out of luck. Their tent had been shredded, their supplies burnt.

“It was back at camp, when they should have been safe, that the fatal blow fell. The snow in one spot becomes a riot of confusion – doused in blood. Buffoons in hunting pink would have made a less grisly mess!

“It was there, on the edge of this melee, that their bodies were discovered. Frozen, with bloodied knuckles, bruised skin, and broken teeth suggesting that, in this moment of *extremis*, they had fought for their lives – fought like wild animals – with an enemy that left no tracks behind. No signs at all. And curiouser still was the fact that, in the midst of this life-or-death battle, they found the time to tear off their remaining clothes, for their naked corpses were found lying beside their be-grimed undershirts.

“But, Oh! Watson! What turned the rescue party sick to the stomach wasn’t the horror of the scene. No, they were hardened men, fresh from military service. What shocked them were the victim’s expressions. Naked terror. That’s how and they described it. Pure, naked terror.”

“Good Lord!” I exclaimed, horrified. “Wolves? Bears?” I had no idea what wildlife might make its home in these frosty uplands.

"The men had guns. It's unlikely they would have been caught unawares."

"So it's murder, then?"

"It is possible." He paused, lips pursed, as though running through all the permutations of the puzzle. "There are factions upon factions. Anything is possible. Although if murder it is, it's one of the strangest I've ever encountered. The bodies have been kept on ice and I hope, my dear Watson, to employ your expertise here."

"And what if it is the First Congress?"

"Mycroft feels that highly unlikely. They're intellectuals, not revolutionaries, but a pogrom against them would suit many. Foreign agents, as well as those within the country, who fear change. We must tread carefully."

It was not unusual for Holmes to be embroiled in the affairs of state but, suddenly, I felt the weight of his words and my mind reeled.

I believe he was sensitive to the fact, for throughout the rest of the journey, he worked hard to keep me distracted. Holmes could be an entertaining companion when the mood took him and, with my dear friend driving the conversation, my misgivings quickly evaporated.

In a few hours, suburban brick changed to well-hedged fields and soon the cry of seagulls could be heard on the wind. The train pulled up at Dover Harbor and we headed for the promenade dock, embarked on the paddle steamer, and from there onto Paris.

The majestic Gare du Nord is one of the world's busiest and perhaps one of its most beautiful stations. London's great eastern terminus, King's Cross, boasts a glass-roofed train shed nearly seven-hundred-feet long and one-hundred-feet high, but it is still a dark and gloomy beast, seeming to trap in both steam and smoke. Paris' grand station is an altogether airier affair, bathed in natural light from rows of soaring windows, and its own glass and cast-iron roof.

Scottish engineering can take some of the credit for the construction, as its vast girders were made in Glasgow, but French design dominates the whole. It's that, I think, which gives it a lightness of touch and an elegance that's lacking from its British counterparts. In truth, London stations are merely the helpmates of the Empire. Paris' are its galleries.

It was night by the time we arrived in the capital, and the station was illuminated by lanes of gently buzzing electric lights which painted the brickwork a subtle yellow hue. Twenty-three statues stand atop the terminus' triumphal arch, each personifying a different European city. It seemed to me like a stage, set as if for a performance, and I had the odd fancy that the statues were actors, waiting in the wings for their cues.

We took the time to purchase refreshments from one of the many vendors milling around the concourse so that it was close to midnight when we boarded that icon of exoticism: The Orient Express.

I later discovered that the price of a direct ticket between Paris and Constantinople was a quarter of the annual income for the average British worker. Whether our passage had been paid for by Holmes, Mycroft, or the Sultan, I never knew, and never asked, content simply to enjoy such unexpected comfort. Indeed, everything was so well appointed – and the day had been so full of activity – that it wasn't long before I was settled between the freshly-starched sheets and drifting gently off to sleep.

I dreamt of strange things. Tin spinning tops, in the shape of whirling dervishes, with a figure in the shadows pressing the top so that each squealed in distress as they spun. Giant eyes hanging in the sky like over-inflated moons, blinking down at my sleeping form. Then myself suffocating under blankets of snow, with Holmes adding ever more layers until I cried out and woke myself with a start.

Holmes was already awake, savoring a pot of fresh coffee. I helped myself to a cup and, as the world slowly came into focus, I regaled him with the details of my nocturnal adventures.

"Well, Watson," he chuckled, as was his habit when in high spirits, "I don't need to be Sigmund Freud to guess the meaning of such fevered nightmares! I have laid it on rather thickly, haven't I, my dear fellow? Murder and intrigue! Certainly enough to give anyone fever-dreams. Perhaps you'll allow me to stand you breakfast to apologize for my appalling behavior in your dream? Burying you alive indeed!" And with a bark of a laugh, he rang for fresh coffee, as I readied myself to face the day.

From the bright-white tablecloths to the glittering water decanters, the dining car was everything the well-heeled traveler might expect, but the menu surpassed itself. The galley – squeezed into one end of the dining car – may have been tiny but the chef's ambition was unbounded. British staples such as haddock, kidneys, kedgeree, porridge, poached egg, and bacon, sat alongside croissant, brioche, freshly-squeezed orange juice, and American dishes such as corn-pone which, despite the unappealing name, turned out to be a type of pancake served with maple syrup.

Having had little food the day before, Holmes and I ate with gusto and sat back to smoke with the blissfully unhurried air of men who, for the time being, had nowhere special to be.

During our long association, I often seen Holmes demonstrate his remarkable observational skills, but this morning his mood was so playful that his pronouncements seemed all the more amazing for the apparent lack of effort he expanded in their making.

"There," he whispered, sotto voce, "what do you make of him? Sharing the table with the Accidental Heiress and the Jilted Lover?"

I scanned the dining carriage but saw no one fitting those descriptions, which clearly delighted my companion.

"Young lady in bird's-egg blue with laughing eyes. She sits, stiffly, like someone at church waiting to be denounced for some wrong-doing by the vicar. And see how she fusses at the lace collar and cuffs? They're too tight, too starched, too new. New pearls as well. A piece of the string from the price tag still clings to the clasp. But that brooch? It's old, well-worn, very expensive. See, there! She glances around the carriage, notices the elderly lady in the gabardine hat, then looks at the brooch as though recalling the one who gave it to her. Look now, how she half-rises to help waitress with the dishes, then stops herself with a blush. She's more used to waiting than being waited on, I think. There – her hands. Neatly clipped nails, ruddy knuckles, a little swollen from relentless washing. A nurse or companion to an invalid, I'd vouch, now left a windfall in a will."

I followed his eye-line to the woman, who did appear woefully uncomfortable among such casual luxury.

"Now . . . there, opposite her. See? The Jilted Lover. Red-rimmed eyes. Dressed without care. See how he continually checks his watch? And in it, a small photograph. See how he smiles and sighs? Even one as unaccustomed to affairs of the heart as I am needs no further clues to tell me this man has a broken heart!

"That leaves the Sallow-Faced Man in the window seat, with the sunken eyes and exorbitant ears. Tell me, what do you make of him?"

I glanced across, scanning for those little clues that Holmes would have found so easily.

"A journalist?" I speculated.

"How so?"

"He's an observer. Interested in what's happening around him, but not partaking. Not a wealthy man, either, which would fit the profession. His cuffs are frayed and – look – the way he counts out the tip. Certainly on a budget. And – yes! As he opened his jacket just then, I saw a notebook. I'd warrant his passage has been paid for by some press agency wanting a piece on the lives of the rich and famous!"

Holmes nodded slowly . "Perfectly sound. But Watson, look again. See the shoes – the soles worn thin. This is a man who does much of his business on foot. See how his eyes dart around the carriage. How he starts at the slightest noise? As you say, he's an observer, but a furtive and highly-strung one. Look how he avoids eye-contact and presses himself into the seat, as though trying to become part of the upholstery. You saw him tipping the waitress, but what you took for penny-pinching was him merely sorting the *francs* from Turkish *lira*.

"Like the young lady, he isn't used to such elegant travel, but he carries an air of authority. Mayhap some of that comes from the small caliber revolver tucked in his pocket. He fingers it almost obsessively, especially whenever he looks in our direction. Or perhaps he carries it for self-defense? I noticed when he entered the carriage that he carries a wound on his shoulder – bullet or knife I cannot tell. Now, remove the whiskers and what have you? Does he remind you of anyone?"

"Why – Lestrade! The man has no physical similarity to the detective we know, but there is something in his bearing that reminds me of the Scotland Yard breed. Yet where Lestrade has loyalty and bull-dog grit, this man seems low and cunning. More than that – I'll vouch he's dangerous."

Holmes fixed his eyes upon me with an amused expression. "That is to be seen. But I think it's safe to say that we've had our first encounter with a member of The Scarlet Sultan's secret police."

Strasbourg, Munich, Vienna, Budapest, and Bucharest all rolled past, and with each arrival and departure, the character of the train shifted. Expressive Mediterraneans were replaced by taciturn Austria-Hungarians and, they, in turn, by neat and formal Asiatics. Hurried businessmen were replaced by wide-eyed tourists, and they in turn, by a more esoteric set. As we drew close to our final destination, it seemed that the whole train now comprised artists, explorers, and spiritualists – a veritable cult of those looking for the un-tangible in the trackless hills of Europe's furthest outpost.

Our meals were enlivened by this constant ebb-and-flow of humanity. Holmes's sharp wit was much employed in its dissection and, notwithstanding our now constant shadow, the journey passed pleasantly.

Constantinople's Sirkeci Station is a place where Europe and Asia collide and its architecture is an appropriate melding of European and Ottoman aesthetics. Swathes of rust-red brick surround wide, arched doorways, and stained-glass windows filter the daylight into colorful splashes of light.

When it opened in 1890, the station was considered a modern marvel. Today its gas lanterns and Austrian tile stoves already seemed quaint compared to the electrified magnificence of Gare du Nord but, even in the grip of winter, it was warm and inviting. Despite the crowds, everything was well-ordered and clean, with the scent of freshly-ground coffee permeating all.

Detective Münif turned out to be a petite man with a carefully trimmed beard, oiled hair, and a precisely-tailored pinstriped suit. He trotted rather than walked, and if it hadn't been for his facial hair and a certain sharpness about the eyes, I'd have taken him for an over-exited schoolboy playing at detective.

He extended his hand, making a ludicrous half-bow and clicking his heels, German-style. I took his hand, which he pumped up and down enthusiastically, his round face gleaming beatifically. "Mr. Watson! I take the liberty, I know!" he laughed, still pumping furiously. "Such an honor! Such an honor!" He bobbed his head once more then turned his attention to Holmes.

"And the detective himself! Such an honor! Such an honor!"

He babbled on in this vein for some time until Holmes managed to interject. "And when will we be meeting the Sultan?"

"No, no! No one sees the Sultan. However – " And here the little man bent down as if to pick up our bags and whispered in a conspiratorial tone, " – the Sultan sees everyone." He inclined his head in the direction of the Sallow-Faced Man who had dogged our tracks since Paris, "if you understand my meaning."

We allowed ourselves to be led to a rather preposterous-looking automobile known as a *limousine*. It wasn't until we were settled in its padded interior – the driver safely partitioned from us in his own separate compartment – that Münif stopped his effusive chatter.

"Oh gentlemen! Forgive me! I find the passion of the moment often overcomes good-sense and decorum. I am very honored to have your assistance in this matter. But I believe I may have mentioned that?" He laughed heartily and Holmes shot me the ghost of a smile before addressing himself to the little Turkish detective.

"Our companion on the train, then? The Sallow-Faced Man?"

Münif chuckled appreciatively. "You mean Tekin? As you have no doubt guessed, he's *hafiye*. Police so secret they keep secrets from themselves!"

"It's all a bit much, don't you think?" I said curtly. "We are here on the request on the Sultan, after all!"

"Oh, please do not judge us too harshly" he replied with such good-grace that I immediately regretted my warm words. "Last month there was an attempt on the Sultan's life. It is not widely known but, since the affair, he stays locked in his palace. I have his trust – as do you, gentlemen – but the *hafiye* trust no one. It suits them to keep the Sultan afraid and isolated. Fortunately, humble Münif knows how such games are played!"

Münif's impish manner was tempered with a quiet self-confidence that quickly won us over. The car sped onwards and upwards. The driver attacked the narrow mountain roads with an alarming lack of concern for either the wildlife or the nerves of his passengers, so that it was with some relief that we finally we reached the tiny hamlet clinging to slopes of Snow Hill.

After a simple but hearty meal in the village cafe, we were led to a roughly-hewn chapel which had been converted into a make-shift morgue – its windows left ajar to keep the bodies chilled.

It was a singular place of blasted stonework and arrow-slit windows that seemed more pagan than Christian in these primordial wilds. Its quietness and remoteness were both calming and unnerving.

The bodies lay upon the bare altar table, their injuries all the more hideous for the alabaster paleness of their dead flesh. Their faces were indeed a vision of terror. Even in death they were horribly contorted and their glassily staring eyes and bared teeth produced such a sinister impression upon my mind that it left me momentarily speechless.

Holmes was not unaffected. His black brows drew down, his forehead contracted, and he stood absorbed in thought for many minutes. When he spoke in was in a tone of hushed reverie.

"The word '*mortuary*'," he began, "has its roots in the Latin '*mortuus*', meaning '*death*'. The French '*morgue*' has an altogether stranger meaning: '*To look at solemnly; to defy*'. Even for one such as myself, who has seen much death, the solemnity of an occasion such as this never leaves me. But '*defy*' is an odd word in this context, don't you think, Watson? Defy: '*To challenge, to resist, to be strange or extreme*'. Life is, perhaps, a constant challenge to death. Every morning that we wake and greet a new day, we resist Death's icy fingers. But is death strange or extreme? I would say no. It is perfectly mundane. A cause and effect. We live – therefore we must die. But here we have death both strange *and* extreme."

I had felt uneasy since that first night aboard the Orient Express, and Holmes's words chilled me such that I went about the little room lighting lanterns, like a child trying to throw off their night-fears.

Finally, when I had steadied myself sufficiently, we began the autopsy.

Münif had provided everything necessary, but informed us that the deceased must remain anonymous, for fear that news of their untimely deaths would precipitate some great crisis. So it was that we began work on two men who we knew only as "*Grey Hair*" and "*White Beard*".

The men were in their forties, stockily built, with muscular inner thighs and glutes, and several enthesophytes – those bony projections that appear at the attachment point of tendons or ligaments, caused by repeated stress. Both of these were suggestive of a lifetime spent in the saddle. Various external wounds, long healed, identified them as military men – so likely cavalry rather than wealthy horse-fanciers.

Holmes's knowledge of pathology was first-rate and, combined with my more practical experience, the chain of events began to reveal themselves.

White Beard had defensive cuts and bruises – imprints of Grey Hair's knuckles were clearly visible on his face. Traces of Grey Hair's skin, found under White Beard's nails, confirmed the truth. Rather than being assailed by a third party, the one man had seemingly attacked the other. The cause of such startling behaviour was soon made clear.

The cheeks, chin, and nose of both victims were mottled, and a purple rash lay over the large joints of the extremities, which was easily distinguished from the normal *livor mortis* seen in dependent areas of the body.

Despite their bloody appearance, none of the wounds were fatal, nor were traces of toxins to be found. Experience had taught me that, often, the more mysterious a puzzle seems, the more mundane the solution, and this appeared to be the case. These men had died of hypothermia, in which extreme instances a person becomes disoriented, confused, and combative. Finally, as vasoconstriction fails, warm blood flows back into the frozen skin, producing a false feeling of extreme warmth. This sensation of burning heat causes the dying man to throw off his clothes – sealing his fate.

We worked together, for the most part in silence, each confident in the other's skills, until finally Holmes exclaimed, "No, no! There are still too many questions!"

"But it is not murder," I replied. "No third party need be tracked and punished. Surely that will serve?"

"No, Watson!" He said with a flash of red-hot energy. "It simply will not do! Let us start at the beginning, not at the end. What drove them to this point? Why did two men leave their tents in the middle of the night, in such a hurry, that they did not bother to arm themselves or dress? Surely the danger must have been great indeed, to put military men in such fear for their lives that they gave no thought to fighting, hiding, or running for aid? Instead they propelled themselves off cliff edges and into trees. And what danger is it that comes in the night and leaves no trace? No, this mystery deepens by the moment."

Holmes's words struck home. Whatever the truth, the dead had told us all they could.

Münif was eager to hear our findings, regarding Holmes with a quiet reverence as my companion outlined our progress.

When he was finished, Münif nodded thoughtfully. Despite the grim nature of the discussion, his face was a picture of unfettered delight, but his eyes told a more interesting tale. I was beginning to suspect that "humble Münif" was not all-together what he appeared.

"Interesting, very interesting!" he said. "You will want to stay a night or two at the victim's camp?"

"Quite so," Holmes replied.

Münif clapped his hands. "I had anticipated such a request!"

"Will you join us?" I asked.

"It has been my dearest wish! But, now, come, you must be weary. There's a room above the cafe which has been secured for you. Call for Baris should you need anything."

I awoke early the next morning. The previous day's adventures had given me another restless night and I was filled with strange forebodings.

Holmes was already awake and it seemed to have been for many hours. He sat on the small bed, cross-legged like some Eastern mystic, his old briar thrust out as a challenge to the day. The coverlet was thrown back and strewn with papers – the bottom sheet covered in pencilled notes!

The air was heavy with tobacco and I crossed to the window to let in a little air. It was as I reached for the casement lock that I glanced down and my heart turned to lead. Sallow-Face!

"Ah" Holmes said languidly. "You've noticed our visitor?"

"Lord! How long has he been here?"

"He's been haunting the courtyard all night. For a secret policeman, he's abominably heavy footed."

"What? Have you been awake all night then?"

"I have, and it has been most instructive. Yet, as to the case . . . I have turned it over and over in my mind and found no explanation that appears adequate."

He gestured vaguely to the papers on the bed. "Everything I have – topographical maps, Münif's notes and photographs. But I don't like it! Everything screams that a crime has been committed. That men were driven into the snow to die. How? Who is this impossible assassin? Where is the evidence?" For a moment his eyes fixed vacantly upon the frost-tinted window then he leapt to his feet with a sudden exclamation. "Come! Daylight is wasting."

I rapidly threw on my clothes and navigated the winding, unlit staircase to find Münif – red faced and panting – already in conference with Holmes in the cafe below.

"It seems, my dear Watson, that Münif has also spotted our clod-footed shadow and has just been in pursuit of the fellow."

"Alas!" the detective said. "He fled. Vanished into trees, like the sneaking wolf he is."

"Should we be worried?" I asked.

For a moment Münif did indeed look worried. Then his round face lit up and he said, with a toothy smile. "Ah, what concern is one plodding *hafiye* when the Baker's Road Men are on the scent!"

It was hard not to find the little man's energetic speech amusing, but when I glanced at Holmes I noted that he looked at the colorful fellow with an icy detachment. What it meant I couldn't discern, for the detective kept us quite occupied for the next hour, as breakfast was served and he outlined the journey we would be making.

I was pleased to discover that the Turks took breakfast as seriously as the British. Doughy, sesame-seed-coated bread, soft goat's cheese, succulent olives, rich molasses, a fragrant bergamot jam, eggs, and spicy beef sausage made a tasty spread. By the time we had eaten, the early morning chill had abated and we were full of fuel for the day's exertions.

The morning was icy-blue and locked in frost. There wasn't a cloud in the sky, and our breath blew out such plumes of smoke that we seemed to be miniature steam engines. The snow lay thick and deep, allowing the use of skis, although the wooded nature of the terrain meant that we must walk with them, Nordic style.

Münif declared that he hadn't seen such weather since he was a child, though he moved through the drifts with an enviable nimbleness.

It wasn't long before I began to fall behind the company, and I was grateful when Holmes slowed his pace to join me.

"Watson," he hissed as I came within ear-shot, "no time to explain, but be on the alert. This is a singular and a dangerous web we have become embroiled in – "

Münif appeared at Holmes's heels like an over-eager puppy. My friend fell instantly silent, leaving my mind to grapple with the significance.

We climbed into the clouds for many hours. The sun shone brightly, at times reflecting off the snow to such effect that I was dazzled. By afternoon, the chill had begun to creep into my boots and beneath my heavy Norfolk. My pack got weightier, and my legs heavier, so that by the time we finally reached the location of the crime, I felt quite spent.

There was little left to indicate the tragedy that had occurred. Weeks of snow had covered what remained of the camp, but that didn't stop Holmes's keen eyes from surveying the scene.

Münif busied himself building a small fire and soon tin mugs of steaming coffee were handed round to all. It was a local blend, bitter in taste, which Münif explained was best taken sweetened with molasses. Holmes seemed to relish the brew and drank one cup after another. I drank it for the warmth it brought but, rather than revive me, I found that it increased my lethargy to the point where I could barely keep my eyes open.

It was then that I glanced at Holmes, who sat furiously blinking, cup discarded at his side, the thick treacly liquid forming a rivulet in the snow. His face was pale and a glitter of moisture sat on his brow. I saw his head fall, dragging his tall form backwards into the snow. A low, buzzing alarm began to sound somewhere in my mind. Vague shapes swirled and swam in warning of some unknowable horror. A sinking fear took possession of me – but it was too late! I heard myself cry out. Then I too followed Holmes into the deep and dreamless sleep that laudanum brings.

What happened next only Holmes can tell, and I report his words as accurately as I can.

"I know well," he began "the taste of laudanum and a few gulps of Münif's coffee told me that the drink had been heavily laced with the drug. I had drunk enough – and quickly – to feel its effects and did, in truth, succumb for some time.

"I awoke to find the little Turk shredding our packs, disposing, I assumed, of anything that might give us shelter or warmth, for it seemed clear that he intended to leave us at the mercy of the elements.

"I lay there, limbs slowly succumbing to the cold, determined to play dead until I could get the upper hand, when suddenly the wind began to rise. With it came a curious noise. I am not, I think, easily unnerved, but there was something about that low keening that stopped the blood in my veins. It continued for some time, creating a sensation of intense pressure about the head. I had the ridiculous impression that something was actually inside my skull trying to claw its way out. At the same time, I felt all control of my body slipping away. My limbs began to twitch, my vision blurred, and soon I could taste my own blood which was flowing so freely from my nose that I was beginning to choke on it. I knew with absolute certainty that if I did not flee from that spot in the instant, I would be a dead man.

"And flee I did, insensible to my surroundings, aware only of the growing terror that the Siren's song brought. I ran like a man possessed, howling, tearing at my hair, limbs thrashing out at foliage which, in my fever, I imagined to be assailants. At times I ran like Alice's Red Queen, seemingly going nowhere. At others, I found myself on familiar London streets, being pursued by I know not who. At one point I saw Münif – though I saw so many things which could not be accounted real, that he too may have been a phantom of the mind. He ran like the very devil was on his heels, quite out-pacing me, his face a picture of madness. In such confusion as I found myself, I would have run straight off the hill-side had not our trustworthy shadow brought me down with doughty rugby tackle."

While Holmes raged and howled on that unforgiving mountain, I slept the sleep of the dead. How long I remained unconscious I couldn't tell. It must have many hours, for when I awoke the moon had already risen. I was chilled, heavy headed, and utterly alone!

Once again the camp was a scene of mayhem – our meagre packs scattered. I saw signs of chaos, of panic, and footprints leading down the hill, which I dared not follow.

My body was weary and stiff, yet my mind was at the highest pitch of tension so that every sound, every motion set my nerves on edge. I sat thus for many hours, half-inclined to head out in search of Holmes, half-afraid that should I move, Holmes would return and miss me in the darkness. Logic told me to stay put, so I did what I could to make a beacon for my friend, setting a fire from lichen and strips of my tattered pack which lit up the mountainside like the flare from a Very gun.

I had just begun to despair when two figures emerged from the tree-line. Never have I seen a more welcome sight: Holmes! And supporting his gaunt figure – not the little Turkish detective, but Sallow-Face himself.

There was no time to wonder what this could mean. I jumped up and, between us, we helped Holmes to the fire. His face was drawn, much bloodied, bruised, and covered in a dozen cuts, but otherwise he seemed unharmed.

It didn't take long for the fire and a tot or two of whisky from my flask to do the trick.

"Watson," he said with more vigor than I could credit, "may I introduce the *real* Detective Münif."

I sat blinking stupidly for some time. "Well, who then was Münif?"

"Why," Holmes coughed out a hollow chuckle, "the *real* Tekin!"

"What? How long have you known?"

"I have suspected *something* for a while. It seemed strange to me that a humble detective should know the identities of the Sultan's most secret police by name. Then there were other smaller things. He called you 'mister', not 'doctor'. He spoke of '*Baker's Road*', not '*Baker Street*'. Regardless of the eccentricities of speech, it seemed unlikely that the real Münif – who was such an admirer – would make such mistakes. To my mind, there seemed something too studied, too dissembling about the character he presented to us. But I didn't have anything to support my suspicions until I spoke to the detective, here, last night."

Not for the first time in our long association I felt at a loss. "Why the deception?"

"I believe he saw in our arrival an opportunity. Already two men close to the Sultan were dead. Should we, too, be found dead – think of the ramifications. Think who could be blamed and fitted for the crime. Remember – Mycroft warned us that the *hafiye* had the First Congress in their sights? If the false Münif spoke one true thing during our association I'd wager it was this: '*It suits the* hafiye *to keep the Sultan afraid and isolated*'."

"Did he not imagine the real Münif would arrive to unmask him?"

Our shadow had said little up to this point, but when he spoke it was in the thankfully sober and plain tones of a policeman – quite the contrast to his impersonator! "That would have been difficult, Doctor, for you see, I am dead. Or so he believed. His assassin's bullet very nearly did its job. It was then that I decided to 'lay-low', as the detective novels term it. I am sorry if my appearance on the train unnerved you. If he wanted me out of the way, then it seemed reasonable to assume that he wanted you out of the way too. So I played guard-dog and waited to see what would conspire."

"This is incredible!" I said. "But – wait! We're still no further on. We still don't know what it was that drove Grey Beard and White Hair almost mad with fear."

"And me as well," Holmes added. He sat wrapped in the tattered remains of our camp blankets, a fresh pipe glowing, looking for all the world like he was reclining in his chair at Baker Street rather than perched in alien snowscape. "Now that I've had time to think on it, I'll tell you what I believe. Much is beyond proof.

"You'll remember, perhaps, Tesla's earthquake machine, which nearly caused the death of the great Mark Twain some years back? The device was found to dangerously aggravate anyone who came within close proximity. The low vibrations it created were much like those that make sand dunes appear to sing. The same thing happens when winds rush down elevated slopes at great speeds. I had heard it said in Switzerland that such singing was able to drive a man mad. I think," Holmes continued, rubbing his bruises ruefully, "that we now have good reason to believe the veracity of such tales!"

My friend had once said, "Eliminate the impossible and whatever remains, no matter how improbable, must be the truth – " But what a truth! As we sat, allowing the fire to warm our bones, my mind turned to tales of Homer. To sailors driven to self-destruction by songs carried on the wind. And I marveled at the strangeness of a world that seemingly had such things in it.

Soon the sun had risen, and our little party gathered what kit we could for the journey back to the village. Our progress was a slow but, despite events, I felt lighter than I had for days.

Detective Münif – the *real* Münif – had every confidence that with Tekin dead, the *hafiye* would not dare dispute his account of events. Indeed, everything was tied up so swiftly and neatly that by the next evening we were back at Sirkeci Station, boarding the Orient Express for London.

As we sat that night in the dining car, watching Istanbul slowly disappear from view, Holmes drew my attention to the table opposite. There were the Accidental Heiress and the Jilted Lover, hands clasped across the table in an attitude of complete devotion.

Holmes, naturally, affected his usual half-cynical vein, but to see how this romance had blossomed quickly set me thinking on my own good fortune.

As Holmes had noted, Dr. Freud would have had no difficulties diagnosing the cause of the strange forebodings that had dogged me since this case began. Part of me, I think, had been afraid that I might lose what I had only just won. Yet in three days, I would be back in the arms of dearest wife and, at the thought, I couldn't help but smile and quietly wish this new couple as much happiness as I had found.

> *It happened that at the moment I was clearing up the case which my friend Watson has described as that of the Abbey School, in which the Duke of Greyminster was so deeply involved. I had also a commission from the Sultan of Turkey which called for immediate action, as political consequences of the gravest kind might arise from its neglect.*
>
> – Sherlock Holmes
> "The Blanched Soldier"

NOTES

1. In the 1900's, Constantinople went crazy for detective fiction. The Sultan himself was a huge aficionado.
2. Sand dunes do sing. When Marco Polo first heard it in China, he ascribed the sounds to evil spirits. Similar "songs" have also been reported on steep mountains.
3. Tesla's earthquake machine was, bizarrely, used in 1890 to help his friend, Mark Twain, who was constipated. It's reported that the effects were so dramatic that Tesla feared for his friend's life.
4. Natural or man-made ultra-low frequency sounds (under 10Hz) can cause mental and physical distress when they're powerful enough – and played for long enough. Military experiments with ultra-low frequencies, as part of psy-op operations, have reported that exposure to such sounds can induce fear, vertigo, disorientation, visual distortions, hallucinations, and heart attacks. In nature, *katabatic* winds, which form on steep mountains, may generate similar ultra-low frequency vibrations, and have been suggested as the cause of several mysterious climbing accidents.

Appendix:
The Untold Cases

The following has been assembled from several sources, including lists compiled by Phil Jones and Randall Stock, as well as some internet resources and my own research. I cannot promise that it's complete – some Untold Cases may be missing – after all, there's a great deal of Sherlockian Scholarship that involves interpretation and rationalizing – and there are some listed here that certain readers may believe shouldn't be listed at all.

As a fanatical supporter and collector of pastiches since I was a ten-year-old boy in 1975, reading Nicholas Meyer's *The Seven-Per-Cent Solution* and *The West End Horror* before I'd even read all of The Canon, I can attest that serious and legitimate versions of all of these Untold Cases exist out there – some of them occurring with much greater frequency than others – and I hope to collect, read, and chronologicize them all.

There's so much more to The Adventures of Sherlock Holmes than the pitifully few sixty stories that were fixed up by the First Literary Agent. I highly recommend that you find and read all of the rest of them as well, including those relating these Untold Cases. You won't regret it.

David Marcum

A Study in Scarlet

- Mr. Lestrade . . . got himself in a fog recently over a forgery case
- A young girl called, fashionably dressed
- A gray-headed, seedy visitor, looking like a Jew pedlar who appeared to be very much excited
- A slipshod elderly woman
- An old, white-haired gentleman had an interview
- A railway porter in his velveteen uniform

The Sign of Four

- The consultation last week by Francois le Villard
- The most winning woman Holmes ever knew was hanged for poisoning three little children for their insurance money

- The most repellent man of Holmes's acquaintance was a philanthropist who has spent nearly a quarter of a million upon the London poor
- Holmes once enabled Mrs. Cecil Forrester to unravel a little domestic complication. She was much impressed by his kindness and skill
- Holmes lectured the police on causes and inferences and effects in the Bishopgate jewel case

The Adventures of Sherlock Holmes

"A Scandal in Bohemia"

- The summons to Odessa in the case of the Trepoff murder
- The singular tragedy of the Atkinson brothers at Trincomalee
- The mission which Holmes had accomplished so delicately and successfully for the reigning family of Holland. (He also received a remarkably brilliant ring)
- The Darlington substitution scandal, and . . .
- The Arnsworth castle business. (When a woman thinks that her house is on fire, her instinct is at once to rush to the thing which she values most. It is a perfectly overpowering impulse, and Holmes has more than once taken advantage of it

"The Red-Headed League"

- The previous skirmishes with John Clay

"A Case of Identity"

- The Dundas separation case, where Holmes was engaged in clearing up some small points in connection with it. The husband was a teetotaler, there was no other woman, and the conduct complained of was that he had drifted into the habit of winding up every meal by taking out his false teeth and hurling them at his wife, which is not an action likely to occur to the imagination of the average story-teller.
- The rather intricate matter from Marseilles
- Mrs. Etherege, whose husband Holmes found so easy when the police and everyone had given him up for dead

"The Boscombe Valley Mystery"

NONE LISTED

"The Five Orange Pips"

- The adventure of the Paradol Chamber
- The Amateur Mendicant Society, who held a luxurious club in the lower vault of a furniture warehouse
- The facts connected with the disappearance of the British barque *Sophy Anderson*
- The singular adventures of the Grice-Patersons in the island of Uffa
- The Camberwell poisoning case, in which, as may be remembered, Holmes was able, by winding up the dead man's watch, to prove that it had been wound up two hours before, and that therefore the deceased had gone to bed within that time – a deduction which was of the greatest importance in clearing up the case
- Holmes saved Major Prendergast in the Tankerville Club scandal. He was wrongfully accused of cheating at cards
- Holmes has been beaten four times – three times by men and once by a woman

"The Man with the Twisted Lip"

- The rascally Lascar who runs The Bar of Gold in Upper Swandam Lane has sworn to have vengeance upon Holmes

"The Adventure of the Blue Carbuncle"

NONE LISTED

"The Adventure of the Speckled Band"

- Mrs. Farintosh and an opal tiara. (It was before Watson's time)

"The Adventure of the Engineer's Thumb"

- Colonel Warburton's madness

"The Adventure of the Noble Bachelor"

- The letter from a fishmonger
- The letter a tide-waiter
- The service for Lord Backwater
- The little problem of the Grosvenor Square furniture van
- The service for the King of Scandinavia

"The Adventure of the Beryl Coronet"

NONE LISTED

"The Adventure of the Copper Beeches"
NONE LISTED

The Memoirs of Sherlock Holmes

"Silver Blaze"
NONE LISTED

"The Cardboard Box"

- Aldridge, who helped in the bogus laundry affair

"The Yellow Face"

- The (First) Adventure of the Second Stain was a failure which present[s] the strongest features of interest

'The Stockbroker's Clerk"
NONE LISTED

"The "Gloria Scott"
NONE LISTED

"The Musgrave Ritual"

- The Tarleton murders
- The case of Vamberry, the wine merchant
- The adventure of the old Russian woman
- The singular affair of the aluminum crutch
- A full account of Ricoletti of the club foot and his abominable wife
- The two cases before the Musgrave Ritual from Holmes's fellow students

"The Reigate Squires"

- The whole question of the Netherland-Sumatra Company and of the colossal schemes of Baron Maupertuis

The Crooked Man"
NONE LISTED

The Resident Patient"

- [Catalepsy] is a very easy complaint to imitate. Holmes has done it himself.

<u>"The Greek Interpreter"</u>

- Mycroft expected to see Holmes round last week to consult me over that Manor House case. It was Adams, of course
- Some of Holmes's most interesting cases have come to him through Mycroft

<u>"The Naval Treaty"</u>

- The (Second) adventure of the Second Stain, which dealt with interest of such importance and implicated so many of the first families in the kingdom that for many years it would be impossible to make it public. No case, however, in which Holmes was engaged had ever illustrated the value of his analytical methods so clearly or had impressed those who were associated with him so deeply. Watson still retained an almost verbatim report of the interview in which Holmes demonstrated the true facts of the case to Monsieur Dubugue of the Paris police, and Fritz von Waldbaum, the well-known specialist of Dantzig, both of whom had wasted their energies upon what proved to be side-issues. The new century will have come, however, before the story could be safely told.
- The Adventure of the Tired Captain
- A very commonplace little murder. If it [this paper] turns red, it means a man's life . . . .

<u>"The Final Problem"</u>

- The engagement for the French Government upon a matter of supreme importance
- The assistance to the Royal Family of Scandinavia

The Return of Sherlock Holmes

<u>"The Adventure of the Empty House"</u>

- Holmes traveled for two years in Tibet (as) a Norwegian named Sigerson, amusing himself by visiting Lhassa [*sic*] and spending some days with the head Llama [*sic*]
- Holmes traveled in Persia
- . . . looked in at Mecca . . .

- . . . and paid a short but interesting visit to the Khalifa at Khartoum
- Returning to France, Holmes spent some months in a research into the coal-tar derivatives, which he conducted in a laboratory at Montpelier [*sic*], in the South of France
- Mathews, who knocked out Holmes's left canine in the waiting room at Charing Cross
- The death of Mrs. Stewart, of Lauder, in 1887
- Morgan the poisoner
- Merridew of abominable memory
- The Molesey Mystery (Inspector Lestrade's Case. He handled it fairly well.)

"The Adventure of the Norwood Builder"

- The case of the papers of ex-President Murillo
- The shocking affair of the Dutch steamship, *Friesland*, which so nearly cost both Holmes and Watson their lives
- That terrible murderer, Bert Stevens, who wanted Holmes and Watson to get him off in '87

"The Adventure of the Dancing Men"

NONE LISTED

"The Adventure of the Solitary Cyclist"

- The peculiar persecution of John Vincent Harden, the well-known tobacco millionaire
- It was near Farnham that Holmes and Watson took Archie Stamford, the forger

"The Adventure of the Priory School"

- Holmes was retained in the case of the Ferrers Documents
- The Abergavenny murder, which is coming up for trial

"The Adventure of Black Peter"

- The sudden death of Cardinal Tosca – an inquiry which was carried out by him at the express desire of His Holiness the Pope
- The arrest of Wilson, the notorious canary-trainer, which removed a plague-spot from the East-End of London.

"The Adventure of Charles Augustus Milverton"

NONE LISTED

"The Adventure of the Six Napoleons"

- The dreadful business of the Abernetty family, which was first brought to Holmes's attention by the depth which the parsley had sunk into the butter upon a hot day
- The Conk-Singleton forgery case
- Holmes was consulted upon the case of the disappearance of the black pearl of the Borgias, but was unable to throw any light upon it

"The Adventure of the Three Students"

- Some laborious researches in Early English charters

"The Adventure of the Golden Pince-Nez"

- The repulsive story of the red leech
- . . . and the terrible death of Crosby, the banker
- The Addleton tragedy
- . . . and the singular contents of the ancient British barrow
- The famous Smith-Mortimer succession case
- The tracking and arrest of Huret, the boulevard assassin

"The Adventure of the Missing Three-Quarter"

- Henry Staunton, whom Holmes helped to hang
- Arthur H. Staunton, the rising young forger

"The Adventure of the Abbey Grange"

- Hopkins called Holmes in seven times, and on each occasion his summons was entirely justified

"The Adventure of the Second Stain"

- The woman at Margate. No powder on her nose – that proved to be the correct solution. How can one build on such a quicksand? A woman's most trivial action may mean volumes, or their most extraordinary conduct may depend upon a hairpin or a curling-tong

The Hound of the Baskervilles

- That little affair of the Vatican cameos, in which Holmes obliged the Pope

- The little case in which Holmes had the good fortune to help Messenger Manager Wilson
- One of the most revered names in England is being besmirched by a blackmailer, and only Holmes can stop a disastrous scandal
- The atrocious conduct of Colonel Upwood in connection with the famous card scandal at the Nonpareil Club
- Holmes defended the unfortunate Mme. Montpensier from the charge of murder that hung over her in connection with the death of her stepdaughter Mlle. Carere, the young lady who, as it will be remembered, was found six months later alive and married in New York

The Valley of Fear

- Twice already Holmes had helped Inspector Macdonald

His Last Bow

"The Adventure of Wisteria Lodge"

- The locking-up Colonel Carruthers

"The Adventure of the Red Circle"

- The affair last year for Mr. Fairdale Hobbs
- The Long Island cave mystery

"The Adventure of the Bruce-Partington Plans"

- Brooks . . .
- . . . or Woodhouse, or any of the fifty men who have good reason for taking Holmes's life

"The Adventure of the Dying Detective"

NONE LISTED

"The Disappearance of Lady Frances Carfax"

- Holmes cannot possibly leave London while old Abrahams is in such mortal terror of his life

"The Adventure of the Devil's Foot"

- Holmes's dramatic introduction to Dr. Moore Agar, of Harley Street

"His Last Bow"

- Holmes started his pilgrimage at Chicago . . .
- . . . graduated in an Irish secret society at Buffalo
- . . . gave serious trouble to the constabulary at Skibbareen
- Holmes saves Count Von und Zu Grafenstein from murder by the Nihilist Klopman

The Case-Book of Sherlock Holmes

"The Adventure of the Illustrious Client"

- Negotiations with Sir George Lewis over the Hammerford Will case

"The Adventure of the Blanched Soldier"

- The Abbey School in which the Duke of Greyminster was so deeply involved
- The commission from the Sultan of Turkey which required immediate action
- The professional service for Sir James Saunders

"The Adventure of the Mazarin Stone"

- Old Baron Dowson said the night before he was hanged that in Holmes's case what the law had gained the stage had lost
- The death of old Mrs. Harold, who left Count Sylvius the Blymer estate
- The compete life history of Miss Minnie Warrender
- The robbery in the train de-luxe to the Riviera on February 13, 1892

"The Adventure of the Three Gables"

- The killing of young Perkins outside the Holborn Bar
- Mortimer Maberly, was one of Holmes's early clients

"The Adventure of the Sussex Vampire"

- *Matilda Briggs*, a ship which is associated with the giant rat of Sumatra, a story for which the world is not yet prepared
- Victor Lynch, the forger
- Venomous lizard, or Gila. Remarkable case, that!

- Vittoria the circus belle
- Vanderbilt and the Yeggman
- Vigor, the Hammersmith wonder

<u>"The Adventure of the Three Garridebs"</u>

- Holmes refused a knighthood for services which may, someday, be described

<u>"The Problem of Thor Bridge"</u>

- Mr. James Phillimore who, stepping back into his own house to get his umbrella, was never more seen in this world
- The cutter *Alicia*, which sailed one spring morning into a patch of mist from where she never again emerged, nor was anything further ever heard of herself and her crew.
- Isadora Persano, the well-known journalist and duelist who was found stark staring mad with a match box in front of him which contained a remarkable worm said to be unknown to science

<u>"The Adventure of the Creeping Man"</u>

NONE LISTED

<u>"The Adventure of the Lion's Mane"</u>

NONE LISTED

<u>"The Adventure of the Veiled Lodger"</u>

- The whole story concerning the politician, the lighthouse, and the trained cormorant

<u>"The Adventure of Shoscombe Old Place"</u>

- Holmes ran down that coiner by the zinc and copper filings in the seam of his cuff
- The St. Pancras case, where a cap was found beside the dead policeman. Merivale of the Yard, asked Holmes to look into it

<u>"The Adventure of the Retired Colourman"</u>

- The case of the two Coptic Patriarchs

About the Contributors

The following contributors appear in this volume:

The MX Book of New Sherlock Holmes Stories
Part XXIV – Some More Untold Cases (1895-1903)

Brian Belanger is a publisher and editor, but is best known for his freelance illustration and cover design work. His distinctive style can be seen on several MX Publishing covers, including *Silent Meridian* by Elizabeth Crowen, *Sherlock Holmes and the Menacing Melbournian* by Allan Mitchell, *Sherlock Holmes and A Quantity of Debt* by David Marcum, *Welcome to Undershaw* by Luke Benjamen Kuhns, and many more. Brian is the co-founder of Belanger Books LLC, where he illustrates the popular *MacDougall Twins with Sherlock Holmes* young reader series (#1 bestsellers on Amazon.com UK). A prolific creator, he also designs t-shirts, mugs, stickers, and other merchandise on his personal art site: *www.redbubble.com/people/zhahadun.*

Thomas A. Burns, Jr. is the author of the *Natalie McMasters Mysteries*. He was born and grew up in New Jersey, attended Xavier High School in Manhattan, earned B.S degrees in Zoology and Microbiology at Michigan State University, and a M.S. in Microbiology at North Carolina State University. He currently resides in Wendell, North Carolina. As a kid, Tom started reading mysteries with The Hardy Boys, Ken Holt, and Rick Brant, and graduated to the classic stories by authors such as A. Conan Doyle, Dorothy Sayers, John Dickson Carr, Erle Stanley Gardner, and Rex Stout, to name a few. Tom has written fiction as a hobby all of his life, starting with The Man from U.N.C.L.E. stories in marble-backed copybooks in grade school. He built a career as technical, science, and medical writer and editor for nearly thirty years in industry and government. Now that he's truly on his own as a novelist, he's excited to publish his own mystery series, as well as to contribute stories about his second-most-favorite detective, Sherlock Holmes, to *The MX Book of New Sherlock Holmes Stories*.

Craig Stephen Copland confesses that he discovered Sherlock Holmes when, sometime in the muddled early 1960's, he pinched his older brother's copy of the immortal stories and was forever afterward thoroughly hooked. He is very grateful to his high school English teachers in Toronto who inculcated in him a love of literature and writing, and even inspired him to be an English major at the University of Toronto. There he was blessed to sit at the feet of both Northrup Frye and Marshall McLuhan, and other great literary professors, who led him to believe that he was called to be a high school English teacher. It was his good fortune to come to his pecuniary senses, abandon that goal, and pursue a varied professional career that took him to over one-hundred countries and endless adventures. He considers himself to have been and to continue to be one of the luckiest men on God's good earth. A few years back he took a step in the direction of Sherlockian studies and joined the *Sherlock Holmes Society of Canada* – also known as *The Toronto Bootmakers*. In May of 2014, this esteemed group of scholars announced a contest for the writing of a new Sherlock Holmes mystery. Although he had never tried his hand at fiction before, Craig entered and was pleasantly surprised to be selected as one of the winners. Having enjoyed the experience, he decided to write more of the same, and is now on a mission to write a new Sherlock Holmes mystery that is related to and inspired by each of the sixty stories in the original Canon. He currently lives and writes in Toronto and Dubai, and looks forward to finally settling down when he turns ninety.

John William Davis is a retired US Army counterintelligence officer, civil servant, and linguist. He was commissioned from Washington University in St. Louis as an artillery officer in the 101st Air Assault Division. Thereafter, he went into counterintelligence and served some thirty-seven years. A linguist, Mr. Davis learned foreign languages in each country he served. After the Cold War and its bitter aftermath, he wrote *Rainy Street Stories, Reflections on Secret Wars, Terrorism, and Espionage*. He wanted to write about not only true events themselves, but also the moral and ethical aspects of the secret world. With the publication of *Around the Corner*, Davis expanded his reflections on conflicted human nature to our present day traumas of fear, and causes for hope. A dedicated Sherlockian, he's contributed to telling the story of the Great Detective in retirement.

Harry DeMaio is a *nom de plume* of Harry B. DeMaio, successful author of several books on Information Security and Business Networks, as well as the thirteen-volume *Casebooks of Octavius Bear*. He is also a published author for Belanger Books, the Dear Holmes series, and the MX Sherlock Holmes anthologies edited by David Marcum. A retired business executive, former consultant, information security specialist, pilot, disk jockey, and graduate school adjunct professor, he whiles away his time traveling and writing preposterous books, articles, and stories. He has appeared on many radio and TV shows and is an accomplished, frequent public speaker. Former New York City natives, he and his extremely patient and helpful wife, Virginia, and their late, lamented Bichon Frisé, Woof, live in Cincinnati (and several other parallel universes.) They have two sons living in Scottsdale, Arizona and Cortlandt Manor, New York, both of whom are quite successful and quite normal, thus putting the lie to the theory that insanity is hereditary. His e-mail is *hdemaio@zoomtown.com* and you can also find him on Facebook. His books are available on Amazon, Barnes and Noble, directly from MX Publishing and at other fine bookstores. His website is *www.octaviusbearslair.com*

Sir Arthur Conan Doyle (1859-1930) *Holmes Chronicler Emeritus*. If not for him, this anthology would not exist. Author, physician, patriot, sportsman, spiritualist, husband and father, and advocate for the oppressed. He is remembered and honored for the purposes of this collection by being the man who introduced Sherlock Holmes to the world. Through fifty-six Holmes short stories, four novels, and additional Apocryphal entries, Doyle revolutionized mystery stories and also greatly influenced and improved police forensic methods and techniques for the betterment of all. *Steel True Blade Straight.*

Steve Emecz's main field is technology, in which he has been working for about twenty years. Steve is a regular trade show speaker on the subject of eCommerce, and his tech career has taken him to more than fifty countries – so he's no stranger to planes and airports. He wrote two novels (one a bestseller) in the 1990's, and a screenplay in 2001. Shortly after, he set up MX Publishing, specialising in NLP books. In 2008, MX published its first Sherlock Holmes book, and MX has gone on to become the largest specialist Holmes publisher in the world. MX is a social enterprise and supports three main causes. The first is Happy Life, a children's rescue project in Nairobi, Kenya, where he and his wife, Sharon, spend every Christmas at the rescue centre in Kasarani. In 2014, they wrote a short book about the project, *The Happy Life Story*. The second is the Stepping Stones School, of which Steve is a patron. Stepping Stones is located at Undershaw, Sir Arthur Conan Doyle's former home. Steve has been a mentor for the World Food Programme for the last several years, supporting their innovation bootcamps and giving 1-2-1 mentoring to several projects.

Mark A. Gagen BSI is co-founder of Wessex Press, sponsor of the popular *From Gillette to Brett* conferences, and publisher of *The Sherlock Holmes Reference Library* and many other fine Sherlockian titles. A life-long Holmes enthusiast, he is a member of *The Baker Street Irregulars* and *The Illustrious Clients of Indianapolis*. A graphic artist by profession, his work is often seen on the covers of *The Baker Street Journal* and various BSI books.

Jayantika Ganguly BSI is the General Secretary and Editor of the *Sherlock Holmes Society of India*, a member of the *Sherlock Holmes Society of London*, and the *Czech Sherlock Holmes Society*. She is the author of *The Holmes Sutra* (MX 2014). She is a corporate lawyer working with one of the Big Six law firms.

Dick Gillman is an English writer and acrylic artist living in Brittany, France with his wife Alex, Truffle, their Black Labrador, and Jean-Claude, their Breton cat. During his retirement from teaching, he has written over twenty Sherlock Holmes short stories which are published as both e-books and paperbacks. His initial contribution to the superb MX Sherlock Holmes collection, published in October 2015, was entitled "The Man on Westminster Bridge" and had the privilege of being chosen as the anchor story in *The MX Book of New Sherlock Holmes Stories – Part II (1890-1895).*

John Linwood Grant is a writer and editor who lives in Yorkshire with a pack of lurchers and a beard. He may also have a family. He focuses particularly on dark Victorian and Edwardian fiction, such as his recent novella *A Study in Grey*, which also features Holmes. Current projects include his *Tales of the Last Edwardian* series, about psychic and psychiatric mysteries, and curating a collection of new stories based on the darker side of the British Empire. He has been published in a number of anthologies and magazines, with stories range from madness in early Virginia to questions about the monsters we ourselves might be. He is also co-editor of *Occult Detective Quarterly*. His website *greydogtales.com* explores weird fiction, especially period ones, weird art, and even weirder lurchers.

John Atkinson Grimshaw (1836-1893) was born in Leeds, England. His amazing paintings, usually featuring twilight or night scenes illuminated by gas-lamps or moonlight, are easily recognizable, and are often used on the covers of books about The Great Detective to set the mood, as shadowy figures move in the distance through misty mysterious settings and over rain-slicked streets.

Arthur Hall was born in Aston, Birmingham, UK, in 1944. He discovered his interest in writing during his schooldays, along with a love of fictional adventure and suspense. His first novel, *Sole Contact*, was an espionage story about an ultra-secret government department known as "Sector Three", and was followed, to date, by three sequels. Other works include five Sherlock Holmes novels, *The Demon of the Dusk*, *The One Hundred Percent Society*, *The Secret Assassin*, *The Phantom Killer*, and *In Pursuit of the Dead*, as well as a collection of short stories, and a modern detective novel. He lives in the West Midlands, United Kingdom.

Paula Hammond has written over sixty fiction and non-fiction books, as well as short stories, comics, poetry, and scripts for educational DVD's. When not glued to the keyboard, she can usually be found prowling round second-hand books shops or hunkered down in a hide, soaking up the joys of the natural world.

Stephen Herczeg is an IT Geek, writer, actor, and film-maker based in Canberra Australia. He has been writing for over twenty years and has completed a couple of dodgy novels, sixteen feature-length screenplays, and numerous short stories and scripts. Stephen was very successful in 2017's International Horror Hotel screenplay competition, with his scripts *TITAN* winning the Sci-Fi category and *Dark are the Woods* placing second in the horror category. His work has featured in *Sproutlings – A Compendium of Little Fictions* from Hunter Anthologies, the *Hells Bells* Christmas horror anthology published by the Australasian Horror Writers Association, and the *Below the Stairs*, *Trickster's Treats*, *Shades of Santa*, *Behind the Mask*, and *Beyond the Infinite* anthologies from *OzHorror.Con*, *The Body Horror Book*, *Anemone Enemy*, and *Petrified Punks* from Oscillate Wildly Press, and *Sherlock Holmes In the Realms of H.G. Wells* and *Sherlock Holmes: Adventures Beyond the Canon* from Belanger Books.

Roger Johnson BSI, ASH is a retired librarian, now working as a volunteer assistant at the Essex Police Museum. In his spare time, he is commissioning editor of *The Sherlock Holmes Journal*, an occasional lecturer, and a frequent contributor to *The Writings about the Writings*. His sole work of Holmesian pastiche was published in 1997 in Mike Ashley's anthology *The Mammoth Book of New Sherlock Holmes Adventures*, and he has the greatest respect for the many authors who have contributed new tales to the present mighty trilogy. Like his wife, Jean Upton, he is a member of both *The Baker Street Irregulars* and *The Adventuresses of Sherlock Holmes.*

Susan Knight's newest novel from MX publishing, *Mrs. Hudson Goes to Ireland*, is a follow-up to her well-received collection of stories, *Mrs. Hudson Investigates* of 2019. She is the author of two other non-Sherlockian story collections, as well as three novels, a book of non-fiction, and several plays, and has won several prizes for her writing. She lives in Dublin where she teaches Creative Writing. Her next Mrs. Hudson novel is already a gleam in her eye.

John Lawrence served for thirty-eight years as a staff member in the U.S. House of Representatives, the last eight as Chief of Staff to Speaker Nancy Pelosi (2005-2013). He has been a Visiting Professor at the University of California's Washington Center since 2013. He is the author of *The Class of '74: Congress After Watergate and the Roots of Partisanship* (2018), and has a Ph.D. in history from the University of California (Berkeley).

David Marcum plays *The Game* with deadly seriousness. He first discovered Sherlock Holmes in 1975 at the age of ten, and since that time, he has collected, read, and chronologicized literally thousands of traditional Holmes pastiches in the form of novels, short stories, radio and television episodes, movies and scripts, comics, fan-fiction, and unpublished manuscripts. He is the author of over sixty Sherlockian pastiches, some published in anthologies and magazines such as *The Strand*, and others collected in his own books, *The Papers of Sherlock Holmes*, *Sherlock Holmes and A Quantity of Debt*, and *Sherlock Holmes – Tangled Skeins*. He has edited fifty books, including several dozen traditional Sherlockian anthologies, such as the ongoing series *The MX Book of New Sherlock Holmes Stories*, which he created in 2015. This collection is now up to 24 volumes, with more in preparation. He was responsible for bringing back August Derleth's Solar Pons for a new generation, first with his collection of authorized Pons stories, *The Papers of Solar Pons*, and then by editing the reissued authorized versions of the original Pons books, and then volumes of new Pons adventures. He is now doing the same for the adventures of Dr. Thorndyke. He has contributed numerous essays to various publications, and is a member of a number of Sherlockian groups and Scions. He is a licensed Civil Engineer, living in Tennessee with his wife and son. His irregular Sherlockian blog, *A Seventeen Step Program*, addresses various topics related to his favorite book friends (as his son used to call them when he was small), and can be found at *http://17stepprogram.blogspot.com/* Since the age of nineteen, he has worn a deerstalker as his regular-and-only hat. In 2013, he and his deerstalker were finally able make his first trip-of-a-lifetime Holmes Pilgrimage to England, with return Pilgrimages in 2015 and 2016, where you may have spotted him. If you ever run into him and his deerstalker out and about, feel free to say hello!

Sidney Paget (1860-1908), a few of whose illustrations are used within this anthology, was born in London, and like his two older brothers, became a famed illustrator and painter. He completed over three-hundred-and-fifty drawings for the Sherlock Holmes stories that were first published in *The Strand* magazine, defining Holmes's image forever after in the public mind.

Otto Penzler, proprietor of The Mysterious Bookshop in New York City, founded The Mysterious Press in 1975, and publishes e-books through *MysteriousPress.com.* Penzler has won two Edgar Awards, *The Mystery Writers of America*'s Ellery Queen Award, and The Raven. He has been given Lifetime Achievement awards by Noircon and *The Strand Magazine*. He founded two new publishing companies in 2018, Penzler Publishers, reissuing American Mystery Classics in hardcover and trade paperback, and Scarlet, which publishes original psychological suspense novels. He has edited more than sixty anthologies.

Gayle Lange Puhl has been a Sherlockian since Christmas of 1965. She has had articles published in *The Devon County Chronicle*, *The Baker Street Journal*, and *The Serpentine Muse*, plus her local newspaper. She has created Sherlockian jewelry, a 2006 calendar entitled "If Watson Wrote For TV", and has painted a limited series of Holmes-related nesting dolls. She co-founded the scion *Friends of the Great Grimpen Mire* and the Janesville, Wisconsin-based *The Original Tree Worshipers*. In January 2016, she was awarded the "Outstanding Creative Writer" award by the Janesville Art Alliance for her first book *Sherlock Holmes and the Folk Tale Mysteries*. She is semi-retired and lives in Evansville, Wisconsin. Ms. Puhl has one daughter, Gayla, and four grandchildren.

Tracy J. Revels, a Sherlockian from the age of eleven, is a professor of history at Wofford College in Spartanburg, South Carolina. She is a member of *The Survivors of the Gloria Scott* and *The Studious Scarlets Society*, and is a past recipient of the Beacon Society Award. Almost every semester, she teaches a class that covers The Canon, either to college students or to senior citizens. She is also the author of three supernatural Sherlockian pastiches with MX (*Shadowfall*, *Shadowblood*, and *Shadowwraith*), and a regular contributor to her scion's newsletter. She also has some notoriety as an author of very silly skits: For proof, see "The Adventure of the Adversarial Adventuress" and "Occupy Baker Street" on YouTube. When not studying Sherlock, she can be found researching the history of her native state, and has written books on Florida in the Civil War and on the development of Florida's tourism industry.

Brenda Seabrooke's stories have been published in a number of reviews, journals, and anthologies. She has received grants from the National Endowment for the Arts and Emerson College's Robbie Macauley Award. She is the author of twenty-three books for young readers including *Scones and Bones on Baker Street: Sherlock's (maybe!) Dog and the Dirt Dilemma*, and *The Rascal in the Castle: Sherlock's (possible!) Dog and the Queen's Revenge.* Brenda states: "*It was fun to write from Dr. Watson's point of view and not have to worry about fleas, smelly pits, ralphing, or scratching at inopportune times.*"

Jacqueline Silver is the newly-appointed Headteacher of Stepping Stones School. She has developed her career from her early days as an accomplished Drama teacher and has a strong background in school leadership. She has always had a passion for creating nurturing and positive school environments for mixed ability children. Her recent career history has seen her spearhead pastoral care provision at a number of schools where she has also been resolute in her vision for safeguarding, particularly of the most vulnerable children in our society. Since her recent appointment as Headteacher of Stepping Stones School, she can realise her prime personal focus for improving the employability of young people with learning needs. Quality of life, independence, and positive engagement with society are linchpins of Jacqueline's vision for the future. Stepping Stones will flourish under her leadership.

Joseph W. Svec III is retired from Oceanography, Satellite Test Engineering, and college teaching. He has lived on a forty-foot cruising sailboat, on a ranch in the Sierra Nevada Foothills, in a country rose-garden cottage, and currently lives in the shadow of a castle with his childhood sweetheart and several long coated German shepherds. He enjoys writing, gardening, creating dioramas, world travel, and enjoying time with his sweetheart.

Kevin P. Thornton is a seven-time Arthur Ellis Award Nominee. He is a former director of the local Heritage Society and Library, and he has been a soldier in Africa, a contractor for the Canadian Military in Afghanistan, a newspaper and magazine columnist, a Director of both the *Crime Writers of Canada* and the *Writers' Guild of Alberta*, a founding member of *Northword Literary Magazine*, and is either a current or former member of *The Mystery Writers of America, The Crime Writers Association, The Calgary Crime Writers, The International Thriller Writers, The International Association of Crime Writers, The Keys* – a Catholic Writers group founded by Monsignor Knox and G.K. Chesterton – as well as, somewhat inexplicably, *The Mesdames of Mayhem* and *Sisters in Crime*. If you ask, he will join. Born in Kenya, Kevin has lived or worked in South Africa, Dubai, England, Afghanistan, New Zealand, Ontario, and now Northern Alberta. He lives on his wits and his wit, and is doing better than expected. He is not one to willingly split infinitives, and while never pedantic, is on occasion known to be ever so slightly punctilious.

D.J. Tyrer is the person behind Atlantean Publishing, was placed second in the Writing Magazine "Local Reporter" competition, and has been widely published in anthologies and magazines around the world, such as *Disturbance* (Laurel Highlands), *Mysteries of Suspense* (Zimbell House), *History and Mystery, Oh My!* (Mystery & Horror LLC), and *Love 'Em, Shoot 'Em* (Wolfsinger), and issues of *Awesome Tales*, and in addition, has a novella available in paperback and on the Kindle, *The Yellow House* (Dunhams Manor) and a comic horror e-novelette, *A Trip to the Middle of the World*, available from Alban Lake through Infinite Realms Bookstore.
His website is: *https://djtyrer.blogspot.co.uk/*
The Atlantean Publishing website is at *https://atlanteanpublishing.wordpress.com/*

Marcia Wilson is a freelance researcher and illustrator who likes to work in a style compatible for the color blind and visually impaired. She is Canon-centric, and her first MX offering, *You Buy Bones*, uses the point-of-view of Scotland Yard to show the unique talents of Dr. Watson. This continued with the publication of *Test of the Professionals: The Adventure of the Flying Blue Pidgeon* and *The Peaceful Night Poisonings.* She can be contacted at: *gravelgirty.deviantart.com*

The following contributors appear
in the companion volumes:

The MX Book of New Sherlock Holmes Stories

Part XXII – Some More Untold Cases (1877-1887)
and
Part XXIII – Some More Untold Cases (1888-1894)

Ian Ableson is an ecologist by training and a writer by choice. When not reading or writing, he can reliably be found scowling at a clipboard while ankle-deep in a marsh somewhere in Michigan. His love for the stories of Arthur Conan Doyle started when his grandfather gave him a copy of *The Original Illustrated Sherlock Holmes* when he was in high school, and he's proud to have been able to contribute to the continuation of the tales of Sherlock Holmes and Dr. Watson.

Hugh Ashton was born in the U.K., and moved to Japan in 1988, where he remained until 2016, living with his wife Yoshiko in the historic city of Kamakura, a little to the south of Yokohama. He and Yoshiko have now moved to Lichfield, a small cathedral city in the Midlands of the U.K., the birthplace of Samuel Johnson, and one-time home of Erasmus Darwin. In the past, he has worked in the technology and financial services industries, which have provided him with material for some of his books set in the 21st century. He currently works as a writer: Novelist, freelance editor, and copywriter, (his work for large Japanese corporations has appeared in international business journals), and journalist, as well as producing industry reports on various aspects of the financial services industry. However, his lifelong interest in Sherlock Holmes has developed into an acclaimed series of adventures featuring the world's most famous detective, written in the style of the originals. In addition to these, he has also published historical and alternate historical novels, short stories, and thrillers. Together with artist Andy Boerger, he has produced the *Sherlock Ferret* series of stories for children, featuring the world's cutest detective.

Derrick Belanger is an educator and also the author of the #1 bestselling book in its category, *Sherlock Holmes: The Adventure of the Peculiar Provenance*, which was in the top 200 bestselling books on Amazon. He also is the author of *The MacDougall Twins with Sherlock Holmes* books, and he edited the Sir Arthur Conan Doyle horror anthology *A Study in Terror: Sir Arthur Conan Doyle's Revolutionary Stories of Fear and the Supernatural*. Mr. Belanger co-owns the publishing company Belanger Books, which has released numerous Sherlock Holmes anthologies including *Beyond Watson, Holmes Away From Home: Adventures from the Great Hiatus, Sherlock Holmes: Before Baker Street, Sherlock Holmes: Adventures in the Realms of H.G. Wells, Sherlock Holmes and the Occult Detectives, Sherlock Holmes and the Great Detectives*, and *Beyond the Adventures of Sherlock Holmes*. Derrick resides in Colorado and continues compiling unpublished works by Dr. John H. Watson.

S.F. Bennett has, at various times, been an actor, a lecturer, a journalist, a historian, an author and a potter. Whilst some of those things still apply, she has always been an avid collector, concentrating mainly on ephemera and other related items concerning Sherlock Holmes and British science-fiction of the 1970's. To date, she has written articles on aspects of The Canon for *The Baker Street Journal*, *The Sherlock Holmes Journal*, and *The Torr*, the journal of *The Sherlock Holmes Society of the West Country*. When not collecting, she can be found writing science-fiction and mystery stories, and has contributed to several anthologies of new Sherlock Holmes pastiches. Her first novel was *The Secret Diary of Mycroft Holmes: The Thoughts and Reminiscences of Sherlock Holmes's Elder Brother, 1880-1888* (2017). She is also the author of *A Study in Postcards: Sherlock Holmes in the Golden Age of the Picture Postcard* (*Sherlock Holmes Society of London*, 2019).

Bob Bishop is the author of over twenty stage plays, musicals, and pantomimes, several written in collaboration with Norfolk composer Bob McNeil Watson. Many of these theatrical works were first performed by the fringe theatre company of which he was principal director, The Fossick Valley Fumblers, at the Edinburgh Festival Fringe between 1982 and 2000. Amongst these works were four Sherlock Holmes plays, inspired by the playwright's lifelong affection for the works of Sir Arthur Conan Doyle. Bob's other works include the comic novel, *A Tickle Amongst the Cornstalks*, an anthology of short stories, *Shadows on the Blind*, and a number of Sherlock Holmes pastiche novellas. He currently lives with his wife and three poodles in North Norfolk.

Leverett Butts teaches composition and literature at the University of North Georgia. His poetry and fiction have appeared in *Eclectic* and *The Georgia State University Review*. He is the recipient of several fiction prizes offered by the University of West Georgia and TAG Publishing. His first collection of short fiction, *Emily's Stitches: The Confessions of Thomas Calloway and Other Stories*, was nominated for the 2013 Georgia Author of the Year Award in Short Fiction. The collection of the first two volumes of his *Guns of the Waste Land* was nominated in 2016, and the third volume of the series won honorable mention in the 2018 Georgia Independent Author of the Year Award in historical fiction. He recently completed the fourth and final volume, *Desinence*. He lives in Carrollton, Georgia, with his wife, son, their Jack Russell terrier, and an antisocial cat.

Chris Chan is a writer, educator, and historian. He works as a researcher and "International Goodwill Ambassador" for Agatha Christie Ltd. His true crime articles, reviews, and short fiction have appeared (or will soon appear) in *The Strand*, *The Wisconsin Magazine of History*, *Mystery Weekly*, *Gilbert!*, *Nerd HQ*, Akashic Books' *Mondays are Murder* web series, *The Baker Street Journal*, and *Sherlock Holmes Mystery Magazine*. His latest book is *Sherlock and Irene: The Secret Truth Behind "A Scandal in Bohemia"*

Leslie Charteris was born in Singapore on May 12th, 1907. With his mother and brother, he moved to England in 1919 and attended Rossall School in Lancashire before moving on to Cambridge University to study law. His studies there came to a halt when a publisher accepted his first novel. His third one, entitled *Meet the Tiger*, was written when he was twenty years old and published in September 1928. It introduced the world to Simon Templar, *aka* The Saint. He continued to write about The Saint until 1983 when the last book, *Salvage for The Saint*, was published. The books, which have been translated into over thirty languages, number nearly a hundred and have sold over forty-million copies around the world. They've inspired, to date, fifteen feature films, three television series, ten radio series, and a comic strip that was written by Charteris and syndicated around the world for over a decade. He enjoyed travelling, but settled for long periods in Hollywood, Florida, and finally in Surrey, England. He was awarded the Cartier Diamond Dagger by the *Crime Writers' Association* in 1992, in recognition of a lifetime of achievement. He died the following year.

Mike Chinn lives in Birmingham UK with his wife Caroline and their guinea pigs. He has published over sixty short stories, some of which have found their way into two collections: *Give Me These Moments Back* (The Alchemy Press, 2015) and *Radix Omnium Malum* (Parallel Universe Publications, 2017). He has edited three volumes of *The Alchemy Press Book of Pulp Heroes* (2012, 2013 and 2014) and *Swords Against the Millenium* (2000) for The Alchemy Press. The first publication of his Damian Paladin collection, *The Paladin Mandates* (The Alchemy Press, 1998), was short-listed for the British Fantasy Award in 1999, and a second Paladin collection, *Walkers in Shadow*, was published by Pro Se Publications in 2017 (who are due to republish an expanded and revised edition of *The Paladin Mandates* in 2020). He sent Sherlock Holmes to the Moon in *Vallis Timoris* (Fringeworks, 2015), and in 2018 Pro Se published his first Western: *Revenge is a Cold Pistol.*

Barry Clay is a graduate of Shippensburg University with a BA in English. He's dug ditches, stocked grocery shelves, tutored for room and board, cleaned restrooms, mopped floors, taught cartooning, worked in a bank, asked if you'd like fries with that (and cooked the fries to boot), ordered carpet for cars, and worked commission sales at Sears. Currently, he is a thirty-two year veteran of the Federal employee workforce. He has been writing all his life in different genres, and he has written thirteen books ranging from Christian theology, anthologies, speculative fiction, horror, science fiction, and humor. His Sherlockian volumes include *The Darkened Village* and *The Leveson-Gower Theft.* He volunteers as conductor of a local student orchestra and has been commissioned to write music. His first two musicals were locally produced. He is the husband of one wife, father of four children, and "Opa" to one granddaughter. He is honored to have been asked to contribute to this collection.

Ian Dickerson was just nine years old when he discovered The Saint. Shortly after that, he discovered Sherlock Holmes. The Saint won, for a while anyway. He struck up a friendship with The Saint's creator, Leslie Charteris, and his family. With their permission, he spent six weeks studying the Leslie Charteris collection at Boston University and went on to write, direct, and produce documentaries on the making of *The Saint* and *Return of The Saint,* which have been released on DVD. He oversaw the recent reprints of almost fifty of the original Saint books in both the US and UK, and was a co-producer on the 2017 TV movie of *The Saint*. When he discovered that Charteris had written Sherlock Holmes stories as well – well, there was the excuse he needed to revisit The Canon. He's consequently written and edited three books on Holmes' radio adventures. For the sake of what little sanity he has, Ian has also written about a wide range of subjects, none of which come with a halo, including talking mashed potatoes, Lord Grade, and satellite links. Ian lives in Hampshire with his wife and two children. And an awful lot of books by Leslie Charteris. Not quite so many by Conan Doyle, though.

Matthew J. Elliott is the author of *Big Trouble in Mother Russia* (2016), the official sequel to the cult movie *Big Trouble in Little China*, *Lost in Time and Space: An Unofficial Guide to the Uncharted Journeys of Doctor Who* (2014), *Sherlock Holmes on the Air* (2012), *Sherlock Holmes in Pursuit* (2013), *The Immortals: An Unauthorized Guide to* Sherlock *and* Elementary (2013), and *The Throne Eternal* (2014). His articles, fiction, and reviews have appeared in the magazines *Scarlet Street*, *Total DVD*, *SHERLOCK*, and *Sherlock Holmes Mystery Magazine*, and the collections *The Game's Afoot*, *Curious Incidents 2*, *Gaslight Grimoire*, *The Mammoth Book of Best British Crime 8*, and *The MX Book of New Sherlock Holmes Stories – Part III: 1896-1929.* He has scripted over 260 radio plays, including episodes of *Doctor Who*, *The Further Adventures of Sherlock*

Holmes, *The Twilight Zone*, *The New Adventures of Mickey Spillane's Mike Hammer*, *Fangoria's Dreadtime Stories*, and award-winning adaptations of *The Hound of the Baskervilles* and *The War of the Worlds*. He is the only radio dramatist to adapt all sixty original stories from The Canon for the series *The Classic Adventures of Sherlock Holmes*. Matthew is a writer and performer on *RiffTrax.com*, the online comedy experience from the creators of cult sci-fi TV series *Mystery Science Theater 3000* (*MST3K* to the initiated). He's also written a few comic books.

Tim Gambrell lives in Exeter, Devon, with his wife, two young sons, three cats, and now only four chickens. He has previously contributed stories to *The MX Book of New Sherlock Holmes Stories*, and also to *Sherlock Holmes and Dr Watson: The Early Adventures* and *Sherlock Holmes and The Occult Detectives*, also from Belanger Books. Outside of the world of Holmes, Tim has written extensively for Doctor Who spin-off ranges. His books include two linked novels from Candy Jar Books: *Lethbridge-Stewart: The Laughing Gnome – Lucy Wilson & The Bledoe Cadets*, and *The Lucy Wilson Mysteries: The Brigadier and The Bledoe Cadets* (both 2019), and *Lethbridge-Stewart: Bloodlines – An Ordinary Man* (Candy Jar, 2020, written with Andy Frankham-Allen). He's also written a novella, *The Way of The Bry'hunee* (2019) for the Erimem range from Thebes Publishing. Tim's short fiction includes stories in *Lethbridge-Stewart: The HAVOC Files 3* (Candy Jar, 2017, revised edition 2020), *Bernice Summerfield: True Stories* (Big Finish, 2017) and *Relics . . . An Anthology* (Red Ted Books, 2018), plus a number of charity anthologies.

Paul D. Gilbert was born in 1954 and has lived in and around London all of his life. His wife Jackie is a Holmes expert who keeps him on the straight and narrow! He has two sons, one of whom now lives in Spain. His interests include literature, ancient history, all religions, most sports, and movies. He is currently employed full-time as a funeral director. His books so far include *The Lost Files of Sherlock Holmes* (2007), *The Chronicles of Sherlock Holmes* (2008), *Sherlock Holmes and the Giant Rat of Sumatra* (2010), *The Annals of Sherlock Holmes* (2012), *Sherlock Holmes and the Unholy Trinity* (2015), *Sherlock Holmes: The Four Handed Game* (2017), and *The Illumination of Sherlock Holmes* (2019).

Paul Hiscock is an author of crime, fantasy, and science fiction tales. His short stories have appeared in several anthologies and include a seventeenth century whodunnit, a science fiction western, and a steampunk Sherlock Holmes story. Paul lives with his family in Kent, England, and spends his days chasing a toddler with more energy than the Duracell Bunny. He mainly does his writing in coffee shops with members of the local NaNoWriMo group, or in the middle of the night when his family has gone to sleep. Consequently, his stories tend to be fuelled by large amounts of black coffee. You can find out more about his writing at *www.detectivesanddragons.uk.*

John Linwood Grant *also has a poem in Part XXIII*

Denis Green was born in London, England in April 1905. He grew up mostly in London's Savoy Theatre where his father, Richard Green, was a principal in many Gilbert and Sullivan productions, A Flying Officer with RAF until 1924, he then spent four years managing a tea estate in North India before making his stage debut in *Hamlet* with Leslie Howard in 1928. He made his first visit to America in 1931 and established a respectable stage career before appearing in films – including minor roles in the first two Rathbone and Bruce Holmes films – and developing a career in front of and behind the microphone during the golden age of radio. Green and Leslie Charteris met in 1938 and struck up a lifelong friendship. Always busy, be it on stage, radio, film or television, Green passed away at the age of fifty in New York.

Arthur Hall *also has a story in Part XXIII*

Christopher James was born in 1975 in Paisley, Scotland. Educated at Newcastle and UEA, he was a winner of the UK's National Poetry Competition in 2008. He has written three full length Sherlock Holmes novels, *The Adventure of the Ruby* Elephant, *The Jeweller of Florence*, and *The Adventure of the Beer Barons*, all published by MX.

In the year 1998 **Craig Janacek** took his degree of Doctor of Medicine at Vanderbilt University, and proceeded to Stanford to go through the training prescribed for pediatricians in practice. Having completed his studies there, he was duly attached to the University of California, San Francisco as Associate Professor. The author of over seventy medical monographs upon a variety of obscure lesions, his travel-worn and battered tin dispatch-box is crammed with papers, nearly all of which are records of his fictional works. To date, these have been published solely in electronic format, including two non-Holmes novels (*The Oxford Deception* and *The Anger of Achilles Peterson*), the trio of holiday adventures collected as *The Midwinter Mysteries of Sherlock Holmes*, the Holmes story collections *The First of Criminals*, *The Assassination of Sherlock Holmes*, *The Treasury of Sherlock Holmes*, *Light in the Darkness, The Gathering Gloom*, *The Travels of Sherlock Holmes*, and the Watsonian novels *The Isle of Devils* and *The Gate of Gold*. Craig Janacek is a *nom de plume*.

Steven Philip Jones has written over sixty graphic novels and comic books including the horror series *Lovecraftian*, *Curious Cases of Sherlock Holmes*, the original series *Nightlinger*, *Street Heroes 2005*, adaptations of *Dracula*, several H. P. Lovecraft stories, and the 1985 film *Re-animator*. Steven is also the author of several novels and nonfiction books including *The Clive Cussler Adventures: A Critical Review*, *Comics Writing: Communicating With Comic Book* , *King of Harlem*, *Bushwackers*, *The House With the Witch's Hat*, *Talisman: The Knightmare Knife*, and *Henrietta Hex: Shadows From the Past.* Steven's other writing credits include a number of scripts for radio dramas that have been broadcast internationally. A graduate of the University of Iowa, Steven has a Bachelor of Arts in Journalism and Religion, and was accepted into Iowa's Writer's Workshop – M.F.A. program.

Susan Knight *also has a story in Part XXII*

David Marcum *also has stories in Parts XXII and XXIII*

Stephen Mason has been the Third Mate (President) of *The Crew of the Barque* Lone Star scion society in Dallas/Fort Worth for over seven years. He is also the Chair of the Communications Committee for *The Beacon Society*, a national educational scion society. With Joe Fay and Rusty Mason, he produces the *Baker Street Elementary* comic strip each week, the first adventures of Sherlock Holmes and John Watson.

Mark Mower is a member of the *Crime Writers' Association*, *The Sherlock Holmes Society of London*, and *The Solar Pons Society of London*. He writes true crime stories and fictional mysteries. His volumes of Holmes pastiches include *A Farewell to Baker Street*, *Sherlock Holmes: The Baker Street Case-Files*, and *Baker Street Legacy* (all published by MX Publishing) and he has contributed multiple stories to the ongoing *The MX Book of*

New Sherlock Holmes Stories. He has also had stories in two anthologies by Belanger Books: *Holmes Away From Home: Adventures from the Great Hiatus – Volume II – 1893-1894* (2016) and *Sherlock Holmes: Before Baker Street* (2017). More are bound to follow. Mark's non-fiction works include *Bloody British History: Norwich* (The History Press, 2014), *Suffolk Murders* (The History Press, 2011) and *Zeppelin Over Suffolk* (Pen & Sword Books, 2008).

Will Murray has been writing about popular culture since 1973, principally on the subjects of comic books, pulp magazine heroes, and film. As a fiction writer, he's the author of over 70 novels featuring characters as diverse as Nick Fury and Remo Williams. With the late Steve Ditko, he created the Unbeatable Squirrel Girl for Marvel Comics. Murray has written numerous short stories, many on Lovecraftian themes. Currently, he writes The Wild Adventures of Doc Savage for Altus Press. His acclaimed Doc Savage novel, *Skull Island*, pits the pioneer superhero against the legendary King Kong. This was followed by *King Kong vs. Tarzan* and two Doc Savage novels guest-starring The Shadow. *Tarzan, Conqueror of Mars*, a crossover with John Carter of Mars, was just published. *www.adventuresinbronze.com* is his website.

This work represents **Richard Paolinelli**'s fifth published Sherlock Holmes pastiche. He began his writing journey as a freelance writer in 1984 and gained his first fiction credit serving as the lead writer for the first two issues of the Elite Comics sci-fi/fantasy series, *Seadragon*. Following a twenty-year newspaper writing career, he returned to his fiction writing roots and has since published several novels, two non-fiction sports books, and has appeared in several anthologies. His novel, *Escaping Infini*ty, was a 2017 Dragon Award Finalist for Best Sci-Fi novel. He also writes weekly short fiction on his website, *www.richardpaolinelli.com*.

Tracy J. Revels *also has stories in Parts XXII and XXIII*

Roger Riccard of Los Angeles, California, U.S.A., is a descendant of the Roses of Kilravock in Highland Scotland. He is the author of two previous Sherlock Holmes novels, *The Case of the Poisoned Lilly* and *The Case of the Twain Papers*, a series of short stories in two volumes, *Sherlock Holmes: Adventures for the Twelve Days of Christmas* and *Further Adventures for the Twelve Days of Christmas*, and the new series *A Sherlock Holmes Alphabet of Cases,* all of which are published by Baker Street Studios. He has another novel and a non-fiction Holmes reference work in various stages of completion. He became a Sherlock Holmes enthusiast as a teenager (many, many years ago), and, like all fans of The Great Detective, yearned for more stories after reading The Canon over and over. It was the Granada Television performances of Jeremy Brett and Edward Hardwicke, and the encouragement of his wife, Rosilyn, that at last inspired him to write his own Holmes adventures, using the Granada actor portrayals as his guide. He has been called "The best pastiche writer since Val Andrews" by the *Sherlockian E-Times.*

Jane Rubino is the author of *A Jersey Shore* mystery series, featuring a Jane Austen-loving amateur sleuth and a Sherlock Holmes-quoting detective, *Knight Errant, Lady Vernon and Her Daughter*, (a novel-length adaptation of Jane Austen's novella *Lady Susan*, co-authored with her daughter Caitlen Rubino-Bradway, *What Would Austen Do?*, also co-authored with her daughter, a short story in the anthology *Jane Austen Made Me Do It, The Rucastles' Pawn, The Copper Beeches from Violet Turner's POV*, and, of course, there's the Sherlockian novel in the drawer – who doesn't have one? Jane lives on a barrier island at the New Jersey shore.

Geri Schear is a novelist and short story writer. Her work has been published in literary journals in the U.S. and Ireland. Her first novel, *A Biased Judgement: The Diaries of Sherlock Holmes 1897* was released to critical acclaim in 2014. The sequel, *Sherlock Holmes and the Other Woman* was published in 2015, and *Return to Reichenbach* in 2016. She lives in Kells, Ireland.

Award-winning author **Dr. Liese Sherwood-Fabre** doesn't remember a time she didn't know of Sherlock Holmes – be it the old Basel Rathbone movies, Tom and Jerry in deerstalker hats, or the original Conan Doyle tales. During her thirty-plus years as a federal employee, Dr. Sherwood-Fabre worked and lived in various countries, including Mexico and Russia, finding inspiration for stories based on events taking place around her. She garnered a prestigious Pushcart nomination for a short story inspired by her experiences in Mexico, and having lived through the tumultuous years of Russia's budding democracy, her first published novel, *Saving Hope*, centered around an unemployed Russian microbiologist who must choose between saving her daughter's life or working with a former KGB agent to stop the sale of bioweapons to Iran. After returning to the United States, Dr. Sherwood-Fabre revived her early interest in Sherlock Holmes and the Victorian period. For the past six years, she has shared her knowledge with other Sherlockians by contributing regularly to several society newsletters, as well as the prestigious *Baker Street Journal* and *Canadian Holmes* publications. Besides her own recently launch series *The Early Case Files of Sherlock Holmes*, she has contributed to Sherlockian anthologies through *Mocha Memoirs* and *The Crew of the Barque Lone Star* scion – and now MX Publishing. Visit her Website *www.liesesherwoodfabre.com* for more about her publications and to sign up for her newsletter.

Shane Simmons is the author of the occult detective novels *Necropolis* and *Epitaph*, and the crime collection *Raw and Other Stories*. An award-winning screenwriter and graphic novelist, his work has appeared in international film festivals, museums, and lectures about design and structure. He was born in Lachine, a suburb of Montreal best known for being massacred in 1689 and having a joke name. Visit Shane's homepage at *eyestrainproductions.com* for more.

Denis O. Smith's first published story of Sherlock Holmes and Doctor Watson, "The Adventure of The Purple Hand", appeared in 1982. Since then, numerous other such accounts have been published in magazines and anthologies both in the U.K. and the U.S. In the 1990's, four volumes of his stories were published under the general title of *The Chronicles of Sherlock Holmes*, and, more recently his stories have been collected as *The Lost Chronicles of Sherlock Holmes* (2014), *The Lost Chronicles of Sherlock Holmes Volume II* (2016), *The Further Chronicles of Sherlock Holmes* (201). He also wrote a Holmes novel, *The Riddle of Foxwood Grange* (2017). Born in Yorkshire, in the north of England, Denis Smith has lived and worked in various parts of the country, including London, and has now been resident in Norfolk for many years. His interests range widely, but apart from his dedication to the career of Sherlock Holmes, he has a passion for historical mysteries of all kinds, the railways of Britain and the history of London.

Robert V. Stapleton was born and brought up in Leeds, Yorkshire, England, and studied at Durham University. After working in various parts of the country as an Anglican parish priest, he is now retired and lives with his wife in North Yorkshire. As a member of his local writing group, he now has time to develop his other life as a writer of adventure stories. He has recently had a number of short stories published, and he is hoping to have a couple of completed novels published at some time in the future.

Dacre Stoker is the great-grand-nephew of Bram Stoker, and the international best-selling co-author of *Dracula the Un-Dead* (Dutton, 2009), and *Dracul* (Putnam 2018). Dacre is also the co-editor (with Elizabeth Miller) of *The Lost Journal of Bram Stoker: The Dublin Years* (Robson Press, 2012). A native of Montreal, Canada, Dacre taught Physical Education and Sciences for twenty-two years, in both Canada and the U.S. He has participated in the sport of Modern Pentathlon as an athlete and a coach at the international and Olympic levels for Canada for twelve years. He currently lives in Aiken, SC, and together with his wife Jenne, they manage The Bram Stoker Estate.

Tim Symonds was born in London. He grew up in Somerset, Dorset, and Guernsey. After several years in East and Central Africa, he settled in California and graduated Phi Beta Kappa in Political Science from UCLA. He is a Fellow of the *Royal Geographical Society*. He writes his novels in the woods and hidden valleys surrounding his home in the High Weald of East Sussex. Dr. Watson knew the untamed region well. In "The Adventure of Black Peter", Watson wrote, "*the Weald was once part of that great forest which for so long held the Saxon invaders at bay*." Tim's novels are published by MX Publishing. His novels include *Sherlock Holmes and the Nine Dragon Sigil. Sherlock Holmes and The Sword of Osman, Sherlock Holmes and the Mystery of Einstein's Daughter, Sherlock Holmes and the Dead Boer at Scotney Castle*, and *Sherlock Holmes and the Case of The Bulgarian Codex*. His collection of Holmes short stories is called *A Most Diabolical Plot.*

Kevin P. Thornton *also has a story in Part XXII*

William Todd has been a Holmes fan his entire life, and credits *The Hound of the Baskervilles* as the impetus for his love of both reading and writing. He began to delve into fan fiction a few years ago when he decided to take a break from writing his usual Victorian/Gothic horror stories. He was surprised how well-received they were, and has tried to put out a couple of Holmes stories a year since then. When not writing, Mr. Todd is a pathology supervisor at a local hospital in Northwestern Pennsylvania. He is the husband of a terrific lady and father to two great kids, one with special needs, so the benefactor of these anthologies is close to his heart.

Jan van Koningsveld was born in Emden, Germany, having both the German and the Dutch citizenship. He has been a fan of Sherlock Holmes and Dr. Watson since 1982, when a TV series starring Geoffrey Whitehead and Donald Pickering was aired in Germany. The first Holmes story that he read was *A Study in Scarlet*. In his study, he has a library containing more than 1,000 books regarding Sherlock Holmes, and he is a collector of different versions of *The Hound of the Baskervilles* in different languages. He is married and father of three children, works as an account and instructor, and is the author of the books *The Mental Calculator's Handbook* (with Dr. Robert Fountain) and *Become a Human Calendar in just 7 Days*. He is the organizer of multiple events regarding Mental Calculation (such as the World Championships for students), and also a tutor for workshops, all non-profit. HE is the creator and maintainer of the Pi World Ranking List (since 2001) *www-pi-world-ranking-list.com* and the holder of more than twenty world records in Mental Calculation, a 4-time World Cup winner, and a 2-time Memoriad winner. He is a consultant for German TV shows regarding math, and has made several appearances on German and Dutch TV shows. His German website is: *www.janvankoningsveld.com*

Margaret Walsh was born Auckland, New Zealand and now lives in Melbourne, Australia. She is the author of *Sherlock Holmes and the Molly-Boy Murders*, *Sherlock Holmes and the Case of the Perplexed Politician*, and *Sherlock Holmes and the Case of the London Dock Deaths*, all published by MX Publishing. Margaret has been a devotee of Sherlock Holmes since childhood and has had several Holmesian related essays printed in anthologies, and is a member of the online society *Doyle's Rotary Coffin*. She has an ongoing love affair with the city of London. When she's not working or planning trips to London. Margaret can be found frequenting the many and varied bookshops of Melbourne.

I.A. Watson is a novelist and jobbing writer from Yorkshire who cut his teeth on writing Sherlock Holmes stories and has even won an award for one. His works include *Holmes and Houdini*, *Labours of Hercules*, *St. George and the Dragon* Volumes 1 and 2, *Women of Myth*, and the non-fiction essay book *Where Stories Dwell*. He pens short detective stories as a means of avoiding writing things that pay better. A full list of his many works published works appears at:
http://www.chillwater.org.uk/writing/iawatsonhome.htm

Marcia Wilson *also has a story in Part XXIII*

The MX Book of New Sherlock Holmes Stories
Edited by David Marcum
(MX Publishing, 2015-   )

"This is the finest volume of Sherlockian fiction I have ever read, and I have read, literally, thousands." – Philip K. Jones

"Beyond Impressive . . . This is a splendid venture for a great cause!
– Roger Johnson, Editor, *The Sherlock Holmes Journal,*
The Sherlock Holmes Society of London

Part I: 1881-1889
Part II: 1890-1895
Part III: 1896-1929
Part IV: 2016 Annual
Part V: Christmas Adventures
Part VI: 2017 Annual
Part VII: Eliminate the Impossible (1880-1891)
Part VIII – Eliminate the Impossible (1892-1905)
Part IX – 2018 Annual (1879-1895)
Part X – 2018 Annual (1896-1916)
Part XI – Some Untold Cases (1880-1891)
Part XII – Some Untold Cases (1894-1902)
Part XIII – 2019 Annual (1881-1890)
Part XIV – 2019 Annual (1891-1897)
Part XV – 2019 Annual (1898-1917)
Part XVI – Whatever Remains . . . Must be the Truth (1881-1890)
Part XVII – Whatever Remains . . . Must be the Truth (1891-1898)
Part XVIII – Whatever Remains . . . Must be the Truth (1898-1925)
Part XIX – 2020 Annual (1882-1890)
Part XX – 2020 Annual (1891-1897)
Part XXI – 2020 Annual (1898-1923)
Part XXII – Some More Untold Cases (1877-1887)
Part XXIII – Some More Untold Cases (1888-1894)
Part XXIV – Some More Untold Cases (1895-1903)

In Preparation
Part XXV – 2021 Annual

. . . and more to come!

The MX Book of New Sherlock Holmes Stories

Edited by David Marcum

(MX Publishing, 2015-)

Publishers Weekly says:

Part VI: *The traditional pastiche is alive and well . . . .*

Part VII: *Sherlockians eager for faithful-to-the-canon plots and characters will be delighted.*

Part VIII: *The imagination of the contributors in coming up with variations on the volume's theme is matched by their ingenious resolutions.*

Part IX: *The 18 stories . . . will satisfy fans of Conan Doyle's originals. Sherlockians will rejoice that more volumes are on the way.*

Part X: . . . *new Sherlock Holmes adventures of consistently high quality.*

Part XI: . . . *an essential volume for Sherlock Holmes fans.*

Part XII: . . . *continues to amaze with the number of high-quality pastiches . . .*

Part XIII: . . . *Amazingly, Marcum has found 22 superb pastiches . . . This is more catnip for fans of stories faithful to Conan Doyle's original*

Part XIV: . . . *this standout anthology of 21 short stories written in the spirit of Conan Doyle's originals.*

Part XV: *Stories pitting Sherlock Holmes against seemingly supernatural phenomena highlight Marcum's 15th anthology of superior short pastiches.*

Part XVI: *Marcum has once again done fans of Conan Doyle's originals a service.*

Part XVII: *This is yet another impressive array of new but traditional Holmes stories.*

Part XVIII: *Sherlockians will again be grateful to Marcum and MX for high-quality new Holmes tales.*

Part XIX: *Inventive plots and intriguing explorations of aspects of Dr. Watson's life and beliefs lift the 24 pastiches in Marcum's impressive 19th Sherlock Holmes anthology*

Part XX: *Marcum's reserve of high-quality new Holmes exploits seems endless.*

Part XXI: *This is another must-have for Sherlockians.*

The MX Book of New Sherlock Holmes Stories

Edited by David Marcum

(MX Publishing, 2015-   )

MX Publishing

MX Publishing is the world's largest specialist Sherlock Holmes publisher, with several hundred titles and over a hundred authors creating the latest in Sherlock Holmes fiction and non-fiction.

From traditional short stories and novels to travel guides and quiz books, MX Publishing caters to all Holmes fans.

The collection includes leading titles such as *Benedict Cumberbatch In Transition* and *The Norwood Author*, which won the 2011 *Tony Howlett Award* (Sherlock Holmes Book of the Year).

MX Publishing also has one of the largest communities of Holmes fans on *Facebook*, with regular contributions from dozens of authors.

www.mxpublishing.co.uk (UK) and *www.mxpublishing.com* (USA)